GOTHIC

LOST ATLANTIS SHORT STORIES

ANTHOLOGY OF NEW & CLASSIC TALES

Foreword by Dr. Jennifer Fuller

FANTASY

FLAME TREE PUBLISHING

This is a FLAME TREE Book

Publisher & Creative Director: Nick Wells
Project Editor: Gillian Whitaker

Publisher's Note: Due to the historical nature of the classic text, we're aware that there may be some language used which has the potential to cause offence to the modern reader. However, wishing overall to preserve the integrity of the text, rather than imposing contemporary sensibilities, we have left it unaltered.

FLAME TREE PUBLISHING
6 Melbray Mews, Fulham,
London SW6 3NS, United Kingdom
www.flametreepublishing.com

First published 2023

23 25 27 26 24
1 3 5 7 9 10 8 6 4 2

ISBN: 978-1-80417-585-9
Special ISBN: 978-1-80417-338-1

The cover image is created by Flame Tree Studio based on artwork by Slava Gerj and Gabor Ruszkai.

A copy of the CIP data for this book is available from the British Library.

Printed and bound in China

GOTHIC

LOST ATLANTIS SHORT STORIES

ANTHOLOGY OF NEW & CLASSIC TALES

Foreword by Dr. Jennifer Fuller

FLAME TREE PUBLISHING

FANTASY

Contents

GOTHIC

LOST ATLANTIS SHORT STORIES

ANTHOLOGY OF NEW & CLASSIC TALES

Foreword by Dr. Jennifer Fuller

FLAME TREE PUBLISHING

FANTASY

Foreword: Lost Atlantis Short Stories

IN HER POEM 'One Art', Elizabeth Bishop (1911–79) eloquently reflected on how humans experience loss. The poem meditates on items the poet has lost, beginning with small trinkets and building to much larger ones, from cities to rivers to an entire continent. This increasingly hyperbolic listing of lost things leads to the realization that humanity can survive what seems to be insurmountable amounts of loss. As Bishop well articulates, loss is part of the human condition and all of us, to varying degrees, are seeking to regain the precious value of something we once had, something lost to time or change or one misguided choice.

Yet, while it would seem loss would only serve our melancholic moods, loss is also a source of great inspiration. We humans yearn for lost civilizations, for lost peoples, those who have endured beyond our understanding and survive only in the realms of imagination. And perhaps no location is so synonymous with loss in the literary imagination as the fabled city of Atlantis. In the myth of Atlantis, the Greeks invoked a city of dreams, a place where all citizens lived in harmony and the palaces and temples were beyond comparison.

Plato first introduced us to Atlantis in his philosophical works *Timaeus* and *Critias*, which are collections of conversations between wise men in Athens. It is Critias himself who tells the story of the lost city, presented to him by his grandfather who had heard in his travels of an enormous island, ringed by mountains and sea, far beyond the known world. This island was sacred to the sea god and was full of fertile crops and guarded by fearsome warriors. Yet the kings of Atlantis were not satisfied, and set off on a quest to conquer all the Mediterranean world. Angered at their pride and destruction, the gods punished Atlantis, cursing it and all its people to sink beneath the waves, forever lost.

Yet, even in Critias's version of the story, the island is already a part of myth and legend. The story largely takes place a long time ago in a kingdom far, far away – the language we instinctively recognize as part of fairy tales and fantasy. The goal of his story is not to find a missing place but to reflect on a lost part of ourselves, to wonder what the world could be outside of our daily experience.

This idea of the lost world beneath the waves, the city of Atlantis, inspired authors long after Plato. Thomas More used it as a blueprint for his fictional *Utopia* (which importantly translates to 'no place'), and authors from Charlotte Perkins Gilman to Jules Verne to Clark Ashton Smith continued to build upon the idea of the civilization lost but not forgotten. And modern writers continue the story in settings as diverse as the mythical island of television's *Lost* to the Afrofuturist realm of Wakanda – humans remain fascinated by the city of the imagination and enthralled (and occasionally horrified) by the hope of one day discovering it.

This anthology both reclaims and re-imagines the lost city of Atlantis, exploring the idea of the perfect society lost to time in a host of iterations. We present classic authors who used the city as a touchstone to imagine paradises and dystopias, and modern writers who use the Atlantis tale to envision the possibility of new worlds and new societies, but also delve into interior worlds (like Bishop's lost continent). In these stories we will discover the full range of both individual and civic ambition, not only to consider what we have lost, but to build a vision of what we could be, if only we have the courage to embrace the art of loss.

Dr. Jennifer Fuller

Publisher's Note

BEYOND the Pillars of Hercules, we are told by Plato, lies the fabled Atlantis, sunk forever beneath the sea as divine punishment for the corrupted behaviour of its citizens. This allegory of hubris has sparked the imaginations of writers over the centuries, with stories not just of the land itself, and its people, but of what it represents and reflects back onto us. For this reason, in this fascinating addition to our Gothic Fantasy series, we begin the collection with Plato's *Critias*, setting the scene for the rich retellings and reimaginings that follow. The theme invites a wide range of interpretations, which can be seen across the classic stories as well as those by modern authors. Our intention has been to include the notion of Atlantis in its various forms: places of great riches, healing, sanctuary, or unattainable perfection, and the sense of these paradises lost. Consistently, it is the pursuit, the desire and yearning for these that drive the story, from Algernon Blackwood's bewitched, 'sand-haunted' narrator to Francis Bacon's plan of an ideal commonwealth.

Once again, our call for submissions was met with a great response from authors. We partnered with Daniella Blechner of Conscious Dreams Publishing to widen our reach on submissions, and it was a huge task to choose a selection of stories that sit well together alongside the older fiction. On the new side, as well as Atlantean adventures, we have stories of Ys, Tír na nÓg, the Lost City of Z, Mohenjo Daro, Kumari Kandam, Meroe, and a modern-day quest for Avalon – to mention just a few. As these newer contributions unearth ancient cities, dream up utopian existences and explore mythology from around the world, they prove interesting to compare to the older tales. Above all, we hope this anthology shows how, over two thousand years later, Atlantis continues to inspire powerful narratives examining the nature of humanity in entertaining and original ways.

Critias

Plato (translated by Benjamin Jowett)

PERSONS OF THE DIALOGUE: Critias, Hermocrates, Timaeus, Socrates.

TIMAEUS: How thankful I am, Socrates, that I have arrived at last, and, like a weary traveller after a long journey, may be at rest! And I pray the being who always was of old, and has now been by me revealed, to grant that my words may endure in so far as they have been spoken truly and acceptably to him; but if unintentionally I have said anything wrong, I pray that he will impose upon me a just retribution, and the just retribution of him who errs is that he should be set right. Wishing, then, to speak truly in future concerning the generation of the gods, I pray him to give me knowledge, which of all medicines is the most perfect and best. And now having offered my prayer I deliver up the argument to Critias, who is to speak next according to our agreement.

CRITIAS: And I, Timaeus, accept the trust, and as you at first said that you were going to speak of high matters, and begged that some forbearance might be shown to you, I too ask the same or greater forbearance for what I am about to say. And although I very well know that my request may appear to be somewhat ambitious and discourteous, I must make it nevertheless. For will any man of sense deny that you have spoken well? I can only attempt to show that I ought to have more indulgence than you, because my theme is more difficult; and I shall argue that to seem to speak well of the gods to men is far easier than to speak well of men to men: for the inexperience and utter ignorance of his hearers about any subject is a great assistance to him who has to speak of it, and we know how ignorant we are concerning the gods. But I should like to make my meaning clearer, if you will follow me. All that is said by any of us can only be imitation and representation. For if we consider the likenesses which painters make of bodies divine and heavenly, and the different degrees of gratification with which the eye of the spectator receives them, we shall see that we are satisfied with the artist who is able in any degree to imitate the earth and its mountains, and the rivers, and the woods, and the universe, and the things that are and move therein, and further, that knowing nothing precise about such matters, we do not examine or analyse the painting; all that is required is a sort of indistinct and deceptive mode of shadowing them forth. But when a person endeavours to paint the human form we are quick at finding out defects, and our familiar knowledge makes us severe judges of any one who does not render every point of similarity. And we may observe the same thing to happen in discourse; we are satisfied with a picture of divine and heavenly things which has very little likeness to them; but we are more precise in our criticism of mortal and human things. Wherefore if at the moment of speaking I cannot suitably express my meaning, you must excuse me, considering that to form approved likenesses of human things is the reverse of easy. This is what I want to suggest to you, and at the same time to beg, Socrates, that I may have not less, but more indulgence conceded to me in what I am about to say. Which favour, if I am right in asking, I hope that you will be ready to grant.

SOCRATES: Certainly, Critias, we will grant your request, and we will grant the same by anticipation to Hermocrates, as well as to you and Timaeus; for I have no doubt that when his turn comes a little while hence, he will make the same request which you have made. In order, then, that he may provide himself with a fresh beginning, and not be compelled to say the same things over again, let him understand that the indulgence is already extended by anticipation to him. And now, friend Critias, I will announce to you the judgment of the theatre. They are of opinion that the last performer was wonderfully successful, and that you will need a great deal of indulgence before you will be able to take his place.

HERMOCRATES: The warning, Socrates, which you have addressed to him, I must also take to myself. But remember, Critias, that faint heart never yet raised a trophy; and therefore you must go and attack the argument like a man. First invoke Apollo and the Muses, and then let us hear you sound the praises and show forth the virtues of your ancient citizens.

CRITIAS: Friend Hermocrates, you, who are stationed last and have another in front of you, have not lost heart as yet; the gravity of the situation will soon be revealed to you; meanwhile I accept your exhortations and encouragements. But besides the gods and goddesses whom you have mentioned, I would specially invoke Mnemosyne; for all the important part of my discourse is dependent on her favour, and if I can recollect and recite enough of what was said by the priests and brought hither by Solon, I doubt not that I shall satisfy the requirements of this theatre. And now, making no more excuses, I will proceed.

Let me begin by observing first of all, that nine thousand was the sum of years which had elapsed since the war which was said to have taken place between those who dwelt outside the pillars of Heracles and all who dwelt within them; this war I am going to describe. Of the combatants on the one side, the city of Athens was reported to have been the leader and to have fought out the war; the combatants on the other side were commanded by the kings of Atlantis, which, as I was saying, was an island greater in extent than Libya and Asia, and when afterwards sunk by an earthquake, became an impassable barrier of mud to voyagers sailing from hence to any part of the ocean. The progress of the history will unfold the various nations of barbarians and families of Hellenes which then existed, as they successively appear on the scene; but I must describe first of all the Athenians of that day, and their enemies who fought with them, and then the respective powers and governments of the two kingdoms. Let us give the precedence to Athens.

In the days of old, the gods had the whole earth distributed among them by allotment. There was no quarrelling; for you cannot rightly suppose that the gods did not know what was proper for each of them to have, or, knowing this, that they would seek to procure for themselves by contention that which more properly belonged to others. They all of them by just apportionment obtained what they wanted, and peopled their own districts; and when they had peopled them they tended us, their nurselings and possessions, as shepherds tend their flocks, excepting only that they did not use blows or bodily force, as shepherds do, but governed us like pilots from the stern of the vessel, which is an easy way of guiding animals, holding our souls by the rudder of persuasion according to their own pleasure; – thus did they guide all mortal creatures. Now different gods had their allotments in different places which they set in order. Hephaestus and Athene, who were brother and sister, and sprang from the same father, having a common nature, and being united also in the love of philosophy and art, both obtained as their common portion this land, which was naturally adapted for wisdom and virtue; and there they implanted brave children of the soil, and put into their minds the order of government; their names are preserved, but their actions have disappeared by reason of the destruction of those who received the tradition, and the lapse of ages. For when there were any survivors, as I have already said, they were men who dwelt in the mountains; and they were ignorant of the art of writing, and had heard only the names of the chiefs of the land, but very little about their actions. The names they were willing enough to give to their children; but the virtues and the laws of their predecessors, they knew only by obscure traditions; and as they themselves and their children lacked for many generations the necessaries of life, they directed their attention to the supply of their wants, and of them they conversed, to the neglect of events that had happened in times long past; for mythology and the enquiry into antiquity are first introduced into cities when they begin to have leisure, and when they see that the necessaries of life have already been provided, but not before. And this is the reason why the names of the ancients have been preserved to us and not their actions. This I infer because Solon said that the priests in their narrative of that war mentioned most of the names which are recorded prior to the time of Theseus, such as Cecrops, and Erechtheus, and Erichthonius, and Erysichthon, and the names of the women in like manner. Moreover, since military pursuits were then common to men and women, the men of those days in accordance with the custom of the time set up a figure and image of the goddess in full armour, to be a testimony that all animals which associate together, male as well as female, may, if they please, practise in common the virtue which belongs to them without distinction of sex.

Now the country was inhabited in those days by various classes of citizens; – there were artisans, and there were husbandmen, and there was also a warrior class originally set apart by divine men. The latter dwelt by themselves, and had all things suitable for nurture and education; neither had any of them anything of their own, but they regarded all that they had as common property; nor did they claim to receive of the other citizens anything more than their necessary food. And they practised all the pursuits which we yesterday described as those of our imaginary guardians. Concerning the country the Egyptian priests said what is not only probable but manifestly true, that the boundaries were in those days fixed by the Isthmus, and that in the direction of the continent they extended as far as the heights of Cithaeron and Parnes; the boundary line came down in the direction of the sea, having the district of Oropus on the right, and with the river Asopus as the limit on the left. The land was the best in the world, and was therefore able in those days to support a vast army, raised from the surrounding people. Even the remnant of Attica which now exists may compare with any region in the world for the variety and excellence of its fruits and the suitableness of its pastures to every sort of animal, which proves what I am saying; but in those days the country was fair as now and yielded far more abundant produce. How shall I establish my words? And what part of it can be truly called a remnant of the land that then was? The whole country is only a long promontory extending far into the sea away from the rest of the continent, while the surrounding basin of the sea is everywhere deep in the neighbourhood of the shore. Many great deluges have taken place during the nine thousand years, for that is the number of years which have elapsed since the time of which I am speaking; and during all this time and through so many changes, there has never been any considerable accumulation of the soil coming down from the mountains, as in other places, but the earth has fallen away all round and sunk out of sight. The consequence is, that in comparison of what then was, there are remaining only the bones of the wasted body, as they may be called, as in the case of small islands, all the richer and softer parts of the soil having fallen away, and the mere skeleton of the land being left. But in the primitive state of the country, its mountains were high hills covered with soil, and the plains, as they are termed by us, of Phelleus were full of rich earth, and there was abundance of wood in the mountains. Of this last the traces still remain, for although some of the mountains now only afford sustenance to bees, not so very long ago there were still to be seen roofs of timber cut from trees growing there, which were of a size sufficient to cover the largest houses; and there were many other high trees, cultivated by man and bearing abundance of food for cattle. Moreover, the land reaped the benefit of the annual rainfall, not as now losing the water which flows off the bare earth into the sea, but, having an abundant supply in all places, and receiving it into herself and treasuring it up in the close clay soil, it let off into the hollows the streams which it absorbed from the heights, providing everywhere abundant fountains and rivers, of which there may still be observed sacred memorials in places where fountains once existed; and this proves the truth of what I am saying.

Such was the natural state of the country, which was cultivated, as we may well believe, by true husbandmen, who made husbandry their business, and were lovers of honour, and of a noble nature, and had a soil the best in the world, and abundance of water, and in the heaven above an excellently attempered climate. Now the city in those days was arranged on this wise. In the first place the Acropolis was not as now. For the fact is that a single night of excessive rain washed away the earth and laid bare the rock; at the same time there were earthquakes, and then occurred the extraordinary inundation, which was the third before the great destruction of Deucalion. But in primitive times the hill of the Acropolis extended to the Eridanus and Ilissus, and included the Pnyx on one side, and the Lycabettus as a boundary on the opposite side to the Pnyx, and was all well covered with soil, and level at the top, except in one or two places. Outside the Acropolis and under the sides of the hill there dwelt artisans, and such of the husbandmen as were tilling the ground near; the warrior class dwelt by themselves around the temples of Athene and Hephaestus at the summit, which moreover they had enclosed with a single fence like the garden of a single house. On the north side they had dwellings in common and had erected halls for dining in winter, and had all the buildings which they needed for their common life, besides temples, but there was no adorning of them with gold and silver, for they made no use of these for any purpose; they took a middle course between meanness and ostentation, and built modest houses in which they and their children's children grew old, and they handed them down to others who were like themselves, always the same. But in summer-time they left their gardens and gymnasia and dining halls, and then the southern side of the hill was made use of by them for the same purpose. Where the Acropolis now is there was a fountain, which was choked by the earthquake, and has left only the few small streams which still exist in the vicinity, but in those days the fountain gave an abundant supply of water for all and of suitable temperature in summer and in winter. This is how they dwelt, being the guardians of their own citizens and the leaders of the Hellenes, who were their willing followers. And they took care to preserve the same number of men and women through all time, being so many as were required for warlike purposes, then as now – that is to say, about twenty thousand. Such were the ancient Athenians, and after this manner they righteously administered their own land and the rest of Hellas; they were renowned all over Europe and Asia for the beauty of their persons and for the many virtues of their souls, and of all men who lived in those days they were the most illustrious. And next, if I have not forgotten what I heard when I was a child, I will impart to you the character and origin of their adversaries. For friends should not keep their stories to themselves, but have them in common.

Yet, before proceeding further in the narrative, I ought to warn you, that you must not be surprised if you should perhaps hear Hellenic names given to foreigners. I will tell you the reason of this: Solon, who was intending to use the tale for his poem, enquired into the meaning of the names, and found that the early Egyptians in writing them down had translated them into their own language, and he recovered the meaning of the several names and when copying them out again translated them into our language. My great-grandfather, Dropides, had the original writing, which is still in my possession, and was carefully studied by me when I was a child. Therefore if you hear names such as are used in this country, you must not be surprised, for I have told how they came to be introduced. The tale, which was of great length, began as follows:

I have before remarked in speaking of the allotments of the gods, that they distributed the whole earth into portions differing in extent, and made for themselves temples and instituted sacrifices.

And Poseidon, receiving for his lot the island of Atlantis, begat children by a mortal woman, and settled them in a part of the island, which I will describe. Looking towards the sea, but in the centre of the whole island, there was a plain which is said to have been the fairest of all plains and very fertile. Near the plain again, and also in the centre of the island at a distance of about fifty stadia, there was a mountain not very high on any side. In this mountain there dwelt one of the earth-born primeval men of that country, whose name was Evenor, and he had a wife named Leucippe, and they had an only daughter who was called Cleito. The maiden had already reached womanhood, when her father and mother died; Poseidon fell in love with her and had intercourse with her, and breaking the ground, inclosed the hill in which she dwelt all round, making alternate zones of sea and land larger and smaller, encircling one another; there were two of land and three of water, which he turned as with a lathe, each having its circumference equidistant every way from the centre, so that no man could get to the island, for ships and voyages were not as yet. He himself, being a god, found no difficulty in making special arrangements for the centre island, bringing up two springs of water from beneath the earth, one of warm water and the other of cold, and making every variety of food to spring up abundantly from the soil. He also begat and brought up five pairs of twin male children; and dividing the island of Atlantis into ten portions, he gave to the first-born of the eldest pair his mother's dwelling and the surrounding allotment, which was the largest and best, and made him king over the rest; the others he made princes, and gave them rule over many men, and a large territory. And he named them all; the eldest, who was the first king, he named Atlas, and after him the whole island and the ocean were called Atlantic. To his twin brother, who was born after him, and obtained as his lot the extremity of the island towards the pillars of Heracles, facing the country which is now called the region of Gades in that part of the world, he gave the name which in the Hellenic language is Eumelus, in the language of the country which is named after him, Gadeirus. Of the second pair of twins he called one Ampheres, and the other Evaemon. To the elder of the third pair of twins he gave the name Mneseus, and Autochthon to the one who followed him. Of the fourth pair of twins he called the elder Elasippus, and the younger Mestor. And of the fifth pair he gave to the elder the name of Azaes, and to the younger that of Diaprepes. All these and their descendants for many generations were the inhabitants and rulers of divers islands in the open sea; and also, as has been already said, they held sway in our direction over the country within the pillars as far as Egypt and Tyrrhenia. Now Atlas had a numerous and honourable family, and they retained the kingdom, the eldest son handing it on to his eldest for many generations; and they had such an amount of wealth as was never before possessed by kings and potentates, and is not likely ever to be again, and they were furnished with everything which they needed, both in the city and country. For because of the greatness of their empire many things were brought to them from foreign countries, and the island itself provided most of what was required by them for the uses of life. In the first place, they dug out of the earth whatever was to be found there, solid as well as fusile, and that which is now only a name and was then something more than a name, orichalcum, was dug out of the earth in many parts of the island, being more precious in those days than anything except gold. There was an abundance of wood for carpenter's work, and sufficient maintenance for tame and wild animals. Moreover, there were a great number of elephants in the island; for as there was provision for all other sorts of animals, both for those which live in lakes and marshes and rivers, and also for those which live in mountains and on plains, so there was for the animal which is the largest and most voracious of all. Also whatever fragrant things there now are in the earth, whether roots, or herbage, or woods, or essences which distil from fruit and flower, grew and thrived in that land; also the fruit which admits of cultivation, both the dry sort, which is given us for nourishment and any other which we use for food – we call them all by the common name of pulse, and the fruits having a hard rind, affording drinks and meats and ointments, and good store of chestnuts and the like, which furnish pleasure and amusement, and are fruits which spoil with keeping, and the pleasant kinds of dessert, with which we console ourselves after dinner, when we are tired of eating – all these that sacred island which then beheld the light of the sun, brought forth fair and wondrous and in infinite abundance. With such blessings the earth freely furnished them; meanwhile they went on constructing their temples and palaces and harbours and docks. And they arranged the whole country in the following manner:

First of all they bridged over the zones of sea which surrounded the ancient metropolis, making a road to and from the royal palace. And at the very beginning they built the palace in the habitation of the god and of their ancestors, which they continued to ornament in successive generations, every king surpassing the one who went before him to the utmost of his power, until they made the building a marvel to behold for size and for beauty. And beginning from the sea they bored a canal of three hundred feet in width and one hundred feet in depth and fifty stadia in length, which they carried through to the outermost zone, making a passage from the sea up to this, which became a harbour, and leaving an opening sufficient to enable the largest vessels to find ingress. Moreover, they divided at the bridges the zones of land which parted the zones of sea, leaving room for a single trireme to pass out of one zone into another, and they covered over the channels so as to leave a way underneath for the ships; for the banks were raised considerably above the water. Now the largest of the zones into which a passage was cut from the sea was three stadia in breadth, and the zone of land which came next of equal breadth; but the next two zones, the one of water, the other of land, were two stadia, and the one which surrounded the central island was a stadium only in width. The island in which the palace was situated had a diameter of five stadia. All this including the zones and the bridge, which was the sixth part of a stadium in width, they surrounded by a stone wall on every side, placing towers and gates on the bridges where the sea passed in. The stone which was used in the work they quarried from underneath the centre island, and from underneath the zones, on the outer as well as the inner side. One kind was white, another black, and a third red, and as they quarried, they at the same time hollowed out double docks, having roofs formed out of the native rock. Some of their buildings were simple, but in others they put together different stones, varying the colour to please the eye, and to be a natural source of delight. The entire circuit of the wall, which went round the outermost zone, they covered with a coating of brass, and the circuit of the next wall they coated with tin, and the third, which encompassed the citadel, flashed with the red light of orichalcum. The palaces in the interior of the citadel were constructed on this wise: – In the centre was a holy temple dedicated to Cleito and Poseidon, which remained inaccessible, and was surrounded by an enclosure of gold; this was the spot where the family of the ten princes first saw the light, and thither the people annually brought the fruits of the earth in their season from all the ten portions, to be an offering to each of the ten. Here was Poseidon's own temple which was a stadium in length, and half a stadium in width, and of a proportionate height, having a strange barbaric appearance. All the outside of the temple, with the exception of the pinnacles, they covered with silver, and the pinnacles with gold. In the interior of the temple the roof was of ivory, curiously wrought everywhere with gold and silver and orichalcum; and all the other parts, the walls and pillars and floor, they coated with orichalcum. In the temple they placed statues of gold: there was the god himself standing in a chariot – the charioteer of six winged horses – and of such a size that he touched the roof of the building with his head; around him there were a hundred Nereids riding on dolphins, for such was thought to be the number of them by the men of those days. There were also in the interior of the temple other images which had been dedicated by private persons. And around the temple on the outside were placed statues of gold of all the descendants of the ten kings and of their wives, and there were many other great offerings of kings and of private persons, coming both from the city itself and from the foreign cities over which they held sway. There was an altar too, which in size and workmanship corresponded to this magnificence, and the palaces, in like manner, answered to the greatness of the kingdom and the glory of the temple.

In the next place, they had fountains, one of cold and another of hot water, in gracious plenty flowing; and they were wonderfully adapted for use by reason of the pleasantness and excellence of their waters. They constructed buildings about them and planted suitable trees, also they made cisterns, some open to the heaven, others roofed over, to be used in winter as warm baths; there were the kings' baths, and the baths of private persons, which were kept apart; and there were separate baths for women, and for horses and cattle, and to each of them they gave as much adornment as was suitable. Of the water which ran off they carried some to the grove of Poseidon, where were growing all manner of trees of wonderful height and beauty, owing to the excellence of the soil, while the remainder was conveyed by aqueducts along the bridges to the outer circles; and there were many temples built and dedicated to many gods; also gardens and places of exercise, some for men, and others for horses in both of the two islands formed by the zones; and in the centre of the larger of the two there was set apart a race-course of a stadium in width, and in length allowed to extend all round the island, for horses to race in. Also there were guard-houses at intervals for the guards, the more trusted of whom were appointed to keep watch in the lesser zone, which was nearer the Acropolis; while the most trusted of all had houses given them within the citadel, near the persons of the kings. The docks were full of triremes and naval stores, and all things were quite ready for use. Enough of the plan of the royal palace.

Leaving the palace and passing out across the three harbours, you came to a wall which began at the sea and went all round: this was everywhere distant fifty stadia from the largest zone or harbour, and enclosed the whole, the ends meeting at the mouth of the channel which led to the sea. The entire area was densely crowded with habitations; and the canal and the largest of the harbours were full of vessels and merchants coming from all parts, who, from their numbers, kept up a multitudinous sound of human voices, and din and clatter of all sorts night and day.

I have described the city and the environs of the ancient palace nearly in the words of Solon, and now I must endeavour to represent to you the nature and arrangement of the rest of the land. The whole country was said by him to be very lofty and precipitous on the side of the sea, but the country immediately about and surrounding the city was a level plain, itself surrounded by mountains which descended towards the sea; it was smooth and even, and of an oblong shape, extending in one direction three thousand stadia, but across the centre inland it was two thousand stadia. This part of the island looked towards the south, and was sheltered from the north. The surrounding mountains were celebrated for their number and size and beauty, far beyond any which still exist, having in them also many wealthy villages of country folk, and rivers, and lakes, and meadows supplying food enough for every animal, wild or tame, and much wood of various sorts, abundant for each and every kind of work.

I will now describe the plain, as it was fashioned by nature and by the labours of many generations of kings through long ages. It was for the most part rectangular and oblong, and where falling out of the straight line followed the circular ditch. The depth, and width, and length of this ditch were incredible, and gave the impression that a work of such extent, in addition to so many others, could never have been artificial. Nevertheless I must say what I was told. It was excavated to the depth of a hundred feet, and its breadth was a stadium everywhere; it was carried round the whole of the plain, and was ten thousand stadia in length. It received the streams which came down from the mountains, and winding round the plain and meeting at the city, was there let off into the sea. Further inland, likewise, straight canals of a hundred feet in width were cut from it through the plain, and again let off into the ditch leading to the sea: these canals were at intervals of a hundred stadia, and by them they brought down the wood from the mountains to the city, and conveyed the fruits of the earth in ships, cutting transverse passages from one canal into another, and to the city. Twice in the year they gathered the fruits of the earth – in winter having the benefit of the rains of heaven, and in summer the water which the land supplied by introducing streams from the canals.

As to the population, each of the lots in the plain had to find a leader for the men who were fit for military service, and the size of a lot was a square of ten stadia each way, and the total number of all the lots was sixty thousand. And of the inhabitants of the mountains and of the rest of the country there was also a vast multitude, which was distributed among the lots and had leaders assigned to them according to their districts and villages. The leader was required to furnish for the war the sixth portion of a war-chariot, so as to make up a total of ten thousand chariots; also two horses and riders for them, and a pair of chariot-horses without a seat, accompanied by a horseman who could fight on foot carrying a small shield, and having a charioteer who stood behind the man-at-arms to guide the two horses; also, he was bound to furnish two heavy-armed soldiers, two archers, two slingers, three stone-shooters and three javelin-men, who were light-armed, and four sailors to make up the complement of twelve hundred ships. Such was the military order of the royal city – the order of the other nine governments varied, and it would be wearisome to recount their several differences.

As to offices and honours, the following was the arrangement from the first. Each of the ten kings in his own division and in his own city had the absolute control of the citizens, and, in most cases, of the laws, punishing and slaying whomsoever he would. Now the order of precedence among them and their mutual relations were regulated by the commands of Poseidon which the law had handed down. These were inscribed by the first kings on a pillar of orichalcum, which was situated in the middle of the island, at the temple of Poseidon, whither the kings were gathered together every fifth and every sixth year alternately, thus giving equal honour to the odd and to the even number. And when they were gathered together they consulted about their common interests, and enquired if any one had transgressed in anything, and passed judgment, and before they passed judgment they gave their pledges to one another on this wise: – There were bulls who had the range of the temple of Poseidon; and the ten kings, being left alone in the temple, after they had offered prayers to the god that they might capture the victim which was acceptable to him, hunted the bulls, without weapons, but with staves and nooses; and the bull which they caught they led up to the pillar and cut its throat over the top of it so that the blood fell upon the sacred inscription. Now on the pillar, besides the laws, there was inscribed an oath invoking mighty curses on the disobedient. When therefore, after slaying the bull in the accustomed manner, they had burnt its limbs, they filled a bowl of wine and cast in a clot of blood for each of them; the rest of the victim they put in the fire, after having purified the column all round. Then they drew from the bowl in golden cups, and pouring a libation on the fire, they swore that they would judge according to the laws on the pillar, and would punish him who in any point had already transgressed them, and that for the future they would not, if they could help, offend against the writing on the pillar, and would neither command others, nor obey any ruler who commanded them, to act otherwise than according to the laws of their father Poseidon. This was the prayer which each of them offered up for himself and for his descendants, at the same time drinking and dedicating the cup out of which he drank in the temple of the god; and after they had supped and satisfied their needs, when darkness came on, and the fire about the sacrifice was cool, all of them put on most beautiful azure robes, and, sitting on the ground, at night, over the embers of the sacrifices by which they had sworn, and extinguishing all the fire about the temple, they received and gave judgment, if any of them had an accusation to bring against any one; and when they had given judgment, at daybreak they wrote down their sentences on a golden tablet, and dedicated it together with their robes to be a memorial.

There were many special laws affecting the several kings inscribed about the temples, but the most important was the following: They were not to take up arms against one another, and they were all to come to the rescue if any one in any of their cities attempted to overthrow the royal house; like their ancestors, they were to deliberate in common about war and other matters, giving the supremacy to the descendants of Atlas. And the king was not to have the power of life and death over any of his kinsmen unless he had the assent of the majority of the ten.

Such was the vast power which the god settled in the lost island of Atlantis; and this he afterwards directed against our land for the following reasons, as tradition tells: For many generations, as long as the divine nature lasted in them, they were obedient to the laws, and well-affectioned towards the god, whose seed they were; for they possessed true and in every way great spirits, uniting gentleness with wisdom in the various chances of life, and in their intercourse with one another. They despised everything but virtue, caring little for their present state of life, and thinking lightly of the possession of gold and other property, which seemed only a burden to them; neither were they intoxicated by luxury; nor did wealth deprive them of their self-control; but they were sober, and saw clearly that all these goods are increased by virtue and friendship with one another, whereas by too great regard and respect for them, they are lost and friendship with them. By such reflections and by the continuance in them of a divine nature, the qualities which we have described grew and increased among them; but when the divine portion began to fade away, and became diluted too often and too much with the mortal admixture, and the human nature got the upper hand, they then, being unable to bear their fortune, behaved unseemly, and to him who had an eye to see grew visibly debased, for they were losing the fairest of their precious gifts; but to those who had no eye to see the true happiness, they appeared glorious and blessed at the very time when they were full of avarice and unrighteous power. Zeus, the god of gods, who rules according to law, and is able to see into such things, perceiving that an honourable race was in a woeful plight, and wanting to inflict punishment on them, that they might be chastened and improve, collected all the gods into their most holy habitation, which, being placed in the centre of the world, beholds all created things. And when he had called them together, he spake as follows—[*]

* *The rest of the Dialogue of Critias has been lost.*

A Promise in Bronze

Ash Arya

***JUST AS** the wheel of Time neither stops nor slows down for anyone, so the soul of Time neither melts nor is moved by individual events and actions. Time watches passively as civilizations come and go, letting Nature take over in the wake of one to clean house for the next. It's then up to those who inhabit this dominion of Time to leave their mark upon it.*

Kalaa appreciated the sight of the arcade, abuzz once more. The citadel walls were whole again, taller than before. The floodwaters that'd invaded the lower city were gone, the Sumerians who'd been asked to delay their monthly visit were back. It was time for business again.

"It's very hot, sweetling." Kalaa caught a petite claw reaching for her famed mango pudding, blowing on the earthen vessel to convey her point. "Why don't we wait for your Elder to pay for it while it cools down?"

She beamed as the boy ran and fetched an older woman, probably a mother. A merchant ought to know the speech of her customers and Kalaa deemed herself a *thorough trader*.

A thorough trader thriving in one of the largest urban centers of the Harappan world, at that.

At noon, panting between plating a loaf of venison and stirring the meat-and-herbs stew, Kalaa marveled at the seemingly endless influx of traders. *This* was the kind of deluge she appreciated.

Two more days of such footfall and I shall finally be able to commission some bangles…

"Excuse me. Please…" a rough voice, bordering on despair, cut through Kalaa's mental bookkeeping. She turned to see a broad-shouldered woman, a few years her senior, dressed in a knee-length wrap and a breastband that suited her curvaceous body all too well. She wore a new-looking pair of jute shoes but was entirely devoid of ornaments. Not even a headdress to cover those flowing locks, matted from travel. "I was told I could get some food here," stuttered she.

Kalaa assumed a smug look, "Even if you hadn't been *told*…" She pointed to the array of dishes, prepared and unprepared, then smiled awkwardly, loathing herself for her idiotic response.

But the stunning foreigner was unheeding of Kalaa's buffoonery, herself in the throes of hesitance. "I have nothing to trade. Gave my last quartz to secure passage on the ship."

An intrigued Kalaa immediately wanted to prod into the foreigner's story. But the thorough-trader-Kalaa only asked, "Didn't they give you any food along the way?"

"They did. I just," the foreigner tarried somewhat reluctantly, "ate it all."

Kalaa smiled to ease the sting of her embarrassed confession. "I enjoy food too."

The relief in the foreigner's round, brown eyes made Kalaa's heart skip a beat. For a second she considered offering the woman some food for free.

A thorough trader except when confronted by a dazzling woman, her own voice taunted.

Behind the woman, a queue was building up. Kalaa thought fast while scooping up some pudding and dolloping it on a circular vessel she'd made out of banyan leaves. "I can't just give you free food," she whispered, subtly indicating the prying ears. She couldn't risk the whole shipload of foreigners walking up to her with sob stories in exchange for free food.

"Of course not," the traveler flushed, announcing loudly, "I mean to pay you back."

Kalaa's brow puckered. Debts were something which the city traders only accepted of native citizens. It was unheard of to extend credit even to a fellow Harappan who came from outside the citadel. A *foreigner* then was a dubious gamble. "What, on your next visit?"

"No, I..." The traveler hesitated some more before sighing and declaring. "I'm here to stay."

"Stay?" Kalaa wondered if she'd gotten her word-meanings mixed up, only to realize that the words weren't spoken in the foreigners' language but *hers*. "Why?"

The traveler now addressed only her, in *her* Harappan dialect.

"The *priestess* said this is where I belong. That this is where I'll find a home."

"Priestess?" Kalaa echoed, unfamiliar with the lone foreign word the traveler had used amidst a rather fine flow of Harappan ones. Kalaa only now noticed that her skin too appeared darker than the other foreigners. Closer to her own...

"Important woman," explained the traveler, "Wise woman."

Despite her curt words, Kalaa caught the vulnerability in her eyes. She nodded, whispering in Harappan, "Well, if a wise woman sent you." Then, squaring her shoulders, she spoke loudly in Sumerian, "Even though you're *staying*, I still can't give you free food. I *can* give you however, a chance to earn your keep. You can help me and get yourself a meal of your choosing."

A slight smile appeared on the traveler's drawn face. "I can pick anything?"

Kalaa nodded, amused. "Know that the duration of your service will be weighed against your purchases." As the woman eagerly accepted her terms and asked for some mango pudding, Kalaa felt a strange sense of pride in herself and her work. Trying to keep her tone light, she taunted, "Quite the taste you have. I should inform you this is my priciest dish and alone will cost you the entirety of an hour's service."

"That's fine," the woman laughed, her first, "I shall pay for it with unmatched assistance."

She did. By sundown, not only had Kalaa taken full advantage of the foreigners' influx, rather she'd done so with novel precision. One that took her a step closer to her beautiful bronze bangles. She told the foreigner – *Mishrakeshi* – as much when she closed shop.

* * *

Mishrakeshi gleefully accepted her day's last earnings, barley cakes and chicken soup.

The slim Harappan girl watched intently as she bagged her dinner, twirling a lock of curly hair on a long finger as she asked, "Where will you stay? I don't suppose you have lodgings?"

Her hands froze on her jute satchel. She panicked, until she saw a gleam in Kalaa's eyes. "I'm petrified of incurring more debt from you," she jested, bones aching from the day's work.

Not that Kalaa looked any less fatigued. "Yet, it's inevitable. You won't find work right away, outsider that you are. But you *will* need food tomorrow..." she trailed off, probably having noticed her wince. Yet, she boldly asked, "You didn't think this through, did you?"

Mishrakeshi sighed, mumbling only, "They didn't want me there," before pursing her lips anew.

She couldn't bear to speak of it, even to a near-stranger. The priestess had told her to forget her otherness and talking about it was certainly not the way to do so.

It was then somewhat relieving to hear Kalaa say, "You can stay at my house."

Equal parts surprised and fatigued, Mishrakeshi accepted the offer at once.

Soon they were immersed in the crowd exiting the arcade in the upper city and fanning out into the many rectilinear lanes leading into the residential lower city. Rows and columns of double-storied houses organized in straight lines, each street a systematic replica of the other.

Trees lined the sidewalks which were separated from the middle path with a... very narrow tunnel with dark water flowing through it.

"What are these tunnels… these cracks?" Mishrakeshi was unsure if these were the right words.

Kalaa, though, easily articulated her confusion. "Drains. They often surprise the foreigners."

"*Drains*? What are they for?"

"They carry away the sewage from the houses. Wastewater, human refuse, and such."

The very idea produced galling images in Mishrakeshi's head. "You defecate in your homes?"

"Not just anywhere!" Kalaa exclaimed back. "We have a room for it. A very small room with a very small hole in it and that's the *only* place we relieve ourselves in."

Mishrakeshi felt both stupid and confused as she mumbled, "Oh."

Kalaa scoffed, "Never ask this to anyone else or you won't be *belonging* here anytime soon."

Despite Kalaa's lack of malice, her words hurt and Mishrakeshi couldn't hide her sorrow.

Kalaa hurriedly changed the subject. "My house is just in the next street. Luckily for you, I've just moved out of my parental home and in with my sisters. Or else you'd be answering a dozen questions from each one of my six parents."

Mishrakeshi tripped over her own feet. "How many—"

"Err… six. Two Mas, four Pitas." Kalaa answered, steadying her by the elbow. "It's called a family," she pressed. "They aren't all always there—"

"How do you tell who your real Ma and Pita are? I'm just curious." Mishrakeshi asked after due consideration. *It isn't rude if it's coming from a place of genuine curiosity, she told herself. And if there's no place for my curiosity here then it's doubtful there'd be a place for me.*

Kalaa, thankfully, was unperturbed. "They all are."

"But – biologically?" she let the question hang, giving Kalaa the option to ignore her enquiry.

At length, the dark-eyed girl shrugged. "What does it matter?"

That meagre but earnest reply reduced Mishrakeshi's apprehensions a great deal.

So, matching Kalaa's smile as they resumed their walk, she prodded, "How many sisters?"

"Two," Kalaa chirped. "Ameeyati and Sabrivalla."

"Just two?" Mishrakeshi smirked, "I was preparing myself to greet a house full of gorgeous Harappan belles like yourself." She felt the embarrassment from those words only when a blush traveled over Kalaa's round face and colored her high cheekbones.

Yet, Kalaa sounded unfazed, "You still should. For, between Amee Didi's sworn partners and Sabri's lover visiting, we do have a full house. I hope you won't mind?"

Mishrakeshi instantly shook her head. "I've lived in crammed spaces all my life. I'm just so grateful you'd let me intrude upon your space…" Ever mediocre with words, she took Kalaa's hand and clasped it between both of hers, hoping to convey how she valued her kindness.

The girl only jested, "I need not your gratitude, Mishri ji, for I have your impeccable assistantship. I shall like to avail of it as long as I can. It's been a pleasure to meet you."

Mishrakeshi suspected, or hoped, those last words to be more than a jest.

She, on her part, replied earnestly, "Likewise."

* * *

Kalaa admired Mishrakeshi's unending surprise over the city's workings. In the last six days, she'd used her leisure hours to show Mishrakeshi most of their metropolis. From the Great Granary to the cattle farms and foundries in the upper city, to the Gathering Circles where the elders convened, and the fields on the periphery of the lower city. Mishrakeshi loved it all.

So, last night, Kalaa took her along on her jaunt to the bronzesmith – having finally collected enough bronze to have herself made a small set of bangles. Four were what she ultimately obtained. They felt like forty. Moreover, the place gladdened Mishrakeshi beyond expectations.

The only place Kalaa had left to show her was the one she was taking her to now.

The ceremony to thank Mother Nature for giving them enough strength to cope with the flood. The celebratory ritual at the Great Bath.

"So many people. Everyone looks so enthusiastic," Mishrakeshi murmured.

Seeing her glee, Kalaa refrained from saying that there were actually *fewer* people than usual. This month's flood, the third this year, had made three whole families migrate to the relative security of Lothal. It petrified Kalaa to see people she'd known all her life leaving so abruptly.

"So what do we do in this ceremony—" Mishrakeshi's question was cut off by a gasp, just as they rounded the high wall encompassing the Great Bath. She gaped wide-eyed at the rectangular stepwell, slowly taking in the people descending into the freshwaters.

"Come along," Kalaa nudged her when she remained frozen, removing her jewels, and placing the ensemble among a heap on one of the dry, top slabs. "We're to join them."

"Join them?" the alarm in Mishrakeshi's voice made Kalaa halt. "Like so?" she demanded, indicating Kalaa's tiny form, naked save the cowry-string around her neck and the wrap around her waist.

Kalaa perceived discomfort on her new friend's part. "That's the ritual," she cautiously drawled, adding quickly, "You don't have to—"

"Good," Mishrakeshi inserted, "Because I shan't."

Kalaa cocked her head to a side, "Might I ask why?"

"Why?" Mishri echoed wide-eyed, "They'll all *look*. That's why!"

Kalaa couldn't contain the ensuing scoff. "You are pretty, Mishri ji. But not that much. They're here for Ma Nature, not you. Even if they needed diversion, they each have their own," she indicated the paired off youths and adults who comprised the majority of the gathering.

Mishrakeshi, though, was unmoved. "I shall wait for you here to finish your ritual," she declared, fisted hands crossed over her chest.

Kalaa laughed. "Very well. Maybe next time."

"Not unless Ma Nature herself drags me by the scruff of my neck and shoves me into that pool."

Kalaa winced. "Oh, careful what you wish for. There are just too many stairs there. Maybe we could ask Ma Nature to give you enough courage and inclination to come voluntarily."

"Sounds unlikely."

"So does a wanderer finding a home. You managed that well enough."

A startled Mishrakeshi frowned incredulously, "Have I?"

Kalaa simply took her hand and placed her bangles on it. "Take care of my hard-earned treasure until I return, won't you?" She dashed away without giving Mishrakeshi a chance to respond.

* * *

Mishrakeshi gawked after Kalaa as she carefully descended the wet steps and joined five youths sporting on a deep end of the pool.

She couldn't fathom how they felt no apprehensions, no fear of prying eyes, frolicking like that.

However, she soon realized that true to Kalaa's claims, there was no disconcerting ogling.

But they'd look at me, for I'm different, Mishrakeshi's brain prompted, recalling the sad sight of the villagers bidding her adieu. They'd grieved her departure but deemed it inevitable. For she had a wanderer's blood. Gritting her teeth, she recalled the Priestess' words:

Forget you are different and different you no longer will be. Craft your belonging and all the universe shall aid you in becoming worthy.

Mishrakeshi wondered if the old woman had only said those words to ease her pain, to give her hope long enough to get her out of their village. But then her gaze fell on the bangles in her hand. Seeing them, she understood. Whether by fate or by sheer stupidity, this was where she now was. These were the people who'd taken her into their city, the girl who'd fed her and given her shelter, the youths who now waved to her from the pool. Waving back, she smiled down at the bangles.

Perhaps she could make the Priestess' words come true.

* * *

Kalaa pestled the lapis lazuli in the noon's silence, admiring the blue stone being pulverized while Amee Didi prepared the resin and the beeswax to make the dye for her shop.

The foreign traders never tired of the blue brilliance. Nor did Kalaa.

"What's going on with that foreigner-not-foreigner of yours? A quaint creature, that one." Amee Didi broke the silence.

"She *is*," Kalaa gleefully agreed, recalling all she'd seen and heard from the aspiring Harappan in the last two weeks, ending with, "Do you know what she did yesterday?"

Didi theatrically shoved away her equipment and placed her chin on one hand.

Kalaa laughed and began. "You heard of the travelers from the far-off country, yes? Tall, broad shouldered, males all," she squeezed her nose. "The arcade was awash with them, but none could understand what they wanted. For an entire hour, trade was sluggish. I was losing all hope of business when, lo and behold, Mishri ji begins yelling at the top of her lungs. Gibberish that means nothing to me. But it meant something to the foreigners who began ambling towards my stall. In no time, I was running to prepare more pudding, more stew, more *everything*. Other vendors came to *borrow* Mishri—"

"Quite the wonder," Amee Didi cut in, smiling crookedly, "So, you gave her the day off?"

"She quite deserves it." Kalaa felt compelled to add, "I don't always need assistance. Actually, I never needed it before she showed up. Besides, *she needs* time, to secure herself the apprenticeship she's been eyeing. Leena, the bronzesmith, is a tough nut to crack."

"Right, and how'd she do that between working with you until late noon and loitering around the city with you until sunset."

Kalaa frowned, "I'm just showing her around."

"And dragging her to community rituals. Baths and dances and whatnot."

"Someone must. She's new here."

"And bringing her to family dinners."

"Well, the woman wants so badly to belong—" Kalaa bit her lip, mortified. "I've said nothing."

"Yes, you have. Explain?" Amee Didi raised a brow. "Either you tell me, and we pestle this down with the blue or I ask *her*—"

"Don't you dare," Kalaa pointed the pestle threateningly at Didi, then sighed, "It's just something she said. *Refusing* vehemently to say more." It was the truth, for despite her unsubtle prodding, Mishrakeshi persistently shot down all her enquiries about her life in Sumer.

As if reading her disappointment, Didi threw a piece of resin at her, saying, "Best not to prod. She'll share it with you if she sees you as worthy."

Those words made a nest in Kalaa's mind. "You're actually right," she mumbled. She didn't know what'd be *worthy* in Mishrakeshi's eyes, but she dearly hoped she'd be it, someday.

* * *

Mishrakeshi woke one morning, three months into her stay at the apprentices' residence, with a dreadful realization.

She'd spent an entire month living under Kalaa's roof, often eating a meal beyond her daily earnings. She'd used Sabri's cinnabar to paint her face and Amee's lapis lazuli to dye her skirt.

And she'd never repaid the pudding-girl or her sisters for any of it! That had to be remedied.

She had to give Kalaa something. And she wanted it to be something special, at least for her if not for her sisters. Her best piece of work perhaps?

But artistic grandeur isn't something to be coerced into existence by agitated minds.

Which is why, when she went to meet Kalaa the next day at one of the Gathering Circles in the lower city, Mishrakeshi brought her not a seminal work of art but just some two dozen varieties of that 'bangle' ornament that she admired so much, clumsily bundled up in her spare garment.

Unable to come up with anything truly ingenious, she'd simply melted her practice bronze, collected over months, to make those bangles, engraved with commonplace motifs.

She hadn't expected them to make Kalaa squeal until passersby began to eye them askance.

"But these are just brilliant! All the bangles I could want! And how finely you've engraved all these motifs onto them."

"It's really rather amateurish," Mishrakeshi stuttered, looking around in embarrassment.

"Rubbish! I've never seen such craftsmanship. I would've said so the other day itself when you brought me those *bowls* to use for my pudding. Mishri," she grasped her hand when she was done putting all the twenty-four bangles on, "how're you so good at this?"

Seeing Kalaa eyeing her in amazement and keen to know the story of her being, Mishrakeshi felt a rush of warmth. First time in years, she didn't fear judgement, and so gladly shared her tale.

"My mother was a sculptor from hereabouts. A wanderer in Sumer. She traveled far and wide. Until she had me and settled down in one of the small villages. They loved her, almost like family. She taught their children the art of sculpting from metal and from clay. These motifs you like so much came like breath to her. Sadly, at the time she died of a fever, the village had a new headwoman. One who wasn't very keen on our family, especially me, for I was past twenty and unclaimed. Not to mention my *foreign* appearance. Plus, Ma had created enough sculptors among the villagers. There was no need for me, only to get rid of me. There were those who opposed but the headwoman was so… hostile. By the end, I myself chose to leave."

Kalaa, sitting across from her on a stone, listened patiently all along. Mishrakeshi, at one point, had risen to walk around, hard pressed to continue when she saw her words sadden Kalaa. She was facing the opening of the woods ahead when Kalaa turned her by the elbow and took her in her arms. "I'm sorry you had to endure that. But I must tell you one thing. The loss is all theirs." She said emphatically, cupping Mishrakeshi's face, holding her gaze.

A surprised laugh escaped her, and she leaned in. "And the gain is all mine, I suppose? To have found this land and this home?"

"Indeed," Kalaa ran a thumb over her jaw. "Yours. And mine," she whispered, a moment before drawing her lips in a lingering kiss. A kiss deep enough to fulfill the Priestess' prophecy.

* * *

Kalaa couldn't fathom the force of nature that was Mishrakeshi.

Courting her was proving to be an intrigue like none other. One day she'd deem herself a slave to Kalaa's whims while on others she'd decline every proposition she made.

It took her months to realize that Mishri's temperament was linked intrinsically to her artistic success and failure. There was something she wanted to make, she'd told Kalaa, something that'd both survive her and immortalize her, but she knew not what it was to be. Kalaa barely even knew what those words meant.

They weren't however as perplexing as seeing Mishrakeshi walking up to her...

At the Great Baths. On a ritual evening. Removing her necklace...

"Are you... really doing this?" she asked when Mishri came to a halt in front of her, placing her necklace and amulet beside Kalaa's. Mishrakeshi's response was a coy smile. Kalaa's own turned teasing, "They'll *look* at you, you know?" she quoted her mad words.

Never expecting a grin in return. Mishrakeshi bent her lips to Kalaa's ears and whispered, "As long as you're one of them, I really don't mind."

* * *

Mishrakeshi hadn't expected to find her home and her inspiration in a single, lithe girl.

Yet ultimately, she did.

The realization dawned suddenly as she sat on the porch in the wee hours of morning, musing how she'd gone from being a guest in Kalaa's home, fawned on and treated with formality, to a part of the family, casually handed out chores at feasts and dinners. All in a few months...

"You didn't wake me," Kalaa's voice rang in the doorway behind her.

Mishri recalled she was supposed to awaken Kalaa before dawn so she could make the mango pudding for Amee Didi's journey. Wincing, she turned to apologize.

But the sight that greeted her took her breath away.

In that space between their home and the world stood her Kalaa, clad only in her bangles – the four bought by her and the twenty-four of Mishri's making – and the cowry necklace that was Mother Nature's insignia. With her hair in a hurried bun and a hand on her hip, she looked ethereal. Her head tilted backwards ever so slightly and the miniscule bend in her knee rendered her indignation madly endearing.

It was watching her, like this, that Mishrakeshi concluded, "You really are."

Kalaa frowned, "What?"

"Kalaa," Mishrakeshi whispered, "Craft-manifest. My craft," she murmured, pulling Kalaa onto her lap and kissing her heartily.

"Well," Kalaa pecked her cheek before leaving, "Now I *must* see you put *your Kalaa* to use."

* * *

Kalaa did. A year later.

The occasion was a solemn one, frighteningly so, for Kalaa. They were leaving for Lothal.

The floods had become an incessantly recurring phenomena in the last few months. The city could no longer recuperate at its earlier rate. It was losing its brilliant sheen.

It was among such tumultuous circumstances that Mishrakeshi gave Kalaa a piece of her Kalaa.

She uttered no vows, made no grand claims, but simply promised to stay by Kalaa's side in times good and bad, and placed on her hand a tiny piece of metal.

Kalaa herself, cast in bronze, no bigger than the palm of her hand.

The belonging Mishri had crafted for herself. The promise that assuaged all of Kalaa's fears.

Mishrakeshi called it a memory captured by her heart, a testament to her Kalaa, her home.

The world – unaware of the lovers in the lost metropolis – would call her *The Dancing Girl of Mohenjo Daro*.

The New Atlantis

Francis Bacon

WE SAILED from Peru (where we had continued for the space of one whole year), for China and Japan, by the South Sea; taking with us victuals for twelve months; and had good winds from the east, though soft and weak, for five months space, and more. But the wind came about, and settled in the west for many days, so as we could make little or no way, and were sometime in purpose to turn back. But then again there arose strong and great winds from the south, with a point east, which carried us up (for all that we could do) towards the north; by which time our victuals failed us, though we had made good spare of them. So that finding ourselves, in the midst of the greatest wilderness of waters in the world, without victuals, we gave ourselves for lost men and prepared for death. Yet we did lift up our hearts and voices to God above, who showeth his wonders in the deep, beseeching him of his mercy, that as in the beginning he discovered the face of the deep, and brought forth dry land, so he would now discover land to us, that we might not perish.

And it came to pass that the next day about evening we saw within a kenning before us, towards the north, as it were thick clouds, which did put us in some hope of land; knowing how that part of the South Sea was utterly unknown; and might have islands, or continents, that hitherto were not come to light. Wherefore we bent our course thither, where we saw the appearance of land, all that night; and in the dawning of the next day, we might plainly discern that it was a land; flat to our sight, and full of boscage; which made it show the more dark. And after an hour and a half's sailing, we entered into a good haven, being the port of a fair city; not great indeed, but well built, and that gave a pleasant view from the sea: and we thinking every minute long, till we were on land, came close to the shore, and offered to land. But straightways we saw divers of the people, with bastons in their hands (as it were) forbidding us to land; yet without any cries of fierceness, but only as warning us off, by signs that they made. Whereupon being not a little discomforted, we were advising with ourselves, what we should do.

During which time, there made forth to us a small boat, with about eight persons in it; whereof one of them had in his hand a tipstaff of a yellow cane, tipped at both ends with blue, who came aboard our ship, without any show of distrust at all. And when he saw one of our number, present himself somewhat before the rest, he drew forth a little scroll of parchment (somewhat yellower than our parchment, and shining like the leaves of writing tables, but otherwise soft and flexible,) and delivered it to our foremost man. In which scroll were written in ancient Hebrew, and in ancient Greek, and in good Latin of the school, and in Spanish, these words:

> *Land ye not, none of you; and provide to be gone from this coast, within sixteen days, except you have further time given you. Meanwhile, if you want fresh water or victuals, or help for your sick, or that your ship needeth repairs, write down your wants, and you shall have that, which belongeth to mercy.*

This scroll was signed with a stamp of cherubim: wings, not spread, but hanging downwards; and by them a cross. This being delivered, the officer returned, and left only a servant with us to receive our answer.

Consulting hereupon amongst ourselves, we were much perplexed. The denial of landing and hasty warning us away troubled us much; on the other side, to find that the people had languages, and were so full of humanity, did comfort us not a little. And above all, the sign of the cross to that instrument was to us a great rejoicing, and as it were a certain presage of good. Our answer was in the Spanish tongue; that for our ship, it was well; for we had rather met with calms and contrary winds than any tempests. For our sick, they were many, and in very ill case; so that if they were not permitted to land, they ran danger of their lives. Our other wants we set down in particular; adding, That we had some little store of merchandise, which if it pleased them to deal for, it might supply our wants, without being chargeable unto them. We offered some reward in pistolets unto the servant, and a piece of crimson velvet to be presented to the officer; but the servant took them not, nor would scarce look upon them; and so left us, and went back in another little boat, which was sent for him.

About three hours after we had dispatched our answer, there came towards us a person (as it seemed) of place. He had on him a gown with wide sleeves, of a kind of water chamolet, of an excellent azure colour, fair more glossy than ours; his under apparel was green; and so was his hat, being in the form of a turban, daintily made, and not so huge as the Turkish turbans; and the locks of his hair came down below the brims of it. A reverend man was he to behold. He came in a boat, gilt in some part of it, with four persons more only in that boat; and was followed by another boat, wherein were some twenty. When he was come within a flightshot of our ship, signs were made to us, that we should send forth some to meet him upon the water; which we presently did in our ship-boat, sending the principal man amongst us save one, and four of our number with him.

When we were come within six yards of their boat, they called to us to stay, and not to approach farther; which we did. And thereupon the man, whom I before described, stood up, and with a loud voice, in Spanish, asked, "Are ye Christians?" We answered, "We were"; fearing the less, because of the cross we had seen in the subscription. At which answer the said person lifted up his right hand towards Heaven, and drew it softly to his mouth (which is the gesture they use, when they thank God); and then said: "If ye will swear (all of you) by the merits of the Saviour, that ye are no pirates, nor have shed blood, lawfully, nor unlawfully within forty days past, you may have licence to come on land." We said, "We were all ready to take that oath." Whereupon one of those that were with him, being (as it seemed) a notary, made an entry of this act. Which done, another of the attendants of the great person which was with him in the same boat, after his Lord had spoken a little to him, said aloud: "My Lord would have you know, that it is not of pride, or greatness, that he cometh not aboard your ship; but for that in your answer you declare that you have many sick amongst you, he was warned by the Conservator of Health of the city that he should keep a distance." We bowed ourselves towards him, and answered, "We were his humble servants; and accounted for great honour, and singular humanity towards us, that which was already done; but hoped well, that the nature of the sickness of our men was not infectious." So he returned; and a while after came the Notary to us aboard our ship; holding in his hand a fruit of that country, like an orange, but of colour between orange-tawney and scarlet; which cast a most excellent odour. He used it (as it seemeth) for a preservative against infection. He gave us our oath; "By the name of Jesus, and his merits," and after told us, that the next day, by six of the Clock, in the Morning, we should be sent to, and brought to the Strangers' House (so he called it), where we should be accommodated of things, both for our whole, and for our sick. So he left us; and when we offered him some pistolets, he smiling said, "He must not be twice paid for one labour," meaning (as I take it) that he had salary sufficient of the State for his service. For (as I after learned) they call an officer that taketh rewards, 'twice paid'.

The next morning early, there came to us the same officer that came to us at first with his cane, and told us, he came to conduct us to the Strangers' House; and that he had prevented the hour, because we might have the whole day before us, for our business. "For," said he, "if you will follow my advice, there shall first go with me some few of you, and see the place, and how it may be made convenient for you; and then you may send for your sick, and the rest of your number, which ye will bring on land." We thanked him, and said, "That this care, which he took of desolate strangers, God would reward." And so six of us went on land with him: and when we were on land, he went before us, and turned to us, and said, "He was but our servant, and our guide." He led us through three fair streets; and all the way we went, there were gathered some people on both sides, standing in a row; but in so civil a fashion, as if it had been, not to wonder at us, but to welcome us: and divers of them, as we passed by them, put their arms a little abroad; which is their gesture, when they did bid any welcome.

The Strangers' House is a fair and spacious house, built of brick, of somewhat a bluer colour than our brick; and with handsome windows, some of glass, some of a kind of cambric oiled. He brought us first into a fair parlour above stairs, and then asked us, "What number of persons we were? And how many sick?" We answered, "We were in all (sick and whole), one and fifty persons, whereof our sick were seventeen." He desired us to have patience a little, and to stay till he came back to us; which was about an hour after; and then he led us to see the chambers which were provided for us, being in number nineteen: they having cast it (as it seemeth) that four of those chambers, which were better than the rest, might receive four of the principal men of our company; and lodge them alone by themselves; and the other fifteen chambers were to lodge us two and two together. The chambers were handsome and cheerful chambers, and furnished civilly. Then he led us to a long gallery, like a dorture, where he showed us all along the one side (for the other side was but wall and window), seventeen cells, very neat ones, having partitions of cedar wood. Which gallery and cells, being in all forty, many more than we needed, were instituted as an infirmary for sick persons. And he told us withal, that as any of our sick waxed well, he might be removed from his cell, to a chamber; for which purpose there were set forth ten spare chambers, besides the number we spake of before. This done, he brought us back to the parlour, and lifting up his cane a little (as they do when they give any charge or command), said to us, "Ye are to know, that the custom of the land requireth, that after this day and tomorrow (which we give you for removing of your people from your ship), you are to keep within doors for three days. But let it not trouble you, nor do not think yourselves restrained, but rather left to your rest and ease. You shall want nothing, and there are six of our people appointed to attend you, for any business you may have abroad." We gave him thanks, with all affection and respect, and said, "God surely is manifested in this land." We offered him also twenty pistolets; but he smiled, and only said; "What? twice paid!" And so he left us.

Soon after our dinner was served in; which was right good viands, both for bread and treat: better than any collegiate diet, that I have known in Europe. We had also drink of three sorts, all wholesome and good; wine of the grape; a drink of grain, such as is with us our ale, but more clear: And a kind of cider made of a fruit of that country; a wonderful pleasing and refreshing drink. Besides, there were brought in to us, great store of those scarlet oranges, for our sick; which (they said) were an assured remedy for sickness taken at sea. There was given us also, a box of small grey, or whitish pills, which they wished our sick should take, one of the pills, every night before sleep; which (they said) would hasten their recovery.

The next day, after that our trouble of carriage and removing of our men and goods out of our ship, was somewhat settled and quiet, I thought good to call our company together; and when they were assembled, said unto them; "My dear friends, let us know ourselves, and how it standeth with us. We are men cast on land, as Jonas was, out of the whale's belly, when we were as buried in the deep: and now we are on land, we are but between death and life; for we are beyond, both the old world, and the new; and whether ever we shall see Europe, God only knoweth. It is a kind of miracle bath brought us hither: and it must be little less, that shall bring us hence. Therefore in regard of our deliverance past, and our danger present, and to come, let us look up to God, and every man reform his own ways. Besides we are come here amongst a Christian people, full of piety and humanity: let us not bring that confusion of face upon ourselves, as to show our vices, or unworthiness before them. Yet there is more. For they have by commandment (though in form of courtesy), cloistered us within these wall, for three days: who knoweth, whether it be not, to take some taste of our manners and conditions? And if they find them bad, to banish us straightways; if good, to give us further time. For these men that they have given us for attendance, may withal have an eye upon us. Therefore for God's love, and as we love the weal of our souls and bodies, let us so behave ourselves, as we may be at peace with God, and may find grace in the eyes of this people." Our company with one voice thanked me for my good admonition, and promised me to live soberly and civilly, and without giving any the least occasion of offence. So we spent our three days joyfully, and without care, in expectation what would be done with us, when they were expired. During which time, we had every hour joy of the amendment of our sick; who thought themselves cast into some divine pool of healing; they mended so kindly, and so fast.

The morrow after our three days were past, there came to us a new man, that we had not seen before, clothed in blue as the former was, save that his turban was white, with a small red cross on the top. He had also a tippet of fine linen. At his coming in, he did bend to us a little, and put his arms abroad. We of our parts saluted him in a very lowly and submissive manner; as looking that from him, we should receive sentence of life, or death: he desired to speak with some few of us: whereupon six of us only staid, and the rest avoided the room. He said, "I am by office governor of this House of Strangers, and by vocation I am a Christian priest: and therefore am come to you to offer you my service, both as strangers and chiefly as Christians. Some things I may tell you, which I think you will not be unwilling to hear. The State hath given you license to stay on land, for the space of six weeks; and let it not trouble you, if your occasions ask further time, for the law in this point is not precise; and I do not doubt, but my self shall be able, to obtain for you such further time, as may be convenient. Ye shall also understand, that the Strangers' House is at this time rich, and much aforehand; for it hath laid up revenue these thirty-seven years; for so long it is since any stranger arrived in this part: and therefore take ye no care; the State will defray you all the time you stay; neither shall you stay one day the less for that. As for any merchandise ye have brought, ye shall be well used, and have your return, either in merchandise, or in gold and silver: for to us it is all one. And if you have any other request to make, hide it not. For ye shall find we will not make your countenance to fall by the answer ye shall receive. Only this I must tell you, that none of you must go above a karan," (that is with them a mile and an half) "from the walls of the city, without especial leave."

We answered, after we had looked awhile one upon another, admiring this gracious and parent-like usage; "That we could not tell what to say: for we wanted words to express our thanks; and his noble free offers left us nothing to ask. It seemed to us, that we had before us a picture of our salvation in Heaven; for we that were a while since in the jaws of death, were now brought into a place, where we found nothing but consolations. For the commandment laid upon us, we would not fail to obey it, though it was impossible but our hearts should be enflamed to tread further upon this happy and holy ground." We added, "That our tongues should first cleave to the roofs of our mouths, ere we should forget, either his reverend person, or this whole nation, in our prayers." We also most humbly besought him, to accept of us as his true servants; by as just a right as ever men on earth were bounden; laying and presenting, both our persons, and all we had, at his feet. He said; "He was a priest, and looked for a priest's reward; which was our brotherly love, and the good of our souls and bodies." So he went from us, not without tears of tenderness in his eyes; and left us also confused with joy and kindness, saying amongst ourselves; "That we were come into a land of angels, which did appear to us daily, and prevent us with comforts, which we thought not of, much less expected."

The next day about ten of the clock, the Governor came to us again, and after salutations, said familiarly; "That he was come to visit us"; and called for a chair, and sat him down: and we, being some ten of us (the rest were of the meaner sort, or else gone abroad), sat down with him, And when we were set, he began thus: "We of this island of Bensalem," (for so they call it in their language) "have this; that by means of our solitary situation; and of the laws of secrecy, which we have for our travellers, and our rare admission of strangers; we know well most part of the habitable world, and are ourselves unknown. Therefore because he that knoweth least is fittest to ask questions, it is more reason, for the entertainment of the time, that ye ask me questions, than that I ask you."

We answered; "That we humbly thanked him that he would give us leave so to do: and that we conceived by the taste we had already, that there was no worldly thing on earth, more worthy to be known than the state of that happy land. But above all," (we said) "since that we were met from the several ends of the world, and hoped assuredly that we should meet one day in the kingdom of Heaven (for that we were both parts Christians), we desired to know (in respect that land was so remote, and so divided by vast and unknown seas, from the land where our Saviour walked on earth), who was the apostle of that nation, and how it was converted to the faith?" It appeared in his face that he took great contentment in this our question: he said; "Ye knit my heart to you, by asking this question in the first place; for it sheweth that you first seek the kingdom of heaven; and I shall gladly, and briefly, satisfy your demand.

"About twenty years after the ascension of our Saviour, it came to pass, that there was seen by the people of Renfusa (a city upon the eastern coast of our island), within night (the night was cloudy, and calm), as it might be some mile into the sea, a great pillar of light; not sharp, but in form of a column, or cylinder, rising from the sea a great way up towards heaven; and on the top of it was seen a large cross of light, more bright and resplendent than the body of the pillar. Upon which so strange a spectacle, the people of the city gathered apace together upon the sands, to wonder; and so after put themselves into a number of small boats, to go nearer to this marvellous sight. But when the boats were come within (about) sixty yards of the pillar, they found themselves all bound, and could go no further; yet so as they might move to go about, but might not approach nearer: so as the boats stood all as in a theatre, beholding this light as an heavenly sign. It so fell out, that there was in one of the boats one of the wise men, of the society of Salomon's House; which house, or college (my good brethren) is the very eye of this kingdom; who having awhile attentively and devoutly viewed and contemplated this pillar and cross, fell down upon his face; and then raised himself upon his knees, and lifting up his hands to heaven, made his prayers in this manner.

"'Lord God of heaven and earth, thou hast vouchsafed of thy grace to those of our order, to know thy works of Creation, and the secrets of them: and to discern (as far as appertaineth to the generations of men) between divine miracles, works of nature, works of art, and impostures and illusions of all sorts. I do here acknowledge and testify before this people, that the thing which we now see before our eyes is thy Finger and a true Miracle. And forasmuch as we learn in our books that thou never workest miracles, but to divine and excellent end (for the laws of nature are thine own laws, and thou exceedest them not but upon great cause), we most humbly beseech thee to prosper this great sign, and to give us the interpretation and use of it in mercy; which thou dost in some part secretly promise by sending it unto us.'

"When he had made his prayer, he presently found the boat he was in, moveable and unbound; whereas all the rest remained still fast; and taking that for an assurance of leave to approach, he caused the boat to be softly and with silence rowed towards the pillar. But ere he came near it, the pillar and cross of light brake up, and cast itself abroad, as it were, into a firmament of many stars; which also vanished soon after, and there was nothing left to be seen, but a small ark, or chest of cedar, dry, and not wet at all with water, though it swam. And in the fore-end of it, which was towards him, grew a small green branch of palm; and when the wise man had taken it, with all reverence, into his boat, it opened of itself, and there were found in it a Book and a Letter; both written in fine parchment, and wrapped in sindons of linen. The Book contained all the canonical books of the Old and New Testament, according as you have them (for we know well what the churches with you receive); and the Apocalypse itself, and some other books of the New Testament, which were not at that time written, were nevertheless in the Book. And for the Letter, it was in these words:

"'I, Bartholomew, a servant of the Highest, and Apostle of Jesus Christ, was warned by an angel that appeareth to me, in a vision of glory, that I should commit this ark to the floods of the sea. Therefore I do testify and declare unto that people where God shall ordain this ark to come to land, that in the same day is come unto them salvation and peace and good-will, from the Father, and from the Lord Jesus.'

"There was also in both these writings, as well the Book, as the Letter, wrought a great miracle, conform to that of the Apostles, in the original Gift of Tongues. For there being at that time in this land Hebrews, Persians, and Indians, besides the natives, every one read upon the Book, and Letter, as if they had been written in his own language. And thus was this land saved from infidelity (as the remainder of the old world was from water) by an ark, through the apostolical and miraculous evangelism of Saint Bartholomew." And here he paused, and a messenger came, and called him from us. So this was all that passed in that conference.

The next day, the same governor came again to us, immediately after dinner, and excused himself, saying; "That the day before he was called from us, somewhat abruptly, but now he would make us amends, and spend time with us if we held his company and conference agreeable." We answered, "That we held it so agreeable and pleasing to us, as we forgot both dangers past and fears to come, for the time we hear him speak; and that we thought an hour spent with him, was worth years of our former life." He bowed himself a little to us, and after we were set again, he said; "Well, the questions are on your part."

One of our number said, after a little pause; that there was a matter, we were no less desirous to know, than fearful to ask, lest we might presume too far. But encouraged by his rare humanity towards us (that could scarce think ourselves strangers, being his vowed and professed servants), we would take the hardiness to propound it: humbly beseeching him, if he thought it not fit to be answered, that he would pardon it, though he rejected it. We said; "We well observed those his words, which he formerly spake, that this happy island, where we now stood, was known to few, and yet knew most of the nations of the world; which we found to be true, considering they had the languages of Europe, and knew much of our state and business; and yet we in Europe, (notwithstanding all the remote discoveries and navigations of this last age), never heard of the least inkling or glimpse of this island. This we found wonderful strange; for that all nations have inter-knowledge one of another, either by voyage into foreign parts, or by strangers that come to them: and though the traveller into a foreign country, doth commonly know more by the eye, than he that stayeth at home can by relation of the traveller; yet both ways suffice to make a mutual knowledge, in some degree, on both parts. But for this island, we never heard tell of any ship of theirs that had been seen to arrive upon any shore of Europe; nor of either the East or West Indies; nor yet of any ship of any other part of the world, that had made return from them. And yet the marvel rested not in this. For the situation of it (as his lordship said) in the secret conclave of such a vast sea might cause it. But then, that they should have knowledge of the languages, books, affairs, of those that lie such a distance from them, it was a thing we could not tell what to make of; for that it seemed to us a conditioner and propriety of divine powers and beings, to be hidden and unseen to others, and yet to have others open and as in a light to them."

At this speech the Governor gave a gracious smile, and said; "That we did well to ask pardon for this question we now asked: for that it imported, as if we thought this land, a land of magicians, that sent forth spirits of the air into all parts, to bring them news and intelligence of other countries." It was answered by us all, in all possible humbleness, but yet with a countenance taking knowledge, that we knew that he spake it but merrily, "That we were apt enough to think there was somewhat supernatural in this island; but yet rather as angelical than magical. But to let his lordship know truly what it was that made us tender and doubtful to ask this question, it was not any such conceit, but because we remembered, he had given a touch in his former speech, that this land had laws of secrecy touching strangers." To this he said; "You remember it aright and therefore in that I shall say to you, I must reserve some particulars, which it is not lawful for me to reveal; but there will be enough left, to give you satisfaction."

"You shall understand (that which perhaps you will scarce think credible) that about three thousand years ago, or somewhat more, the navigation of the world (especially for remote voyages), was greater than at this day. Do not think with yourselves, that I know not how much it is increased with you, within these six-score years: I know it well: and yet I say greater then than now; whether it was, that the example of the ark, that saved the remnant of men from the universal deluge, gave men confidence to adventure upon the waters; or what it was; but such is the truth. The Phoenicians, and especially the Tyrians, had great fleets. So had the Carthaginians their colony, which is yet further west. Toward the east the shipping of Egypt and of Palestine was likewise great. China also, and the great Atlantis (that you call America), which have now but junks and canoes, abounded then in tall ships. This island (as appeareth by faithful registers of those times), had then fifteen hundred strong ships, of great content. Of all this, there is with you sparing memory, or none; but we have large knowledge thereof.

"At that time, this land was known and frequented by the ships and vessels of all the nations before named. And (as it cometh to pass) they had many times men of other countries, that were no sailors, that came with them; as Persians, Chaldeans, Arabians; so as almost all nations of might and fame resorted hither; of whom we have some stirps, and little tribes with us at this day. And for our own ships, they went sundry voyages, as well to your straits, which you call the Pillars of Hercules, as to other parts in the Atlantic and Mediterrane Seas; as to Paguin (which is the same with Cambaline), and Quinzy, upon the Oriental Seas, as far as to the borders of the East Tartary.

"At the same time, and an age after, or more, the inhabitants of the great Atlantis did flourish. For though the narration and description, which is made by a great man with you; that the descendants of Neptune planted there; and of the magnificent temple, palace, city, and hill; and the manifold streams of goodly navigable rivers (which as so many chains environed the same site and temple); and the several degrees of ascent, whereby men did climb up to the same, as if it had been a scala coeli, be all poetical and fabulous: yet so much is true, that the said country of Atlantis, as well that of Peru, then called Coya, as that of Mexico, then named Tyrambel, were mighty and proud kingdoms in arms, shipping and riches: so mighty, as at one time (or at least within the space of ten years) they both made two great expeditions; they of Tyrambel through the Atlantic to the Mediterranean Sea; and they of Coya through the South Sea upon this our island: and for the former of these, which was into Europe, the same author amongst you (as it seemeth) had some relation from the Egyptian priest whom he cited. For assuredly such a thing there was. But whether it were the ancient Athenians that had the glory of the repulse and resistance of those forces, I can say nothing: but certain it is, there never came back either ship or man from that voyage. Neither had the other voyage of those of Coya upon us had better fortune, if they had not met with enemies of greater clemency. For the king of this island (by name Altabin), a wise man and a great warrior, knowing well both his own strength and that of his enemies, handled the matter so, as he cut off their land-forces from their ships; and entoiled both their navy and their tamp with a greater power than theirs, both by sea and land: arid compelled them to render themselves without striking stroke and after they were at his mercy, contenting himself only with their oath that they should no more bear arms against him, dismissed them all in safety.

"But the divine revenge overtook not long after those proud enterprises. For within less than the space of one hundred years, the great Atlantis was utterly lost and destroyed: not by a great earthquake, as your man saith (for that whole tract is little subject to earthquakes); but by a particular deluge or inundation; those countries having, at this day, far greater rivers and far higher mountains to pour down waters, than any part of the old world. But it is true that the same inundation was not deep; not past forty foot, in most places, from the ground; so that although it destroyed man and beast generally, yet some few wild inhabitants of the wood escaped. Birds also were saved by flying to the high trees and woods. For as for men, although they had buildings in many places, higher than the depth of the water, yet that inundation, though it were shallow, had a long continuance; whereby they of the vale that were not drowned, perished for want of food and other things necessary.

"So as marvel you not at the thin population of America, nor at the rudeness and ignorance of the people; for you must account your inhabitants of America as a young people; younger a thousand years, at the least, than the rest of the world: for that there was so much time between the universal flood and their particular inundation. For the poor remnant of human seed, which remained in their mountains, peopled the country again slowly, by little and little; and being simple and savage people (not like Noah and his sons, which was the chief family of the earth); they were not able to leave letters, arts, and civility to their posterity; and having likewise in their mountainous habitations been used (in respect of the extreme cold of those regions) to clothe themselves with the skins of tigers, bears, and great hairy goats, that they have in those parts; when after they came down into the valley, and found the intolerable heats which are there, and knew no means of lighter apparel, they were forced to begin the custom of going naked, which continueth at this day. Only they take great pride and delight in the feathers of birds; and this also they took from those their ancestors of the mountains, who were invited unto it by the infinite flights of birds that came up to the high grounds, while the waters stood below. So you see, by this main accident of time, we lost our traffic with the Americans, with whom of, all others, in regard they lay nearest to us, we had most commerce.

"As for the other parts of the world, it is most manifest that in the ages following (whether it were in respect of wars, or by a natural revolution of time), navigation did everywhere greatly decay; and specially far voyages (the rather by the use of galleys, and such vessels as could hardly brook the ocean), were altogether left and omitted. So then, that part of intercourse which could be from other nations to sail to us, you see how it hath long since ceased; except it were by some rare accident, as this of yours. But now of the cessation of that other part of intercourse, which might be by our sailing to other nations, I must yield you some other cause. For I cannot say (if I shall say truly), but our shipping, for number, strength, mariners, pilots, and all things that appertain to navigation, is as great as ever; and therefore why we should sit at home, I shall now give you an account by itself: and it will draw nearer to give you satisfaction to your principal question.

"There reigned in this land, about nineteen hundred years ago, a king, whose memory of all others we most adore; not superstitiously, but as a divine instrument, though a mortal man; his name was Solamona: and we esteem him as the lawgiver of our nation. This king had a large heart, inscrutable for good; and was wholly bent to make his kingdom and people happy. He therefore, taking into consideration how sufficient and substantive this land was to maintain itself without any aid (at all) of the foreigner; being five thousand six hundred miles in circuit, and of rare fertility of soil in the greatest part thereof; and finding also the shipping of this country might be plentifully set on work, both by fishing and by transportations from port to port, and likewise by sailing unto some small islands that are not far from us, and are under the crown and laws of this state; and, recalling into his memory the happy and flourishing estate wherein this land then was; so as it might be a thousand ways altered to the worse, but scarce any one way to the better; thought nothing wanted to his noble and heroical intentions, but only (as far as human foresight might reach) to give perpetuity to that which was in his time so happily established. Therefore amongst his other fundamental laws of this kingdom, he did ordain the interdicts and prohibitions which we have touching entrance of strangers; which at that time (though it was after the calamity of America) was frequent; doubting novelties, and commixture of manners. It is true, the like law against the admission of strangers without licence is an ancient law in the kingdom of China, and yet continued in use. But there it is a poor thing; and hath made them a curious, ignorant, fearful, foolish nation. But our lawgiver made his law of another temper. For first, he hath preserved all points of humanity, in taking order and making provision for the relief of strangers distressed; whereof you have tasted."

At which speech (as reason was) we all rose up and bowed ourselves. He went on.

"That king also, still desiring to join humanity and policy together; and thinking it against humanity, to detain strangers here against their wills, and against policy that they should return and discover their knowledge of this estate, he took this course: he did ordain that of the strangers that should be permitted to land, as many (at all times) might depart as would; but as many as would stay should have very good conditions and means to live from the state. Wherein he saw so far, that now in so many ages since the prohibition, we have memory not of one ship that ever returned, and but of thirteen persons only, at several times, that chose to return in our bottoms. What those few that returned may have reported abroad I know not. But you must think, whatsoever they have said could be taken where they came but for a dream. Now for our travelling from hence into parts abroad, our Lawgiver thought fit altogether to restrain it. So is it not in China. For the Chinese sail where they will or can; which sheweth that their law of keeping out strangers is a law of pusillanimity and fear. But this restraint of ours hath one only exception, which is admirable; preserving the good which cometh by communicating with strangers, and avoiding the hurt; and I will now open it to you. And here I shall seem a little to digress, but you will by and by find it pertinent.

"Ye shall understand (my dear friends) that amongst the excellent acts of that king, one above all hath the pre-eminence. It was the erection and institution of an Order or Society, which we call Salomon's House; the noblest foundation (as we think) that ever was upon the earth; and the lanthorn of this kingdom. It is dedicated to the study of the works and creatures of God. Some think it beareth the founder's name a little corrupted, as if it should be Solamona's House. But the records write it as it is spoken. So as I take it to be denominate of the king of the Hebrews, which is famous with you, and no stranger to us. For we have some parts of his works, which with you are lost; namely, that natural history, which he wrote, of all plants, from the cedar of Libanus to the moss that groweth out of the wall, and of all things that have life and motion. This maketh me think that our king, finding himself to symbolize in many things with that king of the Hebrews (which lived many years before him), honoured him with the title of this foundation. And I am rather induced to be of this opinion, for that I find in ancient records this Order or Society is sometimes called Salomon's House, and sometimes the College of the Six Days Works; whereby I am satisfied that our excellent king had learned from the Hebrews that God had created the world and all that therein is within six days: and therefore he instituting that House for the finding out of the true nature of all things, (whereby God might have the more glory in the workmanship of them, and insert the more fruit in the use of them), did give it also that second name.

"But now to come to our present purpose. When the king had forbidden to all his people navigation into any part that was not under his crown, he made nevertheless this ordinance; that every twelve years there should be set forth, out of this kingdom two ships, appointed to several voyages; that in either of these ships there should be a mission of three of the Fellows or Brethren of Salomon's House; whose errand was only to give us knowledge of the affairs and state of those countries to which they were designed, and especially of the sciences, arts, manufactures, and inventions of all the world; and withal to bring unto us books, instruments, and patterns in every kind: That the ships, after they had landed the brethren, should return; and that the brethren should stay abroad till the new mission. These ships are not otherwise fraught, than with store of victuals, and good quantity of treasure to remain with the brethren, for the buying of such things and rewarding of such persons as they should think fit. Now for me to tell you how the vulgar sort of mariners are contained from being discovered at land; and how they that must be put on shore for any time, colour themselves under the names of other nations; and to what places these voyages have been designed; and what places of rendezvous are appointed for the new missions; and the like circumstances of the practique; I may not do it: neither is it much to your desire. But thus you see we maintain a trade not for gold, silver, or jewels; nor for silks; nor for spices; nor any other commodity of matter; but only for God's first creature, which was Light: to have light (I say) of the growth of all parts of the world."

And when he had said this, he was silent; and so were we all. For indeed we were all astonished to hear so strange things so probably told. And he, perceiving that we were willing to say somewhat but had it not ready in great courtesy took us off, and descended to ask us questions of our voyage and fortunes and in the end concluded, that we might do well to think with ourselves what time of stay we would demand of the state; and bade us not to scant ourselves; for he would procure such time as we desired: Whereupon we all rose up, and presented ourselves to kiss the skirt of his tippet; but he would not suffer us; and so took his leave. But when it came once amongst our people that the state used to offer conditions to strangers that would stay, we had work enough to get any of our men to look to our ship; and to keep them from going presently to the governor to crave conditions. But with much ado we refrained them, till we might agree what course to take.

We took ourselves now for free men, seeing there was no danger of our utter perdition; and lived most joyfully, going abroad and seeing what was to be seen in the city and places adjacent within our tedder; and obtaining acquaintance with many of the city, not of the meanest quality; at whose hands we found such humanity, and such a freedom and desire to take strangers as it were into their bosom, as was enough to make us forget all that was dear to us in our own countries: and continually we met with many things right worthy of observation and relation: as indeed, if there be a mirror in the world worthy to hold men's eyes, it is that country.

One day there were two of our company bidden to a Feast of the Family, as they call it. A most natural, pious, and reverend custom it is, shewing that nation to be compounded of all goodness. This is the manner of it. It is granted to any man that shall live to see thirty persons descended of his body alive together, and all above three years old, to make this feast which is done at the cost of the state. The Father of the Family, whom they call the Tirsan, two days before the feast, taketh to him three of such friends as he liketh to choose; and is assisted also by the governor of the city or place where the feast is celebrated; and all the persons of the family, of both sexes, are summoned to attend him. These two days the Tirsan sitteth in consultation concerning the good estate of the family. There, if there be any discord or suits between any of the family, they are compounded and appeased. There, if any of the family be distressed or decayed, order is taken for their relief and competent means to live. There, if any be subject to vice, or take ill courses, they are reproved and censured. So likewise direction is given touching marriages, and the courses of life, which any of them should take, with divers other the like orders and advices. The governor assisteth, to the end to put in execution by his public authority the decrees and orders of the Tirsan, if they should be disobeyed; though that seldom needeth; such reverence and obedience they give to the order of nature. The Tirsan doth also then ever choose one man from among his sons, to live in house with him; who is called ever after the Son of the Vine. The reason will hereafter appear.

On the feast day, the father or Tirsan cometh forth after divine service into a large room where the feast is celebrated; which room hath an half-pace at the upper end. Against the wall, in the middle of the half-pace, is a chair placed for him, with a table and carpet before it. Over the chair is a state, made round or oval, and it is of ivy; an ivy somewhat whiter than ours, like the leaf of a silver asp; but more shining; for it is green all winter. And the state is curiously wrought with silver and silk of divers colours, broiding or binding in the ivy; and is ever of the work of some of the daughters of the family; and veiled over at the top with a fine net of silk and silver. But the substance of it is true ivy; whereof, after it is taken down, the friends of the family are desirous to have some leaf or sprig to keep.

The Tirsan cometh forth with all his generation or linage, the males before him, and the females following him; and if there be a mother from whose body the whole linage is descended, there is a traverse placed in a loft above on the right hand of the chair, with a privy door, and a carved window of glass, leaded with gold and blue; where she sitteth, but is not seen. When the Tirsan is come forth, he sitteth down in the chair; and all the linage place themselves against the wall, both at his back and upon the return of the half-pace, in order of their years without difference of sex; and stand upon their feet. When he is set; the room being always full of company, but well kept and without disorder; after some pause, there cometh in from the lower end of the room, a taratan (which is as much as an herald) and on either side of him two young lads; whereof one carrieth a scroll of their shining yellow parchment; and the other a cluster of grapes of gold, with a long foot or stalk. The herald and children are clothed with mantles of sea-water green satin; but the herald's mantle is streamed with gold, and hath a train.

Then the herald with three curtesies, or rather inclinations, cometh up as far as the half-pace; and there first taketh into his hand the scroll. This scroll is the king's charter, containing gifts of revenue, and many privileges, exemptions, and points of honour, granted to the Father of the Family; and is ever styled and directed, To such do one our well beloved friend and creditor: which is a title proper only to this case. For they say the king is debtor to no man, but for propagation of his subjects. The seal set to the king's charter is the king's image, imbossed or moulded in gold; and though such charters be expedited of course, and as of right, yet they are varied by discretion, according to the number and dignity of the family. This charter the herald readeth aloud; and while it is read, the father or Tirsan standeth up supported by two of his sons, such as he chooseth. Then the herald mounteth the half-pace and delivereth the charter into his hand: and with that there is an acclamation by all that are present in their language, which is thus much: Happy are the people of Bensalem.

Then the herald taketh into his hand from the other child the cluster of grapes, which is of gold, both the stalk and the grapes. But the grapes are daintily enamelled; and if the males of the family be the greater number, the grapes are enamelled purple, with a little sun set on the top; if the females, then they are enamelled into a greenish yellow, with a crescent on the top. The grapes are in number as many as there are descendants of the family. This golden cluster the herald delivereth also to the Tirsan; who presently delivereth it over to that son that he had formerly chosen to be in house with him: who beareth it before his father as an ensign of honour when he goeth in public, ever after; and is thereupon called the Son of the Vine.

After the ceremony endeth the father or Tirsan retireth; and after some time cometh forth again to dinner, where he sitteth alone under the state, as before; and none of his descendants sit with him, of what degree or dignity soever, except he hap to be of Salomon's House. He is served only by his own children, such as are male; who perform unto him all service of the table upon the knee; and the women only stand about him, leaning against the wall. The room below the half-pace hath tables on the sides for the guests that are bidden; who are served with great and comely order; and towards the end of dinner (which in the greatest feasts with them lasteth never above an hour and an half) there is an hymn sung, varied according to the invention of him that composeth it (for they have excellent posy) but the subject of it is (always) the praises of Adam and Noah and Abraham; whereof the former two peopled the world, and the last was the Father of the Faithful: concluding ever with a thanksgiving for the nativity of our Saviour, in whose birth the births of all are only blessed.

Dinner being done, the Tirsan retireth again; and having withdrawn himself alone into a place, where he makes some private prayers, he cometh forth the third time, to give the blessing with all his descendants, who stand about him as at the first. Then he calleth them forth by one and by one, by name, as he pleaseth, though seldom the order of age be inverted. The person that is called (the table being before removed) kneeleth down before the chair, and the father layeth his hand upon his head, or her head, and giveth the blessing in these words: Son of Bensalem (or Daughter of Bensalem), thy father with it: the man by whom thou hast breath and life speaketh the word: the blessing of the everlasting Father, the Prince of Peace, and the Holy Dove, be upon thee, and make the days of thy pilgrimage good and many. This he saith to every of them; and that done, if there be any of his sons of eminent merit and virtue (so they be not above two), he calleth for them again; and saith, laying his arm over their shoulders, they standing; Sons, it is well ye are born, give God the praise, and persevere to the end. And withall delivereth to either of them a jewel, made in the figure of an ear of wheat, which they ever after wear in the front of their turban or hat. This done, they fall to music and dances, and other recreations, after their manner, for the rest of the day. This is the full order of that feast.

By that time six or seven days were spent, I was fallen into straight acquaintance with a merchant of that city, whose name was Joabin. He was a Jew and circumcised: for they have some few stirps of Jews yet remaining among them, whom they leave to their own religion. Which they may the better do, because they are of a far differing disposition from the Jews in other parts. For whereas they hate the name of Christ; and have a secret inbred rancour against the people among whom they live: these (contrariwise) give unto our Saviour many high attributes, and love the nation of Bensalem extremely. Surely this man of whom I speak would ever acknowledge that Christ was born of a virgin and that he was more than a man; and he would tell how God made him ruler of the seraphims which guard his throne; and they call him also the Milken Way, and the Eliah of the Messiah; and many other high names; which though they be inferior to his divine majesty, yet they are far from the language of other Jews.

And for the country of Bensalem, this man would make no end of commending it; being desirous, by tradition among the Jews there, to have it believed that the people thereof were of the generations of Abraham, by another son, whom they call Nachoran; and that Moses by a secret Cabala ordained the Laws of Bensalem which they now use; and that when the Messiah should come, and sit in his throne at Hierusalem, the king of Bensalem should sit at his feet, whereas other kings should keep a great distance. But yet setting aside these Jewish dreams, the man was a wise man, and learned, and of great policy, and excellently seen in the laws and customs of that nation.

Amongst other discourses, one day I told him I was much affected with the relation I had, from some of the company, of their custom, in holding the Feast of the Family; for that (methought) I had never heard of a solemnity wherein nature did so much preside. And because propagation of families proceedeth from the nuptial copulation, I desired to know of him what laws and customs they had concerning marriage; and whether they kept marriage well and whether they were tied to one wife; for that where population is so much affected, and such as with them it seemed to be, there is commonly permission of plurality of wives.

To this he said, "You have reason for to commend that excellent institution of the Feast of the Family. And indeed we have experience that those families that are partakers of the blessing of that feast do flourish and prosper ever after in an extraordinary manner. But hear me now, and I will tell you what I know. You shall understand that there is not under the heavens so chaste a nation as this of Bensalem; nor so free from all pollution or foulness. It is the virgin of the world. I remember I have read in one of your European books, of an holy hermit amongst you that desired to see the Spirit of Fornication; and there appeared to him a little foul ugly Aethiop. But if he had desired to see the Spirit of Chastity of Bensalem, it would have appeared to him in the likeness of a fair beautiful Cherubim. For there is nothing amongst mortal men more fair and admirable, than the chaste minds of this people. Know therefore, that with them there are no stews, no dissolute houses, no courtesans, nor anything of that kind. Nay they wonder (with detestation) at you in Europe, which permit such things. They say ye have put marriage out of office: for marriage is ordained a remedy for unlawful concupiscence; and natural concupiscence seemeth as a spar to marriage. But when men have at hand a remedy more agreeable to their corrupt will, marriage is almost expulsed. And therefore there are with you seen infinite men that marry not, but chose rather a libertine and impure single life, than to be yoked in marriage; and many that do marry, marry late, when the prime and strength of their years is past. And when they do marry, what is marriage to them but a very bargain; wherein is sought alliance, or portion, or reputation, with some desire (almost indifferent) of issue; and not the faithful nuptial union of man and wife, that was first instituted. Neither is it possible that those that have cast away so basely so much of their strength, should greatly esteem children (being of the same matter), as chaste men do. So likewise during marriage, is the case much amended, as it ought to be if those things were tolerated only for necessity? No, but they remain still as a very affront to marriage. The haunting of those dissolute places, or resort to courtesans, are no more punished in married men than in bachelors. And the depraved custom of change, and the delight in meretricious embracements (where sin is turned into art), maketh marriage a dull thing, and a kind of imposition or tax. They hear you defend these things, as done to avoid greater evils; as advoutries, deflowering of virgins, unnatural lust, and the like. But they say this is a preposterous wisdom; and they call it Lot's offer, who to save his guests from abusing, offered his daughters: nay they say farther that there is little gained in this; for that the same vices and appetites do still remain and abound; unlawful lust being like a furnace, that if you stop the flames altogether, it will quench; but if you give it any vent, it will rage. As for masculine love, they have no touch of it; and yet there are not so faithful and inviolate friendships in the world again as are there; and to speak generally (as I said before), I have not read of any such chastity, in any people as theirs. And their usual saying is, that whosoever is unchaste cannot reverence himself; and they say, that the reverence of a man's self, is, next to religion, the chiefest bridle of all vices."

And when he had said this, the good Jew paused a little; whereupon I, far more willing to hear him speak on than to speak myself, yet thinking it decent that upon his pause of speech I should not be altogether silent, said only this; "That I would say to him, as the widow of Sarepta said to Elias; that he was come to bring to memory our sins; and that I confess the righteousness of Bensalem was greater than the righteousness of Europe." At which speech he bowed his head, and went on in this manner:

"They have also many wise and excellent laws touching marriage. They allow no polygamy. They have ordained that none do intermarry or contract, until a month be past from their first interview. Marriage without consent of parents they do not make void, but they mulct it in the inheritors: for the children of such marriages are not admitted to inherit above a third part of their parents' inheritance. I have read in a book of one of your men, of a Feigned Commonwealth, where the married couple are permitted, before they contract, to see one another naked. This they dislike; for they think it a scorn to give a refusal after so familiar knowledge: but because of many hidden defects in men and women's bodies, they have a more civil way; for they have near every town a couple of pools (which they call Adam and Eve's pools), where it is permitted to one of the friends of the men, and another of the friends of the woman, to see them severally bathe naked."

And as we were thus in conference, there came one that seemed to be a messenger, in a rich huke, that spake with the Jew: whereupon he turned to me and said; "You will pardon me, for I am commanded away in haste." The next morning he came to me again, joyful as it seemed, and said; "There is word come to the Governor of the city, that one of the Fathers of Salomon's House will be here this day seven-night: we have seen none of them this dozen years. His coming is in state; but the cause of his coming is secret. I will provide you and your fellows of a good standing to see his entry." I thanked him, and told him, I was most glad of the news.

The day being come, he made his entry. He was a man of middle stature and age, comely of person, and had an aspect as if he pitied men. He was clothed in a robe of fine black cloth, with wide sleeves and a cape. His under garment was of excellent white linen down to the foot, girt with a girdle of the same; and a sindon or tippet of the same about his neck. He had gloves, that were curious and set with stone; and shoes of peach-coloured velvet. His neck was bare to the shoulders. His hat was like a helmet, or Spanish montera; and his locks curled below it decently: they were of colour brown. His beard was cut round, and of the same colour with his hair, somewhat lighter. He was carried in a rich chariot without wheels, litter-wise; with two horses at either end, richly trapped in blue velvet embroidered; and two footmen on each side in the like attire. The chariot was all of cedar, gilt, and adorned with crystal; save that the fore-end had panels of sapphires, set in borders of gold; and the hinder-end the like of emeralds of the Peru colour. There was also a sun of gold, radiant, upon the top, in the midst; and on the top before, a small cherub of gold, with wings displayed. The chariot was covered with cloth of gold tissued upon blue. He had before him fifty attendants, young men all, in white satin loose coats to the mid leg; and stockings of white silk; and shoes of blue velvet; and hats of blue velvet; with fine plumes of diverse colours, set round like hat-bands. Next before the chariot, went two men, bare-headed, in linen garments down the foot, girt, and shoes of blue velvet; who carried, the one a crosier, the other a pastoral staff like a sheep-hook; neither of them of metal, but the crosier of balm-wood, the pastoral staff of cedar. Horsemen he had none, neither before nor behind his chariot: as it seemeth, to avoid all tumult and trouble. Behind his chariot went all the officers and principals of the companies of the city. He sat alone, upon cushions of a kind of excellent plush, blue; and under his foot curious carpets of silk of diverse colours, like the Persian, but far finer. He held up his bare hand as he went, as blessing the people, but in silence. The street was wonderfully well kept: so that there was never any army had their men stand in better battle-array than the people stood. The windows likewise were not crowded, but every one stood in them as if they had been placed.

When the shew was past, the Jew said to me; "I shall not be able to attend you as I would, in regard of some charge the city hath laid upon me, for the entertaining of this great person." Three days after the Jew came to me again, and said; "Ye are happy men; for the Father of Salomon's House taketh knowledge of your being here, and commanded me to tell you that he will admit all your company to his presence, and have private conference with one of you, that ye shall choose: and for this hath appointed the next day after tomorrow. And because he meaneth to give you his blessing, he hath appointed it in the forenoon."

We came at our day and hour, and I was chosen by my fellows for the private access. We found him in a fair chamber, richly hanged, and carpeted under foot without any degrees to the state. He was set upon a low throne richly adorned, and a rich cloth of state over his head, of blue satin embroidered. He was alone, save that he had two pages of honour, on either hand one, finely attired in white. His under garments were the like that we saw him wear in the chariot; but instead of his gown, he had on him a mantle with a cape, of the same fine black, fastened about him. When we came in, as we were taught, we bowed low at our first entrance; and when we were come near his chair, he stood up, holding forth his hand ungloved, and in posture of blessing; and we every one of us stooped down, and kissed the hem of his tippet. That done, the rest departed, and I remained. Then he warned the pages forth of the room, and caused me to sit down beside him, and spake to me thus in the Spanish tongue.

"God bless thee, my son; I will give thee the greatest jewel I have. For I will impart unto thee, for the love of God and men, a relation of the true state of Salomon's House. Son, to make you know the true state of Salomon's House, I will keep this order. First, I will set forth unto you the end of our foundation. Secondly, the preparations and instruments we have for our works. Thirdly, the several employments and functions whereto our fellows are assigned. And fourthly, the ordinances and rites which we observe.

"The end of our foundation is the knowledge of causes, and secret motions of things; and the enlarging of the bounds of human empire, to the effecting of all things possible.

"The Preparations and Instruments are these. We have large and deep caves of several depths: the deepest are sunk six hundred fathom: and some of them are digged and made under great hills and mountains: so that if you reckon together the depth of the hill and the depth of the cave, they are (some of them) above three miles deep. For we find, that the depth of a hill, and the depth of a cave from the flat, is the same thing; both remote alike, from the sun and heaven's beams, and from the open air. These caves we call the Lower Region; and we use them for all coagulations, indurations, refrigerations, and conservations of bodies. We use them likewise for the imitation of natural mines; and the producing also of new artificial metals, by compositions and materials which we use, and lay there for many years. We use them also sometimes (which may seem strange), for curing of some diseases, and for prolongation of life in some hermits that choose to live there, well accommodated of all things necessary, and indeed live very long; by whom also we learn many things.

"We have burials in several earths, where we put diverse cements, as the Chinese do their porcelain. But we have them in greater variety, and some of them more fine. We have also great variety of composts and soils, for the making of the earth fruitful.

"We have high towers; the highest about half a mile in height; and some of them likewise set upon high mountains; so that the vantage of the hill with the tower is in the highest of them three miles at least. And these places we call the Upper Region; accounting the air between the high places and the low, as a Middle Region. We use these towers, according to their several heights, and situations, for insolation, refrigeration, conservation; and for the view of divers meteors; as winds, rain, snow, hail; and some of the fiery meteors also. And upon them, in some places, are dwellings of hermits, whom we visit sometimes, and instruct what to observe.

"We have great lakes, both salt, and fresh; whereof we have use for the fish and fowl. We use them also for burials of some natural bodies: for we find a difference in things buried in earth or in air below the earth, and things buried in water. We have also pools, of which some do strain fresh water out of salt; and others by art do turn fresh water into salt. We have also some rocks in the midst of the sea, and some bays upon the shore for some works, wherein is required the air and vapour of the sea. We have likewise violent streams and cataracts, which serve us for many motions: and likewise engines for multiplying and enforcing of winds, to set also on going diverse motions.

"We have also a number of artificial wells and fountains, made in imitation of the natural sources and baths; as tincted upon vitriol, sulphur, steel, brass, lead, nitre, and other minerals. And again we have little wells for infusions of many things, where the waters take the virtue quicker and better, than in vessels or basins. And amongst them we have a water which we call Water of Paradise, being, by that we do to it made very sovereign for health, and prolongation of life.

"We have also great and spacious houses where we imitate and demonstrate meteors; as snow, hail, rain, some artificial rains of bodies and not of water, thunders, lightnings; also generations of bodies in air; as frogs, flies, and divers others.

"We have also certain chambers, which we call Chambers of Health, where we qualify the air as we think good and proper for the cure of divers diseases, and preservation of health.

"We have also fair and large baths, of several mixtures, for the cure of diseases, and the restoring of man's body from arefaction: and others for the confirming of it in strength of sinewes, vital parts, and the very juice and substance of the body.

"We have also large and various orchards and gardens; wherein we do not so much respect beauty, as variety of ground and soil, proper for divers trees and herbs: and some very spacious, where trees and berries are set whereof we make divers kinds of drinks, besides the vineyards. In these we practise likewise all conclusions of grafting, and inoculating as well of wild-trees as fruit-trees, which produceth many effects. And we make (by art) in the same orchards and gardens, trees and flowers to come earlier or later than their seasons; and to come up and bear more speedily than by their natural course they do. We make them also by art greater much than their nature; and their fruit greater and sweeter and of differing taste, smell, colour, and figure, from their nature. And many of them we so order, as they become of medicinal use.

"We have also means to make divers plants rise by mixtures of earths without seeds; and likewise to make divers new plants, differing from the vulgar; and to make one tree or plant turn into another.

"We have also parks and enclosures of all sorts of beasts and birds which we use not only for view or rareness, but likewise for dissections and trials; that thereby we may take light what may be wrought upon the body of man. Wherein we find many strange effects; as continuing life in them, though divers parts, which you account vital, be perished and taken forth; resuscitating of some that seem dead in appearance; and the like. We try also all poisons and other medicines upon them, as well of chirurgery, as physic. By art likewise, we make them greater or taller than their kind is; and contrariwise dwarf them, and stay their growth: we make them more fruitful and bearing than their kind is; and contrariwise barren and not generative. Also we make them differ in colour, shape, activity, many ways. We find means to make commixtures and copulations of different kinds; which have produced many new kinds, and them not barren, as the general opinion is. We make a number of kinds of serpents, worms, flies, fishes, of putrefaction; whereof some are advanced (in effect) to be perfect creatures, like bests or birds; and have sexes, and do propagate. Neither do we this by chance, but we know beforehand, of what matter and commixture what kind of those creatures will arise.

"We have also particular pools, where we make trials upon fishes, as we have said before of beasts and birds.

"We have also places for breed and generation of those kinds of worms and flies which are of special use; such as are with you your silk-worms and bees.

"I will not hold you long with recounting of our brewhouses, bake-houses, and kitchens, where are made divers drinks, breads, and meats, rare and of special effects. Wines we have of grapes; and drinks of other juice of fruits, of grains, and of roots; and of mixtures with honey, sugar, manna, and fruits dried, and decocted; also of the tears or woundings of trees; and of the pulp of canes. And these drinks are of several ages, some to the age or last of forty years. We have drinks also brewed with several herbs, and roots, and spices; yea with several fleshes, and white-meats; whereof some of the drinks are such, as they are in effect meat and drink both: so that divers, especially in age, do desire to live with them, with little or no meat or bread. And above all, we strive to have drink of extreme thin parts, to insinuate into the body, and yet without all biting, sharpness, or fretting; insomuch as some of them put upon the back of your hand will, with a little stay, pass through to the palm, and yet taste mild to the mouth. We have also waters which we ripen in that fashion, as they become nourishing; so that they are indeed excellent drink; and many will use no other. Breads we have of several grains, roots, and kernels; yea and some of flesh and fish dried; with divers kinds of leavenings and seasonings: so that some do extremely move appetites; some do nourish so, as divers do live of them, without any other meat; who live very long. So for meats, we have some of them so beaten and made tender and mortified, yet without all corrupting, as a weak heat of the stomach will turn them into good chylus; as well as a strong heat would meat otherwise prepared. We have some meats also and breads and drinks, which taken by men enable them to fast long after; and some other, that used make the very flesh of men's bodies sensibly more hard and tough and their strength far greater than otherwise it would be.

"We have dispensatories, or shops of medicines. Wherein you may easily think, if we have such variety of plants and living creatures more than you have in Europe (for we know what you have), the simples, drugs, and ingredients of medicines, must likewise be in so much the greater variety. We have them likewise of divers ages, and long fermentations. And for their preparations, we have not only all manner of exquisite distillations and separations, and especially by gentle heats and percolations through divers strainers, yea and substances; but also exact forms of composition, whereby they incorporate almost, as they were natural simples.

"We have also divers mechanical arts, which you have not; and stuffs made by them; as papers, linen, silks, tissues; dainty works of feathers of wonderful lustre; excellent dies, and, many others; and shops likewise, as well for such as are not brought into vulgar use amongst us as for those that are. For you must know that of the things before recited, many of them are grown into use throughout the kingdom; but yet, if they did flow from our invention, we have of them also for patterns and principals.

"We have also furnaces of great diversities, and that keep great diversity of heats; fierce and quick; strong and constant; soft and mild; blown, quiet; dry, moist; and the like. But above all, we have heats, in imitation of the Sun's and heavenly bodies' heats, that pass divers inequalities, and (as it were) orbs, progresses, and returns, whereby we produce admirable effects. Besides, we have heats of dungs; and of bellies and maws of living creatures, and of their bloods and bodies; and of hays and herbs laid up moist; of lime unquenched; and such like. Instruments also which generate heat only by motion. And farther, places for strong insulations; and again, places under the earth, which by nature, or art, yield heat. These divers heats we use, as the nature of the operation, which we intend, requireth.

"We have also perspective-houses, where we make demonstrations of all lights and radiations; and of all colours: and out of things uncoloured and transparent, we can represent unto you all several colours; not in rainbows (as it is in gems, and prisms), but of themselves single. We represent also all multiplications of light, which we carry to great distance, and make so sharp as to discern small points and lines. Also all colourations of light; all delusions and deceits of the sight, in figures, magnitudes, motions, colours all demonstrations of shadows. We find also divers means, yet unknown to you, of producing of light originally from divers bodies. We procure means of seeing objects afar off; as in the heaven and remote places; and represent things near as afar off; and things afar off as near; making feigned distances. We have also helps for the sight, far above spectacles and glasses in use. We have also glasses and means to see small and minute bodies perfectly and distinctly; as the shapes and colours of small flies and worms, grains and flaws in gems, which cannot otherwise be seen, observations in urine and blood not otherwise to be seen. We make artificial rainbows, halos, and circles about light. We represent also all manner of reflexions, refractions, and multiplications of visual beams of objects.

"We have also precious stones of all kinds, many of them of great beauty, and to you unknown; crystals likewise; and glasses of divers kinds; and amongst them some of metals vitrificated, and other materials besides those of which you make glass. Also a number of fossils, and imperfect minerals, which you have not. Likewise loadstones of prodigious virtue; and other rare stones, both natural and artificial.

"We have also sound-houses, where we practise and demonstrate all sounds, and their generation. We have harmonies which you have not, of quarter-sounds, and lesser slides of sounds. Divers instruments of music likewise to you unknown, some sweeter than any you have, together with bells and rings that are dainty and sweet. We represent small sounds as great and deep; likewise great sounds extenuate and sharp; we make divers tremblings and warblings of sounds, which in their original are entire. We represent and imitate all articulate sounds and letters, and the voices and notes of beasts and birds. We have certain helps which set to the ear do further the hearing greatly. We have also divers strange and artificial echoes, reflecting the voice many times, and as it were tossing it: and some that give back the voice louder than it came, some shriller, and some deeper; yea, some rendering the voice differing in the letters or articulate sound from that they receive. We have also means to convey sounds in trunks and pipes, in strange lines and distances.

"We have also perfume-houses; wherewith we join also practices of taste. We multiply smells, which may seem strange. We imitate smells, making all smells to breathe out of other mixtures than those that give them. We make divers imitations of taste likewise, so that they will deceive any man's taste. And in this house we contain also a confiture-house; where we make all sweet-meats, dry and moist; and divers pleasant wines, milks, broths, and sallets; in far greater variety than you have.

"We have also engine-houses, where are prepared engines and instruments for all sorts of motions. There we imitate and practise to make swifter motions than any you have, either out of your muskets or any engine that you have: and to make them and multiply them more easily, and with small force, by wheels and other means: and to make them stronger and more violent than yours are; exceeding your greatest cannons and basilisks. We represent also ordnance and instruments of war, and engines of all kinds: and likewise new mixtures and compositions of gun-powder, wild-fires burning in water, and unquenchable. Also fireworks of all variety both for pleasure and use. We imitate also flights of birds; we have some degrees of flying in the air. We have ships and boats for going under water, and brooking of seas; also swimming-girdles and supporters. We have divers curious clocks, and other like motions of return: and some perpetual motions. We imitate also motions of living creatures, by images, of men, beasts, birds, fishes, and serpents. We have also a great number of other various motions, strange for equality, fineness, and subtilty.

"We have also a mathematical house, where are represented all instruments, as well of geometry as astronomy, exquisitely made.

"We have also houses of deceits of the senses; where we represent all manner of feats of juggling, false apparitions, impostures, and illusions; and their fallacies. And surely you will easily believe that we that have so many things truly natural which induce admiration, could in a world of particulars deceive the senses, if we would disguise those things and labour to make them seem more miraculous. But we do hate all impostures, and lies; insomuch as we have severely forbidden it to all our fellows, under pain of ignominy and fines, that they do not show any natural work or thing, adorned or swelling; but only pure as it is, and without all affectation of strangeness.

"These are (my son) the riches of Salomon's House.

"For the several employments and offices of our fellows; we have twelve that sail into foreign countries, under the names of other nations (for our own we conceal); who bring us the books, and abstracts, and patterns of experiments of all other parts. These we call Merchants of Light.

"We have three that collect the experiments which are in all books. These we call Depredators.

"We have three that collect the experiments of all mechanical arts; and also of liberal sciences; and also of practices which are not brought into arts. These we call Mystery-men.

"We have three that try new experiments, such as themselves think good. These we call Pioneers or Miners.

"We have three that draw the experiments of the former four into titles and tables, to give the better light for the drawing of observations and axioms out of them. These we call Compilers.

"We have three that bend themselves, looking into the experiments of their fellows, and cast about how to draw out of them things of use and practise for man's life, and knowledge, as well for works as for plain demonstration of causes, means of natural divinations, and the easy and clear discovery of the virtues and parts of bodies. These we call Dowry-men or Benefactors.

"Then after divers meetings and consults of our whole number, to consider of the former labours and collections, we have three that take care, out of them, to direct new experiments, of a higher light, more penetrating into nature than the former. These we call Lamps.

"We have three others that do execute the experiments so directed, and report them. These we call Inoculators.

"Lastly, we have three that raise the former discoveries by experiments into greater observations, axioms, and aphorisms. These we call Interpreters of Nature.

"We have also, as you must think, novices and apprentices, that the succession of the former employed men do not fail; besides, a great number of servants and attendants, men and women. And this we do also: we have consultations, which of the inventions and experiences which we have discovered shall be published, and which not: and take all an oath of secrecy, for the concealing of those which we think fit to keep secret: though some of those we do reveal sometimes to the state and some not.

"For our ordinances and rites: we have two very long and fair galleries: in one of these we place patterns and samples of all manner of the more rare and excellent inventions in the other we place the statues of all principal inventors. There we have the statue of your Columbus, that discovered the West Indies: also the inventor of ships: your monk that was the inventor of ordnance and of gunpowder: the inventor of music: the inventor of letters: the inventor of printing: the inventor of observations of astronomy: the inventor of works in metal: the inventor of glass: the inventor of silk of the worm: the inventor of wine: the inventor of corn and bread: the inventor of sugars: and all these, by more certain tradition than you have. Then have we divers inventors of our own, of excellent works; which since you have not seen, it were too long to make descriptions of them; and besides, in the right understanding of those descriptions you might easily err. For upon every invention of value, we erect a statue to the inventor, and give him a liberal and honourable reward. These statues are some of brass; some of marble and touch-stone; some of cedar and other special woods gilt and adorned; some of iron; some of silver; some of gold.

"We have certain hymns and services, which we say daily, of Lord and thanks to God for his marvellous works: and forms of prayers, imploring his aid and blessing for the illumination of our labours, and the turning of them into good and holy uses.

"Lastly, we have circuits or visits of divers principal cities of the kingdom; where, as it cometh to pass, we do publish such new profitable inventions as we think good. And we do also declare natural divinations of diseases, plagues, swarms-of hurtful creatures, scarcity, tempests, earthquakes, great inundations, comets, temperature of the year, and divers other things; and we give counsel thereupon, what the people shall do for the prevention and remedy of them."

And when he had said this, he stood up; and I, as I had been taught, kneeled down, and he laid his right hand upon my head, and said; "God bless thee, my son; and God bless this relation, which I have made. I give thee leave to publish it for the good of other nations; for we here are in God's bosom, a land unknown." And so he left me; having assigned a value of about two thousand ducats, for a bounty to me and my fellows. For they give great largesses where they come upon all occasions.

[The rest was not perfected.]

Aging Ivy, Absent Sister

Rose Beardmore

These violent delights have violent ends
And in their triumph die, like fire and powder
Which, as they kiss, consume. The sweetest honey
Is loathsome in his own deliciousness
And in the taste confounds the appetite.
Therefore love moderately.
Romeo and Juliet
Act II, Scene vi, Lines 9–14

BEFORE SHE DEALS the killing blow, Talia looks Marion in the eye. She hesitates. They stand there for a moment, forehead to forehead, while the clash of metal on metal and bodies hitting the ground reverberates all around them. The sky is a violent blue. The sun beats down on the encampment as it goes up in flames, heat from the ground meeting heat from the sky. But Talia does not sweat. She does not pant. She feels the goosebumps rise on her shoulders, and she shakes.

Marion has always been tall. She's always been lovely.

She stands very close and does not move.

"You're my best friend," Talia says quietly. "I love you more than anything else in the world."

She drives the dagger into Marion's stomach and twists methodically, like turning a screwdriver. Marion grunts a little and keels over, her forehead falling on Talia's shoulder.

"No you don't," Marion says through gritted teeth.

Talia can feel her hand wet with blood, resting on Marion's abdomen. The cloth has been soaked right though. It drips into a little puddle between the two of them.

"I'm sorry," Talia says again. She takes the blade out and drives it in once more, lower this time. Marion hisses into her neck. "If it wasn't you, it would've been me."

Marion falls to her knees, and Talia follows. They kneel there together, clutching each other's faces and shoulders, pulling and pushing in some weak semblance of a struggle. Talia brings her hands up to Marion's face, clawing, then settling right under her jaw. The skin is warm and wet with blood. Her pulse fights through the flesh like something with a voice, something with feet that could jump right out of her.

"Please understand," Talia says. "You have to understand."

Marion purses her lips and shakes her head.

"You killed me," she says. "Live with that."

Talia says nothing. She brings her knife to Marion's throat. She slashes it once. The body goes limp and falls to the ground with a sound that she pretends not to hear. Talia bends her arm over her chest, stretching out her left shoulder. There's a cramp building up in the muscle there, one that's been bugging her since she woke up this morning. It loosens.

She walks away stiffly.

When she sees another soldier approaching her with a crossbow, tall and blonde and eyeing her up and down with intent to kill, she whispers *Do it.* There is a pressure in her chest, then a crack. Her breastplate has broken. The feeling goes out of her limbs. She collapses.

Once the smoke has cleared, the wagons carry their bodies away in the same load, pressed against each other in a cold rendezvous. There were summers when Marion and Talia found lips and hips and shoulders like pebbles on a beach, holding them up to the light, grinning with wonder and kissing with childlike eagerness. These things go unitemized, collected from the autumn battlefield without a thought to the significance of seasons prior.

Their bodies rest in a mass grave, right on the coast where the wall ends. And when other lovers find the footholds, grasping the ivy as they murmur confessions and sweet nothings, Talia and Marion stay under the sand, collecting salt and losing their fingernails to the creatures of the sea.

The wall comes down. North and South find peace. But the shore does not give way to hands clawing their way out of the past. It firms with age, and the waves lap over it peacefully, pretending not to know what lies beneath.

But corpses hold secrets under their tongues and between their knuckles. They pass them around like candy wrappers and trading cards. *Talia moved like a lizard through the trees,* they say. *And Marion loved her like a bird loves its prey from above the clouds. Circling. Circling.*

This, they share with each other. The parts that sound like poetry and ring against the hardness of the earth like bells. But they know all the rest—

They know that Talia and Marion met for the first time through a hole in the wall. There were whispers then, too. In childhood, everything sacred feels like a secret. The joy of company is practically unspeakable.

* * *

"Is anyone there?" Marion whispered. She was twelve. Blonde and tall and perpetually sunburnt.

"Yes," said Talia. "I'm here."

"Prove it," said Marion, laughing a little.

"How?" Talia asked.

There was a rustling sound from the other side of the wall. Talia waited for a response.

"Reach in," Marion said. "I have my hand out. Touch it."

Talia pursed her lips. She looked back toward the house. The lights were still on from dinner. She had a little while until she was expected to return for evening tea and bedtime stretches. And it was so dark, so quiet. Nobody would know.

She turned back and put her hands through the hole, trying not to think about the dirt and insects that could be lurking in the darkness. It was cold, and the broken rock scraped against the sides of her palms. She pushed more and more, until the stone reached past her elbow, and she had to stand on her tiptoes to keep her shoulders from bending unnaturally. The wall was thicker than she anticipated.

Finally, Talia felt something warm. The tip of a finger. Two fingers. She pushed her arm even further into the wall and grabbed at Marion's wrist. It was thin. Bony. Marion grabbed back. They held each other like that for a moment, arm-to-arm, in silence. Talia didn't dare breathe. She had never spoken to a Southerner before, let alone touched one.

Marion squeezed her wrist. Once. Twice. Talia laughed a little. She squeezed back.

Marion. *One, two, three.*

Talia. *One, two, three.*

They went on like that for several minutes, playing with the tempo and pressure of touch.

One, two. Wait. Wait. *One, two, three.* Again, repeat. *Your turn.*

They said nothing. There was nothing to tell.

Then, abruptly, there was something sharp, two fingernails pinching the inside of Talia's wrist. She cried out in pain and retracted her hand from the hole, clutching it to her chest and rubbing the damaged skin.

From the other side of the wall, there was a laugh.

"That hurt," Talia said through the hole. "Don't do it again."

"I didn't pinch you *that* hard."

"Yes, you did. It was mean. Apologize," Talia said stiffly.

"No."

She huffed and slid down with her back against the wall. She looked up. The hole was right above her head. It was more obvious, now that she knew it was there. She was surprised she hadn't noticed it earlier, through all her years of playing war games under the thicket of pine trees nearby.

The wall was wide, made of rounded stones and cement, stacked up five meters tall. It was cleaner in the early years of her childhood, when the Northern half of the city could funnel more money into domestic upkeep. They would send men to the border once a month to wash it down and cut the weeds off. Since then, the war took a turn for the worse, and the men stopped showing up. But Talia didn't mind. The wall was covered in vines now. It was a little easier to look at.

But this couldn't have been a symptom of architectural neglect. The hole ran straight through the wall, just wide enough to see to the other side and directly parallel to the ground. Somebody must've drilled it, or beaten the stone in with some kind of power tool.

Talia leaned her head back against the vines. No matter. It wasn't her business. It was probably there for a reason. She would wake up tomorrow morning and pretend she never saw it.

"What's your name?" the girl asked from the other side of the wall.

Talia said nothing. The light in the kitchen went off. The forest went dark. She thought about running back to the house and burying herself in blankets and pillows. But she didn't move.

"My name is Marion," the girl said. "Where are you from?"

Talia remained silent.

"I live right by here," Marion said. "My house is just a short walk from the wall. On the Southern side. You're from the North, right?"

Talia looked down and began picking at her fingernails.

"Well, okay," Marion said. "I'm going back now. I'll be here at the same time tomorrow. See you then?"

A moment passed.

"My name is Talia," Talia said. "See you tomorrow."

She stood and put her face up to the hole. It was dark, and it smelled like dirt and rainwater. But through it, she could see a pair of wide brown eyes. Like a doe. It was Marion, peering through from the South.

Talia flinched a little. She felt the hair rise on the back of her neck. She turned on her heel and ran back to the house, pounding her bare feet against the grass as hard and as fast as she could.

The tea was cold. Ginger and lemon on Tuesdays, always. Josephine and Gregor and Sergio were already halfway done with their cups.

Talia brushed her feet off on the mat and washed her hands. She sat at the table with them and bowed her head apologetically. Mother looked cross. But the rest of them didn't care. Josephine tapped her spoon on the rim of the cup impatiently. She had to get to evening training soon. Talia knew that she never liked being at home for too long. Northerners of a certain age always missed the fight, even when it wasn't kind to them. And Gregor and Sergio were kicking each other under the table. They didn't like the tea without any sugar in it, but Mother made them take it that way regardless. Sugar rations were for birthdays and holidays. Not for greedy little boys.

Talia lay awake that night, staring out the window, toward the South. She wondered if Marion was doing the same thing, on the other side of the wall.

The air was too damp. The sheets stuck to her legs, and the hair at the back of her neck knotted itself against the pillow. She listened to the sound of Gregor and Sergio snoring softly, then the sound of Josephine coming back in and changing into her sleep shirt around midnight. The chorus of rhythmic, unconscious breath settled into the walls like butter, and finally, Talia was able to sleep.

The next morning went about the same as all mornings did. They rose with the sun, then ate bread with strawberry jam and lukewarm coffee, then went off to morning training. They walked in a line, Josephine first, head held high, neck arching like a swan, then Talia, Gregor, and Sergio, all dragging their feet and fighting to keep their eyes open.

The gym was too loud and too bright. Josephine went straight to the combat room, like she always did. Sergio and Gregor went to the jungle set, along with all the other little boys who were too young to play with knives. Talia went to the track and ran laps around the warehouse until she couldn't breathe. When that got boring, she lifted weights by the window. The sky outside was gray and thick with motion. It was going to rain. A hot, miserable rain, probably in the afternoon.

Then school. History, math, science, and battle theory. Talia stared directly forward, watching the lecturer as her eyes went out of focus and the sound of her classmates taking notes faded into a dull buzz in the back of her mind. The tedium was going to kill her.

All the while, she thought only of the wall. Out the back porch, across the lawn, through the forest, behind the thicket of pine trees: the hole in the wall. And Marion looking through it.

The hallways of the schoolhouse were plastered with wartime graphics, mass-produced poster paper bearing images of men and women holding spears. The Southerners were always on the ground, on their backs, bleeding out, with drooping blood red eyes and mouths like fish. There was something distinctly undead about this representation of a person. Marion did not look like that – not in the least bit. Talia wondered if other Southerners might.

For the first time, she wondered about the South, conceptually. How far did it go? Did Southerners go to training compounds, like Talia? Did they go to school? There was no way of knowing. And nobody to ask. Who would even know? It had been ages since the North and South were on stable enough terms to discuss the intricacies of their contrasting cultures – but were they even that different? Really, the proximity must've been worth something: some overlap between plant species, the dishes they cooked on holidays, the time of day they chose to close their curtains.

Talia raised her hand in history class.

"When did we build the wall?" she asked. A silence followed. Then: "Who built the wall?"

"After the Great Collapse about thirty years ago, the Northern Commission for Defense sent an emergency crew to reconstruct a hundred meters of the wall," the boy next to her said loudly. He had a piece of corn stuck in his tooth.

Talia stared at him. Stupidity ran deep in little boys. "I know that," she said. "But who put it up originally?"

He fell silent. So did the rest of the class. The professor stepped in.

"That information isn't available to us," she said. "You might take that up with the Northern Commission for Defense. I'm sure they would know."

Talia sunk down in her chair and looked up at the ceiling. The white tiles shifted into a dreamlike sea of stone and ivy. A pair of eyes, looking back. And open air, on the other side of the world.

When the school day ended, Sergio and Gregor went home to help Mother with the laundry. Talia followed Josephine to the gym, this time joining her in the combat room. She only watched. The older kids were so tall, so strong. All built like birds and leopards, muscled in their shoulders and the bottoms of their thighs, cut and curved in ways that Talia could never imagine on her own body.

Josephine fought like something out of a legend. She chose a long, curved blade to fight with, and it moved as an extension of her wrist, ducking and curving around her opponents without even a tremble, a single moment of hesitation. If she was tired, she didn't show it. She went on like that for hours, pulling surrender out of her challengers like it had been there the whole time, waiting. There was something so deceptively peaceful about that blade, the way it swept through the air, frictionless. When Josephine brought it to her partner's throat for the fifth time, Talia half-expected them to start dancing.

But he rolled his eyes and tapped twice on her arm. Forfeit. He left the mat with his head hung low, and a cheer went up from a group of onlookers.

"That's my sister," Talia whispered to the boy next to her.

"You should be proud," he said. "Your sister is going to win the war."

Talia nodded silently, and she knew he was right.

An hour later, she left the gym without Josephine, running all the way home to escape the impending storm. The air was starting to feel thick against her hair and clothes. A bad sign.

When the sky broke, she went around the house with Mother and Sergio and Gregor, locking all the windows and moving the books and food away from corners of the house that might risk water damage. They ate dinner in silence. Lentils and bread.

Talia watched the clock and prayed that the rain would slow. An hour left. Forty minutes. Twenty. Ten. The rain did not stop, but it lessened. The hard roar of water against the roof eased into a dull pattering.

"I'm going to play outside," Talia announced.

"It's raining," Mother said. "No, you're not."

"I'll bring a coat," Talia mumbled, and grabbed one of Josephine's old ponchos off the rack, dashing out the door and off the back porch before Mother could object.

It was far more difficult to make out the lines of the forest through the wind and the rain, but Talia knew this place like the back of her hand. She could navigate to the wall with her eyes closed.

As promised, Marion was waiting.

"Are you there?" Talia whispered into the hole.

"Yes," Marion said. "I'm here."

Talia put her hand into the wall, and there was Marion's, right where she knew it would be. She squeezed. *One, two, three.* Marion squeezed back. *One, two, three.* They both laughed. The rain was lighter now. Barely a mist.

"Do you know how to climb?" Marion asked.

"Yes," Talia said. "I'm very good at it."

"Not better than me," she said. "I bet I can beat you to the top of the wall."

Talia laughed and pulled her hand back, reaching up to grab one of the thicker vines and jumping as she scrambled to find a foothold. She pulled herself up by her arms desperately, ignoring the rough scratch of the stone and wood against her wrists. She had never climbed anything this high before outside of the gym, where there was always a mat to catch her. But she tried not to think about it. When she finally pulled herself over the top of the wall, Marion was already there, sitting cross-legged.

"You cheated," Talia said, breathing hard.

"Did not," Marion said calmly.

She was taller than Talia expected. Broad in the shoulders and narrow in the face. She had dark blonde hair that curled into a knot at the nape of her neck. Talia had never seen anyone like that before. But then again, she had never seen anyone from the South.

"Nobody knows I'm here," Talia whispered. She didn't know why. But it felt important.

"Me neither," Marion said, and then she laughed a little. "Don't tell, okay?"

"I won't," Talia shook her head. "It's a secret."

They stared at each other for a moment. It was so quiet. And so clear. Talia could recognize the lights of the Northern village. The outline of the schoolhouse. The long path back home. And to the South, new lights. Ones with shapes and colors she didn't recognize. They went on forever, as far as the eye could see.

"I am going to come up here every day for the rest of my life," Talia said.

"Okay," Marion said. "Can I come too?"

"As long as you don't pinch me anymore."

"Okay."

"And don't tell anyone. Not a single soul," Talia warned.

"Okay," Marion said again. "Will you be my friend?"

"Secret friend," Talia smiled. She reached out and grabbed Marion's hand.

One, two, three.

And most days went something like that. The suffocation of training, of school, of meals, of moving about the world and knowing things nobody else knew. And then climbing to the top of the wall and learning them all over again.

Marion had siblings too, with strange names that Talia laughed at. Ruby and Benny and Bash. Ruby, the oldest, who played the guitar and wrote poetry. Benny, who beat everyone at chess. And Bash, who was still learning to speak. They were all destined for the battlefield, too. All Southerners were. Ruby was already getting pretty good at archery, but she fainted at the sight of blood. Talia laughed even harder at that.

They had better food in the South. Or more money to spend on it. Marion was all too willing to steal food right off the dinner table and stuff buns, sandwiches, and candies directly into her coat pockets. Talia ate them all greedily over the edge of the wall. Southern food tasted like wealth. Like winning the war. Also like sugar and fat and some kind of spice that Talia coughed on intermittently.

Marion's thirteenth birthday came in October, then Talia's in November. They drew pictures of each other on leftover notebook paper and played rhyming games.

Marion was far better at words, while Talia was far better at pictures. *Dog* to *bog, speculum* to *pendulum* – none of it came with ease or immediacy. But Talia played the game anyway, closing her eyes and listening to the lilt of Marion's voice as she strung one syllable to the next. She enjoyed this almost as much as her time with a pen and paper. She pushed Marion away by her thigh, positioning her face so the light would catch it properly. The curve of her eyebrow, the sharp point of her nose, both seared themselves into the back of Talia's mind with the setting sun. She drew Marion's face over and over again, from every angle she could reasonably invent on top of the wall. Then, after hours of experimentation, she reached for Marion's hand. The part she knew best.

Hands were the hardest to draw. Especially the creases in the knuckles and the shadows between the veins. But Talia balanced both Marion's hands on her knee and tried not to think about it. The pressure was almost nice. And the feeling of Marion's hands on her leg. That was nice too.

"Are you done yet?" Marion whined as the moon emerged from the coastline.

"No," Talia murmured.

Then, without thinking, she set her drawing down between her legs and took Marion's hands between both of her own. She kissed them both. On the knuckles. On the base of her thumbs. And then, as an afterthought, on both her palms. It was a strange thing to do, and she knew it. But when Talia looked up, Marion was smiling.

Talia bit Marion's left forefinger. Marion shrieked and pulled both her hands back, laughing.

Marion's fourteenth birthday came, then Talia's. For Marion, a marble figurine of a dog, like the strays that roamed the streets in the North. For Talia, a glass ornament that split the light six different ways when she held it up to a window.

"I want a dog when I grow up," Marion said, turning the little figurine over in her hands. "How did you know?"

"Why would you want a dog?" Talia asked. When she thought of dogs, she thought of malnourishment, of dirt caked into fur and pained whimpering from unattended gutters in the middle of the winter.

"For a friend," Marion said. "To play catch with."

"I'm your friend," Talia said. "I'll play catch with you."

"Are you really?" Marion asked sarcastically. "I forgot."

Talia sighed and held her ornament up to the light. It was a prism, and it was sharp in her hand, but not so sharp that it hurt. Just enough to pinch. She turned it around, waiting to catch the right position. Right on time, the light shot through, fracturing into several different hues. An orangey one hit Marion right in the eye.

"Don't be mean," Marion said, squinting as she held a hand up to block the light.

"I'm blinding my enemies," Talia said.

"You're my least favorite enemy," Marion murmured, leaning in to flick Talia on her temple. Talia batted her hand away and flicked her back.

Marion's fifteenth birthday came, then Talia's. They wrote each other letters. Talia put her head in Marion's lap and thought of nothing. Marion put her hands in Talia's hair and whispered about her dreams. It did not matter what the letters said. But Talia kept hers stashed under her pillow, and she read them every time she felt sad. During a particularly long stretch of boredom mid-spring, she memorized her favorite section – *When I think of you, I think of the sound that doves make before they float to the ground. I think of the mole on the right side of your back. I think of all the things I would steal from my own world just to introduce them to yours.*

Marion was always better with words. Talia tried not to remember all the things she'd written – they were ineloquent and clumsy. But true.

When Marion's sixteenth birthday came, she showed Talia a different letter. A summons from the head of the city. It was on thick paper, written with a heavy hand and stamped with a purple seal at the end. Marion had been selected for active service. She would be on the battlefield by next autumn. Talia nodded silently.

"What?" Marion said. "Say something. Please."

"Things are different in the North," Talia explained. "We don't get summoned individually. It's just assumed that we're going to join on our seventeenth birthdays. My sister left two years ago. I'm due for next November."

"Oh," Marion said. "Okay."

Talia watched her. She said nothing. It was so rare that silence fell in the space between them. They had spent so many years filling it with laughter and made-up stories, lying hand-in-hand or head-in-lap and practicing bird calls whenever they ran out of things to say.

Marion grabbed her hand and squeezed. *One, two, three.*

Talia's face stung. She breathed in with a deep shudder. *One, two, three.*

A month later, for Talia's sixteenth birthday, they walked along the top of the wall. It wasn't wide enough for two people to safely travel side-by-side, but Talia could hold Marion's hand from behind and follow along. It was flat and dry and peaceful between the North and South. Nobody lived within half a mile of the wall. An old tradition from the earlier decades of the war, long before both sides ran out of the necessary equipment for bombs.

Marion hummed a song as they went, an old tune that Talia learned as a child.

The gray-eyed morn smiles on the frowning night
Chequering the eastern clouds with streaks of light.

After an hour or so, they reached a lake that lapped right up to the Southern side of the wall. The water was deep and clear right down to the bottom, surrounded in what looked like willow trees. Talia had only ever seen them in books.

Marion knelt and swung her legs over the side of the wall.

"What are you doing?" Talia asked.

"Going down," Marion said. "C'mon, nobody will see. Southerners don't live by the water. Too superstitious."

Talia obliged.

They left their belongings on the grassy shore and tied up their hair. They went into the lake in their undershirts. Talia braced herself, but the water was warm and practically motionless against her skin. They went deeper, until even Marion was up to her shoulders. She grinned, and there were creases around her eyes and mouth. Light bounced off the surface of the water and lit up her eyes, her hair, the outline of her ears. She was the sun. Again and again.

Talia did not know how to swim.

"Close your eyes," Marion said. "Trust me."

Talia nodded and closed her eyes. She felt Marion's arms going around her waist and under her legs. She felt herself being pulled to the surface, lying flat. She was floating.

"Are you there?" Talia asked.

"Yes," Marion said. "I'm here."

And while Talia floated in the water listlessly, Marion told her stories. About her dreams. About fairies living in the forest and the unsuspecting wanderers who fell into their traps. About the things they would do once the war was over. About napping in the middle of the day and eating sugar cubes for breakfast.

They left the water when the sun went down.

Talia walked in front this time, without humming.

Halfway back, Marion stopped. Talia turned back to look at her.

Marion was crying. Silently, but enough that her face glistened red. She wiped her cheeks and grinned in a self-deprecating way.

"I don't want you to fight," she said. "We can run away, or… Please don't go."

Talia shook her head.

"Why not?" Marion whispered.

"I'm good at it," Talia said. "And you will be too. You're going first, anyway."

"I might not."

"But what else is there?"

"This," Marion said. "As long as you want."

Talia did not know what that meant. But she stood there and nodded as if she did.

When Marion pulled her close, she let it happen. She surrendered to the warmth and the inertia and the smell of lake water, turned sweet against her skin. She bent into the impossible goodness of this thing, the one thing she would always have to herself. Marion's lips met hers, and Talia tried not to move. She tried not to breathe too hard. She felt something crack between her temples.

Talia put her hand on the side of Marion's neck and pushed her nose against her cheek, like a failure, like someone too eager for something she knew she could not have. But it was so nice to want something. It was so nice to be wanted back.

They walked home in silence. When they reached the split where Talia always went North and Marion always went South, they stopped. Marion was still crying. Talia thought of shaking her, tickling and poking until she could smile again. She did not. It didn't feel right.

"I don't want to see you again," Marion said, sniffling and wiping her eyes with her sleeve. "Not if you still want to fight."

"I don't understand," Talia said. "That's not fair."

"Yes, it is," Marion whispered. "It's me or the North. Choose."

"That's not what it is."

"Yes. That's exactly what it is."

"It's my birthday," Talia hissed.

"I don't care. I don't want you to die. And I don't want you to kill anyone."

Talia stared at her blankly. Marion looked away and crossed her arms over her chest.

"What else am I supposed to do?" Talia asked.

"Anything else," Marion said, steadily growing louder. "Go swimming. Write stories. Or just sleep all day. It doesn't matter. Most people can get through life without going to war. It's not a requirement."

"Not where I live," Talia said. "That's not an option for me."

"So go somewhere else!" Marion yelled, throwing her arms wide and gesticulating to the open air around them. "Go anywhere else! I'll go with you, I don't care! I'll go!"

Then, as if pushed by an invisible wind, she drew in close to Talia. She put her hands on either side of her face and pressed their noses together.

"Please. Anywhere else," Marion said again. "I will go with you."

"You're being ridiculous," Talia said. She pushed Marion's hands off and turned away. The imprint stayed, the warmth outlined on her cheeks. She ignored it. "I'll see you tomorrow."

"No, you won't."

"Yes, I will," Talia said.

She swung her leg over the side of the wall and made her way down.

The next day, she went to the wall. And the next, and the next, and the next.

Marion was not there.

Winter came and went. Then spring. And summer.

Marion's birthday came in October, like it always did, and still Marion was not there.

On her own seventeenth birthday, Talia reported to the barracks, just an hour's walk outside of the Northern village. Josephine had already been promoted to Captain, and when she walked into the hall, Talia bowed in respect with all the rest of the soldiers. In training, it was an honor when her own sister handed her the weapon she would take to the battlefield.

It was a curved blade. Long and dark gray and shining in the fluorescent light of the compound. Talia turned it over in her palm. It was cold. It was beautiful.

A week later, Talia went to the battlefield with the rest of her troop. When she saw Marion's face through the mob of bodies, she did not turn and run the other way. She charged forward.

* * *

The bodies under the beach know the rest. All except this:

Captain Josephine of the Northern Militia visits home twice a month. It's the only time she gets off duty. Twenty-four hours at a time, like clockwork. While she's there, she helps with the laundry and the dishes. She brings home extra rations, so Sergio and Gregor always have something to look forward to. They're fifteen now – old enough to care more seriously about training. They don't ask for sugar cubes anymore. They ask for hats and jackets with the Northern seal. Dull, discarded blades. Josephine provides what she can.

At the end of October, she does this, and more. She returns home with a medal and a bouquet of vervain. She weeps with Mother and Sergio and Gregor as they assemble a shrine for the absent sister.

They say her name over and over again until it sounds like a prayer. It is.

Talia, be at peace. Talia, leave us. Talia, rest.

Once that is done, once the boys are in bed and Mother has gone back to her reading, Josephine cleans up what is left of dinner, what is left of mourning. Tissues. Trinkets belonging to no one. Letters addressed to a nonexistent place. The house looks bare. Unaffected by the trauma of a child ripped away from the world.

Josephine brushes her hands off on her thighs and exits the house through the back porch. She makes her way over the back lawn, through the forest, past the thicket of pine trees. There is a hole in the wall. Every time she returns, she remembers the agony, the labor that went into it. Every day for two weeks, she would come to this wall with a hammer. Her arms were so sore, she fell behind in training. She was only thirteen then. Now, at twenty, she has to hunch down just to see through it.

"Are you there?" she whispers.

"Yes," Ruby says from the other side of the wall. "I'm here."

"Are you okay?" Josephine whispers. Without realizing it, she cries. Her tears land heavily on the trodden patch of grass beneath her.

"No," Ruby says. "But I'm glad you're here."

The Chilean Bluejacket

A Tale of Easter Island

Louis Becke

ALONE, in the most solitary part of the Eastern Pacific, midway between the earthquake-shaken littoral of Chili and Peru, and the thousand palm-clad islets of the Low Archipelago, lies an island of the days 'when the world was young'. By the lithe-limbed, soft-eyed descendants of the forgotten and mysterious race that once quickened the land, this lonely outlier of the isles of the Southern Seas is called in their soft tongue Rapanui, or the Great Rapa.

A hundred and seventy years ago Roggewein, on the dawn of an Easter Sunday, discerned through the misty, tropic haze the grey outlines of an island under his lee beam, and sailed down upon it.

He landed, and even as the grim and hardy old navigator gazed upon and wondered at the mysteries of the strange island, so this day do the cunning men of science, who, perhaps once in thirty years, go thither in the vain effort to read the secret of an all-but-perished race. And they can tell us but vaguely that the stupendous existing evidences of past glories are of immense and untold age, and show their designers to have been coeval with the builders of the buried cities of Mexico and Peru; beyond that, they can tell us nothing.

Who can solve the problem? What manner of an island king was he who ruled the builders of the great terraced platforms of stone, the carvers of the huge blocks of lava, the hewers-out with rudest tools of the Sphinx-like images of trachyte, whose square, massive, and disdainful faces have for unnumbered centuries gazed upwards and outwards over the rolling, sailless swell of the mid-Pacific?

And the people of Rapa-nui of today? you may ask. Search the whole Pacific – from Pylstaart, the southern sentinel of the Friendlies, to the one-time buccaneer-haunted, far-away Pelews; thence eastward through the white-beached coral atolls of the Carolines and Marshalls, and southwards to the cloud-capped Marquesas and the sandy stretches of the Paumotu – and you will find no handsomer men or more graceful women than the light-skinned people of Rapa-nui.

Yet are they but the survivors of a race doomed – doomed from the day that Roggewein in his clumsy, high-pooped frigate first saw their land, and marvelled at the imperishable relics of a dead greatness. With smiling faces they welcomed him – a stranger from an unknown, outside world, with cutlass at waist and pistol in hand – as a god; he left them a legacy of civilisation – a hideous and cruel disease that swept through the amiable and unsuspicious race as an epidemic, and slew its thousands, and scaled with the hand of Death and Silence the eager life that had then filled the square houses of lava in many a town from the wave-beaten cliffs of Terano Kau to Ounipu in the west.

Ask of the people now, "Whence came ye? and whose were the hands that fashioned these mighty images and carved upon these stones?" and in their simple manner they will answer, "From Rapa, under the setting sun, came our fathers; and we were then a great people, even as the *oneone* [sand] of the beach... Our Great King was it, he whose name is forgotten by us, that caused these temples and cemeteries and terraces to be built; and it was in his time that the forgotten fathers of our fathers carved from out of the stone of the quarries of Terano Kau the great Silent Faces that gaze for ever upward to the sky.... *Ai-A-Ah!* ... But it was long ago.... Ah! a great people were we then in those days, and the wild people to the West called us *te tagata te pito henua* [the people who live at the end of the world] .... and we know no more."

And here the knowledge and traditions of a broken people begin and end.

Chapter I

A SOFT, COOL MORNING in November, 187—. Between Ducie and Pitcairn Islands two American whale-ships cruise lazily along to the gentle breath of the south-east trades, when the look-out from both vessels see a third sail bearing down upon them. In a few hours she is close enough to be recognised as one of the luckiest sperm whalers of the fleet – the brig *Pocahontas*, of Martha's Vineyard.

Within a quarter of mile of the two ships – the *Nassau* and the *Dagget* – the newcomer backs her foreyard and hauls up her mainsail. A cheer rises from the ships. She wants to 'gam', i.e. to gossip. With eager hands four boats are lowered from the two ships, and the captains and second mates of each are soon racing for the *Pocahontas*.

The skipper of the brig, after shaking hands with his visitors and making the usual inquiries as to their luck, number of days out from New Bedford, etc., led the way to his cabin, and, calling his Portuguese steward, had liquor and a box of cigars brought out. The captain of the *Pocahontas* was a little, withered-up old man with sharp, deep-set eyes of brightest blue, and had the reputation of possessing the most fiery and excitable temper of any of the captains of the sixty or seventy American whale-ships that in those days cruised the Pacific from the West Coast of South America to Gaum in the Ladrones.

After drinking some of his potent New England rum with his visitors, and having answered all their queries, the master of the *Pocahontas* inquired if they had seen anything of a Chilian man-of-war further to the eastward. No, they had not.

"Then just settle down, gentlemen, for awhile, and I'll tell you one of the curiousest things that I ever saw or heard of. I've logged partiklars of the whole business, and when I get to Oahu [Honolulu] I mean to narrate just all I do know to Father Damon of the Honolulu *Friend*. Thar's nothing like a newspaper fur showin' a man up when he's been up to any onnatural villainy, and thinks no one will ever know anything about it. So just take hold and listen."

The two captains nodded, and he told them this.

Ten days previously, when close in to barren and isolated Sala-y-Gomez, the *Pocahontas* had spoken the Chilian corvette *O'Higgins*, bound from Easter Island to Valparaiso. The captain of the corvette entertained the American master courteously, and explained his ship's presence so far to the eastward, by stating that the Government had instructed him to call at Easter Island, and pick up an Englishman in the Chilian service, who had been sent there to examine and report on the colossal statues and mysterious terraces of that lonely island. The Englishman, as Commander Gallegos said, was a valued servant of the Republic, and had for some years served in its Navy as a surgeon on board *El Almirante Cochrane*, the flag-ship. He had left Valparaiso in the whale-ship *Comboy* with the intention of remaining three months on the island. At the end of that time a war vessel was to call and convey him back to Chili. But in less than two months the Republic was in the throes of a deadly struggle with Peru – here the commander of the *O'Higgins* bowed to the American captain, and, pointing to a huge scar that traversed his bronzed face from temple to chin, said, "in which I had the honour to receive this, and promotion" – and nearly two years had elapsed ere the Government had time to think again of the English scientist and his mission. Peace restored, the *O'Higgins* was ordered to proceed to the island and bring him back; and as the character of the natives was not well known, and it was feared he might have been killed, Commander Gallegos was instructed to execute summary justice upon the people of the island, if such was the case.

But, the Chilian officer said, on reaching the island he had found the natives to be very peaceable and inoffensive, and, although much alarmed at the appearance of his armed landing party from the corvette, they had given him a letter from the Englishman, and had satisfied him that Dr. Francis T— had remained with them for some twelve months only, and had then left the island in a passing whale-ship, and Commander Gallegos, making them suitable presents, bade them good-bye, and steamed away to Valparaiso.

This was all the polite little commander had to say, and, after a farewell glass of wine, his visitor rose to go, when the captain of the corvette casually inquired if the *Pocahontas* was likely to call at the island.

"I ask you," he said in his perfect English, "because one of my ship's company deserted there. You, senor, may possibly meet with him there. Yet he is of no value, and he is no sailor, and but a lad. He was very ill most of the time, and this was his first voyage. I took him ashore with me in my boat, as he besought me eagerly to do so, and the little devil ran away and hid, or was hidden by the natives."

"Why didn't you get him back?" asked the captain of the *Pocahontas*.

"That was easy enough, but" – and the commander raised his eyebrows and shrugged his shoulders – "of what use? He was no use to the corvette. Better for him to stay there, and perhaps recover, than to die on board the *O'Higgins* and be thrown to the blue sharks. Possibly, senor, you may find him well, and it may suit you to take him to your good ship, and teach him the business of catching the whale. My trade is to show my crew how to fight, and such as he are of no value for that."

Then the two captains bade each other farewell, and in another hour the redoubtable *O'Higgins*, with a black trail of smoke streaming astern, was ten miles away on her course to Valparaiso.

A week after the *Pocahontas* lay becalmed close in to the lee side of Rapa-nui, and within sight of the houses of the principal village. The captain, always ready to get a 'green' hand, was thinking of the chances of his securing the Chilian deserter, and decided to lower a boat and try. Taking four men with him, he pulled ashore, and landed at the village of Hagaroa.

Chapter II

SOME SIXTY OR SEVENTY natives clustered round the boat as she touched the shore. With smiling faces and outstretched hands they surrounded the captain, and pressed upon him their simple gifts of ripe bananas and fish baked in leaves, begging him to first eat a little and then walk with them to Mataveri, their largest village, distant a mile, where preparations were being made to welcome him formally. The skipper, nothing loth, bade his crew not to go too far away in their rambles, and, accompanied by his boatsteerer, was about to set off with the natives, when he remembered the object of his visit, and asked a big, well-made woman, the only native present that could speak English, "Where is the man you hid from the man-of-war?"

There was a dead silence, and for nearly half a minute no one spoke. The keen blue eyes of the American looked from one face to another inquiringly, and then settled on the fat, good-natured features of Varua, the big woman.

Holding her hands, palms upwards, to the captain, she endeavoured to speak, and then, to his astonishment, he saw that her dark eyes were filled with tears. And then, as if moved with some sudden and sorrowful emotion, a number of other women and young girls, murmuring softly in pitying tones, "*E mate! E mate!*" ["Dead! Dead!"] came to his side, and held their hands out to him with the same supplicating gesture.

The captain was puzzled. For all his island wanderings and cruises he had no knowledge of any Polynesian dialect, and the tearful muteness of the fat Varua was still unbroken. At last she placed one hand on his sleeve, and, pointing land-ward with the other, said, in her gentle voice, "Come," and taking his hand in hers, she led the way, the rest of the people following in silence.

For about half a mile they walked behind the captain and his boatsteerer and the woman Varua without uttering a word. Presently Varua stopped, and called out the name of "Taku" in a low voice.

A fine, handsome native, partly clothed in European sailor's dress, stepped apart from the others and came to her.

Turning to the captain, she said, "This is Taku the Sailor. He can speak a little English and much Spanish. I tell him now to come with us, for he has a paper."

Although not understanding the relevancy of her remark, the captain nodded, and then with gentle insistence Varua and the other women urged him on, and they again set out.

A few minutes more, and they were at the foot of one of the massive-stoned and ancient *papaku*, or cemeteries, on the walls of which were a number of huge images carved from trachyte, and representing the trunk of the human body. Some of the figures bore on their heads crowns of red tufa, and the aspect of all was towards the ocean. At the foot of the wall of the *papaku* were a number of prone figures, with hands and arms sculptured in low relief, the outspread fingers clasping the hips.

About a cable length from the wall stood two stone houses – memorials of the olden time – and it was to these that Varua and the two white men, attended now by women only, directed their steps.

The strange, unearthly stillness of the place, the low whispers of the women, the array of colossal figures with sphinx-like faces set to the sea, and the unutterable air of sadness that enwrapped the whole scene, overawed even the unimaginative mind of the rough whaling captain, and he experienced a curious feeling of relief when his gentle-voiced guide entered through the open doorway the largest of the two houses, and, in a whisper, bade him follow.

A delightful sense of coolness was his first sensation on entering, and then with noiseless step the other women followed and seated themselves on the ground.

Still clasping his hand, Varua led him to the farther end of the house, and pointed to a motionless figure that lay on a couch of mats, covered with a large piece of navy-blue calico. At each side of the couch sat a young native girl, and their dark, luminous eyes, shining star-like from out the wealth of black, glossy hair that fell upon their bronzed shoulders, turned wonderingly upon the stranger who had broken in upon their watch.

Motioning the girls aside, Varua released her hold of the white man's hand and drew the cloth from off the figure, and the seaman's pitying glance fell upon the pale, sweet features of a young white girl.

But for the unmistakable pallid hue of death he thought at first that she slept. In the thin, delicate hands, crossed upon her bosom, there was placed, after the manner of those of her faith, a small metal crucifix. Her hair, silky and jet black, was short like a man's, and the exquisitely modelled features, which even the coldness of death had not robbed of their beauty, showed the Spanish blood that, but a few hours before, had coursed through her veins.

Slowly the old seaman drew the covering over the still features, and, with an unusual emotion stirring his rude nature, he rose, and, followed by Varua, walked outside and sat upon a broken pillar of lava that lay under the wall of the *papaku*.

Calling his boatsteerer, he ordered him to return to the beach and go off to the ship with instructions to the mate to have a coffin made as quickly as possible and send it ashore; and then, at a glance from Varua, who smiled a grave approval as she listened to his orders, he followed her and the man she called Taku into the smaller of the two houses.

Round about the inside walls of this ancient dwelling of a forgotten race were placed a number of seamen's chests made of cedar and camphor wood – the *lares* and *penates* of most Polynesian houses. The gravelled floor was covered with prettily-ornamented mats of *fala* [the screw-palm].

Seating herself, with Taku the Sailor, on the mats, Varua motioned the captain to one of the boxes, and then told him a tale that moved him – rough, fierce, and tyrannical as was his nature – to the deepest pity.

Chapter III

"IT IS NOT YET twenty days since the fighting *pahi afi* [steamer] came here, and we of Mataveri saw the boat full of armed men land on the beach at Hagaroa. Filled with fear were we; but yet as we had done no wrong we stood on the beach to welcome. And, ere the armed men had left the boat, we knew them to be the *sipaniola* from Chili – the same as those that came here ten years ago in three ships, and seized and bound three hundred and six of our men, and carried them away for slaves to the land of the Tae Manu, and of whom none but four ever returned to Rapa-nui. And then we trembled again."

(She spoke of the cruel outrage of 1862, when three Peruvian slave-ships took away over three hundred islanders to perish on the guano-fields of the Chincha Islands).

"The chief of the ship was a little man, and he called out to us in the tongue of Chili, 'Have no fear,' and took a little gun from out its case of skin that hung by his side, and giving it to a man in the boat, stepped over to us, and took our hands in his.

"'Is there none among ye that speak my tongue?' he said quickly.

"Now, this man here, Taku the Sailor, speaketh the tongue of Chili, but he feared to tell it, lest they might take him away for a sailor; so he held his lips tight.

"Then I, who for six years dwelt with English people at Tahiti, was pushed forward by those behind me and made to talk in English; and lo! the little man spoke in your tongue even as quick as he did in that of Chili. And then he told us that he came for Farani [Frank].

"Now this Farani was a young white man of Peretania [England], big and strong. He came to us a year and a half ago. He was rich, and had with him chests filled with presents for us of Rapa-nui; and he told us that he came to live a while among us, and look upon the houses of stone and the Faces of the Silent that gaze out upon the sea. For a year he dwelt with us and became as one of ourselves, and we loved him; and then, because no ship came, he began to weary and be sad. At last a ship – like thine, one that hunts for the whale – came, and Farani called us together, and placed a letter in the hands of the chief at Mataveri, and said: 'If it so be that a ship cometh from Chili, give these my words to the captain, and all will be well.' Then he bade us farewell and was gone.

"All this I said in quick words, and then we gave to the little fighting chief the letter Farani had written. When he had counted the words in the letter, he said: '*Bueno*, it is well,' and called to his men, and they brought out many gifts for us from the boat – cloth, and garments for men and women, and two great bags of canvas filled with tobacco. *Ai-A-Ah!* many presents he gave us – this because of the good words Farani had set down in the letter. Then the little chief said to me, 'Let these my men walk where they list, and I will go with thee to Mataveri and talk with the chief.'

"So the sailors came out of the boats carrying their guns and swords in their hands, but the little chief, whose *avagutu* [moustache] stuck out on each side of his face like the wings of a flying-fish when it leaps in terror from the mouth of the hungry bonito, spoke angrily, and they laid their guns and swords back in the boats.

"So the sailors went hither and thither with our young men and girls; and, although at that time I knew it not, she, who now is not, was one of them, and walked alone.

"Then I, and Taku the Sailor, and the little sea-chief came to the houses of Mataveri, and he stayed awhile and spoke good words to us. And we, although we fear the men of Chili for the wrong they once did us, were yet glad to listen, for we also are of their faith.

"As we talked, there came inside the house a young girl named Temeteri, whom, when Farani had been with us for two months, he had taken for wife; and she bore him a son. But from the day that he had sailed away she became sick with grief; and when, after many months, she told me that Farani had said he would return to her, my heart was heavy, for I know the ways of white men with us women of brown skins. Yet I feared to tell her he lied and would return no more. Now, this girl Temeteri was sought after by a man named Huarani, the son of Heremai, who desired to marry her now that Farani had gone, and he urged her to question the chief of the fighting ship, and ask him if Farani would return.

"So I spoke of Temeteri. He laughed and shook his head, and said: 'Nay, Farani the Englishman will return no more; but yet one so beautiful as she,' and he pointed to Temeteri, 'should have many lovers and know no grief. Let her marry again and forget him, and this is my marriage gift to her,' and he threw a big golden coin upon the mat on which the girl sat.

"She took it in her hand and threw it far out through the doorway with bitter words, and rose and went away to her child.

"Then the little captain went back to the boat and called his men to him, and lo! one was gone. Ah! he was angry, and a great scar that ran down one side of his face grew red with rage. But soon he laughed, and said to us: 'See, there be one of my people hidden away from me. Yet he is but a boy, and sick; and I care not to stay and search for him. Let him be thy care so that he wanders not away and perishes among the broken lava; he will be in good hands among the people of Rapa-nui.' With that he bade us farewell, and in but a little time the great fighting ship had gone away towards the rising sun.

"All that day and the next we searched, but found not him who had hidden away; but in the night of the second day, when it rained heavily, and Taku (who is my brother's son) and I and my two children worked at the making of a *kupega* [net], he whom we had sought came to the door. And as we looked our hearts were filled with pity, for, as he put out his hands to us, he staggered and fell to the ground.

"So Taku – who is a man of a good heart – and I lifted him up and carried him to a bed of soft mats, and as I placed my hand on his bosom to see if he was dead, lo! it was soft as a woman's, and I saw that the stranger was a young girl!

"I took from her the wet garments and brought warm clothes of *mamoe* [blankets], and Taku made a great fire, and we rubbed her cold body and her hands and feet till her life came back to her again, and she sat up and ate a little beaten-up taro. When the night and the dawn touched she slept again.

"The sun was high when the white girl awoke, and fear leapt into her eyes when she saw the house filled with people who came to question Taku and me about the stranger. With them came the girl Temeteri, whose head was still filled with foolish thoughts of Farani, her white lover.

"I went to the strange girl, put my arm around her, and spoke, but though she smiled and answered in a little voice, I understood her not, for I know none of the tongue of Chili. But yet she leaned her head against my bosom, and her eyes that were as big and bright as Fetuaho, the star of the morning, looked up into mine and smiled through their tears.

"There was a great buzzing of talk among the women. Some came to her and touched her hands and forehead, and said: 'Let thy trembling cease; we of Rapa-nui will be kind to the white girl.'

"And as the people thronged about her and talked, she shook her head and her eyes sought mine, and hot tears splashed upon my hand. Then the mother of Temeteri raised her voice and called to Taku the Sailor, and said: 'O Taku, thou who knowest her tongue, ask her of Farani, my white son, the husband of my daughter.'

"The young girls in the house laughed scornfully at old Pohere, for some of them had loved Farani, who yet had put them all aside for Temeteri, whose beauty exceeded theirs; and so they hated her and laughed at her mother. Then Taku, being pressed by old Pohere, spoke in the tongue of Chili, but not of Temeteri.

"Ah! She sprang to her feet and talked then! and the flying words chased one another from her lips; and these things told she to Taku: – She had hidden among the broken lava and watched the little captain come back to the boat and bid us farewell. Then when night came she had crept out and gone far over to the great *papaku*, and lay down to hide again, for she feared the fighting ship might return to seek her. And all that day she lay hidden in the lava till night fell upon her again, and hunger drove her to seek the faces of men. In the rain she all but perished, till God brought her feet to this, my house.

"Then said Taku the Sailor: 'Why didst thou flee from the ship?'

"The white girl put her hands to her face and wept, and said: 'Bring me my jacket.'

"I gave to her the blue sailor's jacket, and from inside of it she took a little flat thing and placed it in her bosom.

"Again said old Pohere to Taku: 'O man of slow tongue, ask her of Farani.' So he asked in this wise:

"'See, O White Girl, that is Pohere, the mother of Temeteri, who bore a son to the white man that came here to look upon the Silent Faces; and because he came from thy land, and because of the heart of Temeteri, which is dried up for love of him, does this foolish old woman ask thee if thou hast seen him; for long months ago he left Rapa-nui. In our tongue we call him Farani.'

"The girl looked at Taku the Sailor, and her lips moved, but no words came. Then from her bosom she took the little flat thing and held it to him, but sickness was in her hand so that it trembled, and that which she held fell to the ground. So Taku stooped and picked it up from where it lay on the mat, and looked, and his eyes blazed, and he shouted out '*Aue!*' for it was the face of Farani that looked into his! And as he held it up in his hand to the people, they, too, shouted in wonder; and then the girl Temeteri cast aside those that stood about her, and tore it from his hand and fled.

"'Who is she?' said the white girl, in a weak voice to Taku; 'and why hath she robbed me of that which is dear to me?' and Taku was ashamed, and turned his face away from her because of two things – his heart was sore for Temeteri, who is a blood relation, and was shamed because her white lover had deserted her; and he was full of pity for the white girl's tears. So he said nought.

"The girl raised herself, and her hand caught Taku by the arm, and these were her words: 'O man, for the love of Jesu Christ, tell me what was this woman Temeteri to my husband?'

"Now Taku the Sailor was sore troubled, and felt it hard to hurt her heart, yet he said: 'Was Farani, the Englishman, thy husband?'

"She wept again, 'He was my husband.'

"'Why left he one as fair as thee?' said Taku, in wonder.

"She shook her head. 'I know not, except he loved to look upon strange lands; yet he loved me.'

"'He is a bad man,' said Taku. 'He loved others as well as thee. The girl that fled but now with his picture was wife to him here. He loved her, and she bore him a son.'

"The girl's head fell on my shoulder, and her eyes closed, and she became as dead; and lo! in a little while, as she strove to speak, blood poured from her mouth and ran down over her bosom.

"'It is the hand of Death,' said Taku the Sailor.

"Where she now lies, there died she, at about the hour when the people of Vaihou saw the sails of thy ship.

"We have no priest here, for the good father that was here three years ago is now silent [i.e. dead]; yet did Taku and I pray with her. And ere she died she said she would set down some words on paper; so Alrema, my little daughter, hastened to Mataveri, and the chief sent back some paper and *vai tuhi* [ink] that had belonged to the good priest. So with weak hand she set down some words, but even as she wrote she rose up and threw out her hands, and called out: 'Francisco! Francisco!' and fell back, and was dead."

Chapter IV

THE CAPTAIN of the *Pocahontas* dashed the now fast-falling tears from his eyes, and with his rough old heart swelling with pity for the poor wanderer, took from Taku the sheet of paper on which the heart-broken girl's last words were traced.

Ere he could read it a low murmur of voices outside told him his crew had returned. They carried a rude wooden shell, and then with bared heads the captain and boatsteerer entered the house where she lay.

Again the old man raised the piece of navy blue cloth from off the sweet, sad face, and a heavy tear dropped down upon her forehead. Then, aided by the gentle, sympathetic women, his task was soon finished, and two of his crew entered and carried their burden to its grave. Service there was none – only the prayers and tears of the brown women of Rapa-nui.

Ere he said farewell the captain of the whale-ship placed money in the hands of Varua and Taku. They drew back, hurt and mortified. Seeing his mistake, the seaman desired Varua to give the money to the girl Temeteri.

"Nay, sir," said Varua, "she would but give me bitter words. Even when she who is now silent was not yet cold, Temeteri came to the door of the house where she lay and spat twice on the ground, and taking up gravel in her hand cast it at her, and cursed her in the name of our old heathen gods. And as for money, we here in Rapa-nui need it not. May Christ protect thee on the sea. Farewell!"

The captain of the *Pocahontas* rose and came to the cabin table, and motioning to his guests to fill their glasses, said –

"'Tis a real sad story, gentlemen, and if I should ever run across Doctor Francis, I should talk some to him. But see here. Here is my log; my mate, who is a fancy writist, wrote it at my dictation. I can't show you the letter that the pore creature herself wrote; that I ain't going to show to anyone."

The two captains rose and stood beside him, and read the entry in the log of the *Pocahontas*.

November 28, 187—.

This day I landed at Easter Island, to try and obtain as a 'green' hand a young Chilian seaman who, the captain of the Chilian corvette O'Higgins informed me, had run away there. On landing I was shown the body of a young girl, whom the natives stated to be the deserter. She had died that morning. Buried her as decently as circumstances would permit. From a letter she wrote on the morning of her death I learned her name to be Senora Teresa T—. Her husband, Dr. Francis T—, was an Englishman in the service of the Chilian Republic. He was sent out on a scientific mission to the island, and his wife followed him in the O'Higgins disguised as a blue-jacket. I should take her to have been about nineteen years of age.

SPENCE ELDRIDGE, MASTER

MANUAL LEGASPE, 2ND OFFICER
Brig POCAHONTAS, of Martha's Vineyard, U.S.A.

"Well, that's curious now," said the skipper of the *Nassau*; "why, I knew that man. He left the island in the *King Darius*, of New Bedford, and landed at Ponape in the Caroline Group, whar those underground ruins are at Metalanien Harbour. Guess he wanted to potter around there a bit. But he got inter some sorter trouble among the natives there, an' he got shot."

"Aye," said the captain of the *Dagget*, "I remember the affair. I was mate of the *Josephine*, and we were lying at Jakoits Harbour when he was killed, and now I remember the name too. Waal, he wasn't much account, anyhow."

Ten years ago a wandering white man stood, with Taku the Sailor, at the base of the wall of the great *papaku*, and the native pointed out the last resting-place of the wanderer. There, under the shadow of the Silent Faces of Stone, the brave and loving heart that dared so much is at peace for ever.

The Blindman's World

Edward Bellamy

THE NARRATIVE to which this note is introductory was found among the papers of the late Professor S. Erastus Larrabee, and, as an acquaintance of the gentleman to whom they were bequeathed, I was requested to prepare it for publication. This turned out a very easy task, for the document proved of so extraordinary a character that, if published at all, it should obviously be without change. It appears that the professor did really, at one time in his life, have an attack of vertigo, or something of the sort, under circumstances similar to those described by him, and to that extent his narrative may be founded on fact. How soon it shifts from that foundation, or whether it does at all, the reader must conclude for himself. It appears certain that the professor never related to anyone, while living, the stranger features of the experience here narrated, but this might have been merely from fear that his standing as a man of science would be thereby injured.

The Professor's Narrative

AT THE TIME of the experience of which I am about to write, I was professor of astronomy and higher mathematics at Abercrombie College. Most astronomers have a specialty, and mine was the study of the planet Mars, our nearest neighbor but one in the Sun's little family. When no important celestial phenomena in other quarters demanded attention, it was on the ruddy disc of Mars that my telescope was oftenest focused. I was never weary of tracing the outlines of its continents and seas, its capes and islands, its bays and straits, its lakes and mountains. With intense interest I watched from week to week of the Martial winter the advance of the polar ice-cap toward the equator, and its corresponding retreat in the summer; testifying across the gulf of space as plainly as written words to the existence on that orb of a climate like our own. A specialty is always in danger of becoming an infatuation, and my interest in Mars, at the time of which I write, had grown to be more than strictly scientific. The impression of the nearness of this planet, heightened by the wonderful distinctness of its geography as seen through a powerful telescope, appeals strongly to the imagination of the astronomer. On fine evenings I used to spend hours, not so much critically observing as brooding over its radiant surface, till I could almost persuade myself that I saw the breakers dashing on the bold shore of Kepler Land, and heard the muffled thunder of avalanches descending the snow-clad mountains of Mitchell. No earthly landscape had the charm to hold my gaze of that far-off planet, whose oceans, to the unpracticed eye, seem but darker, and its continents lighter, spots and bands.

Astronomers have agreed in declaring that Mars is undoubtedly habitable by beings like ourselves, but, as may be supposed, I was not in a mood to be satisfied with considering it merely habitable. I allowed no sort of question that it was inhabited. What manner of beings these inhabitants might be I found a fascinating speculation. The variety of types appearing in mankind even on this small Earth makes it most presumptuous to assume that the denizens of different planets may not be characterized by diversities far profounder. Wherein such diversities, coupled with a general resemblance to man, might consist, whether in mere physical differences or in different mental laws, in the lack of certain of the great passional motors of men or the possession of quite others, were weird themes of never-failing attractions for my mind. The El Dorado visions with which the virgin mystery of the New World inspired the early Spanish explorers were tame and prosaic compared with the speculations which it was perfectly legitimate to indulge, when the problem was the conditions of life on another planet.

It was the time of the year when Mars is most favorably situated for observation, and, anxious not to lose an hour of the precious season, I had spent the greater part of several successive nights in the observatory. I believed that I had made some original observations as to the trend of the coast of Kepler Land between Lagrange Peninsula and Christie Bay, and it was to this spot that my observations were particularly directed.

On the fourth night other work detained me from the observing-chair till after midnight. When I had adjusted the instrument and took my first look at Mars, I remember being unable to restrain a cry of admiration. The planet was fairly dazzling. It seemed nearer and larger than I had ever seen it before, and its peculiar ruddiness more striking. In thirty years of observations, I recall, in fact, no occasion when the absence of exhalations in our atmosphere has coincided with such cloudlessness in that of Mars as on that night. I could plainly make out the white masses of vapor at the opposite edges of the lighted disc, which are the mists of its dawn and evening. The snowy mass of Mount Hall over against Kepler Land stood out with wonderful clearness, and I could unmistakably detect the blue tint of the ocean of De La Rue, which washes its base – a feat of vision often, indeed, accomplished by star-gazers, though I had never done it to my complete satisfaction before.

I was impressed with the idea that if I ever made an original discovery in regard to Mars, it would be on that evening, and I believed that I should do it. I trembled with mingled exultation and anxiety, and was obliged to pause to recover my self-control. Finally, I placed my eye to the eye-piece, and directed my gaze upon the portion of the planet in which I was especially interested. My attention soon became fixed and absorbed much beyond my wont, when observing, and that itself implied no ordinary degree of abstraction. To all mental intents and purposes I was on Mars. Every faculty, every susceptibility of sense and intellect, seemed gradually to pass into the eye, and become concentrated in the act of gazing. Every atom of nerve and will power combined in the strain to see a little, and yet a little, and yet a little, clearer, farther, deeper.

The next thing I knew I was on the bed that stood in a corner of the observing-room, half raised on an elbow, and gazing intently at the door. It was broad daylight. Half a dozen men, including several of the professors and a doctor from the village, were around me. Some were trying to make me lie down, others were asking me what I wanted, while the doctor was urging me to drink some whiskey. Mechanically repelling their offices, I pointed to the door and ejaculated, "President Byxbee – coming," giving expression to the one idea which my dazed mind at that moment contained. And sure enough, even as I spoke the door opened, and the venerable head of the college, somewhat blown with climbing the steep stairway, stood on the threshold. With a sensation of prodigious relief, I fell back on my pillow.

It appeared that I had swooned while in the observing-chair, the night before, and had been found by the janitor in the morning, my head fallen forward on the telescope, as if still observing, but my body cold, rigid, pulseless, and apparently dead.

In a couple of days I was all right again, and should soon have forgotten the episode but for a very interesting conjecture which had suggested itself in connection with it. This was nothing less than that, while I lay in that swoon, I was in a conscious state outside and independent of the body, and in that state received impressions and exercised perceptive powers. For this extraordinary theory I had no other evidence than the fact of my knowledge in the moment of awaking that President Byxbee was coming up the stairs. But slight as this clue was, it seemed to me unmistakable in its significance. That knowledge was certainly in my mind on the instant of arousing from the swoon.

It certainly could not have been there before I fell into the swoon. I must therefore have gained it in the meantime; that is to say, I must have been in a conscious, percipient state while my body was insensible.

If such had been the case, I reasoned that it was altogether unlikely that the trivial impression as to President Byxbee had been the only one which I had received in that state. It was far more probable that it had remained over in my mind, on waking from the swoon, merely because it was the latest of a series of impressions received while outside the body. That these impressions were of a kind most strange and startling, seeing that they were those of a disembodied soul exercising faculties more spiritual than those of the body, I could not doubt. The desire to know what they had been grew upon me, till it became a longing which left me no repose. It seemed intolerable that I should have secrets from myself, that my soul should withhold its experiences from my intellect. I would gladly have consented that the acquisitions of half my waking lifetime should be blotted out, if so be in exchange I might be shown the record of what I had seen and known during those hours of which my waking memory showed no trace. None the less for the conviction of its hopelessness, but rather all the more, as the perversity of our human nature will have it, the longing for this forbidden lore grew on me, till the hunger of Eve in the Garden was mine.

Constantly brooding over a desire that I felt to be vain, tantalized by the possession of a clue which only mocked me, my physical condition became at length affected. My health was disturbed and my rest at night was broken. A habit of walking in my sleep, from which I had not suffered since childhood, recurred, and caused me frequent inconvenience. Such had been, in general, my condition for some time, when I awoke one morning with the strangely weary sensation by which my body usually betrayed the secret of the impositions put upon it in sleep, of which otherwise I should often have suspected nothing. In going into the study connected with my chamber, I found a number of freshly written sheets on the desk. Astonished that anyone should have been in my rooms while I slept, I was astounded, on looking more closely, to observe that the handwriting was my own. How much more than astounded I was on reading the matter that had been set down, the reader may judge if he shall peruse it. For these written sheets apparently contained the longed-for but despaired-of record of those hours when I was absent from the body. They were the lost chapter of my life; or rather, not lost at all, for it had been no part of my waking life, but a stolen chapter – stolen from that sleep-memory on whose mysterious tablets may well be inscribed tales as much more marvelous than this as this is stranger than most stories.

It will be remembered that my last recollection before awaking in my bed, on the morning after the swoon, was of contemplating the coast of Kepler Land with an unusual concentration of attention. As well as I can judge – and that is no better than anyone else – it is with the moment that my bodily powers succumbed and I became unconscious that the narrative which I found on my desk begins.

Even had I not come as straight and swift as the beam of light that made my path, a glance about would have told me to what part of the universe I had fared. No earthly landscape could have been more familiar. I stood on the high coast of Kepler Land where it trends southward. A brisk westerly wind was blowing and the waves of the ocean of De La Bue were thundering at my feet, while the broad blue waters of Christie Bay stretched away to the southwest. Against the northern horizon, rising out of the ocean like a summer thunder-head, for which at first I mistook it, towered the far-distant, snowy summit of Mount Hall.

Even had the configuration of land and sea been less familiar, I should none the less have known that I stood on the planet whose ruddy hue is at once the admiration and puzzle of astronomers. Its explanation I now recognized in the tint of the atmosphere, a coloring comparable to the haze of Indian summer, except that its hue was a faint rose instead of purple. Like the Indian summer haze, it was impalpable, and without impeding the view bathed all objects near and far in a glamor not to be described. As the gaze turned upward, however, the deep blue of space so far overcame the roseate tint that one might fancy he were still on Earth.

As I looked about me I saw many men, women, and children. They were in no respect dissimilar, so far as I could see, to the men, women, and children of the Earth, save for something almost childlike in the untroubled serenity of their faces, unfurrowed as they were by any trace of care, of fear, or of anxiety. This extraordinary youthful-ness of aspect made it difficult, indeed, save by careful scrutiny, to distinguish the young from the middle-aged, maturity from advanced years. Time seemed to have no tooth on Mars.

I was gazing about me, admiring this crimson-lighted world, and these people who appeared to hold happiness by a tenure so much firmer than men's, when I heard the words, "You are welcome," and, turning, saw that I had been accosted by a man with the stature and bearing of middle age, though his countenance, like the other faces which I had noted, wonderfully combined the strength of a man's with the serenity of a child's. I thanked him, and said –

"You do not seem surprised to see me, though I certainly am to find myself here."

"Assuredly not," he answered. "I knew, of course, that I was to meet you today. And not only that, but I may say I am already in a sense acquainted with you, through a mutual friend, Professor Edgerly. He was here last month, and I met him at that time. We talked of you and your interest in our planet. I told him I expected you."

"Edgerly!" I exclaimed. "It is strange that he has said nothing of this to me. I meet him every day."

But I was reminded that it was in a dream that Edgerly, like myself, had visited Mars, and on awaking had recalled nothing of his experience, just as I should recall nothing of mine. When will man learn to interrogate the dream soul of the marvels it sees in its wanderings? Then he will no longer need to improve his telescopes to find out the secrets of the universe.

"Do your people visit the Earth in the same manner?" I asked my companion.

"Certainly," he replied; "but there we find no one able to recognize us and converse with us as I am conversing with you, although myself in the waking state. You, as yet, lack the knowledge we possess of the spiritual side of the human nature which we share with you."

"That knowledge must have enabled you to learn much more of the Earth than we know of you," I said.

"Indeed it has," he replied. "From visitors such as you, of whom we entertain a concourse constantly, we have acquired familiarity with your civilization, your history, your manners, and even your literature and languages. Have you not noticed that I am talking with you in English, which is certainly not a tongue indigenous to this planet?"

"Among so many wonders I scarcely observed that," I answered.

"For ages," pursued my companion, "we have been waiting for you to improve your telescopes so as to approximate the power of ours, after which communication between the planets would be easily established. The progress which you make is, however, so slow that we expect to wait ages yet."

"Indeed, I fear you will have to," I replied. "Our opticians already talk of having reached the limits of their art."

"Do not imagine that I spoke in any spirit of petulance," my companion resumed. "The slowness of your progress is not so remarkable to us as that you make any at all, burdened as you are by a disability so crushing that if we were in your place I fear we should sit down in utter despair."

"To what disability do you refer?" I asked. "You seem to be men like us."

"And so we are," was the reply, "save in one particular, but there the difference is tremendous. Endowed otherwise like us, you are destitute of the faculty of foresight, without which we should think our other faculties well-nigh valueless."

"Foresight!" I repeated. "Certainly you cannot mean that it is given you to know the future?"

"It is given not only to us," was the answer, "but, so far as we know, to all other intelligent beings of the universe except yourselves. Our positive knowledge extends only to our system of moons and planets and some of the nearer foreign systems, and it is conceivable that the remoter parts of the universe may harbor other blind races like your own; but it certainly seems unlikely that so strange and lamentable a spectacle should be duplicated. One such illustration of the extraordinary deprivations under which a rational existence may still be possible ought to suffice for the universe."

"But no one can know the future except by inspiration of God," I said.

"All our faculties are by inspiration of God," was the reply, "but there is surely nothing in foresight to cause it to be so regarded more than any other. Think a moment of the physical analogy of the case. Your eyes are placed in the front of your heads. You would deem it an odd mistake if they were placed behind. That would appear to you an arrangement calculated to defeat their purpose. Does it not seem equally rational that the mental vision should range forward, as it does with us, illuminating the path one is to take, rather than backward, as with you, revealing only the course you have already trodden, and therefore have no more concern with? But it is no doubt a merciful provision of Providence that renders you unable to realize the grotesqueness of your predicament, as it appears to us."

"But the future is eternal!" I exclaimed. "How can a finite mind grasp it?"

"Our foreknowledge implies only human faculties," was the reply. "It is limited to our individual careers on this planet. Each of us foresees the course of his own life, but not that of other lives, except so far as they are involved with his."

"That such a power as you describe could be combined with merely human faculties is more than our philosophers have ever dared to dream," I said. "And yet who shall say, after all, that it is not in mercy that God has denied it to us? If it is a happiness, as it must be, to foresee one's happiness, it must be most depressing to foresee one's sorrows, failures, yes, and even one's death. For if you foresee your lives to the end, you must anticipate the hour and manner of your death – is it not so?"

"Most assuredly," was the reply. "Living would be a very precarious business, were we uninformed of its limit. Your ignorance of the time of your death impresses us as one of the saddest features of your condition."

"And by us," I answered, "it is held to be one of the most merciful."

"Foreknowledge of your death would not, indeed, prevent your dying once," continued my companion, "but it would deliver you from the thousand deaths you suffer through uncertainty whether you can safely count on the passing day. It is not the death you die, but these many deaths you do not die, which shadow your existence. Poor blindfolded creatures that you are, cringing at every step in apprehension of the stroke that perhaps is not to fall till old age, never raising a cup to your lips with the knowledge that you will live to quaff it, never sure that you will meet again the friend you part with for an hour, from whose hearts no happiness suffices to banish the chill of an ever-present dread, what idea can you form of the Godlike security with which we enjoy our lives and the lives of those we love! You have a saying on earth, 'Tomorrow belongs to God'; but here tomorrow belongs to us, even as today. To you, for some inscrutable purpose, He sees fit to dole out life moment by moment, with no assurance that each is not to be the last. To us He gives a lifetime at once, fifty, sixty, seventy years – a divine gift indeed. A life such as yours would, I fear, seem of little value to us; for such a life, however long, is but a moment long, since that is all you can count on."

"And yet," I answered, "though knowledge of the duration of your lives may give you an enviable feeling of confidence while the end is far off, is that not more than offset by the daily growing weight with which the expectation of the end, as it draws near, must press upon your minds?"

"On the contrary," was the response, "death, never an object of fear, as it draws nearer becomes more and more a matter of indifference to the moribund. It is because you live in the past that death is grievous to you. All your knowledge, all your affections, all your interests, are rooted in the past, and on that account, as life lengthens, it strengthens its hold on you, and memory becomes a more precious possession. We, on the contrary, despise the past, and never dwell upon it. Memory with us, far from being the morbid and monstrous growth it is with you, is scarcely more than a rudimentary faculty. We live wholly in the future and the present. What with foretaste and actual taste, our experiences, whether pleasant or painful, are exhausted of interest by the time they are past. The accumulated treasures of memory, which you relinquish so painfully in death, we count no loss at all. Our minds being fed wholly from the future, we think and feel only as we anticipate; and so, as the dying man's future contracts, there is less and less about which he can occupy his thoughts. His interest in life diminishes as the ideas which it suggests grow fewer, till at the last death finds him with his mind a *tabula rasa*, as with you at birth. In a word, his concern with life is reduced to a vanishing point before he is called on to give it up. In dying he leaves nothing behind."

"And the after-death," I asked, "is there no fear of that?"

"Surely," was the reply, "it is not necessary for me to say that a fear which affects only the more ignorant on Earth is not known at all to us, and would be counted blasphemous. Moreover, as I have said, our foresight is limited to our lives on this planet. Any speculation beyond them would be purely conjectural, and our minds are repelled by the slightest taint of uncertainty. To us the conjectural and the unthinkable may be called almost the same."

"But even if you do not fear death for itself," I said, "you have hearts to break. Is there no pain when the ties of love are sundered?"

"Love and death are not foes on our planet," was the reply. "There are no tears by the bedsides of our dying. The same beneficent law which makes it so easy for us to give up life forbids us to mourn the friends we leave, or them to mourn us. With you, it is the intercourse you have had with friends that is the source of your tenderness for them. With us, it is the anticipation of the intercourse we shall enjoy which is the foundation of fondness. As our friends vanish from our future with the approach of their death, the effect on our thoughts and affections is as it would be with you if you forgot them by lapse of time. As our dying friends grow more and more indifferent to us, we, by operation of the same law of our nature, become indifferent to them, till at the last we are scarcely more than kindly and sympathetic watchers about the beds of those who regard us equally without keen emotions. So at last God gently unwinds instead of breaking the bands that bind our hearts together, and makes death as painless to the surviving as to the dying. Relations meant to produce our happiness are not the means also of torturing us, as with you. Love means joy, and that alone, to us, instead of blessing our lives for a while only to desolate them later on, compelling us to pay with a distinct and separate pang for every thrill of tenderness, exacting a tear for every smile."

"There are other partings than those of death. Are these, too, without sorrow for you?" I asked.

"Assuredly," was the reply. "Can you not see that so it must needs be with beings freed by foresight from the disease of memory? All the sorrow of parting, as of dying, comes with you from the backward vision which precludes you from beholding your happiness till it is past. Suppose your life destined to be blessed by a happy friendship. If you could know it beforehand, it would be a joyous expectation, brightening the intervening years and cheering you as you traversed desolate periods. But no; not till you meet the one who is to be your friend do you know of him. Nor do you guess even then what he is to be to you, that you may embrace him at first sight. Your meeting is cold and indifferent. It is long before the fire is fairly kindled between you, and then it is already time for parting. Now, indeed, the fire burns well, but henceforth it must consume your heart. Not till they are dead or gone do you fully realize how dear your friends were and how sweet was their companionship. But we – we see our friends afar off coming to meet us, smiling already in our eyes, years before our ways meet. We greet them at first meeting, not coldly, not uncertainly, but with exultant kisses, in an ecstasy of joy. They enter at once into the full possession of hearts long warmed and lighted for them. We meet with that delirium of tenderness with which you part. And when to us at last the time of parting comes, it only means that we are to contribute to each other's happiness no longer. We are not doomed, like you, in parting, to take away with us the delight we brought our friends, leaving the ache of bereavement in its place, so that their last state is worse than their first. Parting here is like meeting with you, calm and unimpassioned. The joys of anticipation and possession are the only food of love with us, and therefore Love always wears a smiling face. With you he feeds on dead joys, past happiness, which are likewise the sustenance of sorrow. No wonder love and sorrow are so much alike on Earth. It is a common saying among us that, were it not for the spectacle of the Earth, the rest of the worlds would be unable to appreciate the goodness of God to them; and who can say that this is not the reason the piteous sight is set before us?"

"You have told me marvelous things," I said, after I had reflected. "It is, indeed, but reasonable that such a race as yours should look down with wondering pity on the Earth. And yet, before I grant so much, I want to ask you one question. There is known in our world a certain sweet madness, under the influence of which we forget all that is untoward in our lot, and would not change it for a god's. So far is this sweet madness regarded by men as a compensation, and more than a compensation, for all their miseries that if you know not love as we know it, if this loss be the price you have paid for your divine foresight, we think ourselves more favored of God than you. Confess that love, with its reserves, its surprises, its mysteries, its revelations, is necessarily incompatible with a foresight which weighs and measures every experience in advance."

"Of love's surprises we certainly know nothing," was the reply. "It is believed by our philosophers that the slightest surprise would kill beings of our constitution like lightning; though of course this is merely theory, for it is only by the study of Earthly conditions that we are able to form an idea of what surprise is like. Your power to endure the constant buffetings of the unexpected is a matter of supreme amazement to us; nor, according to our ideas, is there any difference between what you call pleasant and painful surprises. You see, then, that we cannot envy you these surprises of love which you find so sweet, for to us they would be fatal. For the rest, there is no form of happiness which foresight is so well calculated to enhance as that of love. Let me explain to you how this befalls. As the growing boy begins to be sensible of the charms of woman, he finds himself, as I dare say it is with you, preferring some type of face and form to others. He dreams oftenest of fair hair, or may be of dark, of blue eyes or brown. As the years go on, his fancy, brooding over what seems to it the best and loveliest of every type, is constantly adding to this dream-face, this shadowy form, traits and lineaments, hues and contours, till at last the picture is complete, and he becomes aware that on his heart thus subtly has been depicted the likeness of the maiden destined for his arms.

"It may be years before he is to see her, but now begins with him one of the sweetest offices of love, one to you unknown. Youth on Earth is a stormy period of passion, chafing in restraint or rioting in excess. But the very passion whose awaking makes this time so critical with you is here a reforming and educating influence, to whose gentle and potent sway we gladly confide our children. The temptations which lead your young men astray have no hold on a youth of our happy planet. He hoards the treasures of his heart for its coming mistress. Of her alone he thinks, and to her all his vows are made. The thought of license would be treason to his sovereign lady, whose right to all the revenues of his being he joyfully owns. To rob her, to abate her high prerogatives, would be to impoverish, to insult, himself; for she is to be his, and her honor, her glory, are his own. Through all this time that he dreams of her by night and day, the exquisite reward of his devotion is the knowledge that she is aware of him as he of her, and that in the inmost shrine of a maiden heart his image is set up to receive the incense of a tenderness that needs not to restrain itself through fear of possible cross or separation.

"In due time their converging lives come together. The lovers meet, gaze a moment into each other's eyes, then throw themselves each on the other's breast. The maiden has all the charms that ever stirred the blood of an Earthly lover, but there is another glamor over her which the eyes of Earthly lovers are shut to – the glamor of the future. In the blushing girl her lover sees the fond and faithful wife, in the blithe maiden the patient, pain-consecrated mother. On the virgin's breast he beholds his children. He is prescient, even as his lips take the first-fruits of hers, of the future years during which she is to be his companion, his ever-present solace, his chief portion of God's goodness. We have read some of your romances describing love as you know it on Earth, and I must confess, my friend, we find them very dull.

"I hope," he added, as I did not at once speak, "that I shall not offend you by saying we find them also objectionable. Your literature possesses in general an interest for us in the picture it presents of the curiously inverted life which the lack of foresight compels you to lead. It is a study especially prized for the development of the imagination, on account of the difficulty of conceiving conditions so opposed to those of intelligent beings in general. But our women do not read your romances. The notion that a man or woman should ever conceive the idea of marrying a person other than the one whose husband or wife he or she is destined to be is profoundly shocking to our habits of thought. No doubt you will say that such instances are rare among you, but if your novels are faithful pictures of your life, they are at least not unknown. That these situations are inevitable under the conditions of earthly life we are well aware, and judge you accordingly; but it is needless that the minds of our maidens should be pained by the knowledge that there anywhere exists a world where such travesties upon the sacredness of marriage are possible.

"There is, however, another reason why we discourage the use of your books by our young people, and that is the profound effect of sadness, to a race accustomed to view all things in the morning glow of the future, of a literature written in the past tense and relating exclusively to things that are ended."

"And how do you write of things that are past except in the past tense?" I asked.

"We write of the past when it is still the future, and of course in the future tense," was the reply. "If our historians were to wait till after the events to describe them, not alone would nobody care to read about things already done, but the histories themselves would probably be inaccurate; for memory, as I have said, is a very slightly developed faculty with us, and quite too indistinct to be trustworthy. Should the Earth ever establish communication with us, you will find our histories of interest; for our planet, being smaller, cooled and was peopled ages before yours, and our astronomical records contain minute accounts of the Earth from the time it was a fluid mass. Your geologists and biologists may yet find a mine of information here."

In the course of our further conversation it came out that, as a consequence of foresight, some of the commonest emotions of human nature are unknown on Mars. They for whom the future has no mystery can, of course, know neither hope nor fear. Moreover, everyone being assured what he shall attain to and what not, there can be no such thing as rivalship, or emulation, or any sort of competition in any respect; and therefore all the brood of heart-burnings and hatreds, engendered on Earth by the strife of man with man, is unknown to the people of Mars, save from the study of our planet. When I asked if there were not, after all, a lack of spontaneity, of sense of freedom, in leading lives fixed in all details beforehand, I was reminded that there was no difference in that respect between the lives of the people of Earth and of Mars, both alike being according to God's will in every particular. We knew that will only after the event, they before – that was all. For the rest, God moved them through their wills as He did us, so that they had no more dense of compulsion in what they did than we on Earth have in carrying out an anticipated line of action, in cases where our anticipations chance to be correct. Of the absorbing interest which the study of the plan of their future lives possessed for the people of Mars, my companion spoke eloquently. It was, he said, like the fascination to a mathematician of a most elaborate and exquisite demonstration, a perfect algebraical equation, with the glowing realities of life in place of figures and symbols.

When I asked if it never occurred to them to wish their futures different, he replied that such a question could only have been asked by one from the Earth. No one could have foresight, or clearly believe that God had it, without realizing that the future is as incapable of being changed as the past. And not only this, but to foresee events was to foresee their logical necessity so clearly that to desire them different was as impossible as seriously to wish that two and two made five instead of four. No person could ever thoughtfully wish anything different, for so closely are all things, the small with the great, woven together by God that to draw out the smallest thread would unravel creation through all eternity.

While we had talked the afternoon had waned, and the sun had sunk below the horizon, the roseate atmosphere of the planet imparting a splendor to the cloud coloring, and a glory to the land and sea scape, never paralleled by an earthly sunset. Already the familiar constellations appearing in the sky reminded me how near, after all, I was to the Earth, for with the unassisted eye I could not detect the slightest variation in their position. Nevertheless, there was one wholly novel feature in the heavens, for many of the host of asteroids which circle in the zone between Mars and Jupiter were vividly visible to the naked eye. But the spectacle that chiefly held my gaze was the Earth, swimming low on the verge of the horizon. Its disc, twice as large as that of any star or planet as seen from the Earth, flashed with a brilliancy like that of Venus.

"It is, indeed, a lovely sight," said my companion, "although to me always a melancholy one, from the contrast suggested between the radiance of the orb and the benighted condition of its inhabitants. We call it 'The Blindman's World'." As he spoke he turned toward a curious structure which stood near us, though I had not before particularly observed it.

"What is that?" I asked.

"It is one of our telescopes," he replied. "I am going to let you take a look, if you choose, at your home, and test for yourself the powers of which I have boasted"; and having adjusted the instrument to his satisfaction, he showed me where to apply my eye to what answered to the eye-piece.

I could not repress an exclamation of amazement, for truly he had exaggerated nothing. The little college town which was my home lay spread out before me, seemingly almost as near as when I looked down upon it from my observatory windows. It was early morning, and the village was waking up. The milkmen were going their rounds, and workmen, with their dinner-pails, where hurrying along the streets. The early train was just leaving the railroad station. I could see the puffs from the smoke-stack, and the jets from the cylinders. It was strange not to hear the hissing of the steam, so near I seemed. There were the college buildings on the hill, the long rows of windows flashing back the level sunbeams. I could tell the time by the college clock. It struck me that there was an unusual bustle around the buildings, considering the earliness of the hour. A crowd of men stood about the door of the observatory, and many others were hurrying across the campus in that direction. Among them I recognized President Byxbee, accompanied by the college janitor. As I gazed they reached the observatory, and, passing through the group about the door, entered the building. The president was evidently going up to my quarters. At this it flashed over me quite suddenly that all this bustle was on my account. I recalled how it was that I came to be on Mars, and in what condition I had left affairs in the observatory. It was high time I were back there to look after myself.

* * *

Here abruptly ended the extraordinary document which I found that morning on my desk. That it is the authentic record of the conditions of life in another world which it purports to be I do not expect the reader to believe. He will no doubt explain it as another of the curious freaks of somnambulism set down in the books. Probably it was merely that, possibly it was something more. I do not pretend to decide the question. I have told all the facts of the case, and have no better means for forming an opinion than the reader. Nor do I know, even if I fully believed it the true account it seems to be, that it would have affected my imagination much more strongly than it has. That story of another world has, in a word, put me out of joint with ours. The readiness with which my mind has adapted itself to the Martial point of view concerning the Earth has been a singular experience. The lack of foresight among the human faculties, a lack I had scarcely thought of before, now impresses me, ever more deeply, as a fact out of harmony with the rest of our nature, belying its promise – a moral mutilation, a deprivation arbitrary and unaccountable. The spectacle of a race doomed to walk backward, beholding only what has gone by, assured only of what is past and dead, comes over me from time to time with a sadly fantastical effect which I cannot describe. I dream of a world where love always wears a smile, where the partings are as tearless as our meetings, and death is king no more. I have a fancy, which I like to cherish, that the people of that happy sphere, fancied though it may be, represent the ideal and normal type of our race, as perhaps it once was, as perhaps it may yet be again.

Sand

Algernon Blackwood

Chapter I

AS FELIX HENRIOT came through the streets that January night the fog was stifling, but when he reached his little flat upon the top floor there came a sound of wind. Wind was stirring about the world. It blew against his windows, but at first so faintly that he hardly noticed it. Then, with an abrupt rise and fall like a wailing voice that sought to claim attention, it called him. He peered through the window into the blurred darkness, listening.

There is no cry in the world like that of the homeless wind. A vague excitement, scarcely to be analysed, ran through his blood. The curtain of fog waved momentarily aside. Henriot fancied a star peeped down at him.

"It will change things a bit – at last," he sighed, settling back into his chair. "It will bring movement!"

Already something in himself had changed. A restlessness, as of that wandering wind, woke in his heart – the desire to be off and away. Other things could rouse this wildness too: falling water, the singing of a bird, an odour of wood-fire, a glimpse of winding road. But the cry of wind, always searching, questioning, travelling the world's great routes, remained ever the master-touch. High longing took his mood in hand. Mid seven millions he felt suddenly – lonely.

"I will arise and go now, for always night and day
I hear lake water lapping with low sounds by the shore;
While I stand on the roadway, or on the pavements gray,
I hear it in the deep heart's core."

He murmured the words over softly to himself. The emotion that produced Innisfree passed strongly through him. He too would be over the hills and far away. He craved movement, change, adventure – somewhere far from shops and crowds and motor-'busses. For a week the fog had stifled London. This wind brought life.

Where should he go? Desire was long; his purse was short.

He glanced at his books, letters, newspapers. They had no interest now. Instead he listened. The panorama of other journeys rolled in colour through the little room, flying on one another's heels. Henriot enjoyed this remembered essence of his travels more than the travels themselves. The crying wind brought so many voices, all of them seductive:

There was a soft crashing of waves upon the Black Sea shores, where the huge Caucasus beckoned in the sky beyond; a rustling in the umbrella pines and cactus at Marseilles, whence magic steamers start about the world like flying dreams. He heard the plash of fountains upon Mount Ida's slopes, and the whisper of the tamarisk on Marathon. It was dawn once more upon the Ionian Sea, and he smelt the perfume of the Cyclades. Blue-veiled islands melted in the sunshine, and across the dewy lawns of Tempe, moistened by the spray of many waterfalls, he saw – Great Heavens above! – the dancing of white forms…or was it only mist the sunshine painted against Pelion?… "Methought, among the lawns together, we wandered underneath the young grey dawn. And multitudes of dense white fleecy clouds shepherded by the slow, unwilling wind...."

And then, into his stuffy room, slipped the singing perfume of a wall-flower on a ruined tower, and with it the sweetness of hot ivy. He heard the 'yellow bees in the ivy bloom'. Wind whipped over the open hills – this very wind that laboured drearily through the London fog.

And – he was caught. The darkness melted from the city. The fog whisked off into an azure sky. The roar of traffic turned into booming of the sea. There was a whistling among cordage, and the floor swayed to and fro. He saw a sailor touch his cap and pocket the two-franc piece. The syren hooted – ominous sound that had started him on many a journey of adventure – and the roar of London became mere insignificant clatter of a child's toy carriages.

He loved that syren's call; there was something deep and pitiless in it. It drew the wanderers forth from cities everywhere: "Leave your known world behind you, and come with me for better or for worse! The anchor is up; it is too late to change. Only – beware! You shall know curious things – and alone!"

Henriot stirred uneasily in his chair. He turned with sudden energy to the shelf of guide-books, maps and time-tables – possessions he most valued in the whole room. He was a happy-go-lucky, adventure-loving soul, careless of common standards, athirst ever for the new and strange.

"That's the best of having a cheap flat," he laughed, "and no ties in the world. I can turn the key and disappear. No one cares or knows – no one but the thieving caretaker. And he's long ago found out that there's nothing here worth taking!"

There followed then no lengthy indecision. Preparation was even shorter still. He was always ready for a move, and his sojourn in cities was but breathing-space while he gathered pennies for further wanderings. An enormous kit-bag – sack-shaped, very worn and dirty – emerged speedily from the bottom of a cupboard in the wall. It was of limitless capacity. The key and padlock rattled in its depths. Cigarette ashes covered everything while he stuffed it full of ancient, indescribable garments. And his voice, singing of those 'yellow bees in the ivy bloom', mingled with the crying of the rising wind about his windows. His restlessness had disappeared by magic.

This time, however, there could be no haunted Pelion, nor shady groves of Tempe, for he lived in sophisticated times when money markets regulated movement sternly. Travelling was only for the rich; mere wanderers must pig it. He remembered instead an opportune invitation to the Desert. 'Objective' invitation, his genial hosts had called it, knowing his hatred of convention. And Helouan danced into letters of brilliance upon the inner map of his mind. For Egypt had ever held his spirit in thrall, though as yet he had tried in vain to touch the great buried soul of her. The excavators, the Egyptologists, the archaeologists most of all, plastered her grey ancient face with labels like hotel advertisements on travellers' portmanteaux. They told where she had come from last, but nothing of what she dreamed and thought and loved. The heart of Egypt lay beneath the sand, and the trifling robbery of little details that poked forth from tombs and temples brought no true revelation of her stupendous spiritual splendour. Henriot, in his youth, had searched and dived among what material he could find, believing once – or half believing – that the ceremonial of that ancient system veiled a weight of symbol that was reflected from genuine supersensual knowledge. The rituals, now taken literally, and so pityingly explained away, had once been genuine pathways of approach. But never yet, and least of all in his previous visits to Egypt itself, had he discovered one single person, worthy of speech, who caught at his idea. "Curious," they said, then turned away – to go on digging in the sand. Sand smothered her world today. Excavators discovered skeletons. Museums everywhere stored them – grinning, literal relics that told nothing.

But now, while he packed and sang, these hopes of enthusiastic younger days stirred again – because the emotion that gave them birth was real and true in him. Through the morning mists upon the Nile an old pyramid bowed hugely at him across London roofs: "Come," he heard its awful whisper beneath the ceiling, "I have things to show you, and to tell." He saw the flock of them sailing the Desert like weird grey solemn ships that make no earthly port. And he imagined them as one: multiple expressions of some single unearthly portent they adumbrated in mighty form – dead symbols of some spiritual conception long vanished from the world.

"I mustn't dream like this," he laughed, "or I shall get absent-minded and pack fire-tongs instead of boots. It looks like a jumble sale already!" And he stood on a heap of things to wedge them down still tighter.

But the pictures would not cease. He saw the kites circling high in the blue air. A couple of white vultures flapped lazily away over shining miles. Felucca sails, like giant wings emerging from the ground, curved towards him from the Nile. The palm-trees dropped long shadows over Memphis. He felt the delicious, drenching heat, and the Khamasin, that over-wind from Nubia, brushed his very cheeks. In the little gardens the mish-mish was in bloom.... He smelt the Desert... grey sepulchre of cancelled cycles.... The stillness of her interminable reaches dropped down upon old London....

The magic of the sand stole round him in its silent-footed tempest.

And while he struggled with that strange, capacious sack, the piles of clothing ran into shapes of gleaming Bedouin faces; London garments settled down with the mournful sound of camels' feet, half dropping wind, half water flowing underground – sound that old Time has brought over into modern life and left a moment for our wonder and perhaps our tears.

He rose at length with the excitement of some deep enchantment in his eyes. The thought of Egypt plunged ever so deeply into him, carrying him into depths where he found it difficult to breathe, so strangely far away it seemed, yet indefinably familiar. He lost his way. A touch of fear came with it.

"A sack like that is the wonder of the world," he laughed again, kicking the unwieldy, sausage-shaped monster into a corner of the room, and sitting down to write the thrilling labels: 'Felix Henriot, Alexandria *via* Marseilles.' But his pen blotted the letters; there was sand in it. He rewrote the words. Then he remembered a dozen things he had left out. Impatiently, yet with confusion somewhere, he stuffed them in. They ran away into shifting heaps; they disappeared; they emerged suddenly again. It was like packing hot, dry, flowing sand. From the pockets of a coat – he had worn it last summer down Dorset way – out trickled sand. There was sand in his mind and thoughts.

And his dreams that night were full of winds, the old sad winds of Egypt, and of moving, sifting sand. Arabs and Afreets danced amazingly together across dunes he could never reach. For he could not follow fast enough. Something infinitely older than these ever caught his feet and held him back. A million tiny fingers stung and pricked him. Something flung a veil before his eyes. Once it touched him – his face and hands and neck. "Stay here with us," he heard a host of muffled voices crying, but their sound was smothered, buried, rising through the ground. A myriad throats were choked. Till, at last, with a violent effort he turned and seized it. And then the thing he grasped at slipped between his fingers and ran easily away. It had a grey and yellow face, and it moved through all its parts. It flowed as water flows, and yet was solid. It was centuries old.

He cried out to it. "Who are you? What is your name? I surely know you... but I have forgotten...?"

And it stopped, turning from far away its great uncovered countenance of nameless colouring. He caught a voice. It rolled and boomed and whispered like the wind. And then he woke, with a curious shaking in his heart, and a little touch of chilly perspiration on the skin.

But the voice seemed in the room still – close beside him:

"I am the Sand," he heard, before it died away.

And next he realised that the glitter of Paris lay behind him, and a steamer was taking him with much unnecessary motion across a sparkling sea towards Alexandria. Gladly he saw the Riviera fade below the horizon, with its hard bright sunshine, treacherous winds, and its smear of rich, conventional English. All restlessness now had left him. True vagabond still at forty, he only felt the unrest and discomfort of life when caught in the network of routine and rigid streets, no chance of breaking loose. He was off again at last, money scarce enough indeed, but the joy of wandering expressing itself in happy emotions of release. Every warning of calculation was stifled. He thought of the American woman who walked out of her Long Island house one summer's day to look at a passing sail – and was gone eight years before she walked in again. Eight years of roving travel! He had always felt respect and admiration for that woman.

For Felix Henriot, with his admixture of foreign blood, was philosopher as well as vagabond, a strong poetic and religious strain sometimes breaking out through fissures in his complex nature. He had seen much life; had read many books. The passionate desire of youth to solve the world's big riddles had given place to a resignation filled to the brim with wonder. Anything *might* be true. Nothing surprised him. The most outlandish beliefs, for all he knew, might fringe truth somewhere. He had escaped that cheap cynicism with which disappointed men soothe their vanity when they realise that an intelligible explanation of the universe lies beyond their powers. He no longer expected final answers.

For him, even the smallest journeys held the spice of some adventure; all minutes were loaded with enticing potentialities. And they shaped for themselves somehow a dramatic form. "It's like a story," his friends said when he told his travels. It always was a story.

But the adventure that lay waiting for him where the silent streets of little Helouan kiss the great Desert's lips, was of a different kind to any Henriot had yet encountered. Looking back, he has often asked himself, "How in the world can I accept it?"

And, perhaps, he never yet has accepted it. It was sand that brought it. For the Desert, the stupendous thing that mothers little Helouan, produced it.

Chapter II

HE SLIPPED THROUGH CAIRO with the same relief that he left the Riviera, resenting its social vulgarity so close to the imperial aristocracy of the Desert; he settled down into the peace of soft and silent little Helouan. The hotel in which he had a room on the top floor had been formerly a Khedivial Palace. It had the air of a palace still. He felt himself in a country-house, with lofty ceilings, cool and airy corridors, spacious halls. Soft-footed Arabs attended to his wants; white walls let in light and air without a sign of heat; there was a feeling of a large, spread tent pitched on the very sand; and the wind that stirred the oleanders in the shady gardens also crept in to rustle the palm leaves of his favourite corner seat. Through the large windows where once the Khedive held high court, the sunshine blazed upon vistaed leagues of Desert.

And from his bedroom windows he watched the sun dip into gold and crimson behind the swelling Libyan sands. This side of the pyramids he saw the Nile meander among palm groves and tilled fields. Across his balcony railings the Egyptian stars trooped down beside his very bed, shaping old constellations for his dreams; while, to the south, he looked out upon the vast untamable Body of the sands that carpeted the world for thousands of miles towards Upper Egypt, Nubia, and the dread Sahara itself. He wondered again why people thought it necessary to go so far afield to know the Desert. Here, within half an hour of Cairo, it lay breathing solemnly at his very doors.

For little Helouan, caught thus between the shoulders of the Libyan and Arabian Deserts, is utterly sand-haunted. The Desert lies all round it like a sea. Henriot felt he never could escape from it, as he moved about the island whose coasts are washed with sand. Down each broad and shining street the two end houses framed a vista of its dim immensity – glimpses of shimmering blue, or flame-touched purple. There were stretches of deep sea-green as well, far off upon its bosom. The streets were open channels of approach, and the eye ran down them as along the tube of a telescope laid to catch incredible distance out of space. Through them the Desert reached in with long, thin feelers towards the village. Its Being flooded into Helouan, and over it. Past walls and houses, churches and hotels, the sea of Desert pressed in silently with its myriad soft feet of sand. It poured in everywhere, through crack and slit and crannie. These were reminders of possession and ownership. And every passing wind that lifted eddies of dust at the street corners were messages from the quiet, powerful Thing that permitted Helouan to lie and dream so peacefully in the sunshine. Mere artificial oasis, its existence was temporary, held on lease, just for ninety-nine centuries or so.

This sea idea became insistent. For, in certain lights, and especially in the brief, bewildering dusk, the Desert rose – swaying towards the small white houses. The waves of it ran for fifty miles without a break. It was too deep for foam or surface agitation, yet it knew the swell of tides. And underneath flowed resolute currents, linking distance to the centre. These many deserts were really one. A storm, just retreated, had tossed Helouan upon the shore and left it there to dry; but any morning he would wake to find it had been carried off again into the depths. Some fragment, at least, would disappear. The grim Mokattam Hills were rollers that ever threatened to topple down and submerge the sandy bar that men called Helouan.

Being soundless, and devoid of perfume, the Desert's message reached him through two senses only – sight and touch; chiefly, of course, the former. Its invasion was concentrated through the eyes. And vision, thus uncorrected, went what pace it pleased. The Desert played with him. Sand stole into his being – through the eyes.

And so obsessing was this majesty of its close presence, that Henriot sometimes wondered how people dared their little social activities within its very sight and hearing; how they played golf and tennis upon reclaimed edges of its face, picnicked so blithely hard upon its frontiers, and danced at night while this stern, unfathomable Thing lay breathing just beyond the trumpery walls that kept it out. The challenge of their shallow admiration seemed presumptuous, almost provocative. Their pursuit of pleasure suggested insolent indifference. They ran fool-hardy hazards, he felt; for there was no worship in their vulgar hearts. With a mental shudder, sometimes he watched the cheap tourist horde go laughing, chattering past within view of its ancient, half-closed eyes. It was like defying deity.

For, to his stirred imagination the sublimity of the Desert dwarfed humanity. These people had been wiser to choose another place for the flaunting of their tawdry insignificance. Any minute this Wilderness, 'huddled in grey annihilation', might awake and notice them…!

In his own hotel were several 'smart', so-called 'Society' people who emphasised the protest in him to the point of definite contempt. Overdressed, the latest worldly novel under their arms, they strutted the narrow pavements of their tiny world, immensely pleased with themselves. Their vacuous minds expressed themselves in the slang of their exclusive circle – value being the element excluded. The pettiness of their outlook hardly distressed him – he was too familiar with it at home – but their essential vulgarity, their innate ugliness, seemed more than usually offensive in the grandeur of its present setting. Into the mighty sands they took the latest London scandal, gabbling it over even among the Tombs and Temples. And 'it was to laugh', the pains they spent wondering whom they might condescend to know, never dreaming that they themselves were not worth knowing. Against the background of the noble Desert their titles seemed the cap and bells of clowns.

And Henriot, knowing some of them personally, could not always escape their insipid company. Yet he was the gainer. They little guessed how their commonness heightened contrast, set mercilessly thus beside the strange, eternal beauty of the sand.

Occasionally the protest in his soul betrayed itself in words, which of course they did not understand. "He is so clever, isn't he?" And then, having relieved his feelings, he would comfort himself characteristically:

"The Desert has not noticed them. The Sand is not aware of their existence. How should the sea take note of rubbish that lies above its tide-line?"

For Henriot drew near to its great shifting altars in an attitude of worship. The wilderness made him kneel in heart. Its shining reaches led to the oldest Temple in the world, and every journey that he made was like a sacrament. For him the Desert was a consecrated place. It was sacred.

And his tactful hosts, knowing his peculiarities, left their house open to him when he cared to come – they lived upon the northern edge of the oasis – and he was as free as though he were absolutely alone. He blessed them; he rejoiced that he had come. Little Helouan accepted him. The Desert knew that he was there.

From his corner of the big dining-room he could see the other guests, but his roving eye always returned to the figure of a solitary man who sat at an adjoining table, and whose personality stirred his interest. While affecting to look elsewhere, he studied him as closely as might be. There was something about the stranger that touched his curiosity – a certain air of expectation that he wore. But it was more than that: it was anticipation, apprehension in it somewhere. The man was nervous, uneasy. His restless way of suddenly looking about him proved it. Henriot tried everyone else in the room as well; but, though his thought settled on others too, he always came back to the figure of this solitary being opposite, who ate his dinner as if afraid of being seen, and glanced up sometimes as if fearful of being watched. Henriot's curiosity, before he knew it, became suspicion. There was mystery here. The table, he noticed, was laid for two.

"Is he an actor, a priest of some strange religion, an enquiry agent, or just – a crank?" was the thought that first occurred to him. And the question suggested itself without amusement. The impression of subterfuge and caution he conveyed left his observer unsatisfied.

The face was clean shaven, dark, and strong; thick hair, straight yet bushy, was slightly unkempt; it was streaked with grey; and an unexpected mobility when he smiled ran over the features that he seemed to hold rigid by deliberate effort. The man was cut to no quite common measure. Henriot jumped to an intuitive conclusion: "He's not here for pleasure or merely sight-seeing. Something serious has brought him out to Egypt." For the face combined too ill-assorted qualities: an obstinate tenacity that might even mean brutality, and was certainly repulsive, yet, with it, an undecipherable dreaminess betrayed by lines of the mouth, but above all in the very light blue eyes, so rarely raised. Those eyes, he felt, had looked upon unusual things; 'dreaminess' was not an adequate description; 'searching' conveyed it better. The true source of the queer impression remained elusive. And hence, perhaps, the incongruous marriage in the face – mobility laid upon a matter-of-fact foundation underneath. The face showed conflict.

And Henriot, watching him, felt decidedly intrigued. "I'd like to know that man, and all about him." His name, he learned later, was Richard Vance; from Birmingham; a business man. But it was not the Birmingham he wished to know; it was the – other: cause of the elusive, dreamy searching. Though facing one another at so short a distance, their eyes, however, did not meet. And this, Henriot well knew, was a sure sign that he himself was also under observation. Richard Vance, from Birmingham, was equally taking careful note of Felix Henriot, from London.

Thus, he could wait his time. They would come together later. An opportunity would certainly present itself. The first links in a curious chain had already caught; soon the chain would tighten, pull as though by chance, and bring their lives into one and the same circle. Wondering in particular for what kind of a companion the second cover was laid, Henriot felt certain that their eventual coming together was inevitable. He possessed this kind of divination from first impressions, and not uncommonly it proved correct.

Following instinct, therefore, he took no steps towards acquaintance, and for several days, owing to the fact that he dined frequently with his hosts, he saw nothing more of Richard Vance, the business man from Birmingham. Then, one night, coming home late from his friend's house, he had passed along the great corridor, and was actually a step or so into his bedroom, when a drawling voice sounded close behind him. It was an unpleasant sound. It was very near him too –

"I beg your pardon, but have you, by any chance, such a thing as a compass you could lend me?"

The voice was so close that he started. Vance stood within touching distance of his body. He had stolen up like a ghostly Arab, must have followed him, too, some little distance, for further down the passage the light of an open door – he had passed it on his way – showed where he came from.

"Eh? I beg your pardon? A – compass, did you say?" He felt disconcerted for a moment. How short the man was, now that he saw him standing. Broad and powerful too. Henriot looked down upon his thick head of hair. The personality and voice repelled him. Possibly his face, caught unawares, betrayed this.

"Forgive my startling you," said the other apologetically, while the softer expression danced in for a moment and disorganised the rigid set of the face. "The soft carpet, you know. I'm afraid you didn't hear my tread. I wondered" – he smiled again slightly at the nature of the request – "if – by any chance – you had a pocket compass you could lend me?"

"Ah, a compass, yes! Please don't apologise. I believe I have one – if you'll wait a moment. Come in, won't you? I'll have a look."

The other thanked him but waited in the passage. Henriot, it so happened, had a compass, and produced it after a moment's search.

"I am greatly indebted to you – if I may return it in the morning. You will forgive my disturbing you at such an hour. My own is broken, and I wanted – er – to find the true north."

Henriot stammered some reply, and the man was gone. It was all over in a minute. He locked his door and sat down in his chair to think. The little incident had upset him, though for the life of him he could not imagine why. It ought by rights to have been almost ludicrous, yet instead it was the exact reverse – half threatening. Why should not a man want a compass? But, again, why should he? And at midnight? The voice, the eyes, the near presence – what did they bring that set his nerves thus asking unusual questions? This strange impression that something grave was happening, something unearthly – how was it born exactly? The man's proximity came like a shock. It had made him start. He brought – thus the idea came unbidden to his mind – something with him that galvanised him quite absurdly, as fear does, or delight, or great wonder. There was a music in his voice too – a certain – well, he could only call it lilt, that reminded him of plainsong, intoning, chanting. Drawling was *not* the word at all.

He tried to dismiss it as imagination, but it would not be dismissed. The disturbance in himself was caused by something not imaginary, but real. And then, for the first time, he discovered that the man had brought a faint, elusive suggestion of perfume with him, an aromatic odour, that made him think of priests and churches. The ghost of it still lingered in the air. Ah, here then was the origin of the notion that his voice had chanted: it was surely the suggestion of incense. But incense, intoning, a compass to find the true north – at midnight in a Desert hotel!

A touch of uneasiness ran through the curiosity and excitement that he felt.

And he undressed for bed. "Confound my old imagination," he thought, "what tricks it plays me! It'll keep me awake!"

But the questions, once started in his mind, continued. He must find explanation of one kind or another before he could lie down and sleep, and he found it at length in – the stars. The man was an astronomer of sorts; possibly an astrologer into the bargain! Why not? The stars were wonderful above Helouan. Was there not an observatory on the Mokattam Hills, too, where tourists could use the telescopes on privileged days? He had it at last. He even stole out on to his balcony to see if the stranger perhaps was looking through some wonderful apparatus at the heavens. Their rooms were on the same side. But the shuttered windows revealed no stooping figure with eyes glued to a telescope. The stars blinked in their many thousands down upon the silent desert. The night held neither sound nor movement. There was a cool breeze blowing across the Nile from the Lybian Sands. It nipped; and he stepped back quickly into the room again. Drawing the mosquito curtains carefully about the bed, he put the light out and turned over to sleep.

And sleep came quickly, contrary to his expectations, though it was a light and surface sleep. That last glimpse of the darkened Desert lying beneath the Egyptian stars had touched him with some hand of awful power that ousted the first, lesser excitement. It calmed and soothed him in one sense, yet in another, a sense he could not understand, it caught him in a net of deep, deep feelings whose mesh, while infinitely delicate, was utterly stupendous. His nerves this deeper emotion left alone: it reached instead to something infinite in him that mere nerves could neither deal with nor interpret. The soul awoke and whispered in him while his body slept.

And the little, foolish dreams that ran to and fro across this veil of surface sleep brought oddly tangled pictures of things quite tiny and at the same time of others that were mighty beyond words. With these two counters Nightmare played. They interwove. There was the figure of this dark-faced man with the compass, measuring the sky to find the true north, and there were hints of giant Presences that hovered just outside some curious outline that he traced upon the ground, copied in some nightmare fashion from the heavens. The excitement caused by his visitor's singular request mingled with the profounder sensations his final look at the stars and Desert stirred. The two were somehow inter-related.

Some hours later, before this surface sleep passed into genuine slumber, Henriot woke – with an appalling feeling that the Desert had come creeping into his room and now stared down upon him where he lay in bed. The wind was crying audibly about the walls outside. A faint, sharp tapping came against the window panes.

He sprang instantly out of bed, not yet awake enough to feel actual alarm, yet with the nightmare touch still close enough to cause a sort of feverish, loose bewilderment. He switched the lights on. A moment later he knew the meaning of that curious tapping, for the rising wind was flinging tiny specks of sand against the glass. The idea that they had summoned him belonged, of course, to dream.

He opened the window, and stepped out on to the balcony. The stone was very cold under his bare feet. There was a wash of wind all over him. He saw the sheet of glimmering, pale desert near and far; and something stung his skin below the eyes.

"The sand," he whispered, "again the sand; always the sand. Waking or sleeping, the sand is everywhere – nothing but sand, sand, Sand...."

He rubbed his eyes. It was like talking in his sleep, talking to someone who had questioned him just before he woke. But was he really properly awake? It seemed next day that he had dreamed it. Something enormous, with rustling skirts of sand, had just retreated far into the Desert. Sand went with it – flowing, trailing, smothering the world. The wind died down.

And Henriot went back to sleep, caught instantly away into unconsciousness; covered, blinded, swept over by this spreading thing of reddish brown with the great, grey face, whose Being was colossal yet quite tiny, and whose fingers, wings and eyes were countless as the stars.

But all night long it watched and waited, rising to peer above the little balcony, and sometimes entering the room and piling up beside his very pillow. He dreamed of Sand.

Chapter III

FOR SOME DAYS Henriot saw little of the man who came from Birmingham and pushed curiosity to a climax by asking for a compass in the middle of the night. For one thing, he was a good deal with his friends upon the other side of Helouan, and for another, he slept several nights in the Desert.

He loved the gigantic peace the Desert gave him. The world was forgotten there; and not the world merely, but all memory of it. Everything faded out. The soul turned inwards upon itself.

An Arab boy and donkey took out sleeping-bag, food and water to the Wadi Hof, a desolate gorge about an hour eastwards. It winds between cliffs whose summits rise some thousand feet above the sea. It opens suddenly, cut deep into the swaying world of level plateaux and undulating hills. It moves about too; he never found it in the same place twice – like an arm of the Desert that shifted with the changing lights. Here he watched dawns and sunsets, slept through the mid-day heat, and enjoyed the unearthly colouring that swept Day and Night across the huge horizons. In solitude the Desert soaked down into him. At night the jackals cried in the darkness round his cautiously-fed camp fire – small, because wood had to be carried – and in the day-time kites circled overhead to inspect him, and an occasional white vulture flapped across the blue. The weird desolation of this rocky valley, he thought, was like the scenery of the moon. He took no watch with him, and the arrival of the donkey boy an hour after sunrise came almost from another planet, bringing things of time and common life out of some distant gulf where they had lain forgotten among lost ages.

The short hour of twilight brought, too, a bewitchment into the silence that was a little less than comfortable. Full light or darkness he could manage, but this time of half things made him want to shut his eyes and hide. Its effect stepped over imagination. The mind got lost. He could not understand it. For the cliffs and boulders of discoloured limestone shone then with an inward glow that signalled to the Desert with veiled lanterns. The misshappen hills, carved by wind and rain into ominous outlines, stirred and nodded. In the morning light they retired into themselves, asleep. But at dusk the tide retreated. They rose from the sea, emerging naked, threatening. They ran together and joined shoulders, the entire army of them. And the glow of their sandy bodies, self-luminous, continued even beneath the stars. Only the moonlight drowned it. For the moonrise over the Mokattam Hills brought a white, grand loveliness that drenched the entire Desert. It drew a marvellous sweetness from the sand. It shone across a world as yet unfinished, whereon no life might show itself for ages yet to come. He was alone then upon an empty star, before the creation of things that breathed and moved.

What impressed him, however, more than everything else was the enormous vitality that rose out of all this apparent death. There was no hint of the melancholy that belongs commonly to flatness; the sadness of wide, monotonous landscape was not here. The endless repetition of sweeping vale and plateau brought infinity within measurable comprehension. He grasped a definite meaning in the phrase 'world without end': the Desert had no end and no beginning. It gave him a sense of eternal peace, the silent peace that star-fields know. Instead of subduing the soul with bewilderment, it inspired with courage, confidence, hope. Through this sand which was the wreck of countless geological ages, rushed life that was terrific and uplifting, too huge to include melancholy, too deep to betray itself in movement. Here was the stillness of eternity. Behind the spread grey masque of apparent death lay stores of accumulated life, ready to break forth at any point. In the Desert he felt himself absolutely royal.

And this contrast of Life, veiling itself in Death, was a contradiction that somehow intoxicated. The Desert exhilaration never left him. He was never alone. A companionship of millions went with him, and he *felt* the Desert close, as stars are close to one another, or grains of sand.

It was the Khamasin, the hot wind bringing sand, that drove him in – with the feeling that these few days and nights had been immeasurable, and that he had been away a thousand years. He came back with the magic of the Desert in his blood, hotel-life tasteless and insipid by comparison. To human impressions thus he was fresh and vividly sensitive. His being, cleaned and sensitized by pure grandeur, 'felt' people – for a time at any rate – with an uncommon sharpness of receptive judgment. He returned to a life somehow mean and meagre, resuming insignificance with his dinner jacket. Out with the sand he had been regal; now, like a slave, he strutted self-conscious and reduced.

But this imperial standard of the Desert stayed a little time beside him, its purity focussing judgment like a lens. The specks of smaller emotions left it clear at first, and as his eye wandered vaguely over the people assembled in the dining-room, it was arrested with a vivid shock upon two figures at the little table facing him.

He had forgotten Vance, the Birmingham man who sought the North at midnight with a pocket compass. He now saw him again, with an intuitive discernment entirely fresh. Before memory brought up her clouding associations, some brilliance flashed a light upon him. "That man," Henriot thought, "might have come with me. He would have understood and loved it!" But the thought was really this – a moment's reflection spread it, rather: "He belongs somewhere to the Desert; the Desert brought him out here." And, again, hidden swiftly behind it like a movement running below water – "What does he want with it? What is the deeper motive he conceals? For there is a deeper motive; and it *is* concealed."

But it was the woman seated next him who absorbed his attention really, even while this thought flashed and went its way. The empty chair was occupied at last. Unlike his first encounter with the man, she looked straight at him. Their eyes met fully. For several seconds there was steady mutual inspection, while her penetrating stare, intent without being rude, passed searchingly all over his face. It was disconcerting. Crumbling his bread, he looked equally hard at her, unable to turn away, determined not to be the first to shift his gaze. And when at length she lowered her eyes he felt that many things had happened, as in a long period of intimate conversation. Her mind had judged him through and through. Questions and answer flashed. They were no longer strangers. For the rest of dinner, though he was careful to avoid direct inspection, he was aware that she felt his presence and was secretly speaking with him. She asked questions beneath her breath. The answers rose with the quickened pulses in his blood. Moreover, she explained Richard Vance. It was this woman's power that shone reflected in the man. She was the one who knew the big, unusual things. Vance merely echoed the rush of her vital personality.

This was the first impression that he got – from the most striking, curious face he had ever seen in a woman. It remained very near him all through the meal: she had moved to his table, it seemed she sat beside him. Their minds certainly knew contact from that moment.

It is never difficult to credit strangers with the qualities and knowledge that oneself craves for, and no doubt Henriot's active fancy went busily to work. But, nonetheless, this thing remained and grew: that this woman was aware of the hidden things of Egypt he had always longed to know. There was knowledge and guidance she could impart. Her soul was searching among ancient things. Her face brought the Desert back into his thoughts. And with it came – the sand.

Here was the flash. The sight of her restored the peace and splendour he had left behind him in his Desert camps. The rest, of course, was what his imagination constructed upon this slender basis. Only – not all of it was imagination.

Now, Henriot knew little enough of women, and had no pose of 'understanding' them. His experience was of the slightest; the love and veneration felt for his own mother had set the entire sex upon the heights. His affairs with women, if so they may be called, had been transient – all but those of early youth, which having never known the devastating test of fulfilment, still remained ideal and superb. There was unconscious humour in his attitude – from a distance; for he regarded women with wonder and respect, as puzzles that sweetened but complicated life, might even endanger it. He certainly was not a marrying man! But now, as he felt the presence of this woman so deliberately possess him, there came over him two clear, strong messages, each vivid with certainty. One was that banal suggestion of familiarity claimed by lovers and the like – he had often heard of it – "I have known that woman before; I have met her ages ago somewhere; she is strangely familiar to me"; and the other, growing out of it almost: "Have nothing to do with her; she will bring you trouble and confusion; avoid her, and be warned"; – in fact, a distinct presentiment.

Yet, although Henriot dismissed both impressions as having no shred of evidence to justify them, the original clear judgment, as he studied her extraordinary countenance, persisted through all denials. The familiarity, and the presentiment, remained. There also remained this other – an enormous imaginative leap! – that she could teach him 'Egypt'.

He watched her carefully, in a sense fascinated. He could only describe the face as black, so dark it was with the darkness of great age. Elderly was the obvious, natural word; but elderly described the features only. The expression of the face wore centuries. Nor was it merely the coal-black eyes that betrayed an ancient, age-travelled soul behind them. The entire presentment mysteriously conveyed it. This woman's heart knew long-forgotten things – the thought kept beating up against him. There were cheek-bones, oddly high, that made him think involuntarily of the well-advertised Pharaoh, Ramases; a square, deep jaw; and an aquiline nose that gave the final touch of power. For the power undeniably was there, and while the general effect had grimness in it, there was neither harshness nor any forbidding touch about it. There was an implacable sternness in the set of lips and jaw, and, most curious of all, the eyelids over the steady eyes of black were level as a ruler. This level framing made the woman's stare remarkable beyond description. Henriot thought of an idol carved in stone, stone hard and black, with eyes that stared across the sand into a world of things non-human, very far away, forgotten of men. The face was finely ugly. This strange dark beauty flashed flame about it.

And, as the way ever was with him, Henriot next fell to constructing the possible lives of herself and her companion, though without much success. Imagination soon stopped dead. She was not old enough to be Vance's mother, and assuredly she was not his wife. His interest was more than merely piqued – it was puzzled uncommonly. What was the contrast that made the man seem beside her – vile? Whence came, too, the impression that she exercised some strong authority, though never directly exercised, that held him at her mercy? How did he guess that the man resented it, yet did not dare oppose, and that, apparently acquiescing good-humouredly, his will was deliberately held in abeyance, and that he waited sulkily, biding his time? There was furtiveness in every gesture and expression. A hidden motive lurked in him; unworthiness somewhere; he was determined yet ashamed. He watched her ceaselessly and with such uncanny closeness.

Henriot imagined he divined all this. He leaped to the guess that his expenses were being paid. A good deal more was being paid besides. She was a rich relation, from whom he had expectations; he was serving his seven years, ashamed of his servitude, ever calculating escape – but, perhaps, no ordinary escape. A faint shudder ran over him. He drew in the reins of imagination.

Of course, the probabilities were that he was hopelessly astray – one usually is on such occasions – but this time, it so happened, he was singularly right. Before one thing only his ready invention stopped every time. This vileness, this notion of unworthiness in Vance, could not be negative merely. A man with that face was no inactive weakling. The motive he was at such pains to conceal, betraying its existence by that very fact, moved, surely, towards aggressive action. Disguised, it never slept. Vance was sharply on the alert. He had a plan deep out of sight. And Henriot remembered how the man's soft approach along the carpeted corridor had made him start. He recalled the quasi shock it gave him. He thought again of the feeling of discomfort he had experienced.

Next, his eager fancy sought to plumb the business these two had together in Egypt – in the Desert. For the Desert, he felt convinced, had brought them out. But here, though he constructed numerous explanations, another barrier stopped him. Because he *knew*. This woman was in touch with that aspect of ancient Egypt he himself had ever sought in vain; and not merely with stones the sand had buried so deep, but with the meanings they once represented, buried so utterly by the sands of later thought.

And here, being ignorant, he found no clue that could lead to any satisfactory result, for he possessed no knowledge that might guide him. He floundered – until Fate helped him. And the instant Fate helped him, the warning and presentiment he had dismissed as fanciful, became real again. He hesitated. Caution acted. He would think twice before taking steps to form acquaintance. "Better not," thought whispered. "Better leave them alone, this queer couple. They're after things that won't do you any good." This idea of mischief, almost of danger, in their purposes was oddly insistent; for what could possibly convey it? But, while he hesitated, Fate, who sent the warning, pushed him at the same time into the circle of their lives: at first tentatively – he might still have escaped; but soon urgently – curiosity led him inexorably towards the end.

Chapter IV

IT WAS SO SIMPLE a manoeuvre by which Fate began the innocent game. The woman left a couple of books behind her on the table one night, and Henriot, after a moment's hesitation, took them out after her. He knew the titles – *The House of the Master*, and *The House of the Hidden Places*, both singular interpretations of the Pyramids that once had held his own mind spellbound. Their ideas had been since disproved, if he remembered rightly, yet the titles were a clue – a clue to that imaginative part of his mind that was so busy constructing theories and had found its stride. Loose sheets of paper, covered with notes in a minute handwriting, lay between the pages; but these, of course, he did not read, noticing only that they were written round designs of various kinds – intricate designs.

He discovered Vance in a corner of the smoking-lounge. The woman had disappeared.

Vance thanked him politely. "My aunt is so forgetful sometimes," he said, and took them with a covert eagerness that did not escape the other's observation. He folded up the sheets and put them carefully in his pocket. On one there was an ink-sketched map, crammed with detail, that might well have referred to some portion of the Desert. The points of the compass stood out boldly at the bottom. There were involved geometrical designs again. Henriot saw them. They exchanged, then, the commonplaces of conversation, but these led to nothing further. Vance was nervous and betrayed impatience. He presently excused himself and left the lounge. Ten minutes later he passed through the outer hall, the woman beside him, and the pair of them, wrapped up in cloak and ulster, went out into the night. At the door, Vance turned and threw a quick, investigating glance in his direction. There seemed a hint of questioning in that glance; it might almost have been a tentative invitation. But, also, he wanted to see if their exit had been particularly noticed – and by whom.

This, briefly told, was the first manoeuvre by which Fate introduced them. There was nothing in it. The details were so insignificant, so slight the conversation, so meagre the pieces thus added to Henriot's imaginative structure. Yet they somehow built it up and made it solid; the outline in his mind began to stand foursquare. That writing, those designs, the manner of the man, their going out together, the final curious look – each and all betrayed points of a hidden thing. Subconsciously he was excavating their buried purposes. The sand was shifting. The concentration of his mind incessantly upon them removed it grain by grain and speck by speck. Tips of the smothered thing emerged. Presently a subsidence would follow with a rush and light would blaze upon its skeleton. He felt it stirring underneath his feet – this flowing movement of light, dry, heaped-up sand. It was always – sand.

Then other incidents of a similar kind came about, clearing the way to a natural acquaintanceship. Henriot watched the process with amusement, yet with another feeling too that was only a little less than anxiety. A keen observer, no detail escaped him; he saw the forces of their lives draw closer. It made him think of the devices of young people who desire to know one another, yet cannot get a proper introduction. Fate condescended to such little tricks. They wanted a third person, he began to feel. A third was necessary to some plan they had on hand, and – they waited to see if he could fill the place. This woman, with whom he had yet exchanged no single word, seemed so familiar to him, well known for years. They weighed and watched him, wondering if he would do.

None of the devices were too obviously used, but at length Henriot picked up so many forgotten articles, and heard so many significant phrases, casually let fall, that he began to feel like the villain in a machine-made play, where the hero forever drops clues his enemy is intended to discover.

Introduction followed inevitably. "My aunt can tell you; she knows Arabic perfectly." He had been discussing the meaning of some local name or other with a neighbour after dinner, and Vance had joined them. The neighbour moved away; these two were left standing alone, and he accepted a cigarette from the other's case. There was a rustle of skirts behind them. "Here she comes," said Vance; "you will let me introduce you." He did not ask for Henriot's name; he had already taken the trouble to find it out – another little betrayal, and another clue.

It was in a secluded corner of the great hall, and Henriot turned to see the woman's stately figure coming towards them across the thick carpet that deadened her footsteps. She came sailing up, her black eyes fixed upon his face. Very erect, head upright, shoulders almost squared, she moved wonderfully well; there was dignity and power in her walk. She was dressed in black, and her face was like the night. He found it impossible to say what lent her this air of impressiveness and solemnity that was almost majestic. But there *was* this touch of darkness and of power in the way she came that made him think of some sphinx-like figure of stone, some idol motionless in all its parts but moving as a whole, and gliding across – sand. Beneath those level lids her eyes stared hard at him. And a faint sensation of distress stirred in him deep, deep down. Where had he seen those eyes before?

He bowed, as she joined them, and Vance led the way to the armchairs in a corner of the lounge. The meeting, as the talk that followed, he felt, were all part of a preconceived plan. It had happened before. The woman, that is, was familiar to him – to some part of his being that had dropped stitches of old, old memory.

Lady Statham! At first the name had disappointed him. So many folk wear titles, as syllables in certain tongues wear accents – without them being mute, unnoticed, unpronounced. Nonentities, born to names, so often claim attention for their insignificance in this way. But this woman, had she been Jemima Jones, would have made the name distinguished and select. She was a big and sombre personality. Why was it, he wondered afterwards, that for a moment something in him shrank, and that his mind, metaphorically speaking, flung up an arm in self-protection? The instinct flashed and passed. But it seemed to him born of an automatic feeling that he must protect – not himself, but the woman from the man. There was confusion in it all; links were missing. He studied her intently. She was a woman who had none of the external feminine signals in either dress or manner, no graces, no little womanly hesitations and alarms, no daintiness, yet neither anything distinctly masculine. Her charm was strong, possessing; only he kept forgetting that he was talking to a – woman; and the thing she inspired in him included, with respect and wonder, somewhere also this curious hint of dread. This instinct to protect her fled as soon as it was born, for the interest of the conversation in which she so quickly plunged him obliterated all minor emotions whatsoever. Here, for the first time, he drew close to Egypt, the Egypt he had sought so long. It was not to be explained. He *felt* it.

Beginning with commonplaces, such as "You like Egypt? You find here what you expected?" she led him into better regions with "One finds here what one brings." He knew the delightful experience of talking fluently on subjects he was at home in, and to someone who understood. The feeling at first that to this woman he could not say mere anythings, slipped into its opposite – that he could say everything. Strangers ten minutes ago, they were at once in deep and intimate talk together. He found his ideas readily followed, agreed with up to a point – the point which permits discussion to start from a basis of general accord towards speculation. In the excitement of ideas he neglected the uncomfortable note that had stirred his caution, forgot the warning too. Her mind, moreover, seemed known to him; he was often aware of what she was going to say before he actually heard it; the current of her thoughts struck a familiar gait, and more than once he experienced vividly again the odd sensation that it all had happened before. The very sentences and phrases with which she pointed the turns of her unusual ideas were never wholly unexpected.

For her ideas were decidedly unusual, in the sense that she accepted without question speculations not commonly deemed worth consideration at all, indeed not ordinarily even known. Henriot knew them, because he had read in many fields. It was the strength of her belief that fascinated him. She offered no apologies. She knew. And while he talked, she listening with folded arms and her black eyes fixed upon his own, Richard Vance watched with vigilant eyes and listened too, ceaselessly alert. Vance joined in little enough, however, gave no opinions, his attitude one of general acquiescence. Twice, when pauses of slackening interest made it possible, Henriot fancied he surprised another quality in this negative attitude. Interpreting it each time differently, he yet dismissed both interpretations with a smile. His imagination leaped so absurdly to violent conclusions. They were not tenable: Vance was neither her keeper, nor was he in some fashion a detective. Yet in his manner was sometimes this suggestion of the detective order. He watched with such deep attention, and he concealed it so clumsily with an affectation of careless indifference.

There is nothing more dangerous than that impulsive intimacy strangers sometimes adopt when an atmosphere of mutual sympathy takes them by surprise, for it is akin to the false frankness friends affect when telling 'candidly' one another's faults. The mood is invariably regretted later. Henriot, however, yielded to it now with something like abandon. The pleasure of talking with this woman was so unexpected, and so keen.

For Lady Statham believed apparently in some Egypt of her dreams. Her interest was neither historical, archaeological, nor political. It was religious – yet hardly of this earth at all. The conversation turned upon the knowledge of the ancient Egyptians from an unearthly point of view, and even while he talked he was vaguely aware that it was *her* mind talking through his own. She drew out his ideas and made him say them. But this he was properly aware of only afterwards – that she had cleverly, mercilessly pumped him of all he had ever known or read upon the subject. Moreover, what Vance watched so intently was himself, and the reactions in himself this remarkable woman produced. That also he realised later.

His first impression that these two belonged to what may be called the 'crank' order was justified by the conversation. But, at least, it was interesting crankiness, and the belief behind it made it even fascinating. Long before the end he surprised in her a more vital form of his own attitude that anything *may* be true, since knowledge has never yet found final answers to any of the biggest questions.

He understood, from sentences dropped early in the talk, that she was among those few 'superstitious' folk who think that the old Egyptians came closer to reading the eternal riddles of the world than any others, and that their knowledge was a remnant of that ancient Wisdom Religion which existed in the superb, dark civilisation of the sunken Atlantis, lost continent that once joined Africa to Mexico. Eighty thousand years ago the dim sands of Poseidonis, great island adjoining the main continent which itself had vanished a vast period before, sank down beneath the waves, and the entire known world today was descended from its survivors.

Hence the significant fact that all religions and 'mythological' systems begin with a story of a flood – some cataclysmic upheaval that destroyed the world. Egypt itself was colonised by a group of Atlantean priests who brought their curious, deep knowledge with them. They had foreseen the cataclysm.

Lady Statham talked well, bringing into her great dream this strong, insistent quality of belief and fact. She knew, from Plato to Donelly, all that the minds of men have ever speculated upon the gorgeous legend. The evidence for such a sunken continent – Henriot had skimmed it too in years gone by – she made bewilderingly complete. He had heard Baconians demolish Shakespeare with an array of evidence equally overwhelming. It catches the imagination though not the mind. Yet out of her facts, as she presented them, grew a strange likelihood. The force of this woman's personality, and her calm and quiet way of believing all she talked about, took her listener to some extent – further than ever before, certainly – into the great dream after her. And the dream, to say the least, was a picturesque one, laden with wonderful possibilities. For as she talked the spirit of old Egypt moved up, staring down upon him out of eyes lidded so curiously level. Hitherto all had prated to him of the Arabs, their ancient faith and customs, and the splendour of the Bedouins, those Princes of the Desert. But what he sought, barely confessed in words even to himself, was something older far than this. And this strange, dark woman brought it close. Deeps in his soul, long slumbering, awoke. He heard forgotten questions.

Only in this brief way could he attempt to sum up the storm she roused in him.

She carried him far beyond mere outline, however, though afterwards he recalled the details with difficulty. So much more was suggested than actually expressed. She contrived to make the general modern scepticism an evidence of cheap mentality. It was so easy; the depth it affects to conceal, mere emptiness. "We have tried all things, and found all wanting" – the mind, as measuring instrument, merely confessed inadequate. Various shrewd judgments of this kind increased his respect, although her acceptance went so far beyond his own. And, while the label of credulity refused to stick to her, her sense of imaginative wonder enabled her to escape that dreadful compromise, a man's mind in a woman's temperament. She fascinated him.

The spiritual worship of the ancient Egyptians, she held, was a symbolical explanation of things generally alluded to as the secrets of life and death; their knowledge was a remnant of the wisdom of Atlantis. Material relics, equally misunderstood, still stood today at Karnac, Stonehenge, and in the mysterious writings on buried Mexican temples and cities, so significantly akin to the hieroglyphics upon the Egyptian tombs.

"The one misinterpreted as literally as the other," she suggested, "yet both fragments of an advanced knowledge that found its grave in the sea. The Wisdom of that old spiritual system has vanished from the world, only a degraded literalism left of its undecipherable language. The jewel has been lost, and the casket is filled with sand, sand, sand."

How keenly her black eyes searched his own as she said it, and how oddly she made the little word resound. The syllable drew out almost into chanting. Echoes answered from the depths within him, carrying it on and on across some desert of forgotten belief. Veils of sand flew everywhere about his mind. Curtains lifted. Whole hills of sand went shifting into level surfaces whence gardens of dim outline emerged to meet the sunlight.

"But the sand may be removed." It was her nephew, speaking almost for the first time, and the interruption had an odd effect, introducing a sharply practical element. For the tone expressed, so far as he dared express it, disapproval. It was a baited observation, an invitation to opinion.

"We are not sand-diggers, Mr. Henriot," put in Lady Statham, before he decided to respond. "Our object is quite another one; and I believe – I have a feeling," she added almost questioningly, "that you might be interested enough to help us perhaps."

He only wondered the direct attack had not come sooner. Its bluntness hardly surprised him. He felt himself leap forward to accept it. A sudden subsidence had freed his feet.

Then the warning operated suddenly – for an instant. Henriot *was* interested; more, he was half seduced; but, as yet, he did not mean to be included in their purposes, whatever these might be. That shrinking dread came back a moment, and was gone again before he could question it. His eyes looked full at Lady Statham. "What is it that you know?" they asked her. "Tell me the things we once knew together, you and I. These words are merely trifling. And why does another man now stand in my place? For the sands heaped upon my memory are shifting, and it is *you* who are moving them away."

His soul whispered it; his voice said quite another thing, although the words he used seemed oddly chosen:

"There is much in the ideas of ancient Egypt that has attracted me ever since I can remember, though I have never caught up with anything definite enough to follow. There was majesty somewhere in their conceptions – a large, calm majesty of spiritual dominion, one might call it perhaps. I *am* interested."

Her face remained expressionless as she listened, but there was grave conviction in the eyes that held him like a spell. He saw through them into dim, faint pictures whose background was always sand. He forgot that he was speaking with a woman, a woman who half an hour ago had been a stranger to him. He followed these faded mental pictures, though he never caught them up.... It was like his dream in London.

Lady Statham was talking – he had not noticed the means by which she effected the abrupt transition – of familiar beliefs of old Egypt; of the Ka, or Double, by whose existence the survival of the soul was possible, even its return into manifested, physical life; of the astrology, or influence of the heavenly bodies upon all sublunar activities; of terrific forms of other life, known to the ancient worship of Atlantis, great Potencies that might be invoked by ritual and ceremonial, and of their lesser influence as recognised in certain lower forms, hence treated with veneration as the 'Sacred Animal' branch of this dim religion. And she spoke lightly of the modern learning which so glibly imagined it was the animals themselves that were looked upon as 'gods' – the bull, the bird, the crocodile, the cat. "It's there they all go so absurdly wrong," she said, "taking the symbol for the power symbolised. Yet natural enough. The mind today wears blinkers, studies only the details seen directly before it. Had none of us experienced love, we should think the first lover mad. Few today know the Powers *they* knew, hence deny them. If the world were deaf it would stand with mockery before a hearing group swayed by an orchestra, pitying both listeners and performers. It would deem our admiration of a great swinging bell mere foolish worship of form and movement. Similarly, with high Powers that once expressed themselves in common forms – where best they could – being themselves bodiless. The learned men classify the forms with painstaking detail. But deity has gone out of life. The Powers symbolised are no longer experienced."

"These Powers, you suggest, then – their Kas, as it were – may still—"

But she waved aside the interruption. "They are satisfied, as the common people were, with a degraded literalism," she went on. "Nut was the Heavens, who spread herself across the earth in the form of a woman; Shu, the vastness of space; the ibis typified Thoth, and Hathor was the

Patron of the Western Hills; Khonsu, the moon, was personified, as was the deity of the Nile. But the high priest of Ra, the sun, you notice, remained ever the Great One of Visions."

The High Priest, the Great One of Visions! – How wonderfully again she made the sentence sing. She put splendour into it. The pictures shifted suddenly closer in his mind. He saw the grandeur of Memphis and Heliopolis rise against the stars and shake the sand of ages from their stern old temples.

"You think it possible, then, to get into touch with these High Powers you speak of, Powers once manifested in common forms?"

Henriot asked the question with a degree of conviction and solemnity that surprised himself. The scenery changed about him as he listened. The spacious halls of this former khedivial Palace melted into Desert spaces. He smelt the open wilderness, the sand that haunted Helouan. The soft-footed Arab servants moved across the hall in their white sheets like eddies of dust the wind stirred from the Libyan dunes. And over these two strangers close beside him stole a queer, indefinite alteration. Moods and emotions, nameless as unknown stars, rose through his soul, trailing dark mists of memory from unfathomable distances.

Lady Statham answered him indirectly. He found himself wishing that those steady eyes would sometimes close.

"Love is known only by feeling it," she said, her voice deepening a little. "Behind the form you feel the person loved. The process is an evocation, pure and simple. An arduous ceremonial, involving worship and devotional preparation, is the means. It is a difficult ritual – the only one acknowledged by the world as still effectual. Ritual is the passage way of the soul into the Infinite."

He might have said the words himself. The thought lay in him while she uttered it. Evocation everywhere in life was as true as assimilation. Nevertheless, he stared his companion full in the eyes with a touch of almost rude amazement. But no further questions prompted themselves; or, rather, he declined to ask them. He recalled, somehow uneasily, that in ceremonial the points of the compass have significance, standing for forces and activities that sleep there until invoked, and a passing light fell upon that curious midnight request in the corridor upstairs. These two were on the track of undesirable experiments, he thought.... They wished to include him too.

"You go at night sometimes into the Desert?" he heard himself saying. It was impulsive and miscalculated. His feeling that it would be wise to change the conversation resulted in giving it fresh impetus instead.

"We saw you there – in the Wadi Hof," put in Vance, suddenly breaking his long silence; "you too sleep out, then? It means, you know, the Valley of Fear."

"We wondered—" It was Lady Statham's voice, and she leaned forward eagerly as she said it, then abruptly left the sentence incomplete. Henriot started; a sense of momentary acute discomfort again ran over him. The same second she continued, though obviously changing the phrase – "we wondered how you spent your day there, during the heat. But you paint, don't you? You draw, I mean?"

The commonplace question, he realised in every fibre of his being, meant something *they* deemed significant. Was it his talent for drawing that they sought to use him for? Even as he answered with a simple affirmative, he had a flash of intuition that might be fanciful, yet that might be true: that this extraordinary pair were intent upon some ceremony of evocation that should summon into actual physical expression some Power – some type of life – known long ago to ancient worship, and that they even sought to fix its bodily outline with the pencil – his pencil.

A gateway of incredible adventure opened at his feet. He balanced on the edge of knowing unutterable things. Here was a clue that might lead him towards the hidden Egypt he had ever craved to know. An awful hand was beckoning. The sands were shifting. He saw the million eyes of the Desert watching him from beneath the level lids of centuries. Speck by speck, and grain by grain, the sand that smothered memory lifted the countless wrappings that embalmed it.

And he was willing, yet afraid. Why in the world did he hesitate and shrink? Why was it that the presence of this silent, watching personality in the chair beside him kept caution still alive, with warning close behind? The pictures in his mind were gorgeously coloured. It was Richard Vance who somehow streaked them through with black. A thing of darkness, born of this man's unassertive presence, flitted ever across the scenery, marring its grandeur with something evil, petty, dreadful. He held a horrible thought alive. His mind was thinking venal purposes.

In Henriot himself imagination had grown curiously heated, fed by what had been suggested rather than actually said. Ideas of immensity crowded his brain, yet never assumed definite shape. They were familiar, even as this strange woman was familiar. Once, long ago, he had known them well; had even practised them beneath these bright Egyptian stars. Whence came this prodigious glad excitement in his heart, this sense of mighty Powers coaxed down to influence the very details of daily life? Behind them, for all their vagueness, lay an archetypal splendour, fraught with forgotten meanings. He had always been aware of it in this mysterious land, but it had ever hitherto eluded him. It hovered everywhere. He had felt it brooding behind the towering Colossi at Thebes, in the skeletons of wasted temples, in the uncouth comeliness of the Sphinx, and in the crude terror of the Pyramids even. Over the whole of Egypt hung its invisible wings. These were but isolated fragments of the Body that might express it. And the Desert remained its cleanest, truest symbol. Sand knew it closest. Sand might even give it bodily form and outline.

But, while it escaped description in his mind, as equally it eluded visualisation in his soul, he felt that it combined with its vastness something infinitely small as well. Of such wee particles is the giant Desert born….

Henriot started nervously in his chair, convicted once more of unconscionable staring; and at the same moment a group of hotel people, returning from a dance, passed through the hall and nodded him good-night. The scent of the women reached him; and with it the sound of their voices discussing personalities just left behind. A London atmosphere came with them. He caught trivial phrases, uttered in a drawling tone, and followed by the shrill laughter of a girl. They passed upstairs, discussing their little things, like marionettes upon a tiny stage.

But their passage brought him back to things of modern life, and to some standard of familiar measurement. The pictures that his soul had gazed at so deep within, he realised, were a pictorial transfer caught incompletely from this woman's vivid mind. He had seen the Desert as the grey, enormous Tomb where hovered still the Ka of ancient Egypt. Sand screened her visage with the veil of centuries. But She was there, and She was living. Egypt herself had pitched a temporary camp in him, and then moved on.

There was a momentary break, a sense of abruptness and dislocation. And then he became aware that Lady Statham had been speaking for some time before he caught her actual words, and that a certain change had come into her voice as also into her manner.

Chapter V

SHE WAS leaning closer to him, her face suddenly glowing and alive. Through the stone figure coursed the fires of a passion that deepened the coal-black eyes and communicated a hint of light – of exaltation – to her whole person. It was incredibly moving. To this deep passion was due the power he had felt. It was her entire life; she lived for it, she would die for it. Her calmness of manner enhanced its effect. Hence the strength of those first impressions that had stormed him.

The woman had belief; however wild and strange, it was sacred to her. The secret of her influence was – conviction.

His attitude shifted several points then. The wonder in him passed over into awe. The things she knew were real. They were not merely imaginative speculations.

"I knew I was not wrong in thinking you in sympathy with this line of thought," she was saying in lower voice, steady with earnestness, and as though she had read his mind. "You, too, know, though perhaps you hardly realise that you know. It lies so deep in you that you only get vague feelings of it – intimations of memory. Isn't that the case?"

Henriot gave assent with his eyes; it was the truth.

"What we know instinctively," she continued, "is simply what we are trying to remember. Knowledge is memory." She paused a moment watching his face closely. "At least, you are free from that cheap scepticism which labels these old beliefs as superstition." It was not even a question.

"I – worship real belief – of any kind," he stammered, for her words and the close proximity of her atmosphere caused a strange upheaval in his heart that he could not account for. He faltered in his speech. "It is the most vital quality in life – rarer than deity." He was using her own phrases even. "It is creative. It constructs the world anew—"

"And may reconstruct the old."

She said it, lifting her face above him a little, so that her eyes looked down into his own. It grew big and somehow masculine. It was the face of a priest, spiritual power in it. Where, oh where in the echoing Past had he known this woman's soul? He saw her in another setting, a forest of columns dim about her, towering above giant aisles. Again he felt the Desert had come close. Into this tent-like hall of the hotel came the sifting of tiny sand. It heaped softly about the very furniture against his feet, blocking the exits of door and window. It shrouded the little present. The wind that brought it stirred a veil that had hung for ages motionless....

She had been saying many things that he had missed while his mind went searching. "There were types of life the Atlantean system knew it might revive – life unmanifested today in any bodily form," was the sentence he caught with his return to the actual present.

"A type of life?" he whispered, looking about him, as though to see who it was had joined them; "you mean a – soul? Some kind of soul, alien to humanity, or to – to any forms of living thing in the world today?" What she had been saying reached him somehow, it seemed, though he had not heard the words themselves. Still hesitating, he was yet so eager to hear. Already he felt she meant to include him in her purposes, and that in the end he must go willingly. So strong was her persuasion on his mind.

And he felt as if he knew vaguely what was coming. Before she answered his curious question – prompting it indeed – rose in his mind that strange idea of the Group-Soul: the theory that big souls cannot express themselves in a single individual, but need an entire group for their full manifestation.

He listened intently. The reflection that this sudden intimacy was unnatural, he rejected, for many conversations were really gathered into one. Long watching and preparation on both sides had cleared the way for the ripening of acquaintance into confidence – how long he dimly wondered? But if this conception of the Group-Soul was not new, the suggestion Lady Statham developed out of it was both new and startling – and yet always so curiously familiar. Its value for him lay, not in far-fetched evidence that supported it, but in the deep belief which made it a vital asset in an honest inner life.

"An individual," she said quietly, "one soul expressed completely in a single person, I mean, is exceedingly rare. Not often is a physical instrument found perfect enough to provide it with adequate expression. In the lower ranges of humanity – certainly in animal and insect life – one soul is shared by many. Behind a tribe of savages stands one Savage. A flock of birds is a single Bird, scattered through the consciousness of all. They wheel in mid-air, they migrate, they obey the deep intelligence called instinct – all as one. The life of any one lion is the life of all – the lion Group-Soul that manifests itself in the entire genus. An ant-heap is a single Ant; through the bees spreads the consciousness of a single Bee."

Henriot knew what she was working up to. In his eagerness to hasten disclosure he interrupted –

"And there may be types of life that have no corresponding bodily expression at all, then?" he asked as though the question were forced out of him. "They exist as Powers – unmanifested on the earth today?"

"Powers," she answered, watching him closely with unswerving stare, "that need a group to provide their body – their physical expression – if they came back."

"Came back!" he repeated below his breath.

But she heard him. "They once had expression. Egypt, Atlantis knew them – spiritual Powers that never visit the world today."

"Bodies," he whispered softly, "actual bodies?"

"Their sphere of action, you see, would be their body. And it might be physical outline. So potent a descent of spiritual life would select materials for its body where it could find them. Our conventional notion of a body – what is it? A single outline moving altogether in one direction. For little human souls, or fragments, this is sufficient. But for vaster types of soul an entire host would be required."

"A church?" he ventured. "Some Body of belief, you surely mean?"

She bowed her head a moment in assent. She was determined he should seize her meaning fully.

"A wave of spiritual awakening – a descent of spiritual life upon a nation," she answered slowly, "forms itself a church, and the body of true believers are its sphere of action. They are literally its bodily expression. Each individual believer is a corpuscle in that Body. The Power has provided itself with a vehicle of manifestation. Otherwise we could not know it. And the more real the belief of each individual, the more perfect the expression of the spiritual life behind them all. A Group-Soul walks the earth. Moreover, a nation naturally devout could attract a type of soul unknown to a nation that denies all faith. Faith brings back the gods.... But today belief is dead, and Deity has left the world."

She talked on and on, developing this main idea that in days of older faiths there were deific types of life upon the earth, evoked by worship and beneficial to humanity. They had long ago withdrawn because the worship which brought them down had died the death. The world had grown pettier. These vast centres of Spiritual Power found no 'Body' in which they now could express themselves or manifest.... Her thoughts and phrases poured over him like sand. It was always sand he felt – burying the Present and uncovering the Past....

He tried to steady his mind upon familiar objects, but wherever he looked Sand stared him in the face. Outside these trivial walls the Desert lay listening. It lay waiting too. Vance himself had dropped out of recognition. He belonged to the world of things today. But this woman and himself stood thousands of years away, beneath the columns of a Temple in the sands. And the sands were moving. His feet went shifting with them... running down vistas of ageless memory that woke terror by their sheer immensity of distance....

Like a muffled voice that called to him through many veils and wrappings, he heard her describe the stupendous Powers that evocation might coax down again among the world of men.

"To what useful end?" he asked at length, amazed at his own temerity, and because he knew instinctively the answer in advance. It rose through these layers of coiling memory in his soul.

"The extension of spiritual knowledge and the widening of life," she answered. "The link with the 'unearthly kingdom' wherein this ancient system went forever searching, would be re-established. Complete rehabilitation might follow. Portions – little portions of these Powers – expressed themselves naturally once in certain animal types, instinctive life that did not deny or reject them. The worship of sacred animals was the relic of a once gigantic system of evocation – not of monsters," and she smiled sadly, "but of Powers that were willing and ready to descend when worship summoned them."

Again, beneath his breath, Henriot heard himself murmur – his own voice startled him as he whispered it: "Actual bodily shape and outline?"

"Material for bodies is everywhere," she answered, equally low; "dust to which we all return; sand, if you prefer it, fine, fine sand. Life moulds it easily enough, when that life is potent."

A certain confusion spread slowly through his mind as he heard her. He lit a cigarette and smoked some minutes in silence. Lady Statham and her nephew waited for him to speak. At length, after some inner battling and hesitation, he put the question that he knew they waited for. It was impossible to resist any longer.

"It would be interesting to know the method," he said, "and to revive, perhaps, by experiment—"

Before he could complete his thought, she took him up:

"There are some who claim to know it," she said gravely – her eyes a moment masterful. "A clue, thus followed, might lead to the entire reconstruction I spoke of."

"And the method?" he repeated faintly.

"Evoke the Power by ceremonial evocation – the ritual is obtainable – and note the form it assumes. Then establish it. This shape or outline once secured, could then be made permanent – a mould for its return at will – its natural physical expression here on earth."

"Idol!" he exclaimed.

"Image," she replied at once. "Life, before we can know it, must have a body. Our souls, in order to manifest here, need a material vehicle."

"And – to obtain this form or outline?" he began; "to fix it, rather?"

"Would be required the clever pencil of a fearless looker-on – someone not engaged in the actual evocation. This form, accurately made permanent in solid matter, say in stone, would provide a channel always open. Experiment, properly speaking, might then begin. The cisterns of Power behind would be accessible."

"An amazing proposition!" Henriot exclaimed. What surprised him was that he felt no desire to laugh, and little even to doubt.

"Yet known to every religion that ever deserved the name," put in Vance like a voice from a distance. Blackness came somehow with his interruption – a touch of darkness. He spoke eagerly.

To all the talk that followed, and there was much of it, Henriot listened with but half an ear. This one idea stormed through him with an uproar that killed attention. Judgment was held utterly in abeyance. He carried away from it some vague suggestion that this woman had hinted at previous lives she half remembered, and that every year she came to Egypt, haunting the sands and temples in the effort to recover lost clues. And he recalled afterwards that she said, "This all came to me as a child, just as though it was something half remembered." There was the further suggestion that he himself was not unknown to her; that they, too, had met before. But this, compared to the grave certainty of the rest, was merest fantasy that did not hold his attention. He answered, hardly knowing what he said. His preoccupation with other thoughts deep down was so intense, that he was probably barely polite, uttering empty phrases, with his mind elsewhere. His one desire was to escape and be alone, and it was with genuine relief that he presently excused himself and went upstairs to bed. The halls, he noticed, were empty; an Arab servant waited to put the lights out. He walked up, for the lift had long ceased running.

And the magic of old Egypt stalked beside him. The studies that had fascinated his mind in earlier youth returned with the power that had subdued his mind in boyhood. The cult of Osiris woke in his blood again; Horus and Nephthys stirred in their long-forgotten centres. There revived in him, too long buried, the awful glamour of those liturgal rites and vast body of observances, those spells and formulae of incantation of the oldest known recension that years ago had captured his imagination and belief – the Book of the Dead. Trumpet voices called to his heart again across the desert of some dim past. There were forms of life – impulses from the Creative Power which is the Universe – other than the soul of man. They could be known. A spiritual exaltation, roused by the words and presence of this singular woman, shouted to him as he went.

Then, as he closed his bedroom door, carefully locking it, there stood beside him – Vance. The forgotten figure of Vance came up close – the watching eyes, the simulated interest, the feigned belief, the detective mental attitude, these broke through the grandiose panorama, bringing darkness. Vance, strong personality that hid behind assumed nonentity for some purpose of his own, intruded with sudden violence, demanding an explanation of his presence.

And, with an equal suddenness, explanation offered itself then and there. It came unsought, its horror of certainty utterly unjustified; and it came in this unexpected fashion:

Behind the interest and acquiescence of the man ran – fear: but behind the vivid fear ran another thing that Henriot now perceived was vile. For the first time in his life, Henriot knew it at close quarters, actual, ready to operate. Though familiar enough in daily life to be of common occurrence, Henriot had never realised it as he did now, so close and terrible. In the same way he had never *realised* that he would die – vanish from the busy world of men and women, forgotten as though he had never existed, an eddy of wind-blown dust. And in the man named Richard Vance this thing was close upon blossom. Henriot could not name it to himself. Even in thought it appalled him.

He undressed hurriedly, almost with the child's idea of finding safety between the sheets. His mind undressed itself as well. The business of the day laid itself automatically aside; the will sank down; desire grew inactive. Henriot was exhausted. But, in that stage towards slumber when thinking stops, and only fugitive pictures pass across the mind in shadowy dance, his brain ceased shouting its mechanical explanations, and his soul unveiled a peering eye. Great limbs of memory, smothered by the activities of the Present, stirred their stiffened lengths through the sands of long ago – sands this woman had begun to excavate from some far-off pre-existence they had surely known together. Vagueness and certainty ran hand in hand. Details were unrecoverable, but the emotions in which they were embedded moved.

He turned restlessly in his bed, striving to seize the amazing clues and follow them. But deliberate effort hid them instantly again; they retired instantly into the subconsciousness. With the brain of this body he now occupied they had nothing to do. The brain stored memories of each life only. This ancient script was graven in his soul. Subconsciousness alone could interpret and reveal. And it was his subconscious memory that Lady Statham had been so busily excavating.

Dimly it stirred and moved about the depths within him, never clearly seen, indefinite, felt as a yearning after unrecoverable knowledge. Against the darker background of Vance's fear and sinister purpose – both of this present life, and recent – he saw the grandeur of this woman's impossible dream, and *knew*, beyond argument or reason, that it was true. Judgment and will asleep, he left the impossibility aside, and took the grandeur. The Belief of Lady Statham was not credulity and superstition; it was Memory. Still to this day, over the sands of Egypt, hovered immense spiritual potencies, so vast that they could only know physical expression in a group – in many. Their sphere of bodily manifestation must be a host, each individual unit in that host a corpuscle in the whole.

The wind, rising from the Lybian wastes across the Nile, swept up against the exposed side of the hotel, and made his windows rattle – the old, sad winds of Egypt. Henriot got out of bed to fasten the outside shutters. He stood a moment and watched the moon floating down behind the Sakkara Pyramids. The Pleiades and Orion's Belt hung brilliantly; the Great Bear was close to the horizon. In the sky above the Desert swung ten thousand stars. No sounds rose from the streets of Helouan. The tide of sand was coming slowly in.

And a flock of enormous thoughts swooped past him from fields of this unbelievable, lost memory. The Desert, pale in the moon, was coextensive with the night, too huge for comfort or understanding, yet charged to the brim with infinite peace. Behind its majesty of silence lay whispers of a vanished language that once could call with power upon mighty spiritual Agencies. Its skirts were folded now, but, slowly across the leagues of sand, they began to stir and rearrange themselves. He grew suddenly aware of this enveloping shroud of sand – as the raw material of bodily expression: Form.

The sand was in his imagination and his mind. Shaking loosely the folds of its gigantic skirts, it rose; it moved a little towards him. He saw the eternal countenance of the Desert watching him – immobile and unchanging behind these shifting veils the winds laid so carefully over it. Egypt, the ancient Egypt, turned in her vast sarcophagus of Desert, wakening from her sleep of ages at the Belief of approaching worshippers.

Only in this insignificant manner could he express a letter of the terrific language that crowded to seek expression through his soul.... He closed the shutters and carefully fastened them. He turned to go back to bed, curiously trembling. Then, as he did so, the whole singular delusion caught him with a shock that held him motionless. Up rose the stupendous apparition of the entire Desert and stood behind him on that balcony. Swift as thought, in silence, the Desert stood on end against his very face. It towered across the sky, hiding Orion and the moon; it dipped below the horizons. The whole grey sheet of it rose up before his eyes and stood. Through its unfolding skirts ran ten thousand eddies of swirling sand as the creases of its grave-clothes smoothed themselves out in moonlight. And a bleak, scarred countenance, huge as a planet, gazed down into his own....

Through his dreamless sleep that night two things lay active and awake... in the subconscious part that knows no slumber. They were incongruous. One was evil, small and human; the other unearthly and sublime. For the memory of the fear that haunted Vance, and the sinister cause of it, pricked at him all night long. But behind, beyond this common, intelligible emotion, lay the crowding wonder that caught his soul with glory:

The Sand was stirring, the Desert was awake. Ready to mate with them in material form, brooded close the Ka of that colossal Entity that once expressed itself through the myriad life of ancient Egypt.

Chapter VI

NEXT DAY, and for several days following, Henriot kept out of the path of Lady Statham and her nephew. The acquaintanceship had grown too rapidly to be quite comfortable. It was easy to pretend that he took people at their face value, but it was a pose; one liked to know something of antecedents. It was otherwise difficult to 'place' them. And Henriot, for the life of him, could not 'place' these two. His Subconsciousness brought explanation when it came – but the Subconsciousness is only temporarily active. When it retired he floundered without a rudder, in confusion.

With the flood of morning sunshine the value of much she had said evaporated. Her presence alone had supplied the key to the cipher. But while the indigestible portions he rejected, there remained a good deal he had already assimilated. The discomfort remained; and with it the grave, unholy reality of it all. It was something more than theory. Results would follow – if he joined them. He would witness curious things.

The force with which it drew him brought hesitation. It operated in him like a shock that numbs at first by its abrupt arrival, and needs time to realise in the right proportions to the rest of life. These right proportions, however, did not come readily, and his emotions ranged between sceptical laughter and complete acceptance. The one detail he felt certain of was this dreadful thing he had divined in Vance. Trying hard to disbelieve it, he found he could not. It was true. Though without a shred of real evidence to support it, the horror of it remained. He knew it in his very bones.

And this, perhaps, was what drove him to seek the comforting companionship of folk he understood and felt at home with. He told his host and hostess about the strangers, though omitting the actual conversation because they would merely smile in blank miscomprehension. But the moment he described the strong black eyes beneath the level eyelids, his hostess turned with a start, her interest deeply roused: "Why, it's that awful Statham woman," she exclaimed, "that must be Lady Statham, and the man she calls her nephew."

"Sounds like it, certainly," her husband added. "Felix, you'd better clear out. They'll bewitch you too."

And Henriot bridled, yet wondering why he did so. He drew into his shell a little, giving the merest sketch of what had happened. But he listened closely while these two practical old friends supplied him with information in the gossiping way that human nature loves. No doubt there was much embroidery, and more perversion, exaggeration too, but the account evidently rested upon some basis of solid foundation for all that. Smoke and fire go together always.

"He *is* her nephew right enough," Mansfield corrected his wife, before proceeding to his own man's form of elaboration; "no question about that, I believe. He's her favourite nephew, and she's as rich as a pig. He follows her out here every year, waiting for her empty shoes. But they *are* an unsavoury couple. I've met 'em in various parts, all over Egypt, but they always come back to Helouan in the end. And the stories about them are simply legion. You remember—" he turned hesitatingly to his wife – "some people, I heard," he changed his sentence, "were made quite ill by her."

"I'm sure Felix ought to know, yes," his wife boldly took him up, "my niece, Fanny, had the most extraordinary experience." She turned to Henriot. "Her room was next to Lady Statham in some hotel or other at Assouan or Edfu, and one night she woke and heard a kind of mysterious chanting or intoning next her. Hotel doors are so dreadfully thin. There was a funny smell too, like incense of something sickly, and a man's voice kept chiming in. It went on for hours, while she lay terrified in bed—"

"Frightened, you say?" asked Henriot.

"Out of her skin, yes; she said it was so uncanny – made her feel icy. She wanted to ring the bell, but was afraid to leave her bed. The room was full of – of things, yet she could see nothing. She *felt* them, you see. And after a bit the sound of this sing-song voice so got on her nerves, it half dazed her – a kind of enchantment – she felt choked and suffocated. And then—" It was her turn to hesitate.

"Tell it all," her husband said, quite gravely too.

"Well – something came in. At least, she describes it oddly, rather; she said it made the door bulge inwards from the next room, but not the door alone; the walls bulged or swayed as if a huge thing pressed against them from the other side. And at the same moment her windows – she had two big balconies, and the venetian shutters were fastened – both her windows *darkened* – though it was two in the morning and pitch dark outside. She said it was all *one* thing – trying to get in; just as water, you see, would rush in through every hole and opening it could find, and all at once. And in spite of her terror – that's the odd part of it – she says she felt a kind of splendour in her – a sort of elation."

"She saw nothing?"

"She says she doesn't remember. Her senses left her, I believe – though she won't admit it."

"Fainted for a minute, probably," said Mansfield.

"So there it is," his wife concluded, after a silence. "And that's true. It happened to my niece, didn't it, John?"

Stories and legendary accounts of strange things that the presence of these two brought poured out then. They were obviously somewhat mixed, one account borrowing picturesque details from another, and all in disproportion, as when people tell stories in a language they are little familiar with. But, listening with avidity, yet also with uneasiness, somehow, Henriot put two and two together. Truth stood behind them somewhere. These two held traffic with the powers that ancient Egypt knew.

"Tell Felix, dear, about the time you met the nephew – horrid creature – in the Valley of the Kings," he heard his wife say presently. And Mansfield told it plainly enough, evidently glad to get it done, though.

"It was some years ago now, and I didn't know who he was then, or anything about him. I don't know much more now – except that he's a dangerous sort of charlatan-devil, *I* think. But I came across him one night up there by Thebes in the Valley of the Kings – you know, where they buried all their Johnnies with so much magnificence and processions and masses, and all the rest. It's the most astounding, the most haunted place you ever saw, gloomy, silent, full of gorgeous lights and shadows that seem alive – terribly impressive; it makes you creep and shudder. You feel old Egypt watching you."

"Get on, dear," said his wife.

"Well, I was coming home late on a blasted lazy donkey, dog-tired into the bargain, when my donkey boy suddenly ran for his life and left me alone. It was after sunset. The sand was red and shining, and the big cliffs sort of fiery. And my donkey stuck its four feet in the ground and wouldn't budge. Then, about fifty yards away, I saw a fellow – European apparently – doing something – Heaven knows what, for I can't describe it – among the boulders that lie all over the ground there. Ceremony, I suppose you'd call it. I was so interested that at first I watched. Then I saw he wasn't alone. There were a lot of moving things round him, towering big things, that came and went like shadows. That twilight is fearfully bewildering; perspective changes, and distance gets all confused. It's fearfully hard to see properly. I only remember that I got off my donkey and went up closer, and when I was within a dozen yards of him – well, it sounds such rot, you know, but I swear the things suddenly rushed off and left him there alone. They went with a roaring noise like wind; shadowy but tremendously big, they were, and they vanished up against the fiery precipices as though they slipped bang into the stone itself. The only thing I can think of to describe 'em is – well, those sand-storms the Khamasin raises – the hot winds, you know."

"They probably *were* sand," his wife suggested, burning to tell another story of her own.

"Possibly, only there wasn't a breath of wind, and it was hot as blazes – and – I had such extraordinary sensations – never felt anything like it before – wild and exhilarated – drunk, I tell you, drunk."

"You saw them?" asked Henriot. "You made out their shape at all, or outline?"

"Sphinx," he replied at once, "for all the world like sphinxes. You know the kind of face and head these limestone strata in the Desert take – great visages with square Egyptian head-dresses where the driven sand has eaten away the softer stuff beneath? You see it everywhere – enormous idols they seem, with faces and eyes and lips awfully like the sphinx – well, that's the nearest I can get to it." He puffed his pipe hard. But there was no sign of levity in him. He told the actual truth as far as in him lay, yet half ashamed of what he told. And a good deal he left out, too.

"She's got a face of the same sort, that Statham horror," his wife said with a shiver. "Reduce the size, and paint in awful black eyes, and you've got her exactly – a living idol." And all three laughed, yet a laughter without merriment in it.

"And you spoke to the man?"

"I did," the Englishman answered, "though I confess I'm a bit ashamed of the way I spoke. Fact is, I was excited, thunderingly excited, and felt a kind of anger. I wanted to kick the beggar for practising such bally rubbish, and in such a place too. Yet all the time – well, well, I believe it was sheer funk now," he laughed; "for I felt uncommonly queer out there in the dusk, alone with – with that kind of business; and I was angry with myself for feeling it. Anyhow, I went up – I'd lost my donkey boy as well, remember – and slated him like a dog. I can't remember what I said exactly – only that he stood and stared at me in silence. That made it worse – seemed twice as real then. The beggar said no single word the whole time. He signed to me with one hand to clear out. And then, suddenly out of nothing – she – that woman – appeared and stood beside him. I never saw her come. She must have been behind some boulder or other, for she simply rose out of the ground. She stood there and stared at me too – bang in the face. She was turned towards the sunset – what was left of it in the west – and her black eyes shone like – ugh! I can't describe it – it was shocking."

"She spoke?"

"She said five words – and her voice – it'll make you laugh – it was metallic like a gong: 'You are in danger here.' That's all she said. I simply turned and cleared out as fast as ever I could. But I had to go on foot. My donkey had followed its boy long before. I tell you – smile as you may – my blood was all curdled for an hour afterwards."

Then he explained that he felt some kind of explanation or apology was due, since the couple lodged in his own hotel, and how he approached the man in the smoking-room after dinner. A conversation resulted – the man was quite intelligent after all – of which only one sentence had remained in his mind.

"Perhaps you can explain it, Felix. I wrote it down, as well as I could remember. The rest confused me beyond words or memory; though I must confess it did not seem – well, not utter rot exactly. It was about astrology and rituals and the worship of the old Egyptians, and I don't know what else besides. Only, he made it intelligible and almost sensible, if only I could have got the hang of the thing enough to remember it. You know," he added, as though believing in spite of himself, "there *is* a lot of that wonderful old Egyptian religious business still hanging about in the atmosphere of this place, say what you like."

"But this sentence?" Henriot asked. And the other went off to get a note-book where he had written it down.

"He was jawing, you see," he continued when he came back, Henriot and his wife having kept silence meanwhile, "about direction being of importance in religious ceremonies, West and North symbolising certain powers, or something of the kind, why people turn to the East and all that sort of thing, and speaking of the whole Universe as if it had living forces tucked away in it that expressed themselves somehow when roused up. That's how I remember it anyhow. And then he said this thing – in answer to some fool question probably that I put." And he read out of the note-book:

"'You were in danger because you came through the Gateway of the West, and the Powers from the Gateway of the East were at that moment rising, and therefore in direct opposition to you.'"

Then came the following, apparently a simile offered by way of explanation. Mansfield read it in a shamefaced tone, evidently prepared for laughter:

"'Whether I strike you on the back or in the face determines what kind of answering force I rouse in you. Direction is significant.' And he said it was the period called the Night of Power – time when the Desert encroaches and spirits are close."

And tossing the book aside, he lit his pipe again and waited a moment to hear what might be said. "Can you explain such gibberish?" he asked at length, as neither of his listeners spoke. But Henriot said he couldn't. And the wife then took up her own tale of stories that had grown about this singular couple.

These were less detailed, and therefore less impressive, but all contributed something towards the atmosphere of reality that framed the entire picture. They belonged to the type one hears at every dinner party in Egypt – stories of the vengeance mummies seem to take on those who robbed them, desecrating their peace of centuries; of a woman wearing a necklace of scarabs taken from a princess's tomb, who felt hands about her throat to strangle her; of little Ka figures, Pasht goddesses, amulets and the rest, that brought curious disaster to those who kept them. They are many and various, astonishingly circumstantial often, and vouched for by persons the reverse of credulous. The modern superstition that haunts the desert gullies with Afreets has nothing in common with them. They rest upon a basis of indubitable experience; and they remain – inexplicable. And about the personalities of Lady Statham and her nephew they crowded like flies attracted by a dish of fruit. The Arabs, too, were afraid of her. She had difficulty in getting guides and dragomen.

"My dear chap," concluded Mansfield, "take my advice and have nothing to do with 'em. There *is* a lot of queer business knocking about in this old country, and people like that know ways of reviving it somehow. It's upset you already; you looked scared, I thought, the moment you came in." They laughed, but the Englishman was in earnest. "I tell you what," he added, "we'll go off for a bit of shooting together. The fields along the Delta are packed with birds now: they're home early this year on their way to the North. What d'ye say, eh?"

But Henriot did not care about the quail shooting. He felt more inclined to be alone and think things out by himself. He had come to his friends for comfort, and instead they had made him uneasy and excited. His interest had suddenly doubled. Though half afraid, he longed to know what these two were up to – to follow the adventure to the bitter end. He disregarded the warning of his host as well as the premonition in his own heart. The sand had caught his feet.

There were moments when he laughed in utter disbelief, but these were optimistic moods that did not last. He always returned to the feeling that truth lurked somewhere in the whole strange business, and that if he joined forces with them, as they seemed to wish, he would witness – well, he hardly knew what – but it enticed him as danger does the reckless man, or death the suicide. The sand had caught his mind.

He decided to offer himself to all they wanted – his pencil too. He would see – a shiver ran through him at the thought – what they saw, and know some eddy of that vanished tide of power and splendour the ancient Egyptian priesthood knew, and that perhaps was even common experience in the far-off days of dim Atlantis. The sand had caught his imagination too. He was utterly sand-haunted.

Chapter VII

AND SO HE TOOK PAINS, though without making definite suggestion, to place himself in the way of this woman and her nephew – only to find that his hints were disregarded. They left him alone, if they did not actually avoid him. Moreover, he rarely came across them now. Only at night, or in the queer dusk hours, he caught glimpses of them moving hurriedly off from the hotel, and always desertwards. And their disregard, well calculated, enflamed his desire to the point when he almost decided to propose himself. Quite suddenly, then, the idea flashed through him – how do they come, these odd revelations, when the mind lies receptive like a plate sensitised by anticipation? – that they were waiting for a certain date, and, with the notion, came Mansfield's remark about 'the Night of Power', believed in by the old Egyptian Calendar as a time when the supersensuous world moves close against the minds of men with all its troop of possibilities. And the thought, once lodged in its corner of imagination, grew strong. He looked it up. Ten days from now, he found, Leyel-el-Sud would be upon him, with a moon, too, at the full. And this strange hint of guidance he accepted. In his present mood, as he admitted, smiling to himself, he could accept anything. It was part of it, it belonged to the adventure. But, even while he persuaded himself that it was play, the solemn reality, of what lay ahead increased amazingly, sketched darkly in his very soul.

These intervening days he spent as best he could – impatiently, a prey to quite opposite emotions. In the blazing sunshine he thought of it and laughed; but at night he lay often sleepless, calculating chances of escape. He never did escape, however. The Desert that watched little Helouan with great, unwinking eyes watched also every turn and twist he made. Like this oasis, he basked in the sun of older time, and dreamed beneath forgotten moons. The sand at last had crept into his inmost heart. It sifted over him.

Seeking a reaction from normal, everyday things, he made tourist trips; yet, while recognising the comedy in his attitude, he never could lose sight of the grandeur that banked it up so hauntingly. These two contrary emotions grafted themselves on all he did and saw. He crossed the Nile at Bedrashein, and went again to the Tomb-World of Sakkara; but through all the chatter of veiled and helmeted tourists, the *bandar-log* of our modern Jungle, ran this dark under-stream of awe their monkey methods could not turn aside. One world lay upon another, but this modern layer was a shallow crust that, like the phenomenon of the 'desert-film', a mere angle of falling light could instantly obliterate. Beneath the sand, deep down, he passed along the Street of Tombs, as he had often passed before, moved then merely by historical curiosity and admiration, but now by emotions for which he found no name. He saw the enormous sarcophagi of granite in their gloomy chambers where the sacred bulls once lay, swathed and embalmed like human beings, and, in the flickering candle light, the mood of ancient rites surged round him, menacing his doubts and laughter. The least human whisper in these subterraneans, dug out first four thousand years ago, revived ominous Powers that stalked beside him, forbidding and premonitive. He gazed at the spots where Mariette, unearthing them forty years ago, found fresh as of yesterday the marks of fingers and naked feet – of those who set the sixty-five ton slabs in position. And when he came up again into the sunshine he met the eternal questions of the pyramids, overtopping all his mental horizons. Sand blocked all the avenues of younger emotion, leaving the channels of something in him incalculably older, open and clean swept.

He slipped homewards, uncomfortable and followed, glad to be with a crowd – because he was otherwise alone with more than he could dare to think about. Keeping just ahead of his companions, he crossed the desert edge where the ghost of Memphis walks under rustling palm trees that screen no stone left upon another of all its mile-long populous splendours. For here was a vista his imagination could realise; here he could know the comfort of solid ground his feet could touch. Gigantic Ramases, lying on his back beneath their shade and staring at the sky, similarly helped to steady his swaying thoughts. Imagination could deal with these.

And daily thus he watched the busy world go to and fro to its scale of tips and bargaining, and gladly mingled with it, trying to laugh and study guidebooks, and listen to half-fledged explanations, but always seeing the comedy of his poor attempts. Not all those little donkeys, bells tinkling, beads shining, trotting beneath their comical burdens to the tune of shouting and belabouring, could stem this tide of deeper things the woman had let loose in the subconscious part of him. Everywhere he saw the mysterious camels go slouching through the sand, gurgling the water in their skinny, extended throats. Centuries passed between the enormous knee-stroke of their stride. And, every night, the sunsets restored the forbidding, graver mood, with their crimson, golden splendour, their strange green shafts of light, then – sudden twilight that brought the Past upon him with an awful leap. Upon the stage then stepped the figures of this pair of human beings, chanting their ancient plainsong of incantation in the moonlit desert, and working their rites of unholy evocation as the priests had worked them centuries before in the sands that now buried Sakkara fathoms deep.

Then one morning he woke with a question in his mind, as though it had been asked of him in sleep and he had waked just before the answer came. "Why do I spend my time sight-seeing, instead of going alone into the Desert as before? What has made me change?"

This latest mood now asked for explanation. And the answer, coming up automatically, startled him. It was so clear and sure – had been lying in the background all along. One word contained it:

Vance.

The sinister intentions of this man, forgotten in the rush of other emotions, asserted themselves again convincingly. The human horror, so easily comprehensible, had been smothered for the time by the hint of unearthly revelations. But it had operated all the time. Now it took the lead. He dreaded to be alone in the Desert with this dark picture in his mind of what Vance meant to bring there to completion. This abomination of a selfish human will returned to fix its terror in him. To be alone in the Desert meant to be alone with the imaginative picture of what Vance – he knew it with such strange certainty – hoped to bring about there.

There was absolutely no evidence to justify the grim suspicion. It seemed indeed far-fetched enough, this connection between the sand and the purpose of an evil-minded, violent man. But Henriot saw it true. He could argue it away in a few minutes – easily. Yet the instant thought ceased, it returned, led up by intuition. It possessed him, filled his mind with horrible possibilities. He feared the Desert as he might have feared the scene of some atrocious crime. And, for the time, this dread of a merely human thing corrected the big seduction of the other – the suggested 'super-natural'.

Side by side with it, his desire to join himself to the purposes of the woman increased steadily. They kept out of his way apparently; the offer seemed withdrawn; he grew restless, unable to settle to anything for long, and once he asked the porter casually if they were leaving the hotel. Lady Statham had been invisible for days, and Vance was somehow never within speaking distance. He heard with relief that they had not gone – but with dread as well. Keen excitement worked in him underground. He slept badly. Like a schoolboy, he waited for the summons to an important examination that involved portentous issues, and contradictory emotions disturbed his peace of mind abominably.

Chapter VIII

BUT IT WAS NOT until the end of the week, when Vance approached him with purpose in his eyes and manner, that Henriot knew his fears unfounded, and caught himself trembling with sudden anticipation – because the invitation, so desired yet so dreaded, was actually at hand. Firmly determined to keep caution uppermost, yet he went unresistingly to a secluded corner by the palms where they could talk in privacy. For prudence is of the mind, but desire is of the soul, and while his brain of today whispered wariness, voices in his heart of long ago shouted commands that he knew he must obey with joy.

It was evening and the stars were out. Helouan, with her fairy twinkling lights, lay silent against the Desert edge. The sand was at the flood. The period of the Encroaching of the Desert was at hand, and the deeps were all astir with movement. But in the windless air was a great peace. A calm of infinite stillness breathed everywhere. The flow of Time, before it rushed away backwards, stopped somewhere between the dust of stars and Desert. The mystery of sand touched every street with its unutterable softness.

And Vance began without the smallest circumlocution. His voice was low, in keeping with the scene, but the words dropped with a sharp distinctness into the other's heart like grains of sand that pricked the skin before they smothered him. Caution they smothered instantly; resistance too.

"I have a message for you from my aunt," he said, as though he brought an invitation to a picnic. Henriot sat in shadow, but his companion's face was in a patch of light that followed them from the windows of the central hall. There was a shining in the light blue eyes that betrayed the excitement his quiet manner concealed. "We are going – the day after tomorrow – to spend the night in the Desert; she wondered if, perhaps, you would care to join us?"

"For your experiment?" asked Henriot bluntly.

Vance smiled with his lips, holding his eyes steady, though unable to suppress the gleam that flashed in them and was gone so swiftly. There was a hint of shrugging his shoulders.

"It is the Night of Power – in the old Egyptian Calendar, you know," he answered with assumed lightness almost, "the final moment of Leyel-el-Sud, the period of Black Nights when the Desert was held to encroach with – with various possibilities of a supernatural order. She wishes to revive a certain practice of the old Egyptians. There *may* be curious results. At any rate, the occasion is a picturesque one – better than this cheap imitation of London life." And he indicated the lights, the signs of people in the hall dressed for gaieties and dances, the hotel orchestra that played after dinner.

Henriot at the moment answered nothing, so great was the rush of conflicting emotions that came he knew not whence. Vance went calmly on. He spoke with a simple frankness that was meant to be disarming. Henriot never took his eyes off him. The two men stared steadily at one another.

"She wants to know if you will come and help too – in a certain way only: not in the experiment itself precisely, but by watching merely and—" He hesitated an instant, half lowering his eyes.

"Drawing the picture," Henriot helped him deliberately.

"Drawing what you see, yes," Vance replied, the voice turned graver in spite of himself. "She wants – she hopes to catch the outlines of anything that happens—"

"Comes."

"Exactly. Determine the shape of anything that comes. You may remember your conversation of the other night with her. She is very certain of success."

This was direct enough at any rate. It was as formal as an invitation to a dinner, and as guileless. The thing he thought he wanted lay within his reach. He had merely to say yes. He did say yes; but first he looked about him instinctively, as for guidance. He looked at the stars twinkling high above the distant Libyan Plateau; at the long arms of the Desert, gleaming weirdly white in the moonlight, and reaching towards him down every opening between the houses; at the heavy mass of the Mokattam Hills, guarding the Arabian Wilderness with strange, peaked barriers, their sand-carved ridges dark and still above the Wadi Hof.

These questionings attracted no response. The Desert watched him, but it did not answer. There was only the shrill whistling cry of the lizards, and the sing-song of a white-robed Arab gliding down the sandy street. And through these sounds he heard his own voice answer: "I will come – yes. But how can I help? Tell me what you propose – your plan?"

And the face of Vance, seen plainly in the electric glare, betrayed his satisfaction. The opposing things in the fellow's mind of darkness fought visibly in his eyes and skin. The sordid motive, planning a dreadful act, leaped to his face, and with it a flash of this other yearning that sought unearthly knowledge, perhaps believed it too. No wonder there was conflict written on his features.

Then all expression vanished again; he leaned forward, lowering his voice.

"You remember our conversation about there being types of life too vast to manifest in a single body, and my aunt's belief that these were known to certain of the older religious systems of the world?"

"Perfectly."

"Her experiment, then, is to bring one of these great Powers back – we possess the sympathetic ritual that can rouse some among them to activity – and win it down into the sphere of our minds, our minds heightened, you see, by ceremonial to that stage of clairvoyant vision which can perceive them."

"And then?" They might have been discussing the building of a house, so naturally followed answer upon question. But the whole body of meaning in the old Egyptian symbolism rushed over him with a force that shook his heart. Memory came so marvellously with it.

"If the Power floods down into our minds with sufficient strength for actual form, to note the outline of such form, and from your drawing model it later in permanent substance. Then we should have means of evoking it at will, for we should have its natural Body – the form it built itself, its signature, image, pattern. A starting-point, you see, for more – leading, she hopes, to a complete reconstruction."

"It might take actual shape – assume a bodily form visible to the eye?" repeated Henriot, amazed as before that doubt and laughter did not break through his mind.

"We are on the earth," was the reply, spoken unnecessarily low since no living thing was within earshot, "we are in physical conditions, are we not? Even a human soul we do not recognise unless we see it in a body – parents provide the outline, the signature, the sigil of the returning soul. This," and he tapped himself upon the breast, "is the physical signature of that type of life we call a soul. Unless there is life of a certain strength behind it, no body forms. And, without a body, we are helpless to control or manage it – deal with it in any way. We could not know it, though being possibly *aware* of it."

"To be aware, you mean, is not sufficient?" For he noticed the italics Vance made use of.

"Too vague, of no value for future use," was the reply. "But once obtain the form, and we have the natural symbol of that particular Power. And a symbol is more than image, it is a direct and concentrated expression of the life it typifies – possibly terrific."

"It may be a body, then, this symbol you speak of."

"Accurate vehicle of manifestation; but 'body' seems the simplest word."

Vance answered very slowly and deliberately, as though weighing how much he would tell. His language was admirably evasive. Few perhaps would have detected the profound significance the curious words he next used unquestionably concealed. Henriot's mind rejected them, but his heart accepted. For the ancient soul in him was listening and aware.

"Life, using matter to express itself in bodily shape, first traces a geometrical pattern. From the lowest form in crystals, upwards to more complicated patterns in the higher organisations – there is always first this geometrical pattern as skeleton. For geometry lies at the root of all possible phenomena; and is the mind's interpretation of a living movement towards shape that shall express it." He brought his eyes closer to the other, lowering his voice again. "Hence," he said softly, "the signs in all the old magical systems – skeleton forms into which the Powers evoked descended; outlines those Powers automatically built up when using matter to express themselves. Such signs are material symbols of their bodiless existence. They attract the life they represent and interpret. Obtain the correct, true symbol, and the Power corresponding to it can approach – once roused and made aware. It has, you see, a ready-made mould into which it can come down."

"Once roused and made aware?" repeated Henriot questioningly, while this man went stammering the letters of a language that he himself had used too long ago to recapture fully.

"Because they have left the world. They sleep, unmanifested. Their forms are no longer known to men. No forms exist on earth today that could contain them. But they may be awakened," he added darkly. "They are bound to answer to the summons, if such summons be accurately made."

"Evocation?" whispered Henriot, more distressed than he cared to admit.

Vance nodded. Leaning still closer, to his companion's face, he thrust his lips forward, speaking eagerly, earnestly, yet somehow at the same time, horribly: "And we want – my aunt would ask – your draughtsman's skill, or at any rate your memory afterwards, to establish the outline of anything that comes."

He waited for the answer, still keeping his face uncomfortably close.

Henriot drew back a little. But his mind was fully made up now. He had known from the beginning that he would consent, for the desire in him was stronger than all the caution in the world. The Past inexorably drew him into the circle of these other lives, and the little human dread Vance woke in him seemed just then insignificant by comparison. It was merely of Today.

"You two," he said, trying to bring judgment into it, "engaged in evocation, will be in a state of clairvoyant vision. Granted. But shall I, as an outsider, observing with unexcited mind, see anything, know anything, be aware of anything at all, let alone the drawing of it?"

"Unless," the reply came instantly with decision, "the descent of Power is strong enough to take actual material shape, the experiment is a failure. Anybody can induce subjective vision. Such fantasies have no value though. They are born of an overwrought imagination." And then he added quickly, as though to clinch the matter before caution and hesitation could take effect: "You must watch from the heights above. We shall be in the valley – the Wadi Hof is the place. You must not be too close—"

"Why not too close?" asked Henriot, springing forward like a flash before he could prevent the sudden impulse.

With a quickness equal to his own, Vance answered. There was no faintest sign that he was surprised. His self-control was perfect. Only the glare passed darkly through his eyes and went back again into the sombre soul that bore it.

"For your own safety," he answered low. "The Power, the type of life, she would waken is stupendous. And if roused enough to be attracted by the patterned symbol into which she would decoy it down, it will take actual, physical expression. But how? Where is the Body of Worshippers through whom it can manifest? There is none. It will, therefore, press inanimate matter into the service. The terrific impulse to form itself a means of expression will force all loose matter at hand towards it – sand, stones, all it can compel to yield – everything must rush into the sphere of action in which it operates. Alone, we at the centre, and you, upon the outer fringe, will be safe. Only – you must not come too close."

But Henriot was no longer listening. His soul had turned to ice. For here, in this unguarded moment, the cloven hoof had plainly shown itself. In that suggestion of a particular kind of danger Vance had lifted a corner of the curtain behind which crouched his horrible intention. Vance desired a witness of the extraordinary experiment, but he desired this witness, not merely for the purpose of sketching possible shapes that might present themselves to excited vision. He desired a witness for another reason too. Why had Vance put that idea into his mind, this idea of so peculiar danger? It might well have lost him the very assistance he seemed so anxious to obtain.

Henriot could not fathom it quite. Only one thing was clear to him. He, Henriot, was not the only one in danger.

They talked for long after that – far into the night. The lights went out, and the armed patrol, pacing to and fro outside the iron railings that kept the desert back, eyed them curiously. But the only other thing he gathered of importance was the ledge upon the cliff-top where he was to stand and watch; that he was expected to reach there before sunset and wait till the moon concealed all glimmer in the western sky, and – that the woman, who had been engaged for days in secret preparation of soul and body for the awful rite, would not be visible again until he saw her in the depths of the black valley far below, busy with this man upon audacious, ancient purposes.

Chapter IX

AN HOUR before sunset Henriot put his rugs and food upon a donkey, and gave the boy directions where to meet him – a considerable distance from the appointed spot. He went himself on foot. He slipped in the heat along the sandy street, where strings of camels still go slouching, shuffling with their loads from the quarries that built the pyramids, and he felt that little friendly Helouan tried to keep him back. But desire now was far too strong for caution. The desert tide was rising. It easily swept him down the long white street towards the enormous deeps beyond. He felt the pull of a thousand miles before him; and twice a thousand years drove at his back.

Everything still basked in the sunshine. He passed Al Hayat, the stately hotel that dominates the village like a palace built against the sky; and in its pillared colonnades and terraces he saw the throngs of people having late afternoon tea and listening to the music of a regimental band. Men in flannels were playing tennis, parties were climbing off donkeys after long excursions; there was laughter, talking, a babel of many voices. The gaiety called to him; the everyday spirit whispered to stay and join the crowd of lively human beings. Soon there would be merry dinner-parties, dancing, voices of pretty women, sweet white dresses, singing, and the rest. Soft eyes would question and turn dark. He picked out several girls he knew among the palms. But it was all many, oh so many leagues away; centuries lay between him and this modern world. An indescribable loneliness was in his heart. He went searching through the sands of forgotten ages, and wandering among the ruins of a vanished time. He hurried. Already the deeper water caught his breath.

He climbed the steep rise towards the plateau where the Observatory stands, and saw two of the officials whom he knew taking a siesta after their long day's work. He felt that his mind, too, had dived and searched among the heavenly bodies that live in silent, changeless peace remote from the world of men. They recognised him, these two whose eyes also knew tremendous distance close. They beckoned, waving the straws through which they sipped their drinks from tall glasses. Their voices floated down to him as from the star-fields. He saw the sun gleam upon the glasses, and heard the clink of the ice against the sides. The stillness was amazing. He waved an answer, and passed quickly on. He could not stop this sliding current of the years.

The tide moved faster, the draw of piled-up cycles urging it. He emerged upon the plateau, and met the cooler Desert air. His feet went crunching on the 'desert-film' that spread its curious dark shiny carpet as far as the eye could reach; it lay everywhere, unswept and smooth as when the feet of vanished civilisations trod its burning surface, then dipped behind the curtains Time pins against the stars. And here the body of the tide set all one way. There was a greater strength of current, draught and suction. He felt the powerful undertow. Deeper masses drew his feet sideways, and he felt the rushing of the central body of the sand. The sands were moving, from their foundation upwards. He went unresistingly with them.

Turning a moment, he looked back at shining little Helouan in the blaze of evening light. The voices reached him very faintly, merged now in a general murmur. Beyond lay the strip of Delta vivid green, the palms, the roofs of Bedrashein, the blue laughter of the Nile with its flocks of curved felucca sails. Further still, rising above the yellow Libyan horizon, gloomed the vast triangles of a dozen Pyramids, cutting their wedge-shaped clefts out of a sky fast crimsoning through a sea of gold. Seen thus, their dignity imposed upon the entire landscape. They towered darkly, symbolic signatures of the ancient Powers that now watched him taking these little steps across their damaged territory.

He gazed a minute, then went on. He saw the big pale face of the moon in the east. Above the ever-silent Thing these giant symbols once interpreted, she rose, grand, effortless, half-terrible as themselves. And, with her, she lifted up this tide of the Desert that drew his feet across the sand to Wadi Hof. A moment later he dipped below the ridge that buried Helouan and Nile and Pyramids from sight. He entered the ancient waters. Time then, in an instant, flowed back behind his footsteps, obliterating every trace. And with it his mind went too. He stepped across the gulf of centuries, moving into the Past. The Desert lay before him – an open tomb wherein his soul should read presently of things long vanished.

The strange half-lights of sunset began to play their witchery then upon the landscape. A purple glow came down upon the Mokattam Hills. Perspective danced its tricks of false, incredible deception. The soaring kites that were a mile away seemed suddenly close, passing in a moment from the size of gnats to birds with a fabulous stretch of wing. Ridges and cliffs rushed close without a hint of warning, and level places sank into declivities and basins that made him trip and stumble. That indescribable quality of the Desert, which makes timid souls avoid the hour of dusk, emerged; it spread everywhere, undisguised. And the bewilderment it brings is no vain, imagined thing, for it distorts vision utterly, and the effect upon the mind when familiar sight goes floundering is the simplest way in the world of dragging the anchor that grips reality. At the hour of sunset this bewilderment comes upon a man with a disconcerting swiftness. It rose now with all this weird rapidity. Henriot found himself enveloped at a moment's notice.

But, knowing well its effect, he tried to judge it and pass on. The other matters, the object of his journey chief of all, he refused to dwell upon with any imagination. Wisely, his mind, while never losing sight of it, declined to admit the exaggeration that over-elaborate thinking brings. "I'm going to witness an incredible experiment in which two enthusiastic religious dreamers believe firmly," he repeated to himself. "I have agreed to draw – anything I see. There may be truth in it, or they may be merely self-suggested vision due to an artificial exaltation of their minds. I'm interested – perhaps against my better judgment. Yet I'll see the adventure out – because I *must*."

This was the attitude he told himself to take. Whether it was the real one, or merely adopted to warm a cooling courage, he could not tell. The emotions were so complex and warring. His mind, automatically, kept repeating this comforting formula. Deeper than that he could not see to judge. For a man who knew the full content of his thought at such a time would solve some of the oldest psychological problems in the world. Sand had already buried judgment, and with it all attempt to explain the adventure by the standards acceptable to his brain of today. He steered subconsciously through a world of dim, huge, half-remembered wonders.

The sun, with that abrupt Egyptian suddenness, was below the horizon now. The pyramid field had swallowed it. Ra, in his golden boat, sailed distant seas beyond the Libyan wilderness. Henriot walked on and on, aware of utter loneliness. He was walking fields of dream, too remote from modern life to recall companionship he once had surely known. How dim it was, how deep and distant, how lost in this sea of an incalculable Past! He walked into the places that are soundless. The soundlessness of ocean, miles below the surface, was about him. He was with One only – this unfathomable, silent thing where nothing breathes or stirs – nothing but sunshine, shadow and the wind-borne sand. Slowly, in front, the moon climbed up the eastern sky, hanging above the silence – silence that ran unbroken across the horizons to where Suez gleamed upon the waters of a sister sea in motion. That moon was glinting now upon the Arabian Mountains by its desolate shores. Southwards stretched the wastes of Upper Egypt a thousand miles to meet the Nubian wilderness. But over all these separate Deserts stirred the soft whisper of the moving sand – deep murmuring message that Life was on the way to unwind Death. The Ka of Egypt, swathed in centuries of sand, hovered beneath the moon towards her ancient tenement.

For the transformation of the Desert now began in earnest. It grew apace. Before he had gone the first two miles of his hour's journey, the twilight caught the rocky hills and twisted them into those monstrous revelations of physiognomies they barely take the trouble to conceal even in the daytime. And, while he well understood the eroding agencies that have produced them, there yet rose in his mind a deeper interpretation lurking just behind their literal meanings. Here, through the motionless surfaces, that nameless thing the Desert ill conceals urged outwards into embryonic form and shape, akin, he almost felt, to those immense deific symbols of Other Life the Egyptians knew and worshipped. Hence, from the Desert, had first come, he felt, the unearthly life they typified in their monstrous figures of granite, evoked in their stately temples, and communed with in the ritual of their Mystery ceremonials.

This 'watching' aspect of the Libyan Desert is really natural enough; but it is just the natural, Henriot knew, that brings the deepest revelations. The surface limestones, resisting the erosion, block themselves ominously against the sky, while the softer sand beneath sets them on altared pedestals that define their isolation splendidly. Blunt and unconquerable, these masses now watched him pass between them. The Desert surface formed them, gave them birth. They rose, they saw, they sank down again – waves upon a sea that carried forgotten life up from the depths below. Of forbidding, even menacing type, they somewhere mated with genuine grandeur. Unformed, according to any standard of human or of animal faces, they achieved an air of giant physiognomy which made them terrible. The unwinking stare of eyes – lidless eyes that yet ever succeed in hiding – looked out under well-marked, level eyebrows, suggesting a vision that included the motives and purposes of his very heart. They looked up grandly, understood why he was there, and then – slowly withdrew their mysterious, penetrating gaze.

The strata built them so marvellously up; the heavy, threatening brows; thick lips, curved by the ages into a semblance of cold smiles; jowls drooping into sandy heaps that climbed against the cheeks; protruding jaws, and the suggestion of shoulders just about to lift the entire bodies out of the sandy beds – this host of countenances conveyed a solemnity of expression that seemed everlasting, implacable as Death. Of human signature they bore no trace, nor was comparison possible between their kind and any animal life. They peopled the Desert here. And their smiles, concealed yet just discernible, went broadening with the darkness into a Desert laughter. The silence bore it underground. But Henriot was aware of it. The troop of faces slipped into that single, enormous countenance which is the visage of the Sand. And he saw it everywhere, yet nowhere.

Thus with the darkness grew his imaginative interpretation of the Desert. Yet there was construction in it, a construction, moreover, that was *not* entirely his own. Powers, he felt, were rising, stirring, wakening from sleep. Behind the natural faces that he saw, these other things peered gravely at him as he passed. They used, as it were, materials that lay ready to their hand. Imagination furnished these hints of outline, yet the Powers themselves were real. There *was* this amazing movement of the sand. By no other manner could his mind have conceived of such a thing, nor dreamed of this simple, yet dreadful method of approach.

Approach! that was the word that first stood out and startled him. There was approach; something was drawing nearer. The Desert rose and walked beside him. For not alone these ribs of gleaming limestone contributed towards the elemental visages, but the entire hills, of which they were an outcrop, ran to assist in the formation, and were a necessary part of them. He was watched and stared at from behind, in front, on either side, and even from below. The sand that swept him on, kept even pace with him. It turned luminous too, with a patchwork of glimmering effect that was indescribably weird; lanterns glowed within its substance, and by their light he stumbled on, glad of the Arab boy he would presently meet at the appointed place.

The last torch of the sunset had flickered out, melting into the wilderness, when, suddenly opening at his feet, gaped the deep, wide gully known as Wadi Hof. Its curve swept past him.

This first impression came upon him with a certain violence: that the desolate valley rushed. He saw but a section of its curve and sweep, but through its entire length of several miles the Wadi fled away. The moon whitened it like snow, piling black shadows very close against the cliffs. In the flood of moonlight it went rushing past. It was emptying itself.

For a moment the stream of movement seemed to pause and look up into his face, then instantly went on again upon its swift career. It was like the procession of a river to the sea. The valley emptied itself to make way for what was coming. The approach, moreover, had already begun.

Conscious that he was trembling, he stood and gazed into the depths, seeking to steady his mind by the repetition of the little formula he had used before. He said it half aloud. But, while he did so, his heart whispered quite other things. Thoughts the woman and the man had sown rose up in a flock and fell upon him like a storm of sand. Their impetus drove off all support of ordinary ideas. They shook him where he stood, staring down into this river of strange invisible movement that was hundreds of feet in depth and a quarter of a mile across.

He sought to realise himself as he actually was today – mere visitor to Helouan, tempted into this wild adventure with two strangers. But in vain. That seemed a dream, unreal, a transient detail picked out from the enormous Past that now engulfed him, heart and mind and soul. *This* was the reality.

The shapes and faces that the hills of sand built round him were the play of excited fancy only. By sheer force he pinned his thought against this fact: but further he could not get. There *were* Powers at work; they were being stirred, wakened somewhere into activity. Evocation had already begun. That sense of their approach as he had walked along from Helouan was not imaginary. A descent of some type of life, vanished from the world too long for recollection, was on the way – so vast that it would manifest itself in a group of forms, a troop, a host, an army. These two were near him somewhere at this very moment, already long at work, their minds driving beyond this little world. The valley was emptying itself – for the descent of life their ritual invited.

And the movement in the sand was likewise true. He recalled the sentences the woman had used. "My body," he reflected, "like the bodies life makes use of everywhere, is mere upright heap of earth and dust and – sand. Here in the Desert is the raw material, the greatest store of it in the world."

And on the heels of it came sharply that other thing: that this descending Life would press into its service all loose matter within its reach – to form that sphere of action which would be in a literal sense its Body.

In the first few seconds, as he stood there, he realised all this, and realised it with an overwhelming conviction it was futile to deny. The fast-emptying valley would later brim with an unaccustomed and terrific life. Yet Death hid there too – a little, ugly, insignificant death. With the name of Vance it flashed upon his mind and vanished, too tiny to be thought about in this torrent of grander messages that shook the depths within his soul. He bowed his head a moment, hardly knowing what he did. He could have waited thus a thousand years it seemed. He was conscious of a wild desire to run away, to hide, to efface himself utterly, his terror, his curiosity, his little wonder, and not be seen of anything. But it was all vain and foolish. The Desert saw him. The Gigantic knew that he was there. No escape was possible any longer. Caught by the sand, he stood amid eternal things. The river of movement swept him too.

These hills, now motionless as statues, would presently glide forward into the cavalcade, sway like vessels, and go past with the procession. At present only the contents, not the frame, of the Wadi moved. An immense soft brush of moonlight swept it empty for what was on the way.... But presently the entire Desert would stand up and also go.

Then, making a sideways movement, his feet kicked against something soft and yielding that lay heaped upon the Desert floor, and Henriot discovered the rugs the Arab boy had carefully set down before he made full speed for the friendly lights of Helouan. The sound of his departing footsteps had long since died away. He was alone.

The detail restored to him his consciousness of the immediate present, and, stooping, he gathered up the rugs and overcoat and began to make preparations for the night. But the appointed spot, whence he was to watch, lay upon the summit of the opposite cliffs. He must cross the Wadi bed and climb. Slowly and with labour he made his way down a steep cleft into the depth of the Wadi Hof, sliding and stumbling often, till at length he stood upon the floor of shining moonlight. It was very smooth; windless utterly; still as space; each particle of sand lay in its ancient place asleep. The movement, it seemed, had ceased.

He clambered next up the eastern side, through pitch-black shadows, and within the hour reached the ledge upon the top whence he could see below him, like a silvered map, the sweep of the valley bed. The wind nipped keenly here again, coming over the leagues of cooling sand. Loose boulders of splintered rock, started by his climbing, crashed and boomed into the depths. He banked the rugs behind him, wrapped himself in his overcoat, and lay down to wait. Behind him was a two-foot crumbling wall against which he leaned; in front a drop of several hundred feet through space. He lay upon a platform, therefore, invisible from the Desert at his back. Below, the curving Wadi formed a natural amphitheatre in which each separate boulder fallen from the cliffs, and even the little *silla* shrubs the camels eat, were plainly visible. He noted all the bigger ones among them. He counted them over half aloud.

And the moving stream he had been unaware of when crossing the bed itself, now began again. The Wadi went rushing past before the broom of moonlight. Again, the enormous and the tiny combined in one single strange impression. For, through this conception of great movement, stirred also a roving, delicate touch that his imagination felt as bird-like. Behind the solid mass of the Desert's immobility flashed something swift and light and airy. Bizarre pictures interpreted it to him, like rapid snap-shots of a huge flying panorama: he thought of darting dragon-flies seen at Helouan, of children's little dancing feet, of twinkling butterflies – of birds. Chiefly, yes, of a flock of birds in flight, whose separate units formed a single entity. The idea of the Group-Soul possessed his mind once more. But it came with a sense of more than curiosity or wonder. Veneration lay behind it, a veneration touched with awe. It rose in his deepest thought that here was the first hint of a symbolical representation. A symbol, sacred and inviolable, belonging to some ancient worship that he half remembered in his soul, stirred towards interpretation through all his being.

He lay there waiting, wondering vaguely where his two companions were, yet fear all vanished because he felt attuned to a scale of things too big to mate with definite dread. There was high anticipation in him, but not anxiety. Of himself, as Felix Henriot, indeed, he hardly seemed aware. He was someone else. Or, rather, he was himself at a stage he had known once far, far away in a remote pre-existence. He watched himself from dim summits of a Past, of which no further details were as yet recoverable.

Pencil and sketching-block lay ready to his hand. The moon rose higher, tucking the shadows ever more closely against the precipices. The silver passed into a sheet of snowy whiteness, that made every boulder clearly visible. Solemnity deepened everywhere into awe. The Wadi fled silently down the stream of hours. It was almost empty now. And then, abruptly, he was aware of change. The motion altered somewhere. It moved more quietly; pace slackened; the end of the procession that evacuated the depth and length of it went trailing past and turned the distant bend.

"It's slowing up," he whispered, as sure of it as though he had watched a regiment of soldiers filing by. The wind took off his voice like a flying feather of sound.

And there *was* a change. It had begun. Night and the moon stood still to watch and listen. The wind dropped utterly away. The sand ceased its shifting movement. The Desert everywhere stopped still, and turned.

Some curtain, then, that for centuries had veiled the world, drew softly up, leaving a shaded vista down which the eyes of his soul peered towards long-forgotten pictures. Still buried by the sands too deep for full recovery, he yet perceived dim portions of them – things once honoured and loved passionately. For once they had surely been to him the whole of life, not merely a fragment for cheap wonder to inspect. And they were curiously familiar, even as the person of this woman who now evoked them was familiar. Henriot made no pretence to more definite remembrance; but the haunting certainty rushed over him, deeper than doubt or denial, and with such force that he felt no effort to destroy it. Some lost sweetness of spiritual ambitions, lived for with this passionate devotion, and passionately worshipped as men today worship fame and money, revived in him with a tempest of high glory. Centres of memory stirred from an age-long sleep, so that he could have wept at their so complete obliteration hitherto. That such majesty had departed from the world as though it never had existed, was a thought for desolation and for tears. And though the little fragment he was about to witness might be crude in itself and incomplete, yet it was part of a vast system that once explored the richest realms of deity. The reverence in him contained a holiness of the night and of the stars; great, gentle awe lay in it too; for he stood, aflame with anticipation and humility, at the gateway of sacred things.

And this was the mood, no thrill of cheap excitement or alarm to weaken in, in which he first became aware that two spots of darkness he had taken all along for boulders on the snowy valley bed, were actually something very different. They were living figures. They moved. It was not the shadows slowly following the moonlight, but the stir of human beings who all these hours had been motionless as stone. He must have passed them unnoticed within a dozen yards when he crossed the Wadi bed, and a hundred times from this very ledge his eyes had surely rested on them without recognition. Their minds, he knew full well, had not been inactive as their bodies. The important part of the ancient ritual lay, he remembered, in the powers of the evoking mind.

Here, indeed, was no effective nor theatrical approach of the principal figures. It had nothing in common with the cheap external ceremonial of modern days. In forgotten powers of the soul its grandeur lay, potent, splendid, true. Long before he came, perhaps all through the day, these two had laboured with their arduous preparations. They were there, part of the Desert, when hours ago he had crossed the plateau in the twilight. To them – to this woman's potent working of old ceremonial – had been due that singular rush of imagination he had felt. He had interpreted the Desert as alive. Here was the explanation. It *was* alive. Life was on the way. Long latent, her intense desire summoned it back to physical expression; and the effect upon him had steadily increased as he drew nearer to the centre where she would focus its revival and return. Those singular impressions of being watched and accompanied were explained. A priest of this old-world worship performed a genuine evocation; a Great One of Vision revived the cosmic Powers.

Henriot watched the small figures far below him with a sense of dramatic splendour that only this association of far-off Memory could account for. It was their rising now, and the lifting of their arms to form a slow revolving outline, that marked the abrupt cessation of the larger river of movement; for the sweeping of the Wadi sank into sudden stillness, and these two, with motions not unlike some dance of deliberate solemnity, passed slowly through the moonlight to and fro. His attention fixed upon them both. All other movement ceased. They fastened the flow of Time against the Desert's body.

What happened then? How could his mind interpret an experience so long denied that the power of expression, as of comprehension, has ceased to exist? How translate this symbolical representation, small detail though it was, of a transcendent worship entombed for most so utterly beyond recovery? Its splendour could never lodge in minds that conceive Deity perched upon a cloud within telephoning distance of fashionable churches. How should he phrase it even to himself, whose memory drew up pictures from so dim a past that the language fit to frame them lay unreachable and lost?

Henriot did not know. Perhaps he never yet has known. Certainly, at the time, he did not even try to think. His sensations remain his own – untranslatable; and even that instinctive description the mind gropes for automatically, floundered, halted, and stopped dead. Yet there rose within him somewhere, from depths long drowned in slumber, a reviving power by which he saw, divined and recollected – remembered seemed too literal a word – these elements of a worship he once had personally known. He, too, had worshipped thus. His soul had moved amid similar evocations in some aeonian past, whence now the sand was being cleared away. Symbols of stupendous meaning flashed and went their way across the lifting mists. He hardly caught their meaning, so long it was since, he had known them; yet they were familiar as the faces seen in dreams, and some hint of their spiritual significance left faint traces in his heart by means of which their grandeur reached towards interpretation. And all were symbols of a cosmic, deific nature; of Powers that only symbols can express – prayer-books and sacraments used in the Wisdom Religion of an older time, but today known only in the decrepit, literal shell which is their degradation.

Grandly the figures moved across the valley bed. The powers of the heavenly bodies once more joined them. They moved to the measure of a cosmic dance, whose rhythm was creative. The Universe partnered them.

There was this transfiguration of all common, external things. He realised that appearances were visible letters of a soundless language, a language he once had known. The powers of night and moon and desert sand married with points in the fluid stream of his inmost spiritual being that knew and welcomed them. He understood.

Old Egypt herself stooped down from her uncovered throne. The stars sent messengers. There was commotion in the secret, sandy places of the desert. For the Desert had grown Temple. Columns reared against the sky. There rose, from leagues away, the chanting of the sand.

The temples, where once this came to pass, were gone, their ruin questioned by alien hearts that knew not their spiritual meaning. But here the entire Desert swept in to form a shrine, and the Majesty that once was Egypt stepped grandly back across ages of denial and neglect. The sand was altar, and the stars were altar lights. The moon lit up the vast recesses of the ceiling, and the wind from a thousand miles brought in the perfume of her incense. For with that faith which shifts mountains from their sandy bed, two passionate, believing souls invoked the Ka of Egypt.

And the motions that they made, he saw, were definite harmonious patterns their dark figures traced upon the shining valley floor. Like the points of compasses, with stems invisible, and directed from the sky, their movements marked the outlines of great signatures of power – the sigils of the type of life they would evoke. It would come as a Procession. No individual outline could contain it. It needed for its visible expression – many. The descent of a Group-Soul, known to the worship of this mighty system, rose from its lair of centuries and moved hugely down upon them. The Ka, answering to the summons, would mate with sand. The Desert was its Body.

Yet it was not this that he had come to fix with block and pencil. Not yet was the moment when his skill might be of use. He waited, watched, and listened, while this river of half-remembered things went past him. The patterns grew beneath his eyes like music. Too intricate and prolonged to remember with accuracy later, he understood that they were forms of that root-geometry which lies behind all manifested life. The mould was being traced in outline. Life would presently inform it. And a singing rose from the maze of lines whose beauty was like the beauty of the constellations.

This sound was very faint at first, but grew steadily in volume. Although no echoes, properly speaking, were possible, these precipices caught stray notes that trooped in from the further sandy reaches. The figures certainly were chanting, but their chanting was not all he heard. Other sounds came to his ears from far away, running past him through the air from every side, and from incredible distances, all flocking down into the Wadi bed to join the parent note that summoned them. The Desert was giving voice. And memory, lifting her hood yet higher, showed more of her grey, mysterious face that searched his soul with questions. Had he so soon forgotten that strange union of form and sound which once was known to the evocative rituals of olden days?

Henriot tried patiently to disentangle this desert-music that their intoning voices woke, from the humming of the blood in his own veins. But he succeeded only in part. Sand was already in the air. There was reverberation, rhythm, measure; there was almost the breaking of the stream into great syllables. But was it due, this strange reverberation, to the countless particles of sand meeting in mid-air about him, or – to larger bodies, whose surfaces caught this friction of the sand and threw it back against his ears? The wind, now rising, brought particles that stung his face and hands, and filled his eyes with a minute fine dust that partially veiled the moonlight. But was not something larger, vaster these particles composed now also on the way?

Movement and sound and flying sand thus merged themselves more and more in a single, whirling torrent. But Henriot sought no commonplace explanation of what he witnessed; and here was the proof that all happened in some vestibule of inner experience where the strain of question and answer had no business. One sitting beside him need not have seen anything at all. His host, for instance, from Helouan, need not have been aware. Night screened it; Helouan, as the whole of modern experience, stood in front of the screen. This thing took place behind it. He crouched motionless, watching in some reconstructed ante-chamber of the soul's pre-existence, while the torrent grew into a veritable tempest.

Yet Night remained unshaken; the veil of moonlight did not quiver; the stars dropped their slender golden pillars unobstructed. Calmness reigned everywhere as before. The stupendous representation passed on behind it all.

But the dignity of the little human movements that he watched had become now indescribable. The gestures of the arms and bodies invested themselves with consummate grandeur, as these two strode into the caverns behind manifested life and drew forth symbols that represented vanished Powers. The sound of their chanting voices broke in cadenced fragments against the shores of language. The words Henriot never actually caught, if words they were; yet he understood their purport – these Names of Power to which the type of returning life gave answer as they approached. He remembered fumbling for his drawing materials, with such violence, however, that the pencil snapped in two between his fingers as he touched it. For now, even here, upon the outer fringe of the ceremonial ground, there was a stir of forces that set the very muscles working in him before he had become aware of it....

Then came the moment when his heart leaped against his ribs with a sudden violence that was almost pain, standing a second later still as death. The lines upon the valley floor ceased their maze-like dance. All movement stopped. Sound died away. In the midst of this profound and dreadful silence the sigils lay empty there below him. They waited to be in-formed. For the moment of entrance had come at last. Life was close.

And he understood why this return of life had all along suggested a Procession and could be no mere momentary flash of vision. From such appalling distance did it sweep down towards the present.

Upon this network, then, of splendid lines, at length held rigid, the entire Desert reared itself with walls of curtained sand, that dwarfed the cliffs, the shouldering hills, the very sky. The Desert stood on end. As once before he had dreamed it from his balcony windows, it rose upright, towering, and close against his face. It built sudden ramparts to the stars that chambered the thing he witnessed behind walls no centuries could ever bring down crumbling into dust.

He himself, in some curious fashion, lay just outside, viewing it apart. As from a pinnacle, he peered within – peered down with straining eyes into the vast picture-gallery Memory threw abruptly open. And the picture spaced its noble outline thus against the very stars. He gazed between columns, that supported the sky itself, like pillars of sand that swept across the field of vanished years. Sand poured and streamed aside, laying bare the Past.

For down the enormous vista into which he gazed, as into an avenue running a million miles towards a tiny point, he saw this moving Thing that came towards him, shaking loose the countless veils of sand the ages had swathed about it. The Ka of buried Egypt wakened out of sleep. She had heard the potent summons of her old, time-honoured ritual. She came. She stretched forth an arm towards the worshippers who evoked her. Out of the Desert, out of the leagues of sand, out of the immeasurable wilderness which was her mummied Form and Body, she rose and came. And this fragment of her he would actually see – this little portion that was obedient to the stammered and broken ceremonial. The partial revelation he would witness – yet so vast, even this little bit of it, that it came as a Procession and a host.

For a moment there was nothing. And then the voice of the woman rose in a resounding cry that filled the Wadi to its furthest precipices, before it died away again to silence. That a human voice could produce such volume, accent, depth, seemed half incredible. The walls of towering sand swallowed it instantly. But the Procession of life, needing a group, a host, an army for its physical expression, reached at that moment the nearer end of the huge avenue. It touched the Present; it entered the world of men.

Chapter X

THE ENTIRE RANGE of Henriot's experience, read, imagined, dreamed, then fainted into unreality before the sheer wonder of what he saw. In the brief interval it takes to snap the fingers the climax was thus so hurriedly upon him. And, through it all, he was clearly aware of the pair of little human figures, man and woman, standing erect and commanding at the centre – knew, too, that she directed and controlled, while he in some secondary fashion supported her – and ever watched. But both were dim, dropped somewhere into a lesser scale. It was the knowledge of their presence, however, that alone enabled him to keep his powers in hand at all. But for these two *human* beings there within possible reach, he must have closed his eyes and swooned.

For a tempest that seemed to toss loose stars about the sky swept round about him, pouring up the pillared avenue in front of the procession. A blast of giant energy, of liberty, came through.

Forwards and backwards, circling spirally about him like a whirlwind, came this revival of Life that sought to dip itself once more in matter and in form. It came to the accurate outline of its form they had traced for it. He held his mind steady enough to realise that it was akin to what men call a 'descent' of some 'spiritual movement' that wakens a body of believers into faith – a race, an entire nation; only that he experienced it in this brief, concentrated form before it has scattered down into ten thousand hearts. Here he knew its source and essence, behind the veil. Crudely, unmanageable as yet, he felt it, rushing loose behind appearances. There was this amazing impact of a twisting, swinging force that stormed down as though it would bend and coil the very ribs of the old stubborn hills. It sought to warm them with the stress of its own irresistible life-stream, to beat them into shape, and make pliable their obstinate resistance. Through all things the impulse poured and spread, like fire at white heat.

Yet nothing visible came as yet, no alteration in the actual landscape, no sign of change in things familiar to his eyes, while impetus thus fought against inertia. He perceived nothing formal. Calm and untouched himself, he lay outside the circle of evocation, watching, waiting, scarcely daring to breathe, yet well aware that any minute the scene would transfer itself from memory that was subjective to matter that was objective.

And then, in a flash, the bridge was built, and the transfer was accomplished. How or where he did not see, he could not tell. It was there before he knew it – there before his normal, earthly sight. He saw it, as he saw the hands he was holding stupidly up to shield his face. For this terrific release of force long held back, long stored up, latent for centuries, came pouring down the empty Wadi bed prepared for its reception. Through stones and sand and boulders it came in an impetuous hurricane of power. The liberation of its life appalled him. All that was free, untied, responded instantly like chaff; loose objects fled towards it; there was a yielding in the hills and precipices; and even in the mass of Desert which provided their foundation. The hinges of the Sand went creaking in the night. It shaped for itself a bodily outline.

Yet, most strangely, nothing definitely moved. How could he express the violent contradiction? For the immobility was apparent only – a sham, a counterfeit; while behind it the essential *being* of these things did rush and shift and alter. He saw the two things side by side: the outer immobility the senses commonly agree upon, *and* this amazing flying-out of their inner, invisible substance towards the vortex of attracting life that sucked them in. For stubborn matter turned docile before the stress of this returning life, taught somewhere to be plastic. It was being moulded into an approach to bodily outline. A mobile elasticity invaded rigid substance. The two officiating human beings, safe at the stationary centre, and himself, just outside the circle of operation, alone remained untouched and unaffected. But a few feet in any direction, for any one of them, meant – instantaneous death. They would be absorbed into the vortex, mere corpuscles pressed into the service of this sphere of action of a mighty Body....

How these perceptions reached him with such conviction, Henriot could never say. He knew it, because he *felt* it. Something fell about him from the sky that already paled towards the dawn. The stars themselves, it seemed, contributed some part of the terrific, flowing impulse that conquered matter and shaped itself this physical expression.

Then, before he was able to fashion any preconceived idea of what visible form this potent life might assume, he was aware of further change. It came at the briefest possible interval after the beginning – this certainty that, to and fro about him, as yet however indeterminate, passed Magnitudes that were stupendous as the desert. There was beauty in them too, though a terrible beauty hardly of this earth at all. A fragment of old Egypt had returned – a little portion of that vast Body of Belief that once was Egypt. Evoked by the worship of one human heart, passionately sincere, the Ka of Egypt stepped back to visit the material it once informed – the Sand.

Yet only a portion came. Henriot clearly realised that. It stretched forth an arm. Finding no mass of worshippers through whom it might express itself completely, it pressed inanimate matter thus into its service.

Here was the beginning the woman had spoken of – little opening clue. Entire reconstruction lay perhaps beyond.

And Henriot next realised that these Magnitudes in which this group-energy sought to clothe itself as visible form; were curiously familiar. It was not a new thing that he would see. Booming softly as they dropped downwards through the sky, with a motion the size of them rendered delusive, they trooped up the Avenue towards the central point that summoned them. He realised the giant flock of them – descent of fearful beauty – outlining a type of life denied to the world for ages, countless as this sand that blew against his skin. Careering over the waste of Desert moved the army of dark Splendours, that dwarfed any organic structure called a body men have ever known. He recognised them, cold in him of death, though the outlines reared higher than the pyramids, and towered up to hide whole groups of stars. Yes, he recognised them in their partial revelation, though he never saw the monstrous host complete. But, one of them, he realised, posing its eternal riddle to the sands, had of old been glimpsed sufficiently to seize its form in stone – yet poorly seized, as a doll may stand for the dignity of a human being or a child's toy represent an engine that draws trains....

And he knelt there on his narrow ledge, the world of men forgotten. The power that caught him was too great a thing for wonder or for fear; he even felt no awe. Sensation of any kind that can be named or realised left him utterly. He forgot himself. He merely watched. The glory numbed him. Block and pencil, as the reason of his presence there at all, no longer existed....

Yet one small link remained that held him to some kind of consciousness of earthly things: he never lost sight of this – that, being just outside the circle of evocation, he was safe, and that the man and woman, being stationary in its untouched centre, were also safe. But – that a movement of six inches in any direction meant for any one of them instant death.

What was it, then, that suddenly strengthened this solitary link so that the chain tautened and he felt the pull of it? Henriot could not say. He came back with the rush of a descending drop to the realisation – dimly, vaguely, as from great distance – that he was with these two, now at this moment, in the Wadi Hof, and that the cold of dawn was in the air about him. The chill breath of the Desert made him shiver.

But at first, so deeply had his soul been dipped in this fragment of ancient worship, he could remember nothing more. Somewhere lay a little spot of streets and houses; its name escaped him. He had once been there; there were many people, but insignificant people. Who were they? And what had he to do with them? All recent memories had been drowned in the tide that flooded him from an immeasurable Past.

And who were they – these two beings, standing on the white floor of sand below him? For a long time he could not recover their names. Yet he remembered them; and, thus robbed of association that names bring, he saw them for an instant naked, and knew that one of them was evil. One of them was vile. Blackness touched the picture there. The man, his name still out of reach, was sinister, impure and dark at the heart. And for this reason the evocation had been partial only. The admixture of an evil motive was the flaw that marred complete success.

The names then flashed upon him – Lady Statham – Richard Vance.

Vance! With a horrid drop from splendour into something mean and sordid, Henriot felt the pain of it. The motive of the man was so insignificant, his purpose so atrocious. More and more, with the name, came back – his first repugnance, fear, suspicion. And human terror caught him. He shrieked. But, as in nightmare, no sound escaped his lips. He tried to move; a wild desire to interfere, to protect, to prevent, flung him forward – close to the dizzy edge of the gulf below. But his muscles refused obedience to the will. The paralysis of common fear rooted him to the rocks.

But the sudden change of focus instantly destroyed the picture; and so vehement was the fall from glory into meanness, that it dislocated the machinery of clairvoyant vision. The inner perception clouded and grew dark. Outer and inner mingled in violent, inextricable confusion. The wrench seemed almost physical. It happened all at once, retreat and continuation for a moment somehow combined. And, if he did not definitely see the awful thing, at least he was aware that it had come to pass. He knew it as positively as though his eye were glued against a magnifying lens in the stillness of some laboratory. He witnessed it.

The supreme moment of evocation was close. Life, through that awful sandy vortex, whirled and raged. Loose particles showered and pelted, caught by the draught of vehement life that moulded the substance of the Desert into imperial outline – when, suddenly, shot the little evil thing across that marred and blasted it.

Into the whirlpool flew forward a particle of material that was a human being. And the Group-Soul caught and used it.

The actual accomplishment Henriot did not claim to see. He was a witness, but a witness who could give no evidence. Whether the woman was pushed of set intention, or whether some detail of sound and pattern was falsely used to effect the terrible result, he was helpless to determine. He pretends no itemised account. She went. In one second, with appalling swiftness, she disappeared, swallowed out of space and time within that awful maw – one little corpuscle among a million through which the Life, now stalking the Desert wastes, moulded itself a troop-like Body. Sand took her.

There followed emptiness – a hush of unutterable silence, stillness, peace. Movement and sound instantly retired whence they came. The avenues of Memory closed; the Splendours all went down into their sandy tombs....

The moon had sunk into the Libyan wilderness; the eastern sky was red. The dawn drew out that wondrous sweetness of the Desert, which is as sister to the sweetness that the moonlight brings. The Desert settled back to sleep, huge, unfathomable, charged to the brim with life that watches, waits, and yet conceals itself behind the ruins of apparent desolation. And the Wadi, empty at his feet, filled slowly with the gentle little winds that bring the sunrise.

Then, across the pale glimmering of sand, Henriot saw a figure moving. It came quickly towards him, yet unsteadily, and with a hurry that was ugly. Vance was on the way to fetch him. And the horror of the man's approach struck him like a hammer in the face. He closed his eyes, sinking back to hide.

But, before he swooned, there reached him the clatter of the murderer's tread as he began to climb over the splintered rocks, and the faint echo of his voice, calling him by name – falsely and in pretence – for help.

Erewhon

Chapters XIII–XV

Samuel Butler

[Publisher's Note: Erewhon, an anagram of 'nowhere', is discovered by the narrator while exploring an island in the mid-nineteenth century. After being arrested by the Erewhonians, he is sent to live with an Erewhonian family. There, he learns their ways, and realises it isn't quite the Utopia he expected. We join him as he reflects on their customs.]

Chapter XIII
The Views of the Erewhonians Concerning Death

THE EREWHONIANS regard death with less abhorrence than disease. If it is an offence at all, it is one beyond the reach of the law, which is therefore silent on the subject; but they insist that the greater number of those who are commonly said to die, have never yet been born – not, at least, into that unseen world which is alone worthy of consideration. As regards this unseen world I understand them to say that some miscarry in respect to it before they have even reached the seen, and some after, while few are ever truly born into it at all – the greater part of all the men and women over the whole country miscarrying before they reach it. And they say that this does not matter so much as we think it does.

As for what we call death, they argue that too much has been made of it. The mere knowledge that we shall one day die does not make us very unhappy; no one thinks that he or she will escape, so that none are disappointed. We do not care greatly even though we know that we have not long to live; the only thing that would seriously affect us would be the knowing – or rather thinking that we know – the precise moment at which the blow will fall. Happily no one can ever certainly know this, though many try to make themselves miserable by endeavouring to find it out. It seems as though there were some power somewhere which mercifully stays us from putting that sting into the tail of death, which we would put there if we could, and which ensures that though death must always be a bugbear, it shall never under any conceivable circumstances be more than a bugbear.

For even though a man is condemned to die in a week's time and is shut up in a prison from which it is certain that he cannot escape, he will always hope that a reprieve may come before the week is over. Besides, the prison may catch fire, and he may be suffocated not with a rope, but with common ordinary smoke; or he may be struck dead by lightning while exercising in the prison yards. When the morning is come on which the poor wretch is to be hanged, he may choke at his breakfast, or die from failure of the heart's action before the drop has fallen; and even though it has fallen, he cannot be quite certain that he is going to die, for he cannot know this till his death has actually taken place, and it will be too late then for him to discover that he was going to die at the appointed hour after all. The Erewhonians, therefore, hold that death, like life, is an affair of being more frightened than hurt.

They burn their dead, and the ashes are presently scattered over any piece of ground which the deceased may himself have chosen. No one is permitted to refuse this hospitality to the dead: people, therefore, generally choose some garden or orchard which they may have known and been fond of when they were young. The superstitious hold that those whose ashes are scattered over any land become its jealous guardians from that time forward; and the living like to think that they shall become identified with this or that locality where they have once been happy.

They do not put up monuments, nor write epitaphs, for their dead, though in former ages their practice was much as ours, but they have a custom which comes to much the same thing, for the instinct of preserving the name alive after the death of the body seems to be common to all mankind. They have statues of themselves made while they are still alive (those, that is, who can afford it), and write inscriptions under them, which are often quite as untruthful as are our own epitaphs – only in another way. For they do not hesitate to describe themselves as victims to ill temper, jealousy, covetousness, and the like, but almost always lay claim to personal beauty, whether they have it or not, and, often, to the possession of a large sum in the funded debt of the country. If a person is ugly he does not sit as a model for his own statue, although it bears his name. He gets the handsomest of his friends to sit for him, and one of the ways of paying a compliment to another is to ask him to sit for such a statue. Women generally sit for their own statues, from a natural disinclination to admit the superior beauty of a friend, but they expect to be idealised. I understood that the multitude of these statues was beginning to be felt as an encumbrance in almost every family, and that the custom would probably before long fall into desuetude.

Indeed, this has already come about to the satisfaction of everyone, as regards the statues of public men – not more than three of which can be found in the whole capital. I expressed my surprise at this, and was told that some five hundred years before my visit, the city had been so overrun with these pests, that there was no getting about, and people were worried beyond endurance by having their attention called at every touch and turn to something, which, when they had attended to it, they found not to concern them. Most of these statues were mere attempts to do for some man or woman what an animal-stuffer does more successfully for a dog, or bird, or pike. They were generally foisted on the public by some coterie that was trying to exalt itself in exalting some one else, and not unfrequently they had no other inception than desire on the part of some member of the coterie to find a job for a young sculptor to whom his daughter was engaged. Statues so begotten could never be anything but deformities, and this is the way in which they are sure to be begotten, as soon as the art of making them at all has become widely practised.

I know not why, but all the noblest arts hold in perfection but for a very little moment. They soon reach a height from which they begin to decline, and when they have begun to decline it is a pity that they cannot be knocked on the head; for an art is like a living organism – better dead than dying. There is no way of making an aged art young again; it must be born anew and grow up from infancy as a new thing, working out its own salvation from effort to effort in all fear and trembling.

The Erewhonians five hundred years ago understood nothing of all this – I doubt whether they even do so now. They wanted to get the nearest thing they could to a stuffed man whose stuffing should not grow mouldy. They should have had some such an establishment as our Madame Tussaud's, where the figures wear real clothes, and are painted up to nature. Such an institution might have been made self-supporting, for people might have been made to pay before going in. As it was, they had let their poor cold grimy colourless heroes and heroines loaf about in squares and in corners of streets in all weathers, without any attempt at artistic sanitation – for there was no provision for burying their dead works of art out of their sight – no drainage, so to speak, whereby statues that had been sufficiently assimilated, so as to form part of the residuary impression of the country, might be carried away out of the system. Hence they put them up with a light heart on the cackling of their coteries, and they and their children had to live, often enough, with some wordy windbag whose cowardice had cost the country untold loss in blood and money.

At last the evil reached such a pitch that the people rose, and with indiscriminate fury destroyed good and bad alike. Most of what was destroyed was bad, but some few works were good, and the sculptors of today wring their hands over some of the fragments that have been preserved in museums up and down the country. For a couple of hundred years or so, not a statue was made from one end of the kingdom to the other, but the instinct for having stuffed men and women was so strong, that people at length again began to try to make them. Not knowing how to make them, and having no academics to mislead them, the earliest sculptors of this period thought things out for themselves, and again produced works that were full of interest, so that in three or four generations they reached a perfection hardly if at all inferior to that of several hundred years earlier.

On this the same evils recurred. Sculptors obtained high prices – the art became a trade – schools arose which professed to sell the holy spirit of art for money; pupils flocked from far and near to buy it, in the hopes of selling it later on, and were struck purblind as a punishment for the sin of those who sent them. Before long a second iconoclastic fury would infallibly have followed, but for the prescience of a statesman who succeeded in passing an Act to the effect that no statue of any public man or woman should be allowed to remain unbroken for more than fifty years, unless at the end of that time a jury of twenty-four men taken at random from the street pronounced in favour of its being allowed a second fifty years of life. Every fifty years this reconsideration was to be repeated, and unless there was a majority of eighteen in favour of the retention of the statue, it was to be destroyed.

Perhaps a simpler plan would have been to forbid the erection of a statue to any public man or woman till he or she had been dead at least one hundred years, and even then to insist on reconsideration of the claims of the deceased and the merit of the statue every fifty years – but the working of the Act brought about results that on the whole were satisfactory. For in the first place, many public statues that would have been voted under the old system, were not ordered, when it was known that they would be almost certainly broken up after fifty years, and in the second, public sculptors knowing their work to be so ephemeral, scamped it to an extent that made it offensive even to the most uncultured eye. Hence before long subscribers took to paying the sculptor for the statue of their dead statesmen, on condition that he did not make it. The tribute of respect was thus paid to the deceased, the public sculptors were not mulcted, and the rest of the public suffered no inconvenience.

I was told, however, that an abuse of this custom is growing up, inasmuch as the competition for the commission not to make a statue is so keen, that sculptors have been known to return a considerable part of the purchase money to the subscribers, by an arrangement made with them beforehand. Such transactions, however, are always clandestine. A small inscription is let into the pavement, where the public statue would have stood, which informs the reader that such a statue has been ordered for the person, whoever he or she may be, but that as yet the sculptor has not been able to complete it. There has been no Act to repress statues that are intended for private consumption, but as I have said, the custom is falling into desuetude.

Returning to Erewhonian customs in connection with death, there is one which I can hardly pass over. When anyone dies, the friends of the family write no letters of condolence, neither do they attend the scattering, nor wear mourning, but they send little boxes filled with artificial tears, and with the name of the sender painted neatly upon the outside of the lid. The tears vary in number from two to fifteen or sixteen, according to degree of intimacy or relationship; and people sometimes find it a nice point of etiquette to know the exact number which they ought to send. Strange as it may appear, this attention is highly valued, and its omission by those from whom it might be expected is keenly felt. These tears were formerly stuck with adhesive plaster to the cheeks of the bereaved, and were worn in public for a few months after the death of a relative; they were then banished to the hat or bonnet, and are now no longer worn.

The birth of a child is looked upon as a painful subject on which it is kinder not to touch: the illness of the mother is carefully concealed until the necessity for signing the birth-formula (of which hereafter) renders further secrecy impossible, and for some months before the event the family live in retirement, seeing very little company. When the offence is over and done with, it is condoned by the common want of logic; for this merciful provision of nature, this buffer against collisions, this friction which upsets our calculations but without which existence would be intolerable, this crowning glory of human invention whereby we can be blind and see at one and the same moment, this blessed inconsistency, exists here as elsewhere; and though the strictest writers on morality have maintained that it is wicked for a woman to have children at all, inasmuch as it is wrong to be out of health that good may come, yet the necessity of the case has caused a general feeling in favour of passing over such events in silence, and of assuming their non-existence except in such flagrant cases as force themselves on the public notice. Against these the condemnation of society is inexorable, and if it is believed that the illness has been dangerous and protracted, it is almost impossible for a woman to recover her former position in society.

The above conventions struck me as arbitrary and cruel, but they put a stop to many fancied ailments; for the situation, so far from being considered interesting, is looked upon as savouring more or less distinctly of a very reprehensible condition of things, and the ladies take care to conceal it as long as they can even from their own husbands, in anticipation of a severe scolding as soon as the misdemeanour is discovered. Also the baby is kept out of sight, except on the day of signing the birth-formula, until it can walk and talk. Should the child unhappily die, a coroner's inquest is inevitable, but in order to avoid disgracing a family which may have been hitherto respected, it is almost invariably found that the child was over seventy-five years old, and died from the decay of nature.

Chapter XIV
Mahaina

I CONTINUED my sojourn with the Nosnibors. In a few days Mr. Nosnibor had recovered from his flogging, and was looking forward with glee to the fact that the next would be the last. I did not think that there seemed any occasion even for this; but he said it was better to be on the safe side, and he would make up the dozen. He now went to his business as usual; and I understood that he was never more prosperous, in spite of his heavy fine. He was unable to give me much of his time during the day; for he was one of those valuable men who are paid, not by the year, month, week, or day, but by the minute. His wife and daughters, however, made much of me, and introduced me to their friends, who came in shoals to call upon me.

One of these persons was a lady called Mahaina. Zulora (the elder of my host's daughters) ran up to her and embraced her as soon as she entered the room, at the same time inquiring tenderly after her 'poor dipsomania'. Mahaina answered that it was just as bad as ever; she was a perfect martyr to it, and her excellent health was the only thing which consoled her under her affliction.

Then the other ladies joined in with condolences and the never-failing suggestions which they had ready for every mental malady. They recommended their own straightener and disparaged Mahaina's. Mrs. Nosnibor had a favourite nostrum, but I could catch little of its nature. I heard the words "full confidence that the desire to drink will cease when the formula has been repeated… this confidence is everything…far from undervaluing a thorough determination never to touch spirits again…fail too often…formula a certain cure (with great emphasis)…prescribed form… full conviction." The conversation then became more audible, and was carried on at considerable length. I should perplex myself and the reader by endeavouring to follow the ingenious perversity of all they said; enough, that in the course of time the visit came to an end, and Mahaina took her leave receiving affectionate embraces from all the ladies. I had remained in the background after the first ceremony of introduction, for I did not like the looks of Mahaina, and the conversation displeased me. When she left the room I had some consolation in the remarks called forth by her departure.

At first they fell to praising her very demurely. She was all this that and the other, till I disliked her more and more at every word, and inquired how it was that the straighteners had not been able to cure her as they had cured Mr. Nosnibor.

There was a shade of significance on Mrs. Nosnibor's face as I said this, which seemed to imply that she did not consider Mahaina's case to be quite one for a straightener. It flashed across me that perhaps the poor woman did not drink at all. I knew that I ought not to have inquired, but I could not help it, and asked point blank whether she did or not.

"We can none of us judge of the condition of other people," said Mrs. Nosnibor in a gravely charitable tone and with a look towards Zulora.

"Oh, mamma," answered Zulora, pretending to be half angry but rejoiced at being able to say out what she was already longing to insinuate; "I don't believe a word of it. It's all indigestion. I remember staying in the house with her for a whole month last summer, and I am sure she never once touched a drop of wine or spirits. The fact is, Mahaina is a very weakly girl, and she pretends to get tipsy in order to win a forbearance from her friends to which she is not entitled. She is not strong enough for her calisthenic exercises, and she knows she would be made to do them unless her inability was referred to moral causes."

Here the younger sister, who was ever sweet and kind, remarked that she thought Mahaina did tipple occasionally. "I also think," she added, "that she sometimes takes poppy juice."

"Well, then, perhaps she does drink sometimes," said Zulora; "but she would make us all think that she does it much oftener in order to hide her weakness."

And so they went on for half an hour and more, bandying about the question as to how far their late visitor's intemperance was real or no. Every now and then they would join in some charitable commonplace, and would pretend to be all of one mind that Mahaina was a person whose bodily health would be excellent if it were not for her unfortunate inability to refrain from excessive drinking; but as soon as this appeared to be fairly settled they began to be uncomfortable until they had undone their work and left some serious imputation upon her constitution. At last, seeing that the debate had assumed the character of a cyclone or circular storm, going round and round and round and round till one could never say where it began nor where it ended, I made some apology for an abrupt departure and retired to my own room.

Here at least I was alone, but I was very unhappy. I had fallen upon a set of people who, in spite of their high civilisation and many excellences, had been so warped by the mistaken views presented to them during childhood from generation to generation, that it was impossible to see how they could ever clear themselves. Was there nothing which I could say to make them feel that the constitution of a person's body was a thing over which he or she had had at any rate no initial control whatever, while the mind was a perfectly different thing, and capable of being created anew and directed according to the pleasure of its possessor? Could I never bring them to see that while habits of mind and character were entirely independent of initial mental force and early education, the body was so much a creature of parentage and circumstances, that no punishment for ill-health should be ever tolerated save as a protection from contagion, and that even where punishment was inevitable it should be attended with compassion? Surely, if the unfortunate Mahaina were to feel that she could avow her bodily weakness without fear of being despised for her infirmities, and if there were medical men to whom she could fairly state her case, she would not hesitate about doing so through the fear of taking nasty medicine. It was possible that her malady was incurable (for I had heard enough to convince me that her dipsomania was only a pretence and that she was temperate in all her habits); in that case she might perhaps be justly subject to annoyances or even to restraint; but who could say whether she was curable or not, until she was able to make a clean breast of her symptoms instead of concealing them? In their eagerness to stamp out disease, these people overshot their mark; for people had become so clever at dissembling – they painted their faces with such consummate skill – they repaired the decay of time and the effects of mischance with such profound dissimulation – that it was really impossible to say whether any one was well or ill till after an intimate acquaintance of months or years. Even then the shrewdest were constantly mistaken in their judgements, and marriages were often contracted with most deplorable results, owing to the art with which infirmity had been concealed.

It appeared to me that the first step towards the cure of disease should be the announcement of the fact to a person's near relations and friends. If anyone had a headache, he ought to be permitted within reasonable limits to say so at once, and to retire to his own bedroom and take a pill, without everyone's looking grave and tears being shed and all the rest of it. As it was, even upon hearing it whispered that somebody else was subject to headaches, a whole company must look as though they had never had a headache in their lives. It is true they were not very prevalent, for the people were the healthiest and most comely imaginable, owing to the severity with which ill health was treated; still, even the best were liable to be out of sorts sometimes, and there were few families that had not a medicine-chest in a cupboard somewhere.

Chapter XV
The Musical Banks

ON MY RETURN to the drawing-room, I found that the Mahaina current had expended itself. The ladies were just putting away their work and preparing to go out. I asked them where they were going. They answered with a certain air of reserve that they were going to the bank to get some money.

Now I had already collected that the mercantile affairs of the Erewhonians were conducted on a totally different system from our own; I had, however, gathered little hitherto, except that they had two distinct commercial systems, of which the one appealed more strongly to the imagination than anything to which we are accustomed in Europe, inasmuch as the banks that were conducted upon this system were decorated in the most profuse fashion, and all mercantile transactions were accompanied with music, so that they were called Musical Banks, though the music was hideous to a European ear.

As for the system itself I never understood it, neither can I do so now: they have a code in connection with it, which I have not the slightest doubt that they understand, but no foreigner can hope to do so. One rule runs into, and against, another as in a most complicated grammar, or as in Chinese pronunciation, wherein I am told that the slightest change in accentuation or tone of voice alters the meaning of a whole sentence. Whatever is incoherent in my description must be referred to the fact of my never having attained to a full comprehension of the subject.

So far, however, as I could collect anything certain, I gathered that they have two distinct currencies, each under the control of its own banks and mercantile codes. One of these (the one with the Musical Banks) was supposed to be the system, and to give out the currency in which all monetary transactions should be carried on; and as far as I could see, all who wished to be considered respectable, kept a larger or smaller balance at these banks. On the other hand, if there is one thing of which I am more sure than another, it is that the amount so kept had no direct commercial value in the outside world; I am sure that the managers and cashiers of the Musical Banks were not paid in their own currency. Mr. Nosnibor used to go to these banks, or rather to the great mother bank of the city, sometimes but not very often. He was a pillar of one of the other kind of banks, though he appeared to hold some minor office also in the musical ones. The ladies generally went alone; as indeed was the case in most families, except on state occasions.

I had long wanted to know more of this strange system, and had the greatest desire to accompany my hostess and her daughters. I had seen them go out almost every morning since my arrival and had noticed that they carried their purses in their hands, not exactly ostentatiously, yet just so as that those who met them should see whither they were going. I had never, however, yet been asked to go with them myself.

It is not easy to convey a person's manner by words, and I can hardly give any idea of the peculiar feeling that came upon me when I saw the ladies on the point of starting for the bank. There was a something of regret, a something as though they would wish to take me with them, but did not like to ask me, and yet as though I were hardly to ask to be taken. I was determined, however, to bring matters to an issue with my hostess about my going with them, and after a little parleying, and many inquiries as to whether I was perfectly sure that I myself wished to go, it was decided that I might do so.

We passed through several streets of more or less considerable houses, and at last turning round a corner we came upon a large piazza, at the end of which was a magnificent building, of a strange but noble architecture and of great antiquity. It did not open directly on to the piazza, there being a screen, through which was an archway, between the piazza and the actual precincts of the bank. On passing under the archway we entered upon a green sward, round which there ran an arcade or cloister, while in front of us uprose the majestic towers of the bank and its venerable front, which was divided into three deep recesses and adorned with all sorts of marbles and many sculptures. On either side there were beautiful old trees wherein the birds were busy by the hundred, and a number of quaint but substantial houses of singularly comfortable appearance; they were situated in the midst of orchards and gardens, and gave me an impression of great peace and plenty.

Indeed it had been no error to say that this building was one that appealed to the imagination; it did more – it carried both imagination and judgement by storm. It was an epic in stone and marble, and so powerful was the effect it produced on me, that as I beheld it I was charmed and melted. I felt more conscious of the existence of a remote past. One knows of this always, but the knowledge is never so living as in the actual presence of some witness to the life of bygone ages. I felt how short a space of human life was the period of our own existence. I was more impressed with my own littleness, and much more inclinable to believe that the people whose sense of the fitness of things was equal to the upraising of so serene a handiwork, were hardly likely to be wrong in the conclusions they might come to upon any subject. My feeling certainly was that the currency of this bank must be the right one.

We crossed the sward and entered the building. If the outside had been impressive the inside was even more so. It was very lofty and divided into several parts by walls which rested upon massive pillars; the windows were filled with stained glass descriptive of the principal commercial incidents of the bank for many ages. In a remote part of the building there were men and boys singing; this was the only disturbing feature, for as the gamut was still unknown, there was no music in the country which could be agreeable to a European ear. The singers seemed to have derived their inspirations from the songs of birds and the wailing of the wind, which last they tried to imitate in melancholy cadences that at times degenerated into a howl. To my thinking the noise was hideous, but it produced a great effect upon my companions, who professed themselves much moved. As soon as the singing was over, the ladies requested me to stay where I was while they went inside the place from which it had seemed to come.

During their absence certain reflections forced themselves upon me.

In the first place, it struck me as strange that the building should be so nearly empty; I was almost alone, and the few besides myself had been led by curiosity, and had no intention of doing business with the bank. But there might be more inside. I stole up to the curtain, and ventured to draw the extreme edge of it on one side. No, there was hardly anyone there. I saw a large number of cashiers, all at their desks ready to pay cheques, and one or two who seemed to be the managing partners. I also saw my hostess and her daughters and two or three other ladies; also three or four old women and the boys from one of the neighbouring Colleges of Unreason; but there was no one else. This did not look as though the bank was doing a very large business; and yet I had always been told that everyone in the city dealt with this establishment.

I cannot describe all that took place in these inner precincts, for a sinister-looking person in a black gown came and made unpleasant gestures at me for peeping. I happened to have in my pocket one of the Musical Bank pieces, which had been given me by Mrs. Nosnibor, so I tried to tip him with it; but having seen what it was, he became so angry that I had to give him a piece of the other kind of money to pacify him. When I had done this he became civil directly. As soon as he was gone I ventured to take a second look, and saw Zulora in the very act of giving a piece of paper which looked like a cheque to one of the cashiers. He did not examine it, but putting his hand into an antique coffer hard by, he pulled out a quantity of metal pieces apparently at random, and handed them over without counting them; neither did Zulora count them, but put them into her purse and went back to her seat after dropping a few pieces of the other coinage into an alms box that stood by the cashier's side. Mrs. Nosnibor and Arowhena then did likewise, but a little later they gave all (so far as I could see) that they had received from the cashier back to a verger, who I have no doubt put it back into the coffer from which it had been taken. They then began making towards the curtain; whereon I let it drop and retreated to a reasonable distance.

They soon joined me. For some few minutes we all kept silence, but at last I ventured to remark that the bank was not so busy today as it probably often was. On this Mrs. Nosnibor said that it was indeed melancholy to see what little heed people paid to the most precious of all institutions. I could say nothing in reply, but I have ever been of opinion that the greater part of mankind do approximately know where they get that which does them good.

Mrs. Nosnibor went on to say that I must not think there was any want of confidence in the bank because I had seen so few people there; the heart of the country was thoroughly devoted to these establishments, and any sign of their being in danger would bring in support from the most unexpected quarters. It was only because people knew them to be so very safe, that in some cases (as she lamented to say in Mr. Nosnibor's) they felt that their support was unnecessary. Moreover these institutions never departed from the safest and most approved banking principles. Thus they never allowed interest on deposit, a thing now frequently done by certain bubble companies, which by doing an illegitimate trade had drawn many customers away; and even the shareholders were fewer than formerly, owing to the innovations of these unscrupulous persons, for the Musical Banks paid little or no dividend, but divided their profits by way of bonus on the original shares once in every thirty thousand years; and as it was now only two thousand years since there had been one of these distributions, people felt that they could not hope for another in their own time and preferred investments whereby they got some more tangible return; all which, she said, was very melancholy to think of.

Having made these last admissions, she returned to her original statement, namely, that everyone in the country really supported these banks. As to the fewness of the people, and the absence of the able-bodied, she pointed out to me with some justice that this was exactly what we ought to expect. The men who were most conversant about the stability of human institutions, such as the lawyers, men of science, doctors, statesmen, painters, and the like, were just those who were most likely to be misled by their own fancied accomplishments, and to be made unduly suspicious by their licentious desire for greater present return, which was at the root of nine-tenths of the opposition; by their vanity, which would prompt them to affect superiority to the prejudices of the vulgar; and by the stings of their own conscience, which was constantly upbraiding them in the most cruel manner on account of their bodies, which were generally diseased.

Let a person's intellect (she continued) be never so sound, unless his body is in absolute health, he can form no judgement worth having on matters of this kind. The body is everything: it need not perhaps be such a strong body (she said this because she saw that I was thinking of the old and infirm-looking folks whom I had seen in the bank), but it must be in perfect health; in this case, the less active strength it had the more free would be the working of the intellect, and therefore the sounder the conclusion. The people, then, whom I had seen at the bank were in reality the very ones whose opinions were most worth having; they declared its advantages to be incalculable, and even professed to consider the immediate return to be far larger than they were entitled to; and so she ran on, nor did she leave off till we had got back to the house.

She might say what she pleased, but her manner carried no conviction, and later on I saw signs of general indifference to these banks that were not to be mistaken. Their supporters often denied it, but the denial was generally so couched as to add another proof of its existence. In commercial panics, and in times of general distress, the people as a mass did not so much as even think of turning to these banks. A few might do so, some from habit and early training, some from the instinct that prompts us to catch at any straw when we think ourselves drowning, but few from a genuine belief that the Musical Banks could save them from financial ruin, if they were unable to meet their engagements in the other kind of currency.

In conversation with one of the Musical Bank managers I ventured to hint this as plainly as politeness would allow. He said that it had been more or less true till lately; but that now they had put fresh stained glass windows into all the banks in the country, and repaired the buildings, and enlarged the organs; the presidents, moreover, had taken to riding in omnibuses and talking nicely to people in the streets, and to remembering the ages of their children, and giving them things when they were naughty, so that all would henceforth go smoothly.

"But haven't you done anything to the money itself?" said I, timidly.

"It is not necessary," he rejoined; "not in the least necessary, I assure you."

And yet anyone could see that the money given out at these banks was not that with which people bought their bread, meat, and clothing. It was like it at a first glance, and was stamped with designs that were often of great beauty; it was not, again, a spurious coinage, made with the intention that it should be mistaken for the money in actual use; it was more like a toy money, or the counters used for certain games at cards; for, notwithstanding the beauty of the designs, the material on which they were stamped was as nearly valueless as possible. Some were covered with tin foil, but the greater part were frankly of a cheap base metal the exact nature of which I was not able to determine. Indeed they were made of a great variety of metals, or, perhaps more accurately, alloys, some of which were hard, while others would bend easily and assume almost any form which their possessor might desire at the moment.

Of course everyone knew that their commercial value was nil, but all those who wished to be considered respectable thought it incumbent upon them to retain a few coins in their possession, and to let them be seen from time to time in their hands and purses. Not only this, but they would stick to it that the current coin of the realm was dross in comparison with the Musical Bank coinage.

Perhaps, however, the strangest thing of all was that these very people would at times make fun in small ways of the whole system; indeed, there was hardly any insinuation against it which they would not tolerate and even applaud in their daily newspapers if written anonymously, while if the same thing were said without ambiguity to their faces – nominative case verb and accusative being all in their right places, and doubt impossible – they would consider themselves very seriously and justly outraged, and accuse the speaker of being unwell.

I never could understand (neither can I quite do so now, though I begin to see better what they mean) why a single currency should not suffice them; it would seem to me as though all their dealings would have been thus greatly simplified; but I was met with a look of horror if ever I dared to hint at it. Even those who to my certain knowledge kept only just enough money at the Musical Banks to swear by, would call the other banks (where their securities really lay) cold, deadening, paralysing, and the like.

I noticed another thing, moreover, which struck me greatly. I was taken to the opening of one of these banks in a neighbouring town, and saw a large assemblage of cashiers and managers. I sat opposite them and scanned their faces attentively. They did not please me; they lacked, with few exceptions, the true Erewhonian frankness; and an equal number from any other class would have looked happier and better men. When I met them in the streets they did not seem like other people, but had, as a general rule, a cramped expression upon their faces which pained and depressed me.

Those who came from the country were better; they seemed to have lived less as a separate class, and to be freer and healthier; but in spite of my seeing not a few whose looks were benign and noble, I could not help asking myself concerning the greater number of those whom I met, whether Erewhon would be a better country if their expression were to be transferred to the people in general. I answered myself emphatically, no. The expression on the faces of the high Ydgrunites was that which one would wish to diffuse, and not that of the cashiers.

A man's expression is his sacrament; it is the outward and visible sign of his inward and spiritual grace, or want of grace; and as I looked at the a majority of these men, I could not help feeling that there must be a something in their lives which had stunted their natural development, and that they would have been more healthily minded in any other profession. I was always sorry for them, for in nine cases out of ten they were well-meaning persons; they were in the main very poorly paid; their constitutions were as a rule above suspicion; and there were recorded numberless instances of their self-sacrifice and generosity; but they had had the misfortune to have been betrayed into a false position at an age for the most part when their judgement was not matured, and after having been kept in studied ignorance of the real difficulties of the system. But this did not make their position the less a false one, and its bad effects upon themselves were unmistakable.

Few people would speak quite openly and freely before them, which struck me as a very bad sign. When they were in the room everyone would talk as though all currency save that of the Musical Banks should be abolished; and yet they knew perfectly well that even the cashiers themselves hardly used the Musical Bank money more than other people. It was expected of them that they should appear to do so, but this was all. The less thoughtful of them did not seem particularly unhappy, but many were plainly sick at heart, though perhaps they hardly knew it, and would not have owned to being so. Some few were opponents of the whole system; but these were liable to be dismissed from their employment at any moment, and this rendered them very careful, for a man who had once been cashier at a Musical Bank was out of the field for other employment, and was generally unfitted for it by reason of that course of treatment which was commonly called his education. In fact it was a career from which retreat was virtually impossible, and into which young men were generally induced to enter before they could be reasonably expected, considering their training, to have formed any opinions of their own. Not unfrequently, indeed, they were induced, by what we in England should call undue influence, concealment, and fraud. Few indeed were those who had the courage to insist on seeing both sides of the question before they committed themselves to what was practically a leap in the dark. One would have thought that caution in this respect was an elementary principle – one of the first things that an honourable man would teach his boy to understand; but in practice it was not so.

I even saw cases in which parents bought the right of presenting to the office of cashier at one of these banks, with the fixed determination that some one of their sons (perhaps a mere child) should fill it. There was the lad himself – growing up with every promise of becoming a good and honourable man – but utterly without warning concerning the iron shoe which his natural protector was providing for him. Who could say that the whole thing would not end in a life-long lie, and vain chafing to escape? I confess that there were few things in Erewhon which shocked me more than this.

Yet we do something not so very different from this even in England, and as regards the dual commercial system, all countries have, and have had, a law of the land, and also another law, which, though professedly more sacred, has far less effect on their daily life and actions. It seems as though the need for some law over and above, and sometimes even conflicting with, the law of the land, must spring from something that lies deep down in man's nature; indeed, it is hard to think that man could ever have become man at all, but for the gradual evolution of a perception that though this world looms so large when we are in it, it may seem a little thing when we have got away from it.

When man had grown to the perception that in the everlasting Is-and-Is-Not of nature, the world and all that it contains, including man, is at the same time both seen and unseen, he felt the need of two rules of life, one for the seen, and the other for the unseen side of things. For the laws affecting the seen world he claimed the sanction of seen powers; for the unseen (of which he knows nothing save that it exists and is powerful) he appealed to the unseen power (of which, again, he knows nothing save that it exists and is powerful) to which he gives the name of God.

Some Erewhonian opinions concerning the intelligence of the unborn embryo, that I regret my space will not permit me to lay before the reader, have led me to conclude that the Erewhonian Musical Banks, and perhaps the religious systems of all countries, are now more or less of an attempt to uphold the unfathomable and unconscious instinctive wisdom of millions of past generations, against the comparatively shallow, consciously reasoning, and ephemeral conclusions drawn from that of the last thirty or forty.

The saving feature of the Erewhonian Musical Bank system (as distinct from the quasi-idolatrous views which coexist with it, and on which I will touch later) was that while it bore witness to the existence of a kingdom that is not of this world, it made no attempt to pierce the veil that hides it from human eyes. It is here that almost all religions go wrong. Their priests try to make us believe that they know more about the unseen world than those whose eyes are still blinded by the seen, can ever know – forgetting that while to deny the existence of an unseen kingdom is bad, to pretend that we know more about it than its bare existence is no better.

This chapter is already longer than I intended, but I should like to say that in spite of the saving feature of which I have just spoken, I cannot help thinking that the Erewhonians are on the eve of some great change in their religious opinions, or at any rate in that part of them which finds expression through their Musical Banks. So far as I could see, fully ninety per cent of the population of the metropolis looked upon these banks with something not far removed from contempt. If this is so, any such startling event as is sure to arise sooner or later, may serve as nucleus to a new order of things that will be more in harmony with both the heads and hearts of the people.

The complete and unabridged text is available online, from ***flametreepublishing.com/extras***

Across the River

Leah Cypess

WHEN THE SORCERER walked through the town gates, I was standing with my friends Reuven and Yitzchak in the square, which was not where we were supposed to be. Reuven should have been in the study hall, where his wife had directed him to go. Yitzchak should have been at the market, helping his father. And I should have been resting my voice, since that evening, for the first time, I was going to be allowed to lead the prayers in synagogue – an honor I had been hoping for and practicing for, but that I now, somewhat nervously, wished was not coming so soon.

We were all, mind you, on our way to where we were supposed to be. We were obedient young men, with no inner drive for trouble. Reuven loved his studies, and I loved the taste of prayers in my mouth, the feeling that came when I hit the right accents with the right emotions. Yitzchak, while he did not exactly love trade, certainly appreciated the money he would take home. But we were all still young, and it was a warm lush day with the first hint of summer twining through the breeze. It had been a long time since the three of us had sat together under a teacher's stern eye, and though we saw each other in passing almost every day, we always had something to catch each other up on.

"My wife," Reuven said – he was newly married, and always blushed slightly when he said *my wife* – "tells me her sister is ready for marriage, and her parents are talking to the marriage broker. What do you say, Yitzchak? You won't find a better family."

"Eh," Yitzchak said, lifting a shoulder. "I admire her parents well enough, but I'm not sure I like who my brother-in-law would be."

Reuven made a show of punching him, and I gave them both a sharp look. Not too sharp – I didn't want to appear insulted that *I,* apparently, was not a good marriage prospect for Reuven's wife's sister – but really, we were no longer children. If the rabbi's wife was at market, and saw me behaving like a wild animal, she might mention it to the rabbi, and he might decide I wasn't ready to lead prayers after all.

"I have to go," I said. "I need to practice for tonight."

Yitzchak lifted the corner of his mouth – once he was in a jocular mood, it was hard to get him out of it – but Reuven nodded. "Of course. Are you going to sing one of your own poems?"

"No!" I hadn't even considered it. No one but the two of them and my father had heard my compositions. And though they all assured me my prayer-poems were wonderful, I knew they were just shells of what they could have been. They needed an infusion of words and songs I couldn't yet give them. And though I knew where I could go to find that music, I wasn't ready.

I could not possibly explain. So I said, "It's only my first—"

Then a hush fell over the square, and we turned just in time to see the sorcerer walk through the gate.

He was dressed like a monk, but his cassock cast a shadow darker than itself, so we all knew immediately what he was. He walked past the beggars at the well, past the women herding mules along the street, past the children playing near the walls, straight toward us. The only three Jews in the square.

We should have run. We would have, if he hadn't come so fast. Next thing we knew, he was beside us. His sleeve fell back to reveal a gnarled hand with too-long fingers, and with the knuckles of that hand, he brushed Reuven's cheek.

Reuven let out a small, strangled sound. Yitzchak and I stepped back.

The sorcerer smiled at us, then turned and kept walking, farther into the town.

* * *

News of the sorcerer had been passed along by traders and travelers from the other towns along the Rhine. He was from the east, they said, from the land of the Byzantines, and he was headed back there to help the Byzantine emperor fight the Moors. On his way, he was killing as many Jews – only Jews – as he could.

This was no real surprise to us Jews, though it was quite a relief to our Christian neighbors.

He had already killed many of us. He touched people, and they went home, and then they weakened and died. The travelers were unclear on how long it took.

But they were clear that he never stopped with only one. After Reuven died, there would be dozens more… maybe hundreds. First here in Worms, and then in another town, and another. There was nothing we could do to stop it.

I helped Yitzchak walk Reuven home to his wife and waited with them until the sun dipped low. And then I went to the river.

* * *

Years later, when I was much older and living in another land, I discovered that scholars had been searching for centuries for the Sambatyon River. It puzzled me at first, because of course I had always known where it was. It was right behind my house.

It took me longer than it should have to realize that I was the only one who had ever seen it. Not merely in my hometown – that, I had always known – but in the entire world. That was why others searched for it in distant deserts and faraway jungles. They did not know that the Sambatyon came to those it chose.

By then, I was ashamed to tell them it had chosen me.

The river behind my house wasn't usually the Sambatyon. Normally it was the Rhine, flat and gray, with ripples that were slow and languid, as if they didn't quite have the desire to make it all the way to the sea. As if, like the rest of us, they had nowhere to be but here.

It was only when I was alone, but not *always* when I was alone, that I felt the change: a restless surge within me, as if my mind was a maelstrom, full of thoughts and words and images desperate to get out. As if the prayers I practiced so diligently – prayers that I loved, that I longed to share with my community and devote my life to perfecting – were too rehearsed, too calm. Missing something I could not find in my synagogue or my town.

Then I would go to the river and find it wild and turbulent, waves rearing high above my head and crashing down in a fury of white froth. Rocks the size of a man's fist were tossed among the waves like goose feathers at a slaughter, clashing against each other and smashing the waves into glittering bits of spray.

The violent waters were always blue, a brighter, more crystalline blue than the sky above Worms ever was. And on the other side – which I could glimpse in bits and pieces, scattered and distorted through boulders and froth – I saw no houses and gardens, no chickens or pigs. I saw tents, and long leonine creatures that looked like neither dogs nor cats, and dark-skinned figures in strange white clothes moving among them.

I wanted to see more, but not nearly as much as I wanted to hear their songs – prayers which must be so like, and so unlike, our own. I knew their music would fill the gaps in my own hymns, that if I infused my compositions with their prayers, it would make us whole. Bring us closer to God and to what we should have been. But the river, with its frantic rocks and roars of spray, was unceasingly loud, drowning out any sounds from the other side.

By then, of course, I knew what the river was, though I still didn't know *why* it was what it was. I had learned our history: how a thousand years ago, ten of Israel's twelve tribes were exiled before the rest of us. How they passed through Assyria and found a place, safe and secure, beyond the Sambatyon River: a river that ran wild six days a week, but became calm and smooth between sundown on Friday and nightfall on Saturday.

Living in isolation, the Ten Tribes could atone for the sins that had caused their exile and prepare for their eventual return. They had their own kingdom, their own customs, unchanged over the hundreds of years during which we, descendants of the other two tribes, had mingled with our neighbors and been downtrodden by them. The Ten Tribes had kept their original customs, their unique ways, their native skills.

Which would, I hoped as I watched the waves shoot billows of white spray into the air, include sorcery.

Two boulders crashed against each other, sending shards of wet rock flying. I flinched away, but felt a sharp pain right under my eye. When I touched it, my finger came away with a smudge of blood.

It was the first time anything from the river had touched me. As if it could see the rowboat I had dragged over – borrowed from a sympathetic Christian neighbor – and knew what it meant.

As if the river was warning me.

I did not step back. I was afraid that if I did, the rocks would disappear, and I would be facing only the Rhine: flat and wide and still, with nothing on the opposite bank that couldn't already be found on this side.

The sun touched the horizon, a blaze of orange drawing a host of blue and pink after it.

The rocks fell into the water, a sudden avalanche of deadly splashes. The froth settled into a swirl of bubbles, the ripples going as still as fractured ice.

It was the Sabbath, and on the Sabbath, the Sambatyon River ran smooth and tranquil.

I had thought that in its stillness, it would look ordinary, like any other river. But its sudden serenity looked more unnatural than its usual chaos.

And now, at last, I could hear voices from the other side.

I had dreamed of this moment for so long: my chance to take the music that drifted across the water and weave it into my own prayers. To reunite the Tribes of Israel, in song if not in reality.

Until tonight, I had spent my Friday evenings at synagogue with my father. I went with him even when he said I was too young, in order to pay close attention to the cantor. I had to know the prayers from our side of the river, to know them in my bones, before I could mix them with those from the other side.

They were singing in words I recognized as Hebrew, but so strangely accented that I couldn't make out their meaning. Not that I needed to: I knew what the songs were about. They were singing on their side, as we were on our side – as I should have been, at synagogue – to welcome the Sabbath.

I could have stopped and listened. Could have held those prayers in my mind, to bring back and mingle with my own compositions. Even at that moment, with the palpable terror that was strumming through every Jew in Worms filling my body, I considered it. Just for a few moments. It was what I had been born to do, and surely it wouldn't make a difference...

I thought of Reuven's wan, hopeless face. My shoulder muscles knotted. I drew in a deep breath, closed my eyes, and pushed the boat into the river.

* * *

During the week, it was the rapids and the rocks that kept the Sambatyon impassable. Any attempt to row across it, or even to step into it, would have torn a man's body apart.

On the Sabbath, it was something else that made the river into a barrier: God's law. For a thousand years, no single person from the Ten Tribes had taken advantage of the river's calm. A boat ride, a transgression of the Sabbath, would tear a Jew's soul apart. To them, and to us, it was just as real a blockade as the deadly waves.

Something inside me shrank as I picked up the oars. And yet it was such a simple thing. The river didn't fight me; it was glassy and smooth, stained pink by the sunset. My body didn't fight me; my hands were sweaty but firm around the oars, my arms pulling rhythmically. I thought of all the Jews in my town, of my father's white-streaked beard and my mother's tired smile, of my little sister who climbed trees like she was half-squirrel. She was small and fast and lithe, and had not yet learned to be afraid.

She would learn it today.

In other towns, the sorcerer had killed children as well as adults. Entire families had vanished. In some cases, he had killed all but one, leaving a lone soul to bear all that grief.

The oars dipped in and out of the water, forming ripples that looked like quenched fire. If my soul fought me, I didn't hear it.

Souls can be very quiet, sometimes. That's why we need to raise our voices in prayer.

* * *

A man was waiting for me on the other side of the river. He stood with his arms crossed over his chest, his face set in a forbidding scowl.

I decided not to get out of my boat just yet.

I dug one oar into the bottom of the river and heard a snap – the ground was covered with rocks, not dirt, so there was nothing to dig the oar into. I should have realized.

Since the oar was already broken, I kept pushing until the boat was high enough on the bank that I was pretty sure I wouldn't drift away. Then I pulled the oar – or half of it – into the boat, and laid it carefully next to the few items I had flung in at the last minute: a glass jar, a sack, a woven basket. I was surprised but pleased that my hand did not shake through any of this.

Then I turned to face the man.

He stepped closer, with a little lurch. "You should not be here. You are in violation of the Sabbath."

He spoke in Hebrew. Though his accent was strange, I was able to understand him. His voice was clear and slow and faintly melodic.

My own Hebrew was creaky and limited, used only for prayer and study. But for this, a matter of law, it was not hard to find the words I needed. "It is permitted to violate the Sabbath to save a life."

"Whose life are you saving?"

These words were harder to find. But I managed, in embarrassing fits and starts, to explain. The man listened without changing expression until I reached my point: "We do not know magic anymore, and we do not use weapons. We cannot kill him on our own. We need help. We need someone to cross the river and challenge him."

The man sighed, and I heard his answer in his sigh. "We cannot cross the river."

"To save a life, it is permitted—"

"It's not that. This river is not meant to be crossed." He stepped back, away from the water. Away from me. "Not yet."

I had been thinking this through all day. There were so many arguments, subtle and persuasive, that I could have made. But my limited words would have come out in a tangle, and all I could manage was, "We *need* you."

I put all my despair, all our helplessness, into those three words. The man bowed his head, and I had a moment of hope.

But his eyes remained on mine, and my hope died as I recognized the firmness behind his gaze. It wasn't sadness – or at least, not the type of sadness that would do me any good.

It was regret.

"You need us on this side of the river," he said, "more than you need us on your side."

My hands *were* shaking now, but I managed to pull the glass jar out of the bottom of the boat. I hadn't been certain, when I grabbed all these receptacles, what they might be for. Perhaps some part of me had feared, or known.

"Then give me something," I said, "to take back to my side."

He reached down, pulled a few weeds from the ground, and held them out to me, mud still clinging to their roots.

"Do you have these," he said, "where you come from? They possess healing properties. Perhaps they can help your friend, the one who has already been touched."

I tossed the weeds into the basket, but didn't break his gaze. "What about the rest of us? We will all die, if the sorcerer is not stopped. I need some…" What was the Hebrew for *spell*? "Some *thing*. That I can use to – to fight—"

He was shaking his head even before my words stuttered to a stop.

"You are not a fighter," the man said. "You were not meant to carry *weapons* across this river."

My jaw clenched. "Weapons are what we need."

"We have," he said kindly, "nothing to send with you."

But I didn't need kindness from him. I needed *help*.

"What good are you, then?" I switched to Yiddish; it obviously didn't matter whether he understood me or not. "Why can I see the river, if I was never meant to cross it? Why can I see *you*, if you won't help me? Just to know that you're here? What good does that do for *anyone*?"

From the expression on his face, I thought he might understand me after all. But I didn't wait to hear what he might say, or not say. I turned myself around and used the broken oar to push my boat back into the smooth water.

* * *

It was much harder rowing with only one oar, and with no hope. By the time I reached my side of the river, my shoulders hurt as if the bones inside them had rubbed each other raw.

Which would have been a welcome distraction from the deeper pain in my chest. Except I wasn't distracted at all.

I pulled the boat onto the shore and looked back over the water. I could see the man from the Ten Tribes still standing there, watching me.

I thought of the piece of oar I'd left in the rocks. At nightfall of the next day, when the Sabbath ended and the river started churning, would it be thrown up with the rocks, smashed between them and splintered into shards? Or would it be left behind, a piece of our land not subject to the river's current, to sink into the mud beneath the water and disappear?

Either way, it would be as if I'd never been there.

I took the useless, broken half of the oar and thrust it, too, into the rocks, so hard the wood splintered my hand. I jabbed it again and again, my tears spilling into the water, where they, too, would leave no trace. Finally, I dropped the oar and watched it bob on the surface, which was so clear that I could see the deadly rocks lying heavy and still beneath the glassy water.

A few more plinks on the gentle current, and then nothing. My tears had stopped falling.

I stood staring into the Sambatyon for several minutes. Then I rolled my throbbing shoulders, reached into the water, and started pulling rocks out onto the shore.

* * *

I applied the weeds to Reuven's forehead, and ground some into his water, but they did nothing. Over the Sabbath, he got weaker and weaker.

The sorcerer had not yet attacked any other Jews, possibly because we spent the day enclosed in our homes or praying in our synagogue. According to the travelers' tales, the sorcerer preferred to touch us one at a time, when we were alone.

So I went out alone, after the late-afternoon prayer, under a sky bruised dark blue and purple. I went to the square where I had stood with my friends, dragging my sack along the street. It was filled to bursting with the stones I'd gathered from the river, and it was heavier than I had anticipated. By the time I let go of it, it felt like my shoulders would never recover.

Not that it would matter if I ended up dead.

I was fairly sure the sorcerer would find me. But the sack had slowed me down more than I had expected, and it was later than I had planned; I didn't feel like taking chances. Also, I had spent much of the day listening to Reuven's bride weep, and I was angry.

"Sorcerer!" I shouted into the twilight, in German, which I spoke better than I did Hebrew. "I challenge you to combat!"

I heard him laughing before I saw him coming. I blinked, and there he was: a tall shadow, like the night come early, that solidified into a cowled, black-clad man.

A *man*. But I could not quite convince myself that was what he was. I had left Reuven curled around his own body, shaking and covered with sweat.

"To *combat*?" he repeated, and laughed again. "Have the Jews of the Rhine learned sorcery, then?"

My hands were shaking, too, as I clenched one fist around a slick river stone. But they had been shaking since the night before. I had grown used to it.

"No," I said, and raised my voice so those watching from their windows could hear. *You need us on this side of the river,* the man had said; and though I didn't agree, I understood what he meant. What it had always meant, to know the Ten Tribes existed somewhere, safe and strong and free. "But the Jews on the other side of the Sambatyon have never forgotten it. They will come when we need them."

I flung the rock, with all my strength, at the sorcerer.

All my strength was not a lot; studying to be a cantor does not do much to build one's arm muscles, and mine still hurt from last night's rowing. But my days of playing children's games were not so far behind me, and I still remembered how to aim. The rock flew straight and true, directly at the face within the black cowl.

The sorcerer flung up one hand, palm out, his too-long fingers stretched wide. The rock stopped in midair and hovered several feet in front of him.

He clenched his gnarled hand into a fist and turned it, slowly. With a grinding sound, the rock shattered into pieces, and then into dust. The dust fell, a swift thick sprinkle, to the ground at the sorcerer's feet.

I had expected as much. Even so, his deliberate ease sent fear shooting in sharp quivers through my feet and up my legs.

"Well?" he said. And when I just stood there, the shaking having taken over my entire body, he threw his cowl back so I could see his smile. "Have you nothing more for me?"

I turned and ran.

I heard him laugh behind me, long and slow. I heard his footsteps hit the cobblestones, unhurried but sure.

I did not turn around until I heard him scream.

Training as a cantor does not build muscles, but it builds a very precise sense of time. I need to know just when the sun appears over the horizon, which is when the recitation of the morning prayer is permitted. I need to know the moment the gates of Heaven close on Yom Kippur, which is when my pleas should reach their greatest intensity. I need to be able to judge precisely when the Sabbath begins.

And when it ends.

At the exact right interval after sunset, when the sky was dark enough to reveal three stars, the Sambatyon burst again into fury. Somewhere, behind my house or in another place, the rapids poured up into the sky and crashed down in violent waves.

And the rocks I had dragged from the Sambatyon whirled into the air in turbulent fury, bursting out of my bag, crashing and tossing and smashing, just as the sorcerer leapt over it. Even the droplets of water clinging to them did their best to form waves, hissing and scattering through the air, around and into the black-clad sorcerer.

He only screamed twice, so I think it was quick – that he was dead before the rocks pounded his body into a pulp.

But to be truthful, I can't say I really care.

* * *

The rocks did not continue whirling in the square for long. Away from the river, I suppose, they lost the source of their movement; or perhaps they knew when they were no longer needed. By the time the moon rose, they were jagged and still, piled on the sorcerer's corpse in a broken heap.

Which was just as well. The fact that Jews are mocked for not fighting does not mean we won't also be punished when we do.

I gathered the rocks and threw them into the Rhine. Whether they made their way back home again, I cannot say. I walked by the river several times a week, for many years, but I never saw the Sambatyon again.

I always went on Friday nights, even though it meant giving up the chance to lead prayers. I stood by the gray sluggish water, and closed my eyes, and listened with all my might.

I never heard anything but the faint echo of our own songs. And when I opened my eyes, the river was always dull and gray.

I did find that broken oar, over a decade later, long after I had paid my neighbor for it. I stumbled across it the day before I left Worms to accept a position as the cantor in a much larger synagogue in a city far away. It was an opportunity I had dreamed of for years, so I didn't understand my sudden reluctance to leave. My parents had both passed away years ago, and I lived in a house on the other side of town with my wife and children. Yitzchak had moved to Speyer. Reuven's widow had remarried, and I rarely saw her. There was nothing to hold me here, to this town on the banks of a river I would never cross again.

I had gained some fame, by then, with my own prayer compositions. Some of my poems had spread up and down the river, been adopted by Jews in towns I'd never stepped foot in. Only I knew that my prayers, much as they were admired, were inadequate; that there was something missing, something I could not get down, no matter how hard I labored with pen and parchment. Something no scribe on this side of the river could force quill and ink to express.

A chance I had lost forever. A song neither I nor my people would ever get back.

When I found the broken oar, I turned it over and over in my hands. It was smooth and slick, whittled down by a steady current. I thought of taking it with me.

I left it there, in the mud.

It has been years since I last saw the Rhine. And as for the Sambatyon…

I keep the jar on my lectern, where I can see it when I lead services. I don't need it; my sense of timing has always been excellent. But every once in a while, before I start the Friday night services, I glance over.

And when the water in the jar stops whirling and frothing, and settles into a smooth, tranquil stillness, that is when I begin to pray.

Whispers on the Wind

Niya M.K. Davis

Have you ever sat on a patch of grass and watched the sun filter through the leaves?
Have you ever lifted your hand to that light and felt it kiss your fingertips?
Have you ever felt moved to walk barefoot on mossy ground?
Have you ever felt the earth tremor under the souls of your feet?
Have you ever heard your name dancing on the wind? When you do, you will know your place…

TANI TOOK UP her favourite secluded spot on campus. A huge oak tree tucked away behind the caretaker's cottage. She slipped out of her pumps, set them aside and burrowed her feet into the rich warm soil.

Tani knew she wasn't the first to tuck herself between the safety of its roots, because whittled into its bark were initials. Some covered by moss, others more recent. There were carvings too, elaborate designs, that told a story she was yet to come to the end of. Though she had never as of yet found its beginning.

It was this she now found herself tracing with her fingertips. Have you ever touched something and felt your hand warm to its surface? Felt your palms tingle?

It is a strange but relatable sensation, one I imagine you are experiencing now as you read this. Suggestion, like a root, is a powerful thing.

Tani wasn't like her classmates. Not in the ways that were noticeable, other than the fact that they were. If you looked close enough, really stopped and looked, allowing your vision to truly see, you would notice the slightest of shimmers beneath her skin, the most subtle of highlights around the coils of her hair and a depth behind her eyes that could draw you in or spit you out.

People rarely did notice, and in all honesty Tani liked it that way. She liked being able to slip between shadows of perception and observe rather than partake.

The first time she had found this space, she now knew, was not accidental. She hadn't understood what "There's always one…" had meant on her first meeting with Wilson the caretaker. That is an entirely other story that there simply isn't time to get into. But now, understanding was all she seemed to have, understanding was in fact not what it was at all and the word in itself was a poor expression for the truth that internally resonated as 'knowing'.

The *S* she currently found herself tracing had winding vines with small buds etched into the bark. They began to pulse, shimmering as their petals unfolded. Her scalp tingled and sharp shocks began to ripple across the surface of her skin as roots sprouted from her palms and the soles of her feet. The coils in her hair twisted to become one with the branches of the tree. Her spine was flush with the strength of its trunk. She could feel the dampness of the earth, the moisture in the air, and taste the exchange of every breath through every pore. As the tree breathed, so too did she, and with every breath came a steady flow of information.

Kelly, Beth and Sindara were the first people Tani searched for. She found them as always huddled in the far corner of the great study library. The first time she performed what she now refers to as 'remote location' she had accidentally slipped into another time. A time when the campus only served to expand the minds of men. How interesting it had been to observe their unfiltered thoughts. Even more interesting to discover that some hundred or so years later not much had changed. They still thought about and chased the exact same things. Still held onto stilted perspectives, limited beliefs and a false sense of entitlement.

Beth was the smartest of the bunch. Something about the way her mind tasted always left Tani wanting more. The first time she had filtered through Beth, curiosity had almost kept her trapped, and Beth had shied away for the rest of the day complaining of a migraine. Guilt had twisted inside Tani because she had felt the strain too, trapped as she had been, within her organic being, seeing through her eyes. Though a moment or two in the sunshine and several cups of alkaline water had sorted Tani out in no time. Beth, who never took any days off, was away for two whole days.

Now, Tani had learned to hover, only slightly touching the edges of the consciousness of others. Now, she was able to focus and pluck the exact thoughts she wanted. Tani no longer studied books, she studied people. Flicking through their minds like the pages of a novel. She was still piecing together the strands of her own story, attempting to stretch herself beyond the confines of the campus. Rooting for her own origins. *Why I am* was an obsession that trickled in if she sat long enough and allowed the tendrils of her mind to unravel, but today she had a test to pass, and pass it she would.

"Kelly, you really should open your book." Beth didn't move her eyes from the page she was currently scanning.

"Beth, you worry too much. We have studied till high heaven." Kelly rolled her eyes and met Sindara's.

Tani felt a huge shift in the energy of their group. What was that?

"Today's paper is worth twenty-five per cent of our final." Beth seethed.

"Well, it's not like you need it, in all honesty. What happened to our fun study balance? Half and half?" Kelly pulled out her phone and began scanning her socials.

Sindara looked up at each of them, opened her mouth, closed it again without speaking and lowered her eyes back to the huge volume before her.

The massive oak trembled as Tani found herself laughing at what Sindara hadn't actually said.

The mighty oak across campus rustled and Sindara tilted her head towards the open window. Almost as if she heard someone call her.

"Sindi, you're being weird again." Kelly curled her lip and rolled her eyes. "Stop staring off into space like that, you know it freaks me out."

Being a loner with the ability to remote-view people's interactions had provided Tani with acute insight into the behaviour of others. Naturally she applied this to her social studies. Wowing her teachers with her amazing insight.

Tani, along with several others, including Beth and Sindara, passed the test. Kelly, as anticipated, did not.

"I don't understand why the stupid test is set up to accept your first answer only. It's not fair. I thought I'd get to review my answers." Kelly whined.

"We went over this, in study group, three weeks ago." Beth's frustration was palpable.

Tani paused close by, pretending to search for something in her bag. They didn't notice, never did. She found it interesting to watch the things she already knew were going to play out unfold. "Well, I had things to do."

This was the moment. Tani wasn't sure if not having her own group of friends was the root of her fascination. She didn't like reflecting on her detachments. In this moment she could quite easily make herself the third wheel, disrupt the dynamics of their little squad.

"Err…Kelly, isn't it?" Tani saw herself saying.

Three sets of eyes swivelled around, taking in her existence as though trying to place her.

"Yeah." Kelly's tone was dismissive, and she turned her eyes back towards Beth with a bitter look on her face.

"Why don't you just tell Beth exactly what it was you have been busy doing? I'm sure she'd be so much more inclined to understand if you simply explained that your lack of commitment to studying is due to your overcommitment and worship of her boyfriend's cock."

Three blank faces morphed into one: Sindara's. It was Tani's turn to be still. Looking into dark eyes that sucked her in and away from the scene that she was playing out in her mind.

"Sindara?" Tani's mind whispered her name like a question.

"Tani! Don't do it." Sindara's mind whispered back.

Under Hill, Under Dale

Deborah L. Davitt

***THIS INTERVIEW** seeks to shed light on the fate of the people of Underhill. To that end, we have interviewed Dr. Rebecca Davies, known throughout the world for having 'awakened the residents of Underhill' when she discovered the exclusion field around Glastonbury in September of last year. She's a controversial figure for many reasons. Some call her the most significant anthropologist since Margaret Mead. Others call her a murderer. Dr. Davies, welcome.*

Thank you, Alan, I'm really happy to have the opportunity to set the record straight.

Could you tell us a little about why you were there in the first place? I mean, what was the scientific value of conducting research at a site most dismiss as mythological and without real historic value?

I could sell you the line that half the shopkeepers in the area would use, about crystals drawing me there, or some such. Truth is, I was in my last year of postgraduate study, needed a break from working on my dissertation, had been to a concert, and was walking off the alcohol when I stumbled right through the…

Dome?

Well, 'dome' isn't quite the right word. You called it an 'exclusion field' earlier, but that's not quite right, either.

You cited Douglas Adams in your paper on Underhill – an academic first.

Yes, well…calling it a 'Someone Else's Problem Field' needed attribution, and he got there first. But that's what's kept Underhill and the rest of the world separate for nearly fifteen hundred years. They looked at us, and saw a world that wasn't their problem, and we looked at them, and saw a hill at most. I happened to blunder through a weak spot. Blind luck, really.

But you were uniquely qualified to make what's being called first contact with them, yes?

I wouldn't call it first contact. They weren't aliens. They weren't elves – again, despite what the shopkeepers in the area might tell you while trying to sell you 'genuine Underhill artifacts'. They're humans. The same as you and me. Just…different. But different for explicable reasons of culture and isolation and everything else.

When you first encountered them, and brought their first ambassadors through, there were problems with communication, weren't there?

Well, yes, obviously. They'd gone under the protection of their separation field in Iron Age Britain. Their religious and military leaders at the time spoke medieval Latin, and the common people spoke *Brythonic.* They'd had fifteen hundreds years of isolation, so there was some lingual drift, but they...well, they didn't speak *English.* The best we could do was get some people in from Wales and some linguists specialized in early Celtic dialects, but they...

Had some difficulties?

They laughed, to be honest. When I asked them why, they said that the Underhill folks' accent sounded like Appalachian dialect might to an American.

They sounded like hillbillies?

In a nutshell, yes.

So, you managed to get them communicating with the outside world. We've all seen the videos that capture their...remarkable feats of magic. Something that science has yet to be able to explain.

They explained to me that while they were in their isolation, magic was really the only thing that they studied, as a village. To keep up what they saw as the protective wards that kept the forest and the wolves from encroaching on them. They got really *good* at it over generations.

And yet, in all that time, they never came up with any of the technical achievements of our civilization. No radio, for example. No airplanes.

Well, that's for a couple of reasons. First of all, every advance we've made as a civilization has come about through the trade of ideas. Leonardo da Vinci could have been the smartest man who ever lived, but if he hadn't lived in Renaissance Italy, where trade routes were bringing new ideas, new books, new notions on nearly a daily basis, would he have been an inventor? These people had no one to trade with. No trade in goods. No trade in ideas. And you don't get the notion to communicate better or faster with someone by, say, radio, if you think there's...no one out there to talk to. Or worth talking to, anyway.

That's a telling point. They felt that they were better than the rest of humanity?

Well, they'd been told that they were. For generations. That they were Merlin's chosen people, dedicated to the return of Arthur, and to maintaining the protective wards around the tomb until such time as Arthur was most needed. When you're told for generations that you're the best humanity has to offer, and there's, again, no one around to suggest that you aren't...why wouldn't you believe it?

They also indicated that they were quite wealthy, didn't they?

Yes. That's something that the early reporters fixed on, I'm afraid. The notion that Underhill was filled with 'fairy gold' got locked in some people's heads, and there were...intrusions by outsiders into Underhill as a result.

They weren't wealthy, then?

They had a material that they called 'adamant'. They called it the source of their magical powers.

Was it?

Probably, but a substance that no one else can use has no trade value. It's kind of like handing someone a lead coin. If your government has decided that your coinage is now going to be lead, and the rest of the international community agrees that a lead pound is the same as a pound sterling, it's all fine, but most of us would look at the lead coin and decide it wouldn't even get us something from a vending machine. Value isn't something that *you* determine. It's something that *other people* determine – and in this case, their *adamant* is largely a curiosity. Something to be studied by researchers in the hopes of replicating their powers, but really, no more intrinsic worth than a pebble.

When local residents intruded into Underhill, this resulted in violence, correct?

Yes. I had been trying to minimize their contact with their neighbors. But having bands of local hooligans roving around looking for gold, well. They already felt that their home was sacred ground. They already felt threatened by the outside world. They drew swords and defended themselves against the invaders. There were…some fatalities.

That wasn't the worst of it, though, was it?

No. It wasn't.

Take your time. Can you explain why the residents of Underhill grew ill?

I had been trying to ensure that when their ambassadors came out into our world, that they wore surgical masks, that sort of thing. When the locals went in there…they didn't care about that. They didn't care about germ theory or virus transmission. But these people had been isolated for over a millennium! They had no immunities. They hadn't had a case of the mumps or measles in hundreds of years – those viruses had burned themselves out over time. They had *no disease*. And one of the complete *idiots* who went in there, chasing after fairy gold…he…

Yes?

He had a cold. I mean, it sounds so stupid. But he had the *sniffles*, and they had no immunities. And he killed them. He killed every last one of them. A people that we could have learned so much from, dead. From the oldest man to the youngest baby, inside of a week. They wouldn't even let us bring in doctors, and why should they? All contact with the outside world had brought them was pain – why allow more?

What happened to the man who brought in the disease?

He recovered. Still selling insurance, as I understand it. No charges brought against him for genocide.

Dr. Davies, please, calm yourself.

I am perfectly calm. Do you know what their magistrate told me, as he lay dying?

No.

That we didn't *deserve* to see Arthur return.

Do you think he's still down there?

We've covered the entire village. We haven't found a crypt, if that's what you're asking. If he's there, they're not here to wake him back up for us.

Thank you for your time, Dr. Davies.

The Loot of Bombasharna

Lord Dunsany

THINGS had grown too hot for Shard, captain of pirates, on all the seas that he knew. The ports of Spain were closed to him; they knew him in San Domingo; men winked in Syracuse when he went by; the two Kings of the Sicilies never smiled within an hour of speaking of him; there were huge rewards for his head in every capital city, with pictures of it for identification – *and all the pictures were unflattering*. Therefore Captain Shard decided that the time had come to tell his men the secret.

Riding off Teneriffe one night, he called them all together. He generously admitted that there were things in the past that might require explanation: the crowns that the Princes of Aragon had sent to their nephews the Kings of the two Americas had certainly never reached their Most Sacred Majesties. Where, men might ask, were the eyes of Captain Stobbud? Who had been burning towns on the Patagonian seaboard? Why should such a ship as theirs choose pearls for cargo? Why so much blood on the decks and so many guns? And where was the *Nancy*, the *Lark*, or the *Margaret Belle*? Such questions as these, he urged, might be asked by the inquisitive, and if counsel for the defence should happen to be a fool, and unacquainted with the ways of the sea, they might become involved in troublesome legal formulae. And Bloody Bill, as they rudely called Mr. Gagg, a member of the crew, looked up at the sky, and said that it was a windy night and looked like hanging. And some of those present thoughtfully stroked their necks while Captain Shard unfolded to them his plan. He said the time was come to quit the *Desperate Lark*, for she was too well known to the navies of four kingdoms, and a fifth was getting to know her, and others had suspicions. (More cutters than even Captain Shard suspected were already looking for her jolly black flag with its neat skull-and-crossbones in yellow.) There was a little archipelago that he knew of on the wrong side of the Sargasso Sea; there were but thirty islands there, bare, ordinary islands, but one of them floated. He had noticed it years ago, and had gone ashore and never told a soul, but had quietly anchored it with the anchor of his ship to the bottom of the sea, which just there was profoundly deep, and had made the thing the secret of his life, determining to marry and settle down there if it ever became impossible to earn his livelihood in the usual way at sea. When first he saw it, it was drifting slowly, with the wind in the tops of the trees; but if the cable had not rusted away, it should be still where he left it, and they would make a rudder and hollow out cabins below, and at night they would hoist sails to the trunks of the trees and sail wherever they liked.

And all the pirates cheered, for they wanted to set their feet on land again somewhere where the hangman would not come and jerk them off it at once; and bold men though they were, it was a strain seeing so many lights coming their way at night. Even then…! But it swerved away again and was lost in the mist.

And Captain Shard said that they would need to get provisions first, and he, for one, intended to marry before he settled down; and so they should have one more fight before they left the ship, and sack the sea-coast city of Bombasharna and take from it provisions for several years, while he himself would marry the Queen of the South. And again the pirates cheered, for often they had seen sea-coast Bombasharna, and had always envied its opulence from the sea.

So they set all sail, and often altered their course, and dodged and fled from strange lights till dawn appeared, and all day long fled southwards. And by evening they saw the silver spires of slender Bombasharna, a city that was the glory of the coast. And in the midst of it, far away though they were, they saw the palace of the Queen of the South; and it was so full of windows all looking toward the sea, and they were so full of light, both from the sunset that was fading upon the water and from candles that maids were lighting one by one, that it looked far off like a pearl, shimmering still in its haliotis shell, still wet from the sea.

So Captain Shard and his pirates saw it, at evening over the water, and thought of rumours that said that Bombasharna was the loveliest city of the coasts of the world, and that its palace was lovelier even than Bombasharna; but for the Queen of the South rumour had no comparison. Then night came down and hid the silver spires, and Shard slipped on through the gathering darkness until by midnight the piratic ship lay under the seaward battlements.

And at the hour when sick men mostly die, and sentries on lonely ramparts stand to arms, exactly half-an-hour before dawn, Shard, with two rowing boats and half his crew, with craftily muffled oars, landed below the battlements. They were through the gateway of the palace itself before the alarm was sounded, and as soon as they heard the alarm Shard's gunners at sea opened upon the town, and before the sleepy soldiery of Bombasharna knew whether the danger was from the land or the sea, Shard had successfully captured the Queen of the South. They would have looted all day that silver sea-coast city, but there appeared with dawn suspicious topsails just along the horizon. Therefore the captain with his Queen went down to the shore at once and hastily re-embarked and sailed away with what loot they had hurridly got, and with fewer men, for they had to fight a good deal to get back to the boat. They cursed all day the interference of those ominous ships which steadily grew nearer. There were six ships at first, and that night they slipped away from all but two; but all the next day those two were still in sight, and each of them had more guns than the *Desperate Lark*. All the next night Shard dodged about the sea, but the two ships separated and one kept him in sight, and the next morning it was alone with Shard on the sea, and his archipelago was just in sight, the secret of his life.

And Shard saw he must fight, and a bad fight it was, and yet it suited Shard's purpose, for he had more merry men when the fight began than he needed for his island. And they got it over before any other ship came up; and Shard put all adverse evidence out of the way, and came that night to the islands near the Sargasso Sea.

Long before it was light the survivors of the crew were peering at the sea, and when dawn came there was the island, no bigger than two ships, straining hard at its anchor, with the wind in the tops of the trees.

And then they landed and dug cabins below and raised the anchor out of the deep sea, and soon they made the island what they called shipshape. But the *Desperate Lark* they sent away empty under full sail to sea, where more nations than Shard suspected were watching for her, and where she was presently captured by an admiral of Spain, who, when he found none of that infamous crew on board to hang by the neck from the yard-arm, grew ill through disappointment.

And Shard on his island offered the Queen of the South the choicest of the old wines of Provence, and for adornment gave her Indian jewels looted from galleons with treasure for Madrid, and spread a table where she dined in the sun, while in some cabin below he bade the least coarse of his mariners sing; yet always she was morose and moody towards him, and often at evening he was heard to say that he wished he knew more about the ways of Queens. So they lived for years, the pirates mostly gambling and drinking below, Captain Shard trying to please the Queen of the South, and she never wholly forgetting Bombasharna. When they needed new provisions they hoisted sails on the trees, and as long as no ship came in sight they scudded before the wind, with the water rippling over the beach of the island; but as soon as they sighted a ship the sails came down, and they became an ordinary uncharted rock.

They mostly moved by night; sometimes they hovered off sea-coast towns as of old, sometimes they boldly entered river-mouths, and even attached themselves for a while to the mainland, whence they would plunder the neighbourhood and escape again to sea. And if a ship was wrecked on their island of a night they said it was all to the good. They grew very crafty in seamanship, and cunning in what they did, for they knew that any news of the *Desperate Lark's* old crew would bring hangmen from the interior running down to every port.

And no one is known to have found them out or to have annexed their island; but a rumour arose and passed from port to port and every place where sailors meet together, and even survives to this day, of a dangerous uncharted rock anywhere between Plymouth and the Horn, which would suddenly rise in the safest track of ships, and upon which vessels were supposed to have been wrecked, leaving, strangely enough, no evidence of their doom. There was a little speculation about it at first, till it was silenced by the chance remark of a man old with wandering: "It is one of the mysteries that haunt the sea."

And almost Captain Shard and the Queen of the South lived happily ever after, though still at evening those on watch in the trees would see their captain sit with a puzzled air or hear him mutter now and again in a discontented way: "I wish I knew more about the ways of Queens."

Heart of Atlantan

Nictzin Dyalhis

THERE ARE SINS beyond the urge of the appetites, beyond the desires of the senses. Sins besides which murder is but an idle pastime, and all lesser evils mankind in the frenzy of bestial passions indulge in at expense of their fellows, pale into the category of mere mistakes.

For Man is a creature possessing two natures, a material one which can only transgress the laws of the material plane, and a spiritual one by which he may soar to heights undreamed, or descend to depths unfathomed.

For the sins, follies and mistakes of earth, there is punishment provided, or atonement to be made. But for the sins spiritual there is retribution, grim, lasting, inexorable, and none dare say if it will ever end.

And who sins thus, and is punished, had best welcome his fate, and hope to outwear it with the slow passage of the years, nor seek to escape it, for though he may seem to do so, having found, perchance, the method, yet always remains the Law that in effect says: "As ye sow, so shall ye likewise reap!"

And sin they never so greatly, yet will that awful Law, with inexorable exactitude, requite them in just and perfect measure, proportionate to the harm they have done –

As It has dealt with me!

* * *

Leonard Carman and I sat in my study, smoking and talking as old friends will after long separation. Our conversation ran along the lines of the ancient civilizations, now veiled in the murk of impenetrable mystery.

"And the veil can never be lifted," I mourned. "Nor will these mysteries ever be solved. There are no more Rosetta stones inscribed in unknown tongue together with one familiar to modern scholars. And some of the great lost races and their works passed so long ago that absolutely no traces, however slight, remain to show that ever they lived and moved beneath the sun and moon and stars. Unless," I added, as an afterthought, "science makes greater progress with some form of radio than is now possible."

"I'm not so sure about that," Carman interrupted. "It's barely possible that some fragmentary bits of knowledge *can* be recovered. Perhaps not to the satisfaction of exact science, but still of sufficient interest to satisfy your prying curiosity as well as my perfectly normal interest."

"Wherein do the two differ," I snapped.

"Your curiosity concerns itself with how they lived, what they wore, and the progress they made along the lines of material achievement," he replied, smiling slightly at getting a rise out of me; which, by the way, I had never succeeded in doing with him; for a more equable temper than he possessed, I had never encountered, while mine is short-lived at best, and, also, highly explosive.

"While my normal interest is chiefly concerned with their intellectual attainments, the extent of their knowledge regarding the finer forces of nature and their possible uses," he elucidated.

"Just what are you driving at, Leonard?" I demanded, his words arousing within me a rapidly awakening interest.

"Simply that I believe they progressed along quite other lines than we of this modern age, thus giving rise to the tales of an 'Ancient Wisdom', now lost. And I likewise think that under certain circumstances, it may be recovered, if not wholly, at least in part."

"And the method?" I queried. I was not at all skeptical now. He'd fully convinced me, and I felt, even before he replied that he already had a working basis with which to make an attempt to solve the otherwise unsolvable.

"I can have the method here any evening you may select," he assured me gravely.

"Right now, if that is possible," I stated, and he agreed. He stepped to the phone and called a number, and a moment later – "Otilie?" Apparently the answer was satisfactory, for he asked: "Can you come to where I am, this evening?" Again the response was as he desired, for he gave minute directions for reaching my place. I was curious about this 'Otilie', and showed it, and he increased my mystification by smiling enigmatically, and saying, "Wait."

In about fifteen minutes a taxi stopped before the house. Carman went to the door to admit the strangest-looking being I've ever seen. As I had surmised from the name, 'Otilie' was a woman, but such a woman!

She was a hunchback; wry-necked, with a pronounced squint in her left eye. Her nose had been mashed flat at some time, her mouth hung slackly open, revealing gnarled yellow fangs, and she walked with a decided limp. Add to all this a muddy brown skin and you have the picture. All in all, she was the most unprepossessing figure imaginable – until I noticed her hands. They were beautifully kept, with long tapering fingers, and seemed those of an artist or a musician.

Later, I learned that Otilie was a Finn, and that she was wholly illiterate. But when one looked at those hands and listened to her voice, a clear, bell-like contralto, one forgot all else about Otilie in sheer, downright fascination.

"Get me a stack of paper and a few pencils," Carman demanded. Rapidly he cleared the top of my library table, placed a chair for Otilie, and escorted her to her seat as if she had been an empress.

"Under normal conditions," he explained rapidly, "Otilie cannot read or write. But under other conditions she does some surprising things with automatic writing."

I felt disappointed, let down. So his 'method' was merely automatic writing! I think he saw my feeling reflected in my face, for he smiled tolerantly and told me very gravely:

"Henri, you've known me for a long time, and you know that I do not lie to my friends. When I state that Otilie is phenomenal, and has proven it time and again, to my entire satisfaction, I think that you may well believe it."

"Otilie," and he turned to the queer-looking woman, "do you know anything about Atlantis, or the dead and gone civilizations of antiquity?"

"No," she said. "Otilie knows nothing of those. What do you want to find out? I'll try and see what we can get."

She picked up a pencil, inspecting it critically, laid it flat in her hand, and commenced making long, slow, magnetic passes, stroking the pencil with the fingertips of her right hand. And as she stroked, the pencil, her face, which, despite her grotesquerie, wore an habitual expression of pain and sullen discontent, assumed gradually an abstracted expression, and her usual harsh breathing grew calm and even. The change was so amazing I was dumbfounded. She appeared remote, detached, as if between herself and the ordinary world were measureless gulfs of time, space, and condition.

She ceased stroking the pencil, poised it on a sheet of paper, and nodded slightly at Carman. For a minute or so the pencil moved in aimless figure eights, and Carman looked at me with deepest significance.

Suddenly the pencil started off, apparently by its own volition. Watching closely, I am prepared to state that Otilie's hand followed the pencil, rather than the pencil following her hand.

"Atlantan," it wrote, and paused, again describing figure eights. Yet Carman had queried concerning 'Atlantis'. A second later it wrote "Tekala, priestess of Atlantan," Then, "Kalkan the Golden."

"And who was Tekala?" queried Carman softly.

Otilie's face grew rapt, her eyes lit with an inward fire, her entire figure and features were transformed.

"H-m," grunted Carman. "This is a new one. Never saw Otilie like this before. Wonder what's coming."

We were not long in finding out!

"Who is Tekala?" The deep, mellow tones of Otilie's voice became wistful, dreamy, filled with a strange reverent awe. "She is lovely, beautiful, with all the beauty I never had and can never have! But she says I am to let her speak for herself."

Silence reigned supreme in that quiet study of mine, but Carman and I felt the presence of a fourth personality, one of an alien nature, with a will so terrific in its impact that ours were less than naught beside it.

Added to that was a queer impression of incredible antiquity, plus age-long sorrow, patience beyond human concept, and longing unendurable.

Abruptly the lights dimmed, grew dully red, blinked and went out. Otilie gulped, audibly, Carman whistled softly, and I swore feelingly. Then I noted a faint glow of light close by Otilie and wondered vaguely if she were becoming phosphorescent.

But the glow increased, became a faint aura gradually growing in brilliance to a nimbus whose center was a radiantly, exquisitely beauteous being, formed of tenuous light. It was, at moments, hard to distinguish from its nimbus, while at other moments it became clear and distinct, revealing itself as a form unmistakably feminine in contour, yet robed and shrouded in particles of light, so that its actual apparel was largely a matter of conjecture. Yet there was majesty expressed in that luminous figure, a stateliness shown in the poise of the head, and an air of conscious power compelling respect.

"This," I thought, "is no materialization flummery common to séances, but a genuine apparition – progressed to a stage far in advance of ordinary humanity."

It took me but a second to think thus far, and it took less than that long for our shining visitant to grasp my thought, read it, and appreciate it at its true evaluation. She stared at me for a long minute, then smiled slightly – and oh, the pathos of that smile! It would have wrung the heart of a stone image! It brought a lump to my throat, and caused my eyes to sting and blur with an unaccustomed mist.

And again the radiant vision stared unbelievingly, but then, to my utter surprise, it – or *she*, rather – moved swiftly till the outer edge of her aura was well within a foot of my body, and there she stood, obviously *reading* me as a scientist might study some strange and unusual form of life.

Meantime I gazed up into her face, watching it change from curiosity to understanding, and from that to genuine hope and satisfaction. And I know that I would have given anything and everything I owned could I but lift from her the burden of sorrow, or whatever it was which gave even her smile such wistful pathos.

But apparently our visitor was not as yet completely satisfied, for she moved over beside Carman, her nimbus well nigh touching him. She started, as if surprised, but her expression of doubt lightened somewhat, as does that of one who recognizes an old friend.

One look she cast at Otilie, and that look bespoke absolute pity for the poor ugly travesty, who was watching her with visible adoration writ large in her strange eyes, and again our visitor nodded, as to a friend well liked.

Once more she nodded, vehemently this time, and moved with the speed of light, standing by Otilie's left side. She stretched out her shapely right arm, laying her hand caressingly on Otilie's shoulder. I saw Otilie shudder with ecstasy at the touch, and then her hand began following the pencil, but with a speed I'm positive the poor creature could not have achieved unaided.

But that pencil was bewitched; it was writing in letters and words of liquid golden light! And its first question showed plainly the interest our visitor took in all three of us:

"How are you named, you man of a younger race, who are of so deep intuition that you can read my lost condition in my features; and who holds so great sympathy and pity that you would alleviate my lot, if you could?

"And who are you, man with the calm gray eyes, you to whom emotions are strangers, being replaced by curiosity instead, ever seeking to probe into the secrets of antiquity and the lost lore of the elder races?

"And who are you, little Sister whom I envy, for you have the most precious gift in all the world – freedom, while my body and mind are held helpless prisoners in a dreary prison, not even on the bosom of the kindly earth, but far down in the dim gloom of the bed of old ocean?"

And at that point Carman interrupted. "Lady," he asked in all seriousness, and his very tone bespoke his absolute belief in what she had caused to appear on the paper, "lady, you speak of yourself as being a prisoner, yet you have appeared *here*! And if indeed you indited that message through the hand of Otilie, I ask you to explain how you know our language, if you are of such great antiquity as your appearance implies."

"I am an Atlan," flashed the response on the paper beneath Otilie's hand, "and this is but my projected spirit you do now behold. As to my understanding of your language – bethink you: If I be indeed of so great antiquity as I have claimed, and if I wield sufficient powers to be enabled to appear to you here, then in the course of all the long ages, I have had sufficient time in which to learn it."

Carman nodded, fully satisfied, gave our names: Henri d'Armond, Leonard Carman, and plain Otilie. Then he coolly voiced the same question I was about to ask:

"May we be told—"

"Who I am, and why I thus appear before you? For long I have sought the society of wise men of this day and age who could understand and believe, and perchance, help me to escape an eon-old doom. And it seems that at last I have found my goal – or have I, for I dare not hope too greatly.

"But let me tell you three my tale, which will fully clear up the mystery of the Lost Land – and afterward – who knows? At the least, it may entertain you, and may meet with credence, and perchance I shall feel less lonely thereafter in my prison cell—"

And then, as Carman nodded eagerly, the pencil fairly flew across the pages, and Carman read the words aloud, while Otilie and I hung spellbound on every word as the strangest tale ever told unfolded itself:

* * *

I am Tekala. I am that woman who with a single motion of her hand destroyed a continent and its inhabitants! Truly, a terrible tale to tell in such few words; therefore I will amplify.

It was late in the day, and the sun was slowly sinking to his rest in the calm waters of the great western sea. In the streets of Kalkan the Golden, sacred city of the Sun God, the lights were commencing to gleam; and overhead the silver stars were adorning the purple skies with gorgeous splendor.

I stood beside old Ixtlil the high-priest on the flat top of the highest tower of the great sun temple. The unearthly beauty of the scene held us both, old *paba* [father; priest] and young priestess in breathless enthrallment for a moment. It was a spell I dreaded to break, yet something within me drove me to voice the question which had vexed me for over a year.

"Tell me, O *paba*," I said softly, "who am I, and who my parents, for I never knew them. All I remember is the temple, and naught else know I, and my sister-priestess Malixi taunts me when, daily, we prepare the flowers for the altar. Tell me, O *paba*, and relieve my mind."

Very gravely the old *paba* surveyed me, and I saw in his keen old eyes a twinkle of tolerance for my youth and natural feminine curiosity, which not even the temple discipline could entirely eradicate.

"Tekala, little Daughter of Heaven," he murmured, laying his gentle hand on my bowed head, "it were better that you know not, for it is an evil story; but it is your right to know. Also, there is another reason why you should not, but of that, later. So—

"You are the first-born of wicked King Granat and his no less evil consort, Queen Ayara! But they wanted a man-child, and being what they are, when you disappointed them, you were placed in a boat on a dark, stormy night, and sent adrift, the tide running strongly out at the time. That was some sixteen years gone.

"A fisher-craft picked you up in the dawn, far out of sight of land. The captain, an adherent of the Old Gods, brought you to me, deeming you more than mortal, so beautiful a babe you were, and your robe so richly embroidered.

"The symbol embroidered on that garb of yours told me your identity. So I went straight to the royal palace carrying you in my own arms, whence not king, queen, or the most brutish guardsman dared remove you lest the wrath of the Sun God punish such sacrilege.

"Full into their sneering royal faces I hurled my denunciation of them and their evil ways, prophesying that in a day to come the babe they'd rejected would repay them, unless they accepted the will of the Lords of Life, and reared you as parents should.

"They laughed in my face, bidding me rear the brat, myself, if I wanted her. So, seeing that through them spoke the voice of Destiny – which is above all gods, even the sun and moon – I bowed to them and left their palace. Two sons have come to them since that time, and young demons they are! And I say that when Granat and Ayara pass to their appointed places – which are *not* in the sun-mansions – those two princes will complete the work begun by their parents, and this race of Atlan will be wiped forever from the face of the earth, so thoroughly that naught remains but a tradition!"

The old *paba* lapsed into silence. I felt his eyes probing me, reading my soul. A strange look came on his beautiful old face and he whispered:

"Our Lord the Sun forfend! Let it not be by *her* hand...not hers...not hers!" So low his tone I knew the words were not for my hearing...

From the temple below us arose confused shoutings, thunderous crashes, and a chorus of ear-piercing screams and shrieks from the quarter where dwelt the priestesses. I nearly swooned! But old Ixtlil was a father indeed in that moment. He grasped my shoulder and shook me back to common sense.

"It has come," he said quietly. "The blow falls sooner than I expected, but 'tis ever thus! Now, Tekala, hasten after me, for this temple is no longer a safe place for you."

Down a narrow winding stair he led, and I followed, until I wondered if we would never cease descending. Finally we came into a great circular room, and across this he led into a small crypt.

"This is no time for false modesty," he said sternly. "Take off all your robes immediately."

Dazedly I obeyed. In the center of the little room was a big, flat disk of copper let into the floor, and to that Ixtlil motioned me, and I stepped on it. What he did I know not, but from all directions at once came peculiarly tinted light-rays of purplish hue, beating on my skin like a shower of needles. After a time Ixtlil did something which caused the purple rays to give place to a brilliant flood of light like that of the sun on a clear day.

He pointed to a wide, tall silver mirror against one wall, and I saw myself, and marveled at the magic which had changed the pale gold of my flesh to a brown tint so dark that I looked like any savage maid of the outlands. Even my light brown hair had become blue-black.

Truly the tale of Ixtlil's magic had not stated the half! Men said that he was past-master and sole custodian of all the magic lore and ancient wisdom brought from the stars by the Shining Ones, that he knew the secret of Life. In short, he was believed to be all-wise and all-powerful, but that could not have been true, or – but perhaps it *was* true, and in his mysterious way he worked through my hand, despite his aversion to using me, whom he loved, as an instrument.

He brought a robe fashioned from a beautiful panther-skin, a broad belt of silver bosses and links, a bow and a quiver of arrows, a long-bladed bronze knife, and bade me dress and equip myself. Then he handed me a leathern pouch attached to a beaded baldric so that it hung from my right shoulder to my left hip.

"In this pouch," he stated, "are a full year's supply of tiny food tablets. One will sustain you for an entire day. Also, there is a bottle of jade containing a wine so potent that one drop allays a day's thirst even in the hottest desert. Ten drops on the tongue of a dying man can renew his lease of life for a year, unless his wounds are hopeless. A small box of basanite contains a salve that heals wounds, sores, and bites of insects and reptiles, be they ever so poisonous. This ring" – and he slid an armlet of some dull, white metal lighter than chalk, above my elbow – "will become icy-cold whenever an enemy is nigh, but it will glow, warm and comforting, at the proximity of safety.

"Long ago I foresaw this catastrophe, and made all in readiness against the day of your need. Come now!" He pressed a stud against one wall and a section opened.

"Through that," he commanded. "Follow the passage. It is a long tunnel, and will take all day to traverse. Here is a bundle of torches to light your way. The passage slopes upward, finally, and emerges in the face of a cliff at the edge of the wild lands of Korgan. Wait till the stars proclaim midnight, then retire ten paces inside, sit on the floor, and look out of the opening. A star will apparently hang barely under the arch of the exit. Mark that star well.

"Stay in the tunnel until well after dawn, then survey carefully your surroundings ere you emerge, lest enemies see you, but if all seems clear, strike out across the desert holding to the direction whence the star arose. Keep that as your objective until the hand of Destiny leads, instead. And now, Tekala, princess as well as priestess of Atlantan, go! As for me, I must hasten back to the Great Shrine—"

"Let me return with you," I sobbed. "Send me not from you, O my spiritual father! I can handle bow and knife as well as any young man in Atlantan, thanks to the training we priestesses receive! Surely if danger threatens the Great Shrine of our Lord the Sun, my place is there! Why must *I* be thrust forth into the wild lands of Korgan, the Desert of Demons, while my sisters are privileged to defend the temple? Let me return, I say, and if need be, die—"

"Nay!" his voice was stern, implacable. "That, above all else, you cannot, must not do! In the wild lands, your hands may keep your head, but back in the temple, certain death is your lot! Child, in your veins is the old royal blood of the *Itans*, the ancient kings who founded Atlantan and the Atlan race! Granat and Ayara turned from the pure worship of Sun God and Moon Goddess and the simple offerings of fruits and flowers, to the dark mysteries of Mictla, god of Evil and lord of Darkness! And when King and Queen betook themselves to evil ways, courtiers and populace followed the prevailing fashion.

"And now, Mitcla's wicked priest, Tizoq, has prevailed upon our rulers to allow him and his depraved followers to stamp out the worship of the ancient gods of our race! The old order is doomed, yet in time the destroyers may go too far, and arouse the wrath of the Eternal Ones, and then – remains Tekala, of the Blood-Royal, Queen of Atlantan and all her colonies! And in her hands will lie the power to bring a recalcitrant people back to the pure gods of the Elder Days, and a new and better era will dawn for our race. But for now – again I say: *Go!*"

I sank to my knees, and thence to the floor, prone at his feet, sobbing bitterly. He raised me, blessing me in solemn, holy words, laying his venerable hands on my head; kissed me on my brow, making the signs and symbols of Sun and Moon on my breast with his forefinger, and – abruptly turned and left! Weeping with despair, I turned and entered the tunnel, going straight away from all the life I'd known and loved.

Five days alone in the wild lands of Korgan!

I think most maids would have gone mad in that time, had they been bred as I, in the peace and seclusion of a temple. But now I know what then I did not comprehend – that when old Ixtlil placed his hands on my head and blessed me, he was transmitting a portion of his own spiritual strength and a generous share of his own magic powers to me – and I sorely needed them!

I'd got my direction from the star, and had carefully calculated so that I might hold the same course by night or day. And the white armlet helped in its mysterious way, for whenever I deviated, be it ever so slightly from the direct course, a chill ran up my arm, changing to a warm glow as soon as I rectified my course.

For the first two days I'd foolishly traveled during the hot, daylight hours, but then realized it was overtaxing my body. Wherefore, I rested all the third day in a little patch of shade cast by a clump of stunted bushes, and thereafter I traveled by night.

Idling there as I rested, my mind went back to the temple, and then I began to realize somewhat of Ixtlil's blessing. Gradually I commenced to see clearly. I saw the Ancient Shrine, and the great symbol of our Lord the Sun lying on the floor, battered, bent, its burnished golden surface defiled with dirt and dried blood. The entire place was a wreck. Dead bodies lay in all directions. A priestess I'd known and loved as an elder sister lay naked, slashed and torn. Priests who had died – surely the followers of Tizoq had done their work well in honor of their devil-god.

My soul went sick within me. But I prayed long and earnestly to Sun God and Moon Goddess for the dead whom I'd known since earliest childhood – that they might dwell in his golden mansions by day, and rest in her silver chambers by night, and presently I felt better. But then a dreadful thought arose in my mind, and would not down: What of Ixtlil?

The heat haze of the desert grew dark as I looked. Surely it was not yet night? Then I knew that I was gazing into a crypt beneath Mictla's temple. Dim, gigantic figures, half human, half owl, wholly demon, were sculptured on the walls. Their great round eyes, made of some luminous yellow stone, gave off enough light to see the venerable *paba* with heavy bronze fetters about wrists and ankles, and around his waist a heavy chain.

A prisoner! That kindly old man! And then, more clearly, I saw his face. A prisoner? Nay! A servant of the high gods whom not fetters nor chains could bind. He did but wait whatever was destined, serenely assured that, come what might, at the last he would enter into his reward.

I like, even now, to think that across those drear distances of demon-infested desert he sensed me, knew that I was near him in spirit, for his lips moved, and I am sure that his words were: "Tekala, little sister, you do not forget."

While resting next day a tiny breeze came up, and as I enjoyed its caress – suddenly I heard it! And held my breath in sudden fright, although the armlet gave off no warning chill. It was a strange, wild, sobbing moan rising to a dolorous wail like a lost soul in search of the unattainable. Toward evening the keening died out, but I was shaken by fears and knew not whether to go onward or—

The armlet went cold! I rose to my knees and peered about, but naught could I descry. So I decided it was an intimation I'd best leave that place. Promptly I started, and well for me that I did! Just before darkness fell I glanced back, I knew not why, save that the armlet had not warmed up since its warning chill. I had just topped a rise and stood on the crest of the long sloping ridge of sand, and I could still see the place where I'd spent the long, hot day.

I saw far more than I expected! A dozen figures moved about the spot where I'd lain and slept. Although I could not hear their voices I knew they had correctly interpreted the signs I'd left. And when a bit later they grouped a moment and then started on my trail, I knew my peril. My sole hope lay in the possibility that they could not follow in the night. Which would give me a good ten hours advantage. But I merely deceived myself when I entertained that idea. The ridge whereon I stood ran in a long slant down into a great basin which, in some far-distant era, must have been the bed of some inland sea.

Reaching the floor of the huge bowl I lay flat and stared up at the crest of the ridge standing sharply against the stars. And over the comb of the ridge poured my pursuers. Down there I was invisible to them, but once they reached the floor of the basin, my chances were poor indeed of escaping their keen eyes. I betook myself to precipitate flight, running like a scared cat for at least two hours ere I constrained my racing feet to a slower gait.

Even so, I think they would have overtaken me ere dawn, save that once again that eerie ululation came throbbing and wailing through the night. It bore a distinctly forbidding, angry, menacing tone – yet the armlet on my arm grew warm again, which cheered me immensely.

Deciding that the source of the sound – whatever it might be – was friendly to me, and quite otherwise to my pursuers, I hastened toward it as directly as possible. But it was well after midnight when I first saw, looming dimly against the stars, a tall, indistinct bulk, yet oddly suggestive of the human form. But a human form – so enormous? Never was a statue, even of a god, that big, but ere another hour had passed, I knew it surely for a robed and seated image, female in shape.

Was it a goddess of some forgotten race, pre-human perhaps? Or was it an effigy of some demon holding suzerainty over this desolate land? Speculation availing me nothing, as usual, I pressed forward as if it were a well-known and welcome goal – a sanctuary against those savages who sought to capture me, for what purpose I could surmise only too well!

Dawn revealed that my pursuers were closer than I liked. To my relief I saw that none carried bows, although each carried a long spear and several throwing-knives. But their faces and their bodies! The apes in the royal gardens of Kalkan the Golden were actual beauties by comparison, both in features and figures; the chief difference being that the savages were hairless as to their bodies and of an ashen-gray hue. They were without exception hunchbacked, their necks so short they seemed sunken into the wide shoulders; heavy, squat bodies with long powerfully muscled arms, and short, thick legs with great splay feet.

Finally they drew within bowshot, and I felt that I was done for. Yet still the armlet remained warm, unless I looked back, but in that case it instantly changed. Spread out, crescent-wise, the humped men raced forward, running two bow-lengths to my one. Two I slew with a couple of hard-driven shafts from my bow – and then the horns of the crescent passed me and began closing in. But my armlet stayed warm, and the great figure, which I now could see plainly was hewn from one enormous rough boulder, was but a short distance away. And I felt if I could gain its feet, I'd be safe. But I knew, too, that never could I make it. At the apex of desperation, I halted, arrow nocked, bow half raised, fairly aflame with fury. The humped men hesitated, one or another shifting a foot gradually, sneaking a little nearer – it became evident I was to be taken alive. Then I cursed them. By Sun and Moon, by earth and air and fire. I cursed them by day and by night, sleeping or waking. By famine and pestilence, flood and tempest, by thunder and lightning and wind –

And as that last word fell from my lips a moaning screeching howl ensued! The sands of the desert came alive, rising in dense, dun-hued clouds that swept forward, roaring at terrific velocity. And in the space of a single breath – my pursuers were not! Only a low, crescent-shaped ridge showed where they had stood. Yet not one particle of grit from that hard-driving sandstorm had touched me!

I was all alone, staring dazedly at my work – aye, my work! Over me stole the assurance that old Ixtlil had indeed endowed me with more of his magic power than I was as yet capable of comprehending.

With neither let nor hindrance I walked, albeit somewhat shakily, the remaining distance to the feet of the huge figure of the Old Stone Woman who brooded ever, staring out across the desert, waiting for the world to attain to its supreme wickedness.

That immense figure was, in reality, a vast rock-hewn temple, shaped to the symbolic semblance it bore by the hands of a people so long passed into oblivion that no legend of them remained. The main entrance was between the two feet. The temple proper was wholly under the skirt of the robe and below the waistline. From there up it rose into the air as a high tower, hollow, within which ran a winding stair leading to a chamber occupying the entire head.

It was when I gained that lofty chamber that I learned the source of the mysterious noises; for the winds that blew free up there, even when the desert below lay gasping for lack of a current of moving air – the winds, I repeat, entering through the nostrils and eyeholes and escaping through the parted lips, caused the sounds which had at first terrified me, and after, guided me.

Times there were, as I learned ere all was done, when those winds uttered chants of warning, of prophecy, and once, a soul-shaking shout of triumph. Also, nightly, voices sighed and whispered, and I, listening, learned from them the secrets of the olden days – of magic, of gods and demons, and of the dreams of the ancient dead.

There was no one with whom to associate.

So far as I could ascertain by short trips of exploration in the near vicinity, there never had been a city or village built around the temple. And surely there should have been some traces remaining, for whoever they were who had used that temple, they were giants, judging by the heights of the lifts of the stairs. I was of average height, but while I could with ease tread the steps of the great Sun-temple in Kalkan, there in the old Stone Woman temple I was obliged to raise my foot as if treading two steps at a time!

One room I found in that temple wherein were thin slabs of stone, graven with writings in small characters, bearing no slightest resemblance to our heavy, ornate Atlantan hieroglyphs; yet here again the spiritual gifts of Ixtlil became manifest, for I found that after poring over a slab the better part of a day I was able to read much of it. And after a few more days of study, I read the writings quite freely, much wisdom thus being revealed!

Nearly a year had come and gone since Ixtlil sent me forth through the underground passage from Kalkan the Golden to the wild lands of Korgan. Again and again had I sought out old Ixtlil, throwing myself into that state wherein the sight of the soul views clearly the events taking place at a distance. And always I found him still the captive of Tizoq, still chained in the crypt below the foul temple of Mictla. With practice I'd grown able to comprehend the purport and meanings of conversations without necessity of catching the spoken words. It appeared that Tizoq ever sought to gain by coaxing and threats, some mighty secret from Ixtlil, and ever Ixtlil withstood the desire of Tizoq.

Time and again I contacted my mind with the mind of Ixtlil, beseeching him to unleash his fullest powers and compel Tizoq to release him, that he might fly into the desert and come to where I dwelt in safety and seclusion; but ever Ixtlil made the same reply: "Nay, Tekala, little sister; It may not be!"

Nor would he ever vouchsafe any explanation, but I knew I was beholding a servitor of that mightiest power in the universe, that power which Ixtlil had once spoken of as 'Destiny', and that the eon-old struggle between Good and Evil was in full swing in that darksome crypt. And I bowed my head and wept, for my heart misgave me. I knew that Tizoq was totally mad with hatred and jealousy, for never had he possessed powers such as Ixtlil wielded. That I could sense as clearly as if I were in the damnable temple of Mictla, in the city of Kalkan the Golden, where stood the flat-topped altar beneath the looming effigy of the hybrid devil-god, half man, half owl.

Now with a disembodied consciousness, I could see that a vast concourse of people filled the fane of Evil to overflowing, keeping the temple guards busy maintaining an open aisle all the way from the narrow entrance to the foot of the three steps leading to the broad dais whereon stood the altar itself.

It was a most important ceremonial impending, for I saw my parents, King Granat and Queen Ayara, and with them my two bad brothers, Dokar and Quamac. Then came the blare of trumpets and roll of drums announcing a processional. Tizoq, leading, was followed by his devilish acolytes, in the midst of whom walked Ixtlil.

Despite his bonds he walked with head held high on his finely molded lips a calm smile, in his brilliant eyes a light of pity – not for himself, but for all the world – and surely no great Emperor ever strode to his throne with truer majesty than walked the aged *paba* toward the altar of his adored Sun God's demon enemy, Mictla.

Even the acolytes of the God of Evil betrayed by their attitudes – which sentiment seemed general – that they held this gentle old man in actual dread. For all that he was fettered and surrounded by his enemies who hated and feared him, yet the spell of his spirit dominated them, and they knew it, fearing that at any moment he might loose upon them the unguessable, even as they would have done had conditions been reversed.

The drums and horns increased their din as Ixtlil mounted the three steps, but then the clamor ceased. The great effigy of Mictla appeared to assume life and motion. Its wings unfurled, were outstretched as a canopy over the altar, and from the round, cruel, yellow-gleaming eyes a flood of light poured down, illuminating the scene as plainly as daylight. From the ugly mouth beneath the curved beak came thrice repeated the chilling, evil owl notes.

The *paba* was seized violently, and his naked form stretched on his back atop of Mictla's altar, where he lay staring up into the cruel eyes of the demon.

What humiliation had Tizoq in his malicious mind as he approached the recumbent Ixtlil? The owl-priest raised a hand. Again came three owl-notes from the demon-figure. Five acolytes seized the venerable *paba* – one at each wrist and ankle, and one with both hands clutched in his silvery-white hair. Tizoq raised his right arm on high; in his fist shone a knife whose blade was of ragged-edged volcanic glass. Tizoq's arm swooped down – I strove to shut my eyes by pressing both hands over them. And saw just as clearly! For a moment Tizoq bent above his victim, then turned facing the worshippers, crying:

"Thus deals the god Mictla with the high-priest of his arch-enemy, the Sun God!"

Tizoq held up to view a dripping human heart!

"Behold, ye people! Bow ye before the power of Mictla! Lo, the heart of the first human sacrifice to the new god of Atlantan!"

He turned and flung the pitiful, quivering, sacred thing straight into the open beak of the devil-god.

I know not the words adequate to make plain to other understandings the awful anguish rending my very soul. Ixtlil, the holy one of Atlantan to die thus! My brain, stunned though it was by that sight of horror, was a volcano of hate and wrath, surcharged with desire for such vengeance as would make the devils in Mictlan cower in terror and seek to hide beneath the white-hot rocks of the great Sulphur Sea!

As moves a corpse animated by a life not its own, I rose from my place and started down the winding stair from my chamber in the head of the Old Stone Woman. On the landing level with the huge swell of her breasts, I stood vaguely wondering why I had halted.

Then a small spot of vivid crimson, like a drop of rich blood a-sparkle in the sunshine caught my eye and held my vacant gaze. Hesitant, as one knowing not what she does, I stretched forth a finger and touched that ensanguined spot – and from above, there pealed a thunderous shout of triumph from the lips of the Old Stone Woman. Dully I wondered why. Then a door, hitherto invisible, swung open, revealing a chamber in the left breast. I entered. Eyes still a-stare, I stood striving to understand. Suspended in the air, level with my face, yet upheld by nothing visible, hung a blood-red heart of enormous size which pulsated and beat like any organism, and yet was formed of a single crimson gem!

Directly beneath the beating heart stood a low stone table on which lay a tablet of polished black onyx, and atop of this a bronze mallet. I could have held back from that table as easily as I could have held back from breathing! And as I bent above the onyx tablet, in letters of living flame which faded as soon as noted, there formed the words:

"Tekala! In the day when your heart becomes harder than mine, lift this mallet, and if you dare, smite! Yet remember – vengeance is of the Gods!"

Vengeance…? Smite…!

The flame within my brain roared like the surges of a volcano's angry, molten sea!

Crash!

The pulsating heart of Atlantan burst into a scintillant shower of glittering red slivers at the impact of the mallet in my hand. And ere the tinkle of tiny falling fragments had ceased –

Roar upon roar of thunder, continuous, flash following upon flash of lightning, until the world was all a-glare with purple-white fire. The Old Stone Woman, ponderous as she was, swayed and lurched like a ship on a stormy sea as earthquake shocks added their destructive forces to the universal cataclysm! And *I?* I lay down on the cupped floor within that harsh stone breast, and slept! Aye, like a wearied babe cradled in its mother's comforting bosom! Nor did a single dream disturb me; and as for the tempest's turmoil, and the earthquakes, their din was but a lullaby wooing my sick spirit to deeper, most restful slumber.

How long that slumber lasted I never knew. Time had ceased when I awoke. Above, the skies were black as never midnight had been, and the very foundations of earth were trembling as each shock came with terrific violence.

My mind, inevitably, went out to Kalkan the Golden. Aye, Mictla's foul temple still stood, or at least, a part of it. The great fane was but a heap of tumbled ruins, yet the effigy of the Owl-Man Devil-God was unharmed. And on the ruined dais about the altar, some standing and some crouched, were assembled Tizoq, Granat, Ayara, Dokar, Quamac, and a few of Mictla's evil acolytes and dancing-women. Drawn up in solid ranks before them, facing outward, were the men of the Purple Cohort, the King's own bodyguard – and they were sorely pressed to defend their charges.

Down the streets converging upon the fane came people fleeing in terror before walls of water inexorably flowing inward. The sea had risen – or had the land subsided? The spears of the guards were dripping gouts of crimson, for the dais was the sole refuge, and many strove to reach it.

Even as I gazed, a levin-bolt sped straight from the black vault of heaven. Full on the round head of Mictla's effigy it smote with a vicious crackle – I sensed it, I say, in the distance! The great idol reeled, swayed, lurched far over, then with a dull roar it precipitated itself ponderously on the group occupying the dais. A cloud of dust arose, soon settled by the driving rain. I saw Tizoq, or, rather, his dead, ugly face, peering, hideously convulsed, from beneath a pile of debris. Then the waters reached the place, and naught remained save tossing, tumbling waves a-play with strange flotsam!

The terrific forces unleashed when I shattered the ancient heart of the Old Stone Woman were destroying an old land as well as an ancient people. The awful quakes were rending chasms wide and deep in the bosom of the solid ground, and long dormant earth-fires streamed upward. And ever the sea overcame the land. Shattering explosions took place as water and fire met. The entire continent of Atlantan became the picture of hell let loose. There was not a city left, and even the villages of savages in the wild lands were swallowed up in the vast cracks, or incinerated by leaping, roaring, whistling flames. Yet the Old Stone Woman still stared into space, waiting for a dying world to reach its end. And ever the inward rushing waters were victorious over earth and fire alike.

Atlantan was no more beneath the sun! The great continent with its millions of men, women and children, its temples and colleges and palaces, its gardens and glorious cities and fertile countrysides, its rivers and mountains and lakes and plains, its mines with eon-old hoarded treasures of precious metals and gorgeous gems, Atlantan rests at the bottom of the mighty ocean from which, ages agone, it arose!

And I, whose hand struck the fatal blow bringing all that to pass – because I usurped the prerogative of that awful power, Destiny, I am still alive, nor can I ever die while earth endures; for in the hollow of the harsh breast of the Old Stone Woman, enclosed in a new red crystal heart, by Destiny's inexorable decree, I am compelled to take the place of the old shattered heart of Atlantan, there to remain ever young and undying until Atlantan shall again rise from the sea-slime!

* * *

The writing ceased. We three – Carman, Otilie and I – sat staring at each other, in speechless amazement. Suddenly Otilie sighed softly and slumped to the floor in a dead faint.

"Good Lord!" Carman ejaculated. "The strain was too prolonged for the poor creature! Help me, Henri, to lift her to the table-top."

But Tekala's 'projection' raised a minatory hand. Gliding to where lay the prostrate form, she knelt, placed the palms of her hands on Otilie's temples for a second, and calmly arose, nodding confidently at us.

To our infinite surprise, Otilie awoke none the worse for her experience. Carman attempted to condole with her, but Otilie waved him aside scornfully.

"I'm all right," she stated. "For a minute I was out, no? But the Shining Lady" – as she designated our visitor – "gave me of her strength, and I feel stronger right now than ever in my life! And I would cheerfully go through a greater strain for her any time she needs me!"

Tekala started with surprise, as if she could hardly believe what she heard, but then an expression of absolute love for Otilie came upon her face as she signed her to take up her pencil again.

"It seems," Otilie's hand transcribed. "That I have found three friends, and I have searched the world over, inspired by such hope, but fearing that never should I succeed in my search.

"Tell me, you who are named Leonard, what would you do, were you Tekala?"

"Let me understand you more fully," Carman replied gravely. "Are *you* here, or in the heart of the Old Stone Woman?"

"My undying body is in the breast of the Old Stone Woman," Otilie wrote. "But all which is Tekala's self is *here*! Oh, I tell you that in all the long ages that have passed since the great cataclysm, I have had ample time to develop powers more than mortal! I could, with ease, materialize here and now, for you, but to what avail? Ere long my will would grow wearied and I should again become but a luminous shadow. But, oh! To be free, in a proper, physical body—"

And right there, Carman interrupted:

"If I were you, I would search the wide world over for a suitable body, one young and fair, take possession thereof, and leave my old body right where it is till doomsday!"

"But my punishment – the will of the gods?" Tekala was visibly shocked.

"I'd not worry about the gods," Carman counseled. "The gods passed when Atlantan sank, nor can the lost gods ever return!"

"But where shall I find a body whose tenant is willing to be supplanted? I would not dispossess a soul in whom the love of life runs strongly. And I cannot, will not take a dead body – there are laws I dare not transgress—"

And at that point Otilie interrupted, somewhat diffidently, but decidedly, and in her melodious voice was a queer note of reverence and pleading.

"O Shining Lady! Can you use such an ugly body as mine? For if you can, I pray you, take it! I have nothing to live for! I am so ugly that little children run from me in the streets, and what man so low as to love poor, deformed Otilie? Perhaps with your powers you can make this twisted form straight and my hideous face fair. If so, tell me what to do, O most Beautiful, and I will gladly obey! But one thing do I ask – let there still be enough left of Otilie to remember how ugly she was, and know how beautiful she has become! Lady – Lady Tekala! Help poor Otilie! Set free her soul, and take her warped body and twist it to your own semblance! It would be the sole mercy I ever knew in all my dreary life, and it is mercy that I ask!"

Had Otilie struck Tekala the effect would have been the same! Tekala reeled and almost fell, but recovered her equilibrium and glided to Otilie. Long and earnestly the two looked at each other – the ugliest woman I have ever seen, and the loveliest woman the world has ever beheld – and what silent message passed between them I dare not even surmise.

But obviously both were satisfied, for Tekala bent her regal head and kissed Otilie full on her mouth. Carman and I, watching, saw a look of unearthly ecstasy transfigure Otilie's features, and then the unbelievable happened!

Otilie swayed and fell, lying on her back, and Tekala, standing there, turned about facing us, gradually leaning back and little by little merging herself with the other form lying so still on the floor, until the transformation was accomplished and the two had become one! And we two, staring spellbound, incredulous, saw the poor, twisted body of Otilie straighten, the bosom swell and heave, and the grotesque features slowly bloom into loveliness beyond all words!

Tekala arose from her recumbent position and faced us in triumph, and truly if she had been beautiful before, now she was Beauty's self! She held out her exquisite arms to me – *me*, Henri d'Armond – and her voice that still spoke with Otilie's deep, rich, bell-like resonance, uttered the words I'd hoped to hear, but had never believed possible:

"Henri, my beloved, I am yours, take me!"

In an instant my arms were about her, my lips claiming hers in insatiable hunger – my brain swaying, drunken with happiness, experiencing rapture unearthly –

There came a terrific *crash*! I saw a blaze of unbearable brilliance filled with figures not of earth, and in their midst yet dominant, a great Face, calm, majestic, awful in its inexorable justice. And I knew, even in my stunned and bewildered condition, that I looked full into the sublime countenance of Destiny itself, that power which is above all gods, and which I, a mere mortal, had, in my presumption, defied when I aided Tekala.

At the same moment I experienced an irresistible force snatch her from my arms despite the fervor of my embrace. I heard her voice, heart-broken, calling despairingly:

"Henri! Henri! Never again—"

My senses left me and I fell to the floor, unconscious.

* * *

How long I lay there I cannot say, but when my senses returned – I could see nothing but a blaze of light. Of Leonard Carman there was no trace, nor of Tekala.

Dimly I heard a voice saying in deep contralto tones:

"Mr. d'Armond, are you alive?"

"Who speaks?" I demanded shakily, and heard the welcome reply:

"I, Otilie."

She helped me to my feet. My hand groped until I found hers. I heard her sobbing.

"Are you hurt?" I questioned, stupidly, for I was still dazed.

"Not hurt," she gasped. "But oh, that poor, dear, lovely lady, Tekala! Her gods were not dead, after all, even if Mr. Carman said they were – and they have taken their vengeance upon her – and me! For I am again Otilie, ugly as ever, and you – what have they done to you?"

"I – am blind," I replied shakily. "Nor do I ever expect to see again! Help me to a chair."

Uttering little words of pity and sympathy, she complied, and as I felt her warm tenderness for me in my misfortune flow through me with the touch of her hand, I said, weakly:

"Otilie, I need you! Will you come and live with me and take care of a poor, blind fool?"

"I – I – am so ugly," she sobbed. "But if you need me – and can endure my presence – yes."

Otilie and I were married the next day. After all, I am rich as compared to her and can make life a little more bearable for her in her unfortunate condition. It is purely an arrangement of convenience, yet she takes excellent care of me, forestalling my slightest wish. She at least is happy. Yesterday I heard her singing as she went about the house.

As for myself – I am blind, as I said before. Ten years now I have dwelt in darkness – tortured by memory, and blessed by memory.

Three months ago I saw dimly a dull red light glowing in my everlasting gloom. Later it came again, growing stronger. At first I thought it was my sight returning, and found out that I was wrong. Ultimately it became a crimson glory like incandescent blood. And I knew it for what it really was!

Within the swelling breast of the Old Stone Woman, deep in the ocean's eternal gloom there beats still the great crimson crystal heart. And imprisoned, undying, facing each other yet unable to move, within the pulsating Heart of Atlantan are the two beings I loved, but who, in their arrogance, set at naught the awful fiat of Destiny – ancient priest and ancient priestess, whom Tekala recognized as Ixtlil of old, but yet the Carman I knew who counseled Tekala to her fall, and the priestess Tekala, whom, for so brief a moment I held in my arms, and whose lips I pressed but once ere she was torn from me! And there, undying and unchanging, they wait, wait, wait until Atlantan once more emerges from the depths.

Asylum

Tracy Fahey

THE FIRST TIME she tells me about her homeland, I'm transfixed. It's not the description of the place, or of the people there. It's how *safe* it sounds.

"It's a place where women and children are always welcome, a place for those rejected by the world. A refuge."

"Refuge?" The word is honey in my mouth.

Her face gleams orange in the flickering flames. "Yes. An asylum."

I've heard that word before. A country slowly, grudgingly, opening doors into grey rooms with tired officials, desks piled high with papers. She must see something of this in my face, because she reaches over and takes my hand between her rough ones.

"True asylum," she says gently.

And for the first time in months, a hard knot inside me unravels.

* * *

The class I'm sent to is exactly the horror story I thought it would be.

"Saida Darwish?" She pronounces my name wrongly, but in an exaggerated way to show how hard she's trying. I raise my hand. "And Saida comes from Syria," she says, her voice bright and warm. "Let's all make her feel welcome." A dutiful burst of clapping.

I have to remind myself this was my choice. This was the only option aside from the one on the rough estate I now call home. So I nod, and force a smile at the women in their expensive, stretchy clothes, their pretty make-up. At the men beside them, dutiful and awkward.

Ibrahim. I shiver and huddle inside my dark jilbab. The tight smile stretches my cheeks until they hurt.

The instructor (I think her name is Louise) talks to us in a bright, baby voice. She shows us slides about nutrition and tells us it is important to relax. "Relax and enjoy this precious time," she says, beaming widely, showing her large white teeth. "Now I know most of you already have, but for anyone who hasn't, you need to start thinking about a birth plan. Now, any questions?" I feel her gaze on me; pull the hijab closer around my face.

"Saida," she says slowly and clearly, as if I'm a child. "If you need me to explain anything, let me know." Everyone turns to look at me. I shrink back, shake my head tightly. No.

* * *

On the bus. Tyres plough through puddles, sheeting dirty brown water against the glass. This is the weather I remember from my time in England. Ugly grey skies, damp that soaked through clothes and settled on bone. For a moment I allow myself the luxury of remembering home. Azure skies flecked with puffball clouds. Sun, bright and potent, gilding the windows. The very streets a liquid black haze of heat-mirage. You, drinking coffee outside the café with your friends, laughing, sun-flash on sunglasses, long brown throat smooth against your white shirt collar. Before—

No. My fingers close around my bus ticket, screwing it into a hard little ball. I can't do this. I can't think about this right now.

When I get off the bus I open my hand. My palm is scored with nail marks; an arc of neat purple crescents.

* * *

"You're living here, missus, not Iran!" A woman at the bus-stop; smeared make-up, hard, glittering eyes. Behind her, a bright poster of a sun-dazzled blonde in sunglasses. *ESCAPE. Starring Sorcha Sheil.* From the woman's slack mouth, a low, unpleasant smell of rotting fruit. I don't react. I never do. But my stomach tightens.

I knew it would be like this. Being different. Strange. Marked out as *foreign*, even in the distance. It's my face, my brown skin. My clothes, dark and discreet. Here, the hijab says *I am not like you.* The social workers speak of assimilation, but I know. I see the faces as I move about the city, avid eyes crawling over my face, my jilbab, my covered hair. For the most part, the men look through me. But the women see me, they judge me for my shabby, long dresses; a rejection of their clothing, or a more sinister indicator of my own forced compliance. I know how they see me. Muslim. Oppressed. And they're the kindest generalisations. *Asylum-seeker*, they call me. *Refugee.* An unwanted visitor, here on sufferance.

Here, where I live, they're ruder. Coarser.

I pass by the woman, eyes cast down, a ghost within my clothes. "Go back, if you don't like it here," she calls after me. Her eyes, unfocused. I hold my breath as I walk down the dirty street, keep holding it until I unlock the streaked door, shut it tight behind me. In the darkness of the narrow hall, I let it out – *whoosh* – and it hits me again. The empty place where you should be.

I miss you, habibi. I miss you so much.

No. I didn't know it would be as hard as this.

* * *

I unpack my bag. A net of tangerines, their bright, orange skin the only splash of colour in the dingy kitchen. There's the notebook I brought with me to class. I sit down and flip it open. I've written only two words – 'BIRTH PLAN?'

I sit on the lumpy kitchen chair and look at those capital letters till they swim and dance between the lines. Rain drums on the flat roof.

This was never my plan. I had a birth plan, before. My plan was to have this baby back home in Damascus, in the small hospital beside where I lived. Dr. Amena, who I'd attended, would perform the delivery, her gentle manner and expertise calmly ushering our little one into the world. I would hold this precious bundle in my arms, look up at you, eyes soft with love for this sudden family. Your arms would wrap around us; a magic space, a respite, a refuge. But then—

Well. That was my birth plan.

I unwrap the scarf from my hair and click the kettle on. The pages of my notebook gleam white against the dull wood of the table.

How can I write a plan, when all my plans have failed?

* * *

The next class is just as bad. Worse, maybe. Louise has taken to asking brightly at the end of every edict – "Did you get that, Saida?" We've gone long past the point where I can quietly tell her that I'm fluent in English, that I lived in London for five years, studying law. That my qualifications, at a guess, are higher than hers. No. She looks at me and my worn, dark clothes and sees a poor, ill-educated woman.

"How did you get on with your birth plan?" she asks. Her smile is stretched wide, her eyes crinkled up. She wants everyone to see how *genuine* she is, how kind she is to a poor refugee woman. I look at the information leaflet in front of me for the maternity unit; the image of hospital beds makes me shiver.

"I think I would prefer to have a doula. To give birth at home."

"Oh, *right.*" She arranges her face in a careful, interested expression. "And is that the traditional method back in Syria?" The unspoken addendum 'in your primitive culture' hangs in the air. The other women watch me, covertly.

Not necessarily. I want to tell her I come from a large and cosmopolitan city. That I was a professor, with a book-lined study. I went to concerts, exhibitions. I had a private doctor, dear Amena – she rises in front of me, the last time I saw her, white coat splashed with bright red blood, her face twisted in horror—

I cut away. *Don't think about that.*

Louise is still looking at me expectantly. I give up. "Yes, it is traditional." So she gives me a different information pack with a list of midwifes and doulas. The other women look away, continue talking among themselves.

* * *

Maybe I can't do this, after all? I sit in the coffee shop beside the clinic, delaying my return home to that chill little house. I leaf through the flyers. The prices are outrageous; the thought of the forms to be filled in to try and get financial assistance makes my throat close over. I drink the coffee in tiny, lingering sips. It's weak and brown, not like the rich, beautiful coffee I made at home, the fragile cups of treacle-dark liquid. I think of home – not this cold little place I live in – but my real home. With you. My parents coming to visit; the house alive with the smell of food. I take a breath. Try not to think of those letters I've sent, unanswered.

The steam of the coffee clouds the window beside me. I touch a fingertip to the mist of condensation and trace the letters of your name. إبراهيم. Ibrahim, my love. Tears well up, hot as the coffee.

"Are you OK, love?" A woman sits down beside me; older, her face kind, questioning. "Excuse me." She leans over, puts a hand on my stomach, smiles. "You're going to have a little baby."

I nod, overwhelmed. She glances at the brochures in front of me. "And you're looking for a midwife?"

I clear my throat. "Yes, I am."

Her smile grows wider, radiant. "You've found me. I'm Dorcas."

Could it be this easy? I smile back, uncertainly. I have to ask. "What fee do you charge?"

She looks at me carefully. "Love, you've been through it. I'm happy to help out for nothing."

A spark inside me; a small leap of joy. "Thank you."

Her name is Dorcas Kelly. She is an experienced midwife, she tells me. She's almost retired now; she only takes on 'special cases'. I realise I am one of her special cases, but I don't feel patronised. I feel glad. She asks me practical questions; how far along I am, what medical consultations I've had. She doesn't ask me where I'm from or what I've gone through, and I'm relieved. She just *knows.*

"It's been a long road for you." She takes my number, pats my hand. "But you're in safe hands now," she tells me, and I believe her.

* * *

My next pre-natal class, I sit there, smiling. My homework is done, my birth plan in process. Today Louisa goes round to sit with us, one by one, to 'check in', she says brightly.

"So, Saida, did you have any luck with the leaflets I gave you?"

I consider it. "Not really," I say, and her face falls. "But I did find a midwife who is happy to deliver a home birth."

"Good girl," she says, as if I'm a clever child who has exceeded her expectations. "Who is it?"

"Her name is Dorcas Kelly." There's a silence. Louisa's face is incredulous.

"Dorcas Kelly? I thought she'd retired." Her voice rises, dramatic. "But she's *famous.*"

I'm startled. Louisa stands up. "Class, Saida will be working with Dorcas Kelly as her doula." Murmurs, in-drawn breaths. The women look at me, incredulous. I'm puzzled, nervously smiling. "Why is she famous?"

"She was—" Louisa drops her voice dramatically "*—Sorcha Sheil's midwife.*" Oh. Even I've heard of Sorcha Sheil, the shining blonde movie star from Dublin.

I almost enjoy the class. I can see by their eyes I've risen in their estimation. A few of the women even say goodbye when I leave.

* * *

Dorcas calls me the next day asking to come over.

"Of course." I'm relieved. Part of me thought it was a dream, that someone should be so kind to me. I clean the little house as best I can, sweep and mop the floors, rub down the old kitchen counters. I go out to Poundland, get a cheap tablecloth, some candles, biscuits. I light a small fire in the windy grate; it flickers into uneasy flame.

She knocks to signal her arrival. I open the door, realise with a lurch to my stomach that a group of local kids are outside. "Hey, the Taliban called, they want their clothes back." Loud, uproarious laughter. Dorcas, in her oversized black coat, whips around.

"Get home, you little scutters!"

"What're ya gonna do?" The leader, a tall boy with spiky blond hair.

She narrows her eyes. "I'll curse the lot of you. Don't cross a witch."

They mutter, stroll away, carefully nonchalant.

"*Are* you a witch?" I can't help asking her as I usher her inside. She shakes her head. "Nothing so sinister." She sees my face and laughs. "Something much nicer."

She nods at the window. "Get much of that?"

I bow my head, say nothing. She sighs. "Damn them anyway. And we're meant to be a friendly, welcoming people. This place has changed, and not for the better."

"Was it different when you were young?"

"Maybe," she says. "But I've been away, in a better place." She shakes her head. "Anyway, let's talk more on that later."

* * *

Dorcas checks me out, pronounces me fine and healthy. "Though you could eat more," she says, sipping her tea. "Tell me about your last scan." Wordlessly, I pass over a crumpled photograph. She unfolds it; as she does so, I'm overcome with memories. Your glowing face as you look from me to the photo; the happy disbelief in your eyes. "It's really true, *habibi.* We're having a baby!" Tears come, and I don't try to stop them.

Dorcas lets me cry, drinking her tea quietly. "Tell me about it," she says softly. And I do. Our happy life, before the conflict started. The rising fear, the bombs, the deaths. The bubble of joy that sustained us. That day – that day you went out to buy a pram – "They're on sale," you said, light and happy. A few minutes later; the explosion. Running outside. You, lying on the road, your white shirt a bright, unbelievable red. The hospital. Amena holding me, both of us smeared crimson. Escaping via Lebanon; the long, torturous journey to here.

Without a word, she pulls me to her. I sink into her arms, sobbing. "Poor sweetheart," she murmurs. "You've been through the wars." The Irish phrase is strangely appropriate. "Hush, there."

I let her rock me, the embrace timeless. I feel my grandmother's arms, my mother's arms, tight around me.

"I'll tell you a story, shall I?" It's so unexpected I stop crying, shaking sobs drying into a low whimper. I close my eyes; I'm in my grandmother's house in Aleppo, mint tea perfuming the air.

"Yes please," I whisper. And she does.

* * *

"Once upon a time, there was a lonely, exhausted woman, heavy with child. She was tired of the endless hatred and violence in this world. Late at night she'd lie in bed, stroking her bump, worrying about bringing a child into this place where such horrors lurked.

And one day she heard of a world that was different. A place where women were protected, where babies could grow up in sunshine and peace. It was ruled over by goddesses who preserved a strict boundary between their world and this one. They were an old race, older than ours, and they knew the secrets of happiness. Within this world, women were valued. They were trained in the old ways; making medicine, delivering babies, bringing people together to co-operate, build, make things better. It was a place where women and children were always welcome, a place for those rejected by the world."

I'm transfixed. It's not the description of the place, or of the people there. It's how *safe* it sounds. The baby shifts inside me, as if to agree.

"Where is this magic place?"

She chuckles; I feel the sound reverberate in her chest. "Closer than you think."

"And what happened to the woman?"

Dorcas smiles. "I'll tell you the full story another time. She went there and found refuge."

"A refuge?" The word is honey in my mouth.

Her face gleams orange in the flickering flames. "Yes. An asylum."

"True asylum," she says gently.

And for the first time in months, a hard knot inside me unravels.

* * *

"So what's she like?" Louisa, her face avid.

I resent her new interest in me. "Dorcas is very nice," I say politely.

"Did she mention Sorcha Shein?" One of the blonde mothers.

"No." I duck my head. "We spoke only of medical matters." It's not the truth, but retelling Dorcas' story would be fatal. Too many questions. I sit in silence; disappointment palpable around me.

Later, my social worker calls. I put out the biscuits, make tea. He barely looks at me throughout, focusing instead on a clipboard of questions. *Can you rate the quality of your healthcare?* He chooses not to recognise my pregnancy, though my bump protrudes; a visible reminder. "No tea for me, thanks," he says, ticking off his list.

How are you integrating with the community? The people who call after me on the street, the jeers of the children. But then, Dorcas; that warm hug, the comforting story. "I think – alright. I have a good midwife."

He peers at me through thick glasses. "Well that's good, but more related to the healthcare question." He flips the page back, and I think again of Dorcas and her story. *True asylum.*

* * *

"Can you tell me more about the woman who went to the magical land?" I feel oddly relaxed with Dorcas.

"Sure I can," she says easily. "She was like you, alone and worried. But when she went there she found a place where she was looked after. What a place!" Her voice is dreamy. "Some call it *Tír-na-nÓg*, the land of the ever young. No one gets sick there, the adults don't grow older. All the food they eat is cultivated there; big apples tasting of honey, bread baked from good wheat. Babies thrive there; play in safety, laughing. The sun always shines, the sky always blue."

"And what about the people who created it?" I know it's just a fable, but I can't help it. I want to hear more about this beautiful dream.

Dorcas is quiet. Then – "They are old ones, from an ancient culture. Thousands and thousands of years ago, they were forced underground. But through the caves they found another land; a secret place. It lies not far from this one, and there are more ways to it than you could think. They are the *Tuatha Dé Danann*. Some call them the fae."

"The fae?" I don't even try to pronounce the other one.

"Fairies," says Dorcas. "But not the fairies you might see in children's books. These are older, wiser people."

* * *

I still dream of Syria. How could I not? Home is the place we all return to. But my memories are tainted with fear. Still no replies to my letters. I tell myself it's the postal service, disrupted. But late at night, I can't escape the dark realisation—

So instead I dream of the fairy place. Bright and sunny like my home, but safe. Children play with their mothers, laughing. There are no sirens, no bombs. Instead of picking their way through rubble, women walk in sunshine fields of corn.

* * *

There is a library on the edge of my estate. No one really goes there, when I enter, it's empty, apart from a woman reshelving books.

"I'm looking for something about the fae," I tell her. "Can you help me?" Between Dorcas' visits, I'm hungry for more stories.

"Folklore," she says, as if to herself and wanders off, to return with a slim green volume. *The Irish Fae.*

I'm delighted. "Thank you."

* * *

That night, I'm a lot less thankful. What is this? I recognise some of Dorcas' descriptions – the land of the ever-young, the feasts of good food, the secret land. But the fae? They are like the *djinns* my grandmother warned me about; they are evil spirits, invading houses, kidnapping women and children, stealing souls. I close the book with a shudder.

Is Dorcas? – No. I won't think that. She is a good person, the best person I've met here. Besides, she is famous. People know her. She was the midwife to Sorcha Shein. Reassured, I think about the blonde film star, her radiance and fame dispel the shadows.

That night I try and dream of the magical land, but now it's dark and strangely sinister.

When I go outside the next day, someone has painted 'GO HOME' in crooked red letters on my door. How can I? This is a poor, mean place, but it's my home now.

* * *

I'm meant to go to class, but I don't want to. I call Louisa and tell her I'm sick. It's half-true. My stomach has been upset since I saw that writing on my door, baby whirling in protest. I scrub and scrub but the letters stay, dull pink now, but still visible.

Dorcas is coming over later. I look at the green book beside me and shiver. I'll take it back.

The library has computers. I can go online. Automatically I look for news from Aleppo, but there's nothing but misery. Nothing about the pretty district my family lived in – *live in*, I correct myself automatically, catching my breath at the mistake. To distract myself, I look up Sorcha Sheil. I read news items about her films, the painful divorce from a Hollywood star, her pregnancy. I scroll through her photos on Instagram; film premieres, movie sets, her proud stance in front of a mirror, hand on her bump. There's even a photo of her with an unsmiling Dorcas. She's tagged it #bestmidwifeever. The post has more than a million hearts beside it.

Wait! I frown. No baby photos? She seems to share everything in her life, so why not that? I click on her last post. "I'm taking a break from social media to prepare to welcome #mybelovedbaby. Please respect my privacy."

It's dated three months ago. I go back to the news stories. Nothing since. Though the library is warm, I shiver. *What happened to her?*

* * *

I build the fire mechanically. My brain is numb. I sit back in my chair; encircle my bump, my baby, with a protective arm. Wait for Dorcas.

She's early. I bring her inside, but not before she's noticed the faded pink letters on my door. "You poor dear," she says, and her voice is so warm, so kind, I'm momentarily ashamed of my thoughts.

She sits down, accepts the cup of tea; looks at me shrewdly.

"What is it?"

I abandon my calm. "What happened to her?"

Dorcas takes a long drink of her tea. "Who?"

"Sorcha Sheil. I can't find a trace of her anywhere." I take a deep breath; the words burst forth. "I've been reading about your fae, and I didn't like it – they take women and children! They're *evil*."

"Don't be upset," says Dorcas placidly. "It's bad for the baby." She reaches over, pats my hand. "And don't believe all you read. They get a bad press, the fae, and have done for a long time. It was the Church, you see. They didn't like the way Irish people believed in them. So they put it out that they were fallen angels. Malevolent, looking for souls to steal." She twists up her face in annoyance. "None of that's true. They're always been protectors of human women."

I bite my lip. "Sorcha Sheil?" I ask.

Dorcas sighs. "Poor woman. So beautiful, so talented. But so unhappy. Her husband had left her, journalists camped outside her door. No privacy, ever."

"Did she—" I can't finish the sentence, but Dorcas understands. "Yes. She came back with me. She's happy now. Safe."

I let out a sigh, relief blooming slow. "So she's alright?"

Dorcas smiles. "Of course she is. They're looking after her."

It's so strange. "So you work with them?"

"I do. A long time ago, a faery woman came to me. They had need of a *bean ghlúine*, a midwife like me. It was a difficult birth, they needed help. So I went with her." She raises her face to mine; she is noble in the firelight. "We midwives, we have a sacred task, and we never deny it to anyone in need. So yes, I went with her, and I saw – oh such sights! Such peace and beauty." She closes her eyes.

"And you came back?"

"I did. And since then I've crossed over many times. Sometimes to help them there, sometimes to bring women to them."

"Women like me." It's all clear now.

"Don't be afraid," says Dorcas, her voice soft. "It's a safe place. You and the baby will prosper there. There's no war there, no hatred. It's summer forever; the sun always shines."

I'm lulled by her gentle vision. The wind howls outside. "You've suffered so much here. Surely it's time now to go somewhere to be looked after."

I glance around the small kitchen; the dying fire, the erratic cooker, the surfaces that stay sticky even after I scrub them. "And if I wanted to go, can I come back?"

"Sure you can." She takes my hand. "Don't I pass freely between places? I can bring you back if you want."

I sit, perfectly still, by the fire. And in the silence, your voice, clear in my ear. *Go there, habibi. Be safe.*

I go to the table, scribble a note. *I am gone away to a safer place.* I fold it, slide it into an envelope. Carefully, I write my parents' address, hand the letter to Dorcas. "Will you post this for me?"

"I will, my dear." She looks at me calmly, kindly. "Are you ready and willing?"

I draw in a deep breath, stand up. "I am."

The Exiles

Isobel Granby

IT IS NO USE to narrate the events of a meeting with one of the good neighbours. Those disinclined to believe will be unconvinced, and even those who allow for their presence will consider themselves immune to their draw, thinking it a power that leads weaker folk astray. Only those who have experienced such an encounter for themselves, and followed with the other willingly, will understand, remembering their own surprise at lightly throwing caution to the winds and taking the path of danger.

Those inclined to believe, also, know that no advice can lead them away from such a choice. Whether this is a glamour possessed by the good neighbours that few can ignore, or a fact of the person in question's character, the effect is the same: they do not see the danger until it is too late, even if they think they have been cautious. In the case of Bess, the one concession to common sense that she made was to ask a favour in return.

How the meeting had come about, she had difficulty recalling, once she had stepped aboard the boat and embarked with the prince towards the city that had been lost beneath the waves. Perhaps she had looked in his direction and their eyes had met, or she had spoken to him out of politeness to a stranger, though she herself was strange to that shore, cast on the coast by that most uncivil war which had made England inhospitable. The moment they had spoken to each other, however, she remembered the words of her old Cornish nurse, about the people who lived beyond the ring of hearthlight, who were powerful and elusive and dangerous, and whom she had not wholly believed in, save at night. *You'll know one if you meet one*, she had said. Now Bess found that that was true.

"Will you do me a favour?" he had asked, after introducing himself with a name that seemed carelessly cast on, like a loose shirt – Morvan.

She had agreed, and cursed herself for a fool, adding that he must agree to a favour in return, which he promised. She feared an impossible demand, but he only wished her to listen to a shell that had been cast up from the sea. After a few moments, she handed it back to him, perplexed. "Bells," she said. "Drowned bells." Then, shaking her head – "I don't know why I said that."

Morvan had grown very pale then, and murmured, "Then it is true. The queen has called me back."

What would have been madness now seemed the truth, and she listened to his tale, his voice distant, as if he had recited it to himself often in his exile. Prince of a land long sunken, lost to the city of Ys, the place which years ago had been drowned and yet whose bells still rang above the water for those who heard them. He had been wandering this shore alone, and only in the place between the tides could he take comfort, where he was near again to his world.

"Now she awaits my return," he finished, addressing Bess once more, then turning to the lapping waves. "I am Prince of the Placeless Realm, and I answer your summons, my queen." As he spoke, a boat appeared before his feet, easing up on the sand, and now Bess could remember seeing it, out of the corner of her eye, breaking loose from its moorings and drifting near.

As if in a dream, Bess moved forward, through the surf, and took hold of the boat. "I will come to your city."

He frowned, hesitating. "Few who enter Ys ever leave it."

"I will take what risks await me."

"I will not return. You must find your way alone. It would be unwise."

"Then let me remind you of your promise of a favour. Bring me." His eyes widened and his hands, on the tiller, tightened until the knuckles were white. "And bring me back here afterward."

He relented, for he could not refuse.

* * *

The Breton shore lay behind them, unseen. Bess kept her eyes on the horizon, for if she looked away from that line, or spoke a single word, the land would remain hidden but for the strange lights that danced under the waves. Something in the distance, a stain the colour of a bruise, caught her gaze and held it there. It was not a storm, nor was it land.

She did not blink, she did not turn, she did not speak. The shape grew and shifted, and an outline of high hills formed. At last they came to the strand, a small crescent of white enclaved by black cliffs, all broken and jagged above their heads. She stepped onto the sand and to her relief it did not melt away. She did not close her eyes, though her heart was pounding and her instincts told her to turn back. Her mind pushed against her even as she drew a deep breath full of sea air. It was no different to the shore that she and Morvan had just left, but an impossible distance away.

"You can speak now," he said. He had lost that grave expression, and looked as though he knew not whether to laugh or weep.

"Is this the place, then?" she whispered – as though to do otherwise would be an intrusion on the sanctity of the sunken land. They walked together, side by side, from the beach upward towards the tower that was built into the rock, up a green hill, and along a ragged path that seemed scoured by the sea. A citadel and high walls appeared on the other side, houses and alleyways, like and unlike those of the town she had been living in for months now.

The city was a blend of lavish and decrepit. Barnacles clung to the stones, and the seaweed-strewn streets had been worn down into unwieldy gullies. Yet the walls glimmered with gold, inlaid in curving, elaborate patterns, similar to those she had seen on the ruins near the town, but far more intricate. Flashes of light from the distant lighthouse illuminated the riches of the city of Ys, once the jewel of the coast. The sea had carved out its own pattern on the face of it, scouring and accruing in strange and wonderful shapes. Splendour had been stripped away, and something more marvellous had taken its place.

But the people, who appeared at their windows, or in the alleys, were silent. Perhaps they too were visitors here, thought Bess, and too much afraid to speak; perhaps they were prisoners – but no, they were of Morvan's kind, they shared that certain quality, they seemed at home. To see them anywhere else would be uncanny. They averted their eyes as he passed by.

"They know of my exile," he explained to her in a low voice. "They will let the queen speak to me first."

"Do they fear your return?"

"No, but I fear their welcome." It was the first time he had confessed to being afraid, though he had shown it every time he spoke of the queen. She stretched out a hand, and he took it. They walked in silence together up the still street, past empty, darkened windows. It felt to Bess as though at their arrival a hush had fallen over the city, a new and uncomfortable silence, the silence of being observed.

The feeling increased as they reached the steps of the palace and found the gate open. Someone had expected them, and prepared for their return. His return, she corrected herself. If they never let her go – here she put the thought from her head, or was forced to, as the door to the palace opened and the guards, standing silent to either side, watched them enter. In the still air within, the sound of the great stone door closing behind them echoed.

At the other end of the hall sat the queen.

They approached with the intense concentration required by those who have all eyes upon them. Looking neither to the left nor right, Morvan and Bess walked forth to meet the queen, and stopped a few paces from the throne, gazing up at the woman who sat on it. Power radiated from her, a subtle, irresistible kind that drew all Bess's attention. If she had been attacked just then, by one of the guards who stood to either side of the monarch, or even by an assassin heretofore unseen, she would not have known it until too late. It was not that the queen was unusually striking, or splendidly dressed, but she was sitting utterly still, and she was staring intently at them both.

For several long moments, neither she nor Morvan spoke, and Bess wondered if she should do something to break the silence – cough, or take another step. She was about to speak when the queen rose from the chair, which was made of stone and shell.

"My prince," she said. Morvan knelt, inclining his head.

She stepped closer, and as she approached, Bess noticed a motion out of the corner of her eye; the slight involuntary raising of an arm, then lowering again – as if its owner made to reach for a weapon, but stopped themselves in time. She turned slightly, to see a woman of short stature, with her hair tied back in a sharp braid, a suit of light armour on. A knight, thought Bess; she wore a sword at one hip, a dagger at the other. Her eyes were on the queen and Morvan, and if Bess read her expression correctly, she was concealing intense anger.

Neither the queen nor the prince made any sound, but the queen laid one hand on Morvan's shoulder, and he raised his head, staring into her eyes questioningly. At length he rose.

"I have answered your summons, my queen."

"Welcome, my prince." Now she swept her gaze around the hall, inviting the others to follow her lead. There was a break in the tension that held them there, a subtle but sure exhalation, as though bonds had been loosed – Bess wondered then, as she had not done before, what danger they had been in before the queen's judgment. The knight's expression, to her left, had not softened.

"Rozenn, come, welcome our prince," said the queen, extending a hand to the knight.

"I am glad of your return," she said stiffly. Her slight bow made the hilt of her sword clink against her belt buckle.

"It is a joy beyond my hopes," he replied, equally unconvincing. It was not anger in his voice, by any stretch, but something like fear that Bess detected. She saw in a flash her own country, its polite deceptions, its subtle treasons, until they had spilled out into something bloody and uncontrolled. Her mounting apprehensions were interrupted by the queen's sudden laugh.

"What is this? Who have you brought us?"

"This is a friend," said Morvan quietly. "And I am her protector."

She knew how to conduct herself around royalty, and around dangerous people most of all. Kneeling, she said swiftly, "I am honoured, my queen, to meet you. Such a journey I could never have undertaken alone."

"Indeed," murmured the queen. It sounded like an invitation to continue. Bess held her tongue. Above all she knew when an invitation was a trap.

"She has come at my invitation," Morvan continued, "and she will depart with my blessing."

"No," the queen replied. "She will not depart."

At that, Bess felt her blood freeze. It was a trap, but whose, she now wondered. Morvan's or the queen's? Had the prince known?

"She came of her own free will, and she will leave with it," he protested.

"None may go freely who have seen the city of Ys," she replied with deadly finality. "She is of human kind. It is their lot to wish for impossible things." Bess was reminded of a cat toying with a bird.

Her courage was rising, or perhaps only her temper. "If I promise never to speak of what I have seen, will you not let me go? Perhaps I will forget, perhaps I will think I imagined it."

The queen turned to her, and the knight, still glaring at Morvan, took a step forward and said, "If you send her through the gate, she will forget."

"It is true," the queen said sadly, pensively. "But none has yet passed through it willingly."

"Send me," Bess said. "I will be the first."

Then the knight spoke again – "Send them both."

* * *

It was a sombre party who farewelled the queen and made for the road away from the city. When the queen had declared her judgment, those assembled had been silent, and Bess had been taken from the hall before she could take in what had been decided. There had been severity in the queen's voice but mercy also, a biting kind that was meant as a lesson. Bess would pass through the gate, and Morvan would be the one to send her through, no matter how much she protested. *They always do protest, you know*, the knight, Rozenn, had said with grim satisfaction in her voice. *Take this in case you need it.* She had handed him a sword, thin and flashing in the low lights of the citadel.

Morvan had said no word since they had left the hall. At length Bess asked – "Why does the knight hate you?"

"She doesn't." He looked around to make sure they were not followed. "She resents my welcome, and wishes me dead, but she doesn't hate me. We were friends, once." He stopped abruptly.

They had reached the gate, a great rust-encrusted twist of wrecked iron that had so long ago been the city's destruction. It towered over both of them, even casting a shadow almost to the city. In the weak and watery light it stood stark and black, but the shadow wavered like a mass of seaweed.

"This is where the city fell into the waves," he said with some reverence. "Where the first queen broke the spell that protected the island, and in doing so, forged a new one. Were we to leave through it, we would never return. Our minds would lose the image of it, save in dreams, and even in those dreams, it would be undersea." It was already cold, but in the shadow of the great dark gate Bess felt in her bones a deep and unshakeable chill.

"Then you do not intend to send me through it."

"Did you believe that, even for a second?" She had. His love for this island was visible in every glance, every gesture. To leave it once more might have been impossible.

"You would still fulfil your promise, for I would be safe."

"I never would." His eyes were fixed on the gate, a set expression on his face, though it struck Bess that it was one of fear, not of confidence.

They turned and took a small path that was hidden from view. At last they returned to the green slope that led down to the shore. Wind was singing in the water, and gulls crying overhead, and it was then that Morvan looked as though he might smile, until he turned back towards the city, and saw the knight approaching through the long grass and heather.

"I thought I might find you here." She had walked quickly, from the citadel and not the gate. "You, sweet prince, you may leave as easily as you like," she said almost sadly, "but your captive has seen our city, and must pay the price for it."

"She is not my captive, Rozenn," Morvan said, stepping in front of Bess, and speaking with a coldness that seemed to surprise the knight. She hesitated, drawing her sword.

"The queen's judgment will not be overturned. Nor will you betray her."

"I never betrayed – she is my queen too, friend."

"So you say. And you, newly returned from exile, you wish to cross her again? She will not be so merciful this time."

"Why do you berate me now? I have done you no harm, and we are leaving."

"You were told the terms." Bess felt a fleeting nausea as she recalled the cold air of the gate, and the sword at Morvan's side. He would have needed it. "I will do what you failed to."

Morvan seemed to sway towards his friend, his voice pleading. "You would have me forget it all? You as well?"

"Yes." A hesitation. It was nearly enough – Bess made to shove the boat out from the sand, but at the very moment she moved, the knight drew her sword. "If it comes to forgetfulness or death, I would." The prince hesitated, and Bess fought the instinct to push forth without him. The tide was falling. The boat was feet from the waves, and if this stranger, this man from a world beyond her own, chose to face the renewed wrath of his queen, that was up to him. He had never promised to leave with her. But she would not stay when an escape presented itself.

"I forfeit my own welcome here, in the name of her freedom. I will go with her and I will not return. Is that not enough?"

"It is in ignorance that you offer, friend." Rozenn's voice was deadly soft, an entreaty, but not a surrender to sentiment. "Come back to the queen. Please, come back to the court."

"I will not." He raised his sword but did not strike, and for a moment they stood, tension stretching between them like the strings of a harp, as each waited for the other's provocation. Then – "Fine," from the knight, and a quick, sharp slash that the prince only just blocked, and the battle was joined.

It was a vicious, close fight from the start, both knowing themselves matched. The prince seemed to have the upper hand, desperation spurring his blade, but the knight was methodical and cautious, finding the chance to attack. They did not speak, and as they met once again, Bess sought a weapon of her own. It was no use to sit back and watch. She heard their ragged panting behind her, the struggle continuing, and this gave her hope, reminded her that they were not yet dead, that Morvan was not yet defeated. If she could end the fight, they still had a chance.

Then – the sound of a cry. Bess spun around with an oar in her hand, only to see Morvan sink to the ground. Her blood ran cold for a second. Then she ran them, to where the prince tried to fend off one blow after another. He attempted, twice, to rise to his feet, but the knight was relentless. Bess approached unseen. Swinging the oar, she struck a blow to the back of Rozenn's head, and the knight fell.

Morvan stared at her in astonishment, from where he knelt on the grass. "Thank you," he whispered. She nodded, and made to examine his wound, but he shook his head. "Not now. We must reach the boat, before the tide is out."

Ripping the hem off her petticoat, she twined it around one hand. "Here. We'll bandage that before we go."

"We have no time," he began, then stopped with a gasp. He nodded once, tightly, allowed her to tie the ragged cloth around him as best she could. The sister of a surgeon knew something of wounds, though she chided herself that it was not enough.

She helped Morvan to his feet, slinging one of his arms over her shoulders, feeling for the first time the limits of her own strength. *Come on*, she pleaded silently. *We don't have time for delays.* Her own feet betrayed her at every turn. They were nearly there. The thought took stubborn hold in her mind, a stubborn, repetitive reminder.

"Keep your eyes on the shore, Bess, do not look to me. It is the only way back. Say nothing once we are away." She pushed the boat off from the sand, leapt in, and did not look at him. The horizon was empty, but she kept her eyes on it alone, that blue reverberation in the distance, that blank hollow that would at last resolve itself into land. A gusting of wind followed the boat, nearly capsizing it, and in it were malicious voices. They had been followed. There was nothing for it now. She could not reach to him, and he would die alone, despairing, an exile once more – and then she saw the shoreline.

Still she did not say a word, as she set the boat back ashore, smooth as she could. The feel of the rough sand beneath her shoes was the greatest relief, and it was with difficulty that she kept herself from falling to the ground and kissing it. She helped Morvan from the boat, but he could not stand. She sank with him onto the sand, her arms fast around him, as if that alone kept him from dying.

"They are gone," he said softly, gazing back out to sea, a smile on his face. "They let us go."

"They cannot reach us. Now we must get to town – my brother will help you, he is a surgeon – come with me – or I will carry you." That last was a fruitless promise and they both knew it. He shook his head.

"Lay me down here, Bess, and leave me."

"I must not."

"Between the tides. Remember?" She did, and lowered him to the ground as gently as she could, turning to town with little expectation of help. The world she had fled from was solid beneath her feet once again, and in it was nothing that would save a prince of a lost city. Before leaving the beach, she turned once more towards the shore, a silent farewell.

Bess's blood froze as she saw the figure of the queen bending over him, her hair over her face, her cloak shimmering as though pierced with starlight. Even now she was captivating. Bess stepped forward, ready to push her into the sea, ready to take her on and lose, if it would save Morvan's life, but she stopped suddenly. Whatever the lady was doing, she was not acting out of malice. Her hand was on the prince's forehead, her voice murmuring something, calling out to the tides, asking for the help of her people.

As Bess watched, the queen drew herself up to her full height, and a clear note rang far away, a bell sounding from the depths of the ocean. Then, with one piercing glance at the intruder upon the scene, she took up her cloak and vanished.

The sound of the drowned bell faded, and the sea was quiet. It was then that she noticed that the tide had turned, and now the waves were lifting the boat, threatening to envelop the prince. She knelt by Morvan once more, feeling with relief his pulse beneath her fingers, and made to examine his wound.

There was no wound. Though the sands around him were dark with blood, the wound itself had entirely healed. She had underestimated the queen, before, in thinking her power lay in threats; now she saw that she was just as willing to give life as take it.

"Thank you," she whispered to the wind. There was no answer.

Even as they spoke, Morvan tightened his hand on hers, shifting slightly, and murmured, "My queen." Bess looked back over her shoulder, just in case, but the queen had gone. The beach was silent but for the flapping of the sail and the low seething of the tide.

The Cities We Once Knew

John Linwood Grant

"We came on a road of great length, and a well set-out plaza, besides, in it, and in the middle of the plaza a column of black stone of extraordinary grandeur, on whose summit was a statue of a man with a hand on the left hip and right arm outstretched, pointing with the index finger to the north pole..."
Manuscript 512

13th May
I am not well.

Mosquitoes raise lumps and welts across my upper body and bring a kind of fever; ticks find their way to my ankles, and I have no peroxide left, only sulphur with which to dust my legs. On the sea voyage here, I thought of jaguars, the great cats of the region, and the risk of being torn apart by one, but now – ludicrously – I find myself brought low by the tiniest of God's inexplicable creations.

The mules are also struggling – the heat is dreadful – and yet Francisco is much as he was on the day we left Cuiabá. Perhaps it is because he is *mestiço*, neither fully European nor fully native, and half of this realm already lives within him. He walks ahead, leading the pack beast, and makes the path easier for me; I ride one of the saddle mules when I feel weakest, but otherwise try to match Francisco's stride.

I found the *cerrado* bearable, but we have left that calm savanna and are now deep into untouched forest. Trees and vines crowd even the riverbanks, jealous of the waters which slide unimpeded, mile after mile, through what others have called a green hell. Macaws shriek; white-faced monkeys watch me, and their looks seem scornful.

The nights are not kind. Dreams would not bother me – I have had both fever-dreams and the dreams of a drunk often enough to know their ways. What plagues me here, beneath the trees, is the whispering.

That soft, insidious whispering...

* * *

15th May
I should not have left Canburn and the others in the *cerrado*, though Francisco says that he knows trails which need little cutting – and we are well supplied with gifts, a crucial point. Still, I feel so very alone here, plagued by headaches and dizziness.

I was never alone in London.

"You have good Portuguese, of course, from your time on the Angola expedition in '27?"

That was what the thick-browed dodderers asked when I came before the committee at the Royal Society, and I answered with a minor deception, thinking that when we reached Brazil, it would take little time to freshen up my limited command of the tongue. Once out here, I was reduced to a stammer within a day, confronted by local words and inflections which meant nothing to me.

Francisco speaks Brazilian Portuguese, fluent English, and the Cariban used by the local tribes. I am ashamed, not at my lie, but at his patience with me. And I become more and more aware of my clumsy tread, the frequency with which I snag myself on thorns, or disturb snakes of horrendous size.

"The small ones, *senhor*, they are the ones to fear," he says, and mimics the strike of fangs with two of his fingers. "*Muito venenoso*."

Which only reminds me that the nearest antivenin is in Cuiabá – or São Paulo, a world away.

We see tapir, and peccaries, which I have been told are good eating.

"Will there be native hunters nearby?" I ask when we rest. Despite the partial canopy, the noon sun seeks to boil us.

"Most of them seek fish." He points to where, blurry-eyed, I can just see the river. It is surprisingly blue, unlike the brown, sluggish rivers near São Paulo. "It is rare for them to take animal meat."

I glance at my revolver, imagining the taste of a fresh tapir steak, rather than the salted leathery stuff we carry.

"Can we…?"

"No, *senhor*. Our friends have long memories. If these people hear firearms, they will think only of the *bandeirantes* who used their women, who took and sold their fathers' fathers."

Chastened, I open a can of corned beef. The lianas rustle, their twisted stems – strangling stems – all around us.

Perhaps they are what whisper to me in the night.

* * *

17th May

It was with *bandeirantes* – the explorers, slavers, fortune-hunters of early Brazil – that all this began. With the words of the Portuguese adventurer João da Silva Guimarães, as recorded in Manuscript 512, almost two centuries ago. I have seen that faded manuscript, the crabbed, almost illegible scrawl which describes a magnificent stone city supposed to be far beyond the capacity of Brazil's native peoples to build.

Guimarães states that his ragged band found this city, walked its streets, but it was empty. He thought it abandoned; other tales are told that suggest the inhabitants had only retreated, perhaps to sanctuaries even deeper in the jungle. Who were these city builders?

No one knows, though the usual hints of ancient colonies, of Atlantean descendants, and Phoenicians or Romans swept across the Atlantic, arose in the newspapers and journals. It could not be, people argued, that a home-grown talent might have risen to such heights, for that would mean that dark, jungle-forged skins could contain as much civilisation as European white ones. The walls of Great Zimbabwe had clearly taught them nothing.

Colonel Percy Harrison Fawcett believed in the contents of Manuscript 512; he believed in the lost city of Z (his preferred name for the place), with its great walls and stone arches, its temples, inexplicable writings, and fruitful mines.

For Fawcett there had once been a wise, perfect civilisation here, far from the eyes of modern man – and I suspect that his older brother Edward, the theosophist and occultist, fed and watered such fantasies. Some even said there had been plans for a theosophist paradise to be established on the site of Z, where mystic insights would be found into its people. A change from spiritual messages sent by secret 'masters' out of Tibet, I suppose.

In reality, Percy Fawcett was made of fantasies. Despite his adventurer image, his achievements were limited and his money almost gone when he set out to find Z. Ironically, his disappearance in '25 brought him more fame than he had in life.

Whilst Canburn and the rest map out viable routes into the Mato Grosso, on behalf of the Brazilian government, I have been charged by London with seeking out a pile of mouldering bones, a tribal memory – for I am certain that Fawcett and his two companions are dead. The 'great explorer' probably died not long after his last missive to civilisation, four years ago, but the specific how, the exact where… these questions have fuelled so many fruitless expeditions.

I seek not a city, but a grave.

* * *

18th May

My sight has cleared a little. We are near the headwaters of the Xingu River. Breaking out of a tangle of vines, we discover a clearing by a stream. Three almost naked men stand on the bank, huge bows in their hands, arrows which must be two yards long.

Francisco calls to them in Portuguese, and then in some other tongue.

"They are Kalapalo," he murmurs to me.

I see their catch, by their feet – long, grey fish, some still jerking. Taking steel fish-hooks from my pack, I walk forward, slowly.

"*Para pescar. Para sua*, er… *pescaria*."

The tallest one, his belly hanging over his breech-clout, takes the hooks from my hands; he smiles. His companions smile.

"Kuikuro?" Francisco turns his head, as if searching.

This interests them less. The native points northeast.

"Kuikuro."

I mutter my thanks in Portuguese, and Francisco leads the mules back. Once in cover, we share our first smiles for days. We are close to the tribe which he believes can help me.

* * *

21st May

There were jaguars last night, deep growls nearby, but I was too exhausted to worry. I have to trust Francisco.

His grandmother was Kuikuro, taken by loggers, baptised against her will at the Catedral Senhor Bom Jesus in Cuiabá. Enslaved, would be another word for what was done. So his mother told him once, but she was a *mestiço,* between worlds. He does not even know his grandmother's true name – it was stripped from her by the church, drowned in communion wine, stifled by wafers.

Still, his past – and his skill with languages – gives him confidence that he can guide me.

Late in the morning we cross a narrow tributary, and there is a new enthusiasm in Francisco's step. The longer we are together, the more I wonder if my money is only a nudge, not a reason, for him to guide me. Is this his expedition, not mine?

I hack away at a sapling.

"Others have asked about Fawcett, and discovered little. Why should we succeed?" Not the first time I have asked this question.

Sweat glistens on his black moustache.

"They have asked the wrong people, *senhor*." A lizard, a gleam of amber scales, shoots across in front of us. "The tribes have learned to be careful. Little good comes from speaking to white men, and no good from speaking of secrets. They have songs, and in those songs they name the *itseke*, the spirits above us all. Perhaps *Coronel* Fawcett offended the *itseke*." He gave me a hard look. "A Kalapolo told me this once, when his people were accused of killing your Fawcett."

I am silent. I have heard the stories of hunters and *bandeirantes* murdering people of the Kuikuro and Kalapolo, and of disease spread by settlers; I have listened to tales of Kuhikugu, the remains of settlements in the jungle which are not white men's cities, but are also nothing like the splendour of the city of Z.

Nothing is quite true out here, except that the native peoples have suffered more than any.

Occasionally there is a break in the trees. The monkeys are cautious in these places; where the trees thin, they are watched by the *gavião-real*, the royal hawk, who will take them without warning. And the mosquitoes are back, the sudden whine and then the bites. My dizziness has returned with them.

I have no genuine taste for lost men, or for lost cities. I am here because I would like to be respected, if only for a year or two, to have the better journals seek quotes from me… to lecture to smug faces and count my fees. I would like to be more than I am.

What Fawcett really wanted, I cannot imagine. The same sort of fame? Was this his Atlantis or his El Dorado, his ticket out of relative poverty?

The forest whispers to me, and my bowels loosen.

I should never have come here.

* * *

23rd May

Fear comes with fevered moments. I no longer know if I could find the camp on the *cerrado* where we left Canburn. Should Francisco be injured or die, I will also perish – and no one will send an expedition to find my remains.

My feet and ankles are dry, blistered from the sulphur; Francisco places poultices upon the worst afflicted parts of my arms and legs. It helps, a little. Although I feel confused and light-headed, my body does what is necessary. It walks, it swings a machete, and it defecates quite efficiently. I must thank it one day, if I survive.

"The Kuikuro will have their own medicines," he says.

When we camp for the evening, Francisco gives me brandy, to settle me for sleep.

"*Senhor*, I… I have never been quite this far before, this deep. I could not afford the mules, the gifts…"

I want to be angry, but I am tired, and his dark eyes are honest, fearful in the lantern-light. I indicate that he should finish the brandy.

"Good night, *meu amigo*," I mutter.

What else is there to say? The forest talks enough for both of us each night.

* * *

26th May

A broad trail, and yes, a village – a great clearing with an orderly circle of tall huts, women weaving hammocks, and the laughter of children.

"At last." Francisco's voice betrays his relief.

He walks forward, leaving me with the weary mules, his palms towards the natives. Men whistle and call to each other, turning in our direction. I see spears and bows, but none are raised against us.

I don't know if I had expected some ceremonial welcome or open hostility, but neither occur. An old man shuffles from one of the huge straw-roofed huts, black pigment streaked from his eye sockets to the angles of his jaw, red dots upon his brow. He looks at us, showing broken teeth in some sort of smile. I think.

Tutored, I open the pack on the nearest mule, and spread a blanket with what might make promising offerings – two new machetes, more fish-hooks, a couple of small mirrors and some darning needles. Steel, in a land of fire-hardened wood. I expect that it will rust before a season passes.

The old man comes over, an easy, idle pace, and glances at our gifts. He seems satisfied, and waves over another native, slightly younger, with more complex markings. Francisco speaks in a flood of Portuguese too fast for me to grasp. I hear my name, his, and 'Fawcett'; he points to his own face, and says more, but in Cariban.

"Please, I..." My head spins, and I fall, unconscious.

* * *

27th May

I am in a hammock in a hut; Francisco, the younger man (a chief, or senior hunter?) and a much older stranger are standing over me. Outside it looks to be mid-morning. I must have slept for many hours.

"This is the healer, the shaman," says Francisco. "He is a kind of doctor and a priest, *senhor*."

The healer must have seen sixty, seventy years, and has a scarred leg, which he favours. Leathery hands stroke my cheeks, my arms; he speaks out to a boy, who runs out and returns with a red clay pot. A paste, to be spread over my bites.

"Fawcett," I say, lips dry.

The natives wait.

"A tall white man, a beard, four years ago, with two others. Did he come to this village?"

The shaman looks to the younger chief, who nods.

"The bearded one, alone," says the old man. Occasionally Francisco helps to translate his words into English, but my local Portuguese has improved enough that I understand most of what is said. "He was broken. We worried that he brought the sickness of the *bandeirantes*, but it was not. A snake had chosen him, and the poison spread. We could not help."

So Fawcett's son Jack, and the third man, Rimell, must have died before the village was reached. Fawcett had written that Rimell was in bad shape.

"We called the bearded one Carabranco, monkey with the white face, because we did not have a name to give him. And we listened to his stories. They were important stories – a city with stones as high as trees, very old, made for many, many men. It had metals and stones of great value, and was rich, powerful."

"Had you heard of this before?"

"No. This was a wonderful place, much better than the cities we once knew. Our cities had only earth walls and ditches, ponds where the fish played. His was much greater, maybe like the times when men and *itseke* lived together. Our women sewed *tolo*, new songs, of his place, but we do not share them when the tribes meet, or when strangers come. The women sing them here, among our people only."

I swallow, struggling to follow his words.

"What… what happened to him – Carabranco – at the end?"

"He died. But he was not one of us, and we did not know his ways. We could not bury him outside our huts; we could not call a feast, where the *kaguta* flutes could be played and men might dance for him. What were we to do? He was still searching for his city as he died, calling out for it. We wished to help."

"What did you do?"

"We wished to help," he repeats. "We wondered if the *itseke* built Carabranco's city, but had hidden it from us, because we have done wrong. There are mountains, valleys, beyond counting; rivers we have never swum, forest that is strange even to us. One man cannot search all these places. And so we made him many, that he might continue to look for his fine city."

"You made him many?"

But the shaman does not wish to speak any more.

* * *

29th May

I am feeling a little better.

One of the villagers brings me a woven box, and gestures that I should open it. Inside is, of all things, a tarnished silver cufflink.

"Carabranco," the villager says.

Percy Fawcett came here, to a place beyond our notions of civilisation, and somewhere in his baggage, he had cufflinks.

I begin to laugh, but none of the people around me understand why, not even Francisco.

* * *

1st June

"You can stand?" asks the shaman, not long after dawn.

I slide out of the hammock, cautious, and manage to get to my feet. Francisco is feeding the mules by the river.

"Come, come," he urges, and leads me to the central hut. It is cool inside, but the smell is rank, more than headdresses and the long wooden flutes stored there.

He draws back a woven curtain at one end.

The alcove he exposes is dark, but not too dark. Heaped there are many, many skulls. Jaguar, crab-fox, hawk, capuchin monkey, snake, even the foreparts of huge beetles. Most of the remains are old and almost free of flesh, dried out; a few are more recent, still with skin and sinew attached. But hadn't Francisco told me that the Kuikuro preferred to eat fish?

The shaman takes up the dessicated head of a hawk, its eyes mere sunken pits between the feathers. He mimes tearing his own arm with the beak.

"We gave the bearded one to them, so that he could continue his important search." Putting down the hawk's remains with reverential care, he takes hold of a fox's skull, very gently, and passes it to me. "Each took a part of him. Listen."

My hand trembles as I place the clean white bone against my temple…

Conch shells, when pressed tight to the ear, carry the sounds of the tides; this small skull whispers of endless forest, of a huge, living presence which holds all of us in its grasp, the lianas like reeds and strings, sharing its songs… it is a strand of the voices I have been hearing for so many days.

I hand the skull back, dazed.

His smile broadens. "When we find them again, they tell where they have been. It is how we knew you were coming. And one day, when they reach Carabranco's city, they will come back and speak of it. This shall be added to our songs, and shared with the Kalapolo and the others. We shall hold a great *Kuarup*, and sing to the peoples of mighty walls, and houses of stone."

I stumble, leaning against the wall for support, for I think I understand.

After Fawcett's death, the elders must have hacked his corpse into smaller parts, parcels of tempting flesh. I imagine that they left those parts scattered around the deep forest – left him for the birds, the animals, the insects, to consume and thus carry him with them, after he left this earthly life.

They made him many.

It was how they believed Fawcett could continue looking for the lost city, how he could cover the vastness of the Mato Grosso in a way which no human could ever achieve.

These people care more for Fawcett's work than any committee of geographers or gaggle of gold-hunters back in England. They give honour to a man who may not deserve it. It doesn't matter if the man sought fame or fortune, not to them.

It matters that he believed in the city.

And now they do. They have imagined a great and wonderful place, far better than even their own settlements of the past, and in doing so, they have made Fawcett's fantasy, something foolish, perhaps selfishly pursued and tawdry, into a greater thing.

Somewhere, everywhere, the wild creatures of Brazil search for the lost city of Z.

Perhaps one day they will find it.

We step out into the Brazilian heat. I imagine reporters and adventurers trampling their way into the village clearing; cameras following mining scouts, the trail of misery which follows.

"I will not speak of this to others," I say.

"We know." From his expression, the healer understands enough of the outside world. "Our half-brother would not have brought you to us, if it were otherwise. You would not have lived, if you had not heard the forest speak."

I bow my head. "I will tell the outsiders – my people – that Fawcett is gone, that he is on the wind, like dust."

"It is good." He clasps my arms.

I will have little to recount for Canburn or London's professors and adventurers; I will not be famous, or sought by the papers.

Such things no longer worry me.

I am at peace.

* * *

4th June

Francisco says that he will lead me to 'civilisation' once more when he has visited another nearby village of the Kuikuro. There they are said to have a memory of a woman named Ipia, who was taken more than forty years ago by white men. There is a song about her… about the woman who may be his grandmother. This, then, was his expedition, his quest.

Until my guide returns, the shaman takes me out each day to gather herbs, to help dig roots when his strength fails. Occasionally we find the remains of animals – and if there is a skull, or part of one, I take it up gently, wrapping it in my shirt, and bear it back to the house of ceremonies.

At night I am allowed to sit in there, as long as I do not touch the great *kaguta* flutes. I wait for the whispering to begin, and if I truly listen, I hear of how they seek a perfect city where men, *itseke* and beasts are at peace, where clear, sweet waters flow for every tongue to lap, and vast riches trickle freely between the fingers of every hand. Riches that mean little, for in that place is a greater wealth of spirit – though perhaps neither Guimarães nor Fawcett would understand.

The skulls whisper not of white men's fantasies, but of a place far finer, far more important, constructed by the Kuikuro from the ramblings of fools.

Sometimes I whisper back.

Where the Lost Things Are

David Hankins

LAURA LEANED against the rocky outcropping's only tree and glared down at the West Fields of Atlantis. Forests lined the wheat fields and the sea shimmered beyond a coastal road.

Five years she'd been trapped in the Lost Dimension without hope of returning to New York. Laura gripped her staff and fought against memories of home. Focus. She and Hank were on the lookout for lost people who crossed the dimensional threshold, to scoop them up before the Atlantians found them. Her geek brother had theorized this place, a dimension where all lost people and things go. His theory hadn't included a way home.

A thunderous boom snapped her upright and she scanned the fields.

Hank pointed with his bow. "There." Hank was the one good thing she'd found in the Lost Dimension. He was her rock, a born mountain-man, and she couldn't imagine life without him.

She narrowed her eyes. A young man in a lab coat sprawled in the tall wheat while a boy with a knapsack sloshed out of the surf. What had caused the boom? Transitions were usually silent.

Motion on the coastal road made Laura's jaw clench. An Atlantian patrol's bronze spears and white tunics flashed in the setting sun.

Laura bolted down the hillside, causing a small rockslide. Hank ghosted through the trees beside her, nearly invisible despite his towering size. They stopped at the field's edge to catch their breath, hiding behind soft cypress bushes. The new arrivals stood beside a low stainless-steel platform twenty yards away, their backs turned.

The boy waved his hands, excited. "Dude, that was insane! One second we're in your lab in snowy-ass-Buffalo and then BAM I'm knee-deep in the ocean. How'd you do that? Ooohhhh, you made a teleporter! That's amazing! Is this Hawaii? My friends are gonna be so jealous."

"Andrew, enough!" the man snapped, shoulders hunched. "Yes, it *can* teleport, but that's pushing matter away. Hermes *pulled* us here, so I think we just crossed into the Lost Dimension."

"Huh?"

Laura's breath caught. That lecturing tone sounded like her brother. The man's hair was too shaggy, but Jake had always hunched like that, hiding his height. Laura stepped into the open.

"Jake?" she said, voice low.

"It's like Schrödinger's cat," he continued, not hearing her. "When not observed, lost objects and people can cross dimensions. That phone you lost last week? It was here until you found it. I've sought the Lost Dimension for years, but since one cannot become intentionally lost—"

"Jake!" Laura broke into a run and he spun toward her. Her brother had grown into a man but still exuded social awkwardness.

"Laura?" Jake pushed coke-bottle glasses up his nose.

She crashed into him, wrapping her big brother in a bear hug that made him grunt. She felt like a giddy teenager again, but she didn't care. Her big brother had found her.

Jake disentangled himself. "Mom and Dad said you'd run away, but I *knew* you were in the Lost Dimension. I swore I'd find you, so" – he waved at the platform – "I invented a trans-dimensional portal." He grinned his know-it-all grin. "I named it Hermes."

Laura's breath hitched. "Trans-dimensional portal? You...you can get us home?"

Jake nodded like a bobblehead and pulled her over to Hermes. It was hexagonal, three feet across by eight inches tall. Stainless steel glinted in the waning sunlight.

The distant sound of hooves made Laura's head snap up. The Atlantians. Jake was babbling about grants and disbelieving professors, but she grabbed his sleeve. "We need to leave. Now!"

"Right." He produced a tablet from his lab coat. "Stay close. The transport field extends three feet beyond the platform." Hank sidled up to Laura while the boy Andrew stood opposite.

Jake pressed *enter* on his screen with dramatic flair.

Nothing happened.

Jake blinked at the tablet. "What? I reset—"

"Hurry up, Jake!"

Horsemen appeared on the coastal road and Laura's chest tightened. One shouted, spears pointed, and they charged. She swore, raising Jake's eyebrows, then dragged him toward the tree line.

They made it three yards before Jake face-planted into the wheat. He rolled, clutching his ankle.

"Come on!" Laura yelled as Hank bolted past, dragging Andrew.

Thwunk.

A spear buried itself beside Jake's head and he scrambled up, eyes wide. He hobbled forward and tripped again. Laura eyed the racing horsemen, judging distance. Jake wasn't going to make it.

She gripped her staff, swore, and charged the Atlantians. Thundering hooves and sharp spears bore down on her. Laura deflected the first spear with her staff, sidestepped the second, and whipped her staff into the third rider, unseating him.

A weighted net hit her in the back, knocking her down.

"No!" Jake yelled. Laura drew her knife and slashed at the net. Through the circling horsemen, she saw Jake standing slack-jawed where she'd left him.

"Run!" she yelled.

The riders swung off their mounts and swarmed her. Laura cut free of the net, but another dropped on her. Fists and feet fell with it.

Soon all Laura saw was red blood, brown grass, then darkness.

* * *

Laura woke with a start, bound to a support pole in a large four-post canvas tent. A squat, broad-shouldered man in a belted tunic knelt in the tent's center, caressing Jake's portal.

A cold knot formed in Laura's stomach. Dracontas. The slave-catcher had her again. She licked a bloody lip and glanced around, counting six armed guards in the crackling torchlight. Dracontas saw her move, and rose.

"Welcome back, Laura." His English was heavily accented, though his tone was polished.

Laura climbed to her feet, bruises protesting as she slid her tied wrists up the pole. She refused to look subservient to this snake. "Your English has improved, Dracontas."

He nodded. "After you escaped, I caught a new slave. He was less...entertaining than you" – he flashed a greasy smile – "but a better teacher. He proved himself worthy before I sacrificed him to Poseidon."

Laura clenched her teeth and tested her knots. "I told you, your sacrifices are lost people. Innocents. Not gifts from Olympus for your blood-thirsty perversion of Poseidon."

Dracontas stepped forward, blue eyes twinkling. "The priests would drown you in fire for such blasphemy." Laura flinched when he brushed her hair back. She drew a choppy breath at memories of pain. Six months she'd been his slave.

Never again.

Laura straightened, ready to bite off his fingers. A rustle at the tent flap made Dracontas turn.

Jake and Andrew rushed in and stumbled to a halt before Hermes, waving knives she recognized from Hank's belt. "Laura!" Jake yelled before the guards tackled him and Andrew.

Hank ducked through the tent flap behind them, silent as death, firing arrows as he came. Laura sagged against the post in furious joy. She'd known he'd come – but how dare Hank use Jake as a distraction? Her brother couldn't harm a fly.

Two guards fell to Hank's arrows before Dracontas drew a revolver from his tunic.

"Look out!" Laura yelled, then flinched at the gunshot. Blood exploded from Hank's left shoulder. He spun, bow flying from his grip, then came face-to-face with two guards with drawn swords. Hank grimaced, clutching his injured shoulder. The guards forced him to kneel beside Jake and Andrew.

Dracontas sneered at Laura. "Your replacement taught me much about your world. Even how to use some 'lost things' that I've found." He waggled the pistol. "Who would lose such a powerful weapon? Your people are fools."

He aimed the pistol at each kneeling captive, before settling on Jake. Dracontas kicked Hermes. "What is this device?"

Jake pushed his glasses up, lips pressed tight.

Dracontas thumbed the hammer back with a click. "I won't ask again."

Laura dropped her forehead against the post. "Tell him, Jake."

"It's a...a magic doorway," Jake said, pulling out his tablet and tapping buttons. "It can send you to our world." Hermes whirred to life, vibrating the ground under Laura's feet.

"Show me," Dracontas said, eyes glowing. "Show me your world."

Jake gulped. "It doesn't work."

Dracontas pressed the pistol against Laura's temple. She sucked in a breath.

"Wait!" Jake yelled. "I, uh, forgot to flip the coordinates." He tapped his tablet and Dracontas lowered the pistol.

Laura caught Hank's eye. His mouth was tight and blood streamed down his deerskin jacket, but he gave a shallow nod. He would follow her lead.

Laura gripped the tent pole and slammed both feet into Dracontas's back. He flew into a guard, the revolver went off, and they collapsed in a heap near Andrew. Hank jumped across Hermes and rammed his good shoulder into the tent pole. It splintered with a *crack* and dropped one corner of the tent. Laura and Hank fell together. She slid her wrists free of the pole.

Andrew, who'd been cowering silently, snatched the revolver from Dracontas and jumped onto Hermes. He waved the pistol around, eyes wide, voice cracking. "Get back, you goons, or I swear to God I'll blow you away!" The guards shuffled back as Dracontas rose behind Jake.

Jake, eyes still on his tablet, pumped a fist in triumph. "Got it!" He stood but Dracontas yanked him back. Andrew swung the pistol toward them.

"Stop!" Laura yelled. Everyone froze on the verge of violence. She and Hank sidled up to Hermes, which whirred softly. She eyed Jake.

"I'm glad I found you," he said with a sad smile, then tapped his tablet.

Laura's world imploded with a *whump*. It felt like she, Andrew, and Hank were squeezed into a tennis ball. Then a racket with the strength of God's backswing smacked them into oblivion.

* * *

Laura's world exploded with a *boom.* She slammed into the loamy forest floor, ears ringing. Agony radiated through her body and she sucked ragged breaths. *What the hell, Jake?* Laura spit out moss and rolled over.

Stars winked through rustling leaves, a full moon casting dappled shadows across the sleeping forest. She sat up, inhaled sharply, and looked around.

Hank lay nearby and Andrew groaned beyond him. Laura crawled to Hank and touched his injured shoulder. He flinched, opened his eyes, and tension drained from Laura's chest. Hank was alive.

"You okay, beautiful?" he asked, voice rough. She snorted. Even injured, he was still worried about her. God, she loved him. Laura caressed his beard with still-bound hands.

Andrew sat up and swore. "This doesn't look like Buffalo."

"Nope. We're still in Atlantis," Laura said as she helped Hank sit up. She spied the ridge of Atlantis's Spine, bathed in moonlight. "We're about five miles from where you arrived." She held out her hands. "Give me your pack."

Andrew passed it over, mumbling about Jake's stupid malfunctioning portal.

Laura dug into the pack. "It didn't malfunction. Jake said Hermes was a trans-dimensional portal *and* a teleporter. Hermes isn't here, so it pushed us – teleportation. Ah-ha!" Laura pulled a pocket knife and a hoodie from the pack.

Hank cut her bonds and Laura flung them into the forest. She drew a cleansing breath before slicing the hoodie into strips to bandage Hank's shoulder.

Andrew shoved his hands into his pockets. "I wanna go home."

Shoulder wrapped, Hank moved into the undergrowth toward the Spine. Laura followed. "I'm not leaving Jake with that monster. We need help." Andrew spluttered then stomped after them.

"Help? What help? We're in the middle of the woods!"

Laura let him catch up and threw an arm around the boy's shoulders. "Come on. It's time you met the Raiders, last of the lost colony of Roanoke."

* * *

The moonlit forest was cool as they walked. Laura was glad to hear the calls and rustles of nocturnal life. It meant that no Atlantians were near.

She sighed when Andrew spoke up, silencing the forest around them. "This place looks enormous. How'd you find us?"

"You got lucky," Laura said. "We watch for new arrivals to the Lost Dimension, but only find a handful before the Atlantians do."

"Cool. I thought Roanoke disappeared centuries ago. Wouldn't they be, like, ancient by now?"

Laura chuckled. "Roanoke survived for generations before the Atlantians conquered them. Now we only have one descendent from the original colonists. Ruby practically raised Hank on tales of her ancestors, before dementia took her memory. Now the Raiders are recently lost people who've kept the name."

Andrew eyed Hank as the first rays of dawn pierced the forest. "So...he's a native?"

Laura glanced at Hank who glowered at Andrew. "No," she said. "Twelve years ago, Hank's crazy survivalist papa abandoned him in the woods to 'test him'. Unobserved, Hank crossed over to the Lost Dimension. Now he's the guardian angel of the lost." Hank rolled his eyes but smirked behind his beard.

"Who was the jerk with the gun?"

Laura stopped abruptly. She didn't want to talk about Dracontas, but she'd forgotten about the pistol. She held out a hand. Andrew adopted wide-eyed innocence before deflating and handing it over.

She checked the cylinder. One round left. They'd found guns in the Lost Dimension before, along with keys, wallets, and a surprising number of individual socks, but most guns were rusted wrecks by the time they were found. This could be useful.

They'd reached the foothills of the Spine, so she followed a deer trail upward and changed the subject. "How do you know Jake? Are you his lab assistant?"

"Nah. My grandpa is his academic advisor. I just hang out in the lab after school."

"How'd you end up here?"

Andrew's abrupt silence made Laura stop. She and Hank eyed him and he blushed.

"I…uh, got bored. So I started flipping switches and" – he threw his hands up – "it's not my fault! There was this big red button, and, you know, I kinda pressed it. By accident."

"Jake didn't stop you?"

"Oh, he tried. He was furious! He shoved me and yelled 'get lost'. I tripped over Hermes, everything went *boom,* and then we were here."

They clambered up a narrow shelf along a gray cliff that turned sharply into a ravine. Laura ducked through a narrow tunnel into a limestone cavern. The warm glow of Christmas lights greeted them and a wooden plank beside the entrance said 'Welcome to Roanoke', carved in block letters.

Andrew's jaw dropped, making Laura smile. She loved bringing in newcomers. Twenty-three kids filled the room, watched by the elderly Ruby and her absent smile. The clack of metal on wood echoed across the cavern, teenagers training with an eclectic assortment of swords and staves.

Andrew pointed at the Christmas lights, one eyebrow raised. Laura chuckled. "It took me a long time to figure out power. We have a small windmill wired to an old car battery with spliced phone chargers. It's not much, but we make do with the lost things we find." He blinked and her smile turned to a smirk. "Jake's not the only smart one in the family."

"Where are the adults?" He glanced around. "Kids aren't the only ones who get lost."

Brutal memories flashed through Laura's mind and she grabbed Hank's hand. Her voice became tight. "Adults are more closely watched, harder to rescue. These kids are all we've saved."

A teenage girl sauntered over, sheathing a basket-handled rapier. Tight black cornrows gave her a severe expression. "We expected you sooner."

"Good to see you too, Maddy," Laura said. "This is Andrew." Maddy gave the kid a nod. "Gather the team. My brother came to the Lost Dimension and Dracontas took him. They should be at Poseidon's Temple by now. We'll use the back door."

Maddy's face tightened, but she nodded and spun to the teens. "Raiders of Roanoke, get your gear! We head through the mountain in fifteen minutes. The Fires of Poseidon await."

* * *

The city of Atlantis nestled under sheer cliffs on the far side of the Spine. Poseidon's temple was built into the rock itself on the northern edge of the city where the mountains met the sea.

Worry tightened Laura's chest as the Raiders wended through the mountain's limestone caves, torches and weapons in hand. They'd never tried a daylight raid, but she couldn't wait for darkness. She had to save Jake and his portal. Then they'd all go home.

Home. The very thought made her ache. Her grip tightened on the replacement staff she'd grabbed. *Hold on, Jake.*

Maddy's torch flared as she passed a crack in the wall and the flames blew back toward Andrew.

"Woah! You trying to kill me?" he said, jumping back.

A tongue of flame separated from Maddy's torch and climbed the cave wall to the ceiling where it burned blue and gold before sputtering out.

Andrew paled and Maddy chuckled. "What's the matter, kid? Scared of Poseidon's Breath?"

"Uh, yeah. That was freaky!"

Maddy shrugged. "These caves are riddled with methane vents."

"Methane? As in…cow farts?"

Someone laughed and Laura said, "Don't worry. We'll get more flare-outs, but we've mapped a safe route."

They walked in silence before Andrew asked Laura, "So how'd *you* come to the Lost Dimension?"

The Raiders' silence turned attentive. Laura sighed. "I was kidnapped. I killed the psycho before we reached his secluded cabin, but lost control of his van. We went over a cliff, crossed over, and burned into Atlantis like a meteor." She drew a ragged breath. That was the day she'd met Dracontas. The day she'd been enslaved. "Quiet. We're almost there."

The Raiders doused their torches, dropping the tunnel into near-total darkness. A low rumble and a flickering glow guided them forward. Laura took the lead.

The tunnel turned, revealing the flaming falls of Poseidon's Temple. Thundering water blocked the way, sheathed in eternal fire fed by hidden methane vents at the base of the falls. Water fell while flames climbed. Priests would chain their sacrifices within the falls to burn and drown for their god's pleasure.

Laura pressed her cheek to a damp wall and peered through a rocky gap into the temple, eyes narrowed.

Bright sunlight beamed through an oculus onto a three-story-tall statue of Poseidon that dominated a columned chamber. Jake hunched between Poseidon's feet, fiddling with Hermes.

Beyond him, Dracontas argued with three priests in sea-green robes who clutched barbed tridents. A priest yelled and pointed his trident at Jake. Dracontas shoved the priest and green-robed guards surged into view, sword tips resting on the slave-catcher's neck.

Time to move.

Laura waved Hank forward. He set down a wide plank he'd been carrying and slid it through the falls. Laura dashed through the flaming waters. Methane fire danced on her skin, singeing her before sputtering out.

She was halfway to Poseidon's statue before yells erupted around her. A dozen guards charged from all sides, but Laura ignored them and ran for Jake. Maddy's Roanoke Raiders would handle the guards.

"Laura?" Her brother rose, frowning.

She slid to a stop and grabbed his hand. "Let's go!" Andrew and two teens who'd followed her knelt and struggled to lift Hermes.

"Leave it!" Jake said, throwing his arms up. "The dimensional threshold is impenetrable from—" a trident slammed into his shoulder, throwing him forward.

Laura lunged to catch Jake, dropping her staff, and they fell onto Hermes. Jake screamed, trident tines piercing his chest and arm. Warm blood oozed around Laura's fingers as she tried to slow the bleeding.

No-no-no. Please, no…

Jake clutched her wrist, voice raspy. "At least I got to see you again."

Laura shook her head, fighting tears. "Don't you *dare* give up. You're taking us home."

He coughed, spraying blood. "Can't. I built Hermes to get me lost but I can't make it take us home."

Hank bellowed behind them. Laura whipped around. Dracontas stood over Hank near the Fires of Poseidon, sword stabbed through his leg. Her throat closed. She'd lost track of the battle.

Dracontas whipped his sword free, throwing an arc of blood, then kicked Hank's temple. He collapsed, right arm falling into the flaming falls and dislodging their plank bridge. A sob tore from Laura's throat as Dracontas raised his blade for the killing stroke. "No!"

He paused, his gaze finding hers. "Surrender, slave, and he lives." Slave. Laura's hands twisted in Jake's bloody lab coat and she searched for help.

Half of the Raiders were down. The battered survivors fell back to Hermes, dragging wounded friends. They clustered between Poseidon's feet, blades out like a hedgehog. The guards pressed in.

We've lost.

Emptiness welled in Laura's chest and she slammed a fist into Hermes.

Jake coughed more blood. "Sorry. I never intended…" He waved vaguely.

Realization rocked Laura back. She knew what to do, why Hermes didn't work. She grabbed Andrew. "Jake told you to 'get lost' before Hermes activated, right?"

"Uh, yeah."

Laura eyed Jake. "Hermes reads your neural impulses, doesn't it?"

Jake nodded. "I couldn't get intentionally lost, so I had to bypass—"

Hope built and Laura interrupted. "You've been trying to go home, but Hermes was built to get you lost. Stop thinking about home. To re-cross the dimensional threshold" – she tapped Jake's temple – "intend to get lost from here."

Laura looked back at Hank and drew a sharp breath when he caught her gaze. He had rolled out of the fiery falls and cradled his smoldering arm. Oh, Hank.

Dracontas pressed the bloody sword against Hank's neck, eyes glowing with triumph. "Surrender!"

Laura rose and pushed through the Raiders. Hands raised, she stepped forward and the guards moved aside.

"You win, Dracontas."

"Laura, no!" Jake's yell echoed through the temple.

Laura glanced back but kept walking. "I told you, Jake. Get lost!"

Dracontas wore a gloating grin. Laura was three steps from him when Hermes whirred to life, vibrating the stone floor. She winked at Dracontas, wiping away his grin.

There was a whump and it felt like the hand of Poseidon yanked her backward. Laura hit the floor and spun. Hermes and the Raiders imploded into a tiny dot that disappeared, taking one of the statue's stone legs.

"Yes!" Laura cheered. Jake had done it!

Cracking stone reverberated through the temple and Laura scrambled to her feet. Poseidon twisted, toppling toward the falls. Toward Hank.

Dracontas had kept his footing and swung his sword downward. Laura ran forward, drew the revolver from her pocket, and pulled the trigger.

The pistol jumped, blood flew, and Dracontas spun away.

Laura dove into Hank and they tumbled into the flaming falls. Poseidon crashed down as water and fire washed over them. Laura held Hank close and they tumbled into darkness.

* * *

Two weeks later, Laura sat on her rocky outcropping, gaze roaming the West Fields of Atlantis. The cool wind spoke of changing seasons, though winters here were never severe. Not like Buffalo.

Laura rubbed goosebumps on her scarred arms. Jagged rocks from the underground river they'd dropped into had left their mark before it spat them into the ocean.

Hank eased down beside her, still tender from his wounds. The burns on his right arm were raw but had stopped oozing. "Think he'll come?"

"Give Jake time. He had a punctured lung." Laura kissed Hank's cheek and leaned into him. They breathed the salt air in silence before Laura said, "I've decided."

Hank tensed, his arm tightening around her.

"When Jake returns, I'm staying here, with you." Laura entwined her fingers in his.

"But you wanted to go home."

"Home is where you are." Laura squeezed his hand. "We'll send the rest of the kids and Ruby back, but we're needed here to rescue the lost. I'll ask Jake to schedule regular runs with Hermes. He can bring supplies, then take lost people home."

"Okay." Hank kissed the top of her head. "We stay. But will Jake come?"

Laura gazed out across Atlantis. The wind plucked at her hair. She loved the view from up here. "I have faith in my brother. He got lost once. He'll do it again."

The Dream of a Summer Day

Lafcadio Hearn

Chapter I

THE HOTEL seemed to me a paradise, and the maids thereof celestial beings. This was because I had just fled away from one of the Open Ports, where I had ventured to seek comfort in a European hotel, supplied with all 'modern improvements'. To find myself at ease once more in a yukata, seated upon cool, soft matting, waited upon by sweet-voiced girls, and surrounded by things of beauty, was therefore like a redemption from all the sorrows of the nineteenth century. Bamboo-shoots and lotus-bulbs were given me for breakfast, and a fan from heaven for a keepsake. The design upon that fan represented only the white rushing burst of one great wave on a beach, and sea-birds shooting in exultation through the blue overhead. But to behold it was worth all the trouble of the journey. It was a glory of light, a thunder of motion, a triumph of sea-wind – all in one. It made me want to shout when I looked at it.

Between the cedarn balcony pillars I could see the course of the pretty gray town following the shore-sweep – and yellow lazy junks asleep at anchor – and the opening of the bay between enormous green cliffs – and beyond it the blaze of summer to the horizon. In that horizon there were mountain shapes faint as old memories. And all things but the grey town, and the yellow junks, and the green cliffs, were blue.

Then a voice softly toned as a wind-bell began to tinkle words of courtesy into my reverie, and broke it; and I perceived that the mistress of the palace had come to thank me for the chadai[1], and I prostrated myself before her. She was very young, and more than pleasant to look upon – like the moth-maidens, like the butterfly-women, of Kuni-sada. And I thought at once of death; for the beautiful is sometimes a sorrow of anticipation.

She asked whither I honorably intended to go, that she might order a kuruma for me. And I made answer:

"To Kumamoto. But the name of your house I much wish to know, that I may always remember it."

"My guest-rooms," she said, "are augustly insignificant, and my maidens honourably rude. But the house is called the House of Urashima. And now I go to order a kuruma."

The music of her voice passed; and I felt enchantment falling all about me – like the thrilling of a ghostly web. For the name was the name of the story of a song that bewitches men.

Chapter II

ONCE you hear the story, you will never be able to forget it. Every summer when I find myself on the coast – especially of very soft, still days – it haunts me most persistently. There are many native versions of it which have been the inspiration for countless works of art. But the most impressive and the most ancient is found in the 'Manyefushifu', a collection of poems dating from the fifth to the ninth century. From this ancient version the great scholar Aston translated it into prose, and the great scholar Chamberlain into both prose and verse. But for English readers I think the most charming form of it is Chamberlain's version written for children, in the 'Japanese Fairy-Tale Series', – because of the delicious coloured pictures by native artists. With that little book before me, I shall try to tell the legend over again in my own words.

Fourteen hundred and sixteen years ago, the fisher-boy Urashima Tarō left the shore of Suminoyé in his boat.

Summer days were then as now – all drowsy and tender blue, with only some light, pure white clouds hanging over the mirror of the sea. Then, too, were the hills the same – far blue soft shapes melting into the blue sky. And the winds were lazy.

And presently the boy, also lazy, let his boat drift as he fished. It was a queer boat, unpainted and rudderless, of a shape you probably never saw. But still, after fourteen hundred years, there are such boats to be seen in front of the ancient fishing-hamlets of the coast of the Sea of Japan.

After long waiting, Urashima caught something, and drew it up to him. But he found it was only a tortoise.

Now a tortoise is sacred to the Dragon God of the Sea, and the period of its natural life is a thousand – some say ten thousand – years. So that to kill it is very wrong. The boy gently unfastened the creature from his line, and set it free, with a prayer to the gods.

But he caught nothing more. And the day was very warm; and sea and air and all things were very, very silent. And a great drowsiness grew upon him – and he slept in his drifting boat.

Then out of the dreaming of the sea rose up a beautiful girl – just as you can see her in the picture to Professor Chamberlain's 'Urashima', – robed in crimson and blue, with long black hair flowing down her back even to her feet, after the fashion of a prince's daughter fourteen hundred years ago.

Gliding over the waters she came, softly as air; and she stood above the sleeping boy in the boat, and woke him with a light touch, and said –

"Do not be surprised. My father, the Dragon King of the Sea, sent me to you, because of your kind heart. For today you set free a tortoise. And now we will go to my father's palace in the island where summer never dies; and I will be your flower-wife if you wish; and we shall live there happily forever."

And Urashima wondered more and more as he looked upon her; for she was more beautiful than any human being, and he could not but love her. Then he took one oar, and he took another, and they rowed away together – just as you may still see, off the far western coast, wife and husband rowing together, when the fishing-boats flit into the evening gold.

They rowed away softly and swiftly over the silent blue water down into the south – till they came to the island where summer never dies – and to the palace of the Dragon King of the Sea.

[Here the text of the little book suddenly shrinks away as you read, and faint blue ripplings flood the page; and beyond them in a fairy horizon you can see the long low soft shore of the island, and peaked roofs rising through evergreen foliage – the roofs of the Sea God's palace – like the palace of the Mikado Yuriaku, fourteen hundred and sixteen years ago.]

There strange servitors came to receive them in robes of ceremony – creatures of the Sea, who paid greeting to Urashima as the son-in-law of the Dragon King.

So the Sea God's daughter became the bride of Urashima; and it was a bridal of wondrous splendour; and in the Dragon Palace there was great rejoicing.

And each day for Urashima there were new wonders and new pleasures: wonders of the deepest deep brought up by the servants of the Ocean God; pleasures of that enchanted land where summer never dies. And so three years passed.

But in spite of all these things, the fisher-boy felt always a heaviness at his heart when he thought of his parents waiting alone. So that at last he prayed his bride to let him go home for a little while only, just to say one word to his father and mother – after which he would hasten back to her.

At these words she began to weep; and for a long time she continued to weep silently. Then she said to him: "Since you wish to go, of course you must go. I fear your going very much; I fear we shall never see each other again. But I will give you a little box to take with you. It will help you to come back to me if you will do what I tell you. Do not open it. Above all things, do not open it – no matter what may happen! Because, if you open it, you will never be able to come back, and you will never see me again."

Then she gave him a little lacquered box tied about with a silken cord. [And that box can be seen unto this day in the temple of Kanagawa, by the seashore; and the priests there also keep Urashima Tarō's fishing line, and some strange jewels which he brought back with him from the realm of the Dragon King.]

But Urashima comforted his bride, and promised her never, never to open the box – never even to loosen the silken string. Then he passed away through the summer light over the ever-sleeping sea; and the shape of the island where summer never dies faded behind him like a dream; and he saw again before him the blue mountains of Japan, sharpening in the white glow of the northern horizon.

Again at last he glided into his native bay; again he stood upon its beach. But as he looked, there came upon him a great bewilderment – a weird doubt.

For the place was at once the same, and yet not the same. The cottage of his fathers had disappeared. There was a village; but the shapes of the houses were all strange, and the trees were strange, and the fields, and even the faces of the people. Nearly all remembered landmarks were gone; the Shintō temple appeared to have been rebuilt in a new place; the woods had vanished from the neighbouring slopes. Only the voice of the little stream flowing through the settlement, and the forms of the mountains, were still the same. All else was unfamiliar and new. In vain he tried to find the dwelling of his parents; and the fisherfolk stared wonderingly at him; and he could not remember having ever seen any of those faces before.

There came along a very old man, leaning on a stick, and Urashima asked him the way to the house of the Urashima family. But the old man looked quite astonished, and made him repeat the question many times, and then cried out –

"Urashima Tarō! Where do you come from that you do not know the story? Urashima Tarō! Why, it is more than four hundred years since he was drowned, and a monument is erected to his memory in the graveyard. The graves of all his people are in that graveyard – the old graveyard which is not now used any more. Urashima Tarō! How can you be so foolish as to ask where his house is?" And the old man hobbled on, laughing at the simplicity of his questioner.

But Urashima went to the village graveyard – the old graveyard that was not used any more – and there he found his own tombstone, and the tombstones of his father and his mother and his kindred, and the tombstones of many others he had known. So old they were, so moss-eaten, that it was very hard to read the names upon them.

Then he knew himself the victim of some strange illusion, and he took his way back to the beach – always carrying in his hand the box, the gift of the Sea God's daughter. But what was this illusion? And what could be in that box? Or might not that which was in the box be the cause of the illusion? Doubt mastered faith. Recklessly he broke the promise made to his beloved; he loosened the silken cord – he opened the box!

Instantly, without any sound, there burst from it a white cold spectral vapour that rose in air like a summer cloud, and began to drift away swiftly into the south, over the silent sea. There was nothing else in the box.

And Urashima then knew that he had destroyed his own happiness – that he could never again return to his beloved, the daughter of the Ocean King. So that he wept and cried out bitterly in his despair.

Yet for a moment only. In another, he himself was changed. An icy chill shot through all his blood; his teeth fell out; his face shriveled; his hair turned white as snow; his limbs withered; his strength ebbed; he sank down lifeless on the sand, crushed by the weight of four hundred winters.

Now in the official annals of the Emperors it is written that 'in the twenty-first year of the Mikado Yuriaku, the boy Urashima of Midzunoyé, in the district of Yosa, in the province of Tango, a descendant of the divinity Shimanemi, went to Elysium [*Hōraï*] in a fishing-boat." After this there is no more news of Urashima during the reigns of thirty-one emperors and empresses – that is, from the fifth until the ninth century. And then the annals announce that 'in the second year of Tenchiyō, in the reign of the Mikado Go-Junwa, the boy Urashima returned, and presently departed again, none knew whither.'[2]

Chapter III

THE FAIRY MISTRESS came back to tell me that everything was ready, and tried to lift my valise in her slender hands – which I prevented her from doing, because it was heavy. Then she laughed, but would not suffer that I should carry it myself, and summoned a sea-creature with Chinese characters upon his back. I made obeisance to her; and she prayed me to remember the unworthy house despite the rudeness of the maidens. "And you will pay the kurumaya," she said, "only seventy-five sen."

Then I slipped into the vehicle; and in a few minutes the little grey town had vanished behind a curve. I was rolling along a white road overlooking the shore. To the right were pale brown cliffs; to the left only space and sea.

Mile after mile I rolled along that shore, looking into the infinite light. All was steeped in blue, – a marvelous blue, like that which comes and goes in the heart of a great shell. Glowing blue sea met hollow blue sky in a brightness of electric fusion; and vast blue apparitions – the mountains of Higo – angled up through the blaze, like masses of amethyst. What a blue transparency! The universal colour was broken only by the dazzling white of a few high summer clouds, motionlessly curled above one phantom peak in the offing. They threw down upon the water snowy tremulous lights. Midges of ships creeping far away seemed to pull long threads after them – the only sharp lines in all that hazy glory. But what divine clouds! White purified spirits of clouds, resting on their way to the beatitude of Nirvana? Or perhaps the mists escaped from Urashima's box a thousand years ago?

The gnat of the soul of me flitted out into that dream of blue, 'twixt sea and sun – hummed back to the shore of Suminoyé through the luminous ghosts of fourteen hundred summers. Vaguely I felt beneath me the drifting of a keel. It was the time of the Mikado Yuriaku. And the Daughter of the Dragon King said tinklingly – "Now we will go to my father's palace where it is always blue." "Why always blue?" I asked. "Because," she said, "I put all the clouds into the Box." "But I must go home," I answered resolutely. "Then," she said, "you will pay the kurumaya only seventy-five sen."

Wherewith I woke into Doyō, or the Period of Greatest Heat, in the twenty-sixth year of Meiji – and saw proof of the era in a line of telegraph poles reaching out of sight on the land side of the way. The kuruma was still fleeing by the shore, before the same blue vision of sky, peak, and sea; but the white clouds were gone! – and there were no more cliffs close to the road, but fields of rice and of barley stretching to far-off hills. The telegraph lines absorbed my attention for a moment, because on the top wire, and only on the top wire, hosts of little birds were perched, all with their heads to the road, and nowise disturbed by our coming. They remained quite still, looking down upon us as mere passing phenomena. There were hundreds and hundreds in rank, for miles and miles. And I could not see one having its tail turned to the road. Why they sat thus, and what they were watching or waiting for, I could not guess. At intervals I waved my hat and shouted, to startle the ranks. Whereupon a few would rise up fluttering and chippering, and drop back again upon the wire in the same position as before. The vast majority refused to take me seriously.

The sharp rattle of the wheels was drowned by a deep booming; and as we whirled past a village I caught sight of an immense drum under an open shed, beaten by naked men.

"O kurumaya!" I shouted – "that – what is it?"

He, without stopping, shouted back: – "Everywhere now the same thing is. Much time-in rain has not been: so the gods-to prayers are made, and drums are beaten." We flashed through other villages; and I saw and heard more drums of various sizes, and from hamlets invisible, over miles of parching rice-fields, yet other drums, like echoings, responded.

Chapter IV

THEN I BEGAN to think about Urashima again. I thought of the pictures and poems and proverbs recording the influence of the legend upon the imagination of a race. I thought of an Izumo dancing-girl I saw at a banquet acting the part of Urashima, with a little lacquered box whence there issued at the tragical minute a mist of Kyōto incense. I thought about the antiquity of the beautiful dance, and therefore about vanished generations of dancing-girls, and therefore about dust in the abstract; which, again, led me to think of dust in the concrete, as bestirred by the sandals of the kurumaya to whom I was to pay only seventy-five sen. And I wondered how much of it might be old human dust, and whether in the eternal order of things the motion of hearts might be of more consequence than the motion of dust. Then my ancestral morality took alarm; and I tried to persuade myself that a story which had lived for a thousand years, gaining fresher charm with the passing of every century, could only have survived by virtue of some truth in it. But what truth? For the time being I could find no answer to this question.

The heat had become very great; and I cried –

"O kurumaya! the throat of Selfishness is dry; water desirable is."

He, still running, answered –

"The Village of the Long Beach inside of – not far – a great gush-water is. There pure august water will be given."

I cried again –

"O kurumaya! – those little birds as-for, why this way always facing?"

He, running still more swiftly, responded – "All birds wind-to facing sit."

I laughed first at my own simplicity; then at my forgetfulness, remembering I had been told the same thing, somewhere or other, when a boy. Perhaps the mystery of Urashima might also have been created by forgetfulness.

I thought again about Urashima. I saw the Daughter of the Dragon King waiting vainly in the palace made beautiful for his welcome – and the pitiless return of the Cloud, announcing what had happened – and the loving uncouth sea-creatures, in their garments of great ceremony, trying to comfort her. But in the real story there was nothing of all this; and the pity of the people seemed to be all for Urashima. And I began to discourse with myself thus:

Is it right to pity Urashima at all? Of course he was bewildered by the gods. But who is not bewildered by the gods? What is Life itself but a bewilderment? And Urashima in his bewilderment doubted the purpose of the gods, and opened the box. Then he died without any trouble, and the people built a shrine to him as Urashima Miō-jin. Why, then, so much pity?

Things are quite differently managed in the West. After disobeying Western gods, we have still to remain alive and to learn the height and the breadth and the depth of superlative sorrow. We are not allowed to die quite comfortably just at the best possible time: much less are we suffered to become after death small gods in our own right. How can we pity the folly of Urashima after he had lived so long alone with visible gods.

Perhaps the fact that we do may answer the riddle. This pity must be self-pity; wherefore the legend may be the legend of a myriad souls. The thought of it comes just at a particular time of blue light and soft wind – and always like an old reproach. It has too intimate relation to a season and the feeling of a season not to be also related to something real in one's life, or in the lives of one's ancestors. But what was that real something? Who was the Daughter of the Dragon King? Where was the island of unending summer? And what was the cloud in the box?

I cannot answer all those questions. I know this only, which is not at all new:

I have memory of a place and a magical time in which the Sun and the Moon were larger and brighter than now. Whether it was of this life or of some life before I cannot tell. But I know the sky was very much more blue, and nearer to the world – almost as it seems to become above the masts of a steamer steaming into equatorial summer. The sea was alive, and used to talk – and the Wind made me cry out for joy when it touched me. Once or twice during other years, in divine days lived among the peaks, I have dreamed just for a moment that the same wind was blowing – but it was only a remembrance.

Also in that place the clouds were wonderful, and of colours for which there are no names at all – colours that used to make me hungry and thirsty. I remember, too, that the days were ever so much longer than these days, and that every day there were new wonders and new pleasures for me. And all that country and time were softly ruled by One who thought only of ways to make me happy. Sometimes I would refuse to be made happy, and that always caused her pain, although she was divine; and I remember that I tried very hard to be sorry. When day was done, and there fell the great hush of the light before moonrise, she would tell me stories that made me tingle from head to foot with pleasure. I have never heard any other stories half so beautiful. And when the pleasure became too great, she would sing a weird little song which always brought sleep. At last there came a parting day; and she wept, and told me of a charm she had given that I must never, never lose, because it would keep me young, and give me power to return. But I never returned. And the years went; and one day I knew that I had lost the charm, and had become ridiculously old.

Chapter V

THE VILLAGE OF THE LONG BEACH is at the foot of a green cliff near the road, and consists of a dozen thatched cottages clustered about a rocky pool, shaded by pines. The basin overflows with cold water, supplied by a stream that leaps straight from the heart of the cliff – just as folks imagine that a poem ought to spring straight from the heart of a poet. It was evidently a favourite halting-place, judging by the number of kuruma and of people resting. There were benches under the trees; and, after having allayed thirst, I sat down to smoke and to look at the women washing clothes and the travelers refreshing themselves at the pool, while my kurumaya stripped, and proceeded to dash buckets of cold water over his body. Then tea was brought me by a young man with a baby on his back; and I tried to play with the baby, which said "Ah, bah!"

Such are the first sounds uttered by a Japanese babe. But they are purely Oriental; and in Itomaji should be written *Aba*. And, as an utterance untaught, *Aba* is interesting. It is in Japanese child-speech the word for 'good-bye' – precisely the last we would expect an infant to pronounce on entering into this world of illusion. To whom or to what is the little soul saying good-bye? – to friends in a previous state of existence still freshly remembered? – to comrades of its shadowy journey from nobody knows where? Such theorising is tolerably safe, from a pious point of view, since the child can never decide for us. What its thoughts were at that mysterious moment of first speech, it will have forgotten long before it has become able to answer questions.

Unexpectedly, a queer recollection came to me – resurrected, perhaps, by the sight of the young man with the baby – perhaps by the song of the water in the cliff: the recollection of a story:

Long, long ago there lived somewhere among the mountains a poor wood-cutter and his wife. They were very old, and had no children. Every day the husband went alone to the forest to cut wood, while the wife sat weaving at home.

One day the old man went farther into the forest than was his custom, to seek a certain kind of wood; and he suddenly found himself at the edge of a little spring he had never seen before. The water was strangely clear and cold, and he was thirsty; for the day was hot, and he had been working hard. So he doffed his great straw hat, knelt down, and took a long drink. That water seemed to refresh him in a most extraordinary way. Then he caught sight of his own face in the spring, and started back. It was certainly his own face, but not at all as he was accustomed to see it in the old mirror at home. It was the face of a very young man! He could not believe his eyes. He put up both hands to his head, which had been quite bald only a moment before. It was covered with thick black hair. And his face had become smooth as a boy's; every wrinkle was gone. At the same moment he discovered himself full of new strength. He stared in astonishment at the limbs that had been so long withered by age; they were now shapely and hard with dense young muscle. Unknowingly he had drunk at the Fountain of Youth; and that draught had transformed him.

First, he leaped high and shouted for joy; then he ran home faster than he had ever run before in his life. When he entered his house his wife was frightened, because she took him for a stranger; and when he told her the wonder, she could not at once believe him. But after a long time he was able to convince her that the young man she now saw before her was really her husband; and he told her where the spring was, and asked her to go there with him.

Then she said: "You have become so handsome and so young that you cannot continue to love an old woman; so I must drink some of that water immediately. But it will never do for both of us to be away from the house at the same time. Do you wait here while I go." And she ran to the woods all by herself.

She found the spring and knelt down, and began to drink. Oh! how cool and sweet that water was! She drank and drank and drank, and stopped for breath only to begin again.

Her husband waited for her impatiently; he expected to see her come back changed into a pretty slender girl. But she did not come back at all. He got anxious, shut up the house, and went to look for her.

When he reached the spring, he could not see her. He was just on the point of returning when he heard a little wail in the high grass near the spring. He searched there and discovered his wife's clothes and a baby – a very small baby, perhaps six months old!

For the old woman had drunk too deeply of the magical water; she had drunk herself far back beyond the time of youth into the period of speechless infancy.

He took up the child in his arms. It looked at him in a sad, wondering way. He carried it home, – murmuring to it – thinking strange, melancholy thoughts.

In that hour, after my reverie about Urashima, the moral of this story seemed less satisfactory than in former time. Because by drinking too deeply of life we do not become young.

Naked and cool my kurumaya returned, and said that because of the heat he could not finish the promised run of twenty-five miles, but that he had found another runner to take me the rest of the way. For so much as he himself had done, he wanted fifty-five sen.

It was really very hot – more than 100° I afterwards learned; and far away there throbbed continually, like a pulsation of the beat itself, the sound of great drums beating for rain. And I thought of the Daughter of the Dragon King.

"Seventy-five sen, she told me," I observed; "and that promised to be done has not been done. Nevertheless, seventy-five sen to you shall be given, because I am afraid of the gods."

And behind a yet unwearied runner I fled away into the enormous blaze – in the direction of the great drums.

Footnotes for *The Dream of a Summer's Day*

1. A little gift of money, always made to a hotel by the guest shortly after his arrival.
2. See *The Classical Poetry of the Japanese*, by Professor Chamberlain, in Trübner's *Oriental Series*. According to Western chronology, Urashima went fishing in 477 A.D., and returned in 825.

The Mirrors of Tuzun Thune

Robert E. Howard

A wild, weird clime that lieth sublime
Out of Space, out of Time.
Edgar Allan Poe

THERE COMES, even to kings, the time of great weariness. Then the gold of the throne is brass, the silk of the palace becomes drab. The gems in the diadem sparkle drearily like the ice of the white seas; the speech of men is as the empty rattle of a jester's bell and the feel comes of things unreal; even the sun is copper in the sky, and the breath of the green ocean is no longer fresh.

Kull sat upon the throne of Valusia and the hour of weariness was upon him. They moved before him in an endless, meaningless panorama: men, women, priests, events and shadows of events; things seen and things to be attained. But like shadows they came and went, leaving no trace upon his consciousness, save that of a great mental fatigue. Yet Kull was not tired. There was a longing in him for things beyond himself and beyond the Valusian court. An unrest stirred in him, and strange, luminous dreams roamed his soul. At his bidding there came to him Brule the Spear-slayer, warrior of Pictland, from the islands beyond the West.

"Lord king, you are tired of the life of the court. Come with me upon my galley and let us roam the tides for a space."

"Nay." Kull rested his chin moodily upon his mighty hand. "I am weary beyond all these things. The cities hold no lure for me – and the borders are quiet. I hear no more the sea-songs I heard when I lay as a boy on the booming crags of Atlantis, and the night was alive with blazing stars. No more do the green woodlands beckon me as of old. There is a strangeness upon me and a longing beyond life's longings. Go!"

Brule went forth in a doubtful mood, leaving the king brooding upon his throne. Then to Kull stole a girl of the court and whispered:

"Great king, seek Tuzun Thune, the wizard. The secrets of life and death are his, and the stars in the sky, the lands beneath the seas."

Kull looked at the girl. Fine gold was her hair and her violet eyes were slanted strangely; she was beautiful, but her beauty meant little to Kull.

"Tuzun Thune," he repeated. "Who is he?"

"A wizard of the Elder Race. He lives here in Valusia, by the Lake of Visions in the House of a Thousand Mirrors. All things are known to him, lord king; he speaks with the dead and holds converse with the demons of the Lost Lands."

Kull arose.

"I will seek out this mummer; but no word of my going, do you hear?"

"I am your slave, my lord." And she sank to her knees meekly, but the smile of her scarlet mouth was cunning behind Kull's back and the gleam of her narrow eyes was crafty.

Kull came to the house of Tuzun Thune, beside the Lake of Visions. Wide and blue stretched the waters of the lake, and many a fine palace rose upon its banks; many swan-winged pleasure boats drifted lazily upon its hazy surface and evermore there came the sound of soft music.

Tall and spacious, but unpretentious, rose the House of a Thousand Mirrors. The great doors stood open, and Kull ascended the broad stair and entered, unannounced. There in a great chamber, whose walls were of mirrors, he came upon Tuzun Thune, the wizard. The man was ancient as the hills of Zalgara; like wrinkled leather was his skin, but his cold gray eyes were like sparks of sword steel.

"Kull of Valusia, my house is yours," said he, bowing with old-time courtliness and motioning Kull to a throne-like chair.

"You are a wizard, I have heard," said Kull bluntly, resting his chin upon his hand and fixing his sombre eyes upon the man's face. "Can you do wonders?"

The wizard stretched forth his hand; his fingers opened and closed like a bird's claws.

"Is that not a wonder – that this blind flesh obeys the thoughts of my mind? I walk, I breathe, I speak – are they not all wonders?"

Kull meditated awhile, then spoke. "Can you summon up demons?"

"Aye. I can summon up a demon more savage than any in ghost land – by smiting you in the face."

Kull started, then nodded. "But the dead, can you talk to the dead?"

"I talk with the dead always – as I am talking now. Death begins with birth, and each man begins to die when he is born; even now you are dead, King Kull, because you were born."

"But you, you are older than men become; do wizards never die?"

"Men die when their times come. No later, no sooner. Mine has not come."

Kull turned these answers over in his mind.

"Then it would seem that the greatest wizard of Valusia is no more than an ordinary man, and I have been duped in coming here."

Tuzun Thune shook his head. "Men are but men, and the greatest men are they who soonest learn the simpler things. Nay, look into my mirrors, Kull."

The ceiling was a great many mirrors, and the walls were mirrors, perfectly joined, yet many mirrors of many sizes and shapes.

"Mirrors are the world, Kull," droned the wizard. "Gaze into my mirrors and be wise."

Kull chose one at random and looked into it intently. The mirrors upon the opposite wall were reflected there, reflecting others, so that he seemed to be gazing down a long, luminous corridor, formed by mirror behind mirror; and far down this corridor moved a tiny figure. Kull looked long ere he saw that the figure was the reflection of himself. He gazed and a queer feeling of pettiness came over him; it seemed that that tiny figure was the true Kull, representing the real proportions of himself. So he moved away and stood before another.

"Look closely, Kull. That is the mirror of the past," he heard the wizard say.

Gray fogs obscured the vision, great billows of mist, ever heaving and changing like the ghost of a great river; through these fogs Kull caught swift fleeting visions of horror and strangeness; beasts and men moved there and shapes neither men nor beasts; great exotic blossoms glowed through the grayness; tall tropic trees towered high over reeking swamps, where reptilian monsters wallowed, and bellowed; the sky was ghastly with flying dragons, and the restless seas rocked and roared and beat endlessly along the muddy beaches. Man was not, yet man was the dream of the gods, and strange were the nightmare forms that glided through the noisome jungles. Battle and onslaught were there, and frightful love. Death was there, for Life and Death go hand in hand. Across the slimy beaches of the world sounded the bellowing of the monsters, and incredible shapes loomed through the streaming curtain of the incessant rain.

"This is of the future."

Kull looked in silence.

"See you – what?"

"A strange world," said Kull heavily. "The Seven Empires are crumbled to dust and are forgotten. The restless green waves roar for many a fathom above the eternal hills of Atlantis; the mountains of Lemuria of the West are the islands of an unknown sea. Strange savages roam the elder lands and new lands flung strangely from the deeps, defiling the elder shrines. Valusia is vanished and all the nations of today; they of tomorrow are strangers. They know us not."

"Time strides onward," said Tuzun Thune calmly. "We live today; what care we for tomorrow – or yesterday? The Wheel turns and nations rise and fall; the world changes, and times return to savagery to rise again through the long age. Ere Atlantis was, Valusia was, and ere Valusia was, the Elder Nations were. Aye, we, too, trampled the shoulders of lost tribes in our advance. You, who have come from the green sea hills of Atlantis to seize the ancient crown of Valusia, you think my tribe is old, we who held these lands ere the Valusians came out of the East, in the days before there were men in the sea lands. But men were here when the Elder Tribes rode out of the waste lands, and men before men, tribe before tribe. The nations pass and are forgotten, for that is the destiny of man."

"Yes," said Kull. "Yet is it not a pity that the beauty and glory of men should fade like smoke on a summer sea?"

"For what reason, since that is their destiny? I brood not over the lost glories of my race, nor do I labor for races to come. Live now, Kull, live now. The dead are dead; the unborn are not. What matters men's forgetfulness of you when you have forgotten yourself in the silent worlds of death? Gaze in my mirrors and be wise."

Kull chose another mirror and gazed into it.

"That is the mirror of deepest magic; what see ye, Kull?"

"Naught but myself."

"Look closely, Kull; is it in truth you?"

Kull stared into the great mirror, and the image that was his reflection returned his gaze.

"I come before this mirror," mused Kull, chin on fist, "and I bring this man to life. That is beyond my understanding, since first I saw him in the still waters of the lakes of Atlantis, till I saw him again in the gold-rimmed mirrors of Valusia. He is I, a shadow of myself, part of myself – I can bring him into being or slay him at my will; yet—" He halted, strange thoughts whispering through the vast dim recesses of his mind like shadowy bats flying through a great cavern – "yet where is he when I stand not in front of a mirror? May it be in man's power thus lightly to form and destroy a shadow of life and existence? How do I know that when I step back from the mirror he vanishes into the void of Naught?

"Nay, by Valka, am I the man or is he? Which of us is the ghost of the other? Mayhap these mirrors are but windows through which we look into another world. Does he think the same of me? Am I no more than a shadow, a reflection of himself – to him, as he to me? And if I am the ghost, what sort of a world lives upon the other side of this mirror? What armies ride there and what kings rule? This world is all I know. Knowing naught of any other, how can I judge? Surely there are green hills there and booming seas and wide plains where men ride to battle. Tell me, wizard who is wiser than most men, tell me are there worlds beyond our worlds?"

"A man has eyes, let him see," answered the wizard. "Who would see must first believe."

The hours drifted by, and Kull still sat before the mirrors of Tuzun Thune, gazing into that which depicted himself. Sometimes it seemed that he gazed upon hard shallowness; at other times gigantic depths seemed to loom before him. Like the surface of the sea was the mirror of Tuzun Thune; hard as the sea in the sun's slanting beams, in the darkness of the stars, when no eye can pierce her deeps; vast and mystic as the sea when the sun smites her in such way that the watcher's breath is caught at the glimpse of tremendous abysses. So was the mirror in which Kull gazed.

At last the king rose with a sigh and took his departure still wondering. And Kull came again to the House of a Thousand Mirrors; day after day he came and sat for hours before the mirror. The eyes looked out at him, identical with his; yet Kull seemed to sense a difference – a reality that was not of him. Hour upon hour he would stare with strange intensity into the mirror; hour after hour the image gave back his gaze.

The business of the palace and of the council went neglected. The people murmured; Kull's stallion stamped restlessly in his stable, and Kull's warriors diced and argued aimlessly with one another. Kull heeded not. At times he seemed on the point of discovering some vast, unthinkable secret. He no longer thought of the image in the mirror as a shadow of himself; the thing, to him, was an entity, similar in outer appearance, yet basically as far from Kull himself as the poles are far apart. The image, it seemed to Kull, had an individuality apart from Kull's, he was no more dependent on Kull than Kull was dependent on him. And day by day Kull doubted in which world he really lived; was he the shadow, summoned at will by the other? Did he instead of the other live in a world of delusion, the shadow of the real world?

Kull began to wish that he might enter the personality beyond the mirror for a space, to see what might be seen; yet should he manage to go beyond that door could he ever return? Would he find a world identical with the one in which he moved? A world, of which his was but a ghostly reflection? Which was reality and which illusion?

At times Kull halted to wonder how such thoughts and dreams had come to enter his mind, and at times he wondered if they came of his own volition or – here his thoughts would become mazed. His meditations were his own; no man ruled his thoughts, and he would summon them at his pleasure; yet could he? Were they not as bats, coming and going, not at his pleasure but at the bidding or ruling of – of whom? The gods? The Women who wove the webs of Fate? Kull could come to no conclusion, for at each mental step he became more and more bewildered in a hazy fog of illusory assertions and refutations. This much he knew: that strange visions entered his mind, like flying unbidden from the whispering void of non-existence; never had he thought these thoughts, but now they ruled his mind, sleeping and waking, so that he seemed to walk in a daze at times; and his sleep was fraught with strange, monstrous dreams.

"Tell me, wizard," he said, sitting before the mirror, eyes fixed intently upon his image, "how can I pass yon door? For of a truth, I am not sure that that is the real world and this the shadow; at least, that which I see must exist in some form."

"See and believe," droned the wizard. "Man must believe to accomplish. Form is shadow, substance is illusion, materiality is dream; man is because he believes he is; what is man but a dream of the gods? Yet man can be that which he wishes to be; form and substance, they are but shadows. The mind, the ego, the essence of the god-dream – that is real, that is immortal. See and believe, if you would accomplish, Kull."

The king did not fully understand; he never fully understood the enigmatical utterances of the wizard; yet they struck somewhere in his being a dim responsive chord. So day after day he sat before the mirrors of Tuzun Thune. Ever the wizard lurked behind him like a shadow.

Then came a day when Kull seemed to catch glimpses of strange lands; there flitted across his consciousness dim thoughts and recognitions. Day by day he had seemed to lose touch with the world; all things had seemed each succeeding day more ghostly and unreal; only the man in the mirror seemed like reality. Now Kull seemed to be close to the doors of some mightier worlds; giant vistas gleamed fleetingly; the fogs of unreality thinned; "form is shadow, substance is illusion; they are but shadows" sounded as if from some far country of his consciousness. He remembered the wizard's words and it seemed to him that now he almost understood – form and substance, could not he change himself at will, if he knew the master key that opened this door? What worlds within what worlds awaited the bold explorer?

The man in the mirror seemed smiling at him closer, closer – a fog enwrapped all and the reflection dimmed suddenly – Kull knew a sensation of fading, of change, of merging…

"Kull!" the yell split the silence into a million vibratory fragments!

Mountains crashed and worlds tottered as Kull, hurled back by the frantic shout, made a superhuman effort, how or why he did not know.

A crash, and Kull stood in the room of Tuzun Thune before a shattered mirror, mazed and half blind with bewilderment. There before him lay the body of Tuzun Thune, whose time had come at last, and above him stood Brule the Spear-slayer, sword dripping red and eyes wide with a kind of horror.

"Valka!" swore the warrior. "Kull, it was time I came!"

"Aye, yet what happened?" The king groped for words.

"Ask this traitress," answered the Spear-slayer, indicating a girl who crouched in terror before the king; Kull saw that it was she who first sent him to Tuzun Thune. "As I came in I saw you fading into yon mirror as smoke fades into the sky, by Valka! Had I not seen I would not have believed; you had almost vanished when my shout brought you back."

"Aye," muttered Kull, "I had almost gone beyond the door that time."

"This fiend wrought most craftily," said Brule. "Kull, do you not now see how he spun and flung over you a web of magic? Kaanuub of Blaal plotted with this wizard to do away with you, and this wench, a girl of the Elder Race, put the thought in your mind so that you would come here. Ka-na of the council learned of the plot today; I know not what you saw in that mirror, but with it Tuzun Thune enthralled your soul and almost by his witchery he changed your body to mist—"

"Aye." Kull was still mazed. "But being a wizard, having knowledge of all the ages and despising gold, glory, and position, what could Kaanuub offer Tuzun Thune that would make of him a foul traitor?"

"Gold, power, and position," grunted Brule. "The sooner you learn that men are men whether wizard, king, or thrall, the better you will rule, Kull. Now what of her?"

"Naught, Brule," as the girl whimpered and groveled at Kull's feet. "She was but a tool. Rise, child, and go your ways; none shall harm you."

Alone with Brule, Kull looked for the last time on the mirrors of Tuzun Thune.

"Mayhap he plotted and conjured, Brule; nay, I doubt you not, yet – was it his witchery that was changing me to thin mist, or had I stumbled on a secret? Had you not brought me back, had I faded in dissolution or had I found worlds beyond this?"

Brule stole a glance at the mirrors, and twitched his shoulders as if he shuddered. "Aye, Tuzun Thune stored the wisdom of all the hells here. Let us be gone, Kull, ere they bewitch me, too."

"Let us go, then," answered Kull, and side by side they went forth from the House of a Thousand Mirrors – where, mayhap, are prisoned the souls of men.

None look now in the mirrors of Tuzun Thune. The pleasure boats shun the shore where stands the wizard's house, and no one goes in the house or to the room where Tuzun Thune's dried and withered carcass lies before the mirrors of illusion. The place is shunned as a place accursed, and though it stands for a thousand years to come, no footsteps shall echo there. Yet Kull upon his throne meditates often upon the strange wisdom and untold secrets hidden there and wonders…

For there are worlds beyond worlds, as Kull knows, and whether the wizard bewitched him by words or by mesmerism, vistas did open to the king's gaze beyond that strange door, and Kull is less sure of reality since he gazed into the mirrors of Tuzun Thune.

The Temple's Posthole

M.K. Hutchins

AYIN DUCKED into the temple, one hand wrapped around her ribs, the other one clutching her son's hand. The poor filled this place – some had broken bones, some writhed with yellow snake fever. The priestesses patiently wended through them, administering bandages, salves, and teas.

"It smells funny in here," said her son, Tzi.

A thick, wet cough tensed in Ayin's lungs. She swallowed it. "Temples are a place of reverence. Speak softer."

He rolled his eyes heavenward and sighed loudly. Only seven years old, and so dramatic.

One of the priestesses approached – a pretty woman with a round face. "Welcome to our temple. May the gods see fit to bring you healing."

The cough clawed up Ayin's throat. She dropped Tzi's hand and covered her mouth. She hacked, throat burning. Tzi rubbed her back.

And then the cough faded. Ayin straightened, pulling her hand away. Orange mucous stained it. Before she could find a handkerchief, the young priestess was cleaning her hand with a rag smelling strongly of corn beer. "I need you to sit over here."

Ayin nodded and followed her to a mat of woven palm fronds. Tzi managed to be reverent; he bit his lip and stared at his mother.

The priestess – she said her name was Cham – pressed her ear to Ayin's back and listened. "Have you been to any Xook ruins lately?"

"I'm a looter." She'd been at the ruins of a Xook flintknapping workshop last week, but someone had already used up the magic in the postholes. Two days' trek through the thick of the jungle, and she hadn't even been paid. That seemed to happen a lot, lately.

Cham looked in her throat, felt her pulse, and sighed. "May the gods watch over you, because I can't. I've seen a cough like yours before. In their later buildings, the magic-hating Xook poisoned the bottoms of their postholes."

"I have wet lung, don't I?" Ayin's chest twisted, this time in sinking dread. She'd hoped this was some regular cough.

Cham nodded. "It's not contagious, at least."

Ayin squeezed Tzi's shoulder. Small comfort. Her merchant-minded husband wouldn't return from the trading roads for another half-year at least. If she died in a month, who would care for Tzi? They had no other kin.

"Thank you," Ayin said. She took Tzi's hand and left the smells of cotton, herbs, and sickness behind.

* * *

"So you'll cough up orange slime until you find some good-paying work. Not so bad, right?" Tzi asked. Despite his casual tone, his face pinched with worry.

Ayin wanted to scoop him up, cover his face in kisses, and assure him everything would be sweet as honey. But she'd never been good at lying, at putting on faces. Maybe she'd be a better mother if she were. She shook her head and stayed silent. Tzi scuffed his feet on the dirt road, matching her mood.

If her husband were here, he'd know what to say. Yunen made everyone laugh easily – that's why he'd gone with the caravan to try and make their fortune. A laughing customer is a spending customer. She ached to see his infectious smile again. Too bad they hadn't been able to pay passage for herself and Tzi on the caravan as well.

She should have headed home, but Ayin couldn't resist looking at the cure for her ailment, even though she couldn't afford it. Her feet pulled her deeper into the city, where the thatch and plaster of the houses gleamed new. Women wore shells on their skirts; necklaces of scarlet feathers adorned the men.

"Where are we going?" Tzi asked.

Ayin turned the corner and nodded just ahead. Some six postholes graced the building platform. They'd burned this temple down so recently the air still smelled of smoke, but it had stood and served the poor for ten years – enough time for the soul of the building to develop.

A pair of burly men with obsidian spears stood guard. Here, if you could pay, you could get *real* healing. A gray-haired man with a luxurious cape of blue cotton handed the magician pieces of jade. Ayin's throat tightened. How many months of corn and beans could that buy? Her lungs squeezed, promising a cough. She tried to swallow it.

The caped man pushed a woman forward – much younger than himself, but with the same broad nose. Surely his daughter. A jagged scar marred her forearm. The magician settled her next to one of the postholes, then burned some sweet-smelling copal and chanted.

The postholes glowed. The building's soul remained there, anchored by the strength of the earth, even though the temple itself was gone. Much healing had happened here – and the building's soul remembered that.

A portion of the glow gathered in a ball, then floated upward. The magician chanted louder and it drifted to the girl's arm. It sunk into her skin, removing the scar as it passed.

Ayin's lung burned, then the coughing began anew. Hack after hack, her head swam, desperate for air. Tzi's hand rubbed her back again.

When she felt too weak to breathe, let alone stand, the cough abated. Shakily, she straightened her back. No cloth smelling of corn beer here. She wiped the orange mucus on her skirt.

"Do you have anything to pay for my services?" the magician asked doubtfully.

Ayin didn't have the breath to answer. Tzi did for her. "She's a looter! If you heal her, she'll find you some old, Xook buildings you can use!"

"Pah! Like there are any of those left. Leave, or my guards will remove you."

* * *

Tzi helped her through the streets, back towards the small hut her husband built them before he left. "That magician was a thrice-damned, arrogant bastard."

"*Where* did you learn such words?"

"I used them right, though, didn't I?"

Ayin rubbed the bridge of her nose, trying to push away the threatening headache.

Tzi changed the subject back. "You're a great looter!" His voice bled with indignation. "You can even read Xook. He's an idiot for not healing you."

"Yes, but magicians have already dried up the souls of all the easy-to-find Xook ruins. Work... isn't exactly plentiful."

Ayin bit her lip. She knew of one Xook building, still largely untouched. But the thought of selling the location turned her stomach. The place wasn't safe, and she'd made a promise to keep it secret. No, she'd try to find work some other way. Not that anyone would hire a woman with wet lung.

At last they reached their own neighborhood. The thatched-roof homes were old, but neatly maintained. No one had a reason to burn these down to get at the postholes. Occasionally someone tried to use the poorest huts to curse an enemy, or the postholes of wealthy houses to ensure prosperity, but no one bothered with middling poor.

Would selling the house bring enough money to cure her? Maybe, healthy, she could find a job as a courier or a cotton picker. If she did, they wouldn't have to sleep on the street for long. At least it was the dry season.

"Mother?"

She'd been too busy thinking to even look at their house. A pair of guards stood at her door, each wearing a gleaming wooden pectoral carved with the name Yuknoom, Holy Lord of Kab. Royal guards.

Ayin froze, hand tightening on Tzi's. They weren't looking at her. Run? Lord Yuknoom had ruled less than a year – ever since a pavilion tragically collapsed and killed his father – but he'd already gained a reputation for cruelty.

Maybe these guards were here to offer her work – she *did* read Xook, after all, and the Lord's brother was said to have a library of old Xook codices.

"Mother?" Tzi whispered this time.

Lord Yuknoom had executed more than one person who ignored a summons. Ayin swallowed. Work. Surely they offered work. She hadn't done anything wrong. "Tzi, stay several paces behind me. If they grab me for an arrest, you run. Hide. Understand?"

He nodded, young face so serious that Ayin would have laughed if her stomach wasn't a lump of limestone. She strolled forward. "Royal guards, may I assist you?"

"If you are Ayin, we've come to escort you to the palace of Yuknoom, Holy Lord of Kab."

Ayin exhaled. The palace, not the hearing chambers or the salt mines. "His request honors one so humble as I."

"I *told* you you're a great looter," Tzi said.

"Thanks." What a good son she had.

They followed the guards through the city – past homes, workshops, and turkey pens – up to the palace. She only coughed once, a small splutter she wiped away with the back of her hand.

The Lord himself sat in an open-air pavilion, lounging on a throne of jaguar skin with a cigar in his mouth. His attendants seemed like so much furniture. Tortoise shells and feathers adorned his headdress; jade spools hung from his ears. Cape, skirt, and sandals all burst with color and ornamentation. But Ayin couldn't focus on the riot of color and wealth. Lord Yuknoom's hard, gray eyes were picking her apart.

"You are Ayin?" he asked, words cold.

Her throat threatened to close off. "Yes."

"Your grandmother. She was Xook?"

"So she was raised." Ayin spoke as smoothly as she could. "She was sixteen when the Xook fell."

Lord Yuknoom took a pull at his cigar, then exhaled the smoke. It was rolled fatter than a baby's fist. "Yet you're a looter. Stealing from your own people."

Ayin tensed. How else could she earn a living? All she had was a knowledge of the Xook – her grandmother had raised her.

"My questions bother you?" Lord Yuknoom appeared amused.

"No. I…I didn't realize you wished a reply to your statement. I apologize. Yes, my ancestors are Xook. Yes, I work as a looter."

"I guess that makes you more Kab than Xook."

Tzi glanced nervously between her and the Lord, but thankfully he had the sense to remain silent.

"I suppose it does." Her grandmother didn't like magic, didn't like the practice of burning buildings, but she'd adapted.

Another man strode into the pavilion. He looked much like the Lord, both in face and in the lavish cape and jade pectoral he wore. Ayin bowed low as he passed; Tzi did the same. He spoke a few quiet words with Lord Yuknoom.

"Yes, yes, you can stay," the Lord said.

The newcomer turned and beamed. "I am Prince Kaloomte."

Lord Yuknoom's younger brother, the man rumored to have a Xook library. Ayin's shoulders relaxed. Perhaps he needed another Xook scribe – surely that's why she was here.

"My scribes have read me much that the Xook wrote. But one building always remains… evasive. Mentioned here or there, with never a location, never a description, as if the building were too holy for paper."

He could have forced obsidian down her throat, and the result would have been little different. Ayin's knees shook.

"Perhaps, given the infamous Xook reverence for life, it should not surprise me that they held dearly sacred their temple. Odd, though, that they only had one. And that they kept it isolated from their cities," Prince Kaloomte continued. "Many have looked for it and failed. But as I've searched the mystery out, I've heard rumors. Rumors of a child who fell from a tree and lost both her legs in the process. No temple of ours is old enough or strong enough to restore limbs, but somehow, this little child walked again."

A cough trickled up Ayin's throat. She was that child.

Prince Kaloomte smiled. "Where could healing strong enough to grow legs be found? Only in the Xook temple, centuries old. It took *quite* some time to trace the rumors to you. The granddaughter of a Xook woman. Did you know that your grandmother's mother was a Xook priestess?"

She did.

Lord Yuknoom shifted. Beneath all the finery, she saw what she hadn't at first – his arm was missing. "You will take me to the temple, Ayin. I will reward you handsomely."

She couldn't go back there. For once, Ayin thanked the gods for her wet lung – coughing saved her from answering. Air wouldn't come to her. Dots colored her vision. The ground keeled to the side as warm mucus splattered over her lips.

The world fell dark.

* * *

Little Ayin, you must never come back here, understand? Horrible things will happen. This temple is hidden for a reason. Promise me.

How old had she been? Six, maybe seven? About Tzi's age. Ayin could still taste the horror of falling from that tree. The searing pain that stole her legs. The blistering infection that threatened to take her life.

Grandmother loathed magic as much as the next Xook, but she studied the codices Grandpa, a Kab magician, had used before he passed. Ayin never knew if they married for love, or if Grandma had been some kind of tribute after the war, and she'd never asked.

She remembered the long path to the Xook temple, carried in Grandma's arms on the way in, walking on her way out.

Grandma's eyes gleamed fiercer than jaguar's teeth, making her promise. Promise. *This temple is hidden for a reason.*

She woke to a cool cloth on her head.

"Wet lung. That's nasty stuff." A priestess, in simple homespun white, knelt next to her.

"My son?"

"I'm right here," Tzi said, with an exasperated sigh.

Ayin turned her head. She lay on a mat in the pavilion. Prince Kaloomte had left, but Lord Yuknoom still stared at her with those gray eyes. "It appears that you, too, could make use of the Xook temple. We will leave at dawn tomorrow, before you worsen."

"I...I can't..."

Lord Kaloomte leaned back on his jaguar-skin throne. The cigar was gone. "Can't what? Refusal to obey my command is treason. I will find you, and your near kin, guilty if you prove stubborn."

That could only mean execution. She was already dying, but the hard, gray eyes left no doubt that this man would kill Tzi and her husband, when he returned. Tzi must not have understood, because he still peered down at her, only concerned about the wet lung.

Ayin's breath shook. "The temple...isn't safe."

"Guards." A dozen men appeared at once. "Escort this woman and her son to a guest room. Then fetch my steward; I have preparations to make before we leave."

* * *

In the morning, guards escorted Ayin and Tzi onto a palanquin; they said Lord Yuknoom worried she'd strain her health walking. Did he really think she'd die before they reached the temple? Or was this the easiest way to guard her?

The caravan – two magicians, four dozen guards, and nearly as many porters laden with food and tents – assembled with well-organized quiet. Prince Kaloomte was the only exception. Three small children clung to him, sobbing. He smiled sadly at them, kissed their heads, then embraced the woman behind them – surely his wife – before climbing onto the royal palanquin.

Lord Yuknoom strolled over to Ayin's palanquin, feathered cape swirling against the ground. "I trust you'll prove a helpful guide."

Ayin hugged Tzi to her side, throat tight.

"Tell me which direction we start towards." Lord Yuknoom ordered. He flicked a glance at Tzi, eyes hard with the threat of death.

"West," Ayin spluttered.

Lord Yuknoom nodded and joined his brother on their palanquin.

The caravan quickly traveled through the bustle of the city and out into the countryside, heading towards the jungles and mountains.

"You didn't look happy." Tzi fidgeted with his sandal ties. "About telling Lord Yuknoom which direction to go."

What else could she do? Let them kill her son? Prince Kaloomte had probably already guessed the temple lay westward, towards the heart of Xook lands. "I'm not happy."

Fields flanked either side of the road, some heavy with corn, beans, and squash, some filled with manioc, some stubbled with cotton.

"But…can't this temple heal your cough? Won't Lord Yuknoom make us rich?"

Grandmother hadn't given some idle warning. Like her Xook ancestors, Grandmother revered life dearly, considering murder the worst of crimes and healing the noblest of professions. If there was good to be had at the temple, Grandmother would have carried the infirm on her back to restore their health. But even when she took Ayin, she blindfolded her before they entered the building proper.

Ayin wished the woman was still alive, to stroke her hair and tell her what to do. Instead, she stroked Tzi's hair. He depended on her to take care of them, as much as she wanted to depend on Grandmother right now. "I don't think going to the temple's a good idea."

"You want to be sick?" Tzi gave her a look that seemed to fathom the depth of adults' stupidity.

"No."

"You want to be poor?"

"No."

"Then stop worrying! Why didn't you loot the temple a long time ago?"

Ayin spoke softly. "Grandma didn't want me to."

It began to mist, despite being the dry season. Oddly, the moisture rolled off them and the litter. Ayin frowned at the clean clothes she'd been given. Enchanted. It wasn't uncommon among the well-to-do; pavilion shelters were ubiquitous, cheap to build, and easy to burn. Just some poles and thatch.

Tzi giggled and waved his arms, the mist magically swerving to avoid him.

* * *

The second day, they reached the jungle. Howler monkeys called from the tree tops; tiny white butterflies surrounded a patch of ash where some farmer had tried to clear a field. When they stopped for the night, Lord Yuknoom called her into his tent.

It was nearly as lovely as the palace. Rugs of yellow and green filled the floor; cloth banners of the same obscured the walls. Lord Yuknoom lounged on cushions, Prince Kaloomte kneeling next to him.

Outside, she could hear Tzi laughing. One of the guards had been amusing him with stories. She ached to be out there, on the other side of these cloth walls.

"Which direction do we head tomorrow? We're nearly to the fork in the trail," Lord Yuknoom said.

"Left." But only for a little while. Not that she had to tell them that, now.

Lord Yuknoom peered at her, disgust in his eyes. "You have been granted a chance to help your Lord, and you show this melancholy temperament?"

"Women tend to be attached to their children," Prince Kaloomte intervened. "You did threaten to kill hers."

Lord Yuknoom waved a hand, dismissing her. Ayin bowed, then turned to flee, but the Prince stood. "Perhaps I might divert you into a scholarly discussion?"

"Not in here," Lord Yuknoom grumbled.

Prince Kaloomte bowed his head politely to his brother, then escorted Ayin from the tent. Tzi sat on a fallen tree with the soldier. He waved enthusiastically. Ayin managed a half-hearted smile.

"I'm going to borrow your mother for a moment. Pitz, if you don't mind continuing to keep an eye on him?"

"An eye? We're trading warrior's stories!" Pitz, the soldier, grinned.

"I got a tarantula once!" Tzi chipped in.

Pitz clapped him on the shoulder. "A daring feat!"

Ayin exhaled. At least Tzi was fine, for now. Prince Kaloomte led her to his tent. She hesitated briefly at the threshold. She was a woman. He was of the royalty of Kab. But his face held no untoward intentions. The interior was only slightly less lavish than his brother's. He gestured her to one of the cushions. "It must be hard, to be forced to give up the last undefiled building of your people."

Her people? She'd been raised in Kab. Knew their customs better than she knew those of the Xook. "It's…more about dishonoring the memory of the woman who raised me. My grandmother."

"Sometimes, I wonder if the Xook weren't right, in banning magicians."

Ayin stared at him. Was this some verbal trap?

"We use a building a little while, maybe five or ten years for a soul to develop, and then we burn it. Nothing is constructed to last. Few buildings are erected with beauty in mind. I visited the Xook ruins at Baaknal. The palace there is half-collapsed from looters exposing postholes, but I glimpsed murals, intricately carved roof combs. All hundreds of years old. All beautiful. In Kab, we don't have that kind of history."

Guilt gnawed at her gut. This Kab royal could conjure more grief over the destruction of Xook cities than she could.

"And yet they had one temple. Isolated. Rarely mentioned in texts. Do you…do you know why?" he asked, face cautious.

Prince Kaloomte wasn't what she expected. Lord Yuknoom had a reputation of quick cruelty; she assumed he'd be the same. "I don't. I didn't even see much of it."

He nodded, seemingly relieved. "Good. I'm sorry to keep you from your son – you should go. Sleep well, both of you."

Odd, that he didn't have more questions to ask. Ayin bowed and left.

* * *

The temple is hidden for a reason. Ayin stared into the darkness of her small tent, Tzi breathing loudly in his sleep next to her.

"What reasons, Grandmother?" she whispered silently to the night. She received no answer.

Maybe Prince Kaloomte was right to criticize her. To be Xook, yet aid magicians in destroying their buildings? But that all seemed so long ago. Grandmother, who smelled like mahogany – that was her heritage, her past.

And that wise, fierce woman had told her to stay away. To never come back.

Ayin laid a hand on Tzi's shoulder. "Tzi."

He mumbled in his sleep. Ayin knelt by his ear. "Tzi, you must wake up. Silent now."

He tensed. Awake. Good.

"We can't stay here." Given Lord Yuknoom's threats, they couldn't stay anywhere near Kab once they fled. They'd flee northward, up the caravan road, and find Yunen. Surely they could remain in a northern kingdom, selling goods or some such thing. He'd be delighted to see them again, sooner than expected. Perhaps he'd already made enough to pay a magician to cure her wet lung.

"Why…not?"

"It isn't safe." Not that running through the jungle was particularly safe, either. She wished they had something more than sandals to guard against snakes. "We'll have to move quietly. Can you do that?"

He nodded. What a good son she had. "Where are we going?"

"To your father."

He sat up. It was too dark to see his face, but she could feel the smile radiating off the boy. "Father?"

"Yes." How they'd make it up the caravan road alone, she couldn't fathom. But they couldn't stay here.

Ayin took his hand and pulled him to the tent flaps. The canopy of trees let little starlight through, but she could make out guards encircling the camp, watching for bandits and beasts.

Ayin gritted her teeth. She was an looter, not a warrior. How to get through them? Her eyes drifted skyward. Perhaps if they were very quiet, they could climb up a tree in the middle of camp, then travel from branch to branch until they passed the guards. Perhaps the guards would mistake them for howler monkeys.

It would be dangerous even in daylight. But Ayin couldn't imagine it was more dangerous than the temple.

She stepped into the warm, humid night. A few quiet strides brought her to the base of a large tree, well shielded from view by tents and greenery.

"Up," Ayin whispered, boosting Tzi. He clung for a moment to the trunk above her head, unmoving. Then he climbed, lithe limbs pulling him surely up, more than twice her height above the ground.

Then he screamed and fell. Ayin scrambled to catch him. He crashed into her; they collapsed in a heap on the loamy ground. "Did you break anything?"

"N-no." His voice shook, crying. "Something bit me."

Before Ayin could say another word, the deadly tip of an obsidian spear pricked her throat. "Trying to escape, and clumsily at that. We'll see what Lord Yuknoom wants to do with you."

* * *

But apparently no one dared wake Lord Yuknoom until morning. The guards tossed her in her tent, then surrounded it. She didn't have enough light to look at Tzi's hand, but she ran her fingers over the bump there.

"It burns," Tzi whispered, voice small. "All up my arm."

"Did you see what it was?"

"No. Just this sharp pain and…fire. It's spreading to my chest."

Ayin bit her lip. Likely a gray caterpillar sting. He'd feel like he was on fire for three days, but with enough water, he'd survive. She pulled back the tent flap. "Guards, I need—"

A spear butt cracked into her ribs. Ayin fell back, gasping.

"Mother!" Tzi yelled.

The guard snorted. "Didn't we tell you to stay put?"

Ayin spluttered, felt her ribs. Nothing broken. "I'm sorry, Tzi. I'm sorry."

There was nothing else for it. She made him drink the last of their water flask, then cuddled him, stroked his hair, and told him everything would be fine. Tzi didn't seem convinced; she'd never been good at lying.

* * *

The guards dragged her and Tzi into Lord Yuknoom's tent. Tzi collapsed onto the floor, rubbing his arms. Two dirty trails of perpetual tears ran across his cheeks. He whimpered quietly. Ayin knelt and gathered her son in her lap.

"What's this?" Lord Yuknoom demanded, disgusted. Prince Kaloomte sat by him; each had a steaming cup of atole.

"She tried to escape last night with the boy by climbing up one of the trees in camp."

Pity welled in Prince Kaloomte's soft eyes; derision hardened Lord Yuknoom's face. "Worthless wench! I should have your head here."

"We'll never find the temple if you do," Prince Kaloomte said. "Aren't you determined to get the better of those who cursed you?"

Ayin peered at the empty shoulder anew. Cursed? The postholes of a butchery shop could sever an enemy's limb – but that's why all such buildings were banned. If someone wanted to skin a deer or pluck a turkey, it had to be out of doors or under a lean-to.

"I'd prefer knowing their names and crushing them," Lord Yuknoom muttered, eyes hot with hate.

He hadn't seen them? Only the most talented magicians could affect a person from any distance. Perhaps she shouldn't be surprised that Lord Yuknoom had made powerful enemies.

Prince Kaloomte nodded. "My men are searching for illegal postholes as we speak."

Ayin held Tzi close. He was feverish, shaking. But she didn't dare ask for anything for him – not at this moment.

"You'll continue with us," Lord Yuknoom snapped at her.

Ayin tried not to audibly exhale. He wouldn't kill them outright.

"Your son, however, will be tied up in a tree. Isn't that where you were trying to go?"

Tzi, in his feverish state, didn't seem to hear, but Ayin's throat turned into a desert. "You can't—"

"*Can't?* You seem fond of that word. Of course I can. I could have him gutted here in the tent if I chose." He stared at her, daring her to contradict him again.

Ayin bit her lip hard.

"For his sake, I hope the temple is close. Once you take us safely there, we can return here and let him down."

"A jaguar, or another gray caterpillar, or—"

"Did I give you the impression we were negotiating?"

Ayin clutched Tzi tight. Her boy. Her child. They couldn't have him. She turned to Prince Kaloomte, but his eyes only held sad resignation.

"Guards. Take the boy," Lord Yuknoom commanded.

Panic welled up in her gut. With it, came the cough. She doubled-up, pain flaring from abdomen to throat. Tzi's small hands grasped at her; other hands yanked away. She struggled to hold onto him, to force the cough away, but when she finally regained the ability to breathe, her arms were empty. The orange mucus rolled off her enchanted clothes to the floor.

"You're disgusting," Lord Yuknoom sneered. "Get out."

* * *

Her against Lord Yuknoom's four dozen guards. She had no chance.

"I'm sorry, Grandmother," she whispered to the trees.

Ayin took them to the left fork, then turned from the path. The porters set down the palanquins, then all continued on foot through the dense jungle. Perhaps, if she moved fast enough, they could return to Tzi by nightfall. Lord Yuknoom puffed near the rear of their party. She wished she could inflict more suffering on him.

They twisted between trees, vines, and ferns all morning. Sometimes she had to slide down the steep ground on hand and foot, though her clothes refused to become muddied. Midday, she stopped at a ravine.

Prince Kaloomte strode up alongside her. "It seems you've reached a dead end."

"No. It's down there."

Prince Kaloomte peered over the ravine edge. "I…only see water."

"I'll show you." But first she asked one of the soldiers for a flask. She drank deeply, soothing her throat for the time being, at least.

Hand over hand, she started down the sheer ravine. The guards cried out, but Prince Kaloomte must have said something, for in a moment, they quietly followed her.

She worked slowly, testing her feet against the rock before letting her weight rest on it. At last her feet touched a broad outcropping, midway down. Water lazily flowed over the ravine bottom, ten times her height below.

A narrow opening led into the rock wall – impossible to see from above. "It's here."

The outcropping was just wide enough for two guards to join her.

Lord Yuknoom peered at them from the top of the ravine. "Is it as she says? Is there an entrance?"

One of the guards brushed past her, then returned. "Holy Lord of Kab, there is something down here, but it is too dark to see!"

Ayin swallowed hard, pulse racing. The opening looked like a sideways maw, ready to swallow her. Lord Kaloomte could have this place and whatever disaster it brought. "I've done as you've asked. I want to return to my son."

"Am I healed? I'll take no more insubordination from you," Lord Yuknoom snapped. Then he turned to the guard. "Take her inside."

It smelled like dust, like death. Hardly any light from outside could enter the crooked door. She drank from the flask again, silently apologizing to Grandmother. Perhaps horrible things would happen, but what could be worse than losing Tzi? Grandmother had braved this place to heal her, after all.

The next dozen guards brought torches. The light glittered off stalactites high above them. A family of rats scurried back into the darkness of the cave. But the scenery was hard to stare at, given the large building hunkering in the center of the cave. The flat roof and square stone pillars were as foreboding as they'd been in memory. Figures carved across the roof read, *A Holy Temple, for the Use of Our Gods*.

Ayin took another draw from the flask, to give her hands something to do. When she'd come here before, she'd seen those characters, but hadn't been able to read them. Grandmother had blindfolded her here, told her to be a good girl and not peek.

Prince Kaloomte gawked. "There were no pictures, no descriptions. I can't believe I'm *seeing* this."

"I can't believe you're standing here, when there is work to do," Lord Yuknoom grumbled, pushing ahead. They must have used rope to lower him down. The two magicians followed half a step behind him.

Ayin had hoped to wait outside, but Prince Kaloomte strode up to her. "I'd like you to translate anything we find."

"We…shouldn't go inside."

"Nonsense." He smiled and started forward. Though he hadn't spoken by way of command, Lord Yuknoom's guards seemed all too accustomed to pushing her around. One nudged her legs with his spear butt.

Ayin stumbled forward. She'd leave this place as soon as she could. Gather Tzi. Care for him, while the caterpillar's venom wore away.

She passed under the square doorway. Soldiers filled the spacious interior, some peering down side halls. The walls were made of stone, but in the center rose a dais. A tattered curtain hung around it on three thick poles. The fourth pole had been toppled and burned to reveal a deep posthole, reaching three hand spans into the earth. The magicians chatted excitedly over it.

Ayin couldn't help herself. Morbid curiosity pulled her to the spot. Grandma must have burned it. She'd been healed right here.

The air was musty. It smelled of spider webs. But she was a looter – she'd been in places just as musty, and most of them had more rats.

Then she saw behind the curtain.

The limestone slab was long enough to be a bed, but rose as tall as her waist. The top had a human-shaped impression. Vermin had gnawed away most of the leather straps, but a scrap still remained, here and there, tied through holes on the slab. The stone should have been white, but dark brown stains marred the surface and sides.

Ayin bit her lip. There was writing. That would explain. She asked one of the guards to fetch her a brush from the supplies; he obliged.

Her knees shook as she knelt on the hard dais. Gingerly, she brushed away the grime, revealing a single line of text and a picture. *Man may not kill man. Life's end is for the Gods alone to decide.*

The picture showed a man, strapped to the slab. Another figure, with a God's huge eyes, tore a knife across the bound man's throat. Ayin's stomach heaved. This was no place of healing.

Ayin cleaned the God's face. As she suspected, the art depicted a string behind the head – the face was a mask. This was a priest, killing a man for his gods.

No word of this in all the records she'd seen. No hint. Even here in the temple, they put a curtain around it. Had Grandmother known? She must have, to warn Ayin to stay away.

She heard one of the magicians. "Yes, Lord Yuknoom. Sit there. We're ready to begin."

"No!" Ayin's scream echoed in the vacuous room. One huge room for slitting throats, as if all this emptiness could hide the truth of this place.

Lord Yuknoom glared. "Guards. Cut out her tongue."

"No, look!" Her palms sweated. "This…this is a place of death. Look at this picture, at this altar. If the magicians call up the soul of this building…" Ayin swallowed, hard, as a pair of guards took her arms. *The temple is hidden for a reason.*

Prince Kaloomte held a hand to the guards and turned to his brother. "I believe she's genuinely trying to help. There's a frightening painting there. She's ill, exasperated."

A cough seized her. Not a strong one, but mucus dribbled from her mouth, rolled off her enchanted clothes, and splattered on the floor.

Lord Yuknoom wrinkled his nose, then he caught the image. His gray eyes widened. "Your words may have some truth. But you were healed here, as a child?"

"I…" Ayin couldn't imagine how.

"Guards. Set her by the posthole," Lord Yuknoom commanded.

They yanked her forward and down, between the two magicians.

One had already started burning incense. "Holy Lord, do you mean for us to use the soul of this place on her?"

"Cure her cough," Lord Yuknoom commanded. "Does she not deserve a reward?"

"You can't!" Prince Kaloomte said.

His brother turned, an odd look on his face. "And why not? Do you know something about this building that you haven't spoken before?"

"No." Prince Kaloomte's composure returned immediately. He bowed gracefully. "But what if there is not enough magic left to restore your arm? It is no small magic to grow a limb."

Lord Yuknoom frowned. "Magicians?"

The second, a wiry fellow with an oddly deep voice, answered. "The soul of this building throbs with magic. I imagine it could grow a hundred arms and cure a thousand cases of wet lung."

"Very good. Continue," Lord Yuknoom said. Pity filled the lines in Prince Kaloomte's brow, but he said nothing.

Ayin struggled against the guards' arms. She was more helpless than a one-legged lizard in a child's grasp. Testing the magic on her. Had she expected the brute to be kind? She slumped, helpless, as the magicians chanted. Her knees numbed from waiting – such an old soul required time to coax. She remembered Grandmother doing it, voice soft as a lullaby. These men sounded like a dirge.

The posthole glowed. A cloud of shimmering specks rose from it. They shot into her chest.

Sudden, overwhelming guilt burned in her. Tzi. She hadn't taken care of him. She hadn't protected his life. And she'd endangered the lives of everyone present by leading them here.

She tasted hot blood in her throat. Pain pressed against her. The temple's soul was going to kill her.

But she'd also called out. She'd tried to save Lord Yuknoom's life, even though he threatened hers.

The pain abated. The tang of blood vanished. Her lungs cooled. Ayin stared at her hands. She could breathe properly; the wet lung was gone. What had happened?

"Bah! It works fine. You're a treacherous monkey, to get yourself healed first. Guards, I want her removed so she cannot foul up *my* healing."

"We saw some cells in a side chamber," one of the guards said. "Would that suffice?"

Lord Yuknoom merely waved them away, then settled himself next to the posthole. The magicians began the long process over again.

Alive. How could she be alive? That altar wasn't a decoration.

The guards brought her to a cell – a small square room with a wooden door. They tossed her inside, then barred it.

At least the door had a number of slits, allowing the torchlight into the room. Ayin hugged her arms to her chest. She was alive. Maybe the worst was over. Lord Yuknoom would heal. They'd leave this place. She'd find Tzi.

Ayin exhaled. Then she noticed the walls. Writing. She took her brush and gently cleared the debris.

"You stand accused of the grossest crime: murder. If you are found innocent, we will bathe you, dress you, heal you of any wounds, and set you free into the world. If you are found guilty, your Gods will send you to your afterlife."

The text wrapped around a picture of a meditating man.

This was a *court.* The altar, the executioner's block. She stood in a *prisoner's cell.* One with an admonition to meditate. Some inmate had take the opportunity of his time here to sketch crude anatomy on the man.

No wonder Grandmother dared to take a child here. What crimes could a child be guilty of? This place granted her a pardon, restored her legs.

And then it had taken her wet lung away.

But it had almost killed her first. The building seemed accustomed to taking life. It only relented, only pardoned her, when her memories showed how she'd recently tried to *save* a life.

Lord Yuknoom. If this building's soul judged those who used it, she doubted it would bless a man who left a child strapped to a tree in the jungle. Her stomach twisted. If he died, would the guards send her swiftly after? "Guards. You must stop Lord Yuknoom. He's—"

One of them whacked her door with his spear butt. "Quiet!"

If only Pitz were her guard – he'd seemed like a reasonable man. Ayin frowned. She couldn't remember the last time she'd seen him.

"Using the soul of this building will kill him," she pleaded.

Another bang, followed by, "If you don't sit still, we'll beat you until you do."

Ayin gritted her teeth. Why hadn't she realized what this place was before? The Xook revered life. Of course they wouldn't want to execute criminals in their cities, where killing might turn into a spectacle. A secluded, holy place, watched over by the gods – that suited their needs. They weren't Kab. Weren't so callous as to issue threats by holding a child's life ransom.

Ayin kicked the wall. Surprisingly, part of it gave. This had been a cell – once. Time had begun its work. Perhaps she could dig her way out. She used the handle of her brush and chunked some plaster off.

"Hey! What are you doing in there?"

"I—"

A wail from the main chamber cut her off. Ayin tried to dig faster. The brush snapped in two.

Six more guards entered the hallway. They burst into her cell and ripped her out, dragged her to the main room, then tossed her at Prince Kaloomte's feet.

Lord Yuknoom lay behind him, his throat gaping open and running red with blood.

"You tried to save his life from the dangerous soul of this building." Prince Kaloomte gave her a hand and brought her to her feet. "I cast no blame on you. You have my thanks."

* * *

The guards found something to wrap Lord Yuknoom's corpse in, then hauled it up the cliff. Between the slow carrying of the body and Ayin's quick pace to find Tzi, their party thinned, threading through the jungle like a trail of leaf-cutter ants.

Ayin reached camp at dusk. Tzi sat high in the tree, pale, but looking better than she'd expected. "Mother!"

She ran to the tree. Oddly, a man sat at the base. "Pitz?"

"Prince Kaloomte asked me to stay behind and make sure no jaguars got him."

Ayin frowned, confused.

Pitz shrugged. "It's not like Lord Yuknoom would notice the lack of one man. Did everything go well?"

Ayin shook her head. "Let's get my son down."

* * *

Ayin couldn't sleep. She sat next to Tzi in their tent, finger-combing his hair. In her rush to return to him, she hadn't wasted time on thought.

She had plenty of time now.

Prince – now Lord – Kaloomte had tried to stop Lord Yuknoom from using the soul of the temple on her. He'd left Pitz here to take care of Tzi. Wouldn't that have brought trouble, if Lord Yuknoom returned alive?

Ayin slipped out of her tent and approached Lord Kaloomte's. The guards asked his permission, then let her enter.

Lord Kaloomte's expression was mild, not unfriendly. Ayin bit her lip and seated herself on one of the cushions. "You knew. You knew what kind of place the temple was, before we arrived."

"My library is as extensive as everyone says. Mention of the temple is rare, but I had enough information to hope it would rid Kab of my brother."

She felt cold, hollow inside. "Murderer."

"You're brave, to confront a murderer alone." Even now, his tone was kind. He leaned back and folded his hands over his chest. "My father died a year ago. You know that, yes?"

Ayin nodded.

"Someone burned down his pavilion and staged the scene to look like my father died under a collapsing beam. No such mistake could be made if one saw the knife wounds in his body. And, if one saw the smugness on Yuknoom's face, no one could deny he did it.

"Yuknoom's favorite clothes disappeared afterwards, surely stained with blood. I enlisted a trusted, talented magician and tried to use those postholes to kill Yuknoom in turn. But one murder didn't leave a strong enough memory in the building's soul."

"It took his arm instead," Ayin whispered.

Lord Kaloomte nodded. "He became paranoid, suspicious. I couldn't act directly without risking my head. But if I could find someone who knew where the Xook temple was…in any case, I'm sorry my plots endangered your family."

"You're not telling me this because you're sorry," Ayin said, shoulders stiff, legs ready to run.

"Ayin, the past five rulers gained the lordship through bloodshed. I have three children. If I don't stop this legacy of death, they're either going to kill me or kill each other."

Ayin peered at him. "You think I can help?"

"Yes." He leaned forward, fingers laced together. "How does the temple's posthole *work?*"

"I…I don't know," Ayin faltered. "Maybe it healed me because I've never killed anyone. Or maybe because I'd just tried to save someone's life."

He nodded, thoughtful. "I tried to save your life and your son's. That should be enough. I'm going to institute a healing at the Xook temple as part of the official coronation ceremony. Then no man can earn the throne by murder."

Ayin gaped. "You can't mean to do this! You killed your brother!"

"I brought him to judgment. I think the Xook would approve. I'll return with my court after burying him. If I fail, my oldest son will face the posthole and sit in the lordship, instead. Xook law held all children guiltless. You weren't judged against as a child."

"You'd risk your life? Your son's life?" Her mouth tasted like chalk.

Lord Kaloomte smiled sadly. "This nation has been ruled by killers for too long. I'd risk nearly anything to never see murder in my children's eyes."

"Most children manage to avoid patricide!"

"You don't understand how corrupting power can be."

Ayin shook her head. "So you'd keep and use the immense power of the temple."

"I'll have it guarded."

As if guards were infallible. "My grandmother told me the temple was best left alone. She knew more about it than either of us."

"A Xook woman advises against magic. Why do I find that unsurprising?"

If he'd seen Grandmother's face, he'd understand she'd given no idle warning. "That temple saw more executions than pardons. What happens when it runs out of healing?" She had no words for the knot of dread growing in her chest. "Nothing good will come of your plan."

Lord Kaloomte leaned his head to the side, considering her. "I want to offer you a position among my scholars."

Ayin blinked. Had he not heard her?

"You'd have rooms in the palace, or nearby, if you prefer. You'd be paid well. My brother offered you a reward; I can think of nothing better."

Never worrying about affording a magician's healing. Never worrying about food. Yunen wouldn't have to leave on caravan. It seemed like a dream too lovely to be real. "I can't."

Lord Kaloomte raised an eyebrow.

"The temple should be destroyed. If I joined your scholars, I'd spend all my research trying to convince you."

Lord Kaloomte smiled. "I *enjoy* debate. Perhaps you'll even change my mind."

Ayin bit her lip. This man wasn't like his brother. He'd listen. He might even relent. "If you kill yourself with this new coronation, I want a written reassurance I won't lose my position."

He laughed. "You're blunt. Yes, I can arrange that."

"Thank you."

Lord Kaloomte dismissed her; Ayin bowed politely and left.

When she entered her tent, Tzi stirred. "M-mother?"

"I'm here." She found his hand in the darkness. "How are you feeling?"

"The burning's starting to go down."

She stroked his cheek. Still warm, but not dangerously so. "If you want, I can pay for a magician when we return to the city. You'd be better at once."

Tzi stilled. His voice dropped to a whisper. "You just robbed Lord Kaloomte, didn't you? Did you grab feathers or jade?"

Ayin laughed until her lungs hurt.

The Lost Continent

Chapters VI–VIII

C.J. Cutcliffe Hyne

[Publisher's Note: This classic novel describes events leading up to the fall of Atlantis, recounted by the warrior-priest Deucalion. The beautiful city, ruled by the Empress Phorenice, is prophesied to meet its end as corruption and rebellion surround it. Called back to his homeland, Deucalion must confront the changes that have taken place, and seek to save it from destruction.]

Chapter VI
The Biters of the City Wall

HERE THEN WAS the manner of my reception back in the capital of Atlantis, and some first glimpse at her new policies. I freely confess to my own inaction and limpness; but it was all deliberate. The old ties of duty seemed lost, or at least merged in one another. Beforetime, to serve the king was to serve the Clan of the Priests, from which he had been chosen, and whose head he constituted. But Phorenice was self-made, and appeared to be a rule unto herself; if Zaemon was to be trusted, he was the mouthpiece of the Priests, and their Clan had set her at defiance; and how was a mere honest man to choose on the instant between the two?

But cold argument told me that governments were set up for the good of the country at large, and I said to myself that there would be my choice. I must find out which rule promised best of Atlantis, and do my poor best to prop it into full power. And here at once there opened up another path in the maze: I had heard some considerable talk of rebels; of another faction of Atlanteans who, whatever their faults might be, were at any rate strong enough to beleaguer the capital; and before coming to any final decision, it would be as well to take their claims in balance with the rest. So on the night of that very same day on which I had just re-planted my foot on the old country's shores, I set out to glean for myself tidings on the matter.

No one inside the royal pyramid gainsaid me. The banquet had ended abruptly with the terrible scene that I have set down above on these tablets, for with Tarca writhing on the floor, and thrusting out the gruesome scars of his leprosy, even the most gluttonous had little enough appetite for further gorging. Phorenice glowered on the feasters for a while longer in silent fury, but saying no further word; and then her eyes turned on me, though softened somewhat.

"You may be an honest man, Deucalion," she said, at length, "but you are a monstrous cold one. I wonder when you will thaw?" And here she smiled. "I think it will be soon. But for now I bid you farewell. In the morning we will take this country by the shoulders, and see it in some new order."

She left the banqueting-hall then, Ylga following; and taking precedence of my rank, I went out next, whilst all others stood and made salutation. But I halted by Tarca first, and put my hand on his unclean flesh. "You are an unfortunate man," I said, "but I can admire a brave soldier. If relief can be gained for your plague, I will use interest to procure it for you."

The man's thanks came in a mumble from his wrecked mouth, and some of those near shuddered in affected disgust. I turned on them with a black brow: "Your charity, my lords, seems of as small account as your courage. You affected a fine disbelief of Zaemon's sayings, and a simpering contempt for his priesthood, but when it comes to laying a hand on him, you show a discretion which, in the old days, we should have called by an ugly name. I had rather be Tarca, with all his uncleanness, than any of you now as you stand."

With which leave-taking I waited coldly till they gave me my due salutation, and then walked out of the banqueting-hall without offering a soul another glance. I took my way to the grand gate of the pyramid, called for the officer of the guard, and demanded exit. The man was obsequious enough, but he opened with some demur.

"My lord's attendants have not yet come up?"

"I have none."

"My lord knows the state of the streets?"

"I did twenty years back. I shall be able to pick my way."

"My lord must remember that the city is beleaguered," the fellow persisted. "The people are hungry. They prowl in bands after nightfall, and – I make no question that my lord would conquer in a fight against whatever odds, but—"

"Quite right. I covet no street scuffle tonight. Lend me, I pray you, a sufficiency of men. You will know best what are needed. For me, I am accustomed to a city with quiet streets."

A score of sturdy fellows were detailed off for my escort, and with them in a double file on either hand, I marched out from the close perfumed air of the pyramid into the cool moonlight of the city. It was my purpose to make a tour of the walls and to find out somewhat of the disposition of these rebels.

But the Gods saw fit to give me another education first. The city, as I saw it during that night walk, was no longer the old capital that I had known, the just accretion of the ages, the due admixture of comfort and splendour. The splendour was there, vastly increased. Whole wards had been swept away to make space for new palaces, and new pyramids of the wealthy, and I could not but have an admiration for the skill and the brain which made possible such splendid monuments.

And, indeed, gazing at them there under the silver of the moonlight, I could almost understand the emotions of the Europeans and other barbarous savages which cause them to worship all such great buildings as Gods, since they deem them too wonderful and majestic to be set up by human hands unaided.

Still, if it was easy to admire, it was simple also to see plain advertisement of the cost at which these great works had been reared. From each grant of ground, where one of these stately piles earned silver under the moon, a hundred families had been evicted and left to harbour as they pleased in the open; and, as a consequence, now every niche had its quota of sleepers, and every shadow its squad of fierce wild creatures, ready to rush out and rob or slay all wayfarers of less force than their own.

Myself, I am no pamperer of the common people. I say that, if a man be left to hunger and shiver, he will work to gain him food and raiment; and if not, why then he can die, and the State is well rid of a worthless fellow. But here beside us, as we marched through many wards, were marks of blind oppression; starved dead bodies, with the bones starting through the lean skin, sprawled in the gutter; and indeed it was plain that, save for the favoured few, the people of the great capital were under a most heavy oppression.

But at this, though I might regret it abominably, I could make no strong complaint. By the ancient law of the land all the people, great and small, were the servants of the king, to be put without question to what purposes he chose; and Phorenice stood in the place of the king. So I tried to think no treason, but with a sigh passed on, keeping my eyes above the miseries and the squalors of the roadway, and sending out my thoughts to the stars which hung in the purple night above, and to the High Gods which dwelt amongst them, seeking, if it might be, for guidance for my future policies. And so in time the windings of the streets brought us to the walls, and, coursing beside these and giving fitting answer to the sentries who beat their drums as we passed, we came in time to that great gate which was a charge to the captain of the garrison.

Here it was plain there was some special commotion. A noise of laughter went up into the still night air, and with it now and again the snarl and roar of a great beast, and now and again the shriek of a hurt man. But whatever might be afoot, it was not a scene to come upon suddenly. The entrance gates of our great capital were designed by their ancient builders to be no less strong than the walls themselves. Four pairs of valves were there, each a monstrous block of stone two man-heights square, and a man-height thick, and the wall was doubled to receive them, enclosing an open circus between its two parts. The four gates themselves were set one at the inner, one at the outer side of each of these walls, and a hidden machinery so connected them, that of each set one could not open till the other was closed; and as for forcing them without war engines, one might as foolishly try to push down the royal pyramid with the bare hand.

My escort made outcry with the horn which hung from the wall inviting such a summons, and a warder came to an arrow-slit, and did inspection of our persons and business. His survey was according to the ancient form of words, which is long, and this was made still more tedious by the noise from within, which ever and again drowned all speech between us entirely.

But at last the formalities had been duly complied with, and he shot back the massive bars and bolts of stone, and threw ajar one monstrous stone valve of the door. Into the chamber within – a chamber made from the thickness of the wall between the two doors – I and my fellows crowded, and then the warder with his machines pulled to the valve which had been opened, and came to me again through the press of my escort, bowing low to the ground.

"I have no vail to give you," I said abruptly. "Get on with your duty. Open me that other door."

"With respect, my lord, it would be better that I should first announce my lord's presence. There is a baiting going forward in the circus, and the tigers are as yet mere savages, and no respecters of persons."

"The what?"

"The tigers, if my lord will permit them the name. They are baiting a batch of prisoners with the two great beasts which the Empress (whose name be adored) has sent here to aid us keep the gate. But if my lord will, there are the ward rooms leading off this passage, and the galleries which run out from them commanding the circus, and from there my lord can see the sport undisturbed."

Now, the mere lust for killing excites only disgust in me, but I suspected the orders of the Empress in this matter, and had a curiosity to see her scheme. So I stepped into the warder's lodge, and on into the galleries which commanded the circus with their arrow-slits. The old builders of the place had intended these for a second line of defence, for, supposing the outer doors all forced, an enemy could be speedily shot down in the circus, without being able to give a blow in return, and so would only march into a death-trap. But as a gazing-place on a spectacle they were no less useful.

The circus was bright lit by the moonlight, and the air which came in to me from it was acrid with the reek of blood. There was no sport in what was going forward: as I said, it was mere killing, and the sight disgusted me. I am no prude about this matter. Give a prisoner his weapons, put him in a pit with beasts of reasonable strength, and let him fight to a finish if you choose, and I can look on there and applaud the strokes. The war prisoner, being a prisoner, has earned death by natural law, and prefers to get his last stroke in hot blood than to be knocked down by the headsman's axe. And it is any brave man's luxury either to help or watch a lusty fight. But this baiting in the circus between the gates was no fair battle like that.

To begin with, the beasts were no fair antagonists for single men. In fact, twenty men armed might well have fled from them. When the warder said tigers, I supposed he meant the great cats of the woods. But here, in the circus, I saw a pair of the most terrific of all the fur-bearing land beasts, the great tigers of the caves – huge monsters, of such ponderous strength that in hunger they will oftentimes drag down a mammoth, if they can find him away from his herd.

How they had been brought captive I could not tell. Hunter of beasts though I had been for all my days, I take no shame in saying that I always approached the slaying of a cave-tiger with stratagem and infinite caution. To entrap it alive and bring it to a city on a chain was beyond my most daring schemes, and I have been accredited with more new things than one. But here it was in fact, and I saw in these captive beasts a new certificate for Phorenice's genius.

The purpose of these two cave-tigers was plain: whilst they were in the circus, and loose, no living being could cross from one gate to the other. They were a new and sturdy addition to the defences of the capital. A collar of bronze was round the throat of each, and on the collar was a massive chain which led to the wall, where it could be payed out or hauled in by means of a windlass in one of the hidden galleries. So that at ordinary moments the two huge beasts could be tethered, one close to either end of the circus, as the litter of bones and other messes showed, leaving free passage-way between the two sets of doors.

But when I stood there by the arrow-slit, looking down into the moonlight of the circus, these chains were slackened (though men stood by the windlass of each), and the great striped brutes were prowling about the circus with the links clanking and chinking in their wake. Lying stark on the pavement were the bodies of some eight men, dead and uneaten; and though the cave-tigers stopped their prowlings now and again to nuzzle these, and beat them about with playful paw-blows, they made no pretence at commencing a meal. It was clear that this cruel sport had grown common to them, and they knew there were other victims yet to be added to the tally.

Presently, sure enough, as I watched, a valve of the farther gate swung back an arm's length, and a prisoner, furiously resisting, was thrust out into the circus. He fell on his face, and after one look around him he lay resolutely still, with eyes on the ground passively awaiting his fate. The ponderous stone of the gate clapped to in its place; the cave-tigers turned in their prowlings; and a chatter of wagers ran to and fro amongst the watchers behind the arrow-slits.

It seemed there were niceties of cruelty in this wretched game. There was a sharp clank as the windlasses were manned, and the tethering chains were drawn in by perhaps a score of links. One of the cave-tigers crouched, lashed its tail, and launched forth on a terrific spring. The chain tautened, the massive links sang to the strain, and the great beast gave a roar which shook the walls. It had missed the prone man by a hand's breadth, and the watchers behind the arrow-slits shrieked forth their delight. The other tiger sprang also and missed, and again there were shouts of pleasure, which mingled with the bellowing voices of the beasts. The man lay motionless in his form. One more cowardly, or one more brave, might have run from death, or faced it; but this poor prisoner chose the middle course – he permitted death to come to him, and had enough of doggedness to wait for it without stir.

The great cave-tigers were used, it appeared, to this disgusting sport. There were no more wild springs, no more stubbings at the end of the massive chains. They lay down on the pavement, and presently began to purr, rolling on to their sides and rubbing themselves luxuriously. The prisoner still lay motionless in his form.

By slow degrees the monstrous brutes each drew to the end of its chain and began to reach at the man with out-stretched forepaw. The male could not touch him; the female could just reach him with the far tip of a claw; and I saw a red scratch start up in the bare skin of his side at every stroke. But still the prisoner would not stir. It seemed to me that they must slack out more links of one of the tigers' chains, or let the vile play linger into mere tediousness.

But I had more to learn yet. The male tiger, either taught by his own devilishness, or by those brutes that were his keepers, had still another ruse in store. He rose to his feet and turned round, backing against the chain. A yell of applause from the hidden men behind the arrow-slits told that they knew what was in store; and then the monstrous beast, stretched to the utmost of its vast length, kicked sharply with one hind paw.

I heard the crunch of the prisoner's ribs as the pads struck him, and at that same moment the poor wretch's body was spurned away by the blow, as one might throw a fruit with the hand. But it did not travel far. It was clear that the she-tiger knew this manoeuvre of her mate's. She caught the man on his bound, nuzzling over him for a minute, and then tossing him high into the air, and leaping up to the full of her splendid height after him.

Those other onlookers thought it magnificent; their gleeful shouts said as much. But for me, my gorge rose at the sight. Once the tigers had reached him, the man had been killed, it is true, without any unnecessary lingering. Even a light blow from those terrific paws would slay the strongest man living. But to see the two cave-tigers toying with the poor body was an insult to the pride of our race.

However, I was not there to preach the superiority of man to the beasts, and the indecency and degradation of permitting man to be unduly insulted. I had come to learn for myself the new balance of things in the kingdom of Atlantis, and so I stood at my place behind the arrow-slit with a still face. And presently another scene in this ghastly play was enacted.

The cave-tigers tired of their sport, and first one and then the other fell once more to prowling over the littered pavements, with the heavy chains scraping and chinking in their wake. They made no beginning to feast on the bodies provided for them. That would be for afterwards. In the present, the fascination of slaughter was big in them, and they had thought that it would be indulged further. It seemed that they knew their entertainers.

Again the windlass clanked, and the tethering chains drew the great beasts clear of the doorway; and again a valve of the farther door swung ajar, and another prisoner was thrust struggling into the circus. A sickness seized me when I saw that this was a woman, but still, in view of the object I had in hand, I made no interruption.

It was not that I had never seen women sent to death before. A general, who has done his fighting, must in his day have killed women equally with men; yes, and seen them earn their death-blow by lusty battling. Yet there seemed something so wanton in this cruel helpless sacrifice of a woman prisoner, that I had a struggle with myself to avoid interference. Still it is ever the case that the individual must be sacrificed to a policy, and so as I say, I watched on, outwardly cold and impassive.

I watched too (I confess it freely) with a quickening heart. Here was no sullen submissive victim like the last. She may have been more cowardly (as some women are), she may have been braver (as many women have shown themselves); but, at any rate, it was clear that she was going to make a struggle for her life, and to do vicious damage, it might be, before she yielded it up. The watchers behind the arrow-slits recognized this. Their wagers, and the hum of their appreciation, swept loudly round the ring of the circus.

They stripped their prisoners, before they thrust them out to this death, of all the clothes they might carry, for clothes have a value; and so the woman stood there bare-limbed in the moonlight.

She clapped her back to the great stone door by which she had entered, and faced fate with glowing eye. Gods! there have been times in early years when I could have plucked out sword and jumped down, and fought for her there for the sheer delight of such a battle. But now policy restrained me. The individual might want a helping hand, but it was becoming more and more clear that Atlantis wanted a minister also; and before these great needs, the lesser ones perforce must perish. Still, be it noted that, if I did not jump down, no other man there that night had sufficient manhood remaining to venture the opportunity.

My heart glowed as I watched her. She picked a bone from the litter on the pavement and beat off its head by blows against the wall. Then with her teeth she fashioned the point to still further sharpness. I could see her teeth glisten white in the moonrays as she bit with them.

The huge cave-tigers, which stood as high as her head as they walked, came nearer to her in their prowlings, yet obviously neglected her. This was part of their accustomed scheme of torment, and the woman knew it well. There was something intolerable in their noiseless, ceaseless paddings over the pavement. I could see the prisoner's breast heave as she watched them. A terror such as that would have made many a victim sick and helpless.

But this one was bolder than I had thought. She did not wait for a spring: she made the first attack herself. When the she-tiger made its stroll towards her, and was in the act of turning, she flung herself into a sudden leap, striking viciously at its eye with her sharpened bone. A roar from the onlookers acknowledged the stroke. The cave-tiger's eye remained undarkened, but the puny weapon had dealt it a smart flesh wound, and with a great bellow of surprise and pain it scampered away to gain space for a rush and a spring.

But the woman did not await its charge. With a shrill scream she sped forward, running at the full of her speed across the moonlight directly towards that shadowed part of the encircling wall within whose thickness I had my gazing place; and then, throwing every tendon of her body into the spring, made the greatest leap that surely any human being ever accomplished, even when spurred on by the utmost of terror and desperation. In an after day I measured it, and though of a certainty she must have added much to the tally by the sheer force of her run, which drove her clinging up the rough surface of the wall, it is a sure thing that in that splendid leap her feet must have dangled a man-height and a half above the pavement.

I say it was prodigious, but then the spur was more than the ordinary, and the woman herself was far out of the common both in thews and intelligence; and the end of the leap left her with five fingers lodged in the sill of the arrow-slit from which I watched. Even then she must have slipped back if she had been left to herself, for the sill sloped, and the stone was finely smooth; but I shot out my hand and gripped hers by the wrist, and instantly she clambered up with both knees on the sills, and her fingers twined round to grip my wrist in her turn.

And now you will suppose she gushed out prayers and promises, thinking only of safety and enlargement. There was nothing of this. With savage panting wordlessness she took fresh grip on the sharpened bone with her spare hand, and lunged with it desperately through the arrow-slit. With the hand that clutched mine she drew me towards her, so as to give the blows the surer chance, and so unprepared was I for such an attack, and with such fierce suddenness did she deliver it, that the first blow was near giving me my quietus. But I grappled with the poor frantic creature as gently as might be – the stone of the wall separating us always – and stripped her of her weapon, and held her firmly captive till she might calm herself.

"That was an ungrateful blow," I said. "But for my hand you'd have slipped and be the sport of a tiger's paw this minute."

"Oh, I must kill some one," she panted, "before I am killed myself."

"There will be time enough to think upon that some other day; but for now you are far enough off meeting further harm."

"You are lying to me. You will throw me to the beasts as soon as I loose my grip. I know your kind: you will not be robbed of your sport."

"I will go so far as to prove myself to you," said I, and called out for the warder who had tended the doors below. "Bid those tigers be tethered on a shorter chain," I ordered, "and then go yourself outside into the circus, and help this lady delicately to the ground."

The word was passed and these things were done; and I too came out into the circus and joined the woman, who stood waiting under the moonlight. But the others who had seen these doings were by no means suited at the change of plan. One of the great stone valves of the farther door opened hurriedly, and a man strode out, armed and flushed. "By all the Gods!" he shouted. "Who comes between me and my pastime?"

I stepped quietly to the advance. "I fear, sir," I said, "that you must launch your anger against me. By accident I gave that woman sanctuary, and I had not heart to toss her back to your beasts."

His fingers began to snap against his hilt.

"You have come to the wrong market here with your qualms. I am captain here, and my word carries, subject only to Phorenice's nod. Do you hear that? Do you know too that I can have you tossed to those striped gate-keepers of mine for meddling in here without an invitation?" He looked at me sharp enough, but saw plainly that I was a stranger. "But perhaps you carry a name, my man, which warrants your impertinence?"

"Deucalion is my poor name," I said, "but I cannot expect you will know it. I am but newly landed here, sir, and when I left Atlantis some score of years back, a very different man to you held guard over these gates." He had his forehead on my feet by this time. "I had it from the Empress this night that she will tomorrow make a new sorting of this kingdom's dignities. Perhaps there is some recommendation you would wish me to lay before her in return for your courtesies?"

"My lord," said the man, "if you wish it, I can have a turn with those cave-tigers myself now, and you can look on from behind the walls and see them tear me."

"Why tell me what is no news?"

"I wish to remind my lord of his power; I wish to beg of his clemency."

"You showed your power to these poor prisoners; but from what remains here to be seen, few of them have tasted much of your clemency."

"The orders were," said the captain of the gate, as though he thought a word might be said here for his defence, "the orders were, my lord, that the tigers should be kept fierce and accustomed to killing."

"Then, if you have obeyed orders, let me be the last to chide you. But it is my pleasure that this woman be respited, and I wish now to question her."

The man got to his feet again with obvious relief, though still bowing low.

"Then if my lord will honour me by sitting in my room that overlooks the outer gate, the favour will never be forgotten."

"Show the way," I said, and took the woman by the fingers, leading her gently. At the two ends of the circus the tigers prowled about on short chains, growling and muttering.

We passed through the door into the thickness of the outer wall, and the captain of the gate led us into his private chamber, a snug enough box overlooking the plain beyond the city. He lit a torch from his lamp and thrust it into a bracket on the wall, and bowing deeply and walking backwards, left us alone, closing the door in place behind him. He was an industrious fellow, this captain, to judge from the spoil with which his chamber was packed. There could have come very few traders in through that gate below without his levying a private tribute; and so, judging that most of his goods had been unlawfully come by, I had little qualm at making a selection. It was not decent that the woman, being an Atlantean, should go bereft of the dignity of clothes, as though she were a mere savage from Europe; and so I sought about amongst the captain's spoil for garments that would be befitting.

But, as I busied myself in this search for raiment, rummaging amongst the heaps and bales, with a hand and eye little skilled in such business, I heard a sound behind which caused me to turn my head, and there was the woman with a dagger she had picked from the floor, in the act of drawing it from the sheath.

She caught my eye and drew the weapon clear, but seeing that I made no advance towards her, or move to protect myself, waited where she was, and presently was took with a shuddering.

"Your designs seem somewhat of a riddle," I said. "At first you wished to kill me from motives which you explained, and which I quite understood. It lay in my power next to confer some small benefit upon you, in consequence of which you are here, and not – shall we say? – yonder in the circus. Why you should desire now to kill the only man here who can set you completely free, and beyond these walls, is a thing it would gratify me much to learn. I say nothing of the trifle of ingratitude. Gratitude and ingratitude are of little weight here. There is some far greater in your mind."

She pressed a hand hard against her breasts. "You are Deucalion," she gasped; "I heard you say it."

"I am Deucalion. So far, I have known no reason to feel shame for my name."

"And I come of those," she cried, with a rising voice, "who bite against this city, because they have found their fate too intolerable with the land as it is ordered now. We heard of your coming from Yucatan. It was we who sent the fleet to take you at the entrance to the Gulf."

"Your fleet gave us a pretty fight."

"Oh, I know, I know. We had our watchers on the high land who brought us the tidings. We had an omen even before that. Where we lay with our army before the walls here, we saw great birds carrying off the slain to the mountains. But where the fleet failed, I saw a chance where I, a woman, might—"

"Where you might succeed?" I sat me down on a pile of the captain's stuffs. It seemed as if here at last that I should find a solution for many things. "You carry a name?" I asked.

"They call me Nais."

"Ah," I said, and signed to her to take the clothes that I had sought out. She was curiously like, so both my eyes and hearing said, to Ylga, the fan-girl of Phorenice, but as she had told me of no parentage I asked for none then. Still her talk alone let me know that she was bred of none of the common people, and I made up my mind towards definite understanding. "Nais," I said, "you wish to kill me. At the same time I have no doubt you wish to live on yourself, if only to get credit from your people for what you have done. So here I will make a contract with you. Prove to me that my death is for Atlantis' good, and I swear by our Lord the Sun to go out with you beyond the walls, where you can stab me and then get you gone. Or the—"

"I will not be your slave."

"I do not ask you for service. Or else, I wished to say, I shall live so long as the High Gods wish, and do my poor best for this country. And for you – I shall set you free to do your best also. So now, I pray you, speak."

Chapter VII
The Biters of the Walls (Further Account)

"YOU WILL SET me free," she said, regarding me from under her brows, "without any further exactions or treaty?"

"I will set you free exactly on those terms," I answered, "unless indeed we here decide that it is better for Atlantis that I should die, in which case the freedom will be of your own taking."

"My lord plays a bold game."

"Tut, tut," I said.

"But I shall not hesitate to take the full of my bond, unless my theories are most clearly disproved to me."

"Tut," I said, "you women, how you can play out the time needlessly. Show me sufficient cause, and you shall kill me where and how you please. Come, begin the accusation."

"You are a tyrant."

"At least I have not paraded my tyrannies in Atlantis these twenty years. Why, Nais, I did but land yesterday."

"You will not deny you came back from Yucatan for a purpose."

"I came back because I was sent for. The Empress gives no reasons for her recalls. She states her will; and we who serve her obey without question."

"Pah, I know that old dogma."

"If you discredit my poor honesty at the outset like this, I fear we shall not get far with our unravelling."

"My lord must be indeed simple," said this strange woman scornfully, "if he is ignorant of what all Atlantis knows."

"Then simple you must write me down. Over yonder in Yucatan we were too well wrapped up in our own parochial needs and policies to have leisure to ponder much over the slim news which drifted out to us from Atlantis – and, in truth, little enough came. By example, Phorenice (whose office be adored) is a great personage here at home; but over there in the colony we barely knew so much as her name. Here, since I have been ashore, I have seen many new wonders; I have been carried by a riding mammoth; I have sat at a banquet; but in what new policies there are afoot, I have yet to be schooled."

"Then, if truly you do not know it, let me repeat to you the common tale. Phorenice has tired of her unmated life."

"Stay there. I will hear no word against the Empress."

"Pah, my lord, your scruples are most decorous. But I did no more than repeat what the Empress had made public by proclamation. She is minded to take to herself a husband, and nothing short of the best is good enough for Phorenice. One after another has been put up in turn as favourite – and been found wanting. Oh, I tell you, we here in Atlantis have watched her courtship with jumping hearts. First it was this one here, then it was that one there; now it was this general just returned from a victory, and a day later he had been packed back to his camp, to give place to some dashing governor who had squeezed increased revenues from his province. But every ship that came from the West said that there was a stronger man than any of these in Yucatan, and at last the Empress changed the wording of her vow. 'I'll have Deucalion for my husband,' said she, 'and then we will see who can stand against my wishes.'"

"The Empress (whose name be adored) can do as she pleases in such matters," I said guardedly; "but that is beside the argument. I am here to know how it would be better for Atlantis that I should die?"

"You know you are the strongest man in the kingdom."

"It pleases you to say so."

"And Phorenice is the strongest woman."

"That is beyond doubt."

"Why, then, if the Empress takes you in marriage, we shall be under a double tyranny. And her rule alone is more cruelly heavy than we can bear already."

"I pass no criticism on Phorenice's rule. I have not seen it. But I crave your mercy, Nais, on the newcomer into this kingdom. I am strong, say you, and therefore I am a tyrant, say you. Now to me this sequence is faulty."

"Who should a strong man use strength for, if not for himself? And if for himself, why that spells tyranny. You will get all your heart's desires, my lord, and you will forget that many a thousand of the common people will have to pay for them."

"And this is all your accusation?"

"It seems to be black enough. I am one that has a compassion for my fellow-men, my lord, and because of that compassion you see me what I am today. There was a time, not long passed, when I slept as soft and ate as dainty as any in Atlantis."

I smiled. "Your speech told me that much from the first."

"Then I would I had cast the speech off, too, if that is also a livery of the tyrant's class. But I tell you I saw all the oppression myself from the oppressor's side. I was high in Phorenice's favour then."

"That, too, is easy of credence. Ylga is the fan-girl to the Empress now, and second lady in the kingdom, and those who have seen Ylga could make an easy guess at the parentage of Nais."

"We were the daughters of one birth; but I do not count with either Zaemon or Ylga now. Ylga is the creature of Phorenice, and Phorenice would have all the people of Atlantis slaves and in chains, so that she might crush them the easier. And as for Zaemon, he is no friend of Phorenice's; he fights with brain and soul to drag the old authority to those on the Sacred Mountain; and that, if it come down on us again, would only be the exchange of one form of slavery for another."

"It seems to me you bite at all authority."

"In fact," she said simply, "I do. I have seen too much of it."

"And so you think a rule of no-rule would be best for the country?"

"You have put it plainly in words for me. That is my creed today. That is the creed of all those yonder, who sit in the camp and besiege this city. And we number on our side, now, all in Atlantis save those in the city and a handful on the priests' Mountain."

I shook my head. "A creed of desperation, if you like, Nais, but, believe me, a silly creed. Since man was born out of the quakings and the fevers of this earth, and picked his way amongst the cooler-places, he has been dependent always on his fellow-men. And where two are congregated together, one must be chief, and order how matters are to be governed – at least, I speak of men who have a wish to be higher than the beasts. Have you ever set foot in Europe?"

"No."

"I have. Years back I sailed there, gathering slaves. What did I see? A country without rule or order. Tyrants they were, to be sure, but they were the beasts. The men and the women were the rudest savages, knowing nothing of the arts, dressing in skins and uncleanness, harbouring in caves and the tree-tops. The beasts roamed about where they would, and hunted them unchecked."

"Still, they fought you for their liberty?"

"Never once. They knew how disastrous was their masterless freedom. Even to their dull, savage brains it was a sure thing that no slavery could be worse; and to that state you, and your friends, and your theories, will reduce Atlantis, if you get the upper hand. But, then, to argue in a circle, you will never get it. For to conquer, you must set up leaders, and once you have set them up, you will never pull them down again."

"Aye," she said with a sigh, "there is truth in that last."

The torch had filled the captain's room with a resinous smoke, but the flame was growing pale. Dawn was coming in greyly through a slender arrow-slit, and with it ever and again the glow from some mountain out of sight, which was shooting forth spasmodic bursts of fire. With it also were mutterings of distant falling rocks, and sullen tremblings, which had endured all the night through, and I judged that earth was in one of her quaking moods, and would probably during the forthcoming day offer us some chastening discomforts.

On this account, perhaps, my senses were stilled to certain evidences which would otherwise have given me a suspicion; and also, there is no denying that my general wakefulness was sapped by another matter. This woman, Nais, interested me vastly out of the common; the mere presence of her seemed to warm the organs of my interior; and whilst she was there, all my thoughts and senses were present in the room of the captain of the gate in which we sat.

But of a sudden the floor of the chamber rocked and fell away beneath me, and in a tumult of dust, and litter, and bales of the captain's plunder, I fell down (still seated on the flagstone) into a pit which had been digged beneath it. With the violence of the descent, and the flutter of all these articles about my head, I was in no condition for immediate action; and whilst I was still half-stunned by the shock, and long before I could get my eyes into service again, I had been seized, and bound, and half-strangled with a noose of hide. Voices were raised that I should be despatched at once out of the way; but one in authority cried out that, killing me at leisure, and as a prisoner, promised more genteel sport; and so I was thrust down on the floor, whilst a whole army of men trod in over me to the attack.

What had happened was clear to me now, though I was powerless to do anything in hindrance. The rebels with more craft than any one had credited to them, had driven a galley from their camp under the ground, intending so to make an entrance into the heart of the city. In their clumsy ignorance, and having no one of sufficient talent in mensuration, they had bungled sadly both in direction and length, and so had ended their burrow under this chamber of the captain of the gate. The great flagstone in its fall had, it appeared, crushed four of them to death, but these were little noticed or lamented. Life was to them a bauble of the slenderest price, and a horde of others pressed through the opening, lusting for the fight, and recking nothing of their risks and perils.

Half-choked by the foul air of the galley, and trodden on by this great procession of feet, it was little enough I could do to help my immediate self much less the more distant city. But when the chief mass of the attackers had passed through, and there came only here and there one eager to take his share at storming the gate, a couple of fellows plucked me up out of the mud on the floor, and began dragging me down through the stinking darkness of the galley towards the pit that gave it entrance.

Twenty times we were jostled by others hastening to the attack, either from hunger for fight, or from appetite for what they could steal. But we came to the open at last, and half-suffocated though I was, I contrived to do obeisance, and say aloud the prescribed prayer to the most High Gods in gratitude for the fresh, sweet air which They had provided.

Our Lord the Sun was on the verge of rising for His day, and all things were plainly shown. Before me were the monstrous walls of the capital, with the heads of its pyramids and higher buildings showing above them. And on the walls, the sentries walked calmly their appointed paces, or took shelter against arrows in the casemates provided for them.

The din of fighting within the gate rose high into the air, and the heavy roaring of the cave-tigers told that they too were taking their share of the melee. But the massive stonework of the walls hid all the actual engagement from our view, and which party was getting the upper hand we could not even guess. But the sounds told how tight a fight was being hammered out in those narrow boundaries, and my veins tingled to be once more back at the old trade, and to be doing my share.

But there was no chivalry about the fellows who held me by my bonds. They thrust me into a small temple near by, which once had been a fane in much favour with travellers, who wished to show gratitude for the safe journey to the capital, but which now was robbed and ruined, and they swung to the stone entrance gate and barred it, leaving me to commune with myself. Presently, they told me, I should be put to death by torments. Well, this seemed to be the new custom of Atlantis, and I should have to endure it as best I could. The High Gods, it appeared, had no further use for my services in Atlantis, and I was not in the mood then to bite very much at their decision. What I had seen of the country since my return had not enamoured me very much with its new conditions.

The little temple in which I was gaoled had been robbed and despoiled of all its furnishments. But the light-slits, where at certain hours of the day the rays of our Lord the Sun had fallen upon the image of the God, before this had been taken away, gave me vantage places from which I could see over the camp of these rebel besiegers, and a dreary prospect it was. The people seemed to have shucked off the culture of centuries in as many months, and to have gone back for the most part to sheer brutishness. The majority harboured on the bare ground. Few owned shelter, and these were merely bowers of mud and branches.

They fought and quarrelled amongst themselves for food, eating their meat raw, and their grain (when they had it) unground. Many who passed my vision I saw were even gnawing the soft inside of tree bark.

The dead lay where they fell. The sick and the wounded found no hand to tend them. Great man-eating birds hovered about the camp or skulked about, heavy with gorging, amongst the hovels, and no one had public spirit enough to give them battle. The stink of the place rose up to heaven as a foul incense inviting a pestilence. There was no order, no trace of strong command anywhere. With three hundred well-disciplined troops it seemed to me that I could have sent those poor desperate hordes flying in panic to the forest.

However, there was no very lengthy space of time granted me for thinking out the policy of this matter to any great depth. The attack on the gate had been delivered with suddenness; the repulse was not slow. Of what desperate fighting took place in the galleries, and in the circus between the two sets of gates, the detail will never be told in full.

At the first alarm the great cave-tigers were set loose, and these raged impartially against keeper and foe. Of those that went in through the tunnel, not one in ten returned, and there were few of these but what carried a bloody wound. Some, with the ruling passion still strong in them, bore back plunder; one trailed along with him the head of the captain of the gate; and amongst them they dragged out two of the warders who were wounded, and whom revenge had urged them to take as prisoners.

Over these two last a hubbub now arose, that seemed likely to boil over into blows. Every voice shouted out for them what he thought the most repulsive fate. Some were for burning, some for skinning, some for impaling, some for other things: my flesh crept as I heard their ravenous yells. Those that had been to the trouble of making them captive were still breathless from the fight, and were readily thrust aside; and it seemed to me that the poor wretches would be hustled into death before any definite fate was agreed upon, which all would pass as sufficiently terrific. Never had I seen such a disorderly tumult, never such a leaderless mob. But, as always has happened, and always will, the stronger men by dint of louder voices and more vigorous shoulders got their plans agreed to at last, and the others perforce had to give way.

A band of them set off running, and presently returned at snails' pace, dragging with them (with many squeals from ungreased wheels) one of those huge war engines with which besiegers are wont to throw great stones and other missiles into the cities they sit down against. They ran it up just beyond bowshot of the walls, and clamped it firmly down with stakes and ropes to the earth. Then setting their lean arms to the windlasses, they drew back the great tree which formed the spring till its tethering place reached the ground, and in the cradle at its head they placed one of the prisoners, bound helplessly, so that he could not throw himself over the side.

Then the rude, savage, skin-clad mob stood back, and one who had appointed himself engineer knocked back the catch that held the great spring in place.

With a whir and a twang the elastic wood flung upwards, and the bound man was shot away from its tip with the speed of a lightning flash. He sang through the air, spinning over and over with inconceivable rapidity, and the great crowd of rebels held their breath in silence as they watched. He passed high above the city wall, a tiny mannikin in the distance now, and then the trajectory of his flight began to lower. The spike of a new-built pyramid lay in the path of his terrific flight, and he struck it with a thud whose sound floated out to us afterwards, and then he toppled down out of our sight, leaving a red stain on the whiteness of the stone as he fell.

With a roar the crowd acknowledged the success of their device, and bellowed out insults to Phorenice, and insults to the Gods: a poor frantic crowd they showed themselves. And then with ravening shouts, they fell upon the other captive warder, binding him also into a compact helpless missile, and meanwhile getting the engine in gear again for another shot.

But for my part I saw nothing of this disgusting scene. I heard the bolt grate stealthily against the door of the little temple in which I was imprisoned, and was minded to give these brutish rebels somewhat of a surprise. I had rid myself of my bonds handily enough; I had rubbed my limbs to that perfect suppleness which is always desirable before a fight; and I had planned to rush out so soon as the door was swung, and kill those that came first with fist blows on the brow and chin.

They had not suspected my name, it was clear, for my stature and garb were nothing out of the ordinary; but if my bodily strength and fighting power had been sufficient to raise me to a vice-royalty like that of Yucatan, and let me endure alive in that government throughout twenty hard-battling years, why, it was likely that this rabble of savages would see something that was new and admirable in the practice of arms before the crude weight of their numbers could drag me down. Nay, I did not even despair of winning free altogether. I must find me a weapon from those that came up to battle, with which I could write worthy signatures, and I must attempt no standing fights. Gods! but what a glow the prospect did send through me as I stood there waiting.

A vainer man, writing history, might have said that always, before everything else, he held in mind the greater interests before the less. But for me – I prefer to be honest, and own myself human. In my glee at that forthcoming fight – which promised to be the greatest and most furious I had known in all a long life of battling – I will confess that Atlantis and her differing policies were clean forgot. I should go out an unknown man from the little cell of a temple, I should do my work, and then, whether I took freedom with me, or whether I came down at last myself on a pile of slain, these people would guess without being told the name, that here was Deucalion. Gods! what a fight we would have made!

But the door did not open wide to give me space for my first rush. It creaked gratingly outwards on its pivots, and a slim hand and a white arm slipped inside, beckoning me to quietude. Here was some woman. The door creaked wider, and she came inside.

"Nais," I said.

"Silence, or they will hear you, and remember. At present those who brought you here are killed, and unless by chance someone blunders into this robbed shrine, you will not be found."

"Then, if that is so, let me go out and walk amongst these people as one of themselves."

She shook her head.

"But, Nais, I am not known here. I am merely a man in very plain and mud-stained robe. I should be in no ways remarkable."

A smile twitched her face. "My lord," she said, "wears no beard; and his is the only clean chin in the camp."

I joined in her laugh. "A pest on my want of foppishness then. But I am forgetting somewhat. It comes to my mind that we still have unfinished that small discussion of ours concerning the length of my poor life. Have you decided to cut it off from risk of further mischief, or do you propose to give me further span?"

She turned to me with a look of sharp distress. "My lord," she said, "I would have you forget that silly talk of mine. This last two hours I thought you were dead in real truth."

"And you were not relieved?"

"I felt that the only man was gone out of the world – I mean, my lord, the only man who can save Atlantis."

"Your words give me a confidence. Then you would have me go back and become husband to Phorenice?"

"If there is no other way."

"I warn you I shall do that, if she still so desires it, and if it seems to me that that course will be best. This is no hour for private likings or dislikings."

"I know it," she said, "I feel it. I have no heart now, save only for Atlantis. I have schooled myself once more to that."

"And at present I am in this lone little box of a temple. A minute ago, before you came, I had promised myself a pretty enough fight to signalise my changing of abode."

"There must be nothing of that. I will not have these poor people slaughtered unnecessarily. Nor do I wish to see my lord exposed to a hopeless risk. This poor place, such as it is, has been given to me as an abode, and, if my lord can remain decorously till nightfall in a maiden's chamber, he may at least be sure of quietude. I am a person," she added simply, "that in this camp has some respect. When darkness comes, I will take my lord down to the sea and a boat, and so he may come with ease to the harbour and the watergate."

Chapter VIII
The Preacher from the Mountains

IT WAS LONG ENOUGH since I had found leisure for a parcel of sleep, and so during the larger part of that day I am free to confess that I slumbered soundly, Nais watching me. Night fell, and still we remained within the privacy of the temple. It was our plan that I should stay there till the camp slept, and so I should have more chance of reaching the sea without disturbance.

The night came down wet, with a drizzle of rain, and through the slits in the temple walls we could see the many fires in the camp well cared for, the men and women in skins and rags toasting before them, with steam rising as the heat fought with their wetness. Folk seated in discomfort like this are proverbially alert and cruel in the temper, and Nais frowned as she looked on the inclemency of the weather.

"A fine night," she said, "and I would have sent my lord back to the city without a soul here being the wiser; but in this chill, people sleep sourly. We must wait till the hour drugs them sounder."

And so we waited, sitting there together on that pavement so long unkissed by worshippers, and it was little enough we said aloud. But there can be good companionship without sentences of talk.

But as the hours drew on, the night began to grow less quiet. From the distance someone began to blow on a horn or a shell, sending forth a harsh raucous note incessantly. The sound came nearer, as we could tell from its growing loudness, and the voices of those by the fires made themselves heard, railing at the blower for his disturbance. And presently it became stationary, and standing up we could see through the slits in the walls the people of the camp rousing up from their uneasy rest, and clustering together round one who stood and talked to them from the pedestal of a war engine.

What he was declaiming upon we could not hear, and our curiosity on the matter was not keen. Given that all who did not sleep went to weary themselves with this fellow, as Nais whispered, it would be simple for me to make an exit in the opposite direction.

But here we were reckoning without the inevitable busybody. A dozen pairs of feet splashing through the wet came up to the side of the little temple, and cried loudly that Nais should join the audience. She had eloquence of tongue, it appeared, and they feared lest this speaker who had taken his stand on the war engine should make schisms amongst their ranks unless some skilled person stood up also to refute his arguments.

Here, then, it seemed to me that I must be elbowed into my skirmish by the most unexpected of chances, but Nais was firmly minded that there should be no fight, if courage on her part could turn it. "Come out with me," she whispered, "and keep distant from the light of the fires."

"But how explain my being here?"

"There is no reason to explain anything," she said bitterly. "They will take you for my lover. There is nothing remarkable in that: it is the mode here. But oh, why did not the Gods make you wear a beard, and curl it, even as other men? Then you could have been gone and safe these two hours."

"A smooth chin pleases me better."

"So it does me," I heard her murmur as she leaned her weight on the stone which hung in the doorway, and pushed it ajar; "your chin." The ragged men outside – there were women with them also – did not wait to watch me very closely. A coarse jest or two flew (which I could have found good heart to have repaid with a sword-thrust) and they stepped off into the darkness, just turning from time to time to make sure we followed. On all sides others were pressing in the same direction – black shadows against the night; the rain spat noisily on the camp fires as we passed them; and from behind us came up others. There were no sleepers in the camp now; all were pressing on to hear this preacher who stood on the pedestal of the war engine; and if we had tried to swerve from the straight course, we should have been marked at once.

So we held on through the darkness, and presently came within earshot.

Still it was little enough of the preacher's words we could make out at first. "Who are your chiefs?" came the question at the end of a fervid harangue, and immediately all further rational talk was drowned in uproar. "We have no chiefs," the people shouted, "we are done with chiefs; we are all equal here. Take away your silly magic. You may kill us with magic if you choose, but rule us you shall not. Nor shall the other priests rule. Nor Phorenice. Nor anybody. We are done with rulers."

The press had brought us closer and closer to the man who stood on the war engine. We saw him to be old, with white hair that tumbled on his shoulders, and a long white beard, untrimmed and uncurled. Save for a wisp of rag about the loins, his body was unclothed, and glistened in the wet.

But in his hand he held that which marked his caste. With it he pointed his sentences, and at times he whirled it about bathing his wet, naked body in a halo of light. It was a wand whose tip burned with an unconsuming fire, which glowed and twinkled and blazed like some star sent down by the Gods from their own place in the high heaven. It was the Symbol of our Lord the Sun, a credential no one could forge, and one on which no civilised man would cast a doubt.

Indeed, the ragged frantic crew did not question for one moment that he was a member of the Clan of Priests, the Clan which from time out of numbering had given rulers for the land, and even in their loudest clamours they freely acknowledged his powers. "You may kill us with your magic, if you choose," they screamed at him. But stubbornly they refused to come back to their old allegiance. "We have suffered too many things these later years," they cried. "We are done with rulers now for always."

But for myself I saw the old man with a different emotion. Here was Zaemon that was father to Nais, Zaemon that had seen me yesterday seated on the divan at Phorenice's elbow, and who today could denounce me as Deucalion if so he chose. These rebels had expended a navy in their wish to kill me four days earlier, and if they knew of my nearness, even though Nais were my advocate, her cold reasoning would have had little chance of an audience now. The High Gods who keep the tether of our lives hide Their secrets well, but I did not think it impious to be sure that mine was very near the cutting then.

The beautiful woman saw this too. She even went so far as to twine her fingers in mine and press them as a farewell, and I pressed hers in return, for I was sorry enough not to see her more. Still I could not help letting my thoughts travel with a grim gloating over the fine mound of dead I should build before these ragged, unskilled rebels pulled me down. And it was inevitable this should be so. For of all the emotions that can ferment in the human heart, the joy of strife is keenest, and none but an old fighter, face to face with what must necessarily be his final battle, can tell how deep this lust is embroidered into the very foundations of his being.

But for the time Zaemon did not see me, being too much wrapped in his outcry, and so I was free to listen to the burning words which he spread around him, and to determine their effect on the hearers.

The theme he preached was no new one. He told that ever since the beginning of history, the Gods had set apart one Clan of the people to rule over the rest and be their Priests, and until the coming of Phorenice these had done their duties with exactitude and justice. They had fought invaders, carried war against the beasts, and studied earth-movements so that they were able to foretell earthquakes and eruptions, and could spread warnings that the people might be able to escape their devastations. They are no self-seekers; their aim was always to further the interest of Atlantis, and so do honour to the kingdom on which the High Gods had set their special favour. Under the Priestly Clan, Atlantis had reached the pinnacle of human prosperity and happiness.

"But," cried the old man, waving the Symbol till his wet body glistened in a halo of light, "the people grew fat and careless with their easy life. They began to have a conceit that their good fortune was earned by their own puny brains and thews, and was no gift from the Gods above; and presently the cult of these Gods became neglected, and Their temples were barren of gifts and worshippers. Followed a punishment. The Gods in Their inscrutable way decreed that a wife of one of the Priests (that was a governor of no inconsiderable province) should see a woman child by the wayside, and take it for adoption. That child the Gods in their infinite wisdom fashioned into a scourge for Atlantis, and you who have felt the weight of Phorenice's hand, know with what completeness the High Gods can fashion their instruments.

"Yet, even as they set up, so can they throw down, and those that shall debase Phorenice are even now appointed. The old rule is to be re-established; but not till you who have sinned are sufficiently chastened to cry to it for relief." He waved the mysterious glowing Symbol before him. "See," he cried in his high old quavering voice, "you know the unspeakable Power of which that is the sign, and for which I am the mouthpiece. It is for you to make decision now. Are the Gods to throw down this woman who has scorned Them and so cruelly trodden on you? Or are you to be still further purged of your pride before you are ripe for deliverance?"

The old priest broke off with a gesture, and his ragged white beard sank on to his chest. Promptly a young man, skin clad and carrying his weapon, elbowed up through the press of listeners, and jumped on to the platform beside him. "Hear me, brethren!" he bellowed, in his strong young voice. "We are done with tyrants. Death may come, and we all of us here have shown how little we fear it. But own rulers again we will not, and that is our final say. My lord," he said, turning to the old man with a brave face, "I know it is in your power to kill me by magic if you choose, but I have said my say, and can stand the cost if needs be."

"I can kill you, but I will not," said Zaemon. "You have said your silliness. Now go you to the ground again."

"We have free speech here. I will not go till I choose."

"Aye, but you will," said the old man, and turned on him with a sudden tightening of the brows. There was no blow passed; even the Symbol, which glowed like a star against the night, was not so much as lifted in warning; but the young man tried to retort, and, finding himself smitten with a sudden dumbness, turned with a spasm of fear, and jumped back whence he had come. The crowd of them thrilled expectantly, and when no further portent was given, they began to shout that a miracle should be shown them, and then perchance they would be persuaded back to the old allegiance.

The old man stooped and glowered at them in fury. "You dogs," he cried, "you empty-witted dogs! Do you ask that I should degrade the powers of the Higher Mysteries by dancing them out before you as though they were a mummers' show? Do you tickle yourselves that you are to be tempted back to your allegiance? It is for you to woo the Gods who are so offended. Come in humility, and I take it upon myself to declare that you will receive fitting pardon and relief. Remain stubborn, and the scourge, Phorenice, may torment you into annihilation before she in turn is made to answer for the evil she has put upon the land. There is the choice for you to pick at."

The turmoil of voices rose again into the wetness of the night, and weapons were upraised menacingly. It was clear that the party for independence had by far the greater weight, both in numbers and lustiness; and those who might, from sheer weariness of strife, have been willing for surrender, withheld their word through terror of the consequence. It was a fine comment on the freedom of speech, about which these unruly fools had made their boast, and, with a sly malice, I could not help whispering a word on this to Nais as she stood at my elbow. But Nais clutched at my hand, and implored me for caution. "Oh, be silent, my lord," she whispered back, "or they will tear you in pieces. They are on fire for mischief now."

"Yet a few hours back you were for killing me yourself," I could not help reminding her.

She turned on me with a hot look. "A woman can change her mind, my lord. But it becomes you little to remind her of her fickleness."

A man in the press beside me wrenched round with an effort, and stared at me searchingly through the darkness. "Oh!" he said. "A shaved chin. Who are you, friend, that you should cut a beard instead of curling it? I can see no wound on your face."

I answered him civilly enough that, with 'freedom' for a watchword, the fashion of my chin was a matter of mere private concern. But as that did not satisfy him, and as he seemed to be one of those quarrelsome fellows that are the bane of every community, I took him suddenly by the throat and the shoulder, and bent his neck with the old, quick turn till I heard it crack, and had unhanded him before any of his neighbours had seen what had befallen. The fierce press of the crowd held him from slipping to the ground, and so he stood on there where he was, with his head nodded forward, as though he had fallen asleep through heaviness, or had fainted through the crushing of his fellows. I had no desire to begin that last fight of mine in a place like this, where there was no room to swing a weapon, nor chance to clear a battle ring.

But all this time the lean preacher from the mountains was sending forth his angry anathemas, and still holding the strained attention of the people. And next he set forth before them the cult of the Gods in the ancient form as is prescribed, and they (with old habit coming back to them) made response in the words and in the places where the old ritual enjoins. It was weird enough sight, that time-honoured service of adoration, forced upon these wild people after so long a period of irreligion.

They warmed to the old words as the high shrill voice of the priest cried them forth, and as they listened, and as they realised how intimate was the care of the Gods for the travails and sorrows of their daily lives, so much warmer grew their responses.

"… WHO STILLED THE BURNING OF THE MOUNTAINS, AND MADE COOL PLACES ON THE EARTH FOR US TO LIVE! – PRAISE TO THE MOST HIGH GODS."

"WHO GAVE US MASTERY OVER THE LESSER BEASTS AND SKILL OF TEN TIMES TO PREVAIL! – PRAISE TO THE MOST HIGH GODS…."

"WHO GAVE US MASTERY OVER THE LESSER BEASTS AND SKILL OF TEN TIMES TO PREVAIL! – PRAISE TO THE MOST HIGH GODS…."

It thrilled one to hear their earnestness; it sorrowed one to know that they would yet be obdurate and not return to their old allegiance. For this is the way with these common people; they will work up an enthusiasm one minute, and an hour later it will have fled away and left them cold and empty.

But Zaemon made no further calls upon their loyalty. He finished the prescribed form of sentences, and stepped down off the platform of the war engine with the Symbol of our Lord the Sun thrust out resolutely before him. To all ordinary seeming the crowd had been packed so that no further compression was possible, but before the advance of the Symbol the people crushed back, leaving a wide lane for his passage.

And here came the turning point of my life. At first, like, I take it, everyone else in that crowd, I imagined that the old man, having finished his mission, was making a way to return to the place from which he had come. But he held steadily to one direction, and as that was towards myself, it naturally came to my mind that, having dealt with greater things, he would now settle with the less; or, in plainer words, that having put his policy before the swarming people, he would now smite down the man he had seen but yesterday seated as Phorenice's minister. Well, I should lose that final fight I had promised myself, and that mound of slain for my funeral bed. It was clear that Zaemon was the mouthpiece of the Priests' Clan, duly appointed; and I also was a priest. If the word had been given on the Sacred Mountain to those who sat before the Ark of the Mysteries that Atlantis would prosper more with Deucalion sent to the Gods, I was ready to bow to the sentence with submissiveness. That I had regret for this mode of cutting off, I will not deny. No man who has practised the game of arms could abandon the promise of such a gorgeous final battle without a qualm of longing.

But I had been trained enough to show none of these emotions on my face, and when the old man came up to me, I stood my ground and gave him the salutation prescribed between our ranks, which he returned to me with circumstance and accuracy. The crowd fell back, being driven away by the ineffable force of the Symbol, leaving us alone in the middle of a ring. Even Nais, though she was a priest's daughter, was ignorant of the Mysteries, and could not withstand its force. And so we two men stood there alone together, with the glow of the Symbol bathing us, and lighting up the sea of ravenous faces that watched.

The people were quick to put their natural explanation on the scene. "A spy!" they began to roar out. "A spy! Zaemon salutes him as a Priest!"

Zaemon faced round on them with a queer look on his grim old face. "Aye," he said, "this is a Priest. If I give you his name, you might have further interest. This is the Lord Deucalion."

The word was picked up and yelled amongst them with a thousand emotions. But at least they were loyal to their policy; they had decided that Deucalion was their enemy; they had already expended a navy for his destruction; and now that he was ringed in by their masses, they lusted to tear him into rags with their fingers. But rave and rave though they might against me, the glare from the Symbol drove them shuddering back as though it had been a lava-stream; and Zaemon was not the man to hand me over to their fury until he had delivered formal sentence as the emissary of our Clan on the Sacred Mount. So the end was not to be yet.

The old man faced me and spoke in the sacred tongue, which the common people do not know. "My brother," he said, "which have you come to serve, Deucalion or Atlantis?"

"Words are a poor thing to answer a question like that. You will know all of my record. According to the Law of the Priests, each ship from Yucatan will have carried home its sworn report to lay at the feet of their council, and before I went to that vice-royalty, what I did was written plain here on the face of Atlantis."

"We know your doings in the past, brother, and they have found approval. You have governed well, and you have lived austerely. You set up Atlantis for a mistress, and served her well; but then, you have had no Phorenice to tempt you into change and fickleness."

"You can send me where I shall see her no more, if you think me frail."

"Yes, and lose your usefulness. No, brother, you are the last hope which this poor land has remaining. All other human means that have been tried against Phorenice have failed. You have returned from overseas for the final duel. You are the strongest man we have, and you are our final champion. If you fail, then only those terrible Powers which are locked within the Ark of the Mysteries remains to us, and though it is not lawful to speak even in this hidden tongue of their scope, you at least have full assurance of their potency."

I shrugged my shoulders. "It seems that you would save time and pains if you threw me to these wolves of rebels, and let them end me here and now."

The old man frowned on me angrily. "I am bidding you do your duty. What reason have you for wishing to evade it?"

"I have in my memory the words you spoke in the pyramid, when you came in amongst the banqueters. 'PHORENICE,' was your cry, 'WHILST YOU ARE YET EMPRESS, YOU SHALL SEE THIS ROYAL PYRAMID, WHICH YOU HAVE POLLUTED WITH YOUR DEBAUCHERIES, TORN TIER FROM TIER, AND STONE FROM STONE, AND SCATTERED AS FEATHERS BEFORE A WIND.' It seems that you foresee my defeat."

The old man shuddered. "I cannot tell what she may force us to do. I spoke then only what it was revealed to me must happen. Perhaps when matters have reached that pass, she will repent and submit. But in the meanwhile, before we use the more desperate weapons of the Gods, it is fitting that we should expend all human power remaining to us. And so you must go, my brother, and play your part to the utmost."

"It is an order. So I obey."

"You shall be at Phorenice's side again by the next dawn. She has sent for you from Yucatan as a husband, and as one who (so she thinks, poor human conqueror) has the weight of arm necessary to prolong her tyrannies. You are a Priest, brother, and you are a man of convincing tongue. It will be your part to make her stubborn mind see the invincible power that can be loosed against her, to point out to her the utter hopelessness of prevailing against it."

"If it is ordered, I will do these things. But there is little enough chance of success. I have seen Phorenice, and can gauge her will. There will be no turning her once she has made a decision. Others have tried; you have tried yourself; all have failed."

"Words that were wasted on a maiden may go home to a wife. You have been brought here to be her husband. Well, take your place."

The order came to me with a pang. I had given little enough heed to women through all of a busy life, though when I landed, the taking of Phorenice to wife would not have been very repugnant to me if policy had demanded it. But the matters of the last two days had put things in a different shape. I had seen two other women who had strangely attracted me, and one of these had stirred within me a tumult such as I had never felt before amongst my economies.

To lead Phorenice in marriage would mean a severance from this other woman eternally, and I ached as I thought of it. But though these thoughts floated through my system and gave me harsh wrenches of pain, I did not thrust my puny likings before the command of the council of the Priests. I bowed before Zaemon, and put his hand to my forehead. "It is an order," I said. "If our Lord the Sun gives me life, I will obey."

"Then let us begone from this place," said Zaemon, and took me by the arm and waved a way for us with the Symbol. No further word did I have with Nais, fearing to embroil her with these rebels who clustered round, but I caught one hot glance from her eyes, and that had to suffice for farewell. The dense ranks of the crowd opened, and we walked away between them scathless. Fiercely though they lusted for my life, brimming with hate though they made their cries, no man dared to rush in and raise a hand against me. Neither did they follow. When we reached the outskirts of the crowd, and the ranks thinned, they had a mind, many of them, to surge along in our wake; but Zaemon whirled the Symbol back before their faces with a blaze of lurid light, and they fell to their knees, grovelling, and pressed on us no more.

The rain still fell, and in the light of the camp fires as we passed them, the wet gleamed on the old man's wasted body. And far before us through the darkness loomed the vast bulk of the Sacred Mountain, with the ring of eternal fires encincturing its crest. I sighed as I thought of the old peaceful days I had spent in its temple and groves.

But there was to be no more of that studious leisure now. There was work to be done, work for Atlantis which did not brook delay. And so when we had progressed far out into the waste, and there was none near to view (save only the most High Gods), we found the place where the passage was, whose entrance is known only to the Seven amongst the Priests; and there we parted, Zaemon to his hermitage in the dangerous lands, and I by this secret way back into the capital.

The complete and unabridged text is available online, from *flametreepublishing.com/extras*

Trouble in Paradise

Karl Sade

THE FOLLOWING *are translations of selected writings by an alleged ancient Tamil scribe who went by the name Karanamudalvar. These scriptures were written on olai (chemically treated palm leaves that were used like paper) and contain the writer's unfiltered thoughts in a Tamil dialect that seems to be older than the oldest recorded Tamil writings. However, the writer could very well be fictitious – there are no records of him or his writings in any literature or historical documents, and these palm leaf bundles are said to have suddenly appeared on the doorstep of the Saraswathi Mahal Library (a library in Tanjore, South India that has been collecting palm leaf manuscripts for centuries) on 26th December 2021. According to Dr. P.S. Mahalingam, the director of the institute, two tribal boys from the fishing hamlets of Kanyakumari arrived that morning, carrying a damp gunny sack filled with Karanmudalvar's manuscripts. They reported having found them at a mythical underwater temple while returning from a fishing trip on the 24th of December. They demanded five hundred rupees for their find (converts to six dollars and twelve cents in USD), which the library refused, so they dumped the sack and left. Although the incident looked like an elaborate practical joke, especially because the olai could be no more than thirty years old, on taking a closer look it became apparent that the palm leaves are much thicker and resemble the descriptions of a gigantic palm species known in Tamil literature as Kundal Panai, which went extinct during the last ice age, about twelve thousand years ago. Regardless of the gimmicks and/or mysteries that surround the origins of the manuscripts, the writer's insights seem to hold a great deal of literary value which is why we have decided to publish them. Here are a few key points you ought to know before we dive into the writings – Karanamudalvar was a citizen of Kumari Kandam, a mythical continent situated below present-day India, that spanned from Africa to Australia, and is said to have disappeared after the big flood before the last ice age had begun. The period predates the Vedas and Hinduism, so the God Shiva in these manuscripts seems to be a slightly different version of the forms that are currently worshipped. There also seems to have been a social hierarchy in place that propagated a smooth and peaceful functioning of society, but descriptions of formal caste systems do not exist in these writings. And lastly, every manuscript is made up of two olais, and every olai consists of about four hundred words. We hope you enjoy the read.*

Manuscript Number 26 – On Dreams and Writing

Olai 1

I'VE BEEN HAVING these uneasy visions in my sleep but I've never written about them for I have not had the guts to do so. It takes courage to write, the process of writing can be violent sometimes. Mistake me not – I don't consider the pointed end of the ezhuthu aani [stylus] digging into the olai as violence. I can only compare this aspect of my scribbles to the poultry's claw scratching the mud while they feed. The violence is experienced when the words I scribble become desperate attempts to expose the Shiva [meaning abyss here] that lurks within, by dragging it out into the light and forcing it upon the outside world. This idea makes writing seem like a prophesying tool, which is not the meaning I intend to convey, and it's a dangerous idea that I fear would fall into the hands of the conniving lawmakers. They could easily turn this into a justification to prohibit the oppressed lower-class citizens of Kumari Kandam from writing by deeming our scripts as curses of the animistic damned. The reason this empire is successful is because of the peace, and it's peaceful because the lower classes are yet to understand their oppression and the upper class is yet to resort to blatant violence, and everybody respects and believes these lawmakers because we all fall prey to their holy and intellectual appearances. Anything that they can't explain is not categorized as unexplainable, rather these so-called educated upper classes irrationally blame Shiva for it all. To expose their arrogance and devoid them of their growing powers, the citizens of our Tamil country need to start becoming radically rational critical thinkers, and for this, we'd need to start accepting the incompleteness and irrationality of existence. This doesn't mean we lazily conclude that all matters are incomplete; we should strive to expand the horizons of knowledge, for there is nothing else worth doing in life.

Olai 2

The reason I fear these specific visions is that I am petrified when I see them. I am often alone in these dreams, usually after having abandoned a family member, and having scurried inland. My hands are shaking as I write about it [his shivers were visible in his handwriting. We aren't sure if it was done purely for dramatic effect], and not so much out of fear, but out of awe. My awe-stricken body in my dreams is unable to move, and I am frozen in Kala [time/darkness] as I observe the phenomena that unfold in front of me. Only once do I remember running from it in vain and I never know how it all ends, for I always wake up with a violent jolt. What I see in those dreams is that the coastline grows vertically, to touch the skies, and it grows so tall that it has touched the sun and begins to extinguish it. The sea dims the morning light and turns everything blueish gray, and it roars as it grows larger and larger and reaches the point where the water wall begins to collapse on the people of Kumari Kandam. I know what some people would say about this vision, they'd say it's a memory that has been passed on from the first fish that had experienced such massive waves, but what if this is a danger I'm able to foretell? What if it is a metaphor for my excesses that are about to get me and the people of my country? What if the large wave is my madness, my rage, my greatness that is going to engulf all things mediocre? As much as I fear that vision, I am fond of the way it feels when I watch the wall collapse. Interpret it however you want, for I believe any interpretation of such visions is valid. But the most irrational interpretation of this dream, according to me, would be that a really big wave is going to engulf Kumari Kandam.

Manuscript Number 29 – On Love and Relationships

Olai 1

THE ELDERS SAY that Mandakani's birth stars and mine are aligned in ways that have never been seen in Kumari Kandam's history. This is all the elders spoke about for weeks leading up to the marriage, and my marriage to this fair-skinned beauty was probably one of the best processions organized by our societal class. These elders promised me magical nights and divine family life, that Mandakani and I were going to be one, like the fusion of the masculine and feminine in Shiva. I had experienced one such connection before, but never with Mandakani. It was with Yedhugiri. Yedhugiri was a neighbor of mine growing up, and her father, like my father, was a sewage cleaner – their role in society was to make sure that the town's sewage lines never clogged. As the story goes, Yedhugiri's father contracted a disease on the job that killed him, and the mother passed away within days from grief. The mother's cremation was the last time I'd seen the girl; I still remember her as a plump little doll, dark-skinned and with a mole on her chin, with big round eyes, staring at me as my father covered the deceased's body in perfumed, cow dung patties. I was told that a relative had taken her away. On the day I turned seventeen, my elder brothers lied to my parents, saying they were taking me on a pilgrimage, and they took me to the village of Kamadenu. The village was known for the erotic processions that took place there and the temples were decorated with carvings of copulations and orgies, where each pose was devoted to a certain animistic God. I must admit I landed with a little bit of a fever looking at those sculptures. My brothers taught me what needed to be done when I encountered a woman, and they introduced me to the temple maid to practice. That is when I met the girl again. She was still plump and dark, with big eyes and a fat nose. This is where my society had brought a little orphaned girl from the lower class; they made her a sacred prostitute. Though disgusted by what had happened to her, I spent the night with her and enjoyed every bit of it. She had learned to transcend and experience the higher dimensions and absolute bliss through sex, and undulate her consciousness on waves of raptures. I know she did for I experienced it with her. She had also learned to lie, for she told me it was only me that she'd experienced that with.

Olai 2

Procreation with Mandakani on the other hand, though she is considered much more beautiful and her body is deemed more desirable, is quite the opposite experience. To me, the time I spend with her ends up feeling like a forced and mundane interaction between two bodies and I'm not speaking of procreating alone. I know it's indecent and unfair of me to compare these two ladies, but the point I am trying to make here, or the question that I hold with this thought, is where are all those elders' predictions and promises based on reading stars? If they are as wise as they like to be perceived, why then would they send an orphan child into prostitution? The elders hate being questioned, and that is probably the primary reason for the existence of the unwritten rule against questioning elders. Directly confronting them about this would simply make me an ungrateful villain in their eyes. I don't deny that a society where the young ones learn from old wisdom seems to hold a certain peace, but also, I feel that these old ones have no clue what they are talking about – they simply chant words that have been passed on. The thing is, Kumari Kandam has faced no wars, no famines, and no diseases for so long that the older generations have not had the experience required for wisdom, and they have nothing to pass on to us other than their fears and family names. I wish things had happened differently with Yedhugiri, I wish my parents had taken her to live with us. It saddens me when I think of her – she thinks that spreading her legs for depraved men is God's work, that her services are divine. Would she feel the same if she were to spread her legs for gold rather than God? End of the day, it all feels like stories we tell our lazy selves to feel better.

Manuscript Number 33 – On Arrogance and Weakness

Olai 1

MANDAKANI'S MOTHER is from the warrior class of society. Her father, my mamanar [father-in-law] is a sewage cleaner just like my father. He supposedly saved his mamanar's life, which is why the old warrior gifted him his daughter. It's been at least five generations since Kumari Kandam has been at war; hence these useless warrior classes have evolved to become lawmakers. And the more time that passes without war, the weaker their identity gets. The weaker their identity gets, the more they've got to discriminate to maintain their image in society. We've had two centuries of peace now, and it's the kind of peace the Gods dream of, the kind of peace that has turned stories of courage and valor into stale myths. You'd never hear of marriages between classes such as Mandakani's parents in present times, the warrior classes can't afford to mix and lose their identity. They have no real courage or valor to strengthen their position, they just have their bloodline to hold on to. An empire's peace with its neighboring empires comes only at the cost of civil conflict – I can smell our society's internal turmoil breeding and I can hear our echoes of neurosis. Today is the first time I experienced them in the form of blatant discrimination. Mandakani's cousin, whom she would have married if she were from a full-blooded warrior class, Mahamudra, invited me to our communal baths. I must admit, I was an idiot for going – just because someone invites you doesn't mean you go. But I did have my reason. I wanted to break away from the city's shit stains that my family name bears, and I wanted to be recognized as the writer that I am, so, any opportunity to socialize and get my name out there is an opportunity I thought was worth taking. So, I went. It's also getting unusually cold in the country and a hot soak in the sulfur bath sounded like a comforting idea.

Olai 2

I don't remember a time when I had to walk through my town wearing footwear. Footwear used to be only for the forests and the cold stone floors of the fortresses. You didn't need to protect your feet while walking on the mud streets of our towns; our towns are considered temples. It has become so cold now that you can't walk without slippers and not fall sick. I walked past the mud houses and took the route that goes past the Murthakoil [eldest/oldest temple]. This is my favorite temple because it is not spoiled by the colorful paint the newer temples are covered with. Though the old route is the longest route to the Periyakoil [big/main temple], it is the most beautiful to take, with the green Koladri river running by. I watched Mahamudra and his entourage ride the coracle downstream to the bathhouse. I am pretty sure they saw me, but they did not bother to stop or wave. I should've turned around then and there, but still I shamelessly went. I met them at the baths, and their faces carried the smirks I expected to see – I'd never been humiliated like this before. There were three boys my age and two elder men. They spoke of how the dry skin from their groins and the boggers from their noses go down the drain only to be cleaned by my kind. They told me how the mundane cleaning jobs had made people born into this profession less capable of intellect, and how our families are descendants of uncultured and tribal sub-humans. What I hate about that whole incident is that I didn't react to the insults. I could not do so for I was brought up with the same narratives by my very own kit and kin, being told that we were all inherently inferior to them. Objectively speaking, I was physically the biggest of them all, and even though they are warriors, they haven't worked like me, their hands are not like mine, and they are soft; I've been cleaning their shit when they were playing fight in their training institutes for as long as I remember. And intellectually speaking, I'd leave their gurus in the dust with my mental acrobatics; I've pushed thoughts in ways they can't even imagine, yet I sat there and let them smear my face with their feces. You won't believe how ashamed of myself I am and I can't help but contemplate suicide.

Manuscript Number 34 - On Shiva

Olai 1

WRITING is the only thing keeping me alive. For some reason, I seem to think that my thoughts are worth recording; maybe that's the very reason I despise the upper classes; maybe I feel intellectually superior to them just the way they feel inherently superior to me. But I'd never ill-treat those lesser beings the way I see them ill-treat the lower classes. Their oppressions are becoming blatantly visible and are getting harsher as the days go by. The other day, for instance, I had gone to attend a lecture by Mahamudra – the idiot has taken up writing and he was going to speak about Shiva. The lecture was a substandard bore, to say the least. The idiot kept referring to Shiva as a 'he', while Shiva is a genderless concept that's beyond personification. And it was no lecture, but a recital of devotional love poems to his God. After he recited the poems, he deciphered them for his audience. Not that they were highly encrypted scripts, but what kind of writer would shamelessly stand in front of their audience and clarify their work? Moreover, the language he writes in is so weak; Tamil is not spoken like that. There is strength, aggression, and vulgarity in the language. You speak the tongue with gumption, not like a coward in love. The people, my beautiful people of this paradise country, threw flowers at the idiot for it. He is no writer and I couldn't afford to have his scripts passed on to my people. I had to kill him. So I followed him back to his house after the lecture. He had a lady walk behind him, all the way to his little palace, with a broom tied to her back that touched the ground to sweep away her footprints. I'd never seen such a thing before, so after reaching Mahamudra's little palace I sneaked into the servant's quarter to meet her. The lady was none other than Yedhugiri. She said she'd come to the city to see me and was caught and sold as a slave. I asked her what the broom was for, and she told me that Mahamudra had instructed her to wear it at all times. He'd told her that it was a sin to print her feet on the sacred grounds of Kumari Kandam, and so she needed a broom to constantly wipe her presence off the earth. I gave her a sip of my Somra [either an opiate or a hallucinogen that was consumed like alcohol], gulped a few sips myself, and spoke to her about Shiva.

Olai 2

The amount of filth we people carry in our hearts – no matter how peaceful our civilizations! We'll never cease to be disgusting, and our collectives will never cease to reflect our innate sicknesses. I gave Yedhugiri the lecture Mahamudra had failed to give that evening. I told her that she is a Shiva, and to be Shiva she has to cut her societal ties, for she is her own puppet master and she is her puppet. I pulled out my ezhuthu aani and carved the Shiva lingam [the symbolic representation of Shiva] into her arm. I told her that it symbolizes the masculine and the feminine that lurks within her, and to be her true self requires their unison. I fed her more Somra and watched her break apart as I explained to her that spreading her legs for strangers was not God's work, and that her society had forced her into prostitution. To get her to pull herself back together, I told her Kala [time] was as much of an illusion as life was, and to be Shiva meant she was beyond time and material; that she had nothing to live for and nothing to die for, and that she was nothing and nothing could happen to her. I had just finished engraving the lingam into her arm when Mahamudra walked in. Seeing all the blood and hearing all the wailing, he charged at me. Yedhugiri picked up the ezhuthu aani from my hands and punctured the man to death. She then tore out her broom, sat on the cadaver, and stabbed the broomsticks into the hundred holes she had made, while she meditated. The only beauty I've witnessed in culture is when the oppressed fight back against their oppressors. By morning, people had flooded that palace and I was able to convince them all that Yedhugiri had turned into Shiva and punished the man for her ill treatment. The general public seemed to have bought that story. They were also terrified to go to her – she looked like an angry goddess, and they probably would have made her one by now. I drank more Somra, went to the Murthakoil, meditated, and bathed in Koladri. The water was almost ice.

* * *

Post Script

The night before this article got sent out to be published and printed, we received a phone call from the Saraswathi Mahal Library saying that the boys who had brought the scripts had returned with another. They said they found this one too at the mythical underwater temple, and that this was a new manuscript. The leaf that this one has been written on is from a palm from the Indonesian breed. The passage is short and seems to have been scribbled in a hurry. Also, the olai seems to be brand new.

Manuscript 35 – The Last Manuscript

I AM WRITING for the first time in decades. I had given up my writing, and my desire for greatness, and I gave up more than that. I gave up my family, Mandakini, Kumari Kandam, I gave it all away and I walked further East carrying only my writings. I've now reached Sundaland [present-day Java and Sumatra]; I was standing on the Karyamukti hill temple a couple of days ago when I witnessed my dreams come true. I watched the wall of water engulf all of the lands below and I am sure Kumari Kandam has drowned too, I can feel it. And it is getting very cold here, everything is freezing, but I could not get myself to burn my writings for warmth. I threw it all down the void chamber in the temple. They say it's a teleportation vent – people jump into it but you can never hear them land. I am writing this only to remember what writing felt like and it doesn't feel like much. I can't remember what all that fuss was about. Anyway, it's time for me to throw this into the void chamber and I'll be jumping in after. I've got to say, those big waves were beautiful.

All the Time in the World

Silas Leavitt

IN THE MYTHIC AGE, before humanity ceased their endless wanderings and settled down to raise crops and grow cities, there lived a tribe that could step through Time. In the now, Time is a river. It flows ever onward in one direction. But in those days, Time was a vast ocean.

The Agbo learned that if they were cunning and quick and moved without fear, they could step back and forth between the past, present, and future. Though it little mattered what lessons they took from the past or knowledge they gleaned from the future, as all times were the same. Day after day, season after season, humankind strode across the plain in the endless round. But even in the mythic age, things still changed. Nothing stayed the same forever.

Among the Agbo there was a man called Aleph. He lived with his tribe on the boundless plains that defined humanity's early existence. The Agbo roamed the Earth, hunting game large and small with the great gift of humankind: persistence. Aleph, born with one leg twisted and bent, could not keep up with the other hunters. He stayed with the camp crafting tools and mixing poultices, work just as important for survival. He had no fear of going hungry. Not only did the Agbo take care of their own, but his lover Ome was a mighty hunter who always brought back an extra kill.

Ome stood tall and broad-shouldered, with a great mane of dreaded hair that reached down past his hips. Many women asked to lie with him, so they may bear strong children and thus strengthen the tribe. Ome did his duty, but Aleph held his heart. Many nights they would stretch out away from the central fire and watch the great river of the sky flow by.

Always they talked.

Aleph had many ideas. They spilled out like a torrent, tumbling to the ground to be replaced by others shining behind his eyes. As a hunter, Ome knew the value of patience and perseverance. He often counseled Aleph, saying "Only one idea at once, my heart. See it through, then start anew."

"There are so many to choose from," Aleph would laugh. "It is hard to know where to begin."

His ideas ran from the useful to the absurd. A curved wooden stick he'd carved to hold a spear-butt allowed Ome to cast his dart farther and faster than all the other hunters. They mocked him at first, but after Ome struck an Auroch from over two-hundred paces away, all the others clamored for Aleph to make them one too.

Often, he thought of new ways of knapping the flint the tribe used for tools. He'd check the future each time to see if he succeeded, but knowledge is no substitute for real experience. After he tried a few ways and failed, the elders banned him from wasting their supplies. Change could be powerful, but everyone, even Ome, agreed that tradition was more important.

Aleph's wildest and most often expressed idea was that Time was a living thing. He thought that by tracking its movements he could one day find a way to capture it, even control it. That last he expressed only to Ome, knowing his lover would always take him seriously when others mocked.

Truthfully, Aleph didn't know what he would do with Time if he did catch it. It wasn't like a wildebeest or an Auroch that they could eat, a jackal they must chase away from kills, or even a crocodile they must flee. It was its own thing, both old and new.

The Agbo had an ephemeral relationship with Time. While they could step through it and around it, as if it wasn't there, they couldn't grasp it. Aleph himself had done the same on many occasions, looking back to see the first meeting of his parents or ahead to check on his experiments. He couldn't change the past nor touch the future. But then, what would he want to change or to touch?

Ome and Alpeh lived many years this way, every day a little different, every day the same. Together, they were happy, and the tribe grew in number and strength.

Then a day came when Ome did not return from a hunt.

The other hunters did, and their tale was one strange to the tribe's ears.

The group had made several kills, stalking their prey for miles in the usual manner. They'd been about to turn back, when hunters from another tribe appeared, one Aleph's tribe was unfamiliar with. They outnumbered Ome and the other hunters, two for every one.

Nervous, the Agbo checked the future. The strangers were not interested in talking. Instead of attempting to communicate, they would club down any of the Agbo they caught. The only way for them to escape was for someone to sacrifice themselves. Ome volunteered. The others fled, not looking back. The needs of the tribe came first, and one man could be lost where a whole hunting party could not be.

Aleph understood, but he could not forgive. Rather than keen his grief with the rest of the tribe, he retreated to a nearby cave he sometimes used as a workshop. Unlike the others, he could not believe Ome was gone forever. Surely one day, his heart would return. Frantic, Aleph stepped further and further into the future, searching for the moment that this was true.

The moment did not appear. Turning to the past, Aleph tried in desperation to warn Ome, then to tell himself to warn Ome. Nothing worked. Past, present, and future may have been one, yet only the present was within reach. If he wanted to touch the past and change the future, he must trap Time and bend it to his will.

The next few months Aleph worked without rest. The other Agbo wondered why he would not grieve with them but left him alone to express sadness his own way. As with all his wildest ideas, Aleph knew only Ome could appreciate his plan. And so, Aleph worked in silence.

The steps of this plan were simple. No one could see Time; to be found, it must first be measured.

Aleph started with a large stick, the straightest he could find. Next, he planted it on a large flat plain, where nothing could block the sun. Then, he waited. The following day, Aleph traced the shadow of the stick as the sun moved across the sky. It made a shallow arc. By inspecting the position of the shadow along this arc, he could find when he was in course of the day.

Not trusting his own gait, Aleph measured the arc with his hands. End over end he laid his long fingers down. At each step he affixed another, shorter stick, then, using the side of his hand, calculated the distance the sun moved in the sky as the shadow moved from stick to stick. The sun moved four finger-widths in the time it took for the shadow to reach a new stick.

Now Aleph knew something no Agbo had ever learned before: there were twelve Hands of Time in a day, and four Fingers in each Hand. The Agbo were impressed with this knowledge and chatted excitedly as they applied it to their waking hours. They learned it took exactly two Fingers of Time to reach the river for water and return to their camp, and nearly four Hands of Time for the hunt to return.

Aleph was not satisfied. He still could not change the past nor look far enough in the future to see Ome's return. By checking his future using the Sun-stick, Aleph counted just how many Hands he could look forward.

It was fewer than he had believed.

In the not far Past, the tribe used to be able to check up on their children and children's children, though never beyond their own death. Now, Aleph could only see to the start of the next season. His attempt to capture Time was working.

As Aleph worked, word of his Sun-stick spread. The Agbo were friendly with many tribes in the area, and they shared their resources, discoveries, and knowledge with one another. Across the plains, Sun-sticks sprouted up like mushrooms after a rain. Some used a different angle for the central stick, others tried using natural pillars of stone. A few even tried to apply the same principles to the moon, with mixed results. Everywhere there were people, a new attempt was made to capture Time.

By the Agbo's fires, Aleph focused on dividing Time into smaller and smaller increments. From Hands and Fingers, he moved on to Nails and Half-Nails. He made as many discrete intervals as he could. Finally, Aleph decided that he could wait no longer. The moment arrived for the final step in his plan to capture Time.

First, he took a long string made of spun Auroch gut and tied it to the central stick and the first stick of the arc. Then he wove it through all the other markers, Hands, Fingers, and Nails and tied the string back to the central stick, enclosing the whole arc. Checking the future, Aleph was startled to realize he could now only see Hands away from himself.

The future was closing in.

Curious, Aleph probed at the blankness. It was like someone had set a wall around Time. Seeing this as a sign of his success, Aleph sat down to wait. While he waited, he daydreamed of Ome's return, of how it would be to feel his arms again. When the sun reached the highest point on the arc, his shadow and the stick's shadow flowed together. Aleph stepped into the arc and began to dance.

First, he shuffled back and forth, stamping out the rhythm of the Agbo's hunting dance despite the pain in his injured leg. As he moved, Aleph flickered himself between the past, the present, and the future. Each glimpse of Ome filled him with joy, and each moment without him filled him with sorrow. He flickered faster.

No Agbo had ever done so many jumps through Time so quickly – for what would be the purpose – yet Aleph didn't stop. All around him in Time, a great and soundless wind wailed. The Sun-sticks rattled in place, but beyond the curve of the arc the grass lay still. The breeze roared into a furious windstorm. Inside the arc and outside of Time, Aleph's hair whipped free of its braids and the leather skins he wore began to tear.

He continued his dance.

A shimmer filled the air. Liquid light pooled on the ground around him, splashing over his feet. Still he danced.

He knew nothing but movement, felt nothing but Ome's arms around him, there and gone and there and gone again.

A rip formed in the air. Empty nothing that hungered always to be filled. The rupture grew and grew, sucking greedily on the light of the world.

"Aleph." Ome's voice, clear as if his lover stood beside him. "Aleph, you must stop."

For the first time, Aleph's steps faltered. He looked around, confused. "Ome?" He asked, hesitant. "I can't see you."

"I am here," Ome said. "As I have been and always will be. Aleph, you must stop."

"I have to bring you back." Unheeded tears soaked Aleph's beard. "I must capture Time."

"Aleph, you cannot. Trying to control Time is tearing it apart. Look!"

And Aleph looked. He saw the Sun-sticks spread throughout the plains, trapping Time's ocean and driving it forward. He saw the spread of humanity, carrying trapped Time with them throughout the world. Ever moving forward, they sought new ways to trap Time and keep it for themselves, but the more they tried to trap it, the more it slipped through their fingers. Nearer at hand, Aleph saw the tear he'd made in the present. Small right now, but it would grow and grow until everything was it and it was everything and all was empty.

"What have I done?" He whispered. "Ome, what have I done?"

"The rip must be sealed," said Ome, ever attentive to the task at hand, "though it can never be mended fully."

"What must I do?"

"Take it within yourself and hold it, forever."

And so Aleph reached out. He pulled the rift into himself and himself into the rift, nestling it into the cracks in his heart where Ome once had lived.

Crying out in fear and pain, he felt Ome's arms around his neck, his chest pressed up against his back. In the solace of his lover's touch, Aleph bound the rift with strong rope woven from his soul and his determination to be with Ome once again.

The wind slowed, then stopped. Around him the liquid light sank into the earth and fled up into the sky. All lay still once more. The sun resumed its movement across the sky.

Aleph lay exhausted in the center of his Sun-stick's arc, a great crescent weal burned into his chest. Lips touched his, and he heard Ome's voice again. "Until we next meet, my love."

Tears streaming down his face, Aleph rose to his feet and staggered from the arc. He tried to step through to the past, to hear Ome speaking to him in the circle once more but found nothing to step into. Suddenly frantic, he checked the future and found that it, too was blank.

He had captured Time. And now, captive, it could only flow in one direction. Only the present held him now. Aleph sank to his knees and wept.

Finally, with no notion of how many Hands had passed, Aleph heard Ome's last words once more in his mind. And so, Aleph returned to his people, who welcomed his return with open arms. Though some blamed him for the loss of their connection to Time, most understood they had all been complicit. Together, they shared their grief for Ome, and for the captured Time. But not all was lost – for though they could no longer see the past, still it lived in their memories.

Aleph himself lived across many more seasons, for as long as the rift was bound within his heart, he was both in Time and outside of it. Some say he still lives today. He sits, still as a statue on a great rock formation out on the plains, and he waits. For though Time now roars as a mighty river, all rivers flow toward the sea. One day, he shall look upon Ome's smiling face again.

The City of Warrior Queens

Kwame M.A. McPherson

I STAGGERED as I crested the last hill. I knew it was the last one because of the green vegetation spread below. I reeled, put a dry, calloused hand to shade my eyes and tried to stare into the distance. That failed. I saw only greenness, nothing in detail. Behind me, miles of golden sand were deceiving to look at, not that I could do so for any length of time due to the sun's rays bouncing off the small grains that might blind me. Instead of being a misleading carpet, the sand undulated just like its cousin – the open sea. Mother Nature's children peaked and troughed like true relatives.

A sword was heavy on my waist as I fell flat on my face. Sand smothered my nose, until I could not breathe. Slightly turning my head, I grasped the little oxygen I could. The sun tortured my body and I was burning, thirsty and hungry. I had lost my canteen and a swollen tongue filled my mouth. I gave up on touching my cracked lips. It made no sense touching them for touching's sake. It was said the human body could not last more than five days without water; I guess those five days had yet to pass, since I was still in the land of the living. I wished I had scorpion armour or desert rat fur, at least then I would be protected from the unforgiving element beating down on me.

I shut my eyes. Tiredness tore me apart, I could not walk anymore but I needed to make it, I needed to get to the jungle. My fingers dug into the sand and I dragged my wracked body inch by inch. Rolling would be easier but I was too weak to do even that. I needed to think of something else…

…It had taken us six months. Six months of leaving our loved ones, family, friends and homes behind. Six months on seas as rough as can be, with waves as tall as the tallest ship's mast or as calm as smooth glass. Six months of hot suns, lashing rains or brilliant white moons. Six whole months of running out of food and relying on spearing, or blasting with explosives, fish or the occasional shark. Six months of a stinking, rancid ship, clothes and men. It was six months of living hell.

I had stood on the ship's bow and watched *Voyager* slice through the water. I had closed my eyes and plastered in my mind a picture of green rolling hills with its shades of jade, and the deep valleys with a clear river meandering to the far-flung ocean. I had rubbed a hand over my eyes and said I needed to keep those images alive, especially those of Diane. I saw her laughing from my tickling as she rolled around on a carpet of grass. Her long, dark dreadlocks mixing with the green of the grass and thick smiling lips, revealing white even teeth. Her deep brown eyes seemed to dance above high cheekbones. Our picnic finished, we had frolicked at the top of Strawberry Hill and gawped at the breathtaking view below us – the red tiled roofs of the up-down village houses, the narrow cobbled streets, the small pond in the town centre… those depictions, I needed to cement in my mind. I had shaken my head of the memories, then opened my eyes to see the scenery had not changed. It was the same wide expanse of blue sea, and a long, consistent blue sky. Until we made land…

We were attacked as soon as we came ashore. Fighting a running battle with natives we could not see. The silently thrown stones, arrows and spears decimated my men, leaving me as the only survivor. I ran for my life and straight into this desert…

I clawed like a sand spider and wondered why I was even here. Once, I raised my head to see how far I was from the cool emerald overhang of trees, and it seemed like I had not moved at all. In my mind, I cursed. I swore at the map in my pocket. I swore at the financial backers waiting for their wealth in gold. I swore at the men who followed me on this terrible misadventure. I cursed the sun and the scorpion that crawled across my back, so I dared not move. My breath came in pants. My world was darkening. I was unable to stop it. I wondered if death would be a welcome reprieve.

Suddenly, a shadow blocked the sunlight. Squinting, I glimpsed up at a silhouette and tried raising one hand but failed. I uttered an obscenity at it, and then ever so slowly fell into the welcoming gloom.

* * *

My eyes fluttered open; immediately I covered them. A light intruded my senses. With a hand over my eyes, I gradually took it away and blinked furiously while my sight adjusted. I surveyed the area around me. It was lavish. A room of some kind, though the furnishings were not what I was accustomed to – white walls, lots of material with gold trimmings. A brilliant beam bathed the room through large windows. There was a chair made of a shiny black material and silver support, not the wooden type I knew. In the middle of the room was a table covered in a cloth with gold trimmings, and on one wall a sizeable mirror. Murals depicting animals and forest scenery were on every wall. The smell of something sweet permeated around me. It was a mixture of fragrances I could not place.

I moved, instantly jumping from the structure where I had been lying. I had never seen any contraption like it before. It looked like a bed but bounced. I was used to reeds and leaves. Touching it, I pressed down, feeling it move. I gasped.

Glancing in the mirror, I gawked and stared at my reflection. Aside from my sunken jaw and eye sockets, I stroked my clean face and smiled at the missing stubble. Someone had cleaned me up; even my hands and feet were smooth. In amazement, I stared at my hands. Looking over myself, I wondered what I was wearing. It was made of a material I had never seen or touched before: soft and gentle on my skin. Lovingly, I rubbed it against my face. Diane would wear this. I searched for my clothes and weapon.

The map! Where was the map? And my sword?

Rushing to one of the windows I gazed out and inhaled.

I was in a city of some kind. The magnificent buildings and bizarre carriages, like my room, were nothing like I had ever seen before. Structures stretched skywards and the windows sparkled in the sun. In the distance I saw a large pyramid; it seemed to fill the horizon. People moved from one direction to the next. I massaged my eyes a few times. I had never seen carriages with entirely wooden wheels. I wondered where I was.

"Hello! Hello! Captain Munroe?" A woman's voice.

I heard my name but couldn't see who was speaking. Frantically, I wondered what kind of magic was at work. *Was I dead and in heaven?*

Tentatively, I backed into a corner. I needed to see who was coming and find a way to defend myself. I called out, "Who is this? Where are you?"

She laughed. It put me at ease. The laugh was light and airy, the kind that made you trust the laugher.

"I'm at your door," she chuckled again, "walk over to the rectangle lines; press the right square and you'll see me."

I followed her instructions and a vision appeared in the door. Or what I thought was a door. Unbelievable.

Cute, oval face, thick lips and nose, hazel eyes and hair that reminded me of Diane's. Like hers, it was brushed below the stranger's shoulders. Her complexion had me bemused. It was smooth on the eye and I was sure flawless to the touch.

Quietly, the door slid aside and a rush of heat dashed in. I suddenly realised that the room was cooler than the outside and wondered how that was done. She gracefully glided by me and I caught a scent of some kind. Whenever she moved, her robe flowed, accentuating her curves. I made her out to be early thirties, but that was hard to tell with her unspoiled skin. Her movements reminded me of Diane – once again. Gold bracelets covered her wrists and ankles, and an ornate-designed gold necklace was around her neck. Wide with small details. My interest was piqued. What she was wearing was why I was here. Not wanting to be too obvious or make her uncomfortable, I stared for just a brief moment.

She was dressed in a long white gown, and I was stunned at the patterns, piping and designs. I had seen the motifs before. On a journey to Africa, the West Coast, I met people from the Ashanti tribe and they wore the same decorated garments. Based on our navigations now, I knew we were nowhere near the West Coast. Of medium height, she looked much better in the flesh. I was right about her skin and a part of me wanted to touch her.

Curious, I stepped outside, into the heat and onto a corridor. I walked over to a barrier. Looking over the obstacle I hastily jumped back and quickly returned into the room. Everything was as real as the woman in my room. The door slid shut.

She watched me and a smile played on her lips, as if what she knew was the biggest secret. Her grin radiated warmth. She was captivating.

"Where am I? What is this place? And where are my clothes and sword?"

She beamed. "We found you on the sands. You almost died."

"*We?*"

"Welcome to Meroe. Our custodians found you on their regular patrol."

"Meroe? Custodians?" I remembered the stories of Meroe, a dominant and prominent city in the sixth century. It was a great city in the Sudan, said to be one of the wealthiest in the world. Not only was it known to have over two hundred pyramids, it was also known as 'The City of Warrior Queens'. I stared at my guest, then outside. I wanted to ask her about her jewellery but refrained. It was not the right time.

Questions congregated in my head. *Where is this magnificent place? Who are these people? Where did they come from? Where am I?* It troubled me. The stories I had heard, from the old seadogs and other seafarers in the many ports I visited, were about various cities that appeared and then suddenly disappeared. Meroe was one. Yet here Meroe was, well and good in the eighteenth century.

"You know I've many questions?" I said, walking to one of the windows. "I've never seen a place like this before and I've seen many, many places." Then it occurred to me. "How do you even know my name? I don't know yours?"

She nodded, smiled. "And they'll have to wait until you've eaten and met The Elders. Follow me."

In my excitement, I had forgotten how hungry I was. Chuckling, I nodded. "You're right. I'm hungrier than a warthog. If you know what a warthog is?" She laughed, nodding. I added, "At least if I'm to follow you, I do need to know your name?"

"Princess Abena."

We walked out, along the corridor and to another door. It slid open, and we entered. Abena said it was an elevator. A small room with large numbers displayed above the door. I clung to the sides of the room's wall to her amusement. She said "ground" and as quickly as I blinked we were there, with a slight bump. I noticed where I had been was on the 23rd floor. Alighting, the city from the ground was even more outstanding. One behind the other, carriages went in opposite directions to unseen destinations, the animals trotting along harried with a lash from a tree-branch whip held by the driver. The roads were paved and wide. The buildings, taller than when I first saw them, made me look foolish with my head lolled back, staring skyward one minute then scrambling to look about us the next. Ahead of me, Abena giggled with abandon at my strange antics. We passed other people and each time we did, they stopped and bowed. She definitely was a real princess. Without the graces.

Catching up with her, I walked in step. "Princess Abena, tell me about this place. Tell me about you? When I passed out on the sand…what happened? One thing too," I paused, looking around, "where are the men? I don't see any."

She cocked her head to look at me. "I'm the daughter of a higher order and next heir to the throne. You're going to meet The Elders, they'll tell you more."

She was not giving in. I shrugged. "Ok."

I got the feeling she was hiding something from me again as she continued: "We're the perfect society. One where there's no greed, crime, envy, selfishness, hate, wars. Any negativity of any kind is no longer tolerated here. Everything you see around you has been created through sacrifice and love…"

We crossed at an intersection. A woman in armour stood in the very centre directing the wheeled vehicles. I found it amusing and stared at the spectacle while we passed. When she raised her hands the carriages stopped. I shook my head in awe.

Abena continued. "It took hundreds of years to cleanse ourselves of the thoughts that permeated our citizens back then. Eventually we had a huge exodus of many…and maybe that's how you came by the map?"

The map! I halted; she kept walking then stopped and pointed to a splendid building set back from the street. It was a palace. Huge pillars supported a peaked façade entrance. No windows. Only broad marble steps and a really wide door. Closer to the construction, the large pillars and walls were made of marble. Two sentries – women – stood on either side of the doorway. They held long lances and swords on their hips, and wore helmets and armour. Big lanterns made of gold were above their heads, flames dancing in them. I took note.

In unison, the sentries bowed their heads. I jokingly queried while we climbed the steps, "This where you live?"

Heading down a long corridor, Abena chortled, "We had this palace built for the people to have a place where they can come and meet with their elders."

"These elders are held in reverence by your people?" I asked.

"They are. They're the ones who have had the vision to protect and guide us." She waited by another doorway. "You'll be served food here. I'll get The Elders."

I nodded and watched her move effortlessly down the passageway. I also noticed more golden lanterns on the walls. I grinned. I needed to know more about their gold.

Inside the room, two more sentries stood by the door. The room was as extravagant as my space. Giant curtains, white with gold trimmings, stretched from a very high ceiling to the floor. On one wall, sun filtered through a large open window. More golden lanterns, fire atop. A long table with high-back padded seats was off-centre in the room. I counted ten on both sides and two at either end. A woman sentry quietly stood pointing beside one of the seats at one end of the table.

I walked over, smiled and joked. "There only women here in this beautiful city?"

The sentry ignored me and I sat. This chair felt familiar; I had one like it in my own home. As I sat, a door at the far end of the room opened and a train of women entered, holding trays of food. They placed them in a row on one side of the table and stood back, each woman in turn serving me. I had enough food selection to last me a lifetime and wondered about my men who had died. The food was delicious, compensating for the many days I was in the wilderness, every single lost pound finally won back. Holding high a huge goblet filled with a drink I had never tasted before,

I made a toast. It had a sweet taste and was good. Looking at the guard I said cheers, showed her the glass and downed the liquid in one go. Finished, I slouched in my seat, stuffed.

Immediately, as the women trailed out with partially or completely finished food, Abena entered through the main door, and behind her were ten women, all dressed in different coloured robes. Only their eyes were obvious since a veil covered their mouths and noses. The tallest wore a deep blue robe with gold trimmings, and I quickly figured she was the leader. I guess these were The Elders.

They sat to my right, occupying all the seats. And I was correct; the tallest of the group sat opposite me, way down the table. She removed her veil and the other women followed suit.

She bowed her head before looking me in the eye and speaking eloquently, "Captain Munroe. Welcome to Meroe. My name is Queen Mother Assantewaa and we sincerely hope your stay thus far has been to your comfort and approval. Should you need anything, please do not hesitate to let Abena know. You're our guest."

Abena avoided my appreciative stare and nod.

"I've nothing but great things to say about my stay, and I sincerely thank you for saving my life," I said. "Tell me, I was told that Meroe no longer existed after the sixth century?"

I looked at the line of beautiful women. They were all stunning, and Queen Mother Assantewaa moreso. Chocolate skin, close-cropped hair, long face and firm lips, her demeanour was one of calm. But her dark eyes stared right through me and a couple of times I needed to glance away. Dusky and deep, it was hard to ascertain her thoughts and I had the feeling she knew mine before I even made them.

Mother Assantewaa warmly chuckled. "We moved."

I and the women all laughed. I noted it was genuine and not strained.

Standing, she walked and stood by one wall. Pulling a long golden rope suspended from the ceiling, a large gold-trimmed sheet unfurled to reveal a massive mural with images of all kinds. I recognised it as something I had once seen on a pyramid wall in Kemet. A story in images. I was staring at the story of Meroe.

She began at an image of a mountain and a blue river meandering down a valley. It reminded me of home. She said it was where the Meroe people originated. Covering the pictorial journey, I learned about the wars won and lost, the kings and queens, their rise and falls, the exoduses and movement of the entire population. I questioned out of interest and noted her answers. It was about midway in her story when I saw what looked like a golden hill. At the bottom of the hill men laid prostrate on the ground, spears and swords scattered about.

I asked, pointing, "What happened there?"

"The men became greedy," she said, matter-of-factly, with a quick glance in my direction.

I pressed. "Is that why there are no men now? I haven't seen any anywhere."

Queen Mother Assantewaa slowly turned to observe me. "That's right. You're our guest and in the morning we'll escort you to the river with a boat well laden for your trip to the sea. In the meantime, Abena will show you around so you can see how well we have done."

I nodded. I guess I had outlasted my welcome. I wondered if I was fortunate to be alive. "I thank you for your hospitality, Queen Mother. And for saving my life."

She bowed her head, and waved a hand. A woman suddenly appeared with my sword and clothes. Men's clothes. She handed them to me.

I hesitated. "Er, Queen Mother. I've a question." I was uncertain on how to proceed but did anyway. "How do you know my name?"

Her eyes bored into mine. "The map you carried. It was stolen from us." And while walking to the main door, she said, "You came to me in a vision."

By hand, Abena ushered me from the room and gave me a palace tour. It was interesting enough with its many ornate and lovely decorated rooms. I didn't know what to make of Queen Mother's statement and forgot it in my eagerness.

"I was instructed to take you to our inner sanctum," she said.

We walked along another long corridor, golden-lit lanterns showing us the way and sentries bowing as we passed. She still held my hand, it was cool and nice.

"Inner sanctum?"

"Yes."

"What do you mean?"

"You'll see," she grinned and clutched my hand tighter. I wondered if the lack of male interaction meant my presence was exciting for her. We headed down a number of stairs and into a dungeon. Two guards stood by a high wooden door at the far end. It looked thick. One held a large ring and opened it. We entered an enormous chamber and everywhere I looked, in open containers and more containers, was gold. I struggled to hide my excitement.

"Nice," was all I could manage.

"This is Meroe," Abena muttered in awe.

"And will be yours one day," I added. She shied away.

"It's the people's. The women." She suddenly grabbed my hand. "Come. It's time to return you to your room. You've a long day tomorrow."

Walking out of the palace, I was surprised to see an evening moon climbing into the sky. The street was quiet. Abena was more talkative, but I hardly listened, my mind on the gold. Our walk was uneventful and we soon reached my building and the room.

"Where's the river from here, Abena?"

She pointed to the west. The moon and stars confirmed the direction.

"Thank you. For everything. I enjoyed the food and our tour. And learning about Meroe." I gave her a rapid peck on the cheek. She giggled and covered her mouth. Even in the moonlight I could see the spark in her eyes. If this was any other time… but I was leaving in the morning and there were things to do tonight. I watched her watch me while she retreated to the elevator.

I was not going to sleep. Dressed in the attire I had been given, I belted my sword around my waist. Taking it out, I saw it had been cleaned and sharpened. I re-sheathed it. Watching the moon, I waited. And waited. As it passed its zenith, I made my move. I took the table sheet, tore strips into rough holdalls and tied them to my waist.

I silently made it to the street, staying in the shadows on my way to the palace. The silent sentries stood still as I darted away to the side and the window I saw earlier. Tall enough, I stretched, my fingers grabbing the bottom sill. Using all of my strength I scrambled up, steadied on the edge and then quietly jumped into the room. There was no fire in the lanterns.

I drew my sword. Hereon in I would be the pirate I was.

Bent double, I sprinted for the main door. Metres away, I stopped. The lanterns had unexpectedly ignited, flames licking high. The entire chamber became radiant, and standing by the walls The Elders scrutinised me; Queen Mother Assantewaa and Princess Abena in the centre. Abena looked crestfallen. They were all armed. With swords.

I grimaced, and wondered if I would ever tickle Diane again.

Waters of Avalon

Damien Mckeating

THE SEASON OF MISTS had turned the world to a purgatory. Through the damp air stood the crooked black markers of rising stones and the jagged, skeletal hands of slumbering trees reaching up from the ground.

If the ghost of Avalon was anywhere, it was here. Buried under years of time and myth. Shrouded in its own story.

Abi walked along the sodden path, mud squelching around her boots, water beading on her waterproof jacket and dripping from the peak of the hood.

A figure appeared in the mist. A shade in the shape of a man. Some otherworldly being come to carry her off to the fabled land where Arthur rested. Or so she hoped.

"Abigail Walker?" the figure said. It was a short, balding man, with a gentle smile. His glasses were thick with mist droplets. He was bundled up in waterproofs that stretched over the generosity of his middle-age.

"Abi," she corrected him. "Are you Professor Kane?"

"Call me John," he replied, coming closer and offering his hand for her to shake. "Typical British weather, eh." He chuckled. "Be drizzling by mid-morning, hammering it down by lunch, and then tipping it down in the evening."

"I'm not here for the weather," she replied.

"Oh, I think you might be."

"I want to find Avalon."

"Yes, you explained as much in your email." He turned and gestured into the shrouded world. "You can't see the Tor right now, not even the tower, but it's there. Do you know it used to be an island?"

"Yes," Abi said. "Avalon."

"Do you know it's an island again?" He gave a shrewd look. "All thanks to the climate crisis. Late autumn to early spring, you can't reach the Tor without a boat."

Abi swiped at the lock of blonde hair that had fallen out of her hood and stuck to her face. "That's important," she said, not quite raising it to a question. The Professor seemed to be a man who enjoyed lording his knowledge.

"The past re-created," he said. "If you want to walk the old ways, you have to find them. A quest worthy of one of the knights of the round table." He studied her again. "Is that what you're after? Looking to recapture some of Britain's old glory? Looking for the king who was promised?"

"Yes."

"Don't go chasing paradise," John said. He took his glasses off and tried to wipe the water away. All he achieved was a smear of liquid on the lens. He tutted as he replaced them. "This world is all we've got, imperfect as it is."

"My son is dying," Abi said.

John blinked. He chewed at his lower lip. "There's a pub just up the way. We should talk some more."

* * *

The Hound and Basket made a good show of its stonework and ancient timber. A real fire was burning and it baked the room to a near insufferable heat. Dampness rose up from the drinkers in curling mists.

Abi sat across from John in a secluded booth. They were at the far end of the pub from the fire, but could still feel its prickling heat.

"It's a form of childhood dementia," Abi explained. "He's lost his speech, some cognitive ability, some gross and fine motor skills. He's begun to degenerate at an increased rate. He's nine years old now but we don't believe he'll live beyond his early teens. By then he'll probably be incapable of walking or even chewing food."

She said it all as a matter-of-fact. Her heart had been torn apart so much she was sure it was now a mass of scar tissue.

John seemed on the verge of speaking. Instead, he took off his glasses and polished them on his sweater sleeve; a physical tic he repeated so often Abi was surprised he had any lenses left.

"What's his name?"

"Michael."

"And you think Avalon holds the key to his cure?" he asked, looking over his glasses at her as he perched them back on his nose. "King Arthur was a warrior, not a doctor."

"He went to Avalon to heal. Maybe they could heal my son." Abi sipped at the orange juice she'd ordered. It was sharp and bitter and left a bad taste in her mouth.

"They were warriors," John insisted. "Their world was one of war, not of peace. There was no perfection, in Camelot or in Avalon."

"They fought for a better world," Abi said. "Paradise is the goal but the journey is war. You have to be prepared to fight to make things better for everyone. They did. They found the grail."

"Ah," said John.

"And other things. Celtic legend is filled with healing cauldrons."

"You think they're in Avalon?"

"Yes."

"Drink from the mystic cup and be healed?"

"Why not?" Abi scowled. "It could be magic or medicine, I don't know. They could be knights, fairies or aliens, I don't know. You ingest something and it heals you, whether it's mana from heaven or an antibiotic."

John cleaned his glasses again. He wiped sweat from his forehead. "An advanced society hidden in our mythology." He gave a little chuckle. "Not an unheard-of theory. Mystical beings waging war across the fabric of our reality." He gave another laugh. "This is folly, Miss Walker. You're seeing this idea through the eyes of grief and creating some perfect world that you believe can help you."

"A perfect world is one where I don't outlive my child."

"Such a phrasing tempts fate," John replied sadly. "The natural order of things is not as set as we think. Children do not always outlive their parents."

"I'll find it without you then."

She stood to leave and he stopped her with an outstretched hand, pausing short of actually touching her.

"Please," he said. "You sound so certain. I have to ask: how can you be so positive that it exists?"

Abi looked down at him from where she stood. "Because I have Excalibur," she said.

* * *

John had implored, begged, her to tell him more. To show him the sword. There was a desperation to his voice, but no disbelief. She didn't think he doubted her for a second. He knew it was all true and he knew the way to Avalon, Abi was certain of it.

In the end he had succumbed. He would show her where the path to Avalon had been. Or was. And she would show him Excalibur.

Abi prepared herself. Much like she imagined the knights of old had done, she spent the night in meditation. She could not sleep. The end of her quest was in sight, but there was still so much to be done. There were things she was contemplating, things that might need to be done, that she would not forgive herself for. But nothing was beyond her if it would save Michael.

She watched him sleeping. He was restful, for the most part. Tucked up in his animals-of-the-world duvet. Sometimes a flicker of pain would flash across his face and he would twist in his sleep. Part of his condition meant there was an accumulation of waste material around his joints and in parts of his brain; the kind of things that a body usually cleaned away.

She had watched him lose so many things. His words had been taken from him. His movement was being taken away. He couldn't feed himself anymore.

Closing her eyes against the tears, she reached out into the night and felt the weight of Excalibur in her hand. The sword was always there, and always not. It existed in a fold of reality. She could summon it to her at will, because it was hers. The Lady of the Lake had gifted it to her and now she was bound to the blade.

The presence of the sword was reassuring. A reminder of how far she had already come.

Was this how the knights felt? Had they sought the grail for themselves, for glory, or because they believed it could make things better for someone else?

Like the ailing Fisher King trapped in his castle, Abi looked at Michael trapped in his own ailing body.

She wouldn't fail him.

She couldn't.

There were no prayers for her to say. She wanted no part in heaven. She was struck by the stories of soldiers who return from war unable to adjust to society again. Men and women locked out of the very thing they were trying to save. Forever outside the gates of heaven.

If that was the price, she would pay it.

Excalibur disappeared back into its own reality. There was a legend that the sword should only be drawn if it was intended to be used, otherwise it would lose its power. She had little doubt that she would use the sword before this was done.

There would be blood on the road to Avalon.

* * *

Abi returned to the Tor with Michael. He was big for his age. He was dressed head to toe in waterproofs and giggled as he splashed around in the mud. The rain hammered down on them, like the world was determined to drown itself.

Abi stayed on guard. She had always been protective of Michael, but now she felt it more than ever. At the end of their journey they were vulnerable. Exposed.

"Can't see it again, but you know it's there," said John as he approached. He gestured through the downpour, towards the Tor, but smiled at Abi.

Abi flinched. Her hand flexed, clenching around the sword that wasn't yet there. John had gotten much closer than she'd have liked without her noticing. The world was damp and washed out in white; you couldn't see far at all.

"Hello, Michael," John called, seeing Abi's son stomping in puddles.

Michael spared him a glance, a look towards his mum, and then continued to stomp.

"You've brought him with you," John said, a pained look on his face.

"It's for his benefit," Abi said.

"You have the sword?" he asked. When Abi nodded, he started to walk and gestured for her to follow. "Then let's go on a little way. We can get somewhat closer before we have to start swimming." He chuckled.

The path was beyond waterlogged. It had all been fenland and marsh hundreds of years ago and it was going back that way. St Michael's tower, at the top of the Tor, stood on an island now, until the summer drought hit and dried up the land.

Walking through the white mist, drenched from the rain, Abi could feel herself in another time and place. In the same way that Excalibur came to her, this was a liminal space. Reality could be folded. You could step through, if you knew the path.

They were so close now. So close.

She could feel John looking at her, his eyes assessing the folds of her clothing, silently calculating.

"The sword isn't real," he said.

"The sword is real," Abi replied.

"You're not carrying a sword, unless Excalibur is more of a letter opener than a legendary blade." He mulled over his ideas in silence for a few steps. "It's hidden, then," he said.

"Always hidden and always here."

"Like Avalon," he said, so softly it was almost a sigh.

The ground under their feet was softer and yielded to their feet. Puddles and mud squelched up around their boots. Michael stomped onwards, threatening to lose a wellie with every slurping step.

Ahead of them a tree loomed through the gloom. It was bare and spindly, rising up out of the water as an act of defiance. There was a dilapidated wooden boot tied to it, maybe big enough for one adult to sit in. Abi noticed it floated on the thin layer of water, with only ripples of rainwater inside.

"We haven't reached the high-water mark yet," John observed. "That will come later in the season."

"This is the path," Abi observed, unwilling to yield a question to him.

"It might be better if we think of it as a gate, or a lock. Something that requires a key to open it. A sword, for example," he said with a nonchalant shrug of his shoulders. "Who are you?"

"A scion of the Round Table," Abi replied, her voice level and firm. They were at the threshold. She would not waver now. "A descendent of Galahad."

"The celibate, monastic knight," John replied with a raised eyebrow. "Unlikely."

"These are unlikely times." Abi stared into the mist and across the water. Sound travelled strangely here. Echoes came back to her as splashes, whispers, snatches of music and distant voices. For a moment the Tor felt crowded with people, but she was certain they were alone.

"I always preferred his father, Lancelot," John continued. "The unfaithful knight. His betrayal, of course, led to the end of the knights and Arthur's vision."

Abi turned her gaze on him. "And who are you?" She stood taller. She was strong, fit and capable. She was worthy of wielding the sword. The portly academic in front of her was no worthy match.

"The blood of Mordred," he said, holding out his hands with his palm up, as if to expose the blood in his veins. "The one who was denied his true birth-right. Give me the sword."

"Michael," Abi said cheerfully. "Let's get in the boat." She turned side-on to John, keeping him in view as she helped a gleeful Michael climb into the small vessel.

"Give me the sword," John repeated, his voice harsh and flat. "I deserve to reach the island. It should be mine."

Abi reached out her hand and Excalibur was there. John faltered and gasped, his eyes growing wide as he looked on the blade of legend.

In the surrounding mists rose a susurrus of delicate, insidious whispers. Abi saw black shapes swirl and coalesce into cowled figures, wraiths in the grey-world between realities.

"Think," John implored. "Not for yourself, but for the boy. When you're gone, who will protect him? You can't stop us. Don't make us hurt you. Or him."

Abi placed her hand on Excalibur's hilt. "I think of nothing but him," she said and pulled the blade free.

Excalibur came into the world with a shriek of light. It blazed, refracted and dazzled through the haze and rain. Abi twirled the blade and with a whisper it sliced through the rope binding the boat.

"Stay in the boat, Michael," Abi said.

Michael giggled and splashed in the rainwater lying on the boat's bottom.

Abi faced John and the approaching wraiths; four grey smears of terror etched into the ghost-white world.

John took a step towards her. "You're a mother," he said. "I understand you need to protect him. But it's done. Give me the sword."

Abi sneered at his condescension, but he kept coming.

"You're no killer," he said, a palm raised in a peaceful gesture, his jowls beaded with mist and sweat.

He was wrong. The blade could not be drawn and unused without losing its power. Abi understood that. She knew what unsheathing Excalibur meant.

She was ready.

John was not.

Abi darted forward and slashed across his waist. He fell back, face pale, mouth open in silent shock, blood welling up over the hands crossed at his paunch.

The wraiths flooded towards her.

Abi backed into the water.

She swung Excalibur in a wide arc, holding back the writhing shapes as they swirled and sought to reach her.

She stepped again. Water flooded over her boots.

She stabbed towards a wraith, sent it reeling as the blade touched its ephemeral form, then swung the sword to keep the others back.

They screeched at her.

Rain fell.

Cold water lapped her legs.

The boat bumped against her thighs.

"Michael," she said.

"Ah!" Michael cried. He used to say "Mama," not so long ago. Now he made his sounds and smiled, his eyes lit up with joy, enjoying whatever game his mother was playing.

Abi smiled through tears and rain, took another step towards the boat, and felt the ground drop away from her.

The waters closed over her head.

The drop was impossible. The flooded land transformed into something deep and dark. Abi kicked hard, dragging the sword up with her, and broke the surface.

There was white all around them.

Silence.

Water slapped at the boat. Michael giggled. Abi clung to the side and dropped Excalibur onto the vessel.

"Sit down, Michael," she said. "Stay in your seat."

She gasped and shivered.

And they approached.

Three figures out of the gloom. Their elfin beauty was a charm against the gloom and they lit up the world around them. Three women, hooded and cloaked in white, walking on the surface of the water.

They knelt to receive the boat, and in their faces was the kindly expression of a teacher disappointed with their favourite student.

Michael giggled and reached for them. One of the women smiled and touched his hand with her own.

"Save him," Abi said. "Please. I know who you are, Morgan." She was gratified to see one of the women turn. "You saved Arthur. Save my son."

"There is no wound in your son," Morgan replied, her dark eyes on Abi, her calmness alien.

"He's dying."

"As are we all," Morgan said. She knelt, looking down to Abi who clung to the boat.

"Then what good are you?" Abi sobbed.

"Many seek the path to Avalon."

"Just him," Abi said. "I don't care about me. It's not for me. It's for him."

Forever outside of heaven, she thought to herself. But a price worth paying to know he would be well.

The three women looked at each other and a silent agreement was made.

"Avalon is not for you," Morgan said to Abi.

"No," Abi agreed.

"Then let him go."

Abi sobbed again. She clung to the boat and took Michael's hand. "I love you," she said. "I love you so much. They'll make you better. You'll be alive. You'll have a full life. I love you."

She couldn't say goodbye. The word stuck in her throat. She let go of the boat and it drifted away from her.

In a heartbeat, sooner than she'd thought, they were lost in the mist.

Abi felt her limbs go numb. She was cold and tired. She kicked, reached out, and then the waters of Avalon closed over her head.

Forgotten

John Moralee

I WAS EATING my breakfast with a strong, wake-me-up coffee when my husband came into the crowded mess hall, looking around for me. Like many of the other scientists on the Antarctic base, Gunther had not shaved for six months because a thick beard kept his face warm whenever he ventured outside. He looked like a blond werewolf as he sat beside me and opened his laptop, showing me a video from a drone flight over a glacial region suffering the greatest melting.

"I've found something incredible," he said in a low voice so nobody else would hear. "This was recorded yesterday by one of the drones in Zone H. It was flying over the ice sheet, which you can see has changed dramatically since we last saw it. There are hundreds of meltwater lakes, but that's not what caught my attention. Here it comes. Get ready to have your mind blown."

The drone had flown along the melting edge of the glacier, where the global rise in temperature had melted the ice into a series of spectacular waterfalls and blue-water lakes. As the ice sheet broke apart, one side of a wall of black rock had been exposed.

"Look at that rock," Gunther said. "It's too straight to be natural, Agatha. It's absolutely vertical and featureless. It's a wall, hidden under the ice for thousands of years. A wall!"

Though my mind was fuzzy from being up too early, I agreed with my husband's assessment. There was a wall – *in the middle of Antarctica*. I felt the sudden thrill of a new discovery. For years we had been part of a science team monitoring and analysing the effect of climate change on the world's coldest and least studied continent. That meant living on a small research station for several months at a time, a test of mental and physical endurance. To find something so unexpected made me light-headed. I stared at the images, grinning. The sight woke me up completely. My mind ran calculations based on the thickness of the ice sheet.

"That's at least two kilometres high," I said. "How long is it?"

"I don't know – but the exposed part is at least thirty kilometres long."

"What's a wall doing there?"

"I think it's protecting a lost city," Gunther said. "It could be Atlantis or Ultima Thule. All the legends appear to be based on fact. There was a civilisation here before us and they lived in Antarctica. This is a Nobel Prize-winning discovery!"

His bright-blue eyes gleamed with excitement. Gunther had always dreamed of winning a Nobel Prize. In his mind, he was probably writing his acceptance speech and imagining what he could spend the money on. I loved his enthusiasm, but sometimes it could make him impetuous. Nobody had ever won a Nobel Prize for an archaeological discovery – no matter how profound – but I didn't want to hurt my husband's ego by saying so. A few minutes of video filmed at a long distance didn't prove he had discovered a lost city – just a very straight wall of black rock.

"Don't jump to conclusions," I said. "We don't know what it is yet. We're scientists. We don't assume *anything*."

"Oh, Agatha, come on," he said. "What else could it be?"

"We need to check it out thoroughly before forming conclusions. We don't want to be like the guys who said they'd discovered cold fusion. They were proved wrong and ruined their careers. At the moment, all we have is something unexplained. It could be a natural formation."

Gunther sighed. "You're right. We have to look into this *discreetly*. If it is part of a hidden city, like I suspect, I don't want someone else taking credit for its discovery. We must keep this to ourselves until we learn more. Don't tell the others. We'll investigate this ourselves first, then report our findings."

"That's not the protocol," I said. "We're part of a team."

"Forget protocol. Zone H is under my purview. I need to see it with my own eyes before reporting this. We can take a helo to the location. Finish your breakfast, then join me for a ride out there. Today we make history!"

I sighed. "Okay. Just us. For now."

He grinned like a little kid. "I love you."

As he hurried off to make preparations, I had misgivings. Breaking protocol was dangerous and stupid, but he was right about what would happen. Instead of us getting to see the wall in a few hours, we'd waste days with bureaucratic nonsense.

With hindsight, we should have shared the information with the others before leaving the base, but I kept it a secret.

* * *

The helicopter was ready when I left the base. The sky was a clear bright blue – ideal for flying. Gunther was waiting in the pilot's seat. He was a fully qualified pilot with twenty thousand hours of experience. "I told anyone who asked me that we're taking core samples this morning. Nobody wanted to come along, so we're free."

"That's great."

I knew we were breaking the rules, but I was just as excited as Gunther at the prospect of discovering something amazing. Like my husband, I wanted to see the wall for myself before reporting it.

It was a fine day with no predicted weather problems, which made it easy to reach Zone H following the drone's flight path. I started filming with a digital camera, wanting to capture everything once we arrived.

My first impression of the mysterious wall was that it looked like a black line drawn on a white sheet of paper. It was a little underwhelming. But as we got closer, I could see how unnatural it was to have a straight line of rock poking out the side of a melting glacier. Meltwater had carved a vast crevasse across the ice sheet. The smooth black side of the wall extended for several kilometres east and west. Gunther flew lower, so we were hovering over it. Then he carefully descended into the crevasse for a closer view. A river of blue meltwater was below me. The wall extended under the surface for as far as I could see.

"It looks like black granite, but I can't be sure without getting a sample. Can you land on the ice so we can get a closer look?"

"Yes," Gunther said. "Hold on."

My stomach flipped as he pulled back on the stick. We rose over the wall and swooped over the glacier, looking for a place to land. After a couple of minutes, Gunther chose a flat area three hundred metres from the crevasse's edge. The ice was firm and didn't crack under the weight of the helicopter. We quickly unloaded equipment, including climbing gear. Then we very carefully approached the edge, securing a rope so I could climb down, while Gunther stayed above, keeping me anchored. I rappelled down the ice until I reached the wall. It was obsidian black and shiny – not granite at all.

"Hey! It's not granite!"

"What is it then?"

"Don't know."

I touched it with a gloved hand. Very smooth. It felt like metal. I was reluctant to chip away at its perfection, but I needed a sample. I removed a chisel and hammer from my belt. I hit the chisel against the rock, expecting it to break off a small piece. But the chisel did nothing to the wall. It didn't even dent the surface.

It did have an unexpected effect. I heard a deep metallic clang like the doleful ringing of a huge brass bell. The sound travelled along the wall and faded away, but not before triggering a sudden, violent cracking of the ice above me.

I heard my husband shouting a warning, but it was too late. A huge block of ice had sheared off the crevasse. It was falling towards me. I screamed and did the only thing possible to save myself. I pushed away from the wall and released my tether, plunging down into the meltwater river just ahead of the deadly avalanche. I hit the water so hard my breath was knocked out of me. All around me, the water churned with the impact of fallen ice. Something hit me and pushed me down. The fallen ice was above me, blocking my way to the surface. I was caught in a current and spun around, losing all sense of up and down. Everything was blue or black. Air escaped my lungs and bubbled around me. I tried to swim upwards, chasing the bubbles, but I was hit by something and dragged deeper. Tumbling ice was above me. I slammed into something and felt myself being thrown around in an undercurrent. The dark wall loomed ahead. And something darker. An opening in the wall. A cave-black tunnel. Leading somewhere. Taking me... to the other side.

Darkness overwhelmed me.

* * *

Light. Bright, painful sunlight. It was everywhere, blasting through my closed eyelids. Blinking and coughing, my senses returned slowly. The last thing I remembered was drowning in utter darkness. But I was alive and somewhere else. My lungs were coughing up water, but I was in fresh, warm air, breathing in blessed oxygen.

Where was I?

I sat up and tried to make sense of my surroundings, but my eyes were too sensitive to the light. A pair of sunglasses would have helped. I shielded my eyes from the glare before opening them, giving my pupils time to adjust to the brightness. I could see no sun. The whole sky was a uniform brightness, heating my body, drying my clothes rapidly after my near-drowning. The air smelled of blooming flowers and fields after a summer shower.

I appeared to be on the sandy shore of a crystal-clear pool on the edge of a tropical jungle, with a grand, roaring waterfall on the far side. The water was coming out of a huge pipe attached to the black wall – so it was not a natural phenomenon. The wall looked like the side of an endless cliff from my position. Above it was the cloudless sky filled with sparkling gossamer threads. The threads – no longer than an eyelash – shimmered in the sun. They were all around me, seemingly moving in random ways, as though caught by a breeze.

I had obviously been ejected from the pipe into the pool, where I'd been very lucky to survive the fall. It was clear my entrance into this strange land could not also function as an exit because the water was flowing too fast for me to swim in the other direction, even if I could find a way up to the pipe's entrance. I wondered where the water flowed after filling the pool. It looked like it had disappeared into the jungle.

I stood and looked around, seeing enormous trees and exotic plants that reminded me of prehistoric ferns. Some looked like massive angiosperms. The vegetation was extremely dense, making it impossible to see beyond my local area. The gossamer threads formed a pink mist in the higher branches, shining like stars.

I thought of Gunther on the other side of the wall, watching me disappear under tonnes of ice. My husband would assume I was dead, because he did not know about the entrance. I had no way of communicating with him. What would he do? He'd probably contact the research station, but there was nothing anyone could do to rescue me.

I had to find my bearings and work out what to do next. First, I had to obtain a general idea of my environment from a higher perspective. Luckily, I had my climbing equipment, which I could use to climb one of the trees. Each tree had a thick, firm bark that looked solid enough to hold my crampons. I tested one and began climbing. I was soon at a heady height, climbing up and up like Jack on his beanstalk. Breathless, I reached a wide branch near the top, where I rested and gazed in wonder at the land inside the wall.

From my vantage point, I could see the wall was not straight as I'd first believed. It was gently curved, enclosing a circular area many, many kilometres across. I estimated the wall enclosed an area ten times as big as New York. With the thickest layer of gossamer threads below me, I could also see the bright sky was not a uniform colour. It had a subtle, grid-like pattern. It was some kind of light-emitting material forming a roof over this world. I was stunned to realise I was inside a dome.

The jungle was just a small part of my new environment – a ring of lush green around a city of golden towers, stepped gardens and gleaming glass wonders. Evidently, the city and the dome had been created by a civilisation with a level of technology far beyond humankind's current level. I felt like I was looking at the future, not something built in the distant past. Every building looked as beautiful and delicate as an ice sculpture. At the city's heart, the spear-like buildings rose as high as the sky. The upper echelons were obscured by pink clouds.

Stunned by my discovery, I knew the city had to be my next destination.

* * *

I emerged from the jungle onto a wide thoroughfare made of translucent stone, through which I could see an under-city of exotic buildings, lakes and rivers. There were many tiers to the city, all lit by the constant roof-light, all visible through each other, like a complex glass sculpture twisting and reflecting the artificial sunlight. I passed dozens of weird buildings on my left and right. I approached some of the oddest ones and found they all had no doors, which made it easy to explore inside. The walls were illuminated like the dome itself, though the light was not as blinding. I was sure I saw shifting patterns wherever I looked that had some meaning, some significance, but they were too fleeting to focus on. I felt the joy of being a little girl again as I ran from one building to another, constantly surprised by the enigmatic beauty of it all. The buildings were as magnificent as cathedrals. Art and sculptures of unfathomable skill drew my attention. Whoever or whatever had designed them had the talent of Michelangelo. I wondered about their purpose.

By the scale of the architecture, I calculated everything had been built by a race much taller and thinner than humans. The doorways and stairways were elongated for a society at least twice my height.

As I explored, I worried how the city inhabitants would react to an uninvited visitor if they were not dead. I was *technically* trespassing.

One thing was bothering me. Everywhere was silent and empty. Where were the city's inhabitants? Were they all dead? Was this city a giant mausoleum?

The city *appeared* eerily deserted, and yet I didn't feel as though I was alone. I had the subtle sensation of being observed. Someone or something was out there, watching me.

The thoroughfare was one of many converging on a central tower that rose up higher than all the rest, vanishing into the pink clouds. I walked towards it, seeing a huge archway leading inside. Curiosity made me enter.

My footsteps echoed as I walked into a vaulted chamber. Rainbow-hued light streamed in from a dozen directions towards an object on the floor. The object was a crystal monolith, where the light sources combined to a single point at its base. The light pulsed. As I moved closer, a stream of pink gossamer particles whirled around the monolith, forming a silent, undulating wave like a flock of starlings. They settled on the surface, covering it in a pink layer. Suddenly, the monolith's surface shimmered and transformed into a liquid metal, reflecting my own image.

I stared at myself, hearing a musical whisper, like the sound of a billion tiny voices singing a prayer.

My mirror image stepped out of the monolith, becoming as real as me. I gasped and froze, too stunned to react. My mirror image walked towards me with languid grace. She stopped two metres away, her eyes glittering with pink motes.

"Welcome, Agatha Arnesson," she said in a voice that sounded like my own through an auto-tuner. "I am pleased to meet you, human-child."

"Who are you?" I said.

"You can call me Mi-lo-hee. That means 'friend' in the Ancient Language, though it is not my real name. I do not have one name. I am many. Think of me as an ambassador. I am everything that wants to greet you – a collective of billions. My people have created me so we can communicate in your language. We have been observing and analysing you since you entered our domain. The monolith behind me built me as your exact copy so you would feel comfortable."

I wasn't very comfortable seeing another version of myself. "What exactly are you?"

"You can call us the Lost Tribe," Mi-lo-hee said. "Once, we were a biological species like yours, living on the Earth in the Ancient Times. We used to live in large cities on the single super-continent that you know as Pangaea. Unfortunately, our world was endangered by natural disasters like volcanic eruptions and meteorite impacts – so we built domed cities designed to protect us. Only this one survived the last global extinction event. We designed our home to provide the energy and resources to sustain our population, as long as we did not reproduce and evolve. That was unacceptable to us – so we did the only thing possible. We gave up our flesh bodies for another state of existence. As you would say in your language, we uploaded our minds into nano-machines. Now there are countless billions of us, living in harmony, living forever in the safety of our dome. But now the status quo has been changed. Human-child, your presence has endangered us all."

"I don't understand. Why have I endangered you?"

"We have studied your brain to learn about you. We know your species is violent and dangerous."

"Not all of us."

"No, not all. We see you are a kind and caring individual. But some humans are not. And they would not like knowing another intelligent life form lives on your planet. They would fear us. They would suspect us of being dangerous because we are no longer like you. They would attack us and start a war that you could not win, but which would cost many of your lives. We have seen in your mind what your kind has done to the world beyond our border. The melting ice caps are merely a symptom of insane self-destructive behaviour. Your kind are destroying the planet with greed and ignorance. That is why your presence here is a problem. We can't let you return to your world now that you know of our existence. You must stay here as our honoured guest. Forever."

My mirror image didn't say it like a threat, but it felt like one. "No, no. With respect, you can't make me stay. I have a husband and a life outside. You must let me go back home. I promise I won't tell anyone about your world."

"We have already debated the options," Mi-lo-hee said. "The risk of exposure is unacceptable."

"Isn't it too late for that already? My husband has seen the wall. He will report it and others will come to investigate. This place is no longer a secret, even if you keep me here. It is better if you let me go so I can make the world understand. I know there are bad and ignorant people out there – but there are so many good ones, too. It sounds like you are letting fear control you, too. Imagine what we can achieve together. You don't have to live in this dome any longer. You can join the human race and reach for the stars."

Mi-lo-hee considered my words for a few seconds, which was probably the equivalent of a thousand years in human terms.

"We have debated your suggestion," she said. "There is a huge risk doing as you request. Humans are flawed – physically and mentally. Your species is immature. Many humans will never accept the Lost Tribe as equals. However, it is only a matter of time before our dome becomes visible to your satellites once the ice melts above our home. We are running out of time, anyway. Therefore, we have changed our decision. You can leave us, Agatha Arnesson. You can be our ambassador to your people."

"Thank you," I said. "You won't regret it, I promise. We can make the whole planet a better place – together."

"Come with me," Mi-lo-hee said, taking my hand. I followed her to a glass elevator that took us up to the top of the tower. I stepped out onto a platform at a dizzying height over the city. The roof was nearly touchable.

"What are we doing up here?" I said. I was slightly worried she intended to throw me off.

"We are making a new exit," she said.

A hole appeared in the sky over me, revealing a layer of ice up to the surface of the ice sheet. A drill powered into the ice and cut a neat hole. Then a ladder extruded from the tower.

Mi-lo-hee released my hand. "This will take you back to your world. As you would say, I wish you luck."

I thanked her again before ascending the ladder. When I reached the surface, I crawled onto the ice, hoping to see Gunther. I was worried he would have gone, but the helicopter was not far away. I was happy he'd not abandoned me. My husband was talking on the radio, looking frantic. He did not see me. I ran towards him, waving and calling his name, until he heard me. He opened the door and stared at me like he'd seen a ghost.

"You're alive?" He grabbed me to make sure I wasn't just a dream. "You're alive!" He was weeping with joy. "I thought you'd drowned. How did you survive?"

"It's a long story," I said, laughing with relief. "One that will change the world."

Scavengers

Barry Neenan

ELEVEN CENTURIES of silence came to an abrupt end as the explosives caved in the sandstone wall.

Dust older than several extant languages, dust that had outlasted empires and economies, billowed along the ancient streets. It rose in a wave, blasted forward in a rolling momentum.

The motion didn't last. The dust drifted only for a few moments, too heavy and comfortable to go far. The echoes of the blast rang out, amplified by the cavernous space. But the sheer distance to the rocky ceiling above also provided plenty of space for the sound to get lost, which it promptly did.

Silence settled back on the city of Asoc-Rac. It didn't last.

"See! I told you!"

On the other side of the wall, standing the minimum recommended distance away from her explosives, was a woman. She grinned ear to ear.

"That was beautiful! Couldn't've gone better!"

Standing in her shadow was another woman. "Ohmygod," she squeaked.

"I said," yelled the first, over the ringing in her ears, "'That went really well!'"

Her partner was hugging herself. "Oh my god," she said, slower and, reflexively, louder.

"Yeah! No side effects or anything!"

There was a pause. The first woman continued to grin, and the second continued to stare and tremble and chew her thumbnail.

"…Let's wait until we can hear again, I think!"

They took a few minutes.

Jackie Calloway, erstwhile explosives expert, found a nice flat rock and sat for a while. The hole she had made was too dark to see into, the cavern beyond untouched by the portable lights she had set up, but she peered in nonetheless. Everything had gone to plan so far, on what she knew would be a momentous day for them both. It was all she could do to pace herself. But the city had waited this long for them. It wasn't going anywhere.

Sometimes, Molly couldn't quite recognize the impulsive dropout who had abandoned their shared course. She had doubts about Jackie's career as an 'adventure guide', but she had to admit 'the Jackal' carried herself with newfound expertise. A girl Molly vividly remembered as the terror of every party on campus had gotten her down here safely, demonstrating a thorough knowledge of what not to do when spelunking several storeys under sea level.

But then she did something like blow a hole in a priceless archaeological find.

"I really, really hope that was the right idea…!"

"Of course it was," replied Jackie, without turning. "You said it yourself. The reason no one found this place – before you and your nifty, uh, bat-scream-thing—"

"Seismic reflection," muttered Molly. Another reflex.

"Right. Course. No one found this place, until you seismically reflected a bat-scream down here, because the rock was too thick on every side. How else were we supposed to get in?"

"I don't know!" Molly paced and paced, fiddling with the light on her helmet. The beam went from wide and weak to intensely tight, alternating under her twitching fingers. "That was a question for the scientific community, wh—"

Jackie laughed, short and sharp. It echoed in the cave. "They had their chance! None of those jokers believed you. You and me just proved every one of them wrong."

With a sudden, graceful motion, Jackie was back on her feet. She intercepted Molly and took her by the shoulders, forcibly ending her pacing.

"You did it, girl! And now that you're here, all you can do is freak out? Take a moment! You won!"

No one had understood their friendship, truncated as it was by Jackie's sudden but inevitable exit. Molly remembered the jokes about the Jackal being followed around by a timid little mouse.

But maybe Jackie was on to something by invoking echolocation. Molly may have been a mouse, and may have always remained one. But Asoc-Rac was real. She had actually unearthed it. With a discovery like this, she was a mouse that could fly.

Molly took a breath. Then she managed a smile. "One person believed me. And she's going to get glowing praise in the acknowledgments of all my papers."

"How much cash is that worth?" she replied, but the subtle way her grin widened gave her away.

They were soon underway. Jackie checked their lights and gear. Only the essentials would be brought on this first exploration. Helmets, lights, masks for the dust. Molly didn't even want to bring in tools. Not until she knew what she was dealing with, at least.

Jackie had plenty of her own equipment. She'd be leaving the remaining explosives back here, unattended, under a tarp. She knew what she was doing. At least, she thought so.

Then she led Molly to the opening. It didn't look so bad up close. Things had stabilised, with no obvious damage to anything significant. And just beyond…

"Well?" Jackie waited behind her. "I'm not gonna step in first. That honour's all yours, soon-to-be-Doctor Rhodes."

"Th-thanks, Mz. Calloway." Molly's voice came out small, but she did appreciate the levity. It helped her cope with the overwhelming feelings she was grappling with.

Her boot made contact with the dust of Asoc-Rac.

Another step, and another, and she was completely out of the cave. She was here. She was standing in a city of myth.

Jackie sidled in after her, and gave a low whistle. They were still underground, but the tight passages they had navigated were dwarfed by the city's sandstone tomb. They stood among simple, blocky buildings that may have been homes, or shops, but that wasn't all. In the distance, the cityscape peaked in a central district of curving towers.

"Would you look at that…! It really is an entire buried city. But how could it ever…?"

She trailed off when she noticed Molly was absolutely not listening.

Her hands shook. She had been right all along. The readings from her seismic reflection had seemed so outlandish. Unlike Jackie, she could forgive all her peers and superiors who insisted it must have been a mistake. But she still wasn't ready to be faced with the truth. Molly Rhodes, humble postgraduate researcher, had uncovered an entire lost city.

The possibilities were staggering. It was hard to breathe, not simply because of the mask. Where could she even begin? With a thorough examination, obviously, but with an eye to what? And with whom? She would need a team, a full complement of researchers to assist her, but first she would need proof, but that would require announcing her find to at minimum the academic community but more probably the entire—

"Hey, Mol? You still with me?"

Molly made herself take a breath. Even constrained by the mask, it helped. "Yeah. I'm – I'm just—"

"How about," said Jackie, getting close without crowding her, "we take a little stroll downtown? That sound good to you?

More breaths. Steady. "Perfect. Yes. Let's find the centre. That would be a good start."

"After you."

Every footstep echoed here. After so much stillness, the slightest motions of the two scavengers felt muffled. The silence was as thick as the dust. After so long, it had become choking, almost solid. Impossible to break.

"So, uh…! What are you hoping to find? Anything in particular?"

Molly was overstimulated. Her feet were carefully picking their way down a street that her mind was trying to fathom no one had walked on for centuries, as her eyes strained against the dark to make out details. Now she was supposed to talk, too? "It… Well. So much, really. I researched everything I could about Asoc-Rac before we got here, but the information was…"

"All old and flowery, yeah. Myths. It's like finding out Saint Nick really did move to the North Pole."

"Not quite…"

"No, it is."

Molly sniffed, praying that Jackie wouldn't ruin this with her chatter. But when they made it to the central plaza, they both fell silent.

The streets were cramped and uneven. Much like any other city, from any period in history. But they opened out to an agora that seemed perfectly circular. All the architecture of Asoc-Rac funnelled to this central point.

Five towers, of varying heights but shared design, stood before them like the world's largest fairy ring. Stone mushrooms reaching in vain for the sky.

"Incredible…" Molly's voice felt even smaller. "To think these are still standing after all this time…"

Jackie knew this was an important sight, one she was very privileged to see first-hand. But she preferred the look of wonder in her companion's eyes. "Well?" she smirked, indicating the empty archway carved into the nearest, tallest tower. "Why not wander inside?"

Her smirk died when, wordlessly, Molly began to move forward.

"Oh, Mol, honey, I was joking." Easily outpacing her, Jackie planted herself between Molly and the tower. "There's no way that's safe. Let's stay outside for now, okay?"

Molly hesitated. Jackie's idea made sense. She wished it didn't.

She didn't make eye contact. Instead, her gaze was aimed over Jackie's shoulder, at the entrance to the tower. Even with her light shining directly at it, the interior was a total mystery. The darkness was as thick and immovable as the stone around it.

"We've come this far," she said. Quiet but firm. "I need to go further."

"I get you're enthusiastic, but it's seriously a bad idea to enter any of these structures. They could collapse right onto us."

"They haven't collapsed in centuries, Jackie."

"Haven't had visitors that long, either. C'mon, there's so much else to look at! Don't you wanna find a nice, uh, piazza or something?"

Her smile faded. Molly's eyes were still fixed. She knew how important this trip was, but seeing her friend so overwhelmed was unpleasant. Worse, being brushed off after working so hard stung.

But Molly was intent. She could hear the city calling to her. She alone had believed in it. She alone had found it! She was on the precipice of something huge. It was time to take the last step forward.

"No. I need to get in there." She finally pulled her eyes away, meeting her friend's gaze. "Please, Jackie."

Jackie looked away, giving herself time to think; giving herself space from those big, dark eyes. "Fine," she said. "But if I trust you on this, you gotta trust me too. If I say we should leave, that's it, alright?"

Molly nodded. Without a word, she entered the archway.

Her guide was close behind. She tried to trust Molly's judgement, but it was hard. This woman had been seriously inconvenienced less than two hours ago by an elderly spider. Now she was so quiet, so serious.

But Jackie had believed in this trip from the beginning, so she followed Molly into the tower. Two feeble flashlights illuminated the interior for the first time in centuries.

"My god…" breathed Molly.

The tower had lain untouched for all that time. There was nothing to disturb the mural.

"Uh," said Jackie. "What is that?"

Molly didn't reply. She was instantly enraptured. It was easy to infer that these buildings were significant, but she had never realised just how monumental they were. This city, her city, was more special than she ever could've dreamed.

Both of them craned their necks, following the pattern as it wrapped around and around the tower wall, spiralling upwards apparently without limit. Jackie squinted against the darkness, her jaw set. Molly's eyes had never been wider.

"Okay," said Jackie finally, accepting her question would be ignored. "Is this, uh, what you wanted…?"

"It's better. Much, much better." Molly dumped her backpack on the floor, recreating the earlier explosion of dust in miniature, and rifled hungrily for her sketchbook. "I… I'll have no trouble convincing people to come back. Not when they see this."

"Wouldn't a photo be better…?"

Molly grunted. An afterthought. Pencil in shaking hand, she set to work.

Jackie had readied herself for this moment. She knew her expertise didn't extend past the city walls, and she had been prepared to stand back and let Molly do her thing. In fact, she had looked forward to it. But this wasn't what she pictured.

People who remembered Jackie's student years often struggled with her new career. She knew Molly did. But there was no contradiction between the girl she had been and the woman she had become. The Jackal had survived every inadvisable situation she had thrown herself into. She had cultivated a daredevil's instincts for survival.

Those instincts were screaming.

"Mol," she said, as calmly as she could. "I think it's time we headed back."

Molly kept sketching.

"Molly. I said—"

"I heard you," she replied, without turning. Without stopping.

"Then let's go already."

"I'll catch up."

"No, Molly. We're both going. I'm your guide, and—"

She barked out a laugh. Still sketching. "Oh! Suddenly you're in charge, huh?"

Jackie could only blink.

"Don't pretend you know what you're talking about. You're just a dropout, for god's sake. I won't let you ruin this for me."

It was uncharacteristic of Molly. Scary. But the anger was helpful. "I do know what I'm talking about," said Jackie, as she closed in. "I know about staying alive. I know what can kill you! And neither of us can answer one simple question—"

Molly shrieked as Jackie slapped the sketchbook out of her hands.

"How did this city die?!"

The sketchbook struck the ground. It echoed far too loudly.

That was the point Jackie's trepidation turned to outright fear. The city was still. It was silent. But she would not assume it was empty.

Molly was caught, torn between reclaiming her sketchbook and yelling at Jackie and always, always returning her eyes to that mural. She wasn't about to move.

Jackie dealt with her last dregs of doubt. What if she was wrong? She had been wrong before, plenty of times. So be it. She just wanted the chance to be wrong again.

Knowing Molly wouldn't listen to her, she acted directly instead. She grabbed the smaller woman and ran.

"What are you doing?! We're so close to— I was about to— Get off me, you idiot!"

Her protests, and their unsteady, pounding footsteps, should have echoed. They didn't. Asoc-Rac suddenly felt far too small. It was cramped around them, the walls closing in. Unwilling to relinquish its first guests in centuries.

Molly tugged and tugged against the other woman's grip. "Why are you doing this to me? Why do you always have to ruin everything! I hate you, you jealous, stupid piece of—!"

Jackie didn't reply. She was in a flow state, wholly focused on her task. This city was a deep, deep lake, and she was going to bring Molly back to the surface. No matter how much she thrashed in her arms.

Thrash she did. Molly was shouting things Jackie never would have pictured her learning, let alone screaming in a friend's face. She tuned them all out. Her only concern was surviving. Her only focus was on catching sight of the entrance she had made, with the lights and equipment and sanity they had left there.

Maybe she was too focused. It took her completely by surprise when something knocked her off her feet.

Three terrible things happened in tandem. She landed ribs-first against the stone floor, knocking the air from her. Her helmet protected her head, but with a tinkle of broken glass the light was snuffed. And Molly slipped from her grip.

The darkness fell in immediately. She should have been able to see Molly's flashlight at least, but the abrupt vanishing of her own gave her eyes no chance to adjust. She sucked in a breath through her mask.

"Mol—"

Jackie had a storied history. She had been kicked in the stomach. She had also once been struck by a cinder block.

What happened next felt very much like reliving both those memories simultaneously.

She crashed against a stone wall, the only silver lining the fact her backpack absorbed some of the impact. As pain blossomed through her torso, it felt much harder to breathe. The injury hadn't been that severe, though. Not yet, anyway.

No, Jackie was panicking. She was going to die down here, in the dark. Worse, Molly would too.

She couldn't see what was attacking her. For all she knew, she was entirely surrounded. How she spent these final moments was vital.

Some of it was instinctive. She curled up, protecting her stomach from further hits, and she shifted her legs, striving to at least die on her feet. But all of that was automatic. There was only one thing on her mind.

"Molly!" She shouted as loud as she could. An act of defiance against the thick, crushing silence. "You keep running for the exit! I swear to god, you'd better—"

Another impact. This one caught her arms instead, but it was still enough to cut her off. She couldn't even tell what was hitting her. It didn't feel like a fist, or a foot. But the third and fourth and fifth blow were delivered with the kind of unsteady brutality she thought was exclusive to humanity.

Jackie was brave. She tried to be brave to the last. Knowing she'd never get that chance to stand back up, and aware that any blind attempts at retribution would just leave her vulnerable, she resigned herself. She shut her eyes and thought of Molly.

It didn't last. An uneven sound caught her attention – footsteps, getting closer. Fearing the worst, Jackie opened her eyes—

—and was met with a blinding flash.

There was a half-second of clarity. The comprehensible mid-point between total darkness and pure white. Brief as it was, the image was burned into Jackie's retinas. She had little doubt about what she saw.

Nothing.

Nothing had been looming over her. Nothing had been kicking her, over and over, with a dogged intent to add her corpse to the city's long history.

There was certainly nothing there now. Nothing on all sides. Nothing but her.

"Jackie!"

She felt familiar hands scrabble at her shoulders, too panicked to help her stand. The intense beam of her light brought Molly's face to the edge of visibility.

"Jackie, are you okay? I— I'm really—"

"Had hangovers worse than this," she said, and meant it. "Arms hurt like hell, but I can keep going. You?"

"I'm fine. Listen, I'm—"

"I know."

Jackie pulled herself to her feet, pawing at the wall behind her without the slightest hint of archaeological guilt.

"You sure you don't want to go back to your precious mural?"

"What?" Jackie could make out Molly rapidly blinking. "No. No. I want to leave."

"Yeah," she said, all too aware they were surrounded on all sides by nothing. "Lead the way."

She took Molly's hand, holding it tight, and they went. It wasn't the sprinting pace Jackie had set earlier. Now they moved with the deliberate, steady momentum hikers used to distance themselves from predators. Screaming and flailing could have earned another round of kicks.

Jackie didn't know. She wasn't sure of anything. For all she knew, they'd return to the exact site of the explosion to find a perfectly smooth cave wall. Nothing. But despite the ache in her arms, her grip on Molly never wavered. That much she could do.

In fact, she was faring better than her friend. She could feel a tremble through their connection, and Molly's breathing was uneven. It could have been the exertion. She knew it wasn't.

"You're doing great," she murmured. "Just a little further. That's it." If she spoke with enough calm certainty, she could convince them both.

It paid off. They both saw the walls around them start to sharpen. Felt their eyes adjust to another light source. "There!" said Molly. "Just ahead. Should we—?"

"Yeah," said Jackie, who was already moving forward. "Pick up the pace!"

The last few metres were a mad dash. Jackie braced herself for another blow, another unseen assault. She refused to let go of Molly. Not this time.

It never came. They reached the threshold. Passed it. Their footsteps echoed loudly in their little cavern, suddenly loud. All their equipment was right where they left it. Jackie moved, immediately, for the extra explosives.

Molly sucked in a breath. "Th-that was…"

"Yeah."

"That place… Jackie, I'm so…"

"I know." Soft.

Molly looked like she was on the verge of tears. Jackie wanted to chalk that up to raw relief. She didn't.

"We'll talk about it," she promised, "once we've got a roof over our heads. Okay?"

"Okay."

"For now," she said, trying to find words that wouldn't sound insane to her own ears, "why don't we… close the door we made? I know you're the researcher here, not me, but—"

"No." Molly found herself. Stood firm. "You're the safety expert. We'll do what you think is best."

"Great! Because I say we bury this whole place."

Jackie nodded to herself. Almost business-like. Almost normal.

"Give me just a second. I've got enough to cave in this chamber, which is our best option."

"Um, Jackie…"

"I know, I know. Someone's going to come back here eventually, maybe even us if we have the stomach for it, but—"

"No. That's not what I was asking."

Molly met her gaze. There was a certainty in her eyes Jackie had rarely seen from her.

"Can I light the fuse?"

Jackie paused. Then, despite the pain and adrenaline and unanswered questions, she rediscovered her grin. "Any time you want, hon."

Another blast. Another long, long silence.

Sunken Cities

Douglas Newton

Chapter I

THE DISASTER came suddenly. The sea was quite smooth. The air was thick and hot, and so windless that every sail hung back. All weather conditions were fair. The only indication of anything unusual was the coppery mist that magnified the moon and turned it to orange.

I didn't see the first wave, for I was taking my trick below. Vampage said it was as high as Popocatépetl and travelling at the rate of a thousand miles an hour. Knowing Vampage for the precise scientist he is, one can gauge the moral effect of that wave on him.

Luckily we were practically bow on, and the schooner went up the watery slope of this marine mountain in a dizzy swoop. That was where I woke. Coming out of a dream in which I was climbing a wall like a human fly, I found myself shooting through the air. I landed on what I thought was the floor, but it wasn't, as I found when I discovered my foot through the frame of one of Vampage's Inca drawings, which hung on the forward bulkhead, near the ceiling.

I did find the floor a minute later, for the schooner righted. She also began to jump and pitch like a mad horse. We were in the rough water at the top of the wave, and were getting the worst of it.

On deck I saw the most nerve-destroying sight I have ever looked upon. The sea all about us was lashed to an incredible fury. It whirled and tossed into waves that looked like spouting mountains.

From the look of things we were in the heart of a tornado – only there wasn't any tornado. There was no wind. I think that unnerved me most – that terrible, tearing sea, which threatened to swamp us any moment, behaving as it did under a serene and windless sky.

As I rocked and slithered, and was kicked hither and thither by the great slaps of the sea, I crawled, drenched and holding on for life, toward Vampage at the wheel. He was holding on to that crazy wheel with the concentration of a giant; but he was able to gasp in no great voice, so still was the air:

"Earthquake – submarine upheaval – get sail off her, Warren – wind presently."

I clawed forward on the wild and bucking deck. I yelled for our three kanakas, but none came, so I let the mainsail down at a run. There wasn't so much risk, as there was no wind. One of the men, Toao, came up then, and began to stow the big sail. His teeth were chattering, and he let me know why. The two other men had gone overboard.

Before I could get to the jib, wind hit us. It did the work for me. It blew the canvas right out of its bolt eyes, and for the moment I thought we were finished.

We heeled, and the sea seemed to flow right over us, unopposed. Then we kicked out of it into a night still serene, though I could see massed clouds hurling forward like armies of devils on the charge.

We ought to have been swamped out and drowned a score of times during the next two or three hours, but by a series of miracles we were not. I need not describe what happened to us during that time. Vampage and I clung to the wheel, trying to keep the schooner before the wind, and wondering when the end would come. About three o'clock in the morning we thought it had. The fury of the waters, now no more distinguishable than pale gleams in the intense darkness, seemed to redouble until the whole world raved insanely. There came a series of crashes, bumps, whirlings, heavings, and poundings.

I had the foolish impression that we were turned over and over like a pebble rolling along the floor. To this day I can't say whether that was what happened. I heard Vampage's voice bawling, close to my ear:

"Hit – something – surely?"

I knew instinctively that our mast and most of our rail had gone. I also knew instinctively that no other human being had ever gone through such an experience; and then, quite suddenly, things were almost deadly calm.

Not really deadly calm, for the wind still howled over us – but it *was* over us. We didn't understand it, but we seemed to have been forced into a pocket of dead calm, a little hole in the storm.

The schooner was on even keel, and so steady that we seemed fixed on something – a sand bank, we thought. This was confirmed by the fact that, though strained and leaking, the water did not gain, but maintained a level that was actually below our waterline.

It was too dark to see anything, and we were too much exhausted to care whether we were going to die or not. When we found that the storm no longer touched us, we simply flopped down on the deck and slept.

Chapter II

THE HOT GLARE of the sun woke both of us practically at the same time, and we opened our eyes to a world in full daylight. We saw that the reason why the sun hadn't waked us an hour earlier was that it had only just struck down on us from over a high cliff.

I was staring, amazed, at that unexpected high cliff wall, when Vampage cried in a tone of amazement:

"By Jove, it is the Wahine Rock!"

I turned and followed Vampage's eyes to the skyline, and there, sure enough, towered the profile of that lonely and little known ocean mountain top – the Wahine Rock.

I was quite as startled as Vampage. We had been sailing for the Wahine Rock. We wanted to study the megalithic remains there. We had a theory that we could connect up the great stone fortresses and gigantic heads on the isolated and uninhabited Wahine with finds made of ancient civilisations in a certain remote valley of the Andes.

My surprise, however, was not at finding that the curious tempest of the night had carried us safely to the very point we wanted to reach. It was a more astounding thing than that. It was that the Wahine Rock was no longer the Wahine Rock.

The Wahine, as I have indicated, is – or was – no more than the summit of a mountain thrusting itself over sea level, as the St. Paul's Rock in the Atlantic does. It was – I had better keep it to 'was' – well outside of the trade routes. It had practically no vegetation, and was the most desolately isolated of all the lonely Pacific islands.

In fact, nobody would dream of visiting it save archaeologists like ourselves, who were interested in the few but remarkably well preserved ruins on the slopes of the rock. These ruins – forts constructed of huge slabs of stone, houses of the same nature, and colossal statues – have been half covered by the sea, indicating that in some previous age the Wahine Rock must have been of greater extent, and that it has been submerged in some nature disturbance of the sea bed.

And there lay the reason of our astonishment. The Wahine Rock was no longer the Wahine Rock. It was an island of fair size. That which had once been sunk by some great convulsion had emerged from the sea, thanks to the earthquake that had done its best to wreck us.

We were lying in a deep estuary between high cliffs, on one side, and on the other a beach and slopes leading up to the crest which we both knew – since we had visited the place – to be the old top of the Wahine. We could also see weeds and deep water incrustations leading up to the old waterline, which was now nearly a mile above us.

The seaward end of our estuary was blocked by a bar of slimy shingle, which every wave submerged. We must have been flung right over that bar by the great waves – luckily, for the bar broke the force of the breakers and left us in smooth water. We could see that the schooner itself rested on a bank of shingle that curved up out of unimaginable depths.

"Jove!" cried Vampage. "There's no doubt about it! That which an earthquake once buried under the sea, an earthquake has restored." He stared up to where the old stone houses and platforms cut the sky. "And, Warenne," he said in a shaking voice, "I believe that that accident is going to give us the greatest find in the annals of archaeology!"

"Meaning exactly?"

"Look!" he whispered, and his fingers sketched the outline of the great prehistoric structures. "They continue underwater, as every reputable expert thought. Those few remains on the old Wahine are but the topmost buildings, and there are others down the slopes. Look at the massing of them! Why, my boy, there are thousands of buildings – a veritable city!"

His excitement had got hold of me now. He was right in saying that there was no doubt about it. Massing all the way up the slope from the beach, greened by sea slime, but, on the whole, curiously free from marine growth, were the buildings of what must have once been a large city.

We could make out, even from that distance, the unmistakable solid bulk of the great block stone houses and platforms, built, it seemed, by giants, who cut their huge stones so cunningly that the walls held firm for ages, though cement was never used. I could see, on great platforms, rows of huge images, some nearly forty feet high, some with the round crowns worn by similar images on Easter Island. The entire mass of houses and platforms and images was built up the mountainside in a way made familiar to us by the Inca remains in Peru and Chile. There was no doubt that a prehistoric city had come to light.

A marvellous find for us! Fragmentary remains of a splendid unknown race, or races, are found all over the Pacific from Easter Island to the Carolines; but they are only fragment, giving mere hints of a departed people whose secret is lost. Here, before our eyes, was a complete city.

"And if it was as suddenly engulfed as it was vomited up again into daylight," Vampage said, "then we ought to find in those houses priceless memoirs of human existence – implements, vessels, ornaments, furniture, perhaps; many traces of a vanished civilisation – I say!"

He took a step forward and peered.

"Did you see something, too?" I said breathlessly.

"What do you think you saw?" Vampage asked me.

"It's absurd," I said, shamefaced. "I thought I saw something *walking*!"

He frowned .

"Then I'm absurd, too," he muttered. "That's what I thought I saw."

"Up there by that platform of images?"

"No, down there – by that building that looks like a temple."

"Somebody walking?"

"Yes, upright."

We stared at each other. How could anything that walked upright be on that un inhabited rock only just emerged from the depths of the sea?

"No good being fanciful," I said, with a forced laugh. "We're not the only people who could be wrecked here."

"No," he replied. "No, that is an explanation; but – but it was bare skin, I thought."

"And very white skin – very."

"Yes," he said. "Might be natives."

"Might," I said; "only we're well in the belt of the dark Melanesians. I didn't think – it didn't strike me as a human being who'd lost its clothes, either."

"Ah! You boggle at the sex, too!"

"The hair, I thought, was long and – and, well, I couldn't help thinking that the figure was womanly."

"We're letting our nerves trick us," he said decisively. "It could be nothing but survivors from a wreck. If so, we'd better give them a hail."

We both shouted at the top of our lungs. Our voices rang like thunder against the cliff, boomed and echoed up through the massy stone walls of the once sunken city. We paused, breathless, with hammering hearts, and listened.

There arose a most extraordinary sound – a weird sound. It was a frightened, thin wailing. It rose and fell shrilly, musically, as if tangled with its own echoes. It was a queer, pitiable, flutelike, birdlike sound.

"Birds!" said Vampage, in the voice of a man glad to set his fears at rest. "Look!"

A host of birds rose up from one quarter of the island. They flew screaming upward; with a thousand white flashes of wings.

"Gulls, mostly – but there are vultures there!" I cried. "What the deuce are they doing here?"

"Feeding on the dead fish that couldn't escape when the island was heaved up out of the sea," replied Vampage.

"Do vultures feed on fish?" I asked.

"I don't know," he said slowly, completely puzzled; "but obviously they made that sound."

He said that, I know, because he wanted to convince himself; but he failed. I wasn't convinced, either. It might have been a bird noise, of course, only – only there had been something creepily human in that wailing.

"Anyhow, there's been no answering shout," he went on doggedly. "What is more, I haven't seen any more – walking. Have you?"

"Not a sign. The place seems dead."

"It is dead," he said resolutely. "We've been nerve-shaken fools, Warenne. The flash of a bird wing, or the play of the sunlight on a flapping weed, has deceived us."

I said nothing. Perhaps it was better to think we had been deceived. All the same, I wasn't.

"Anyhow, we'd better get ashore to look around," Vampage suggested.

"How?" I asked. "Our only boat is smashed, and we haven't enough broken bits to build a raft."

"We'll swim, naturally."

I looked into the deep, black waters of the estuary that yesterday must have been the best part of a mile under the surface.

"Of course we'll swim," I said. "We can't miss looking at that town – only, well, I'm just wondering exactly what sort of sea monsters lurk down there."

"None, I hope," he answered with a shudder. "If there had been any, we should have seen them floating dead on the water. The change from the deep sea to the surface would probably have killed them. At the same time, we can't take risks."

Chapter III

WE TOOK as few risks as possible.

Leaving Toao to deal with the leaks in the hull of the schooner – surprisingly few, thank goodness – we went ashore. We used a grating lashed to a couple of empty boxes as a sort of raft. Vampage stood on it with his automatic in his left hand and a boat hook in his right. His business was to watch for the rise of sea monsters. I swam and pushed the raft along. I did this not because I was braver, but because I am a good swimmer.

We had, I suppose, about two hundred and thirty yards to go. We had covered two-thirds of the distance when I heard Vampage gasp. I looked up, and saw him staring over my shoulder into the sea, with the most extraordinary look on his face. It wasn't terror. It was a look of astonishment, bewilderment, and fascination combined. He peered into the water with enthralled eyes, not attempting to defend me against anything.

I stopped kicking, and floated. "What is it?" I cried.

As I spoke, something touched me. It touched the calf of my leg, and ran over it with a gentle pressure, as if to feel it. It passed to the duck trousers I was wearing, tucked above the knee. It tugged gently at them, as if to appraise their texture. It slid up, fingering my belt, and then my silk shirt.

It was uncanny, that touch, but not alarming. It was as if the small hand of a curious child or girl was trying to discover what I was made of. It was a touch as gentle and as delicate as a caress. I wasn't afraid, but suddenly this thing, this hand, took a firm hold of my shirt and began to tug me downward.

I shouted and kicked. Vampage became galvanised into life. He leaned over and beat on the water with the flat of the boat hook. I noticed that he beat the surface only, striking nowhere near where the thing that held me must be.

The thing left in a flurry. I could feel the water swirl about me as it went rapidly; and I, too, went rapidly, pushing Vampage on his platform through the water at the best speed I knew.

Panting on the slimy beach, I stared at Vampage, whose face was a most curious study.

"What was it?" I demanded.

"I wonder if I've gone mad?" he said.

"You've not," I said; "and one way to keep sane is to tell me what it was."

His answer was staggering.

"Do you believe in the mermaid myth, Warenne?" was what he said.

I sat up, dumbfounded. Was he mad, after all?

I asked myself that, and somehow I wasn't sure of the answer.

"That was what I saw, or thought I saw," he said more or less incoherently. "A girl rising through the water – hair floating out like a dark cloud – white shoulders – very white breasts – white arms touching you – hands—"

"A fish tail?" I cried, half scoffing, half serious.

"Legs," he said. "I saw calves, and small feet, very slender, very white. Oh, you're laughing at me, Warenne; and perhaps you're right. Perhaps I am mad; only that's what I thought I saw."

"That's what I thought I felt," I said soberly enough.

I explained my sensations of something plucking at me like a human hand.

No, we couldn't answer the riddle then and there; yet somehow, though the thing was impossible, we had to take it seriously. Vampage had seen. I had felt.

"There was something queer about the neck and throat," said Vampage, elaborating his vague description; "something that looked like fish gills. The flesh seemed curiously transparent, with a beautiful pearly transparency. I thought I saw others, too, in the depths, hovering, as if not so daring as this – this girl. There were pale, pointed faces and dark eyes looking up. White, dim shapes and clouds of hair floating."

We turned it over and over, getting no farther.

"We can't answer that problem by sitting down over it. We may by exploring. Come on!" I said, at last.

I put on thick boots and buckled on the pistol and the big cutting knife that had been carried on the raft, and we made our way up to the city.

The first group of houses we came to told us that we had made a find indeed. They were the authentic dwellings of an ancient and extinct civilisation. It was, however, impossible to examine or enter them. They were choked with sea undergrowth, shell and coral incrustations, and the like. We might have been discouraged, had it not been evident that higher up the mountainside the structures were freer.

We went up through a whole belt of the ancient buildings. Then we came to a break, and crossed what must have been, at one time, a sea beach. Above this we went through another belt of houses and platforms, which was less overgrown than the first. The entrances of the houses were still choked, but the seaweeds and corals were more recent, and not so thick.

Out of this belt, again, we mounted what must have been not so much a beach but a harbour basin. The vast mortised walls that edged it had obviously been quays and dockside structures. Indeed, Vampage pointed to some short upright pillars, which might have been used as bollards for the tying up of ships, or of the great war canoes of the past.

Again we were in a belt of houses partly choked with the weeds and accumulations of years under the sea, but again definitely clearer and less deeply grown. Again we walked through this to what must have once been a beach, fronting a fourth group of houses. It was when we came to this that Vampage stopped and cried out:

"I have it! Do you see what happened, Warenne? This island was swallowed gradually. There were four definite subsidences. Why, it is written as plainly as if it were set down in words. Look there! They built on that cliff across the estuary, too.

"The lowest city, naturally, was the first to go underwater, when something happened in the vast subterranean unknown, and the earth crust holding up this portion of the globe settled down. How many centuries ago that happened, Heaven alone knows. It might have been thousands of years before the first kings of ancient Egypt were ruling. The people of that lower town who escaped, or who had fled to the upper heights at the first rumble of the earthquake, built the next town against the next beach, just above the new water level.

"How long that new city, that new race, that new civilisation lasted we can't say, but in time that, too, was swallowed, as the mountain on which it was built settled once more. Again the survivors built a new city, which stood for centuries, perhaps; but again the mountain sank deeper, and again the city was drowned. Then they built this last city, which is before us, Warenne – their final holding place. They live there – how long? Then, and not many hundred years ago, from the look of it, their island sank again. All was buried under the sea, save the few ruins on the mountain top that we knew as the Wahine Rock; and with that final submergence the people and their civilisation vanished utterly."

"Are you sure?" I asked. He looked sharply at me.

"Perhaps their civilisation has left its history to be read by us, Warenne," he said.

"I was thinking," said I, "of the people themselves."

He gasped a little, and shuddered.

"Better not," he said. "That way madness lies."

I knew what he meant by that. He meant we must ignore the things we thought we had seen – and felt.

Chapter IV

WE TURNED and entered the last city of the drowned civilisation. From what was obviously a harbour basin, set with marvellous quays built of great stone blocks, we mounted, by magnificent broad steps, to the town.

The quays were splendidly spacious, with floors that must once have been as true as a ballroom. The bollards were unmistakable now, and Vampage pointed out ringbolts let into the stone surface. He hacked at one with his knife until barnacles, slime, and metal came away.

"Looks like a bronze alloy," he said. "Very like that Inca stuff we found among those hidden people."

I thrilled. We had spent eight months in a remote valley of the Andes, among a people never discovered since the days of the Spaniards. We had seen buildings, ideographic script, implements, weapons, religious and social ceremonies. We had studied a language which seemed to us to give the key to the secret of an ancient civilisation that must have spread all over the Pacific from Peru to the Java Sea – and even beyond, through Africa and India, back to the civilisations of the Mediterranean, perhaps.

Then we had sailed out to find other remains that could be coordinated with our discoveries; and here, by mighty accident, we had perhaps stumbled on the archaeological treasure house that would tell us everything. Although I am not going into details, they being scientific and dry, I will say that at every step we seemed to see things that confirmed our theory.

The quay was guarded by a gigantic inner wall. We passed through it, under a heavy pylon gate of the type that seems to link the monuments of ancient Egypt with those of prehistoric Mexico and Peru. We walked along high-walled, windowless streets of massive stone houses – streets that might equally well have been those of Cuzo or Thebes in very early times.

We went into a small temple tomb and saw a seated effigy that might have been an ancient Inca or a Ptolemy. The walls were covered with incised picture writing, and there were little guardian gods about, some with bird or animal heads. The writing, I will admit, showed distinct traces of the Melanesian bird cult, but the wall backing of the statue was Inca – a great metal sun, of solid gold, as the point of Vampage's knife showed. A wonderful find – the key to an age-old mystery!

In the houses, we discovered no furniture, but many trinkets and vessels, vases in human shape or animal form, the little statuettes of fused mercury and gold that only the Incas had the secret of working, and writings in ideographic script. I cannot go into the details here.

What soon impressed itself on us most deeply, however, was not a matter of archaeology. Even on the quay we had noticed it. In the little temple itself, Vampage spoke of it.

"The place is much too clean!" he cried.

"I've been waiting for you to say that," I replied. "It has been worrying me. There's no marine growth at all – no seaweed, very few barnacles, no coral at all. Apart from this slight green slime, the place is well preserved."

"Too well preserved," said Vampage. "It's been under the sea for many years, to human knowledge. It may have been submerged for centuries. It ought to have a growth over it as thick as on the bottom of a lagoon; whereas—"

"Whereas," I said slowly and evenly, "it looks as if it had been carefully swept, weeded, and scoured – carefully tended."

"Carefully tended, at the bottom of the sea! My dear fellow, don't be a madman! Who could have—"

He stopped, gasped, stared at me. He knew what I meant.

"We mustn't think of it," he groaned. "Come on – we'll explore."

But we didn't really explore: when we reached what must have been the great central square of the city, all thought of exploration was swept away.

As we stepped into this vast place, amid cyclopean walls, the birds rose up. A host, ten thousand screaming birds, filled the air. They were gulls, mostly, but there were several vultures. The vultures worried me a little.

"Dead fish," said Vampage in a voice which he tried to keep steady. "See them all round by the wall? This square acted like a great trawl as the island lifted out of the sea. No way of getting out save through those four gates, and the rush of the escaping water drove the fish against the stonework and killed them. The gulls are having the catch of their existence!"

"The vultures," I said shakily, "rose from that corner over there."

Vampage threw a quick look at me, and went pale. Perhaps I did, too. We both felt that we were on the verge of abnormal discoveries. Nevertheless, we went straight across the square to the carrier that I had indicated.

And there we saw the people.

There were four of them – two men, a boy, and a young girl. They were all dead. They, too, had been flung against the stonework by the force of the departing water and killed. I heard Vampage's breath coming quickly as we looked down at those pitiable figures, and I knew he was recognising the creatures he had seen under the water when that shy, curious hand had touched me.

They were slender people, as, nude as any savages; but we knew that that was not so because they were savages, but because their habitual element demanded freedom from clothing. The only vestige of garment, if one could call it such, was a belt. On one man and the boy, it was a thing of twisted seaweed. The other man had a belt of metal strips and links, beautifully enamelled. We had seen the brother of that belt among the Andean valleys.

The woman's belt was more what one would expect of her sex. From it, after the fashion of a short kilt, were suspended brightly coloured streamers of seaweed. The use of the belts – even the boy's and the woman's was obvious – for each carried a short, daggerlike sword. One of these was of obsidian; two were of some sort of flinty coral. The man with the metal belt carried a weapon of metal alloy. All the weapons were constructed for stabbing. Underwater, of course, a cutting stroke is almost impossible.

The bodies before us were short and fine-limbed, but their chests were abnomally large, with the breadth one finds among mountain people and others who have to make the most of an inadequate atmosphere. All four had good features. We recognised them as the features of that hidden race among whom we had lived in the Andes. The nose was high-bridged, the forehead broad, the cheek structure slightly Asiatic.

On the other hand, the mouth was curiously copious and loose, as if accustomed to folding tightly, to shut out some dangerous element. The nostrils, distended now, had a strange rubbery look, as if built to contract to nothing as well as to expand at will. The eyes, slightly protuberant, though not unattractive, had the curious look that one ascribes to a fish.

The skin was very white, indeed – blanched, in fact; yet for all that it had a transparency which, in the girl, reached a lovely pearly luster. The girl, indeed, was quite beautiful. Small-boned and slender, with a luxuriant head of hair, she had the appearance of those delicate and exquisite elfin women drawn by Arthur Rackham, the English artist.

Undeniably these were human beings, and yet—

Vampage bent to the nearest male, and spread out the man's toes, which were very long. The webbing between them was as pronounced as a sea bird's. So, too, was the webbing between the fingers. Some South Sea tribes, which live half their days in the water, have this webbing – grown through the course of generations of habit – but none have it in so marked a degree as these people.

And there was another thing. Vampage pointed to the man's throat. I saw the strange structure which he had declared the mermaid had had in her throat – gills – the gills of a fish.

Undeniably these were human beings, but human beings modified, through the course of centuries, to live in an alien element – to live in the water, like fishes.

We didn't speak as we stared down at those mermen. We didn't dare. A thousand questions and demands for explanation thronged our minds, but we dare not voice them, for wonder, horror, and distress held us.

"These are not myths," said Vampage, in a hollow voice. "They died only a few hours ago in that terrible upheaval."

"That means they were living in this city – living as citizens in a submarine world. "By Jove, that is the reason why these buildings are so well kept, why they are free from weed-growths, and are scoured!"

"It's madness!" cried Vampage. "We daren't think of it. It's against nature!"

"The mermaids you saw coming from the depths to me are still living as these people lived yesterday," I persisted.

"Madness!" groaned Vampage. "Here, let's get on and see if we can find the answer to the riddle before our brains crack!"

Chapter V

WE WENT ON to the summit, and to those gigantic remains which were once the only things that stood above the sea level. We saw now that this last and highest group of ruins was part of the outskirts of the city we were in.

One huge structure we had particularly desired to examine. We had meant to cut or blast away some of the great stones, for on our previous visit we had seen that it was impossible to get into it from the land side. We quickened our steps to it, for we now perceived that the falling away of the sea revealed great doors leading into it from the vast platform on which it stood.

As we went forward, Vampage stopped.

He pointed to a curiously worn hollow in the rock where the old waterline had been.

"What do you make of that, Warenne?"

"So you've noticed those places, too!" I said. "I've already decided what they are. Did you observe that two of them had roughly hacked steps? Yes? Well, then, I guess you'll agree with me that those hollows are landing places. The people climbed upon dry land there. From the look of it, they did so regularly and often."

"Yes," he said. "Undoubtedly that is what it means; and yet we saw no signs of such people when we were here last, and I've never met anybody who did."

"No," I said. "They hid, of course; but the fact seems obvious that they did – perhaps had to – come out on dry land at times."

"Like seals," said Vampage.

"Like seals, only they have those gills, and can stay underwater longer than seals."

By this time we had reached the great platform. We entered one of the big doors in the vast stone structure, more than half of which had stood above the sea on our previous visit. We had brought torches for just this type of exploration, but we needed them less than we anticipated.

Climbing a smooth ramp, we came out on a wide floor that must have shelved out of the sea until it was above the water level. From a hundred natural or cunningly contrived crevices in the massive wall and the roof towering above us, the sun shot down intensely golden beams. The place was swimming with a soft, gold, dusty light.

At first we were confused by the dusk. As our eyes became accustomed to it, our wonder overwhelmed us. Vampage put the reason of it into words.

"Good Heavens!" he muttered. "It's like one of the great community huts of the South Seas. Look at those divisions, and the things hanging in them – women's skirts of coloured seaweed – images, utensils. There's a rack of those swords hanging up. Over there is undoubtedly a couch of seaweed. By Jove, this was the community house. They came in here for the night – couldn't sleep underwater, I suppose. The sea is only half their home, and this was used for the other half of life."

"Not was," I said softly. "It is. They are in here now. Can't you feel them? Can't you hear them?"

The feeling of many presences was unmistakable. I had the sense of scores of eyes looking at me from the gloom. These sea people were gathered in the darkness, watching us.

Vampage felt it, too, I could see. Both of us heard it – the rustlings, the queer, sibilant noises. Our eyes turned instinctively to a dark bay in the vast building. Vampage's arm shot out, and he flashed the light of his powerful torch into the gloom.

The immediate result was flurry and panic. We heard the scared bird wailings that had startled us back on the schooner. We heard scufflings and the rush of bodies. We saw white forms scuttling across and out of the bright rays of the torch. Yes, the sea people were there and alive – and humanly frightened!

Vampage called in a level voice to reassure them, and made a step forward. Immediately one of the stone knives came flying through the air – very badly thrown, but its intent obvious. Vampage switched off his torch, and we retreated toward the nearest door.

"Better get out of this!" he said. "We've disturbed and frightened them. They may attack us, and we don't want to shoot them. Better get out, and let them get used to us and our good intentions gradually."

We backed out, down the ramp, to the platform outside in the sunlight; and there the accident happened.

Twenty of these strange amphibians had run out of the community house and upon the platform. In the sunlight, their courage had come back. Most of them being women and girls, their curiosity had got the better of them. They stood, a delicate, lovely, and fairylike group, looking anxiously and eagerly at the doorway through which they expected us to emerge. They stood, beautifully poised in their slender grace, ready to run, yet eager to see.

They did not realise that we had come out of another door until we were very close to them. Then their panic was profound. They turned and scuttled like so many startled pixies across the great platform. I have never seen a more beautiful sight, as their slender limbs twinkled, and their pearly skins shone in the sun, while their long hair floated behind them, shining like lovely sea wrack.

Then, with a shrill cry, one frail girl stumbled over an unevenness in the platform, staggered, and fell. She lay still, stunned, and the rest vanished.

We ran up to the poor, delicate thing. In my arms she seemed indeed as unsubstantial as a fairy. I never saw so delicate, so pointed and piquant, a little face. The beauty of it thrilled me. She had suffered a heavy blow on the temple, and lay cold in my arms.

I forced just a drop or two from my brandy flask between her teeth – sharp, pointed little teeth. Her soft little shoulders shuddered, and she opened her eyes. She looked into my eyes for a minute, and then shrank away from me in fear, fighting to escape.

I smiled at her and let her go. I said over and over again the ancient word, the token of friendship, which we had learned in the mountains of Peru.

She seemed to understand either my word or my smile. She hesitated; then panic came over her again. She wriggled upright from my knee and tried to run. I let her have her own way absolutely, making no effort to hold her; but she was too dizzy to go far, and there was a gash on her shin that must be paining her. After three strides she sank down again, hiding her face in her arms.

We did nothing at all, but simply left her alone. In a minute her shoulders stopped shuddering. She even stole a look at us. We sat squatting, smiling at her.

In another half minute she turned, her full face to us. Though she was trembling, both curiosity and reassurance were getting the better of her. Crouching, supporting herself by one slender arm, she faced us while she examined us steadily. I uttered the word of friendship again, and held up bare hands – the simplest gesture of peaceful intentions.

She sat up. She was conquering herself, or her curiosity was. She gave a half smile – a lovely, pixy smile. Then she grew afraid again, and dragged her stone stabbing sword from her girdle.

We smiled again. We lifted our own big cutting knives, and carefully put them down on the platform, away from us.

Then she really did smile. With a delicious little gesture she put her weapon away, and allowed us to approach.

We made motions to show that we wanted to attend to her injured leg, and I took it into my hand.

She watched, frightened but interested, while I gently washed the wound with water from my bottle. She giggled when I dusted boracic powder upon the cut. She was in raptures when I put a patch of gold-beater's skin over the wound, and bound the slender, delicate limb with an anklet of soft lint. It was a new trinket for her.

Her courage had come back completely. Her elfin smile came perpetually. Her thin, fine fingers played over my hands, punching them gently, to see if they were real flesh.

My clothes amazed her. Tugging at my shirt, and finding it wasn't tight skin, she gave bird laughs of wonder. The bright, slightly futuristic silk handkerchief in the breast pocket of my shirt filled her with amazement. When I gave it to her she was in a transport of delight. She suddenly flung her arm around my neck, with the abandoned gesture of a child, and gave me a little hug. Then, springing to her feet, she turned and waved the handkerchief, like a flag, at the others.

There must have been two score of the sea people on the platform by this time, half of them men. The women kept at a timid distance, and hid as much as possible. The men stood a good way off, with their queer swords in their hands, hesitating between flight and attack. The gestures of the girl we had succoured reassured them, but still they would not come near.

The girl limped toward them, calling to them as she went. This was our first proof that they had a spoken language. She used distinct words, and though we did not understand, we felt that some of them, at least, had root sounds very like the language we had studied among the hidden people of the Andes.

Still the others would not come forward, and the girl, smiling at us, looked back and forward, at a loss. We merely smiled and waved our hands to her, and left her to her companions.

It was no good hurrying things, we knew. We must allow the girl to tell the others that we were friendly and harmless, and leave them alone ourselves until they had become accustomed to the idea of us.

We thought we had plenty of time in front of us – months, probably, of the most wonderful study and discovery.

Chapter VI

ONE HAPPENING, at least, on the way down to the schooner warned us that we might be wrong.

We were on the beach between the second and third of the once submerged cities, when the world began to tremble under our feet. It was a sharp and horrible sensation. The motion threw us flat. We heard the birdlike screaming of the amphibians, around us, and knew that they, too, were terror-stricken. And no wonder. For the space of a minute and a half the very earth swayed and rocked, buckled and heaved – and then was quite still again.

"Another shock!" said Vampage, as we climbed to our feet. "I don't think we are finished with these earthquakes yet. It seems to me that before we start thinking about studying these ruins, we'd better satisfy ourselves that the schooner is still seaworthy."

"You don't mean you think the island may sink under the sea again, Vampage?"

"I hope not, for the discoveries we are to make. But it did so before, and may do it again, and it would be wise for us to make sure that we ourselves possess something capable of floating."

That was the first untoward thing that happened to us as we hurried down to the sea. The second was physically still more fearsome, though perhaps less momentous.

We had gained the lowest of the belts of houses – the city that must have been submerged to a depth of nearly a mile before the earthquake heaved the island above the sea again. Making our way through a wilderness of branching coral and massed and decaying marine growths, we saw something stir in a pool of water and slime. We stopped and looked, and a monster crab rose and attacked us.

The mere sight of him made me sick with horror. He was a loathsome brute. His legs were tall and spidery, like stilts, and they lifted him at least four feet from the ground. His blotched white body was enormous. His big fixed eyes stared straight into mine with cold voracity.

He came with a jump and a sharp, scuttling run that was groggy, but full of the beastliest intention. His enormous nippers poked out at me, and the froth of hungry desire bubbled out of his mouth. I was helpless with a nauseating fright.

Vampage killed the brute with a single upward stroke of his big cutting knife. The knife, in fact, went clean through its body, with such force that it fell apart.

"A deep sea crab," said Vampage, as we examined the monster. "No armour, and as soft as pulp. It was probably dying, from the change from deep sea pressure to air. He'd be an ugly customer in his own element, though."

"Yes," I said, "and it seems to me that there may be other and still uglier creatures flung up by that earthquake. We'd be wise to have the rifle with the exploding bullets ready for action."

Chapter VII

WHEN WE REACHED the seashore, we found that, slight though the earthquake tremor had been, it had wrought astonishing changes. The first knowledge of this came from the fact that a strong sea was pounding and swirling up the estuary, which told us that the shingle bar that had protected it had sunk. It was evident that in that tremor the island must have subsided at least five feet.

We were naturally anxious for the schooner, but we soon found that Toao had been quite adequate to meet the situation. Floated off the shingle bed by the dropping of the land, he had allowed the drive of the incoming sea to carry him up the inlet, where, choosing his moment, he had made the impetus carry him around a long range of old buildings stretching out into the estuary like a breakwater. He had been carried right across the smooth water here, and had grounded the schooner on a smooth, sandy flat.

He was up to his waist in water, when we arrived, examining the hull of the schooner for leaks. He had already cut away the tangle of ropes that bound the broken mast to the vessel.

He was a very calm Polynesian, Toao, and he told us that with a very little patching the schooner would be quite sea-worthy. And in fact we found this out while we worked on the hull, as we did nearly all that afternoon.

Toao was quite undisturbed by fear of earthquakes or death, but the sight of the amphibians filled him with superstitious terror. He told us that they had been swimming about the ship ever since we left it. They had climbed out on the rocks or floated, face and shoulders showing, as if they sought to allure him. He had been so much afraid that he had been on the point of barricading himself in a cabin, when the earthquake tremor had frightened all of them away.

"Why were you afraid of them?" we asked.

"But of course, lords," he answered. "Did they not want to drag me down to the death? That is what they always do."

"You know all about these people, then?" said I.

"Certainly! This is the place whence come the Women of the Beaches. That is why it is called the Wahine Rock – the Woman's Rock. All through the islands they are known. Have you not heard the story? There are certain bays with lovely beaches, which these women haunt."

"They can't haunt," said Vampage, grinning. "They're human – flesh and blood. Only spirits can haunt."

"Whatever they are," insisted Toao, not at all shaken, "they are not as people of this world. They haunt these beaches, waiting for men. If men go upon the beaches, then they show themselves, and, because they are beautiful the men love them; they are dragged under the waters and are gone forever."

"We know that fairy tale," I said smiling; "but I don't think it has anything to do with the people here."

"This is called the Wahine Rock for no other reason," declared Toao. "They have been seen here by men of our race."

So these amphibians had been seen on the Wahine before, by natives! All the same, we were not at all inclined to think that these people had anything to do with the familiar South Sea legend of the Women of the Beaches.

"There are men among the people here, too, Toao," Vampage told him.

"Of course," he admitted. "They are those they have pulled under the sea."

"But they are all white," I argued, "not dark, like the people of the islands, and they have high bones in their noses, like ours."

"It is the sea that changes them," said Toao, unconsciously quoting Shakespeare.

Toao held to his definite opinion, but we could not agree with him. Why should we? His theory was fantastic, while we knew that we were facing decisive facts.

Here before us, in these four submerged cities, was evidence of a civilisation going back for very many centuries – perhaps for uncountable centuries. The people we had seen showed the strain not of the Polynesian or even of the older negroid type, but a rarer, white race. They were, in fact, akin to the very high type that we had found in the hidden Andean valleys, and we were convinced that they were the remnant of a tremendous and highly cultured people who had dominated the greater portion of the two Americas, and probably the whole Pacific belt also.

"I'm thrilled, Warenne," said Vampage. "I really do believe we are on the verge of the greatest historical discovery of the age. I feel that if not from these amphibian people themselves, then certainly from their ruins, we shall solve the riddle that has so greatly puzzled every archaeologist who has studied the question of extinct American civilisations."

"I confess," I smiled, "I am thinking, at present, more of the people themselves."

"*She* was certainly a very lovely little thing," he answered slyly.

"Very lovely," I said blushing; "and because she is so lovely, she helps me to concentrate on the human and personal side of the matter. Why is she amphibian? What condition of things forced her and her kind into a physical shape in which she can, and perhaps must of necessity, live in two elements – water as well as air?"

"Perhaps you have answered that yourself, Warenne," he said. "Necessity did it. I've been thinking on those lines this afternoon, and I believe it is the only answer. Besides, everything conspires to that end. Take, first, the four submerged cities. The four – or there may even have been more – separate catastrophes that gradually drowned what may have been a thickly populated island kingdom, must have assured the people of their ultimate doom. The disasters probably happened at long intervals – indeed, they must have done so; but nevertheless, the race that was gradually forced up the mountainside by successive submergences must have seen that there would come a day when the island would be completely, or almost completely, engulfed. They were a cultured, a brilliant, and perhaps, in their way, a scientific race. Let us agree that their history taught them what, logically, would be the end of their island home. They knew, that is, that a final earthquake would sink their kingdom – or most of it – under the sea. They prepared themselves to survive such an end."

"The best preparation, Vampage, would be to take ship and search out a more stable island or mainland," I jeered.

"*We* think so," he said. "Did they? I think not. Indeed, facts prove not. They did not take ship and go away, for they are still here. Possibly they had arrived at the conclusion that the whole world was to disappear under the seas. The subsidence of other islands, maybe, made them feel that. We can see for ourselves that they must have prepared themselves to survive in a world that was merely water, and apparently they succeeded."

"But, my dear Vampage!" I cried. "Do you mean to tell me you think that ordinary, normal people deliberately trained themselves to be half fish, half human?"

"Deliberately, or by force of circumstances, they have become half fish, half men, haven't they?"

"But, you're talking about a physical impossibility!"

"Am I? Surely not. Don't we know half a dozen tribes between here and the Australian coast which, from constant swimming and traffic with the sea, have developed a definite webbing on their feet and hands? These people only carry that webbing a stage further."

"That doesn't explain the gills. We don't know any tribe with gills like fishes, do we?"

"We don't know, though, that quite a number of children are born with gills, Warenne. Indeed, it's not so very strange, for it is an established fact that the rudimentary organs of the fish exist in all of us. Is it inconceivable, then, that constant training to live an underwater life might have redeveloped those gills which all men have? It may have come about through the evolution of centuries."

"They may always have been like that," I said.

"That is a theory quite as fantastic as mine, Warenne," he returned; "and I don't think it holds good. Did you observe those great carven images? Did you notice the image we saw in the temple?"

"Not closely," I admitted.

"If you had, you might not have used that argument. Not a single statue showed signs of gills rudimentary or otherwise. The gods of their system, then, handed down, as they were, from past ages, were like other dwellers on the earth. They had no gills. Why? Because the men who first carved these gods hadn't gills, and reproduced the human form as they saw it."

I was silent. The argument seemed final.

Chapter VIII

WE WERE AT DINNER, and we sat in the growing dusk, thinking of the strange life of these amphibians on the island. We sat there until the sun was almost down. Suddenly we were aroused by an outcry from Toao, on the deck. We rushed up, only just evading the Polynesian's charge as he ran to cover. On deck we realised why he had bolted. The ship was surrounded by women – the siren women, Toao thought.

It was really a wonderful and beautiful sight – and amazingly fantastic, too, if you like. The schooner, now properly caulked, lay out about a cable from land; and all around us were the women – scores of them, old and young, mature and as slender and girlish as dryads.

They paddled gently, keeping themselves perfectly upright, their milk-white shoulders and breasts and their pearly arms lying on the shining water. About them and behind, their hair floated gloriously, weedlike but magical. Their pointed, elfin faces were turned to us, and their eyes looked shadowy and shining.

They were laughing at us with little bird sounds, raising slender, lovely, eerie arms that seemed to draw us!

"By Jove!" I said with a beating heart, looking on that ring of delicate and uncanny loveliness. "It does look as if Toao was right. They seem like siren women enticing us into the deep!"

Vampage's voice came unnaturally cold – I suppose he saw the effect on me.

"Don't be an ass, Warenne. They've merely come to pay their respects and express their gratitude. See their votive offerings."

I saw that they had brought us presents. Along the side of the ship lay an amazing array. There were brilliantly scaled fish – veritable rainbows – in soft nests of wondrous seaweeds. There were shining pearly shells, branches of prismatic coral, strange stones that glittered, fine woven fishnets of seaweed, eating fish in piles, shells that were like horns, a score of wonders. They had brought their best offerings to us, the things that seemed to them the crown of beauty and utility.

"I believe they think we're gods!" I cried in an excited voice, drinking in the smiles of the women all around.

"Let 'em," said Vampage harshly, "as long as they don't find out we're far too human."

I laughed jeeringly, but I knew he was right. There was something about these fragile things that seemed to intoxicate me with a dangerous fairy allure.

One swam close, calling to *me* in her birdlike voice; and she was most delicate and beautiful. I leaned towards her. Varnpage put his hand on my arm.

"It's all right," I said. "It's the little girl we helped this morning. Isn't she a dear? I say, isn't it etiquette to return presents? We'd better open up one of those cases of trinkets we brought for trade."

"I think *you'd* better do it," said Vampage grimly.

"Perhaps you're right," I laughed unsteadily. "I'm beginning to understand why Ulysses tied himself to the mast when he was in the neighbourhood of ladies like these."

When I came back with the trade goods, Vampage, scientific old stick that he was, was squatting as near to the water as he could, with three women floating quite close. He was patiently trying them out with simple, primary words of the dialect we had learned up in the valleys of the Andes.

"I believe we're right, Warenne!" he cried with excitement.

Fancy being excited about a dialect when three lovely faces, with lovely shoulders to match, were floating a foot away!

"I'm sure these are the same people. Their inflection is shriller, stressed differently, and there are deviations in accent and meaning, but there is undoubtedly a common root. Listen!"

But there was to be no listening. The exquisite sea creatures had caught sight of the articles I carried in my hands, and they raised such a twittering and bird calling, such a laughing and cooing that the solemn subject of language roots was swept right away. Even Vampage had to join in distributing bead necklaces and armlets, bits of brightly coloured cloth, and the two dozen other gaudy things of our line of trade.

The moon was up before we were through with it all and all the women had swum off, twittering, with their loot – that is, all save one. She remained looking up at me, slender, exquisite, lovely, her little hand grasping a broken bit of rail, her body half out of the water, so that she could see me the better. She was the girl I had aided.

I stood looking down at the sheer white beauty of her as the moon shone down over her. Pointed face, lovely and alluring; hair as dark as night, making a tent over the pearl of shoulders and breast; dark, mysterious eyes shining out of shadows up to mine. I was thrilled, intoxicated. I couldn't tear myself away.

She put up a hand, and I caught it. It was cold, but soft and thrilling. It pressed mine, it pulled gently, gently. My blood pounded, and I half yielded, moving toward the side of the schooner.

Vampage's hand caught me tight at the elbow, and his voice said harshly:

"Don't be a fool! *You haven't gills.*"

I came to myself. I bent down, kissed the tiny hand, laughed and waved adieu. Then I went pointedly down below.

* * *

I came up again presently, and sat quietly in the night.

Yes, they went ashore to sleep. I saw white forms moving in the moonlight, white forms stretched out in sleep. I saw on a nearby rock, sitting like an exquisite statue, watching me, a white form. I thought I heard singing, gentle, soft, birdlike singing that might be wind in the rigging. Singing that seemed to have a call; a deep sea call.

I wondered if here was the secret of all the legends of the sirens. Was this, perhaps, the remnant of a race that existed and was known in the days when myth was made? Did the ancients know them to be sirens, and real? Was there a truer explanation of their existence than Vampage's theory?

They called – they seemed to pull at my heartstrings, bidding me plunge into the sea to get to them. Their beauty, their singing bird notes, seemed to overpower my will. I stood up.

Vampage heard me. He came up solidly, told me that it was impossible to sleep below, and sat lolling against the stump of the mast. He dissipated all myth and mystery with his powerful presence, and with his even more powerful tobacco.

Chapter IX

THERE WERE OTHER THINGS to disturb us that night. We had another earthquake shock. It was short and sharp. There were amazing crashing and bangings – the noises of earth, splitting and heaving. We seemed to be lifted up and dropped a terrific distance, then whirled hither and thither.

For half an hour we were in utter chaos, and I felt that our last hour had come. Then, quite amazingly, we settled, gently rocking on the bosom of a calm sea. It was amazing, because with the shock, a storm had developed again, and we could hear an ocean inferno raging elsewhere; but we were untroubled. We rode calmly, not even feeling the wind greatly.

We saw why when we awoke the next morning. The earthquake had done terrible things to the Wahine Rock. The great cliff which I described previously as being between us and the open sea had either crumbled away or been engulfed again. Only a low, rocky, splintered surface lifted between us and the angry ocean. It more than kept the breakers from us – it had locked us in. Part of it had fallen across the mouth of the estuary, and we were now on a lake completely landlocked.

That meant a great danger for us, I'll admit, but we spent less time in considering it, just then, than in examining the effects of the shock on the Wahine Rock. It was ghastly to look at that. Nearly half of the island had been swallowed once more by the sea, two of the cities had vanished again, and the water was covering most of the houses of the third. Of the amphibians themselves we saw not a sign. They had either taken shelter higher up the mountain, or gone underwater, where they would be safe from the storm.

Our own desires, as a matter of fact, made demands on us. We saw that if we were not lucky, the greatest historical find of the age would be snatched from us. Any time now there might come another shock that would drown the last city, with its marvellously scoured and preserved remains. That was the idea which obsessed us, even to the exclusion of our own danger and the fate of the strange amphibian people.

We went below to eat a hasty breakfast, ordering Toao to do his best to move the schooner in toward the now distant mountain slope. When we came on deck, we were close in against the colossal walls of the third town, with the waves of our lake beating gently against them. I was standing by to cast a rope to the housetops at the water's edge, and Vampage was taking the tiller, when something happened.

First, like a flight of flying fish, there came shooting right out of the depths a score of white forms. They came leaping and darting to the surface; they wheeled and flashed and scattered like fish fleeing from some cannibal enemy. It was a moment before we realised that we were watching the amphibians flying for their lives.

Their shoulders flashed white out of the water, their long hair streaming, and they hurled themselves upon the land. More and more of them came darting upward and landward. Once ashore, they all ran for their lives. In a trice the sea and the foreshore must have been peopled by some two hundred darting and panic-stricken things.

Then, with a heave and a monstrous bulge, the water of the lake was disturbed. A wave seemed to burst its way up from the very depth of the sea, sending great ripples all over the inlet, and rocking the schooner. Vampage sprang forward and threw the anchor over to the nearest building, with his eyes on the water.

The sea heaved and boiled, and from the bowels of the world a vast purple back heaved into sight. It seemed long, rounded, wrinkled, and shining, like the back of a great elephant; but there was a vile, sickly colour about it that caught at the throat with disgust. There was a smell, too – a foul, musty smell of immemorial slime.

The disgusting slimy mass heaved itself out of the water. I saw an immense, long, beastly, pulpy bladder of a body, with arms that lashed the water in a mad fury.

Vampage swore, and backed hurriedly toward the companion.

"What is it?" I howled. "What the devil is it?"

"A squid!" he shouted back. "A deep sea octopus! The earthquake kicked it from the bottom to its wrong level. Heaven help us if that monster ever gets a feeler on us! I'm off for the rifle and the explosive bullets."

I stood rooted to the deck with horror. I have seen squids before. I hate them even when they are of ordinary size; but this was gigantic. Perhaps I am exaggerating, but it seemed to me to be bigger than an elephant. It was fabulous. I've never seen anything to approach it. There are no squids of that monstrous and repulsive size in ordinary waters.

This had grown and bloated in the dim, dark caverns at the bottom of the sea. It had lurked there evilly, under the pressure of deep water. Only the force of an earthquake, perhaps, could have heaved the brute to the top.

I watched it lashing out in fury, churning the lake with its mighty feelers. The amphibian people darted hither and thither, in the water and out of it to escape. I thought they would all get away, but one, coming toward us, stumbled amid the growth on a housetop.

With a dart like that of a great spider, the monster flung himself sheer across the water. His long arms rushed into the air, uncoiling like flung ropes. Most of them missed, but one didn't. A tentacle snapped and gripped around a leg – a leg that had a lint bandage on it. The girl screamed and fell, clutching at growths of weed to hold herself against the deadly pull.

The squid, finding her resistant, pulled itself toward her. It slid over the water with evil effortlessness. Other tentacles curled out, gripping solidly here and there. It settled back to pull. I could see its devil face, its cold immobile eyes, its sack-like and horrid mouth.

It pulled, and the girl slipped, screaming. She stabbed at the sucker that held her, with her absurd stone dagger. She dropped the dagger, to clutch at the weeds with both hands again. Her eyes were fixed on me – on me.

The brute monster was pulling inexorably, sure of its prey. I was paralysed by the horror of it. Vampage was standing at my side now, cool, steady. He sighted his rifle at the thick of the body, so as to have all the flabby mass in the line of the bullet. He fired.

The mountainside above us rang and roared with the explosion, and with the crash of the bullet detonating inside the squid. I saw fragments of the pulpy flesh fly, but it was like shooting into a jelly, for all the effect it had.

The noise of the explosion nearly did the mischief. The girl screamed in fright, and all the others screamed at the clamour of the rifle and its echoes. She let go, and the monster pulled.

Vampage's second shot rang out, and his third. Each went home and burst, shattering the flacid mass. The brute was lashing the water with its long arms, but one tentacle held, dragging at the girl.

A fourth shot! I jumped upon the nearest point of land – the roof of the great house the girl was on – and ran, scrambling over the weeds, towards her. She was giving in. The strain of that terrible pull was too much. She had yielded hopelessly, and was being dragged along to that horrible maw. Her slender arms were locked across her eyes.

I slashed with my knife at the tentacle that held her leg. Three savage cuts, and still it was holding on and pulling. The huge, fetid body was hideously close, making me sick.

I slashed again. Another feeler shot uncurling through the air towards me, hissing past my face, missing me by an inch only.

A fifth and a sixth explosive bullet sank into the very substance of that loathsome brute and tore it to pieces. My last slash severed the feeler, but I'll admit that the deadly steadiness of Vampage's shooting did as much to save the girl as my efforts.

The octopus slid off into deep water as its feeler parted. I managed to get the girl to the schooner – she was limp with fright. But we were not yet through with the squid. It reappeared, churning the water into a mad foam. Vampage fired and the great pulpy carcass was blown into fragments before our eyes.

At the tenth shot, the brute seemed to realise from which direction its death was coming. With a gigantic effort it hurled its huge, torn mass right out of the water toward the schooner. I held my breath. Its tentacles were actually upon the rail – one was curling around the mast. It might drag the vessel down into the depths!

Vampage fired again. With admirable coolness he shot straight at the horny mass about the mouth, and the bullet exploded there with shattering effect. A cloud of ink burst from the brute, and the water was clouded for yards; but when it cleared the squid had gone, sunk right out of sight.

Chapter X

THE GIRL WAVED assurance to her companions and they came stealing over the half-submerged housetops towards us, gathering about the schooner. They had been frightened by the shooting.

Vampage had pushed the vessel off a little way.

"If they come crowding aboard," he explained, "they're likely to sink us."

There were, all told, between two and three hundred of the amphibians. All of them, males and females, were between the ages of infanthood and, I should say, thirty-five. We had begun to think that no member of this strange race ever reached the age of forty, when a group of oldish men, surrounding one even older, came through the crowd to the edge of the nearest housetop.

The oldest man wore a diadem of beautiful enamel and gold work, and carried a clublike sceptre that made Vampage open his eyes with pleasure. There was reason. That peculiar crown, and the sceptre, were the traditional badges of royalty in that ancient valley of the Andes that I have so often mentioned.

"The aged king," Vampage muttered to me, "and his court of priests, wise men, and advisers – and not one of them over fifty! This race is obviously at the end of its run, and we have come just in time."

These old men, in their forties, were wrinkled and shrunk like ancients. They carried all the marks of a degenerating strain. They walked as near to the schooner as possible, while all the other amphibian folk drew back, so that not even the kingly shadow should touch them – a taboo as ancient as the islands.

Since these rulers wanted to speak with us, Vampage ordered Toao to pull the schooner close inshore by the warp.

"We'll have audience with his majesty, Warenne," he said, smiling with anticipation. "A great chance for us! He or some of his courtiers may be scholars. The priests, perhaps, may be full of historic lore. We may have a unique opportunity for learning things!"

"I'll leave that side to you, for the present," I replied. "I'm more inclined to take a few private lessons in their language. I seem to have a unique opportunity for that, too!"

I glanced down at the girl we had rescued. She was sitting in an attitude of half terrified wonder, looking at my watch in her hand. Vampage grinned.

"You're a frivolous devil, Warenne," he said. "Always ready to let exact science slide, if there's a chance of a little philandering! However, I don't know that you're altogether wrong this time. Flirtation is the oldest method of language study."

He was right enough there. I had the happiest day with the dainty and delightful girl. She was really lovely – half fairy, half mermaid, strangely abnormal, and yet human enough. She was full of bird twitterings and raptures as I showed her over the schooner.

Fire frightened her a little, and the smoke of my pipe awed her. I gave her a biscuit, and she thought it was an amulet, until I bit a piece myself. Timidly she followed my example, and then spat it out, in disgust. Its sweetness revolted the taste of a creature who lived in salt water.

Our clothes and the fact that our fingers and toes – I was barefoot – were not webbed, and that we hadn't gills, were things to marvel over constantly. She would not believe that I could not dive under the water, and remain under as long as she could. She was unmistakably grieved at my refusal to dive overboard with her and explore the underwater world. She thought I did not like her well enough.

But I didn't indulge *that* folly. If I got into the deeps with her, she would probably hold me down until I came to the death which Toao insisted was the inevitable end of all who coquetted with such sirens. Her superior swimming powers would master me, and she would hold me under quite innocently, not recognising that I was differently constructed.

I therefore remained resolutely on deck and above water. In spite of her seductions, I spent a really happy day – the happy day I would spend with a queer but adorable girl, who was as unaffected and playful as a child.

Of course, there were strange moments. To find that every now and then she began to pant in the heat, and only recovered after diving into the sea, and disappearing from sight for ten or even twenty minutes, was disturbing. To watch her swimming languidly ten feet under water, and turning on her back and blowing a playful stream of bubbles at me; or to see her suddenly dart like a flash and catch a fish, and hold it and let it go – or, as she did on one occasion come back to the schooner with it and calmly eat it – all this was curious indeed.

It was a bizarre, extravagant, and yet strangely beautiful experience. After a delightful day in the company of that delicate and dainty creature, I can well understand how it is that the myth of the mermaid has always had an alluring and lovely fascination for the race of earthbound men. Strange, isn't it, that it is always sea maidens, mermaids, never air maids, that call to us? Well, I understand now why that is. This exquisite little creature put a spell on me.,

Chapter XI

BESIDES, my time wasn't all spent unprofitably. When Vampage returned, I had a notebook vocabulary of phonetic words, taken down as the girl spoke them, which was ahead of anything he had managed.

"Made a good beginning," he said of himself, "but it was very tiring, and not too pleasant."

"I saw that being the guest of kings and prelates wasn't going to be as pleasant as staying at home," I told him, with a grin. "There was method in my frivolity. What did they do to you?"

"First thing they took me into a big, dark building up in the top town, sat me on a sort of altar, and wailed at me."

"Good Lord! They were making a god of you," I gasped.

"Something like that," he said sourly. "I was uncomfortable, and the proceedings very tedious. It was too dark to make out anything clearly. They don't need light, those – those fishes! They can see in the dark. And I dared not do anything, for fear of scaring them. Then we all went along to that big community house – to the king's chamber in it, I take it. There I was supposed to enjoy a sumptuous banquet. Ugh! It was really a trifle too revolting!"

"I know, Maura – that's the name of the girl, as far as she pronounces it – gave me an exhibition of the local appetite. It is simple but disturbing, eh? You just catch your fish, and eat it then and there. Made me shudder to see those sharp white teeth of hers at work!"

"There was that, of course. All the fish was raw, but there were trimmings, too – queer-looking sea fungus and weeds, horrible jellyfish, sea slugs, and so on. I might have stood up to them cooked; but to bolt them just as nature made them, and some of them alive – ugh! It'll take me a long time to get over it. If I wasn't famished now, I couldn't bear the sight of food!"

It grew very hot and still and sultry as we examined my vocabularies on deck after dinner. Vampage scowled every now and then at the sullen, coppery sky.

"I hope it will give us our chance, after all."

"Hope what will?" I asked, seizing the opportunity to roll a napkin ring along the deck to Maura, who was sitting where our rail had broken down, her feet paddling the water.

"This darned earth disturbance," Vampage growled. "I don't think we're done with these earthquakes, but I do hope that the next will keep off until we have finished our work."

"I hope so, too," I agreed, watching Maura's transports of delight as she handled the shining ring of filigree silver. "I doubt whether we could develop gills as rapidly and as effectively as these amphibians did!"

But Vampage, being a scientist, had no time to think of his own safety.

"We're on the verge of an epoch-making discovery, Warenne," he said. "There is no doubt about that. This vocabulary of yours proves it. It's a first-rate day's work!"

"Oh, a little frivolous humanity is a good servant to science," I grinned.

"Yes," he said, so seriously that I wanted to shout with laughter. "That vocabulary of yours has made the first step in a stupendous discovery, I verily believe. You can see for yourself that it has a definite affinity with the dialect we picked up in Peru. Certain things are called by practically the same word, if we allow for the slight difference in accent. That links up with the things we saw in the upper town here – the script writing, the wall paintings, the images, the vases."

"And the features of the people themselves," I said softly, as I looked at Maura.

"Yes, the features of the people themselves, too. By Jove, it all fits in, Warenne! I'll swear they are the same race. I'll swear that we have hit upon the first people, the earliest civilisation, of the Western Hemisphere. Think of it, Warenne! We have unearthed the secret of a great cultured race that dominated, perhaps, from the Peruvian mountains to New Zealand – an empire that ruled all the scattered islands. Perhaps they weren't scattered islands then, but large tracts of land, or even one vast continent. Who knows what these earthquakes may have done with physical geography?"

"In any case," I said dryly, "it is not the duty of a true scientist to weave fairy tales about it. We must still consider them as having always been islands, unless we find differently."

"And we will!" he cried enthusiastically. "Don't you see that, Warenne? The whole history of this unknown and fabled race is ours to read. We've found our Rosetta stone, only it happens to be alive, human, and vocal. Those vocabularies of yours, the additional ones we will collect and perfect through conversations with these people, the translations of the wall writing. They will give us – why, Warenne, we shall be able to read the hidden history of half the universe! The Easter Island ideographs will no longer puzzle us, as they have puzzled all the archaeologists until now. We'll translate the unreadable carvings of Yucatan. Do you understand, Warenne? We've found a new world, a new history. We are on the verge of gigantic discoveries that may rewrite the entire story of the universe!"

"Yes," I agreed. "It's a big thing – mighty big."

"It's the biggest thing of our time," he bellowed, "and it's ours, if those confounded earthquakes will only keep off."

I didn't answer that. I was looking at Maura. She was standing up, and her dryad breast was panting. She looked at me with frightened eyes, and then gazed wildly away across the water. We heard a strange sound – the wailing of fear and woe, the cries of frightened birds.

Maura made a step as if to dive. Then she hesitated, and flung out hands inviting me – a beautiful, heart-rending gesture. Oh, I wanted to go to her, but I knew it meant death, and I shook my head.

She cried out to me a poignant, appealing, warning sentence. The few words I could make out in it seemed to be "hungry monster", "devils", "bowels of the ocean". She wanted me to flee from the anger of that monster to safety. I knew I could not escape as she wished me to, and I shook my head.

The wailing, the calling from the amphibian people, rose insistent, demanding. She gave one agonised look at me, uttered a despairing cry, hid her face in her slender arms and vanished over the side.

Vampage and I stared at each other.

"She said," I muttered huskily, "something about the monster who dwells in the bowels of the ocean."

"The earthquake, of course," Vampage interrupted. "They know – they feel it coming. Better batten everything down, and be ready to cut the warp."

Chapter XII

THE EARTHQUAKE came less than an hour later. I don't think I need to describe it. I know I don't want to describe it, because of what it was, because of what it meant.

It was worse than the upheaval that had uncovered the sunken cities of the dead world. We were tossed through a night and a day in a hell of water, with a great wind trying to blow us under.

Exactly what happened is a mystery. All I know is that as the earth split and gaped, and engulfed the land that was known as the Wahine Rock, we were somehow caught and tossed out of immediate danger by the raging sea that poured across the vanishing land.

Why we didn't shatter against some rock, some projecting portion of the solid old houses, I don't know. I sometimes think we were too insignificant to be destroyed. We simply floated like a microscopic chip on the raging flood. We were whirled and tossed in every direction, but we floated.

Three days later we were still floating, but not quite so well. In fact, the seams had opened again, and the schooner was gaining water at a pace that made our agonised pumping look useless.

However, things were different. Whereas for two days we had been upon a starkly empty ocean, now we were wondering whether the tramp steaming towards us would reach us first, or the schooner sink first. Needless to say, since you are reading this plain narrative, the tramp won.

The steamer had caught the edge of the earthquake disturbance, but the skipper could tell us nothing. He thought it to have been just an ordinary storm.

As he was making for the Chile coast, we had to wait in what patience we could. It wasn't a first-class patience. My notebook with the vocabulary had been reduced to pulp in the story, and Vampage was nearly out of his wits at finding that the greatest discovery of the age, which had been ours to grasp, had been snatched away.

Perhaps I felt with him, but I don't know. I feel that my own anxiety was a personal one. It was not the loss of a dead history, but of a living entity, that filled me with anxiety.

I needn't draw out the agony. We discovered, as everyone who reads newspapers knows, that the earthquakes had been the worst ever known in that region, and that the Peruvian and Chilean coast had suffered horribly, and also the islands far out in the Pacific. We sat quaking as the press gave us daily information of shorelines changed and of whole communities wiped out.

Then came the news we had expected and feared – just a short paragraph, a report from a ship surveying the damage of the earthquake. That paragraph ended our hopes. It told us about the Wahine Rock. It told us that there was now no Wahine Rock.

The Wahine had vanished entirely. The last terrestrial foothold of that unknown race had at last sunk beneath the sea. It was gone. It was wiped out. No longer would it be entered on charts, even as a reef.

Vampage is inconsolable. It left him broken to have that wonderful chance of a lifetime, that tremendous contribution to history archaeology, wiped out at a single sweep.

I am inconsolable, too – not because of that dead history, but because of a living girl.

Maura! I wonder about her. Was she killed?

Had her race been exterminated? Or do she and her people skim the undersea levels, slender, beautiful, mystic, keeping alive in the minds of frightened men the mystery and the terror of the legend of the Sirens?

I wonder if Maura still haunts South Sea beaches looking for me. If I only knew, I know where I would go.

A Poison of Bodies Beneath the Water

Spencer Orey

ANOTHER BARRAGE of glowing boulders struck the water around the ship, until one finally burst through with a spray of wood and flailing bodies. Watching from the depths, I already wanted to intercept the survivors, to slit their throats, to seize some small revenge against these surface dwellers who dared pollute the sea with poisonous magic. The corpses would remain on the seafloor, but their blood, at least, could diffuse to feed other creatures.

My sister Loliea held me tight at her side. "Not long."

She was right. To go now, with boulders still raining down – when the ship itself was beginning to rain down too, splintering into pieces that cascaded into the water like glowing arrows – would be too dangerous.

Soon, survivors would launch in little boats. Others would swim for the coast only to drown in the harsh currents, unless we bled them first. Years earlier, ships had sailed the other direction. Those had been warships, filled with shining metal-armored soldiers. Most had returned. Afterward, the flow of these pathetic smaller ships had begun. We assumed the warships had left behind such terrible desolation that the conquered had grown desperate enough to seek refuge in the land of their conquerors. Those that we bled were not soldiers, for they bore no weapons or armor. Most were already close to death, haggard bodies clothed in rags. But when their ships burst apart, it no longer mattered who they'd been. They became dirty flesh, poison in the sea, a threat to be eliminated here so that our city could stay pure.

Three small boats deployed from the sinking ship, fewer than usual.

More boulders, glowing so bright that even from the depths I saw them ripple through the air above, plummeted to strike. One detonated into the first boat, and bodies struck the water, already dead. Some of them glowed where they'd been hit. The second boat escaped the barrage to continue with its course, but it wouldn't survive long. Loliea released her hold on me, beckoning me forward.

Instead, I watched the third boat.

A glowing bubble slowly lowered around the boat, enclosing it completely. Then the bubbled boat submerged, descending into the depths, into our territory. I expected it to head toward land, but instead, it turned away, but not in the direction it had come. It had a different destination.

"A new poison," Loliea said. "They'd spread their filth."

So we had the same idea. "I will take care of the boat," I said.

"Do not draw close until you can be certain of safety. I would not lose you to the rot," she said. "Good hunting, sister. I will meet you back in the city."

With a flick of my tail, I was off.

To touch the glowing bubble around the boat would mean my death. Everything glowing like that was poisonous to sea creatures. We knew it to be surface magic but called it the rot, and even one rotten touch could rob us of our lives underwater by destroying our gills and fins. With each glowing boulder, with each repelled ship, the seafloor grew more devastated. Once, coral had thrived here. Now, it was a graveyard, littered with glowing wreckage, bones, and rocks, devoid of life.

I kept my distance at first, in case more boulders launched in pursuit. The boat was the brightest thing in the sea and easy to follow. I knew the area well, a shivering kelp forest that stretched to the undersea mountain and its sacred caves. The boat lowered enough to brush one long strand, and the kelp shrank away as if bitten, then withered and detached, floating free.

As long as that bubble persisted, there was little I could do. I swam closer in search of an opening.

I counted nine figures on the boat. Only nine.

The one in the middle was responsible for the glowing bubble. They held a staff, and the bubble grew out from it, around the ship. A wizard.

The other eight were children. Most sat wide-eyed, clutching onto each other. A few were crying.

I understood where the ship was headed.

Inside the undersea mountain was a sacred cave where my people had first shed their disgusting land flesh, where we'd become mer. I'd learned of the cave as a small hatchling but had never journeyed there. It was a place as sacred as it was shameful, a marker of a time when we hadn't belonged in the sea. The wizard should not have known about it. My people do not share our myths, but perhaps there'd been a traitor long ago, before we'd learned to defend our borders.

In stories, the cave's magic only worked on the young. It could transform these children, but not this wizard who'd saved them from shipwreck and then sought one last impossible chance for their safety.

Unworthy, unwelcome children. If I let them swim free of the mountain, they'd pollute my people as much as their glowing magic poisoned the sea. Better to dispose of them before they transformed.

My understanding also gave me an easy opening. The wizard wanted the children to join my people. All I had to do was act welcoming.

I hid my knife in its holster on my back. Then I swam above the ship, close enough for them to see the silhouette of my tail. I couldn't hear the children, but I saw a few of them reach their hands to their disgusting little mouths in gasps of recognition. I waved. I darted over their boat again.

A couple of children tugged on the wizard's robe, pointing at me. I could see her better now too. Weary. Jaw clenched. Hands clasped on the staff to maintain the spell. What horrors had they all faced that had driven them to cross unfriendly waters? Did the wizard know she was protecting the only survivors of the ship? To be responsible for those small broken lives would be an unbearable weight. All I had to do was cause her to slip enough to break the bubble. At this depth, the force of the water alone would be enough to crush them all.

So I danced for them. I mimicked pulling at the wizard's robe and long braid of hair. I even mimicked pushing her staff, but the children must have been warned against anything like that.

The undersea mountain loomed larger, darkening the water with its shadow. The wizard held absolutely unyielding in focus, no matter how many children I convinced to help with the distraction. Perhaps it would be best to wait inside the cave, where the exhausted wizard would have to drop her spell to let the children out. To let them inside would be shameful, but it was best to heed Loliea's warning and protect myself in the hunt.

I waved to the children and then darted ahead.

The cave mouth was far larger than I'd imagined, with a current of its own, pulling me closer. It was a cave that wanted to be visited. Past the mouth, the opening became a rocky tunnel into the mountain. The walls twinkled with true magic, illuminating barnacles and algae. This was my people's magic, not the foul glowing poison of the surface dwellers. A magic that fostered life.

I swam past massive statues, ancient tributes to our transformation. They'd been sculpted by the first mer artisans, the same who'd built our city.

I followed the tunnel to a wide cylindrical passage up into the heart of the mountain where the water grew soothing warm against my scales. I ascended. The walls twinkled brighter, a sign of powerful magic. The children could transform here, if I didn't stop them.

Above, I saw a shimmer of the surface. Just below it, a stone staircase led up out of the water to a sculpted bowl. This could only be the site of transformation, where my ancestors had given up their legs to become something far greater. There could be nothing more sacred.

Beautiful twinkling light cascaded from the bowl, promising magic. Then, a poisonous glow tainted the water too. The boat was rising. It was time.

I again pretended to welcome the children. I waved. I darted through the water. The children waved back at me, jumping in place. Good. Let them be excited. Let them trust me. All I needed was for the wizard to lower the bubble.

I had just long enough to evaluate the wizard before the boat surfaced. She was on one knee, breathing heavily, still gripping her staff. She looked to be almost out of strength.

I stuck my head above the water. It was disgusting to be in the air, to feel water run down my hair and face and neck, to feel my skin start to dry.

Worst of all, above the hum of the poison bubble, I heard the laughter of the children. I waved for them to jump into the water. They waved for me to join them.

The boat pulled closer to the bowl where the children could be transformed. And yet, as I'd suspected, the bowl was too high to be reached from the boat. They'd have to enter the water first, to swim to the stairs and climb from there. All I had to do was wait.

The wizard staggered.

The bubble dropped. All poisonous light suddenly vanished, leaving only the perfect twinkle of the cave.

Children cheered and rushed to the railing, rocking the boat.

"Sister, stay back," the wizard called out. "They belong here, as much or more than we do."

Sister?

That could explain how she knew about the cave. So, the wizard had once been mer. She'd been one of my sisters, but she'd returned the surface. She'd traded her people away to learn the secrets of poison. A traitor.

She'd see the error of her ways when I gutted her. She'd understand the folly of choosing lesser lifeforms, of betraying her kind.

I reached for my knife.

The wizard spun my way, staff pointed. I dove underwater. A glowing ray of light sizzled past where I'd been and hissed against the stone wall.

In the open sea, I would have hidden under the boat, then arced over the side to begin the slaughter. But in water this pure, this clear, it was hard to hide. I dodged another ray of light. It burst apart a statue, one of the timeless treasures of my people. I dodged again, easily. I belonged in this place, but she was an outsider now. Her strength would give out first.

No rays of light followed. I surfaced warily, ready to dart away.

A few of the children had grabbed the wizard's arms and were screaming at her to stop.

"Please help!" I called to them. "She wants to hurt me!"

"That mermaid is not your friend!" the wizard yelled. She shrugged off the children and fired again. I didn't even have to move. Her aim was off, and the ray looked thinner than ones before.

One child screamed, "Don't hurt her!" Another child tackled the wizard in the legs. She wobbled, and the whole boat rocked with her.

"Stop it, everyone! Ageminna is the one keeping us safe!" an older girl said.

The boat rocked as children pushed each other.

"Quick, children, dive into the water!" I called. "I'll catch you." I opened my arms wide.

"No! All of you stay back!" The wizard raised her staff, and the bubble of light began to bloom out to cover the boat.

But a little girl locked eyes with me, face bright with trust. She stepped onto the railing and opened her arms.

"Pull her back!" the wizard yelled.

Two children reached for her, but they were too slow. The girl jumped into the water.

I stayed out of reach. A cloud of dirt wafted off of her, polluting this sacred place. Time to see if she could swim.

A ray of light seared past me.

"Stop!" one of the children yelled.

A deeper splash. The wizard was in the water. A child had pushed her in. Wonderful.

I pulled out my knife. The wizard's robes floated around her, blocking her vision, but she spun, striking with her staff, trying to hit me. But we were in the air no longer. This was my people's rightful domain, my birthright.

I surged forward with my knife but only managed to slice the sleeve of her robe before she raised her staff and a glowing bubble bloomed out. I ducked away.

Another splash, then more, from children jumping in. The boat rocked more, then tipped over, and suddenly all of the children were in the water.

The girl who'd jumped in first was swimming for the stairs. Foul creature. How dare these dirty little things dream of becoming like me, of being worthy to live in the depths.

I darted forward with my knife and struck the girl through the back of her shoulder. It was easy. I darted away and struck another child in the chest, knife sliding smoothly through that small sternum. The other children began to panic and scream in realization, but that only made things easier. They stayed in place. I struck another child in the gut. Only five to go, plus the wizard.

Light flared from behind me, and I darted to the side. It was bold to fire at me like that, to risk hitting children. But no ray came. I spun and saw the wizard clutching a child under her arm, frantically trying to break the surface. One of them must not have been able to swim. In the rescue attempt, the wizard must have lost her grip on the staff. It floated near her in the water, still glowing faintly.

This was my chance. I flicked my tail and surged forward. The wizard swam in little lurching strokes, burdened by her robe and the little body clutched close. I grabbed her braid and ripped my knife down her back. She screamed, bubbles of air pouring out of her, but even then, she kept trying to raise the drowning child to the surface.

I stabbed her again, and she sank backward.

Now my task would be far easier. I adjusted my grip on my knife and twisted to find which of my targets was closest.

There was a flare of light. Pain seared into my side. The older girl who'd tried to keep the others in line had prodded me with the staff. Little fool. I snarled and stabbed, punching my knife through her arm.

But I felt the poison enter me, even from that small touch. The rot. It was already scorching from my side up to my shoulder. I lurched in the water, losing control. With a sharp pinch, my gills sealed.

I ignored the children. I had to save myself first before I could rid us of their pollution. But what could I do? The rot was so terribly fast.

Poison sizzled down my tail. My scales began to itch, then flake away, and leaving behind soft flesh. And then my tail ripped into legs.

Despite the agony, I still had a chance. If I climbed the stairs, I could breathe the foul air. After, I could figure out how to transform back. I pulled myself through the water with just my arms and reached the surface long enough to take a shameful breath of air.

The bowl was full of children. I reached for the stone stairs, and the bowl released a torrent of twinkling bubbles that blocked my sight. I kept clawing forward. My hand hit the stone hard. I gasped in pain but managed to grasp onto the side of the stairs.

Something pulled at me from behind. I twisted, trying to fight, and found the wizard. Whether she'd die first from bleeding or drowning, she'd caught me. She wrapped her arm around my neck and pulled again, and I lost my grip on the stairs. This wizard, this traitor who'd once been one of my sisters, pulled me down, away from the children. And I could do nothing but watch.

We drifted past two statues, standing together, arms linked. One had a tail. The other had legs. They were together, a monument to transformation, to a shared heritage.

And then, above me, I saw the new mer.

They darted through the water, collecting the children I'd hurt, helping them into the bowl. My vision darkened, but I saw the bowl release more bubbles, saw the hurt ones return to water, restored. Now they'd venture into the sea. With their very survival, they'd destroy the purity I'd fought to preserve.

And they were beautiful. The little monsters had transformed into something not pure, but perfect.

The New Gulliver

Barry Pain

Chapter I

(The first few pages of the account of his travels by Mr. Lemuel Gulliver, junior, have unfortunately been damaged by fire and are for the most part illegible. They contain reference to a sea-fog and to a shipwreck. He appears to have escaped by swimming, and his record of the number of days he spent in the water and the distance covered verges upon the incredible. His statement that he lived principally upon the raw flesh of those sharks which made the mistake of attacking him will also be accepted with reserve by those who remember the latitude in which the Island of Thule is traditionally placed. The legible and consecutive manuscript begins with his arrival at the island.)

I NOW WRUNG the water from my clothes as well as I might, and spread them on the rocks in the sun. After an hour, perhaps, I was so far recovered from my exertions that I thought I might now see what manner of island this was to which my ill-chance had brought me. Donning my clothes again I climbed up the low cliff.

The land that now lay before me appeared to be for the most part flat and bleak in character. There were long stretches of sand and coarse grass, and here and there a group of stunted shrubs. Presently, in the far distance, by the aid of my perspective-glass, I made out several cultivated plots, but nowhere could I detect any building which might serve as a human habitation. At one point, which I guessed to be about two miles away, a column of smoke arose, as if from the interior of the earth. This I imagined to be of volcanic origin, but it puzzled me not a little that the land should be under cultivation and that yet I could find not so much as a single house or cottage.

So intent was I upon my survey of the distance that I did not note the approach of a human being until I heard the footsteps close beside me. I speak of it as a human being, but in many respects the creature differed from humanity as previously known to me. Particularly noticeable was its manner of progression. It walked very slowly and laboriously on all fours, the arms being longer and the legs shorter than in the normal man. Its body was clothed in two garments of a thick grey woollen material, and loose boots with tops of a similar material, but with leather soles, were worn both on the hands and feet. The size of the head was disproportionately large and seemed too heavy for the slender neck. It was bald save for a fringe of scanty grey hair. Large spectacles of high magnifying power distorted the eyes, and the toothless mouth was absurdly small. The grotesque object was more likely to inspire laughter than fear, for the body was small and its movements slow and feeble, but indeed it showed not the slightest sign of hostility.

"I see," said the creature, "that you are from the old world. Who are you?" He spoke in a gentle voice and with an accent not unlike that which we call American.

"My name is Lemuel Gulliver, a shipwrecked mariner, at your service. Will you tell me what island this is on which I find myself, and to whom I am speaking."

"The island is Thule – Ultima Thule – the one spot of earth that has emerged from barbarism. Chance has done great things for you in bringing you here."

He slipped one hand out of its boot, removed his big spectacles, and blinked his weak eyes. I watched him narrowly. His face was hairless. It might have been the face of an old woman or of an old man. A look of cunning now crept over it.

"I think," he said, "that I grasp your difficulty. You may speak of me as a man; but for beings of the first class, to which I belong, sex is abolished. It was perhaps the worst of nature's evils that our triumphant civilisation in the process of centuries overcame."

"But in that case," I said, "your race, or that class of it to which you belong, must be rapidly dying out."

"It is undoubtedly dying out," said the strange creature with a complacent smile, "but less rapidly than a barbarian would suppose. Increased knowledge has brought with it increased longevity. I am myself one hundred and ninety-two years of age. The end must come, of course, but after all, why not?"

As I looked at him I did not from the aesthetic point of view see why not. The creature had replaced the spectacles now, and lay at full length on the sand, as if wearied by the standing position. He went on speaking:

"Death in the individual is, of course, to some extent a confession of failure. It means inability, mostly due to ignorance, to adapt oneself to one's environment. Death of a race may be quite a different matter – an exhaustion of utility. However that may be, it is clear that the last of us to survive will represent the highest possible development of human potentiality. I speculate sometimes on the question of who the ultimate survivor will be. It may possibly be Professor YM6403 of the Outer Office. Some think so. I believe he thinks so himself. On the other hand, I may be the last survivor. However, there are still some thousands of us in existence, and for the present these disquisitions may appear to you idle."

My clothes were damp and I was chilly, hungry, and tired. His jabber about professors and survivors had no interest for me. I ventured to point out to him that I was at present in urgent need of rest and refreshment.

He rose on all fours again, and did so with extreme awkwardness. "True," he said. "I will attend to it. We are hospitable people, though it is seldom that a stranger visits us. I will proceed at once to conduct you to my house."

"Your house? I fear that must be at some great distance, for there is no house in sight."

For a moment he looked puzzled, and then light dawned again in his short-sighted eyes.

"I see your mistake," he said. "You come from the old world, where the old type of house is still in existence. The history of the old world is the special study of my friend, the Professor. But of course there is general knowledge that every educated being may be supposed to possess, and I know the type of house you mean. I have seen pictures of it in the museum. Now in Thule, when many centuries ago aviation became the cheapest and most popular form of transit, it also became obviously impossible that we should have houses above ground. Aviation is a source of danger to such houses, and the houses themselves were dangerous to the aviator. Our buildings are all subterranean. We avoid danger of every kind. We dislike risk. You cannot see my house to which I am taking you, but as a matter of fact it is less than a quarter of a mile away."

He went so slowly that I had to abate my usual pace, lest I should outstrip my guide. As he moved, he looked a little like a very small tired elephant.

"Aviation," I said. "I suppose that with you that has been carried to a great point of perfection."

"On the contrary," he said, "it is superseded. It is a back number. We no longer use it. But we have seen no reason to change our style of domicile, which possesses many advantages."

"And what is it?" I asked, "that has superseded aviation?"

"It is the power to dissipate and subsequently reconstruct identically at some different point the atoms of any organism or group of organisms."

"I don't think I understand," I said.

"It is natural that you should not. However, here we are at my house."

It looked to me rather as if we had come to an ordinary well, the interior of which was occupied by a spiral descending incline.

"You will observe," he said, "that when I am weary of exertion and return to my house, I descend. In the old type of house it was customary to ascend."

I should calculate that we descended some thirty-five or forty feet below the surface. At this point we were confronted by a perfectly ordinary door with a brass knocker on it and an electric light above it. On the door were painted the letters and figures MZ04. He opened the door with a small latchkey, which he produced from one of his boots. The keyhole and the handle were placed at such a height that it was easy for him to reach them without assuming the erect position. We went through into a small hall, brightly lit and containing no furniture but a door-mat, on which my guide wiped his four boots carefully. He then requested me to come with him into the dining-room, as indeed I was by no means reluctant to do.

On entering this room, however, I was disappointed, for it bore no resemblance whatever to a dining-room, and there was no look of good cheer about it. Its walls were lined with shelves, and the shelves were filled with numbered bottles containing what looked like small pills. In the middle of the room, immediately under the light, was a low table, on which were a row of small aluminium cups and a leather-bound book. There was no other furniture of any description.

"You are looking for a chair perhaps," said my host presently. "We have none. To stand erect on the feet is a precarious position, and to sit is hardly less precarious. We avoid all risk. On all fours or in a recumbent position one is safe. However, if you would like to sit on the floor, pray do so, while I make up the prescription which you require."

I sat down on the floor, which was very hard and discouraging. I did not greatly like that use of the word 'prescription', and my inner man cried rather for butcher's meat than for chemist's stuff. However, a man must take his adventures as he finds them.

My guide slipped his hands out of his boots and consulted the volume on the table. "From long use," he said meditatively, "I know most of the numbers by heart; but I cannot recall what is taken for a chill caused by prolonged submersion in sea-water. I have never had occasion to use it. Ah, here we are! Number one hundred and one."

He took down the bottle which bore that number, and dropped one pill from it into an aluminium cup. I noticed that the shelves were all placed low on the wall. But indeed the whole of the appointments and furniture of the house was adapted for beings who used the quadrupedal position. I noticed, moreover, both now and afterwards, what very little furniture there was in these houses. The hatred of superfluity was a marked characteristic of the people of Thule.

My host took down one bottle after another from the shelves, talking as he did so. Each bottle had an ingenious stopper, which allowed one pill, and only one, to fall out each time that the bottle was reversed.

"I have never eaten shark, cooked or uncooked," said my host, "but I should imagine that a diet confined to this meat would give an excess of nitrogen. We correct that with one of number eighteen. To this I add our ordinary repast – numbers one, two, and three – a corrective for exhaustion from number sixty-four, and a pill of a narcotic character from sixty-eight."

He handed me the little aluminium cup with the pills in it. "I think," he said, "that is all you require."

"I am extremely thirsty," I said.

"No civilised man eats and drinks at the same time." He whisked down another bottle and dropped one more pill into my cup. "You will find," he said, "that little addition will remove all sensation of thirst. You shall drink when the right time comes."

I took my pills obediently and was now conducted by him into a much smaller room on the same level. I afterwards saw other subterranean houses in the island. They were all alike in plan, and the rooms were all small and so low that when I stood erect I could easily touch the ceiling with my hand. The total absence of decoration, and the simplicity and scarcity of the furniture, were not specially characteristic of my host. Aesthetic pleasure was very slightly appreciated by any of the first-class beings in Thule.

A pneumatic mattress lay at one end of the room which we had now entered, and there were two dials on the wall, each provided with a moving hand. There was no other furniture of any kind.

"There is your bed," said my host. "Now sleep."

"I should hardly have called it a bed," I said dubiously.

"It is not the barbarian idea of a bed. We abandoned bed-clothes of every description long ago. They are not hygienic. All that is necessary is to raise the temperature of the room in which the sleeper lies. This you can easily do by altering the hand on the first of these dials, which controls the heat. It stands at present at fifteen. When I sleep I generally put it up to twenty. We will try it at twenty, and you can advance it farther if you find yourself chilly. The other dial controls the lighting and gives you five degrees of light down to absolute darkness."

"I wonder," I said, "if I might have my clothes dried. They are still damp, I fear."

He looked at my garments with marked distaste.

"If you will put them outside the door," he said, "I will see that they are thrown into the refuse-destructor, and will order proper clothes to be provided for you in their place. You will sleep for one hour, and shortly after that I shall return. By the way, how comes it that you speak our language?"

"I speak English," I said.

"English," he said meditatively. "English. I have heard that word somewhere. No, don't explain. I can easily obtain the information."

He now left me. I put the hand on the heat dial at twenty-five. Although I had no clothes of any description, I felt pleasantly warm, and in spite of the excitement caused by the novelty of my experience, I soon fell asleep. This may be ascribed either to the fatigues I had undergone or to the potency of the drugs administered to me.

Chapter II

WHEN I AWOKE, it seemed to me that I must have slept for some six or eight hours, yet it had been but one hour only. I felt perfectly refreshed and well. I had shut off nearly all the light before falling asleep, and I now groped my way to the light dial and moved the hand round until the room was brightly illuminated. The silence of the place was remarkable; it was almost as if I had been in an uninhabited house. I opened the door of my room a little way, and was pleased to find a bundle of clothes awaiting me outside. I brought the bundle in and investigated it. At first sight it looked as if some mad and malicious tailor had made two pairs of trousers out of a material suitable for an overcoat. The reason of course was that the suit had been made with a view to the conformation and habits of the natives of this curious island. They wear two garments only, and therefore require them to be of considerable thickness, and their arms are of about the same length as their legs. (The difference in our own case is much less than most people imagine.) I soon put the two garments on, and found that they fitted me well enough if I rolled back the sleeves to leave my hands free. I was also provided with a pair of boots similar to those my host wore. They were too large for me, but could be kept on by a buckle and strap fastening at the ankle.

I now made some examination of the room itself. The walls and ceiling were covered with a hard shiny substance, which I at first thought to be paint, but afterwards decided to be of the nature of our water-glass. The usual right-angles between floor and walls and ceiling were in every case softened into a curve, which I recognised to be an advantage from the point of view of cleanliness. The floor itself was covered with the same material as the walls and ceiling, but in this case had a minute corrugation all over it, to prevent slipping. In the middle of the floor was a small grating, about one foot square. As I inspected this, a fan below it began to whirl rapidly, but without the slightest sound. As I was looking at it my host knocked and entered. I was pleased to see that he brought with him a sealed bottle and two aluminium cups that would have held about half a pint apiece.

"We now drink," he said briefly.

"An excellent idea," I began, but he immediately bade me to be quiet, saying that it was not customary to talk while drinking was in progress.

He divided the contents of the bottle (not quite fairly) between the two cups. He gave himself the advantage of the choice and finished his drink at a draught. I followed his example and found that I was drinking distilled water. At this I was somewhat disappointed, but the more disposed to forgive him for the injustice of the division.

"And now, my friend," he said, "we can talk."

"Then," I replied, "you will perhaps tell me what is the reason for the custom which prevents you from taking your drink in a sociable manner. In the country from which I come we like to sit and chat over our glass."

"So it was here also in the dark ages," said my host. "At that time our drink was for the most part of an alcoholic character, and it was found that the more one talked, the more one drank; and the more one drank, the more one talked. It was a vicious circle of foolishness and ill-health, and the practice was made illegal. Alcoholic drink is quite unknown now among the first-class beings of Thule. But the custom of not speaking when one drinks, although we now only drink water, still remains. It is one of the many instances in which the ritual has survived the religion."

I pointed now to the grating in the floor. "A ventilator, I suppose."

"Exactly. It is actuated once every hour for two minutes. It draws out carbon dioxide, which being heavier than air is in the lower part of the room, and at the same time draws in fresh air through the corresponding grating in the ceiling, which communicates with a shaft to the open. The great point about it is that it is absolutely noiseless. Our study of longevity has shown us that irritation is one of its deadliest enemies. The noise of an electric fan is irritating, especially in a bedroom. I dare say the crude appliances you have in the old world still whir or clatter."

"I notice that all your electric lights are fixed in the ceiling itself. Is there any reason for this?"

"Naturally. Anything which hangs may subsequently fall. We do not court dangers. It is curious that you should mention it, because I was speaking of this point only last week to my friend, the Professor. He showed me a picture of an old-world chandelier. He also told me it was the custom in England and other uncivilised parts of the world to daub oil-paints on a piece of canvas. This was surrounded by a heavy frame and was suspended on walls. It was called a framed picture. You will find nothing so reckless here. By the way, I have found out about England. I cross-spoke to the Outer Office, and they told me it was a piece of land at the back of Scotland."

I found later that 'to cross-speak' meant in Thule to send a wireless message.

"The mention of the Professor," my host continued, "reminds me that today is his birthday and mine. On this day I generally make him a ceremonial visit, and I shall be pleased to take you with me. As a specimen you will interest him."

"Might I ask what you mean by the Outer Office?"

"The Central Office deals with utilitarian knowledge and is separated into Controls. I, for instance, am at the head of the Heat and Light Control. The Outer Office deals with academical knowledge, and our friend is the Professor of Old-World History. The Inner Office decides questions of justice. But there is no time just now to explain our simple constitution to you. We should be starting for the Professor's house."

"One more point," I said. "May I ask your name? I should have done so before."

"We do not have names. Beings of the first class have a distinguishing formula, and only use names for plants and the lower animals. The second-class beings, the workers, may possibly use names among themselves, but of that I have no knowledge. My own distinguishing formula is MZ04, and as no two people have the same formula, much confusion is prevented. By the way, your hair is untidy."

"Naturally," I said. "I was going to speak of it."

"And your hands are not clean. That is as it should be. You are now ready to pay a ceremonial call. You perhaps don't understand. All our houses are on the same pattern, and each is provided with a fitted room for the purposes of the bath and the toilet. But when we pay a ceremonial call, it is our invariable custom to do so in a soiled and dishevelled condition. On arriving we make ourselves clean and tidy in our host's toilet-room. This is done by way of compliment. It implies that he possesses conveniences which we do not."

"It seems to me singularly foolish, if I may say so."

"From one point of view all compliments are foolish, but from the point of view of longevity all compliments are wise. They have a slightly emollient effect. We recognise this so much that we even employ at times professional optimists."

"Won't you tell me about them?"

"It is a very simple matter. If a being of the first class gets worried and depressed, he knows that this is lowering his vitality and lessening the period of his life. This knowledge only tends to increase the worry. He therefore sends at once to the Central Office for a professional optimist. The optimist comes and talks. He slightly emphasises all that is most favourable in the being's circumstances. He dwells on the strong points in his character. He listens to his stories. He shows himself impressed by his abilities. We have but a few of these professional optimists, and they are extremely well paid – that is to say, their power of ordering from the Central Office is very considerable."

"Some of this seems to me rather childish," I said. "And some of it I do not understand."

"You, a barbarian, can hardly be expected to grasp at once the refinements of a higher civilisation. You will do so gradually. Now, please, I have only just time to see the Professor before I keep my appointment at the Heat and Light Control. Come along, please."

We passed up the spiral slope, my host going very slowly and breathing heavily. The Professor's house was scarcely a hundred yards away, and I think we took nearly five minutes to get to it. The outward appearance was precisely similar to that of the house we had just quitted. When we reached the outer door my guide knocked once. The door immediately opened, as if of itself, and we passed into an empty hall. From this a door led us into a large room devoted to the purposes of the bath and the toilet. I subsequently found that in all these subterranean houses this room was the largest. I remarked to my guide that no servant had admitted us, and there seemed to be no one to introduce us into the presence of the Professor.

"There are no servants," said my companion. "We have the second class, the workers, but we should not admit them to live in our houses. We have so far simplified life that one being can very well look after one house, his own. As a matter of fact two second-class beings are sent from the Hygienic Control of the Central Office every morning to clean each house, but it is a question whether this should continue. We are discussing it. It looks just a little like luxury, and luxury is dangerous to longevity. Why should we have a servant to announce us? If the Professor knows the visitor, it is not necessary. If he does not know him, the visitor can supply the information just as well as the servant. If the Professor had not wished to receive, the outer door would not have opened."

We did not find the Professor in the first room we entered, but in the dining-room, where he was taking pills out of one of those small aluminium cups. He went on taking his pills and we watched in solemn silence until he had finished. In appearance the Professor closely resembled my guide, but his fringe of hair was darker and more abundant, and something in his face seemed to betoken a love of study rather than high practical ability. I now witnessed another curious piece of etiquette.

"I hope you are ill," said my guide genially.

"Wrong absolutely," said the Professor, "but I trust that you yourself are suffering from some malignant disease."

"Nothing of the kind," said MZ04.

Subsequent inquiries showed me the reason for this. The principle was that the guest should take the earliest opportunity to make his host feel in a superior position. Therefore etiquette required the guest to arrive unkempt, as if he did not possess the conveniences which his host had at his disposal. It also required him to make an obviously false statement as to his host's health, in order that his host might have the power of correcting him. A well-bred host, such as the Professor, immediately replied by giving his guest a similar opportunity to correct and in consequence to feel in the superior position.

They now exchanged rather ponderous compliments on their respective birthdays. But in spite of their politeness I somehow got the impression that these two beings were in strong antagonism to one another, and that however much the emotions might be discouraged in Thule, feelings of jealously still existed.

"On this auspicious occasion," said the Professor, "it is generally my custom to make you some slight offering. I have placed a power to read a manuscript to your order at the Central Office."

"I thank you sincerely," said MZ04. "I had intended to do the same thing, but I think I have found something even more to your taste." He pointed at me with his booted hand. "Here," he said, "is rather a curious thing that I have found. You make a study of the old world and might be interested in it. I have no use for such curios myself and am happy to present it to you. In many respects – notably in its foolish use of the erect position – it resembles our second-class beings, but I believe it to be a genuine old-world relic."

"I am of the same opinion," said the Professor, "and I am obliged to you for your generosity. Can it talk?"

"Fluently," said MZ04, "but with a bad accent."

I now said very decisively that I was a free man, that I did not belong to either of them, and that I absolutely declined to be handed as a slave or a chattel from one to the other. I repeated this in varying terms more than once. They took not the slightest notice of it, but waited patiently till I had finished.

"I am busy today at the Heat and Light Control," said MZ04. "I fear that I must now leave you."

"Going to walk?" asked the Professor.

"No. I have taken my exercise for today. I shall disintegrate."

Even as I looked at him, his substance became a smoky shadow, shimmering and vibrating. It grew rapidly fainter and fainter until it had vanished altogether.

Chapter III

"AND NOW," said the Professor, "before we go any further there is one point on which I wish to be assured. You came from the house of MZ04 just now?"

"I did."

"Did you observe in him as he came up to slope from his front-door any tendency to puff and blow?"

"He certainly did seem slightly short of breath."

"Poor fellow! Poor fellow! It breaks my heart to hear it. I don't give him another hundred years to live. Sad that so intelligent a being should be snuffed out like a candle."

The Professor did not look in the least as if it had broken his heart. So far as I was able to judge he seemed rather pleased than not.

"That being settled," he continued, "I may now devote myself to you. You made some protests just now, based, as most protests are, on ignorance. You are not going to be a slave. You may regard me as your host. I shall treat you as a guest and I shall look upon you as a curiosity. Tell me at once what I can do for you."

"I want to know where I am. I want to know the history of this place – the meaning of first-class and second-class beings – how sex came to be abolished – what is implied by a power of order from the Central Office. I have been here but a few hours and I find everything puzzling and incomprehensible."

"This," said the Professor, "is Thule. I cannot give you its exact geographical relation to the world, for it has no geographical relation. How do you imagine that you came here?"

I gave him some account of the shipwreck and of my fight with the sharks, showing him in proof my large clasp-knife, which, together with my perspective-glass and some other trifles, I had found means to secrete in the clothing provided for me by my former host.

"I have no doubt," said the Professor, "that you speak with sincerity. But you are wrong. That is not how you came here. Nor shall I put you in possession of the actual facts, or you would be able to use them to ensure your return. You are not a prisoner, but at present I wish to detain you. And now, if you will, I will give you roughly and in as few words as possible a sketch of our history and constitution. This being in the nature of a lecture, I shall lie down. It is the custom in this country for every lecture or public speech to be delivered in a recumbent position, the greatest physical ease being consistent with the greatest mental concentration. Come to the sleeping-room."

He led the way to a room provided with a pneumatic mattress. It was in all respects the counterpart of the room I had seen at my former host's house. He stretched himself on this mattress, and as there was plenty of room I saw no reason why I should not do the same. He noticed it and approved.

"You are wise," he said. "Your carcass will now cease to attract your attention and you will be able to attend to me."

He lay on his back with his eyes fixed on the ceiling, and his two long arms crossed over his protuberant stomach. Presently he began to speak in a solemn and magisterial voice, as if he were addressing a large class. I did from time to time interrupt him with question or remark, but have not thought it worth while to place such interruptions on record.

"To understand the conditions of Thule at the present day we must go back to the great social upheaval of centuries ago. At that time the equality of all men was claimed and the community of property. Successful agitation backed by armed force carried the matter. Community of property does to some extent remain to this day, although a more civilised view of the value of property is now held by us. But within a very few years of the social upheaval the fallacy of universal equality declared itself. It is a rare thing for two men to be facially alike, and no two men are ever equal in all respects. Such inequalities soon declared themselves. We had on the one side a minority who contributed more to the State in actual benefit than they received from it, and on the other side a majority who received more from the State than they contributed to it. The minority naturally became a discontented class, and healthy discontent produces activity. The majority, getting more than they gave, were quite satisfied with the state of affairs. They babbled of the blessings of an assured democracy. They took no trouble with themselves. They thought they were at the end of the social revolution when they were only at the beginning of it.

"The formation of a secret society, including most of the minority, was the natural result. You must not make the mistake of confusing this minority with the old aristocracy. The old aristocracy was based on lineage and wealth. The minority of which I speak was based on mind. They were the people who could acquire knowledge and could use knowledge. They included in their number some members of the old upper classes, but many also of the old lower classes. The aim of the secret society which they formed was not only the acquisition of knowledge, principally of a practical character, but also the seclusion of it. The members were sworn not to impart the secrets of the society to any of the great but inactive majority. In this secret society we have the origin of what are now called first-class beings. In the glutted and lazy democracy who formed the majority we have the origin of what we call second-class beings – beings who today are permitted to acquire no other knowledge whatever than that which is necessary for the work which they do under compulsion from us. At this moment by far the greater number of them are unable to read or to write or to perform the simplest operations of arithmetic.

"It is of course a commonplace of the text-books that no social evolution follows exactly on lines laid down and planned. The secret society, which was known as the Crypt, was formed originally for the purposes of self-defence. The only means by which a few superior beings could protect themselves against the aggression of the many inferior was by the possession of secret knowledge. To take a case in point: improvements of the first importance in the accumulation and transmission of electricity were made by a member of the Crypt whose formula was H401. H401 was called upon to specify and to explain what he had done. He produced a written statement which was from the first word to the last abject nonsense veiled in pompous scientific phraseology. It was accepted as perfectly satisfactory and deposited in the archives. Every electrician – every man of sufficient education to detect the fraud – was already a member of the Crypt. With this came the first inkling of the tremendous power which was now in the hands of comparatively few men. By the simplest dislocation of machinery they could deprive the great majority of light and heat, and could, if they would, choose a severe mid-winter for the operation. Many other secrets of knowledge came into the hands of the Crypt. I will not weary you with a catalogue of them, but I will mention one of which our friend MZ04 gave you just now a practical demonstration. I refer to the power to dissipate and subsequently to reconstruct identically at some different point the atoms of any organism or group of organisms. You saw just now how MZ04 dissipated himself as it were into smoke in order to reconstruct himself instantaneously at the Heat and Light Control, over which he presides. It is a secret of this kind which makes one being the master of many armies. This was realised by the Crypt and a course of offensive action was at last decided upon.

"At this juncture the voice of the Crypt was practically the voice of that extraordinary and commanding personality Q666 – a formula that will be for ever remembered in our history. He was not a being of high scientific attainments. His life was irregular. He had neither scruples nor mercy; but he saw clearly the thing to be attained and the means towards it. At his instigation the General National Assembly was declared to be dissolved, and the whole of the second-class beings were enjoined under penalty of death to yield the strictest obedience to the orders of the Crypt as issued.

"The proclamation was received with ridicule by the second class. Democracy had always triumphed and would triumph again. It relied much upon the fact that the army was entirely democratic. That is to say, no officer or man was a member of the Crypt. The army was not deficient in courage. Its officers included even some few men who took their profession seriously. It was confidently anticipated that after a few days of civil war the Crypt would be compelled to submit.

"I have said that Q666 was a being without scruple. His declaration was made in mid-winter and the whole land was ice-bound. And on the night that followed the declaration heat and light were cut off from the dwellings and camps of his opponents. Some thousands died that night and many more in the course of the next few days. The water which they drank was mysteriously tainted and produced death. Their army found no objective for attack, so rapidly, by virtue of that power which I have described, did the members of the Crypt come and go. On the day when the democracy submitted and received the new constitution by which they ranked as second-class beings, they had actually become inferior in numbers to the beings of the first class. The rule which Q666 established remains to this day. Sentimentalists had in the old days clamoured for the abolition of capital punishment. Q666 abolished every other kind of punishment except this. The punishment for idleness after three warnings was death. The punishment for any intentional disobedience was death without any warning at all.

"I have given you quite roughly and simply with little or no detail the story of the struggle between the Crypt and the democracy, ending in the establishment of first-class and second-class beings.

"I have shown how from an attempt to establish universal equality and to abolish all class distinction there came into being two classes between which there was a distinct cleavage – a class of masters and a class of servants. The end of the struggle was only what could have been expected. While all the harnessed forces of wind and tide provided radiance and warmth for the members of the Crypt, their opponents froze in the darkness. The same water that poisoned the democracy that drank it refreshed the masters without injuring them. The old-fashioned disciplined stupid army was powerless against opponents whose mobilisation, swift as lightning, rendered them practically invisible. There is still much to relate to you, but I grow weary of talking. I propose to take you to see my plants."

"Got a nice garden?"

"We have no gardens. I keep my plants as pets here in my house. Without awakening any emotion which might be prejudicial to longevity, they provide a mild interest and a salutary change from more serious occupation. Follow me and I will show you them."

He rose from the mattress and I noticed that he did so with more ease and agility than had characterised the movements of my poor friend MZ04. I followed him to a room so small that it might almost have been called a cupboard. It was intensely lit by a tinted electric light. In it were two tall plants in tubs.

The leaves of the plants were large and of a tropical character. Each had a stem about three feet in height, surmounted by a ball which looked as if it were made of fine silk. The colour of the ball or flower in one case was a peacock-blue and in the other dead black. I noticed a slight movement of the leaves as we entered the room and assigned it to the opening of the door.

"The plant with the blue head is Edward," said my host. "He is rather an affectionate little thing. Observe."

He called Edward twice in a caressing voice, and immediately the stem of the plant bent downwards and the silky blue ball rubbed itself caressingly against my host's cheek. Almost immediately the other plant began to agitate its leaves violently and to waggle its black ball backwards and forwards.

"You observe?" said my guide. "Frederick is jealous."

He gave each of them a little water and we then went back to the sleeping-room again.

"I never saw anything like that in my life before," I said. "Plants with us cannot move of their own volition. They—"

"Surely you mistake," said the Professor. "I am no botanist, but I have made a special study of what went on in the old world, and I think I am correct in saying that there were creeping plants there which moved to find their supports, and plants whose leaves shrivelled up at a touch, and others that actually devoured the insects which formed their sustenance. Almost anything can be done with plants and knowledge. The old world produced many new varieties – some of them of real utility, as for instance the thornless cactus. We have merely gone a little further. We live in solitude and a companion of some kind is a necessity. I think you will find that every first-class being here keeps one or two pet plants."

"You don't keep dogs or cats?"

"We keep nothing which can be both offensive and provocative of strong affection. Cats and dogs, common though they were in the old world, stand condemned under both categories."

Chapter IV

"THIS," said the Professor, "is the hour at which on fine and warm days we go out and bask in the sun. Sunlight is the enemy of disease and the friend of longevity. You would perhaps like to come with me. We shall find many more engaged in the same occupation."

We passed out of the house and up the spiral incline. The scene before me reminded me somewhat of certain stretches of grass in our public parks on a hot day. Here and there on the coarse grass or sand were stretched the grey-clad bodies of beings of the first class. I did not see any engaged in conversation or in reading or even in sleep. They simply lay still in the sun. Some of them had brought rugs with them. One who appeared to be very infirm was carried in a kind of litter by four finely built men who walked erect.

"That," said the Professor, "is the grandson of the great Q666."

"And who are the fine-looking men who are carrying him?"

"Merely second-class beings detailed for the work. Take no notice of them. They will not, of course, venture to remain in our presence."

The four men deposited their master gently on a bed of tufted grass and marched away again without a word. So far as I could compute, there were now some two hundred first-class beings stretched out motionless under the pleasant and vivifying warmth of the sun.

"May we not," I asked as we reposed ourselves, "take this opportunity for some continuation of your lecture? There is still much about which I am curious."

"On what point would you wish me to speak first?"

"I am told that among beings of the first class at any rate sex is abolished."

"Can sex be of interest to any thinking being? It is of no interest at all to me."

"It happens," I said boldly, "to be of the very first interest to myself."

"Very well," said the Professor. "We must withdraw to some distance, so that our voices do not disturb the meditations of others."

I followed him to the spot that he selected. We lay on our backs on the sand and he continued his discourse.

"The practical abolition of sex has with us been a very gradual process extending over centuries. It began with that great social upheaval of which I have already told you. To declare the complete equality of men was to declare the complete equality of the sexes. It ended about one hundred and fifty years ago when the words 'men' and 'women' ceased to be used by first-class beings, and no distinction of sex was admitted. That I think is all you want to know."

"Pardon me," I said. "You give me no explanation whatever."

"The thing explains itself. Take first the case of a male. You will find in him so many factors mental and physical which belong to the race and so many which belong to the individual. In the case of a male the factors which belong to the individual are very much in excess of those which belong to the race. In the female we find the reverse of this. The factors which belong to the race are in her largely in excess of those which belong to the individual. She is the martyr and trustee of humanity. That was the state of affairs before the great social upheaval of which I have spoken. When women began to mix in every business, profession, and sport, a new type of woman very soon declared itself – unusually tall, flat-chested, small in the hips, destitute of femininity. Briefly, the male type and the female type began to assimilate. Now sex assimilation is the death of sex attraction. All that women spent on their individual development they stole from the race. Marriages became rare and where they existed they were frequently sterile. Gradually, all that made man man and all that made woman woman became rudimentary and atrophied until, as I have told you, one hundred and fifty years ago the distinction between man and woman was abolished. Since that time, and indeed for some ten years previous to it, there has been no instance of birth or marriage or love-making among beings of the first class. The last word of civilisation has been reached. It is a splendid consummation."

"Splendid?" I said doubtfully.

"How can you doubt it? Now that the burden of racial responsibility has been cut off from our backs, our longevity is trebled and more than trebled. This may be assigned in part to our increased knowledge and to the fact that we do no laborious or dangerous work. Laborious and dangerous work is confined to the second class. With them, of course, sex still exists. They are a lower order. They breed up children. When the number of workers is deficient we keep those children. When the number tends to be excessive they are destroyed. Have you never thought into what a quandary racial responsibility led men and women in the dark ages? No married man lived as an unmarried man, no married woman as an unmarried woman. Life became a string of compromises and concessions. There were complicated households with nurseries in them. It must be clear to you that the man who works for six people must work just six times as hard as the man who works for himself alone. Work is dangerous. And if work is dangerous, worry is deadly. Worry is enormously increased where there is any emotional attachment. Look how we have simplified things. To one being one house. The emotions never paid for their keep, and it is civilised to get rid of them. Tears are as little known among the first-class beings of Thule as is the gross and unhygienic kiss. The tortures of modesty do not affect us, for where there is no sex distinction there is no modesty. We are emancipated. We are free. Love implies death. The loveless live long. I may tell you that it is whispered already that we are on the edge of discoveries which may make it possible for us to live for ever."

"Well," I said, "I am not constituted as you are. You would hardly expect me to like what you like."

"I do not expect any man from the old world to be civilised. It would not be reasonable. But what objection can you possibly offer to the state of things among the first-class beings here?"

"Well, to take the first point that occurs to me, it seems to me that you must all be most horribly bored."

"Never," said my host emphatically. "Boredom is the result of living too fast. Those who work too hard or those who enjoy too much must in the intervals of their work or enjoyment be bored. Here we have found by experience the exact pace at which one should live. Every one of the first-class beings has an occupation of some kind for which he was originally fitted by training and is now specially fitted by long experience. Take the Central Office alone. It is divided into many Controls and in each Control there are many sections. The being who made me a present of you, our friend MZ04, is at the head of the Heat and Light Control. In that alone there are forty-two sections and each section finds work for two first-class beings. Love never stimulates us to an excess of work. Love never takes our minds from the thing on which we are engaged. We do what we can do well and we do it under the best possible conditions, and we have no entertainments of any kind. How then can we be bored? I have said enough. Let me meditate."

"There is just one thing more I should like to ask."

"What is your name or formula?"

"My name is Lemuel Gulliver."

"Well, Gulliver, we are kindly and hospitable people. For some weeks I shall be keeping you here and obtaining from you first-hand information on various details of life in the old world. You will be catechised for one hour or so a day. You may take your revenge in advance. I will answer one more question."

"You told me that community of property still practically existed among you."

"It does. Money is not used. In proportion to the work he does a first-class being has the power of ordering what he requires from the Central Office. It is an extremely rare thing for any first-class being to order all to which he is entitled. The wisest are those who reduce property to the barest necessities. At a man's death all that he has reverts to the State. Here we have no appalling families. Here no man has to make provision for prodigal sons and worthless daughters. We are free from the insanity of love and we find it more easy to believe in friendship when friendship must always remain unremunerated."

"And still I do not envy you," I said. "You are not free from all emotions yet. I have already found two in existence among you, and they are two which I do not greatly love."

"What are they?" the Professor asked.

"Fear and jealousy."

"Lie still. You disturb my meditations."

For half an hour he remained silent with his eyes closed, but not, I think, asleep. Then rising suddenly on all fours he said that we would return to his dwelling, take our pills and compose ourselves for the night.

"I would make a request to you," I said. "These pills which you take are wonderful and I have already experienced their good effects. But I do not think I could live upon them. Evolution has brought your digestive apparatus to a pitch of perfection that I cannot hope to possess. What can you do for me?"

"Our workers, the beings of the second class, are accustomed to kill an ox, cut off a piece of it, subject it to the action of heat, and then devour it. They make also a drink which has great attractions for them. It has even led them to disobey, and to disobey is of course to die. I am sorry to mention such filthy diet, but I can think of nothing else. After all it might suit an old-world barbarian."

"I think it might suit me admirably."

"Then I will have second-class rations sent you every day from the Central Office. I will cross-speak the Central Office now in order that they may send you a piece of dead animal before you sleep. The one condition I make is that I shall not see you engaged in tearing it to pieces with your teeth. You will take it in your own room."

"And which will that be?"

"Oh," he said carelessly, "I shall keep you in the cupboard with my two other pets, the plants. You shall have a mattress to lie on."

A few minutes later one of the working class brought a covered tray, deposited it just inside the Professor's door, and departed.

"Your food," said the Professor. "Take it to the cupboard."

I did so with pleasure. I found on the tray a plate of excellent cold roast beef and a knife and fork of rough workmanship and some flat hard biscuits. There was also a bottle containing about a quart of strong old ale. With this I was very well satisfied, and stretching myself on my mattress, for which there was barely room in the cupboard, I composed myself to slumber.

Chapter V

I PASSED a wretched night. I cannot assign this to the small size of my sleeping-room, for I was able to stretch myself at full length and the admirable system of ventilation kept the air always fresh. Such sleep as I had was haunted by dreams in which these four-legged human beings figured largely. Early in the morning I rose and switched on the light, hoping that by pacing my cell or the passage without for a few minutes I might again induce sleep. I saw a strange sight. The silky heads of the two plants swayed gently to and fro continuously. Their leaves rose and fell. Somehow they seemed to suggest to me a caged lion.

"You poor devils," I said aloud.

When I had put out the light and stretched myself on the mattress again I felt the silky head of one of these plants rubbing against my cheek. It startled me at first. I touched it with my hand. It was about the size of a man's fist. I felt its thousand fibres vibrating under my touch.

In the morning another covered tray was brought me, precisely the same as on the previous evening. A bad night gives one little appetite for strong ale in the morning and I begged a drink of distilled water from the Professor. I took that opportunity to explain to him the kind of food that I should require in the future, and to beg for some facilities by which I might cook myself a hot dish. This last he refused, but agreed that my evening ration should be brought to me hot in the future.

I remained with the Professor for fifteen days. Every day for about an hour he catechised me closely on the manner of life in my own country – the old world, as he called it. His knowledge and his ignorance alike amused me. For example, he made a drawing of a hansom-cab which was really fairly accurate; but he was under the impression that hansom-cabs were used in Rome at the time of Julius Caesar. All his ideas about dates were wrong and confused, and perpetually I had to correct him. He made notes of all that I told him with an ink pencil.

"You are writing a book on this subject?" I asked him one day.

"I am. That is my duty."

"And when will it be printed and published?"

"Upon the defeat of the democracy and the establishment of first-class and second-class beings, the extremely wise course was taken of breaking up all printing-machines and destroying all books, except those copies, mostly manuscript, which were especially selected for the library of the Central Office. We neither print nor publish."

"Why do you call this a wise course? It seems to me the wildest folly. It is to cheap printing and cheap books that the spread of education in my own country has been largely due."

"Undoubtedly. The question of course is whether the spread of education – or rather what you mean by education – is in any way desirable. It seemed to us that one might as well admit children and fools under no supervision to a menagerie of wild beasts and provide them with the keys of the cages. We respect letters. We consider it a dishonour to letters that books should be cheap or easily obtainable. Here it costs a first-class being more to read one manuscript from the library of the Central Office than it would cost you in your own country for a year's subscription to King Mudie."

I informed him that Mudie was not a king and that I did not know how he had got the idea. He accepted the correction as he always accepted every correction, with considerable irritation.

"It seems to me," he continued, "that you use the word education in a very narrow sense. I myself should say that the whole of our second-class beings were educated. Each is trained to the work that he has to do. We have for instance a group of them who are familiar with the ordinary process of plant culture. They can dig, they can prune, they can plant. They have the education for which they are fitted. They are not versed in those extraordinary modifications which can be produced in plants by chemical changes caused artificially in the nature of the sap. That branch is naturally reserved for beings of the first class. They are taught how to weave and how to make the garments which we all wear. They are taught how to clean our houses in the quickest, most silent and most effective manner. Briefly, they do any work which their intelligence and judgment entitle them to do. Beyond that we do not go. We do not give them knowledge which would be dangerous to them and to us. When you return home, my friend, if ever you do return home, preach to your poor benighted people the inequality of man and the advisability of restricting all really important knowledge to the higher grade."

One day while we were chatting about indifferent subjects he mentioned quite casually that he had been cross-speaking the Central Office and that he found that MZ04 had died that morning.

"I am sorry to hear it," I said. "For after all he received me kindly – fed me and clothed me. When is the funeral?"

"Funeral?" said the Professor. "We have no funerals. The body of MZ04 went into the refuse-destructor hours ago. Death is a confession of failure, a sure proof of a blunder somewhere, and therefore ordinary politeness tells us that we should take as little notice of it as possible."

"Who will take his place?" I asked.

"That has already been decided by the Inner Office."

"You had no ambitions in that direction?"

"None whatever. There is no reason why in addition to my present appointment I should not now be holding a post – and a highly placed post – in the Inner Office. It is merely a want of appreciation and, I am afraid I must add, a certain meanness in the minds of some first-class beings which keeps me a humble professor. However, merit will tell; I can trust to that."

The boasted civilisation of Thule had at any rate not extirpated human vanity. The vanity of the Professor was colossal. No compliment was too gross for him to accept with avidity. His nature was indeed very curious and difficult for a simple man like myself to comprehend. In spite of the casual way in which he spoke of death, I was convinced that he lived in hourly dread of it. In spite of the fact that he spoke of every known form of religion as an idle superstition, and professed the most absolute materialism, I think he was unable to disbelieve entirely in the future life. His nerves were not good. Sometimes in the middle of the night he would tap at the door of the cupboard where I slept and ask me to come out and speak to him. There was always some excuse, and I think the excuse was never the true one. The fact of the case is that the extreme solitude in which most of these first-class beings lived had its inevitable effect upon them. They had, as the Professor observed, no entertainments. They had really no social gatherings. Occasionally one friend would pay a brief and formal visit to another friend, but there was nothing beyond that, When they went abroad for exercise or to bask in the sun, they as a rule passed one another unnoticed.

I was myself the reason why for a time the number of visitors to the Professor's house increased considerably. People came to see me, and he produced me and lectured upon me in terms which were sufficiently humiliating.

"Observe," he would say, "the ludicrous smallness of the head and the short and attenuated forelegs. In this respect one might almost believe him to be a second-class being. He is probably, however, a still lower type. The skin is whiter from deficient pigmentation, and the size of the body is smaller than in a second-class male. In the land from which he comes I find that they learn nothing by experience. The child born into the world there naturally adopts the safe quadrupedal position and has the use of its toes. The creature that we have here can do absolutely nothing with his toes and is uncomfortable in the quadrupedal position. In fact, the deformity of his body prevents him from adopting it easily."

At this point in his lecture he would change to a different language and continue. This second language was used by first-class beings among themselves when they wished to say anything without being understood by those whom they considered their inferiors. In the presence of a second-class being it was that language which the first class always adopted. Among themselves and in my presence they spoke English, except on the occasions when they did not wish me to understand them.

I began to rebel against the kind of life which I was leading. I disliked to be made a curiosity and a show of. The monotony affected me. The horrible familiarities of those two plants in my sleeping-room got on my nerves. I began to hint to the Professor that I must have change and more freedom or that the source of his information would possibly be dried up.

"If you became useless to me," he said carelessly, "you would be killed, of course. You would have failed and your body would go into the refuse-destructor."

"Very likely," I said. "But you would not get the information which you want. And you do want it, you know."

That was my trump card. He really did want to acquire all possible information about what he called the old world. In return for this I was always able to obtain concessions, and I did not fail in this case. I told him that I wished to explore the island, to go right over to the other side of it and see the places where the second class lived and the work they did. At first he tried to dissuade me. He pointed out that the distance to the other side of the island was not less than eight miles, and refused to believe that this would not be beyond my strength. He painted in lurid colours the dangers of the mountain which I should have to cross and of the forests which I should find on the other side. I, however, remained obstinate in my purposes and at last obtained his permission to go, on condition that I returned in ten days and that I never spoke with any second-class being whom I might encounter, lest I should inadvertently betray important knowledge to them. This promise I gave readily enough, but, I must confess, with no intention of keeping it. He gave me some further instructions and a pass written with the ink pencil, which he said would entitle me to protection and help from any first-class being whom I might encounter.

Thus then on a fine sunny morning I started out with no more equipment than I could easily carry on my back. The prospect of adventure lured me. For the first time for days I felt in good temper and spirits.

Chapter VI

THE PROFESSOR had been well within the mark in stating that the breadth of the island was not less than eight miles. By sundown I must have covered thirty miles at least and encamped for the night by the side of a swift and narrow stream. I had still the low hill to cross which the Professor had spoken of as a mountain. In a flat country such as Thule, all hills are mountains.

The Professor's mistakes in regard to time and distance interested me a good deal. I could understand that they rendered him professionally unsuitable for the practical work of the Central Office and that they probably helped to debar him from the post which he desired in the Inner Office. It may be, perhaps, that one cannot have an over-development in one direction without a compensating defect in another. The Professor showed the same anxiety to conceal his want of time-sense that an engine-driver might show to conceal his colour-blindness. After all, instances of this want of time-appreciation are common enough among my own people in dealing with the past. One knows the vagueness with which the ordinary man assigns a fact to the sixteenth or seventeenth century – a fact which in reality belongs to the eighteenth. The further back we go the more vague we become. It is difficult for us to realise that the difference between the tenth and eleventh centuries is a difference of a hundred of those very years which we are now living. So far as the present was concerned, the Professor's time-appreciation was clear and accurate enough. He never forgot the hour at which he should take his pills or his siesta in the sun. Watches were unknown in Thule, but there was a clock in every room, and all clocks were wound and synchronised electrically from the Central Office.

I had never been able to persuade the Professor to tell me where the Central, Outer, and Inner Offices were domiciled. I guessed at first it would be where I saw that shaft of smoke ascending when I landed at the island, but afterwards I saw several other similar smoke columns and assigned them to subterranean factories of some kind. But in the course of my day's ramble I came upon many other features that interested me. I reached a long stretch of fields in which a veritable army of the second class was at work. Each field was numbered and seemed to have its separate gang. Each gang was in the charge of one first-class being. As a rule he lay in the sun with one hand removed from the boot and covered with a rubber glove. In this hand he held a thick rod some three feet in length which seemed to me to be made of aluminium. His quick and watchful eyes surveyed the whole of the field, and every now and then he called out an order to some individual labourer. The order was in every case instantly obeyed. In every one of these fields I was challenged by the overseer with a loud "Who are you?" I replied as the Professor had directed me and showed my pass. I was then allowed to go on unmolested. I may even say that I was treated with kindness. One of these beings had water fetched for me that I might drink. Another, astounded by the distance which I had covered on foot, offered to provide four labourers with a litter to carry me, and seemed surprised to find that I really preferred walking. In many of these fields there was grain ready for harvest – of the same kinds, I think, as we have in our country, but with the ears much larger and heavier and of a very dwarf-like habit. I found barley and oats full grown standing scarcely six inches above the ground.

Beyond these cultivated fields was a gently undulating plain, not unlike common land I have seen in England. The bracken was near waist-high, and often I had to force my way through a tangle of bramble and gorse. This part of the country seemed to be entirely deserted, and with no one to direct me I steered by the sun. After some miles of this I came upon a small clump of elm trees and stretched myself in the shade for food and rest.

As I lay asleep I felt a gentle touch upon my shoulder, and opening my eyes I saw one of the first-class beings. I judged him to be one of the overseers, for from one of his big loose boots an aluminium rod projected.

"Who are you?" he said.

I showed him my credentials. He seemed satisfied.

"Go on your way at once," he said, "and bear well to the right, for here you are in danger."

I could not tell what the danger might be, but thought it best to take his advice. As he trotted away from me I fastened up my pack again and slung it on my back, and almost instantly I saw what the danger was. Out from a dip of the land which had concealed them came a herd of about twenty wild cattle. Their size was enormous. The leader, a white bull, scented or sighted me and charged at once towards me. There was but one thing to do. I gripped a low bough and easily swung myself up into the tree, even in the moment of my activity speculating how long I should be kept there and what would happen to the overseer who had spoken to me and was now scarcely a hundred yards distant. The bull paced round and round the tree, pawing the earth and striking the trunk with his great horns. From my perch I could see that the overseer now stood still. He had slipped one hand out of the boot and now grasped that aluminium rod. At that moment the bull sighted him and charged him. The rest of the herd waited huddled and motionless.

When the bull was within about twenty yards of him the overseer raised his hand and pointed that rod towards the beast. There was a flash as of lightning, a loud crackling sound, and the bull rolled over stone dead. The rest of the herd turned tail and galloped off in panic. Without a word to me the overseer replaced the rod in his boot and went on his way.

I could understand now how one of these beings could easily control a gang of thirty or more of the second-class labourers, and could ensure punctual and complete obedience. Yet, grateful though I was to this overseer, I regarded the beings of his type more with wonder than with admiration. They were a selfish and sterile race. Their mode of walking suggested to me too vividly things that I had seen in the great ape-house in Regent's Park. Physically they were not, according to our notions, to be compared with the second class whom they controlled. Those that I saw of the second class were all men of fine stature. Their skins were darker than the European and of a reddish brown. Their faces were handsome, gloomy, and sombre. They seemed more akin to me than did this four-legged thing with the monstrous head and the death-dealing rod in his boot. But as yet I had spoken to no being of the second class. As I passed through the cultivated fields I was all the time under the eyes of the overseers, and deemed it inadvisable to break through the Professor's injunctions.

I saw nothing more of the wild cattle nor of any living being until I reached the stream beside which I camped for the night. I had been told that on the farther side of the hill I should find a forest and beyond the forest the dwellings of the second class and the sea.

As I lay stretched on my rug I heard beneath me a curious rumbling sound and guessed correctly what it might be. It was commonplace enough – an underground train taking the workers back to their homes. Commonplace, at least, in London, but strange in the environment in which I found it. I slept well, as I ever do in the open on a warm night, and in the morning after a refreshing swim in the stream set out to climb the hill.

Chapter VII

THE AIR WAS CLEAR and from the crest of the hill I obtained a fine view. Beneath me lay a forest that covered, I should imagine, some four or five miles. Beyond was the blue sea, and close to the shore what looked like a small town or village of much the same character as we are familiar with in England. These were the first buildings above ground that I had seen in Thule, and constituted the dwellings of beings of the second class.

The attitude of the first class towards the second was rather puzzling. The restriction of the numbers of the workers was quite ruthless. Children that were not wanted were destroyed as we destroy superfluous kittens, fewer girls than boys being allowed to live. The punishment of death was given for any act of disobedience, and even, after due warning, for carelessness and incompetence. But the workers whom I had seen so far – all men – were evidently well treated. They showed no signs of over-work, or under-feeding, or disease. They were tall, stout fellows, all of them, and evidently in fine condition. Not one of them adopted or attempted to adopt the quadrupedal position. They walked erect, and were obviously the physical superiors of their masters. Doubtless utilitarian views had prevailed with the first-class beings, and they gave such treatment to the second class as would ensure the maximum of effective work from them.

The clothing of the workers was of the same thick woollen material as that of their masters, but of a different colour – a reddish brown. The men threw off their upper garment when working in the fields. It will be remembered that on my arrival I was provided by the late MZ04 with grey garments similar to those worn by the first class. I was thus in the nature of an anomaly to everyone who met me. I walked erect and therefore did not belong to the first-class beings. I wore the grey garments, the sleeves of which had now been abbreviated to suit me, and therefore did not belong to the second class. To tell the truth my stature was inferior to theirs, and would by itself have distinguished me.

Standing on the crest of the hill I made my plans. It was in my mind to get away from this island as soon as might be. In a forest of that extent I might easily lie hidden for weeks, and I doubted if, with all his knowledge and cunning, the Professor would be able to find me. Meanwhile I would establish friendly relations with some of the second class. Living as they did upon the sea-shore, I expected that they would have contrived boats for their own use, and thus I might make my escape. I had the whole day before me, and began now to explore the forest, intending to go on to the village on the shore when the workers had returned in the evening.

I followed the course of the stream that trickled down the hill-side. There was no wind, and except for the burble of the stream and the call of the birds all was still in the forest. Here and there the stream broadened out into wide shady pools, where it seemed to me there might be the chance of tickling a trout. Presently I heard below me a loud splashing. The trees and undergrowth were so thick that I could see but a very little way before me. I still followed the stream in the direction of the sound, but I went with extreme caution, taking care that my footsteps should not be heard. I did not know what danger might not be awaiting me below.

Presently I reached the pool from which the sound had come. Peering through the bushes I saw, seated in a dejected attitude by the edge of the pool, a very beautiful woman. In spite of the fact that she had been swimming, and her long dark hair hung dankly about her brown shoulders – wet hair is ever unbecoming to a woman – her beauty was amazing. The brown shoulders peeped from the heavy folds of the garment which she had thrown round her after her swim. It was of the colour prescribed for beings of the second class. The women of that class wear but one garment – a long piece of stuff like a plaid, that they drape about them. As I came into view she started up and gave a scream of terror.

"Do not be afraid," I called. "I mean you no harm. I will not hurt you."

As she looked at me further she seemed reassured. "I thought," she said, "at first that one of the gods had come to take me."

"What gods?" I asked.

"The gods that walk on four legs and against whom no man can do anything. Your dress is of the same colour that they wear."

"I am no god, but an ordinary man enough – a shipwrecked mariner cast up on this island a few weeks ago, and now planning to escape from it again."

"There is no escape," she said mournfully. "The gods know everything."

"Let me come down and speak with you."

"Come," she said. "I am not afraid any more."

"What do you do here?" I asked, as I sat beside her.

"I have fled from death. It was ordained by the gods that I should die at sundown seven days ago. I escaped and hid myself here. But there is no escape really. Sooner or later they will find me. They never fail. In their coming and going they are unseen. Suddenly before you stands one of the gods, and he points his rod at you and you are dead. It is not possible to hide from those whom one cannot see in their approach."

"Has no one ever escaped?"

"Years ago a girl like myself fled to the forest, and for three months in the summer she lived there. It was I myself who found her lying dead. Her garment over her breast was scorched by the lightning of the gods, and her heart was burned within her. It was all one; for in the winter she would have perished of cold and starvation. I love life. I want every day and hour that I can get. But I have no hopes."

"Tell me, what is your name?"

"To the gods I have no name. When I am at work a number is put upon me; it may be a different number every day. Among my own people I am called Dream."

"And why was it that seven days ago you incurred the anger of your masters and were to die?"

"Seven days ago I had the care of a loom. By sundown so much work was to be finished. It is easy work. Our gods never give the women hard work. All the same, that which is appointed must be done. It was just at the beginning of the first spell of hot weather. The forest called me. It was stronger than I was. When I went to my midday meal I slipped into the forest and swam in the pool, and could not go back to the loom again. After that I dared not go back, for those who have disobeyed die instantly. Such is the will of the gods, and we cannot alter it."

"Listen to me," I said. "Those whom you call gods are not gods. They are descended from those who, many years ago, were men and women just as you are. They are not all-powerful. I myself mean to escape from them. Generations of slavery have crushed your spirit, but in the country from which I come there are no slaves. I shall escape and I shall take you with me."

"You are good. I will do as you say. But how can one escape?"

"In the town on the shore I hope to be able to find a boat."

She looked at me with her dark and lustrous eyes wide open in sheer wonderment.

"What is a boat?" she asked.

Her ignorance I found was not assumed. The making of a boat had been prohibited so long by the beings of the first class that now even the recollection of it had passed from the workers. They regarded the sea with terror. It was the grey liquid wall of their prison-house. To touch it was to die. They bathed in the forest pools, and never in the sea. The fish that they ate were fresh-water fish only. Their masters had told them numberless strange lies about the sea.

"Dream," I said, "there is one thing which I cannot understand. You live in daily terror of these people whom you miscall gods. You are fairly well treated, but you are not free. You live as slaves. Why do you tell me, then, that you want every hour and every minute of life?"

She dipped a bare foot in the water below her, passing it slowly to and fro.

"There is always love," she said pensively.

Chapter VIII

"WHAT do you know of love?" I asked.

She shrugged her pretty shoulders. "Almost nothing, except of the lesser loves – the love of children, the squirrels in the forest."

"Of parents," I suggested.

"No," said Dream decisively. "You cannot love those whom you do not know."

"But how does it happen that you do not know your parents?"

"How should I? Sometimes for two years, sometimes for three – as the gods decide – the child remains with its parents. After that it is taken away from its parents and brought up by the gods. That is the law."

"But these women who have their children taken away from them – how do they bear it?"

"Sometimes they are so sad that they go away into the forest and eat the nightshade and die. More often they weep for a long time and then they forget. When a thing is the law and it cannot be altered, there are very few who become angry or grieved about it. What would be the use? The gods are very careful about the children, you know."

"In what way careful?"

"If a child is weak, sickly, or misshapen, it is killed instantly. If it is unable to learn how to do any work it is killed. The strong which remain are well treated. For some years they do little work, they are well fed, they are healthy and happy."

I thought of the gangs of magnificently built men that I had seen at work in the fields. I looked at the strong and beautiful girl beside me. The drastic methods of the lords of Thule had at least brought about one thing – the highest possible physical condition of the race.

"Tell me," I said, "do your gods interfere also in the matter of marriage?"

She gazed at me with her sincere and wondering eyes. "What is marriage?" she said, in much the same tone as she had inquired what a boat was.

I told her something of the marriage ceremonies existing in my own country, and she was very much amused.

"But why?" she asked; "that is a very great to-do about very little. If a man loves a woman and the woman also loves the man, what more is there to say? Why write down things in books and call many people to a feast?"

"Dream," I said, "you are an immoral heathen."

"Those also are words that I do not know. You will tell me about them."

I did not tell her about them. I had already been rather struck by the curious simplicity of her own speech. Her phrases were at times biblical, though she knew nothing of any religion, and could not have read a bible if she had possessed one.

"And when, as you say, a man and woman love one another, is it customary with you for them to live together for the rest of their lives?"

Dream yawned. I was wearying her.

"It is so strange," she said, "to have to tell you the things that everybody knows. Also what you ask is so funny. Of course people who love live together. Is not that right?"

I hardly knew what to tell her. She had the innocence of the first garden. After all it may be that the notions of right and wrong which are very properly accepted in my own country are not to be imposed upon every people in every form of civilisation. I did not wish to judge her. I therefore changed the subject.

"This evening, Dream, I want you to take me to that town where you all live. I am going to save you and take you away from this island. To do that I must make a boat or a great raft. I must have men to help me."

"I will take you there if you wish, but if I do I shall die immediately. Every day and every night the overseeing gods go up and down there. It is well known that I left my work at the loom, and that I am to die. The gods have said I am to die, and what they say always happens. Any one of them who saw me in the town would point at me with his death-rod and I should fall. Still, no one has ever escaped, and as I must die anyhow, I will take you to the town if this gives you pleasure."

I could not of course hear of this. My first step to secure her safety could not reasonably be a step which would ensure her death. I asked her, however, how these overseeing gods – the police of the town, as I figured it – would recognise her.

"By the pictures," she said. "They have pictures of every one of us. My picture is put up throughout the town on the walls of houses."

"I see," I said. "If I go to the town at all I will go alone. Shall I be in any danger from your people?"

"None. You wear the grey garments. True, you do not walk like a god, and you suffer from short arms, as I do. But would you be safe from the gods themselves?"

"Yes," I said. "I have something that was given to me to show them. It is a sign that they are not to injure me."

"Injure?" she echoed. "The gods injure nobody. They kill when it is necessary, but they do not injure. If one has a crooked spine, or if one falls sick, or if one has lived too long, or if one refuses obedience, as I have done, then of course they must die. It is the law. The gods themselves have told us that in the old days our forefathers were beaten or shut up in prisons or their goods were taken away from them. This was called punishment. We are free from all that. We have food and shelter, we have light and warmth, we have times of work and times of play. No one punishes us. That is why it is our duty to love the gods."

"Who taught you to say that?"

"They taught it me themselves. It is one of the first things that a child learns. But I grow weary of sitting here and telling you the things that everybody knows. Will you come with me through the forest and down to the shore where the caves are where I sleep?"

I assented. She rose up and draped her garment anew about her. As we walked side by side I asked her if she was not afraid of sleeping in the caves. Surely there first of all the gods would go to look for her.

"No," she said. "Never. No god has ever been inside those caves since the creature came out of the sea and lived there."

"What creature?"

"How should I know? It was more than fifty years ago, and none of us live for fifty years. But I have heard the story as it is told by my people. The creature that came out of the sea was something like a serpent, but larger than all serpents. Those who looked into its eyes died of horror. Two of the gods died. It went away into the caves, and no one has ever seen it again. I suppose it still lives there waiting for something. But it is far away in the very heart of the caves where I never go. If I heard it moving I should awake at once, for I sleep but lightly, and so I should save myself. If I could remain always in the caves I need have no fear of the gods, but one must have the sun, and water to swim in, and food to eat. Is that not so?"

I agreed with her. "But," I said, "in the forest you are in constant danger."

"Only on calm days. When the wind blows the gods will not go into the forest. That is well known, but I do not know what the reason is."

I knew perfectly well. I had already learned their fear of something falling on them. Over-civilisation had broken up their nerves and rendered them flaccid and spiritless. They had no reason to fear the wild cattle with the death-rod in their hands. They had no reason to fear the docile race that they had tamed in ignorance to serve them. But the limb of a tree might fall, or a cave might be haunted. I grew to hate these first-class beings, as they called themselves.

She began now to ask me questions about the land from which I had come, and all that I told her was subjected to her barbarian criticism. She was perfectly shocked at hearing of hospitals, and regarded the whole of the medical fraternity as impious. "If those who are weak and sickly are patched up and made to live a little longer, is there not a danger that they will have children who will also be weak and sickly, and so much more trouble be made? We see that this is so with the beasts that we rear, and the plants that we cultivate. Is it not so with men also?"

I had to admit that it was. But I pointed out to her that in my country we regarded many other things besides physical perfection.

"So I have already observed," she said, with almost embarrassing frankness. "Are the women of your country beautiful?"

"Some of them are very beautiful. Some, I fear, are not beautiful at all."

"Then why do they live? It must be very unpleasant. Are any of them more beautiful than I am?"

"I have never seen anyone, Dream, as beautiful as you are."

"Say that again," she said, "it makes a pleasing sound."

I did not say it again. I felt my responsibilities towards this beautiful but wholly barbarous creature. It seemed to me my duty at the very first to purge her mind of her superstitions about that deformed, intelligent, and learned section of humanity in whose divine character she had been taught to believe.

"If your masters are indeed gods, as you say, why did they not destroy the creature from the sea?"

"Two of them went out to kill it, but they saw its eyes and horror overcame them so that they died. After that they saw that this was a very evil creature, and in their wisdom they left it alone."

"They must be poor creatures to be so easily frightened to death. In my country we could not believe in gods that ever die. Yet the very first of your masters that I saw when I reached this island has since died and his body has been burned."

"His body – yes. But he himself still lives. I was taught these things by the gods when I was a child, and it is wrong of you to try and make me think otherwise."

I began to realise the tremendous strength of early impression. I could call to mind that I had seen evidence enough of it before ever I came to Thule. It seemed almost impossible for me – one man – to fight against this crafty and complex organisation of tyranny and slavery that was here blindly accepted. I turned to another of her terrors – her terror of the sea.

"Do you swim well?" I asked her.

She laughed. "One swims as one walks or runs. Why not? You ask such strange things."

"Very well then," I said, "you shall swim in the sea."

"No. The sea is the evil water. If one had only that water to drink, one would die. Is that not so?"

"It is, but—"

"Very well then. We are rightly taught not to touch the sea. You speak to me sometimes very much as if you were a god, and you boast of freedom, and you have come all the way from a far-off country; but you yourself would not dare to enter the sea."

It was my turn to laugh. "I am going to swim in it this evening," I said.

"I implore you not to do it," said Dream.

"I shall come to no harm."

"You will most certainly die."

"You will see that I shall not."

"It would be a pity, because I myself perhaps may escape death yet for a few days longer, and I might begin to love you."

We had now reached the entrance to the caves.

Chapter IX

THE SIDE of the brown sandstone cliff was perforated like a gigantic rabbit warren. I judged the cliffs to be natural in character, but in the labyrinth of passages and rooms upon which one first entered, much artificial work had been done. In places columns of brick upheld the roof, and the walls had been trimmed and levelled by a tool. I guessed – for it was a point upon which Dream could tell me nothing – that the lords of Thule had at one time some intention of making use of these natural excavations, and that they had been frightened from their task by the absurd superstition which Dream had recounted to me. I could not believe in the marvellous amphibious monster that had come out of the sea, and for fifty years or more had lived in the heart of these cliffs.

I told Dream of my doubts, but she was not to be shaken. The track of the animal when it went in had been clearly visible, and no track had been found to show that it had gone out again.

"On what then does it live?" I asked.

"Things that it finds in the water."

"But you tell me that it has never gone back to the sea again."

"Never. But far within the caves – much farther than I have ever gone – there is a great lake. It lives there. I will take you to a place where you can hear the roar of the water falling into the lake. Follow me closely or you may lose yourself."

She took me through many winding passages until she reached a point where she knelt and put her ear to the ground. She made me do the same. I could certainly hear the sound of running water below me, but that did not prove the existence of the lake, much less of the monster that was supposed to inhabit the lake. I told her this, and she did not like it.

"When you found me in the forest," she said, "I was very sad because I had spoken to no one for many days, and I was to die and there was no escape. Then because of your companionship and because you seem to hope and to fear nothing, I became lifted up again. It is necessary for you to think as I think, or I shall grow sad again. Therefore you must believe in the great serpent."

"We will not speak of him. Show me where you sleep."

She took me by a passage that rapidly grew narrower until I could hardly force my way into the chamber beyond. It was a simple sleeping-apartment containing a bed of dried bracken and nothing more.

"Yes," she said, "I chose this place because the passage was so narrow and the great serpent which was in the lake was so big. Here he could not get to me."

"And how do you manage about food?"

"I have plenty – far too much. Every night some one or other of my people brings food and puts it at the entrance of the cave. They do not go near to the cave because they believe in the serpent, not being so wise as you are. I would not go into the cave myself were it not that I have to die anyhow."

"But do your gods permit this?"

"I do not know. They do not care to come very near to the caves. I myself think that they do know that food is brought to me and do not wish to prevent it. They have only one punishment. They would not starve me slowly. They would point the death-rod at me and burn my heart out in an instant. But you remind me that I have become very hungry after my swim. You also must think as I do and be hungry too, and we will eat together."

She showed me another room nearer to the entrance where she kept her supplies. They were simple enough. There was a pile of thin sweet biscuit and another pile of dried fruit. This in colour and flavour was like a raisin, but four times the size.

"That grows in the forest," said Dream. "In the autumn when the fresh fruit is ripe it is very good indeed. I shall not live to pick any more of it, and for that I am very sorry."

She was still, I think, rather offended with me for my disbelief in the creature that came out of the sea, but on the whole we chatted amicably enough. I can see now that I did a clumsy thing in thus suddenly and crudely trying to upset a tradition in which she had grown up. It is not perhaps very desirable to shake the faith of anybody in anything, unless that faith be distinctly and immediately harmful. I am a simple seaman and unused to missionary work, and it is small wonder that I bungled it.

After we had feasted, Dream went off to her bed of bracken and I once more climbed the hill to watch the sea. All that afternoon I watched, using at times my perspective-glass, but never once could I make out a sail.

I may admit that my plans were now changed and that the change was entirely due to the strong fascination which Dream had for me – far stronger than I cared to let her know at present.

I no longer cared to explore the town or to find out more of the condition of the workers than Dream herself could tell me. I had decided to throw in my lot with her and, if it were possible, to save her from the cruel death with which she was threatened. How I was to do this I did not know. I could only wait and see what chance might offer itself.

I cut bracken for my bed, and laden with this I made my way back to the cave again. There Dream awaited me and all traces of her ill-humour had vanished. I did not insist on my swim in the sea that night, lest it should pain her further. We sat and talked together until the stars came out. It was the first time since I had been on the island that I had looked up at the stars. I could find nothing that I recognised. I wondered where in the world or out of the world I now found myself. The problem did not disturb me greatly. It was pleasant to sit and hear Dream's recital of her story of the squirrel that she captured and tamed. Her voice was curiously soft and caressing.

Soon she went back to her bed and I spread my bracken in the door of the cave and lay down. It was in the night that her people came to bring her food, and I wished if possible to see them and to speak with them.

But this experiment turned out ill. I had slept but an hour when I was awakened by a footfall, and looking out from the cave I saw striding towards me a man who bore a tray on his head. But when he was within a hundred yards of the cave he set the tray down and turned back again. I called out that I was a friend and would speak with him, but I do not think he understood what I said, and the sound of a strange voice filled him with terror. He ran off at the top of his speed.

Early that morning I had my swim in the sea, but on my return I said nothing to Dream about it. I told her, however, how the man had run away when he heard my voice the night before.

"You did not do this very well," said Dream. "You told me that you did not wish to go to the town any more and that you would remain with me. But it seems that I am not enough and that you do wish to speak with others. Very well then. This night I will watch outside the cave and I will go to the man who brings the food and I will bring him in to you. He is, I think, a man who loves me very much indeed."

I told her that I had changed my mind and did not wish to see the man. A brisk wind was blowing and we spent most of the day in the forest together. Again from time to time I scanned the horizon with my perspective-glass, and again with no result whatever. I wondered in what deserted sea this island might be placed. Throughout the day Dream was silent and thoughtful, but she was in no immediate fear, knowing that on such a day her gods would not enter the forest. Next morning I went for my swim in the sea again, and on my return Dream told me that she knew what I had done. She had seen me swimming far out.

"Why did you not tell me you had done this?"

"I feared to disturb your mind."

"I am not a child and am not to be treated as a child. I can think as you think about the sea if I like. I dare do anything that you dare to do."

I told her that I had no doubt of it. Rain fell for the greater part of that day and we remained in the cave talking. She told me of the life she had led and of the laws by which her people were governed.

I have said that I had begun to hate the lords of Thule – the first-class beings as they designated themselves – the gods, as the poor ignorant workers supposed them to be. I hate them still. I despise their sexless emasculate nervousness. I despise their want of the warmer sins and their subjection to the colder. I despise their selfishness even while I admire their wisdom.

Yet, if I am to speak honestly, their despotism – not benevolent and wholly self-interested – produced a finer race of workers than is to be found in my own country today. They were better fed, better clothed, better housed. They were healthier – disease was almost unknown – and they were happier. I use the last word deliberately. The cruelty with which they were treated – and to our modern minds it was abominable cruelty – was after all not capricious cruelty. It proceeded on laws as immutable as the laws of nature. The mother of the weakling who saw her child destroyed at any rate knew why; and when the lightning strikes the best and most promising of us we do not know why. Every man was specially trained for special work, and his own inclination was always taken into account; for the greater the inclination, the greater – as a rule – the aptitude. The view taken of women was definitely animal, and only in exceptional cases were women allowed to live beyond the age of forty-five. On the other hand, no woman was worked hard; women who were about to be mothers or had recently become mothers, were treated with a delicate consideration far beyond anything to be found in our Factory Acts; and no woman was influenced in her choice of a mate by vulgar claims of a financial or social character. The children were free from the thwarting and snubbing and the curse of competitive examination which we are pleased to call education. Each child was taught a few essentials very thoroughly. The training was in each case individual and based on a clever study of the child's nature. If reading or writing or arithmetic was unnecessary for the work which the child would ultimately be called upon to do, then none of these things was taught. It might almost be said that the children were spoiled. But they learned early the immutable and inexorable nature of the laws imposed on their race.

Towards the close of this day Dream became once more sad and depressed. Suddenly she rose and said that she was going back to her own people in the town.

"But," I said, "you know that this means death."

"There is one thing worse than death which may happen to a woman. It is useless for you to try to prevent me. If I cannot go to the town, then tomorrow I shall eat the poison berries in the forest."

I had intended, if ever I could find the way, to take Dream back with me to my own country and there to marry her. It seemed to me now that there was no hope of this. I make no defence of what I said or did. I do not know if under those circumstances any defence is needed. But I told Dream that she need not seek the death-rod of her gods or the poison berries of the forest, because the one thing which is worse than death had not happened to her.

Chapter X

THERE FOLLOWED sixteen days of such great and idyllic happiness that for that alone it seems worthwhile to have lived my life. Dream lost her terror of the sea and every morning swam out with me. Sometimes we would catch trout in the forest pools, and these I would clean and cook in the manner I had learned in the South Seas, on hot stones and ashes, getting fire from the sun by means of the lens of my perspective-glass. But this we could only hazard on days when the wind blew strongly, lest the smoke of our fire should signal our whereabouts. I was not able to shake Dream's belief in the creature that came out of the sea, but she seemed no longer to have any fear of that or of anything.

"When death comes," she said, "it will come to both of us. Every day is a gain. Yet, when one cannot possibly be happier, it is not hard to die. One has drunk the wine of life."

I had it in my mind to attempt some further exploration of the caves. In this I had been so far prevented by the fact that we had no means of lighting ourselves. It was on the morning of the sixteenth day that I found in the forest wood of a very resinous character which I guessed would make good torches. I got me a store of this and carried it down to the cave, telling Dream what I meant to do.

"I shall go with you," she said. Nor could I dissuade her from it.

We kept a small fire burning at the entrance to the cave that day, and when the sun had gone down we lit our torches from the fire and started off, taking no other equipment than my clasp-knife and a lump of chalk with which to mark our way in the labyrinth.

We soon reached a point where but two roads were left, each so wide and lofty that a coach and four might easily have been driven along it. One of these roads led upwards, and I made no doubt emerged on the farther side of the hill. The other one struck more abruptly downward, and this was the road which we took. Here, if it existed at all, I should find the subterranean lake. As we went on, the noise of falling water became more and more distinct. I was excited by the adventure and eager to see more.

Presently the road widened into a vast hall, so vast that our torches could not illumine the farthest recesses of it. And here it was as well that I looked carefully to each step, for I found myself suddenly on the edge of a precipice. Lying flat on my stomach and holding out my torch, I could see a vast stretch of black water below, into which at one end a cataract thundered. In the middle of this lake there projected something which looked like a smooth boulder of rock. I wondered what it might be.

"We have plenty of torches?" asked Dream.

"Plenty."

"Then we will see what it is."

She waved her torch round her head till it was all ablaze and then flung it down. It fell on that great mass in the middle of the lake. The mass turned slowly over, showing shaggy hair matted with slime. The smell of burning hair came up to us and with it a deep groan that seemed to shake the cave.

We fled in panic. I must indeed ascribe it to chance and to no courage of my own that I kept my grip of the torch. We did not even pause to look at the chalk marks we had made for our guidance, and in consequence found ourselves lost for a while in the labyrinth of passages at the entrance to the cave. At last we found the way out and made our way to the forest. There we spent the remainder of the night, wakeful and talking of the wonders we had seen. It was the last night that we spent together.

The sun had scarcely risen when I saw a few feet away from us a little smoke flickering over the powdered soil.

"What is that?" I asked.

"That is the end," said Dream. "We shall die together."

Rapidly the smoke, which did not rise and disperse, became more opaque, vibrating until it took solid shape. Before us leered the misshapen head and bright beady eyes of the Professor.

His right hand covered with a rubber glove slipped out of the boot and drew forth the death-rod.

"The stranger dies first," he said, and pointed the rod at me. Dream clung to me. I felt a sensation as of fire in my throat.

And now comes what seems to me – though it may not so seem to others – the strangest part of my story. Passing through a kind of swoon, I found myself gently rocked as on board a ship. Opening my eyes I saw two men bending over me. One of them held a glass containing brandy to my lips.

"You see?" said a voice triumphantly. "The beggar's alive and I win my bet."

I found afterwards that I was on board the steamship *Hermione* bound from Alexandria to Cardiff with a cargo of cotton seed. I had been found senseless at the bottom of an open boat. I was treated with plenty of rough kindness and brought back to my own country; but over the story which I told them the crew shook their heads gravely.

Since then nothing of import happened to me until I was brought to this great barrack-like place where I now live in fair comfort. There are many doctors here and many guests. Some of the guests, I fear, have an aberration of the intellect, for they say strange things. I am well contented. I have lived my life. But since no one will listen to my marvellous experiences in the island of Thule – or if they listen at all make a jest of them – I have written them down here for the service of another and a wiser generation.

A Dweller on Two Planets, or The Dividing of the Way

Part III, Chapter IV: The Fall of Atlantis

Phylos the Thibetan

[Publisher's Note: One of the most famous nineteenth-century texts on Atlantis, this book was presented as a true account by the author, who claimed he had channelled the spirit of Phylos the Thibetan. In it, Atlantean culture is described as technologically and scientifically advanced. This extract covers the height of the action, as the city makes preparations for the foretold deluge.]

Chapter IV
The Fall of Atlantis

AGAIN we looked over Atlantis, and saw many things else. The Zailm time possessed a peculiar interest. I saw that dim, distant past, a past old in the earth and ancient when Earth was yet a babe in the cradle of time. Atl, chiefest of the prehistoric races, numbering at home in Poseid, and abroad in the colonies, almost three hundred millions of souls; Atl, known through the olden earth as Atlan, Queen of the Seas, and her people as Children of Incal, i. e., 'Of the Sun', and as the Sons of God. How are the mighty fallen! For now I behold her ancient site as part of the bed of the restless sea, covered with ocean ooze and slime, and to be known as the haunt of man only through the clear vision of the perfected eyes which scan astral records. Again the scene was presented so that we saw it as the eyes of my poor, weak, and pitifully mortal personality of Zailm had seen it. There was stately Caiphul, the Royal; and there, far away, and not so stately, Marzeus, its towers and turrets and chimneystacks and lofty buildings marking where had stood the greatest of Atlan manufacturing centers, where the machine shops and the mills had been which supplied Poseid with vailx, and naims, and all sorts of machines and instruments; with the products of the looms, the cereals and endless articles of use, and of art. Over a million artisans there by day, but by night scarce fifty thousand, all gone by car or vailx to their homes anywhere from fifty to a hundred miles away, a few minutes' ride. And all this to perish because of man's iniquity, a few short hundreds of years later. Here and there I caught glimpses of canals, distributing either natural rivers or streams, or the product of aqua-aerial generators, such as Zailm had a small model of in his last days in Umaur.

We saw the world as Zailm saw it: Suern, with its millions of people; Necropan, with its ninety-odd millions; Europe, then a barbarian land, only about one-sixth its present area; and Asia, not so large in extent then as now, but containing over a half million of souls. But the sparkling, brilliant civilization which was more than peer of even proud today, that was glorious Atl! Eleven hundred millions of people, civilized or but semi-civilized, and as many more scattered over the continent and islands of the seas who were utter barbarians – such was the world of Zailm, generally viewed. The numbers of the human race, and especially their increase during several generations, has appalled the pessimists. But the greatest of pessimists, Malthus, need have felt no alarm had he but known. Because:

The world goes up and the world goes down,
And the sunshine follows the rain.

There are a varying number of people always in the world; now more, now less; for as a soul comes to Earth (having been in devachan) a soul passes from Earth into devachan. But now two come while one goes, or two go while one comes, relatively. Wherefore the world is apparently encroaching upon the sources of supply, or again the supply of all things exceeds demand. But only a fixed number of Human Rays went forth from the Father, and only so many have Life, or ever will have. But these come and go as the tides ebb and flow, now on Earth, now in Heaven. Malthusians need not fear.

Zailm had been my personality.

Thirty centuries later, approximately, we saw again this land. But how changed. Now had Caiphul lost something. Not the tangible matter visible to earthly men – no, this was not gone. But the men we saw were not the high, lofty, noble-souled men known to Zailm and to Anzimee. And when manhood suffers decadence, degradation, all nature with which he has to do also sensibly alters for the worse. Marzeus, the city of manufacturing arts, was no more; it had gone down before corruption. Art had not suffered so much as had science. But the science which drew upon the mysterious forces of Nature the 'navaz' – this had so far disappeared that airships were forgotten, or at most were semi-mythical history. So were many other instruments which Zailm. had known – the naima, those wonderful, wireless, combined telephonic and photographic image transmitters. And the vocaligrapha, the caloriveyant instruments and the water-generators – all were lost in the night of time. But the men of the twentieth century shall find them all again. Twenty-eight decades of centuries hath Day now here continued, and soon it shall be proclaimed,

"The evening and the morning are the seventh day." Ye who hear all my message are the men and the women of this new day, and shall inherit all things from our Father forever. And the full eventide of that day which cometh shall behold you caught up 'into the heavens' to escape the end of all things, when the earth also, and the works that are therein, shall be burned up.

But I should deal with the past, not with the future. The seeds of corruption sown in the hearts of men by the Evil One, master over Mainin, germinated and throve, and then began, some centuries after the time of Gwauxln and Zailm, a long, steadily downward course which weakened the self-respect, manhood and womanhood of Poseid, a loss revealed in countless ways, culminating in national depravity and ruin.

It was upon one of these phases of ruin that we next gazed. We saw a woman upon whose face rested a light almost divine in the power of its transfiguring beauty. Her slight figure seemed not so much of Earth as of Heaven. The loose robe of gray which she wore fluttered in the breeze, the long tresses of brown hair, unrestrained, swept back from the glorious face, on which sat pity and despair, yet mingled with a wonderful radiance of appealing, entreating, agonized hope that some might hear and turn away from the course they were following. Her appeal assumed that most perilous form, for the champion, which an appeal can assume, that of sharp denunciation. She denounced the hideous system of blood-sacrifice in religion as being in diametrical opposition to right, to God, to man, and responsible for the corruption of the people. At this, the priests among the crowd uttered hoarse cries of rage. In a voice, the astral record of which rings yet, and forever, for those who have ears to hear such psychic tones, she cried, from her high place on the pedestal of the monument, twenty feet from the ground and the upturned faces below:

"Oh, ye! Think ye that Incal will accept the blood of innocent animals for your crimes? Whose sayeth this doth lie! Incal, God, will never take blood of anything, nor symbol of any sort which placeth an innocent in a guilty one's stead! And the Incalithlon, and the Holy Seat, and the Maxin Light axe dishonored whenever a priest layeth an animal on the Teo Stone, and striketh a knife to its heart, tears it out and tosses it as sacrifice into the Unfed Light. Yea, the Unfed Light doth truly destroy it instantly. But think ye because of this that merciful Incal is pleased. O ye brood of vipers, ye priests that are charlatans and sorcerers?'

An angry Incali stooped as she uttered this, and picked up a jagged bit of stoneware. In front of him was a litter borne by sad-visaged slaves. On this, reclining amidst soft silken cushions, was a woman of languorous beauty, the very impersonation of shameless abandon. In the warm, tropical atmosphere she lay, innocent of any covering, except that the heavy waves of the hair of her beautiful, if wicked, head partially concealed her nakedness. The shameless sight did not attract notice because of its shamelessness; the only attention bestowed by the dense and wrathful crowd around her was that of sensual admiration from one or another. Such sights were all too common in these last days of Atl. Seeing the priest pick up the sherd, this woman said:

"What wouldst thou with it?"

"Naught," answered the priest.

"Naught, forsooth! I know thou wouldst throw it at yon blasphemer, if thou hadst courage!"

"Courage, I lack not," was the sullen reply.

A voice in the surging crowd now called out that the blasphemer of religion ought to be sacrificed on the Teo, Stone, and her heart given to the Maxin.

"Listen to that! The people and the Incali would be with thee," said the wanton. "Throw the piece, and see if perchance thou mightest not reach the game."

The ecclesiastic raised his hand back, and poised the missile, while the crowd nearest him gazed with eager eyes. Then the cruel bit of pottery hurtled through the air towards the fair speaker overhead. Her temple was presented, and the missile she might have avoided had she noted its coming, struck full on the dainty mark. With a cry of pain she threw up her hands, reeled, and then fell outwards, downwards, the twenty feet to the hard pavement below. The crowd, which had hushed an instant, now uttered fierce growls, and those nearest ran to the victim of the coward priest. Several of the sacerdotal caste picked the poor body up, and carrying it by the feet, arms and hair, quite as if the assault had been preconcerted, instead of being the work of one miserable fiend, started off to the Incalithlon, whose vast pyramid loomed not far away.

"See!" said Phyris, "the first human sacrifice in Caiphul! Me, even me, they slew, for trying to stem the tide of depravity and ecclesiastical criminality. I repeated to them the prophecy of the Maxin, and they heeded not, but slew me. For that woman was my personality when I reincarnated, three thousand years after thou, as Zailm, did leave me, as Anzimee."

With a strange ecstacy of crime, the priests, scarce an instant pausing, placed the still unconscious victim on the Teo. Then the chief priest, still called the Incalix, stepped from the Holy Seat, as it once had truly been. By the side of the victim he stopped and profaned not God, but Man, by a prayer to God; for no man can injure God except through injuring Man. Then he threw open the gray robe and bared the white breast. Swiftly he raised aloft the keen edged knife, then smote. A shudder shook the reviving victim, who was about recovering consciousness. The murderer then tore out the quivering heart and cast it into the Unfed Light, where it disappeared and made no sign. Then the flesh was divided piecemeal amongst the murderous crowd, together with the bloodstained garments. But the most of the blood had run into a depression in the Teo, made for sacrificial blood. To this the priests added liquor, and in maddened frenzy quaffed the mixture from golden goblets. The scene was sickening, and I felt my very being revolt! And that poor murdered woman, a virgin

– who had given her life to rescue her nation from sin – that was she, who had long centuries before been Anzimee, and now was Phyris, part of myself, and I part of her being, for our Spirit was one reunited. I could forgive the crime I looked back upon, for the criminals knew not what they did. And they have suffered for it, and yet shall suffer, for it is their karma. When Death, the conqueror of all mortals, garnered his harvest in Atl, these souls, which had sown sin and grown tares, were reaped by the Great Reaper, and the tares were sown with the good wheat when next those souls reincarnated. And they have had to glean and uproot as they could, and so must continue to tear up the evil weeds till every one be uprooted. Then will they have atoned unto God. There is time enough, lives enough, but O friends, none to waste!

After this human sacrifice the thirst for blood which the people manifested became unappeasable. They demanded the life of the priest who struck down the woman, for they were not yet accustomed to the rights the Incali had so newly arrogated, those of human sacrifice. They claimed that he had really murdered the woman, that they were unprepared to go so far, that therefore he who threw the missile must die. The tumult became so violent, and insurrection seemed so imminent, that the wretched priest was dragged out and offered by his fellows as the woman had been. But now came the denouement. When the high priest turned to cast the heart of the last victim into the Maxin, he staggered as if struck, his hand fell by his side, the heart dropped on the pavement, and the stricken man fell forward unconscious! The tall taper of the Unfed Light was gone; the Maxin book was gone! In its place stood a human form, that of a Son of the Solitude. In his left hand was a sword, in his right a pen.

"Behold, the day of destruction is at hand which was foretold ages ago! Atlan shall be no more beheld by the sun in his whole course for the sea shall swallow you all! Attend ye!"

Then the dread apparition vanished. But the Unfed Light came not again. The people fled, shrieking, leaving the priest who had fainted lying on the floor. It was as well, for when venturesome ones came into the Incalithlon many days later he still lay as he fell, for he was dead. In his greater knowledge, for wicked as he was he yet was chief, he knew, sorcerer that he was, that there really was a power of right which was destined to bring the corruption of Poseid low and uproot the hideous mockery of sin enslaving the nation. And in his knowledge his soul had gone forth from his body in desperate fear, to return no more.

But the stupid sensualism of the masses, finding that after a few years nothing terrible occurred, gradually lapsed till worse than before, for human sacrifices became common, lust, gluttony and drunkenness ran riot, and the moral night's deep darkness closed in yet more blackly.

One man and his family who lived apart partook not of the general wickedness. True, he and his mate, like the ordinary people about him, were not married, save as the higher animals monogamize. Nor were his sons and their wives any better. But blood sacrifice he nor they would do. And when the monarch proclaimed that all must worship according to the new standard, and sacrifice babes and women, these men, giants in stature, and far superior, any one of them, to a dozen of the corrupt slaves of the Rai, refused to obey the mandate. Fruits and treasure they offered, but not blood. In his seclusion the father, Nepth, had a revelation. It came from the Sons of the Solitude, who were nowise altered from the ancient high standard, but Nepth thought it direct from God. The revelation was but a repetition of the prophecy of doom, but the knowledge of that prophecy having been centuries neglected, bore to Nepth all the force of a new revelation. So he came to know of the coming destruction of Atl, he and his sons. And they considered how to escape. Vailx were unknown. Nepth and his sons were unskilled builders. But they received instructions from the befriending Sons of the Solitude, who came to them in astral shape. And so these better men of Atlantis began to build a great vessel. It was clumsy, but secure, and had room to receive several of all kinds of useful animals found in Atl, and to simple ignorant Nepth these constituted every animal on earth, for he knew nothing of other lands across seas, scarce knew of the provinces in Incalia or Umaur, for in these last days communication was not closely kept up. His neighbors and friends jeered and reviled him as a blasphemer, and he and his sons as men crazed. But the years lapsed, and the great ark of refuge grew, until one day it was complete. Then Nepth and his sons provided it with ample stores, and they took the animals from the pens wherein they had placed them as they captured them in years past. Indeed, most of these animals had been born in captivity and were tame, so long had Nepth carried on all works together, not knowing just when the dread prophecy was to be fulfilled. The final preparations were none too soon completed. Only a few days elapsed ere the earth shook and trembled in a frightful manner. Rivers left their beds, or sank through vast crevices in the earth; mountains shook till they were left as hills, and

Bowed their tall heads to the plain.

A crevice opened close by the vessel of refuge, and the river which, half a mile wide, had flowed past to the ocean, fifty miles away, now poured with a mighty roar into the opening. For three days this awful turmoil continued. A man came, beseeching for admittance. But Nepth said: "Nay, thou wouldst never believe in other days. I told thee then this land should sink under the seas, and thou didst revile me. Now go thy way and tell all thou dost meet that 'Nepth spake truly.'"

Three days of horror, and three nights. Death stalked through the land, for the mountains fell on the plains and floods swept unrestrained. But the worst was to come. On the morning of the fourth day it seemed as if the rains of heaven would drown all, yet the thundering and turmoil was not lessened. The gates of heaven and of the great deep were yet to be broken, and the continent, yea, much also of the world to be drowned. The people not yet destroyed were myriad, and were gathered in the high places. Suddenly it seemed as if the foundations of the world were withdrawn, for by one frightful, universal motion the lands left unflooded began to sink. With never a pause to the hideous, sickening sensation, all things sank, down, down, down – one, two, a dozen feet! Then a period of rest. The rains, which came in sheets, instead of drops; the wild blasts of furious wind; the sinking motion – all ceased while men might count a score. One score, two, three, yet no resumption. The wretched people, hidden in such poor shelter as they could find and dared avail themselves of, began to breathe easier – perhaps the fearful ruin was at last stayed! But, no! A slight tremble, scarcely noticeable after the mad three days, and then with one swift leap down to death the great continent of Atlantis sank as a stone sinks in water! Not a paltry dozen feet, nor even a hundred, but almost a mile it sunk at one horrible bound!

Nepth? In the middle of the third day his vessel of refuge had floated to the ocean on an outgoing rush of the floods, and there the winds had carried him until, when Atl sped down to death, he and his storm-beaten ark were a couple of hundred miles away. A very few other people had been similarly forced seawards, and these, after weary weeks, at last came around the southern promontory of Africa, and drifted northeasterly, to land on the west coast of Umaur. Here, too, the destruction had left but a few miserable survivors. But the few hundreds thus left founded the race which, repopulating that land, was found by Pizarro after many centuries upon centuries had elapsed. And a few thus became many. They would not permit blood sacrifice, but yet, like Nepth, offered fruits to Incal, and retained the name, slightly modified, so as to be Inca, a name bestowed upon their rulers. A few survivors landed further north, and repopulated the land conquered by Cortez, the Spaniard, a few short centuries ago. But these heeded not the lesson, for no sooner were they landed on the desolated shores than they slew a woman as a thanksgiving for their escape. But Nepth? For many days his vessel drifted over the silent seas, with only the ceaseless roar of rain upon the roof to break the stillness. At last the vessel grounded. He knew not where he was, for he was an ignorant man. But the aspect of things was changed wholly. When at last he descended, and let loose his living freight, though he knew it not, he was in Asia. This land had not suffered as other lands, but yet floods had covered all the western part of Asia. The eastern portions, and what there was of Europe and America, had not remained inundated after the quick subsidence of the enormous tidal-wave, which, thirteen hundred feet in height, swept outward from Atlantis' site upon the recoil of the engulfing ocean. Thus closed the scene for us; the great deluge was over.

Then Phyris and I turned to other phases of the mysterious, past. These, though not less interesting, may not enter these pages. Rai Gwauxln was come to be Mendocus, while Rai Ernon of Suern was with us now, Mol Lang. Sohma was that, Son of the Solitude whom I took on my vailx when I was Zailm, away from Suern. So we saw the interweaving of the life lines. Then we saw the course of the lost soul, Mainin, from remote ages when Atlantis was not known in the earth, a sin-laden man then, until we found him, serving Satan, an outcast from human ranks, blasted thence by that Son of God, 'first fruit of them that (had reincarnated) slept'.

Looking, we saw that early Rai of Poseid, him of the Maxin Stone and the Unfed Light, the Lawgiver. We knew him for the Christ, illumining man then, and later as Buddha, and again overshining that greater than Buddha, the Nazarene. "Before Abraham was, I am." Whosoever the Christ-Spirit entereth into and abideth in, becometh a Son of God, and equal with Gautama; but into no one will it enter who doth not travel the Path. That mighty One blasted Mainin. Yet we saw that because Mainin had crossed our life then, I was thereby made the instrument of mercy to him by Christ, and that occasion was yet to come.

Back of the time of Zailm we gazed upon a scene on the great continent of Lemuria, or Lemorus. We saw a great house built of stone, standing on a grassy sward, a plain, over which roamed herds of cattle, and queer little horses, having three toes to each foot and high shoulders. Far to the east was a blue mountain range, beyond that a great ocean. But between the manse and mountains flashed a silvery lake. Within the house were many people, servitors all to two people, a woman and her son. Gloom overspread all faces, the gloom of blood. To a chief among subordinates the son gave orders. This slave, grim, ferocious, a very incarnation of cruelty, attracted my notice. His brown skin was swarthy, his hands talon-like. Only a breech-cloth apparelled him. Receiving his orders, he disappeared, but soon came again, pushing two manacled people, plainly of a different race from any there. One was a youth, lithe, erect, rather haughty of mien, his hair brown, his features symmetrical; that individuality of twenty-three thousand years ago is now Sohma. The other captive was a fair girl, sister to the youth, it seemed. Her beauty was delicate, but voluptuous. The fierce, cruel eyes, gleaming like live coals from under the shaggy brows of the master of the house, lighted with admiration as he saw the girl. His heavy-set figure, his coarse jaw, thick neck, and round, shaven head, all fitted him to be master of the brutish crowd around him. This man extended his hand as if to touch the captive maiden. She shrank away, and drew her figure erect in a queenly scorn.

"Ha! Unyielding as ever!" quoth the master. "We shall see."

He nodded to the chief slave, who threw the captive boy on a sort of altar beside him. He bound him. But the victim said firmly: "Sister, yield not; die first." Her eyes shone with an awful light of horror.

"Stop his voice," exclaimed the master; and the slave, nothing loath, cut out the poor boy's tongue!

"Beast!" hissed the girl to the master.

"Ha!" he replied, "I will prove that true," and he struck the bared breast of the tongueless lad with his own dagger, and tearing out the heart, threw it at the sister's feet. A goblet of the blood was caught and the master's mother, a priestess, who stood by the block, took it and gazed into it. Then she said:

"The gods say that the girl also must die."

"Say they so? By all the powers I will not obey," shouted the master. "Not though my troops of war fail, and the King fails!"

"My son," said the priestess, "thou mayest not avoid this sacrifice and live, say the gods."

"No? Then the gods be served. Give me that knife." He felt its keen edge, and then asked, without taking his eyes from the weapon, "Say the gods yet so?"

"Even yet," said the priestess.

"Bind the maid," and his orders were obeyed, though the girl had fainted. The executioner laid his ear to her breast; a faint smile relaxed his features, and he said in his soul, "She is dead." He laid his hand on her breast, stood erect and said:

"Accept, ye gods, this sacrifice."

An instant the knife glittered overhead, the next he had buried it in his own heart. So had the heart that knew no mercy yielded to love; the stern warrior was dead. The gods must have blood, he thought, but he gave his own. What personality was he, was the girl, dead from horror? Myself! and Phyris!

The complete and unabridged text is available online, from *flametreepublishing.com/extras*

To Selareme

Erica Ruppert

THE DLSARII came out of the glare of the sun, swaying across the scrub on the high backs of the grey dlkii. The great beasts were patient and oddly graceful. Their massy silhouettes were distorted by the flapping banners that draped them, making the dlkii seem like winged things rather than the ponderous earthbound creatures they were. The caravan was still too far off for any watchers to make out the riders. But Thes knew they were there, just out of reach, and his stomach clenched in anticipation of their arrival.

Years ago, after the war had cooled, the Dlsarii had resumed their wandering. They went back to their old trades and left the attempts at rebuilding to the rest. Thes's father often said they were the smart ones in this, that the war had changed things so much that the world could not continue as it had been. Still, Thes's family stayed in Miridaj, and rebuilt what they could.

The mountains that the Dlsarii crossed were the uneven edge of the horizon, melted into haze. Thes had never been that far out of the city, although his father had told him of wandering as far as their foothills when he was young and wild. Thes was at his heart afraid to venture so far from the sheltering city walls. He would never speak it, though, never admit even in the silent darkness of his bed that the vastness of the plains and mountains made him seem too small to survive it. He joked and boasted to his friends, but he never would venture out.

When morning came the Dlsarii were there, just outside the city. Their parti-colored tents had blossomed overnight from the dry fields. Thes went with a pack of other children to stare from the ends of the streets. Safe among the crowd, he shaded his eyes and watched the Dlsarii go about their unpacking.

"What do you think they've got?" he said to his friend Ems as they stood elbow to elbow.

Ems shoved him lightly, maintaining dominance.

"What do you think? Probably cloth and jewelry, decorations and stuff. Same every year, my dad says."

"They don't come every year," Thes said.

"Well, they used to," Ems said.

Eventually the pack of children dissolved back into the city. Thes kicked at the dirt as he walked back to his father's shop. He let himself in to the narrow, cluttered room, put on the heavy leather apron and gloves, and began to file away the rough burrs on the edges of a cut pipe.

In the afternoon his father came in and dismissed him. The Dlsarri were in town. He should go up to the market place to see them.

The sun was hot, and the streets glistened where they had been oiled to keep the dust down. Thes dawdled, wanting to string out the excitement. Then he reached the open square, and stopped in the shade of a shop awning.

Thes stared, fascinated, at the Dlsarii families that drifted through the market. They were golden brown like good bread, with light eyes and hair the colour of bones. Men and women alike wore their hair long and loose and decorated with tiny, colored glass beads that made music as they walked. Their clothes were hemmed with bells and copper mirrors. They moved smoothly and melodically over the broken remnants of pavement, never losing their footing, even the wide-eyed children as they looked around at the strange honeycomb of Miridaj.

When the visitors passed through on their way back to their camp, the normal buzz of the street filled up the empty air behind them. Thes stayed where he was beneath the awning, his face turned east, daydreaming. He always had his eyes on the horizon, waiting for something other to spill over it and change the world. He wondered if this was it. They seemed foreign enough to change things. He could hope.

* * *

Two days passed. Thes had to force the idea of Dlsarii magic out of his head to get anything done, but it still stained his thoughts. He believed he was ready when the girl stopped in front of his father's shop and looked through the clear pane of the door at him where he stood at the buzzing grindwheel. The sparks it threw were like stars in the air. She pressed a hand against the scratched glass, a request.

He put down the mower blade he was sharpening and opened the door for her. She stepped into the tiny, dim shop, pulling her loose clothes close so as not to sweep into the machinery. Her eyes were large and round, pale as ice in her brown face. When she moved, the glass beads threaded through her hair clicked and chimed. Her face was heart-shaped, her mouth small. She was nearly an adult, he thought, probably a year or two from marrying. He wondered that she was there alone.

"I saw you watching my family when we first came," she said.

He looked down at his hands, shy of her after all.

"Are you coming to the trade?"

"I think so," he said. He kept his eyes down.

"You will like it."

His eyes flickered up to her, but he quickly turned away.

"All right," he said.

He heard the door open and ease shut again. He went back to his work.

* * *

She smiled when she saw him at the trade, and left a younger girl with the pile of carpets she had been minding. Thes left his father haggling over a dress for his mother and walked over to meet her.

"What is your name?" she asked him.

"Thes. Albourin."

"Mine is Qarathamlimolo."

Thes stayed silent, afraid to mangle it.

"Lim," she said. "Just say 'Lim'."

"Lim," he repeated, and she smiled again. Her eyes were as clear as water.

She glanced back over her shoulder at the girl. A Miridajian man was folding back the rugs carefully, looking at the patterns.

"I will meet you in a few days, when the trade slows. Look for me."

She did not glance back at him as she walked away.

* * *

When Lim at last came for him it was half a month later. She rapped sharply on the glass door at midday. He startled and peered through the clouded glass, and threw away the remains of his lunch when he recognized her. He had thought she would not come, that she had been teasing him. His face grew hot, but he opened the door.

She waited in the street for him, under the beating sun.

"Thes," she said. "Let's walk."

Her mouth made his name into music. He wanted her to keep talking, to turn the dry city into wonder, to decorate the cramped streets with the bells of her tongue. She led him toward the wide dry fields, humming softly in cadence to their steps. Thes struggled to find a topic of conversation.

"What is over the mountains?" he said at last.

"Which mountains?" she said.

There were only the mountains before them. His temper flared, but he choked it down. Perhaps she was not mocking him.

"There," he said, pointing at the horizon.

She glanced after his gesture.

"Selareme," she said. "If you go far enough."

"How far?" he said. This was news, a fixed point. If it had a name he could get there.

"Years," she said.

"Years is not a distance," he said, angry now, his voice rising.

She did not seem to recognize his anger. Her cool eyes remained on the distant mountains.

"The dlkii take years to bring us here from Selareme. We could not make the journey without them. How else should we measure it?"

"An engine caravan—"

"We have no engines," she said, over him. "I think you have no engines, either, but you have the memory of them."

"You don't know," he said. "We have engines. My father has one. I will get to Selareme without your stupid beasts."

She turned to him, then, her pale eyes empty.

"It is farther than you think," she said, and walked away from him across the dusty fields to her caravan.

Thes kicked at the pebbles beneath his feet.

She stopped and looked back.

"Are you coming?"

He scuffed at the dirt again for a few seconds before he followed her. The tiny bells on her clothing sang as she walked, and the wind pressed the loose folds against her legs and belly. Thes could not keep his eyes away from the shape of her.

The camp was quiet in the day's heat, and she led him around its skirts to an area behind the tents where the massive dlkii drowsed in the shade.

"Here," she said, and took his hand to place against a beast's warm hide. Thes rubbed his palm across the dlkii's flank, feeling the rough hair and loose skin. Even in the dust the animals smelled of grass.

"And here," she said, pulling his hand away from the animal's side and pressing it over her breast. She pushed into him, working her leg between his to get closer. He flushed, excited and embarrassed and unsure of where to put his other hand. He bent his head to kiss her but she turned her face away.

"Not that," she said.

Her hands burrowed under his clothes. "Like this," she said, and rocked her hips against him. Thes was too aware of the dlkii's warm breathing behind him, of the sun just beyond the shadows. He shoved her away, at once regretting it. He reached for her but his fingers only brushed her sleeve as she moved back.

She shook her head, and shifted inside her clothing.

"You don't want this? Do you want the other, then?"

He could not tell if she were dismissing him. His fists clenched against his sides.

"Why did you even come here?" he asked sharply. "You don't bring anything but fancy trash, nothing we can even use. Bring engines, if you're going to come. Bring tools, or fuel – not all this decoration."

Qarathamlimolo stood back from him. She reached up and smoothed her pale hair, her loose sleeves sliding down her thin brown arms in pools. Beads glittered and clinked under her hands. Her slender fingers worked free any tangles the wind had made. Thes watched her, angry and compelled. She would not look at him. He realized he had brought her to tears.

Thes left her there among the drowsing dlkii, running back to the familiarity of Miridaj's crumbling walls.

* * *

The Dlsarii would be gone before the rains came and turned the fields to yellow mud. They were packing already, drawing down the banners and folding away any tent not immediately in use. Children gathered to watch them leave as they had to watch them come. Thes watched, too, when he could leave his father's shop. There was a quality of ritual in witnessing the Dlsarii prepare to move on, as if they measured time for Miridaj. Now, the seasons could turn their slow wheel until the Dlsarii came again.

Thes was glad. He wanted to look at the eastern horizon again without seeing the bright tents between him and the mountains. Lim had come to him twice more after he refused her in the tent, but he let her, despite the awkwardness he felt. When she was gone he could let his fumblings with her fade into the dusty past.

He did not expect her to seek him out again. She was a shadow on the door, and then she was in the shop. She seemed always to know when he was alone there. He did not want to be alone with her, not any more.

She held out an oblong package wrapped in white cloth. He took it from her, wary of such gifts.

"It's a set of magnets," she said, not waiting for him to unwrap it. Then she reached into a deep pocket in her coat and pulled out a spool of green-crusted wire. She pressed it into his empty hand.

"Copper," she said. "You can use this, can't you?"

He looked at what he held, and his cheeks grew hot.

"We find things like this," she said. "Remnants. From before."

He closed his fingers around the spool. The metal warmed against his skin. When Thes was a child his father had told him about the fragments of old machines scattered between the cities, and showed him a small, frozen clockwork he had found while digging in the fields.

"This is what you want, isn't it?" she asked.

"Better than beads," he said, putting her gifts down on his workbench. He picked up a chisel and touched it to the spinning grindwheel, shutting her out as she stood there. Her hand lay on the door handle. The wheel whined down into a slow growl as the electricity sputtered and went out. Thes sighed and got out the hand file.

She shrugged, lingering, watching him. "You feed the dlkii and they work. There is no waiting for there to be power."

He stared at her.

"Why haven't you gone, already?" he said, stung.

Her mouth twisted down against tears.

"Soon enough," she said, and disappeared out the door. Bright sun slashed across the floor and was erased as the door swung shut behind her.

* * *

Thes locked the shop door as dusk came down, stood and stretched his cramped shoulders in the still-busy street. His father had left hours ago to tend Thes's mother. The dust was in her lungs. She had been coughing for weeks, it seemed, and was fading. Thes squinted up past the rooftops at the dimming sky. Soon it would rain. It would be better, then.

He dawdled. He didn't want to see his mother yet. His thoughts were still on the bag he had begun packing with extra clothes, food, and tools he would want when he left. If he left. He shook his head. When. *When.*

He had drifted aimlessly toward the end of the street when the pack of boys surged past him, and Ems came to a stuttering halt to grab his arm and drag him into it.

"Dlsarii girl," Ems panted. "Doesn't know she's out too late."

"Where?"

"Next street. We split, catch her that way."

Thes joined the hunt, blood in his eyes, thoughts of his leaving left behind.

They ran her down outside the city, in the grey dusty space between their walls and her caravan. If the Dlsarii heard her scream for help, they never answered. The younger boys swarmed over her, too many to fight. She jangled like chimes, her decorated hair and clothing tangled and ripped by too many hands. Dust smeared across her open mouth as she was driven into the ground, her face painted now in mud. Thes was not surprised to see Qarathamlimolo was the prey. She did not have the sense to stay away. At last she stopped fighting, and they did what they would. Thes closed his eyes, straying back from the scuffle. He did not try to stop them.

* * *

Years slid by under the slow tread of the dlkii before the Dlsarii wound their way back to Miridaj, materializing in the haze of the plains, distilled from the sun. They had crossed many mountain ranges, seen many cities built and rebuilt, passed news among them and traded and intermarried. It was Miridaj's time, again. And so they came.

Miridaj had changed very little. Its walls still slumped in places, its streets were still narrow and petered out into the fields. Thes's parents were long dead. The shop was his. He had not prospered, but he had not failed. He had his own wife, his own children who played in the oiled streets and ran in the dust outside the walls. The children were excited and impatient to see the visitors, but Thes had no interest in watching the Dlsarii come into his city again, dressed like legends as they walked through the market. He still had to work to keep out Lim's ghost.

He waited to leave for home until after he judged the Dlsarii had gone back to their tents. The air was blue with nightfall, and a thin wind had sprung up as the day's temperature cooled. He was surprised by a pale-haired boy waiting across the street from his shop. The boy crossed to meet him, staring flatly. Thes looked into a familiar face. This boy looked like Thes's other sons, but with the wash of his mother's coloring. His eyes were light, but not so icy, his skin tawny but not as brown. He must be around fourteen. Nearly grown. Thes put his hand in his pocket around the heavy clutch of keys there. He nodded slowly at the boy, admitting his claim.

"She told me you'd still be here," the boy said. "She said you'd never find an engine."

Thes frowned, a flicker of annoyance staining him.

"What did she name you?" he asked.

"Tevilsheniesdi," the boy said. Remembered music rolled with the word.

"None of mine in that," Thes said, half to himself.

The boy stood silently, as if waiting for Thes to do something. His eyes were veiled. Thes looked down at his hands. They were scarred and cut, the knuckles like knots. A cart rattled by in the cross street, its rough engine spitting fumes into the air. He looked up, over the boy's head.

"Go back to your mother," he said. "There's nothing here for you."

"She's gone on," the boy said.

"To Selareme?"

"Maybe. Maybe to Deskaniej out north. She leads where she wants."

"Well, then," said Thes.

Dust gritted in his teeth. The wind filled the air with it, and the mask hung around his neck could not filter it all out even if he wore it. After a while in silence he went back inside, leaving Lim's son to stay or go as he wished. Thes knew the boy was his. It was plain in his face. He did not need to stand and stare.

Ilis came in a moment behind him. Thes felt the weight of her eyes on him. He glanced up. She was silhouetted against the doorway, her shadowed face rimmed with yellow lamplight.

"I was wondering why you were so late. The boys said you never came home tonight. They said you let them go to the market alone."

He arranged his tools in neat lines on his workbench. "What do you want, Ilis?"

"Tell me how you come to have a Dlsari son," she said. "Tell me how his mother knew to bring him here, to our doorstep."

"Shut up," he said. "Get out of here."

She leaned against the doorframe, arms crossed tightly at her waist.

"If he stays he is yours alone. I have enough without raising another woman's child."

Thes flipped the switch for the grindwheel, hoping for electricity. The wheel spun slowly for half a turn before it stopped.

"Get out," he said again, but she had already slid out the door into the gathering night. Thes looked out the door at an empty street. The boy was gone. Thes didn't think he'd see that one again.

* * *

The mountains crouched on the far horizon like sleeping cats. The night blurred them, but their weight still pressed up against the starry sky. Thes turned his eyes away from them as he finally left the shop. He told himself they were only hills, and that the Dlsarii in their brightly lit tents had lied about the vastness of the world. He did not believe in Selareme.

Issa and the Gryphon

C.R. Serajeddini

ZAL'ISSA had never entered the forbidden library before.

The boy knew Anshan, the citadel that sat proudly amidst the mountains of Susiana, like a fortune teller might know the patterns that line the palm of their hand. He'd crawled its dusty paths and traced the cracks in its sandstone walls – at times in search of food, other times in search of a place to hide. He had even memorised the rotations of the market stalls, the guards' names, where they lived and where they rested at night. *Nobody* knew Anshan like Issa did.

Yet the library remained a mystery.

Once named the chambers of enlightenment, King Saam had shuttered its magnificent doors the same day his wife died giving birth to their stillborn child. Still, the building stood defiant under the watchful eyes of the granite gryphon roosting upon its roof. The Sina'mru, wise and benevolent. It had been a decade since the people of Anshan saw a real gryphon, but Issa searched the sky each night, and sometimes, he imagined its shadow flickering over the stars in the north.

Tearing his eyes from the stone beast, Zal'Issa edged closer to the building's side door, brushing slender fingers over its glazed bricks of many colours as he moved. He peered through the gap into the dark library. As his eyes adjusted, Issa caught sight of a figure silhouetted in warm lantern-light.

The librarian.

To enter the library was a crime worthy of the king's wrath. It was the librarian's duty to punish anyone who dared.

And tonight, Issa would steal from it.

Zal'Issa swallowed a sudden wave of nausea. *It is forbidden,* he'd pleaded with the apothecary.

Your very existence *is forbidden, zal. From your ghostly hair to your corrupt eyes, red and full of malice. Do you know what happens to zal children like you?*

The venom in Arsalan's croaking words echoed in Issa's mind and sent his pulse drumming against his ears – its rhythm reminding him of the magi's dafs when they circled their bonfires at solstice. Issa lowered his cap and wrapped his scarf tight around his neck. Steeling himself against his fears, the boy slipped through the small gap in the door.

The librarian was bent over his desk, and by the way he rocked back and forth, Issa guessed he was pressing marks into wet clay. The boy took slow, deliberate steps, the stone cool beneath his feet. He was used to melting into shadows. If he did not, the sun would punish him. If the sun did not, the people would.

Beyond the alcove is a hidden chamber, and within it a chest, Arsalan had said. *Bring me the item from the chest.*

Issa's gaze landed on an arch, shadow pooling beneath it. When he reached it, he spun into the darkness and took a settling breath before descending the stairs. A large door awaited him at the bottom, just as Arsalan had warned, barred with an iron lock. Retrieving the pin from inside his bag, Issa cupped the lock with one hand and set to work. He sucked in the stale air and felt his skin prickle with goosebumps, only daring to breathe again once the lock came undone, and he was able to push through the door.

Inside, stained glass lanterns hung from the ceiling, the tallow candles within them burning brightly. They cast colourful beams of light against a granite tomb laying in the middle of the chamber.

That, Issa thought, *was unexpected.* He rounded the tomb slowly until he reached a small chest at its foot. It gleamed with a copper so red it reminded Issa of the sun setting during summer solstice. *This is when we are nearest to light, to truth, Zal'Issa,* the magi had taught him. Issa shook away the memory of the magi for the second time that night. He knelt and opened the chest to find a canvas bundle, which he quickly lifted and stuffed into his bag. Next was a clay tablet. Issa picked it up with both hands and ran his fingers over the sharp scratches.

There can be no greater pain for a mother than to lose her child. We hear the Sina'mru's cries above the citadel at night as she searches for her lost one. I hope she finds it soon. Her song fills me with dread for my own child. Peace-bringer, the magi call him, before he is even born.

There, the tablet was broken, the rest of its text lost to time. Issa tucked it into his bag in case the apothecary needed it. All that remained was for him to flee the same way he came in.

Issa had pushed the door to the chamber shut but had not replaced the lock lest it make too much noise. When he reached the top of the stairs, he found the librarian still busy, so he retraced his steps through the shadows.

"I see you there."

Ice flooded Issa's veins; he pressed himself against the wall, barely swallowing the scream rising in his throat.

"It's alright." The librarian sighed. "I know Arsalan sent you. What did the apothecary offer you? Gold? Food? You're not the first thief he's sent, child."

Issa's heart sank. For the first time, he wondered if the apothecary had *not* found him by accident. "What happened to the others?"

"Never mind them. I must say I am impressed, child. I nearly didn't notice you. Come, take a seat." The man gestured to a wooden stool in front of his desk. "What did Arsalan promise you?"

Issa tightened his fists. He had to run. "Perhaps another time."

"Time! Different beings perceive time in different ways. Did you know that?"

"No."

"There's a tree in Vourukasha. It's primordial. It is said that its roots extend so far into the earth, they branch out to touch every living plant in the world. How fleeting must our lives seem, to such an aged being?"

Issa licked his lips and eyed the gap in the door. "The tree does not think, so how could it measure the passage of time? Its long life is wasted."

The librarian chuckled at that. Then the sound of wood scraping against stone tore through the air and warned Issa it was time to run. The boy clenched his jaws and leapt the last few feet towards the door.

"I'm not your enemy!"

Issa slid to a halt, hands gripping the door frame either side, heart kicking against his ribs. He turned slowly and scanned the figure standing by the desk properly for the first time: An old man, not fat, but also not starved. Rich silks draped his shoulders and grey hair fell from beneath his cap. A woven satchel of many colours hung over his shoulder, and a pair of half-moon spectacles sat on the bridge of his nose. Even from here Issa could tell the old man smelt of damp clay and musty parchment.

"I won't stop you from leaving," the librarian said, holding out his hands as though to prove he was unarmed. "But it's impossible for you to steal from this place. Come speak with me, and I won't inform the authorities of your visit."

Issa's mind screamed for him to run, yet curiosity would not let him. "What do you mean, *impossible*?"

The librarian waved his hands in the air dismissively. "The lock is enchanted. It will only open for myself or for the king of Elam. The whole library is enchanted."

Issa frowned. "You're lying."

"How would you know?" The old man cocked his head to one side. "Have you tested the lock? Stolen something?"

Issa tensed. "Enchantments are not real."

"I have stories that might change your mind."

"Stories?"

"There are so many stories locked away in my old brain." The librarian tapped a finger against his temple. "They become a burden if they're not shared."

Issa watched the old man carefully. "You are supposed to punish those who enter the library."

"I never liked the idea of punishments." He grimaced. "Don't tell anyone. I have a reputation to keep."

Issa smiled despite himself. "You are not from Anshan. You sound different." He shook his head. "I do not believe you're from Elam at all. Perhaps not even from Persia."

"Well observed."

Issa stepped closer, but the weight of the satchel against his thigh made him stop. "You're not even from Babylon. Where are you from?"

The librarian's eyes twinkled in the dim lantern light. "Perhaps a more important question, my time-conscious friend, is where are *you* from? Where are you going?" He lifted a finger. "But first, what's your name?"

Issa clutched the strap of his satchel. "Some call me Zal."

"*Pale.* Is that what you call yourself?" The librarian squinted. "You may remove your cap. I'm not afraid of you."

"You should be," Issa whispered. "They say I'm a son of Ahriman."

"The *devil*?" The Librarian turned around casually and returned to his seat. "Are you boasting, or sharing a burden?"

Issa wasn't sure what to say – instead, he removed his cap and approached the desk. Only when the librarian sat and folded his arms across the desk did Issa dare sit on the wooden stool opposite him. The boy placed his satchel on his lap and held it close. "I prefer Issa."

The librarian leaned forward. "A nice name. Do you know what it means?"

Issa shrugged. "The magi named me."

The edge of the librarian's lips quivered, as though he were suppressing a smile. "I don't believe you're a son of Ahriman, Issa. Where I'm from, you're not deemed a demon. Just a boy. Unique, yes. Albino, or zal, as you say, but a boy, nonetheless."

Issa could not hold the burst of bitter laughter that escaped his lips. It echoed around the chamber, mocking him. His chest tightened – a sudden sensation, like vines wrapping around his lungs. "Where is this place?"

The librarian gave a sad smile. "Far away. But you don't belong there."

Issa's gaze flitted to a beam of moonlight creeping through a splintered shutter. At night, when the markets had packed away and the people locked their doors, when even the orioles slept, Issa would dare take off his cap and scarf and walk the streets of the citadel freely. The scents of night-jasmine and baked sand filled his nostrils, making him feel as though the city was dead, and he was the only one left alive. He looked back to the librarian.

"Where do I belong? Is this where I belong? Do you know what will happen to me if I am caught?"

The librarian nodded. "You would be exiled to Hara'borz."

Hara'borz, the frozen mountain at the beginning of time. Issa would become an offering, a sacrifice to the Sina'mru.

"Arsalan promised that if I retrieve something for him, he would provide me with a cure."

"Arsalan lied. Had you stolen what he asked for, he would have called the city guards."

Issa tightened his fists around the bundle in his bag. It was the librarian who was lying, he was sure of it. He had already lied about the not-enchanted lock.

"What about you?" Issa asked. "With this wealth of knowledge, surely you could tell me of a cure."

The old man's eyes softened. "You do not need a cure."

"I'm cursed." Issa scoffed. "Even my own mother hated me. My father wished me dead."

"No, Issa. Your mother did not hate you."

Issa bit his bottom lip to stop it from trembling. The librarian's gaze burnt hot in the dim light, and Issa felt it burning through his soul. "How could you know that?"

"I know many things."

"My only mother is Anshan. Her walls protect me. Lead me to food hidden in the dirt. Anshan is my home, and if I am exiled from my home, I will have nothing."

"Then you act out of fear."

Issa wished desperately that his heart would slow to its normal rhythm. Why hadn't he fled?

"The apothecary found me sleeping in the messenger's stables. He threatened to take me to the guards."

The man had twisted Issa's tunic and spat in his face. He'd dragged him across the sharp dirt path, Issa's knees and arms scraping against the stones until they were raw. When he'd pleaded, Arsalan gave him a choice. *Do you know what happens to zal children like you?*

The librarian lifted his woven satchel from around his shoulders and placed it onto the desk with a thunk. "How about those stories? You can read the first one." He reached into his bag and pulled out a small clay tablet with crumbled corners and slid it across the desk to Issa.

Issa watched with wide eyes. How could the librarian change subjects so easily? When the librarian watched back, his brows raised in anticipation, Issa cleared his throat and read:

"'The Sina'mru resided by the lake atop Hara'borz. Her copper feathers gleamed by moonlight as they did in the sun. Before her desolation, the day upon which she lost her children, she often took flight and visited the realms of men. She spread wisdom and kindness. She protected the weak, and championed the innocent, and her tears brought healing and long life to all in the Citadel of Anshan.'"

Issa stopped at the last word and glanced up at the librarian. The tablet he'd read from inside the chest had mentioned the gryphon's loss too. "What happened to her children?"

The old man grunted. "Perhaps the next tablet will tell us." He reached into his woven satchel and removed another tablet, blowing off a thick layer of dust before sliding it across to Issa.

"'When king Saam heard the gryphon's cry, he assembled a party to travel to Hara'borz. There he found and fought the bandits who had set out for the gryphon. It was too late. Her eggs had perished, and the Sina'mru, that beast that once spread wisdom, now left heartbroken and desolate, turned against all men. They fled, none daring to return to Hara'borz but to leave sacrifices, offerings for the beast.

"'When the king returned, he was informed by his advisors that his wife had died giving birth to their son.'" Issa's heart sank as he remembered the words inscribed into the tablet he'd found. "'The king commanded that a burial chamber be built for his wife and son within the Chambers of Enlightenment, a place that the queen loved most in all the world. They rest under the watchful eyes of a stone Sina'mru. None may disturb them.'"

Issa's voice trembled as he finished the last sentence. He pushed the tablet away and wrapped his hands around his bag. "What did the bandits want with a gryphon?" *What do I have in my bag?*

"I've always suspected Arsalan of sending the bandits. Alas—" he sighed, "—I don't have proof. Have you time for another tale?"

Issa nodded, and the librarian took yet another tablet from his satchel. When Issa felt its weight, he frowned.

"What?"

"You must have strong shoulders," he said, "and a stronger bag. Do you always carry these tablets with you?"

The librarian's mouth curled up into a wide smile. "Read."

"'Gilgamesh, the king of Uruk, travelled far and wide in search of the elixir. In the end, he did not find it in the bottom of the sea, nor in distant lands. He returned to Uruk older, closer to death, and empty handed, yet he was no longer afraid of death. His heart was at peace. Wisdom, Gilgamesh had realised, was a greater gift than immortality.'

"This one was not about the Sina'mru."

The librarian nodded. "Gilgamesh spent years searching for an elixir of immortality, motivated by fear of death. He never found it, Issa. Just as you will never find an elixir to change who you are. Gilgamesh found peace and wisdom. He found that life would not be precious, if it were not so fleeting. And you, child, must not fear who you are. Your distinctiveness is not a weakness, though it makes you a target for those who are ignorant. You can, and you will, I believe, use it to change *their* hearts."

"Change their hearts?" Issa shook his head. "How?"

The librarian's eyes glistened. "You'll find a way."

But Issa already knew the way. The items the apothecary needed for creating his cure sat burning in his lap. "You have shown me that enchantments are not real," he whispered.

"Indeed? Reach into the satchel and take out the next tablet."

Curious, Issa pulled the librarian's colourful satchel towards him, feeling its feather-light weight. "It's empty."

"It looks that way," the librarian said, frowning. "Try anyway."

Issa wasn't sure what the librarian hoped to achieve, but he did as he was told. When his hands fell on rough stone, he froze. The empty bag now felt heavy. "*How*?"

"Read it."

When Issa removed the tablet, he saw that the bottom edge of the stone had crumbled, as though it had once been part of a bigger piece. He recognised it as the tablet he'd stolen, and barely stifled a gasp. Issa ran his fingers over the familiar words again:

There can be no greater pain for a mother than to lose her child. We hear the Sina'mru's cries above the citadel at night as she searches for her lost one.

Issa shot up, knocking his stool against the stone floor and nearly stumbling over it. "I must leave," he blurted.

Issa ran through the cool night until the library was out of sight, then he felt inside his bag for the bundle and sighed in relief when he found it was still there. He started towards the apothecary's home, knowing that the librarian would soon find his enchanted lock unlocked and send the city's guards after him. *It is impossible for you to steal from this place.* Issa scoffed at the memory of the librarian's words. As he neared Arsalan's house, he reached into the bag and lifted the canvas bundle out, and that's when he noticed that the tablet was missing.

What if the librarian had been telling the truth? What if the apothecary planned to trick him?

The librarian is a liar, he told himself, yet his heart remained unconvinced. Issa didn't know how the librarian managed to retrieve the tablet, but it made him wonder why he had not retrieved the bundle in the same way.

Issa peeled back the canvas cloth to reveal the item Arsalan had asked for.

Within lay a granite-dark egg, its copper-veined shell shimmering beneath the starlight. It suddenly felt heavier in his hands, as though knowing what it was brought it to life somehow. *The librarian had suspected Arsalan.*

Issa continued to the apothecary's house. He knocked once, twice, then backed away to a safe distance.

A few moments later, the old man appeared. His expression changed when he spotted Issa, a flicker of surprise passing over his features at the sight of the precious bundle in Issa's hands.

"You found it," he hissed, stepping forward, but before he could get closer, Issa turned and ran.

The boy's feet slapped against the dirt and the apothecary chased him, cursing. Issa did not stop until he reached the third alley from the library, which ended at the back of a tall building. There was nowhere else to go.

"You sent the bandits to get the gryphon's eggs. Many years ago," Issa yelled at Arsalan.

The apothecary snarled. "Give me the egg, boy."

"Tell me, and you may have it," Issa yelled again, his heart hammering in his chest. If he had not calculated his paths correctly, he would end this night dead in the back alleys of Anshan, its dirt paths soaking his blood.

"Yes!" Arsalan hissed. "The gryphon's egg holds unimaginable power. The king found the last remaining one on his way back. But he wouldn't let me have it. He insisted on keeping it *safe*." His eyes softened. "You've done well. Give me the egg, and I'll heal you from your illness."

Issa tucked the egg into his bag. "No," he whispered. Then the sound of footsteps shuffling out from the darkness startled them both. In that moment, Issa was more afraid than he had been in his whole life, but he could not hold his smile as he watched cold realisation dawn on Arsalan's face.

Nobody knew Anshan like Issa did.

The apothecary pointed at Issa. "He's a thief!"

"We heard everything, Arsalan," one of the guards boomed. They surrounded him quicker than Issa could have anticipated. The guard's resthouse was the building behind Issa, and he had known that their shutters would be open.

"He stole from the library!"

"That's impossible, Arsalan."

Issa recognised the new voice, but his heart skipped a beat inside his chest when he saw the librarian.

"The library's enchanted. Only I, the king, or his heir can take from the library. And we all know you delivered the king's stillborn child ten years ago. Didn't you, Arsalan?"

Issa's head swam. He reached for the egg, taking it out and clutching it against his chest. He felt its warmth, traced its copper veins with his fingertips. *There can be no greater pain for a mother than to lose her child.*

"The child is a *zal!*" Arsalan spat, and Issa felt as though the pain in his throat would choke him.

Do you know what happens to zal children like you?

"They go to Hara'borz," Issa whispered.

"What?"

Issa lifted his gaze to find Arsalan, the librarian, and the guards all staring at him. He gripped his cap and threw it off, letting his white hair gleam in the moonlight. "Take me to Hara'borz," Issa yelled. "Take me to Hara'borz, and I will return the gryphon's egg."

And he knew in his heart that the Sina'mru would welcome him.

The Tower Calls

Zach Shephard

LUCY'S BLOODIED FINGERS groped under the starlight, seeking the next handhold in the rock. She pulled herself another few feet up the wall.

High above, the summit loomed: a sharp black edge where the desert's stars stopped. Lucy clung to the rock spire with fading strength, arms trembling. Finishing the climb felt like the longest path to relief. Letting go, however…

She shook dark thoughts away. They scattered without going far, like flies buzzing about her head. She had to focus. Somewhere at the top, the Tower called, whispering promises of a better life.

The call from below was less inviting.

At first it was quiet – just a low growl in the distance. Lucy had heard it throughout the climb, somewhere on the desert clay. It patrolled back and forth like a lion beneath a tree, wondering where its trembling prey had fled.

All at once, the predator figured it out.

The growl turned into a deep roar. A breath rushed up to Lucy like arctic wind, chilling her sweat-slickened skin.

The climb became a sprint. Lucy didn't even look back: she knew what was chasing her. It had been on the hunt her entire life.

In her haste, a mistake: Lucy's legs shot out and she lost her grip. A single hand was all that kept her on the wall. Dangling there in the night, she felt like a fishing lure for the thing below.

The thing. Lucy couldn't help but look.

The formless mass rose like billowing smoke, dark against the blue of night. Its storm-cloud jaws opened, rimmed with pointed, wispy teeth. Lucy flinched, like a dog before a familiar belt. She didn't want to feel that bite. Not again.

She redoubled her efforts, scrambling up the wall. If she could just reach the Tower, she'd be safe. Things were different there – no pain, no monsters. That's what the book had said.

Above, a rainbow glow bled over the cliff's edge, waving like the northern lights. Lucy reached for the shifting colors as though they were a helping hand, there to pull her up.

She heaved herself over the edge. Rolling onto her back, she closed her eyes and smiled through heavy breaths. Safe at last. She'd reached the fabled sanctuary of Dwest, where troubles were a myth and no beast could harm her. The sounds of a bustling crowd turned her head.

A city of dark glass and colorful lights sprawled before her. Sleek buildings flanked the thoroughfare up ahead, their windowed façades twinkling with reflected stars. Lucy recalled her vacation with Zane to the Las Vegas Strip, where carefree pedestrians wandered from one social hotspot to the next. But these weren't normal people milling about. They were starfolk: paper dolls cut from the night sky, protected by the Tower at the end of the road.

The distant pedestrians didn't seem to notice Lucy, but the coyote did.

It was cut from the same cosmic cloth as the people up the street, a sparkling nebula in canine form. Lucy realized the coyote wasn't the only of its kind in the city: others wandered among the starfolk, under the rainbow lights, walking as equals. The one who'd noticed Lucy watched her with shining eyes like a binary star system. She smiled, and it smiled back. Then its eyes went wide, brightening like synchronized supernovas. The coyote yipped, but the warning wasn't fast enough.

It felt like a bear trap clamping over Lucy's leg, just above the ankle. She screamed not from the sensation itself, but from the surprise. The pain was, after all, familiar. She just hadn't expected it. Not in Dwest.

The dark cloud whipped Lucy side to side, raking her across the sandstone in its stormy jaws. It pulled her toward the ledge, like a shark dragging a diver off the boat's ladder. Lucy clawed at the rock. She yelled for help. Someone yelled back.

"Lucy!"

A starry man rushed toward her, the coyote at his side. He reached forth with a constellation-hand. She stretched out to grab it.

...And it was gone, Lucy watching the distance between them stretch into infinity. Over the edge she went, grasping for receding stars. Her scream faded through the desert air, dragged down by the stormy dark.

* * *

Lucy snapped awake. The consuming cloud, wrapped all about her, had been traded for bedsheets. The erstwhile starscape was now the plain darkness of her bedroom ceiling.

She groped for her phone and dialed Zane.

"Well, hi," he said, a familiar smile in his voice.

"I had a bad dream."

The smile switched to concern. "Oh, Noodle – I'm sorry. Tell me about it?"

Lucy did. She struggled through the ending.

"Yikes," Zane said. "I'm starting to wonder if that book was such a good idea."

"Hey," Lucy said, wiping her eyes with a tissue, "I *love* that book. And I haven't thanked you for it recently. So, again: thank you."

"Well I'm glad you like it, but if I'd known it was going to give you nightmares, I would have gotten you something else. Heck, just the other day I saw a great porcelain frog in an antique shop. He was wearing a straw hat and holding a sign that said 'Discount Beets, Next Left'. One of his feet was missing, and some amateur taxidermist had tried to cover it up by supergluing a thimble to the stump. Looked like the little guy had stepped into a bucket and gotten stuck. Yep – in hindsight, I really screwed up. Stumpy the Beet-Peddler would have been a much better three-month anniversary gift. I'm sorry I gave you the Tome of Endless Nightmares instead."

Lucy smiled around her tissue. She shook her head in the dark. "I don't know how you do that."

"Do what?"

"A few minutes ago, I woke up crying. Now I'm laughing. You're magical, Z."

"Hey, not so loud! I'm practicing without a license. The State Sorcery Board is gonna confiscate my wand."

Another smile from Lucy. She pulled the phone away to check the time.

"Hey!" she said. "It's five o'clock. Why are you awake?"

"Because there's this woman I'm crazy about, and I once told her she could call at any time, for any reason."

"Wait. I woke you up at 4:40 in the morning, and you just listened patiently while I rambled on about a stupid dream?"

"Yep."

"And then you cheered me up with jokes?"

"That was the hope."

A silent pause.

"I love you, Z."

"Love you too, Noodle."

Lucy thanked Zane for listening and they said their goodbyes. As she tried getting comfortable again, she felt a sharp pain above her left ankle – right where the dream-beast had clamped down. She sat up and turned the light on. A bead of blood rolled down her leg.

Cursing under her breath, she peeled back the bandage. The bite was two weeks old – it had looked almost healed yesterday. Why was it bleeding again? Being a vet tech was fulfilling work, but the strays were often unpredictable. That dog had seemed so friendly until the nip.

Lucy wiped the blood up with a tissue and reaffixed the bandage. When she went to leave the bed, she spotted the slim book on her nightstand: *The Lost City of Dwest: Legends of the Starfolk*. No copyright page, no publisher. Not even an author's name. Lucy wondered how long Zane had spent scouring the internet for that rare treasure, just so she could learn more about the place from her dreams.

She lay back down and opened the book. Changing the bandage could wait – she had a chapter to re-read.

* * *

The server brought two steaming bowls of ramen to the table. Lucy thanked her, while Mateo got straight to slurping.

"I don't get it," Mateo said, his mouth full. "Even if this dumb city were real, why would you want to go there?"

Where could Lucy start? According to the book, Dwest was a perfect utopia. The starfolk didn't have a care in the world: no violence, crime, poverty, hunger. They believed everyone was born with a purpose, up for the individual to discover. This passion for life removed any need for currency: the tailors made clothing not to earn a living, but because they loved their craft; the restaurateurs fed the city simply for the joy of cooking. Less desirable roles were handled by machines or magic. And many starfolk lacked a traditional 'job': their purpose was to consume literature, or daydream, or be the light in another's life. No individual's choice was frowned upon, because everyone was content with their own role. All were equal in the Tower.

The Tower – that's where Dwest resided. A tall, narrow spire of rock, like a skyscraper rising from desert clay. The city lay within – not at the top, like in Lucy's dream. Where had she gotten that idea? Maybe she'd just been thinking of Zane, and their Vegas trip had bled into her vision of Dwest. Dreams were strange like that.

There was so much she could have told Mateo about the city in the spire, or the resident starfolk, or their bond with the desert coyotes. But she knew her best friend's attention easily waned, and that he was often less curious than his questions suggested. So she kept the answer simple.

"There's no sadness there," Lucy said. Hunching over a spoonful of ramen, she quietly added: "No dark clouds."

Mateo shrugged, slurping noisily. "Sounds pretty dumb to me. But if it makes you happy, go for it. How're you supposed to find the place?"

"I don't know. The book didn't include a map. I guess I just drive toward the desert and hope for the best."

"Well, you shouldn't go alone. But I can't join because my mom and brother are still fighting. Plus, I just don't want to. So at least make your internet boyfriend go with you."

"Do you think he would?"

"Pretty sure that dude would do anything for you."

Lucy raised an eyebrow. "I thought you didn't like him."

"I don't like anyone. But he at least treats you good."

It was certainly a pleasant thought: going on a road trip with Zane. But he'd just flown out to visit last month. Lucy didn't want to ask him to travel again so soon.

"How *is* your family, anyway?" she asked.

"Same as usual. Fighting over nothing."

"I'll call your brother later. And maybe your mom after that. See what we can figure out."

"Thanks. I'd do it myself, but…"

"But you know I'll take care of it."

"Hey, it's not my fault you're the best at this stuff."

"Don't worry," she said, smiling despite the exhaustion inside. "I've got you."

After lunch Lucy headed to the animal hospital, where she assisted in a canine kidney transplant. It was supposed to be her day off, and the procedure was much more demanding than her usual work, but Dr. Juarez needed the help. By the time she called Zane during her drive home, she was beat.

"It was just a lot," Lucy said, after detailing the day's events. "And I had to stay late to convince Dr. Juarez to go to her therapy tomorrow. She won't do it unless I make her."

"Yikes. Sorry, Noodle. Sounds like you could use some pampering. Want me to come over? There may not be any flights headed your way tonight, but I could probably commandeer one of the ducks from my pond."

Lucy smiled. It would certainly be nice to fall asleep in Zane's arms tonight. Being with him always made the dark cloud more bearable. "You have no idea how much I'd like that. Wish you were here, Z. I'd make you go Dwest-hunting with me."

"Oh, yeah? Been digging into the book more?"

"Mmhm. I know it's probably just a fairy tale, but it seems so real in my dreams. I'd love to go looking for the place, even if I never found it. I just need a break from life."

Lucy turned onto her block, daydreaming of Dwest. She realized Zane was quiet.

"Z? You still there?"

"Yeah, sorry. I was buying a ticket."

"For what?"

"The next duck out of this joint. Mind if I come over this weekend?"

"Wait," Lucy said, parking in front of her house. "Seriously?"

"Well, sure. If you're gonna go seeking out lost civilizations, you should at least have a traveling buddy. Whaddaya say? Together-adventure?"

"Yes! Of course!" Lucy practically skipped up her front walk. There was a paper bag by the door; she looked inside.

"Z," Lucy said. "There's a bowl of orange chicken on my front step. With broccoli and rice. From my favorite place."

"Is it still warm?"

She held the bag to her chest, sighing contentedly. "Yes."

"Oh, good. Then I don't have to send an angry duck to rough-up a delivery driver."

She shook her head in disbelief. "You remembered I had the transplant surgery today. You knew I'd be too exhausted to feed myself."

"I have no idea what you're talking about. Also, sorry it wasn't noodles. But when you said you were having ramen with Mateo, I figured you might want some variety."

"It's perfect. You're too good to me, Z."

"Considering all that you do for other people, you deserve this sort of treatment from everyone. Love you, Noodle. And I'll see you tomorrow."

Lucy stowed her phone and took a deep breath from the bag's dinner-smells. She smiled and stepped inside. As she turned to close the door, she saw a dog across the street, watching from beneath a streetlight. It looked like the stray who'd bit her weeks ago.

"Hey, pal. Did you get loose again?"

The streetlight flickered and went out. Two twinkling sparkles floated in the dark, where the dog's eyes had been. They moved, as of a dog cocking its head.

The light came back on. The sidewalk was empty.

* * *

It was a sound like a wrecking ball crashing into a mountainside. The world shook, jostling Lucy awake.

She sat up on the cold clay earth. A glass obelisk encased her, wide as a living room and stretching into the starry sky. A small campfire at its center illuminated cracks high in the glass. Outside, distant mountains stood like frozen waves atop the desert floor.

Another thunderous slam rattled the world. Chips of glass rained around Lucy. She turned to see a familiar dark cloud, its head tilted sideways to grasp the obelisk with wispy teeth. Eel-shaped, with an eyeless jack-o-lantern head, the thing wriggled about like it wanted to rip the entire structure from the ground. From the way the glass splintered, it was more likely to just snap the obelisk in half.

The cloud released its grip. It fixated on Lucy for a moment, then swam swiftly away through the air. At the edge of vision, it turned.

The cloud covered the distance in an instant, slamming into the obelisk like a battering ram. A crack shot down the glass, forking as it reached the bottom. A triangle-shaped chunk fell out of the wall, leaving a torso-sized hole.

"Hey!" a voice said. "Over here!"

Lucy turned. Outside the obelisk, opposite the cloud, stood a man cut from the night sky: the same one from her dream, who'd tried grabbing her hand as she'd gone over the ledge. He waved his arms to draw the cloud's attention. In his hand was a constellation-sword, its stars and lines burning sharp white.

"Take this to her," he said, kneeling next to a familiar cosmic coyote. He plucked a shining star, marble-sized, from the nebula of his own chest. The coyote took it in its mouth and sprinted around the obelisk, opposite the direction the cloud was now rushing from.

Roiling darkness lunged at the man, thwarted only by a last-second swing of his star-blade. The formless beast recoiled, growling like thunder in the distant canyons. It attacked again and again, each snap of its jaws defended with timely cuts. The star-man kept his back to the obelisk while the cloud darted side to side, looking for an opening.

The coyote came through the triangle-hole on the opposite wall. Lucy knelt and accepted the star from its mouth.

"I don't know what to do with it!" she said. The obelisk shook from a misaimed attack of the cloud. She glanced back at the fight. It wasn't looking good.

The coyote tapped a paw against her chest. Lucy held the star to that spot.

She felt a silvery glow rush through her. Hurricane winds shot from within her core, tilting her head back and thrusting her sternum forward. Her hair danced on the air like groping tendrils.

"My hand!" the man outside yelled. "Take my hand!" He placed a starry palm against the glass, still facing his relentless opponent. Lucy placed hers over it.

Silver starlight flared from the point of connection, so bright it washed out the world. A dark beast growled in pain, hardly audible against the din of the raging storm.

Lucy woke panting. She went to call Zane, but stopped: if she really wanted, she could tell him about the dream tomorrow, in person.

He couldn't get there soon enough.

* * *

Lucy would never forget the day they first met. She especially liked the way Zane told the story.

When I saw her speed-walking up to the airport, I couldn't believe it was finally happening. We'd spent weeks fantasizing about holding each other, and now there she was, just on the other side of the glass, about to make that dream a reality. I looked down at my phone to end our call as Lucy reached the doors. She must have sprinted those last twenty feet, because I didn't even see her final approach.

You'd think I'd regret glancing away, but – no. Things were perfect the way they happened. One moment I was standing alone, and the next my love was up against me, arms wrapped around my torso. Like she'd always been there. Like we'd known each other our entire lives. I kissed her atop the head, and we held each other a long while in silence.

Then came the first words she ever spoke to me in person, her voice muffled against my chest:

"You're real."

If anyone should have been in disbelief, it was me. There's no one in the world like Lucy Hendrake.

Ever since, they'd always greeted each other the same way. Lucy would rush up to Zane, feeling her dark cloud fall further behind with every step. She'd wrap her arms around him and bury her head in his chest. After a time, she'd say, "You're *still* real."

This occasion was no different, with the airport greeting followed by an arm-in-arm walk to Lucy's car. They spent the evening in bed, where they caught up, ate microwaveable mac and cheese, and held each other in tranquil silence. Zane's touch was just as gentle as Lucy remembered. They talked about Dwest as they cuddled, until Lucy drifted off.

The next day they set out for the desert. Zane drove, knowing Lucy had had a long week. When they stopped for gas, he asked the cashier if they knew the way to Dwest. Lucy hugged his arm tight, appreciating him for humoring her.

After a dinner of chicken noodle soup at a roadside diner, Lucy snoozed in the passenger seat. She woke when the ride got bumpy. Rubbing her eyes, she took in the desert scenery.

Dry mountains lay on the horizon like the corpses of slain giants, silhouetted against the starscape. Hoodoos stood as rocky pillars without a roof. Cracked clay zipped by beneath the car, with no road in sight.

"Where are we?" Lucy asked. When Zane didn't answer, she looked his way. He had a racecar driver's grip on the wheel, and his gaze was fixed on the rear-view mirror. Lucy turned.

Through the SUV's back window, she saw it under the starlight: a great dark cloud, distant but closing fast. Its mouth split like an opening bear trap.

"No," Lucy said. "No no no. This isn't real. I'm dreaming."

"Do me a favor?" Zane asked. "Keep your eyes ahead, let me know if I'm gonna drive us into anything. I've got this guy to worry about."

He swerved, jostling Lucy side to side.

"Whoever left a rock there is fired." Zane spared a hand from the wheel to give hers a squeeze. "That's the sort of thing I'm talking about. I'm not a good enough driver to do this on my own. Think you could help me out, Noodle?"

Lucy couldn't find the words, but she did manage a nod.

"Great," Zane said, smiling despite the circumstances. The expression faded as he re-gripped the wheel and navigated them into a small canyon. A deep roar rushed through the channel, vibrating the car's windows. Lucy resisted the impulse to look back.

"I know this is scary," Zane said, "but we're gonna be fine. We always said 'together-everything', right? This is just together-driving. You watch the front, I'll watch the bac—"

"Look out!"

A feline shape pounced from atop the canyon, up ahead. Zane swerved to dodge it, scraping his side of the SUV against the wall. Lucy flew hard into her seatbelt as they crashed to a stop. She and Zane reached for each other.

"Are you okay?" they said.

The sound of a scuffle answered them. Painted red by the brake lights, the cloud swirled about and snapped its jaws at an agile assailant. The panther was slender and lithe, with sharp, angular features, like a geometric statue stretched disproportionately long. It darted around the cloud, twice as quick, dropping low before every pounce.

Zane tried to get the car moving – no luck. He unbuckled his seatbelt. "We've gotta go," he said. "Like, now."

Zane's door was pinned against the canyon wall, so they both exited on Lucy's side. She looked back at the ongoing scuffle. "He saved us," she said.

"Not exactly." Zane climbed onto the SUV's hood. "The cloud is yours. The cat's mine. I don't wanna be around when they figure out they're on the same side."

"*What?*"

Zane stood tall on the hood and reached overhead with one arm. He pounded the side of his fist against the sky, like he was knocking the static out of an old TV set. A shower of stars fell to the ground, outlining a road through the canyon. They were no longer silver when they landed, instead giving off a rainbow glow that softly transitioned through the spectrum.

"Stay on the path," Zane said, taking Lucy's hand. They ran.

Out of the canyon and into the open desert, colorful spots of light waving at either side. The road led to a tower of rock up ahead. Lucy pointed.

"Is that—"

A massive shape careened off an invisible barrier overhead. Colored light rippled from the point of impact, as though someone had thrown a stone into a rainbow pond. The concentric waves outlined an unseen passageway; Lucy felt like she was in an aquarium tunnel. The attacking shape swooped off somewhere.

"Can't slow down," Zane said. "The shield won't hold forever."

The next time the shape came, Lucy saw its approach. It was the same geometric panther as before – carved from turquoise, she now noticed – its head hidden within a toothy black cloud. More cloud wisps snaked about its body like clinging fog, extending into a set of griffin wings. The nightmare-horror dove into the barrier once more, up ahead. Rainbows rippled under its cloud-teeth as it chewed the invisible ceiling. Glassy bits fell like a beaded curtain.

Zane pulled Lucy to a stop.

"Okay," he said. "We may need a different approach."

He flicked his hand out to the side like a magician summoning a card from his sleeve. A sword extended into his grip, made up of diamond-bright stars connected by constellation lines. He charged forward.

"Zane!" Lucy ran after him.

The nightmare-horror made a big enough hole to reach through with one feline arm, coiled in cloud. Zane swung his star-blade into the turquoise paw. The creature retracted with a growl and hiss that came from two different throats. Lucy seized the opportunity and ran by, pulling Zane along with her.

The rocky tower grew nearer. The next time the nightmare-horror attacked, it hit the tunnel hard enough to shake the earth. Zane stumbled and fell outside the path, unaffected by the barrier. His sword clattered to the ground.

Lucy watched the nightmare-horror leap over to Zane's side of the path, landing past him. It turned to face him. Zane froze on his belly, staring at that eyeless, cloudy visage.

"Lucy," Zane said calmly, not taking his gaze off the stalking hunter. "Please stay on the path."

Lucy left the path.

She scooped up the star-blade and put herself between Zane and the pouncing attacker. Her first swing separated two cloudy teeth from the thing's maw, sending them to dissipate on the desert air. Her second carved a new line into the cat's geometric forelimb. It retreated with another growl-hiss, the wound sparkling with stardust. Lucy didn't let the monster out of her sight as she helped Zane up. They got back on the path and ran.

"Lucy?" Zane said as they reached the base of the tower. "I asked you not to leave the path." He moved one hand in an arc before the rock, and a star-lined doorway opened before them. He looked to Lucy. "Thanks for not listening to me."

Through the doorway and into the tower, a sound of shattering glass behind them.

* * *

"All right," Zane said, as a starry-smiled server delivered two hot chocolates to their table outside the cafe. "I have some explaining to do."

"I'll say," Lucy said, gaze raised as she took it all in.

They sat inside the hollow Tower of Dwest, with its rock walls of striped orange-beige. It was like a multi-level shopping mall, with an empty core in the middle and establishments around the edges. Circular platforms of stone rose and lowered through the floors, ferrying starfolk and coyotes between levels. Lucy couldn't count how many stories high the Tower went. The ceiling was a window to the night sky.

"First of all, I'm sorry," Zane said. "I wanted to tell you. I just didn't know how."

"You could have said: 'Hi, I'm Zane. My interests include board games and writing. Also, I'm a star-man from a secret civilization.'"

Zane raised an eyebrow over the brim of his mug.

"Okay," Lucy said. "I can see how that would be a bit much. Especially coming from a man I met in the comments section of my Instagram page. Still. A near-death experience in the desert seems like a weird way to break the news."

"That was definitely not the plan. You shouldn't have been in any danger. That's not how dreams work here."

"I'm gonna need you to explain that."

Zane set his mug down, cupped in both hands. "Dreams feel a little more real in Dwest than in the outside world. Which, for the most part, is great. Problem is, the bad ones get the reality treatment too. But the Tower protects us from nightmares. They get banished to the outside, where they just sort of lurk nearby. They're not a threat unless you plan on leaving the city, and even then, you can't be hurt by someone else's dreams – only your own."

"So I was in danger, then. That cloud was my nightmare."

"That's just it, though. You're not Dwestian. Your dream shouldn't have manifested at all, let alone merged with mine. I don't know how it happened."

Lucy sipped her chocolate. Some of the people around her looked like the starfolk of her dreams – person-shaped pieces of the night sky, full of tiny bright sparkles – but many looked like Zane. Some transitioned from one form to the other as she watched, like a hand-mirror twisted to catch the sun's glare. The coyotes were the same way.

"I really wouldn't have brought you if I'd thought you could've been hurt," Zane said. "I hope you know that."

"I do."

"Hell, for a while I didn't think I'd bring you here at all. We don't exactly advertise the place to outsiders. But after we'd been talking for a while, you said something that really stuck with me: 'The universe sent you to me as a gift. I'm convinced.'"

Lucy remembered the comment. She'd decided one night that the universe had custom-made Zane for her, as an apology for how the last few years of her life had gone. He was just such a perfect fit. It was the only explanation.

"Do you remember how the book said that everyone in Dwest has a purpose?" Zane asked. "I was the exception. I never felt like I had a function here – which led to some dark thoughts. No one's supposed to be sad in Dwest, but every once in a while the feeling would just pounce on me out of nowhere. So I left. Figured I might find my purpose in the outside world. Then I met you. You were absolutely perfect in every way: sweet, brilliant and beautiful, with a great sense of humor. And as if that wasn't enough, you made your comment about the universe – which is a pretty significant subject around these parts." He reached across and took Lucy's hands. "Lucy Hendrake, you are the most compassionate, selfless, loving person I've ever met. If anyone deserves to be happy, it's you. And I think that's my purpose: making you smile."

Lucy dropped her gaze, shaking her head. She smiled. "I don't know if I'm your purpose," she said, "but you sure treat me that way. And I'll be forever grateful for that. Thanks, Z." They leaned across the table and kissed.

The server refreshed the whipped cream on their hot chocolates. A chihuahua came to the table right after, tail wagging.

"Aw," Lucy said. "I can't say no to that face." She gave the dog a spoonful of whipped cream. It licked the silverware clean and trotted off happily. "I didn't know you had other canines here."

"We don't. Coyotes are just tricky."

Lucy looked down the path from the cafe, at the elevator platform. The chihuahua, facing her, went all starscape-sparkly, then morphed into a coyote shape. It winked one shining eye and licked the residual cream from its lips. The elevator carried it away.

"Huh," Lucy said. "Now that I think about it, I started dreaming of Dwest right after that stray bit me."

"I'd made that connection, too. Pretty sure that was no ordinary dog." Zane finished off his drink. "You've probably got star-rabies."

"I guess that would explain why I'm foaming at the mouth." Lucy licked up some whipped cream and stuck out her tongue. Zane laughed. "Is there any cure, Doc?"

He stood and offered a hand. "Let's ask around."

They strolled through Dwest, admiring the art, sampling the snacks, greeting the starfolk they passed. Everyone really did seem happy there, with sadness just a myth from the outside world. The book was right.

The book – Lucy asked about it. Sure enough, it wasn't something Zane had found online. He'd written it himself. It had started as a personal project to get him through a bout of homesickness, and when Lucy had started having her dreams, he'd rushed to finish it for her.

He apologized again for not being truthful from the beginning. He insisted Lucy had every right to be upset, but she understood his position. If he'd claimed to be a star-man from a secret city when they'd first crossed paths, she would have written him off as a deluded internet creep. They both would have missed out on a lot of happy times.

Zane didn't give Lucy a full tour of Dwest: they never reached the bowels of the city, which spread wide beneath the earth. But she saw enough to know this was the place for her. She was in love.

At one of the Tower's higher levels they lay on a cushioned observation pad, admiring the stars above.

"Zane?" Lucy asked, her head on his shoulder.

"Yeah?"

"How do you guys stay hidden here? Your ceiling's a giant window."

Zane stroked her hair idly. "That's actually solid rock," he said. "We just see through it because the night sky is always visible in Dwest."

"Oh." Considering everything else Lucy had encountered today, a magic ceiling was one of the easier things to swallow. "Do you ever worry about people snooping around, though? Getting too close and seeing something they shouldn't?"

"There are a bunch of nightmares roaming around outside, remember? They may only be a physical threat to their original dreamers, but they can sure scare anyone else away. It's sort of like the Banshee of the Badlands, up in South Dakota: we've got plenty of legends here that keep people from getting too nosy. No one needs to know they're harmless illusions."

The Tower shook with a loud crash, like a giant had heaved a boulder into it.

"Like that?" Lucy asked.

Zane sat up. "No," he said. "That was definitely real."

A shape landed on the Tower's transparent roof, erasing a section of stars. Lucy recognized the dark silhouette: it had the long, sharp lines of a panther's body, softened by the occasional streak of cloud slithering about it. The nightmare-horror's wispy wings spread wide as it assailed the Tower with fang and claw.

Lucy and Zane stood. Nearby starfolk gawked at the spectacle, pointing. Coyotes cowered. Bits of rock rained down the Tower's empty center, falling to the sounds of a relentless attack.

"I thought we were safe from nightmares here!" Lucy said. "Is this normal?"

"It sure isn't," Zane said, and ushered her toward an elevator platform.

Lucy kept her eyes on the nightmare-horror as they ran. It stopped attacking and disappeared to the side, going the same direction they were.

"Zane," Lucy said as they stepped onto the platform, "I think it's following—"

An explosion of dust and rock chips shot out from the nearby wall, the entire Tower shaking. Lucy and Zane hunched and covered against the spray. The thing outside struck again and again, its loud crashes joined by the panicked screams of starfolk. The elevator platform tilted with one of the impacts, rendering it immobile. Zane pulled Lucy off. He looked around, as if seeking a plan.

"I have to get outside," Lucy said.

"What?" Zane fixed on her, brows furrowed. "Why?"

"Because it's after me!"

"How do you know—"

"Outsiders don't usually visit Dwest. My nightmare shouldn't have manifested here. Something is attacking a city that's supposed to protect people from bad dreams. There are a lot of things happening here that normally wouldn't, and who's in the middle of it all? Me." Lucy shook her head. "I can't explain why this is happening, but that thing is obviously hunting me. And I'm not going to let it destroy this perfect world to get to me."

Zane pointed a finger at the wall under assault, its fractures growing. "Half of that thing is my nightmare, too. I don't know why it's here, but it's just as much my problem as yours. You're not going anywhere without me."

The solution came to Lucy in a flash. "That's it."

"What?"

"I'm not going anywhere without you. 'Together-everything', remember? I had a dream: there was a glass obelisk, and a star-man with a sword, and—" The Tower shook under a heavy blow, nearly knocking them from their feet. They reached out to steady each other. "There's no time to explain," Lucy said. "I need one of your stars."

"My *what?*"

"You're full of stars. Can you survive with one less?"

"Sure, but—"

"Then hand it over! From there." She tapped his heart with two fingers. "Please, Zane. If you love me, trust me."

Zane looked into her eyes. The Tower continued shaking around them, but in that moment, he didn't seem to notice. Finally, he pulled a sparkling white marble from his chest.

"I know what you're thinking," he said. "People have tried it before. Starfolk have fallen in love with outsiders and wanted them to become a part of Dwest. It doesn't work. The outsiders don't survive."

"And not every dog survives a kidney transplant. But sometimes there's no other choice. And besides – this whole city's built on dreams. Dreams brought me here. Dreams are trying to tear this place apart. And a dream is what told me this is going to work." She held out a waiting palm. "Come on, Z. Together-save-the-world."

Zane dropped his gaze, sighing. He passed the star over. Lucy kissed him.

"Hold my hand?" she said.

"Always."

With the Tower crumbling around them, Lucy pressed Zane's heart-star against her chest. It sunk inward. Everything went blindingly bright, and the world disappeared.

* * *

A big yawn. A bigger stretch. Eyes still closed, but detecting light somewhere beyond. Lucy rolled away from it.

"I told you you wouldn't want to get up this early, Noodle." She felt Zane's lips softly touch her cheek. "Go back to sleep."

Lucy grumbled. "No, I need to go. Mateo's family is probably imploding as we speak."

"And Dr. Juarez won't go to therapy unless you make her."

"Mmhm."

Zane exhaled. Lucy knew from the sound that he was shaking his head. "Look at you. Living in a perfect utopia, and you still can't just relax when someone needs help. The world doesn't deserve you."

They had breakfast at the cafe where they'd first shared a pair of hot chocolates, months earlier. The clear ceiling atop the Tower had long since been repaired, along with the rest of the city. Beyond, the stars had begun their retreat from morning's light.

Lucy and Zane finished their meal and exited the Tower, the doorway in the rock disappearing behind them. She threaded her hand under his arm. They smiled at each other.

"Your turn, or mine?" Zane asked.

"I'll go. It's still a novelty to me."

He gestured widely, as though the stage were hers.

Holding herself to Zane's arm with both hands, Lucy stood on her toes and blew a breath toward the heavens. The lingering stars of morning fell from the brightening sky, drifting to the clay ground. They outlined a rainbow path through the desert, away from the Tower of Dwest.

The couple traversed the road, smiling all the while. They spotted a wounded beast cowering behind a distant rock formation, but paid it no heed. The thing had learned its lesson: as long as Lucy and Zane were together, they were no easy prey.

A Vintage from Atlantis

Clark Ashton Smith

I THANK YOU, friend, but I am no drinker of wine, not even if it be the rarest Canary or the oldest Amontillado. Wine is a mocker, strong drink is raging… and more than others, I have reason to know the truth that was writ by Solomon the Jewish king. Give ear, if ye will, and I shall tell you a story such as would halt the half-drained cup on the lips of the hardiest bibber.

We were seven-and-thirty buccaneers, who raked the Spanish Main under Barnaby Dwale, he that was called Red Barnaby for the spilling of blood that attended him everywhere. Our ship, the *Black Falcon*, could outfly and outstrike all other craft that flew the Jolly Roger. Full often, Captain Dwale was wont to seek a remote isle on the eastward verge of the West Indies, and lighten the vessel of its weight of ingots and doubloons.

The isle was far from the common course of maritime traffic, and was not known to maps or other mariners; so it suited our purpose well. It was a place of palms and sand and cuffs, with a small harbor sheltered by the curving outstretched arms of rugged reefs, on which the dark ocean climbed and gnashed its fangs of white foam without troubling the tranquil waters beyond. I know not how many times we had visited the isle; but the soil beneath many a coco tree was heavy with our hidden trove. There we had stored the loot of bullion-laden ships, the massy plate and jewels of cathedral towns.

Even as to all mortal things, an ending came at last to our visits. We had gathered a goodly cargo, but might have stayed longer on the open main where the Spaniards passed, if a tempest had not impended. We were near the secret isle, as it chanced, when the skies began to blacken; and wallowing heavily in the rising seas we fled to our placid harbor, reaching it by night-fall. Before dawn the hurricane had blown by; and the sun came up in cloudless amber and blue. We proceeded with the landing and burying of our chests of coin and gems and ingots, which was a task of some length; and afterward we refilled our water-casks at a cool sweet spring that ran from beneath the palmy hill not far inland.

It was now midafternoon. Captain Dwale was planning to weigh anchor shortly and follow the westering sun toward the Caribbees. There were nine of us, loading the last barrels into the boats, with Red Barnaby looking on and cursing us for being slower than mud-turtles; and we were bending knee-deep in the tepid, lazy water, when suddenly the captain ceased to swear, and we saw that he was no longer watching us. He had turned his back and was stooping over a strange object that must have drifted in with the tide, after the storm: a huge and barnacle-laden thing that lay on the sand, half in and half out of the shoaling water. Somehow, none of us had perceived it heretofore.

Red Barnaby was not silent long.

"Come here, ye chancre-eaten coistrels," he called to us. We obeyed willingly enough, and gathered around the beached object, which our captain was examining with much perplexity. We too were greatly bewondered when we saw the thing more closely; and none of us could name it offhand or with certainty.

The object had the form of a great jar, with a tapering neck and a deep, round, abdomen body. It was wholly encrusted with shells and corals that had gathered upon it as if through many ages in the ocean deeps, and was festooned with weeds and sea-flowers such as we had never before beheld; so that we could not determine the substance of which it was made.

At the order of Captain Dwale, we rolled it out of the water and beyond reach of the tide, into the shade of nearby palms; though it required the efforts of four men to move the unwieldy thing, which was strangely ponderous. We found that it would stand easily on end, with its top reaching almost to the shoulders of a tall man. While we were handling the great jar, we heard a swishing noise from within, as if it were filled with some sort of liquor.

Our captain, as it chanced, was a learned man.

"By the communion cup of Satan!" he swore. "If this thing is not an antique wine-jar, then I am a Bed-lamite. Such vessels – though mayhap they were not so huge – were employed by the Romans to store the goodly vintages of Falernus and Cecuba. Indeed, there is today a Spanish wine – that of Valdepenas – which is kept in earthen jars. But this, if I mistake not, is neither from Spain nor olden Rome. It is ancient enough, by its look, to have come from that long-sunken isle, the Atlantis whereof Plato speaks. Truly, there should be a rare vintage within, a wine that was mellowed in the youth of the world, before the founding of Rome and Athens; and which, perchance, has gathered fire and strength with the centuries. Ho! my rascal sea-bullies! We sail not from this harbor till the jar is broached. And if the liquor within be sound and potable, we shall make holiday this evening on the sands."

"Belike, 'tis a funeral urn, full of plaguey cinders and ashes," said the mate, Roger Aglone, who had a gloomy turn of thought.

Red Barnaby had drawn his cutlas and was busily prying away the crust of barnacles and quaint fantastic coral-growths from the top of the jar. Layer on layer of them he removed, and swore mightily at this increment of forgotten years. At last a great stopper of earthen-ware, sealed with a clear wax that had grown harder than amber, was revealed by his prying. The stopper was graven with queer letters of an unknown language, plainly to be seen; but the wax refused the cutlas-point. So, losing all patience, the captain seized a mighty fragment of stone, which a lesser man could scarce have lifted, and broke therewith the neck of the jar.

Now even in those days, I, Stephen Magbane, the one Puritan amid that Christless crew, was no bibber of wine or spirituous liquors, but a staunch Rechabite on all occasions. Therefore I held back, feeling little concern other than that of reprobation, while the others pressed about the jar and sniffed greedily at the contents. But, almost immediately with its opening, my nostrils were assailed by an odor of heathen spices, heavy and strange; and the very inhalation thereof caused me to feel a sort of giddiness, so that I thought it well to retreat still further. But the others were eager as midges around a fermenting-vat in autumn.

"'Sblood! 'Tis a royal vintage!" roared the captain, after he had dipped a forefinger in the jar and sucked the purple drops that dripped from it. "Avast, ye slumgullions! Stow the water-casks on board, and summon all hands ashore, leaving only a watch there to ward the vessel. We'll have a gala night before we sack any more Spaniards."

We obeyed his order; and there was much rejoicing amid the crew of the *Black Falcon* at the news of our find and the postponement of the voyage. Three men, grumbling sorely at their absence from the revels, were left on board; though, in that tranquil harbor, such vigilance was virtually needless. We others returned to the shore, bringing a supply of pannikins in which to serve the wine, and provisions for a feast. Then we gathered pieces of drift with which to build a great fire, and caught several huge tortoises along the sands, and unearthed their hidden eggs, so that we might have an abundance and variety of victuals.

In these preparations I took part with no special ardor. Knowing my habit of abstention, and being of a somewhat malicious and tormenting humor, Captain Dwale had expressly commanded my presence at the feast. However, I anticipated nothing more than a little ribaldry at my expense, as was customary at such times; and being partial to fresh tortoise-meat, I was not wholly unresigned to my lot as a witness of the Babylonian inebrieties of the others.

At nightfall, the feasting and drinking began; and the fire of driftwood, with eery witch-colors of blue and green and white amid the flame, leapt high in the dusk while the sunset died to a handful of red embers far on purpling seas.

It was a strange wine that the crew and captain swilled from their pannikins. I saw that the stuff was thick and dark, as if it had been mingled with blood; and the air was filled with the reek of those pagan spices, hot and rich and unholy, that might have poured from a broken tomb of antique emperors. And stranger still was the intoxication of that wine; for those who drank it became still and thoughtful and sullen; and there was no singing of lewd songs, no playing of apish antics.

Red Barnaby had been drinking longer than the others, having begun to sample the vintage while the crew were making ready for their revel. To our wonderment, he ceased to swear at us after the first cupful, and no longer ordered us about or paid us any heed, but sat peering into the sunset with eyes that held the dazzlement of unknown dreams. And one by one, as they began to drink, the others were likewise affected, so that I marveled much at the unwonted power of the wine. I had never before beheld an intoxication of such nature; for they spoke not nor ate, and moved only to refill their cups from the mighty jar.

The night had grown dark as indigo beyond the flickering fire, and there was no moon; and the firelight blinded the stars. But one by one, after an interval, the drinkers rose from their places and stood staring into the darkness toward the sea. Unquietly they stood, and strained forward, peering intently as men who behold some marvelous thing; and queerly they muttered to one another, with unintelligible words. I knew not why they stared and muttered thus, unless it were because of some madness that had come upon them from the wine; for naught was visible in the dark, and I heard nothing, save the low murmur of wavelets lapping on the sand.

Louder grew the muttering; and some raised their bands and pointed seaward, babbling wildly as if in delirium. Noting their demeanor, and doubtful as to what further turn their madness might take, I bethought me to withdraw along the shore. But when I began to move away, those who were nearest me appeared to waken from their dream, and restrained me with rough hands. Then, with drunken, gibbering words, of which I could make no sense, they held me helpless while one of their number forced me to drink from a pannikin filled with the purple wine.

I fought against them, doubly unwilling to quaff that nameless vintage, and much of it was spilled. The stuff was sweet as liquid honey to the taste, but burned like hell-fire in my throat. I turned giddy; and a sort of dark confusion possessed my senses by degrees; and I seemed to hear and see and feel as in the mounting fever of calenture.

The air about me seemed to brighten, with a redness of ghostly blood that was everywhere; a light that came not from the fire nor from the nocturnal heavens. I beheld the faces and forms of the drinkers, standing without shadow, as if mantled with a rosy phosphorescence. And beyond them, where they stared in troubled and restless wonder, the darkness was illumed with the strange light.

Mad and unholy was the vision that I saw: for the harbor waves no longer lapped on the sand, and the sea had wholly vanished. The *Black Falcon* was gone, and where the reefs had been, great marble walls ascended, flushed as if with the ruby of lost sunsets. Above them were haughty domes of heathen temples, and spires of pagan palaces; and beneath were mighty streets and causeys where people passed in a never-ending throng. I thought that I gazed upon some immemorial city, such as had flourished in Earth's prime; and I saw the trees of its terraced gardens, fairer than the palms of Eden. Listening, I heard the sound of dulcimers that were sweet as the moaning of women; and the cry of horns that told forgotten glorious things; and the wild sweet singing of people who passed to some hidden, sacred festival within the walls.

I saw that the light poured upward from the city, and was born of its streets and buildings. It blinded the heavens above; and the horizon beyond was lost in a shining mist. One building there was, a high fane above the rest, from which the light streamed in a muddier flood; and from its open portals music came, sorcerous and beguiling as the far voices of bygone years. And the revelers passed gayly into its portals, but none came forth. The weird music seemed to call me and entice me; and I longed to tread the streets of the alien city, and a deep desire was upon me to mingle with its people and pass into the glowing fane.

Verily I knew why the drinkers had stared at the darkness and had muttered among themselves in wonder. I knew that they also longed to descend into the city. And I saw that a great causey, built of marble and gleaming with the red luster, ran downward from their very feet over meadows of unknown blossoms to the foremost buildings.

Then, as I watched and listened, the singing grew sweeter, the music stranger, and the rosy luster brightened. Then, with no backward glance, no word or gesture of injunction to his men, Captain Dwale went slowly forward, treading the marble causey like a dreamer who walks in his dream. And after him, one by one, Roger Aglone and the crew followed in the same manner, going toward the city.

Haply I too should have followed, drawn by the witching music. For truly it seemed that I had trod the ways of that city in former time, and had known the things whereof the music told and the voices sang. Well did I remember why the people passed eternally into the fane, and why they came not forth; and there, it seemed, I should meet familiar and beloved faces, and take part in mysteries recalled from the foundered years.

All this, which the wine had remembered through its sleep in the ocean depths, was mine to behold and conceive for a moment. And well it was that I had drunk less of that evil and pagan vintage than the others, and was less besotted than they with its luring vision. For, even as Captain Dwale and his crew went toward the city, it appeared to me that the rosy glow began to fade a little. The walls took on a wavering thinness, and the domes grew insubstantial. The rose departed, the light was pale as a phosphor of the tomb; and the people went to and fro like phantoms, with a thin crying of ghostly horns and a ghostly singing. Dimly above the sunken causey the harbor waves returned; and Red Barnaby and his men walked down beneath them. Slowly the waters darkened above the fading spires and walls; and the midnight blackened upon the sea; and the city was lost like the vanished bubbles of wine.

A terror came upon me, knowing the fate of those others. I fled swiftly, stumbling in darkness toward the palmy hill that crowned the isle. No vestige remained of the rosy light; and the sky was filled with returning stars. And looking oceanward as I climbed the hill, I saw a lantern that burned on the *Black Falcon* in the harbor, and discerned the embers of our fire that smoldered on the sands. Then, praying with a fearful fervor, I waited for dawn.

Twenty Thousand Leagues Under the Sea

Part II: Chapters IX–XI

Jules Verne

[Publisher's Note: In this famous adventure under the sea, a group of men encounter Captain Nemo and his futuristic submarine. The troubled captain lives in exile, secretly roaming the seas, so the men are unable to leave. With Nemo, they visit a number of underwater realms, including the lost city of Atlantis, as covered in this extract.]

Chapter IX
A Vanished Continent

THE NEXT MORNING, the 19th of February, I saw the Canadian enter my room. I expected this visit. He looked very disappointed.

"Well, sir?" said he.

"Well, Ned, fortune was against us yesterday."

"Yes; that Captain must needs stop exactly at the hour we intended leaving his vessel."

"Yes, Ned, he had business at his bankers."

"His bankers!"

"Or rather his banking-house; by that I mean the ocean, where his riches are safer than in the chests of the State."

I then related to the Canadian the incidents of the preceding night, hoping to bring him back to the idea of not abandoning the Captain; but my recital had no other result than an energetically expressed regret from Ned that he had not been able to take a walk on the battlefield of Vigo on his own account.

"However," said he, "all is not ended. It is only a blow of the harpoon lost. Another time we must succeed; and tonight, if necessary—"

"In what direction is the Nautilus going?" I asked.

"I do not know," replied Ned.

"Well, at noon we shall see the point."

The Canadian returned to Conseil. As soon as I was dressed, I went into the saloon. The compass was not reassuring. The course of the Nautilus was S.S.W. We were turning our backs on Europe.

I waited with some impatience till the ship's place was pricked on the chart. At about half-past eleven the reservoirs were emptied, and our vessel rose to the surface of the ocean. I rushed towards the platform. Ned Land had preceded me. No more land in sight. Nothing but an immense sea. Some sails on the horizon, doubtless those going to San Roque in search of favourable winds for doubling the Cape of Good Hope. The weather was cloudy. A gale of wind was preparing. Ned raved, and tried to pierce the cloudy horizon. He still hoped that behind all that fog stretched the land he so longed for.

At noon the sun showed itself for an instant. The second profited by this brightness to take its height. Then, the sea becoming more billowy, we descended, and the panel closed.

An hour after, upon consulting the chart, I saw the position of the Nautilus was marked at 16° 17' long., and 33° 22' lat., at 150 leagues from the nearest coast. There was no means of flight, and I leave you to imagine the rage of the Canadian when I informed him of our situation.

For myself, I was not particularly sorry. I felt lightened of the load which had oppressed me, and was able to return with some degree of calmness to my accustomed work.

That night, about eleven o'clock, I received a most unexpected visit from Captain Nemo. He asked me very graciously if I felt fatigued from my watch of the preceding night. I answered in the negative.

"Then, M. Aronnax, I propose a curious excursion."

"Propose, Captain?"

"You have hitherto only visited the submarine depths by daylight, under the brightness of the sun. Would it suit you to see them in the darkness of the night?"

"Most willingly."

"I warn you, the way will be tiring. We shall have far to walk, and must climb a mountain. The roads are not well kept."

"What you say, Captain, only heightens my curiosity; I am ready to follow you."

"Come then, sir, we will put on our diving-dresses."

Arrived at the robing-room, I saw that neither of my companions nor any of the ship's crew were to follow us on this excursion. Captain Nemo had not even proposed my taking with me either Ned or Conseil.

In a few moments we had put on our diving-dresses; they placed on our backs the reservoirs, abundantly filled with air, but no electric lamps were prepared. I called the Captain's attention to the fact.

"They will be useless," he replied.

I thought I had not heard aright, but I could not repeat my observation, for the Captain's head had already disappeared in its metal case. I finished harnessing myself. I felt them put an iron-pointed stick into my hand, and some minutes later, after going through the usual form, we set foot on the bottom of the Atlantic at a depth of 150 fathoms. Midnight was near. The waters were profoundly dark, but Captain Nemo pointed out in the distance a reddish spot, a sort of large light shining brilliantly about two miles from the Nautilus. What this fire might be, what could feed it, why and how it lit up the liquid mass, I could not say. In any case, it did light our way, vaguely, it is true, but I soon accustomed myself to the peculiar darkness, and I understood, under such circumstances, the uselessness of the Ruhmkorff apparatus.

As we advanced, I heard a kind of pattering above my head. The noise redoubling, sometimes producing a continual shower, I soon understood the cause. It was rain falling violently, and crisping the surface of the waves. Instinctively the thought flashed across my mind that I should be wet through! By the water! In the midst of the water! I could not help laughing at the odd idea. But, indeed, in the thick diving-dress, the liquid element is no longer felt, and one only seems to be in an atmosphere somewhat denser than the terrestrial atmosphere. Nothing more.

After half an hour's walk the soil became stony. Medusae, microscopic crustacea, and pennatules lit it slightly with their phosphorescent gleam. I caught a glimpse of pieces of stone covered with millions of zoophytes and masses of seaweed. My feet often slipped upon this sticky carpet of seaweed, and without my iron-tipped stick I should have fallen more than once. In turning round, I could still see the whitish lantern of the Nautilus beginning to pale in the distance.

But the rosy light which guided us increased and lit up the horizon. The presence of this fire under water puzzled me in the highest degree. Was I going towards a natural phenomenon as yet unknown to the *savants* of the earth? Or even (for this thought crossed my brain) had the hand of man aught to do with this conflagration? Had he fanned this flame? Was I to meet in these depths companions and friends of Captain Nemo whom he was going to visit, and who, like him, led this strange existence? Should I find down there a whole colony of exiles who, weary of the miseries of this earth, had sought and found independence in the deep ocean? All these foolish and unreasonable ideas pursued me. And in this condition of mind, over-excited by the succession of wonders continually passing before my eyes, I should not have been surprised to meet at the bottom of the sea one of those submarine towns of which Captain Nemo dreamed.

Our road grew lighter and lighter. The white glimmer came in rays from the summit of a mountain about 800 feet high. But what I saw was simply a reflection, developed by the clearness of the waters. The source of this inexplicable light was a fire on the opposite side of the mountain.

In the midst of this stony maze furrowing the bottom of the Atlantic, Captain Nemo advanced without hesitation. He knew this dreary road. Doubtless he had often travelled over it, and could not lose himself. I followed him with unshaken confidence. He seemed to me like a genie of the sea; and, as he walked before me, I could not help admiring his stature, which was outlined in black on the luminous horizon.

It was one in the morning when we arrived at the first slopes of the mountain; but to gain access to them we must venture through the difficult paths of a vast copse.

Yes; a copse of dead trees, without leaves, without sap, trees petrified by the action of the water and here and there overtopped by gigantic pines. It was like a coal-pit still standing, holding by the roots to the broken soil, and whose branches, like fine black paper cuttings, showed distinctly on the watery ceiling. Picture to yourself a forest in the Hartz hanging on to the sides of the mountain, but a forest swallowed up. The paths were encumbered with seaweed and fucus, between which grovelled a whole world of crustacea. I went along, climbing the rocks, striding over extended trunks, breaking the sea bind-weed which hung from one tree to the other; and frightening the fishes, which flew from branch to branch. Pressing onward, I felt no fatigue. I followed my guide, who was never tired. What a spectacle! How can I express it? How paint the aspect of those woods and rocks in this medium – their under parts dark and wild, the upper coloured with red tints, by that light which the reflecting powers of the waters doubled? We climbed rocks which fell directly after with gigantic bounds and the low growling of an avalanche. To right and left ran long, dark galleries, where sight was lost. Here opened vast glades which the hand of man seemed to have worked; and I sometimes asked myself if some inhabitant of these submarine regions would not suddenly appear to me.

But Captain Nemo was still mounting. I could not stay behind. I followed boldly. My stick gave me good help. A false step would have been dangerous on the narrow passes sloping down to the sides of the gulfs; but I walked with firm step, without feeling any giddiness. Now I jumped a crevice, the depth of which would have made me hesitate had it been among the glaciers on the land; now I ventured on the unsteady trunk of a tree thrown across from one abyss to the other, without looking under my feet, having only eyes to admire the wild sites of this region.

There, monumental rocks, leaning on their regularly-cut bases, seemed to defy all laws of equilibrium. From between their stony knees trees sprang, like a jet under heavy pressure, and upheld others which upheld them. Natural towers, large scarps, cut perpendicularly, like a 'curtain', inclined at an angle which the laws of gravitation could never have tolerated in terrestrial regions.

Two hours after quitting the Nautilus we had crossed the line of trees, and a hundred feet above our heads rose the top of the mountain, which cast a shadow on the brilliant irradiation of the opposite slope. Some petrified shrubs ran fantastically here and there. Fishes got up under our feet like birds in the long grass. The massive rocks were rent with impenetrable fractures, deep grottos, and unfathomable holes, at the bottom of which formidable creatures might be heard moving. My blood curdled when I saw enormous antennae blocking my road, or some frightful claw closing with a noise in the shadow of some cavity. Millions of luminous spots shone brightly in the midst of the darkness. They were the eyes of giant crustacea crouched in their holes; giant lobsters setting themselves up like halberdiers, and moving their claws with the clicking sound of pincers; titanic crabs, pointed like a gun on its carriage; and frightful-looking poulps, interweaving their tentacles like a living nest of serpents.

We had now arrived on the first platform, where other surprises awaited me. Before us lay some picturesque ruins, which betrayed the hand of man and not that of the Creator. There were vast heaps of stone, amongst which might be traced the vague and shadowy forms of castles and temples, clothed with a world of blossoming zoophytes, and over which, instead of ivy, seaweed and fucus threw a thick vegetable mantle. But what was this portion of the globe which had been swallowed by cataclysms? Who had placed those rocks and stones like cromlechs of prehistoric times? Where was I? Whither had Captain Nemo's fancy hurried me?

I would fain have asked him; not being able to, I stopped him – I seized his arm. But, shaking his head, and pointing to the highest point of the mountain, he seemed to say:

"Come, come along; come higher!"

I followed, and in a few minutes I had climbed to the top, which for a circle of ten yards commanded the whole mass of rock.

I looked down the side we had just climbed. The mountain did not rise more than seven or eight hundred feet above the level of the plain; but on the opposite side it commanded from twice that height the depths of this part of the Atlantic. My eyes ranged far over a large space lit by a violent fulguration. In fact, the mountain was a volcano.

At fifty feet above the peak, in the midst of a rain of stones and scoriae, a large crater was vomiting forth torrents of lava which fell in a cascade of fire into the bosom of the liquid mass. Thus situated, this volcano lit the lower plain like an immense torch, even to the extreme limits of the horizon. I said that the submarine crater threw up lava, but no flames. Flames require the oxygen of the air to feed upon and cannot be developed under water; but streams of lava, having in themselves the principles of their incandescence, can attain a white heat, fight vigorously against the liquid element, and turn it to vapour by contact.

Rapid currents bearing all these gases in diffusion and torrents of lava slid to the bottom of the mountain like an eruption of Vesuvius on another Terra del Greco.

There indeed under my eyes, ruined, destroyed, lay a town – its roofs open to the sky, its temples fallen, its arches dislocated, its columns lying on the ground, from which one would still recognise the massive character of Tuscan architecture. Further on, some remains of a gigantic aqueduct; here the high base of an Acropolis, with the floating outline of a Parthenon; there traces of a quay, as if an ancient port had formerly abutted on the borders of the ocean, and disappeared with its merchant vessels and its war-galleys. Farther on again, long lines of sunken walls and broad, deserted streets – a perfect Pompeii escaped beneath the waters. Such was the sight that Captain Nemo brought before my eyes!

Where was I? Where was I? I must know at any cost. I tried to speak, but Captain Nemo stopped me by a gesture, and, picking up a piece of chalk-stone, advanced to a rock of black basalt, and traced the one word:

ATLANTIS

What a light shot through my mind! Atlantis! The Atlantis of Plato, that continent denied by Origen and Humbolt, who placed its disappearance amongst the legendary tales. I had it there now before my eyes, bearing upon it the unexceptionable testimony of its catastrophe. The region thus engulfed was beyond Europe, Asia, and Lybia, beyond the columns of Hercules, where those powerful people, the Atlantides, lived, against whom the first wars of ancient Greeks were waged.

Thus, led by the strangest destiny, I was treading under foot the mountains of this continent, touching with my hand those ruins a thousand generations old and contemporary with the geological epochs. I was walking on the very spot where the contemporaries of the first man had walked.

Whilst I was trying to fix in my mind every detail of this grand landscape, Captain Nemo remained motionless, as if petrified in mute ecstasy, leaning on a mossy stone. Was he dreaming of those generations long since disappeared? Was he asking them the secret of human destiny? Was it here this strange man came to steep himself in historical recollections, and live again this ancient life – he who wanted no modern one? What would I not have given to know his thoughts, to share them, to understand them! We remained for an hour at this place, contemplating the vast plains under the brightness of the lava, which was some times wonderfully intense. Rapid tremblings ran along the mountain caused by internal bubblings, deep noise, distinctly transmitted through the liquid medium were echoed with majestic grandeur. At this moment the moon appeared through the mass of waters and threw her pale rays on the buried continent. It was but a gleam, but what an indescribable effect! The Captain rose, cast one last look on the immense plain, and then bade me follow him.

We descended the mountain rapidly, and, the mineral forest once passed, I saw the lantern of the Nautilus shining like a star. The Captain walked straight to it, and we got on board as the first rays of light whitened the surface of the ocean.

Chapter X
The Submarine Coal-Mines

THE NEXT DAY, the 20th of February, I awoke very late: the fatigues of the previous night had prolonged my sleep until eleven o'clock. I dressed quickly, and hastened to find the course the Nautilus was taking. The instruments showed it to be still toward the south, with a speed of twenty miles an hour and a depth of fifty fathoms.

The species of fishes here did not differ much from those already noticed. There were rays of giant size, five yards long, and endowed with great muscular strength, which enabled them to shoot above the waves; sharks of many kinds; amongst others, one fifteen feet long, with triangular sharp teeth, and whose transparency rendered it almost invisible in the water.

Amongst bony fish Conseil noticed some about three yards long, armed at the upper jaw with a piercing sword; other bright-coloured creatures, known in the time of Aristotle by the name of the sea-dragon, which are dangerous to capture on account of the spikes on their back.

About four o'clock, the soil, generally composed of a thick mud mixed with petrified wood, changed by degrees, and it became more stony, and seemed strewn with conglomerate and pieces of basalt, with a sprinkling of lava. I thought that a mountainous region was succeeding the long plains; and accordingly, after a few evolutions of the Nautilus, I saw the southerly horizon blocked by a high wall which seemed to close all exit. Its summit evidently passed the level of the ocean. It must be a continent, or at least an island – one of the Canaries, or of the Cape Verde Islands. The bearings not being yet taken, perhaps designedly, I was ignorant of our exact position. In any case, such a wall seemed to me to mark the limits of that Atlantis, of which we had in reality passed over only the smallest part.

Much longer should I have remained at the window admiring the beauties of sea and sky, but the panels closed. At this moment the Nautilus arrived at the side of this high, perpendicular wall. What it would do, I could not guess. I returned to my room; it no longer moved. I laid myself down with the full intention of waking after a few hours' sleep; but it was eight o'clock the next day when I entered the saloon. I looked at the manometer. It told me that the Nautilus was floating on the surface of the ocean. Besides, I heard steps on the platform. I went to the panel. It was open; but, instead of broad daylight, as I expected, I was surrounded by profound darkness. Where were we? Was I mistaken? Was it still night? No; not a star was shining and night has not that utter darkness.

I knew not what to think, when a voice near me said:

"Is that you, Professor?"

"Ah! Captain," I answered, "where are we?"

"Underground, sir."

"Underground!" I exclaimed. "And the Nautilus floating still?"

"It always floats."

"But I do not understand."

"Wait a few minutes, our lantern will be lit, and, if you like light places, you will be satisfied."

I stood on the platform and waited. The darkness was so complete that I could not even see Captain Nemo; but, looking to the zenith, exactly above my head, I seemed to catch an undecided gleam, a kind of twilight filling a circular hole. At this instant the lantern was lit, and its vividness dispelled the faint light. I closed my dazzled eyes for an instant, and then looked again. The Nautilus was stationary, floating near a mountain which formed a sort of quay. The lake, then, supporting it was a lake imprisoned by a circle of walls, measuring two miles in diameter and six in circumference. Its level (the manometer showed) could only be the same as the outside level, for there must necessarily be a communication between the lake and the sea. The high partitions, leaning forward on their base, grew into a vaulted roof bearing the shape of an immense funnel turned upside down, the height being about five or six hundred yards. At the summit was a circular orifice, by which I had caught the slight gleam of light, evidently daylight.

"Where are we?" I asked.

"In the very heart of an extinct volcano, the interior of which has been invaded by the sea, after some great convulsion of the earth. Whilst you were sleeping, Professor, the Nautilus penetrated to this lagoon by a natural canal, which opens about ten yards beneath the surface of the ocean. This is its harbour of refuge, a sure, commodious, and mysterious one, sheltered from all gales. Show me, if you can, on the coasts of any of your continents or islands, a road which can give such perfect refuge from all storms."

"Certainly," I replied, "you are in safety here, Captain Nemo. Who could reach you in the heart of a volcano? But did I not see an opening at its summit?"

"Yes; its crater, formerly filled with lava, vapour, and flames, and which now gives entrance to the life-giving air we breathe."

"But what is this volcanic mountain?"

"It belongs to one of the numerous islands with which this sea is strewn – to vessels a simple sandbank – to us an immense cavern. Chance led me to discover it, and chance served me well."

"But of what use is this refuge, Captain? The Nautilus wants no port."

"No, sir; but it wants electricity to make it move, and the wherewithal to make the electricity – sodium to feed the elements, coal from which to get the sodium, and a coal-mine to supply the coal. And exactly on this spot the sea covers entire forests embedded during the geological periods, now mineralised and transformed into coal; for me they are an inexhaustible mine."

"Your men follow the trade of miners here, then, Captain?"

"Exactly so. These mines extend under the waves like the mines of Newcastle. Here, in their diving-dresses, pick axe and shovel in hand, my men extract the coal, which I do not even ask from the mines of the earth. When I burn this combustible for the manufacture of sodium, the smoke, escaping from the crater of the mountain, gives it the appearance of a still-active volcano."

"And we shall see your companions at work?"

"No; not this time at least; for I am in a hurry to continue our submarine tour of the earth. So I shall content myself with drawing from the reserve of sodium I already possess. The time for loading is one day only, and we continue our voyage. So, if you wish to go over the cavern and make the round of the lagoon, you must take advantage of today, M. Aronnax."

I thanked the Captain and went to look for my companions, who had not yet left their cabin. I invited them to follow me without saying where we were. They mounted the platform. Conseil, who was astonished at nothing, seemed to look upon it as quite natural that he should wake under a mountain, after having fallen asleep under the waves. But Ned Land thought of nothing but finding whether the cavern had any exit. After breakfast, about ten o'clock, we went down on to the mountain.

"Here we are, once more on land," said Conseil.

"I do not call this land," said the Canadian. "And besides, we are not on it, but beneath it."

Between the walls of the mountains and the waters of the lake lay a sandy shore which, at its greatest breadth, measured five hundred feet. On this soil one might easily make the tour of the lake. But the base of the high partitions was stony ground, with volcanic locks and enormous pumice-stones lying in picturesque heaps. All these detached masses, covered with enamel, polished by the action of the subterraneous fires, shone resplendent by the light of our electric lantern. The mica dust from the shore, rising under our feet, flew like a cloud of sparks. The bottom now rose sensibly, and we soon arrived at long circuitous slopes, or inclined planes, which took us higher by degrees; but we were obliged to walk carefully among these conglomerates, bound by no cement, the feet slipping on the glassy crystal, felspar, and quartz.

The volcanic nature of this enormous excavation was confirmed on all sides, and I pointed it out to my companions.

"Picture to yourselves," said I, "what this crater must have been when filled with boiling lava, and when the level of the incandescent liquid rose to the orifice of the mountain, as though melted on the top of a hot plate."

"I can picture it perfectly," said Conseil. "But, sir, will you tell me why the Great Architect has suspended operations, and how it is that the furnace is replaced by the quiet waters of the lake?"

"Most probably, Conseil, because some convulsion beneath the ocean produced that very opening which has served as a passage for the Nautilus. Then the waters of the Atlantic rushed into the interior of the mountain. There must have been a terrible struggle between the two elements, a struggle which ended in the victory of Neptune. But many ages have run out since then, and the submerged volcano is now a peaceable grotto."

"Very well," replied Ned Land; "I accept the explanation, sir; but, in our own interests, I regret that the opening of which you speak was not made above the level of the sea."

"But, friend Ned," said Conseil, "if the passage had not been under the sea, the Nautilus could not have gone through it."

We continued ascending. The steps became more and more perpendicular and narrow. Deep excavations, which we were obliged to cross, cut them here and there; sloping masses had to be turned. We slid upon our knees and crawled along. But Conseil's dexterity and the Canadian's strength surmounted all obstacles. At a height of about 31 feet the nature of the ground changed without becoming more practicable. To the conglomerate and trachyte succeeded black basalt, the first dispread in layers full of bubbles, the latter forming regular prisms, placed like a colonnade supporting the spring of the immense vault, an admirable specimen of natural architecture. Between the blocks of basalt wound long streams of lava, long since grown cold, encrusted with bituminous rays; and in some places there were spread large carpets of sulphur. A more powerful light shone through the upper crater, shedding a vague glimmer over these volcanic depressions for ever buried in the bosom of this extinguished mountain. But our upward march was soon stopped at a height of about two hundred and fifty feet by impassable obstacles. There was a complete vaulted arch overhanging us, and our ascent was changed to a circular walk. At the last change vegetable life began to struggle with the mineral. Some shrubs, and even some trees, grew from the fractures of the walls. I recognised some euphorbias, with the caustic sugar coming from them; heliotropes, quite incapable of justifying their name, sadly drooped their clusters of flowers, both their colour and perfume half gone. Here and there some chrysanthemums grew timidly at the foot of an aloe with long, sickly-looking leaves. But between the streams of lava, I saw some little violets still slightly perfumed, and I admit that I smelt them with delight. Perfume is the soul of the flower, and sea-flowers have no soul.

We had arrived at the foot of some sturdy dragon-trees, which had pushed aside the rocks with their strong roots, when Ned Land exclaimed:

"Ah! sir, a hive! a hive!"

"A hive!" I replied, with a gesture of incredulity.

"Yes, a hive," repeated the Canadian, "and bees humming round it."

I approached, and was bound to believe my own eyes. There at a hole bored in one of the dragon-trees were some thousands of these ingenious insects, so common in all the Canaries, and whose produce is so much esteemed. Naturally enough, the Canadian wished to gather the honey, and I could not well oppose his wish. A quantity of dry leaves, mixed with sulphur, he lit with a spark from his flint, and he began to smoke out the bees. The humming ceased by degrees, and the hive eventually yielded several pounds of the sweetest honey, with which Ned Land filled his haversack.

"When I have mixed this honey with the paste of the bread-fruit," said he, "I shall be able to offer you a succulent cake."

"'Pon my word," said Conseil, "it will be gingerbread."

"Never mind the gingerbread," said I; "let us continue our interesting walk."

At every turn of the path we were following, the lake appeared in all its length and breadth. The lantern lit up the whole of its peaceable surface, which knew neither ripple nor wave. The Nautilus remained perfectly immovable. On the platform, and on the mountain, the ship's crew were working like black shadows clearly carved against the luminous atmosphere. We were now going round the highest crest of the first layers of rock which upheld the roof. I then saw that bees were not the only representatives of the animal kingdom in the interior of this volcano. Birds of prey hovered here and there in the shadows, or fled from their nests on the top of the rocks. There were sparrow hawks, with white breasts, and kestrels, and down the slopes scampered, with their long legs, several fine fat bustards. I leave anyone to imagine the covetousness of the Canadian at the sight of this savoury game, and whether he did not regret having no gun. But he did his best to replace the lead by stones, and, after several fruitless attempts, he succeeded in wounding a magnificent bird. To say that he risked his life twenty times before reaching it is but the truth; but he managed so well that the creature joined the honey-cakes in his bag. We were now obliged to descend toward the shore, the crest becoming impracticable. Above us the crater seemed to gape like the mouth of a well. From this place the sky could be clearly seen, and clouds, dissipated by the west wind, leaving behind them, even on the summit of the mountain, their misty remnants – certain proof that they were only moderately high, for the volcano did not rise more than eight hundred feet above the level of the ocean. Half an hour after the Canadian's last exploit we had regained the inner shore. Here the flora was represented by large carpets of marine crystal, a little umbelliferous plant very good to pickle, which also bears the name of pierce-stone and sea-fennel. Conseil gathered some bundles of it. As to the fauna, it might be counted by thousands of crustacea of all sorts, lobsters, crabs, spider-crabs, chameleon shrimps, and a large number of shells, rockfish, and limpets. Three-quarters of an hour later we had finished our circuitous walk and were on board. The crew had just finished loading the sodium, and the Nautilus could have left that instant. But Captain Nemo gave no order. Did he wish to wait until night, and leave the submarine passage secretly? Perhaps so. Whatever it might be, the next day, the Nautilus, having left its port, steered clear of all land at a few yards beneath the waves of the Atlantic.

Chapter XI
The Sargasso Sea

THAT DAY the Nautilus crossed a singular part of the Atlantic Ocean. No one can be ignorant of the existence of a current of warm water known by the name of the Gulf Stream. After leaving the Gulf of Florida, we went in the direction of Spitzbergen. But before entering the Gulf of Mexico, about 45° of N. lat., this current divides into two arms, the principal one going towards the coast of Ireland and Norway, whilst the second bends to the south about the height of the Azores; then, touching the African shore, and describing a lengthened oval, returns to the Antilles. This second arm – it is rather a collar than an arm – surrounds with its circles of warm water that portion of the cold, quiet, immovable ocean called the Sargasso Sea, a perfect lake in the open Atlantic: it takes no less than three years for the great current to pass round it. Such was the region the Nautilus was now visiting, a perfect meadow, a close carpet of seaweed, fucus, and tropical berries, so thick and so compact that the stem of a vessel could hardly tear its way through it. And Captain Nemo, not wishing to entangle his screw in this herbaceous mass, kept some yards beneath the surface of the waves. The name Sargasso comes from the Spanish word 'sargazzo' which signifies kelp. This kelp, or berry-plant, is the principal formation of this immense bank. And this is the reason why these plants unite in the peaceful basin of the Atlantic. The only explanation which can be given, he says, seems to me to result from the experience known to all the world. Place in a vase some fragments of cork or other floating body, and give to the water in the vase a circular movement, the scattered fragments will unite in a group in the centre of the liquid surface, that is to say, in the part least agitated. In the phenomenon we are considering, the Atlantic is the vase, the Gulf Stream the circular current, and the Sargasso Sea the central point at which the floating bodies unite.

I share Maury's opinion, and I was able to study the phenomenon in the very midst, where vessels rarely penetrate. Above us floated products of all kinds, heaped up among these brownish plants; trunks of trees torn from the Andes or the Rocky Mountains, and floated by the Amazon or the Mississippi; numerous wrecks, remains of keels, or ships' bottoms, side-planks stove in, and so weighted with shells and barnacles that they could not again rise to the surface. And time will one day justify Maury's other opinion, that these substances thus accumulated for ages will become petrified by the action of the water and will then form inexhaustible coal-mines – a precious reserve prepared by far-seeing Nature for the moment when men shall have exhausted the mines of continents.

In the midst of this inextricable mass of plants and seaweed, I noticed some charming pink halcyons and actiniae, with their long tentacles trailing after them, and medusae, green, red, and blue.

All the day of the 22nd of February we passed in the Sargasso Sea, where such fish as are partial to marine plants find abundant nourishment. The next, the ocean had returned to its accustomed aspect. From this time for nineteen days, from the 23rd of February to the 12th of March, the Nautilus kept in the middle of the Atlantic, carrying us at a constant speed of a hundred leagues in twenty-four hours. Captain Nemo evidently intended accomplishing his submarine programme, and I imagined that he intended, after doubling Cape Horn, to return to the Australian seas of the Pacific. Ned Land had cause for fear. In these large seas, void of islands, we could not attempt to leave the boat. Nor had we any means of opposing Captain Nemo's will. Our only course was to submit; but what we could neither gain by force nor cunning, I liked to think might be obtained by persuasion. This voyage ended, would he not consent to restore our liberty, under an oath never to reveal his existence? – an oath of honour which we should have religiously kept. But we must consider that delicate question with the Captain. But was I free to claim this liberty? Had he not himself said from the beginning, in the firmest manner, that the secret of his life exacted from him our lasting imprisonment on board the Nautilus? And would not my four months' silence appear to him a tacit acceptance of our situation? And would not a return to the subject result in raising suspicions which might be hurtful to our projects, if at some future time a favourable opportunity offered to return to them?

During the nineteen days mentioned above, no incident of any kind happened to signalise our voyage. I saw little of the Captain; he was at work. In the library I often found his books left open, especially those on natural history. My work on submarine depths, conned over by him, was covered with marginal notes, often contradicting my theories and systems; but the Captain contented himself with thus purging my work; it was very rare for him to discuss it with me. Sometimes I heard the melancholy tones of his organ; but only at night, in the midst of the deepest obscurity, when the Nautilus slept upon the deserted ocean. During this part of our voyage we sailed whole days on the surface of the waves. The sea seemed abandoned. A few sailing-vessels, on the road to India, were making for the Cape of Good Hope. One day we were followed by the boats of a whaler, who, no doubt, took us for some enormous whale of great price; but Captain Nemo did not wish the worthy fellows to lose their time and trouble, so ended the chase by plunging under the water. Our navigation continued until the 13th of March; that day the Nautilus was employed in taking soundings, which greatly interested me. We had then made about 13,000 leagues since our departure from the high seas of the Pacific. The bearings gave us 45° 37' S. lat., and 37° 53' W. long. It was the same water in which Captain Denham of the Herald sounded 7,000 fathoms without finding the bottom. There, too, Lieutenant Parker, of the American frigate Congress, could not touch the bottom with 15,140 fathoms. Captain Nemo intended seeking the bottom of the ocean by a diagonal sufficiently lengthened by means of lateral planes placed at an angle of 45° with the water-line of the Nautilus. Then the screw set to work at its maximum speed, its four blades beating the waves with in describable force. Under this powerful pressure, the hull of the Nautilus quivered like a sonorous chord and sank regularly under the water.

At 7,000 fathoms I saw some blackish tops rising from the midst of the waters; but these summits might belong to high mountains like the Himalayas or Mont Blanc, even higher; and the depth of the abyss remained incalculable. The Nautilus descended still lower, in spite of the great pressure. I felt the steel plates tremble at the fastenings of the bolts; its bars bent, its partitions groaned; the windows of the saloon seemed to curve under the pressure of the waters. And this firm structure would doubtless have yielded, if, as its Captain had said, it had not been capable of resistance like a solid block. We had attained a depth of 16,000 yards (four leagues), and the sides of the Nautilus then bore a pressure of 1,600 atmospheres, that is to say, 3,200 lb. to each square two-fifths of an inch of its surface.

"What a situation to be in!" I exclaimed. "To overrun these deep regions where man has never trod! Look, Captain, look at these magnificent rocks, these uninhabited grottoes, these lowest receptacles of the globe, where life is no longer possible! What unknown sights are here! Why should we be unable to preserve a remembrance of them?"

"Would you like to carry away more than the remembrance?" said Captain Nemo.

"What do you mean by those words?"

"I mean to say that nothing is easier than to make a photographic view of this submarine region."

I had not time to express my surprise at this new proposition, when, at Captain Nemo's call, an objective was brought into the saloon. Through the widely-opened panel, the liquid mass was bright with electricity, which was distributed with such uniformity that not a shadow, not a gradation, was to be seen in our manufactured light. The Nautilus remained motionless, the force of its screw subdued by the inclination of its planes: the instrument was propped on the bottom of the oceanic site, and in a few seconds we had obtained a perfect negative.

But, the operation being over, Captain Nemo said, "Let us go up; we must not abuse our position, nor expose the Nautilus too long to such great pressure."

"Go up again!" I exclaimed.

"Hold well on."

I had not time to understand why the Captain cautioned me thus, when I was thrown forward on to the carpet. At a signal from the Captain, its screw was shipped, and its blades raised vertically; the Nautilus shot into the air like a balloon, rising with stunning rapidity, and cutting the mass of waters with a sonorous agitation. Nothing was visible; and in four minutes it had shot through the four leagues which separated it from the ocean, and, after emerging like a flying-fish, fell, making the waves rebound to an enormous height.

The complete and unabridged text is available online, from ***flametreepublishing.com/extras***

The Librarian's Secret Society, 1988

Calie Voorhis

"HAVE YOU CONSIDERED a career in the library sciences?"

The classroom was filled with the rich odor of dying leaves, and when the brisk wind stirred amidst the trees of the quad, there came through the open window the heavy scent of a far-off farm bonfire, or the more delicate sandalwood perfume of a passing student.

The question was being addressed to Theca directly, she didn't know why, only knew that she couldn't tear her eyes away from the woman, whose red leather miniskirt, black thigh-high boots, and side-shaved head made her look like the least likely librarian ever. Well, except for the glasses. Those were all horn-rimmed cat's-eye stereotypical and felt like an afterthought to her otherwise punk outfit.

No one raised their hands to answer and Theca kept hers firm on pen and paper and looked away, although her arm itched to be in the air. She wasn't going to be that person anymore. She would wear the proper alligatored Polos, the mandated Gloria jeans, and Malibu Musk, with her hair in precisely feathered wings. She was not the nerd anymore and she reminded herself of that repeatedly as the guest lecturer tried to engage the class, trying not to rub at her eyes, scratchy from new contacts. Finally, she settled into her chair, and as she had always done, opened a book in her memory and lost herself in Madeleine L'Engle once again.

* * *

"Have you ever thought of a career in the library sciences?" The librarian had followed her outside. Theca turned to answer, to tell her, "No," despite her love of books and libraries, and ran into her high school nemesis. She'd known Deedee was here, had been for a year. But campus was large, and in the previous three weeks of classes, she'd never seen her, not once.

"Barf me out," Deedee said, twirling a lock of hair. "But like, do you even wash your hair?" The gaggle of sorority girls, from the most popular of the sororities, Ithos Kai Ithiki, cocked their collective hips and smirked.

"Same old insults," Theca replied. "I'd have thought that after a year here without me you could've come up with something new, but I see you joined the Ikkies."

To the Librarian, waiting by the oak tree, she said, "No."

"What if I could give you all the books?" The Librarian's eyes, magnified by the glasses, darkened.

"Go on, " Deedee interrupted. "Join the rest of the freaks at the library. You're such a wannabe." Another chorus of giggles erupted from her entourage.

Theca remembered when they'd been library girls together, cuddled on a couch and reading *A Wrinkle in Time*, traveling with Meg through the universe.

The hated redness of embarrassment, that old familiar itchy urge to run, swept over her. She'd hoped that Cathedral Mount was big enough to avoid Deedee, that Deedee would've changed in her two years since graduation, that she'd no longer make it her personal goal to humiliate Theca. Once they'd been best friends, but that had ended abruptly in Junior High, when DeeDee had left her for popularity.

"Don't interrupt," the Librarian said. "So rude."

"Bite me," Deedee returned. "Dried-up hag."

Theca wanted to come to the woman's defense. Her legs almost even moved.

"Shhh," the Librarian said, finger pressed to her lips.

And the world stilled. The oak leaves paused in the air, trembling. The sorority girls, stuck with half-open eyes, fingers suspended.

The trees bowed down, and the Librarian's words opened worlds.

"I can give you books," she said. "I can give you *Tristram Shandy*, *Don Quixote*, and *Tom Jones*. The collected works of Fyodor Dostoevsky, and Mark Twain tales never published. The contents of the Library of Alexandria reside in my blood, and further back still, the books from the dawn of time. Join us."

Theca's own fears and hopes froze her. This moment was all she'd ever wanted; the doorway into Narnia, the portal to Wonderland, the eye of the hurricane to Oz.

"What are you?"

"I'm the Librarian," she said, the leaves in the air quivering. "You think me mad and strange, and you wish to be neither, but the books flow through your genes as they do in mine. Come to the library. Present this to the front desk." She held out a card.

Theca's hands stayed at her side.

"Let me give you a taste, then," the Librarian said. In the midst of the stillness, a suspended flaming red maple leaf hovered near a razor cheekbone. "All the books people mean to read, but never get around to."

A quick knife slit on her scarred wrist, a rivulet of blood on paper white skin. A press of her wrist, unexpected to Theca's lips. An inadvertent lick.

Theca tasted books.

Dostoevsky – mice and old leather, and a tinge of Earl Grey tea. All of him, there in her memory now, *Crime and Punishment*, *Demons*, *The Brothers Karamazov*, *Notes from Underground*, and 'White Nights'. All of the Russian, in Russian, which she could read — as if she'd devoured them whole, binged them four days in the stacks, which she'd been known to do. One summer she'd eaten all of Tolkien, storing the elvish woods of Rivendell in her freaky, eidetic memory. This was that, but better. This was her reading Russian. Did she know Russian now?

She tasted another drop of the blood.

And then there was Twain. Stories she hadn't known existed. New stories, that smelled of cigar smoke, with honey-tart satire. This was magic.

The Librarian stroked her cheek, cool hand wiping the last of the blood from Theca's lips. "We need you. More than you know and soon. The Censors' powers are growing. You're quite possibly the key, the one who can open the oldest library of all."

The Librarian tilted her glasses down, her blue eyes pierced her. "The genetic library of Atlantis." She handed Theca a laminated card. "Tomorrow night at 8:00." In a blink, the librarian was gone and the sounds of campus drifted back.

"Take this too," Deedee said, handing her a flyer. "You could be cool. There are times I miss you, you know." The gaggle of girls gave one last giggle and headed into the night, leaving Theca stunned.

* * *

There was no way she was going to the library, even if she had kept the library card, the lamination glossy and sleek under her thumb. The card had her name on, a logo of a book with crossed swords and a temple, and four libraries listed: Damascus, Athens, Byblos, and Cathedral Mount, alongside a sticker with the word 'Temporary' that she couldn't pick off. She didn't want to be a nerd anymore.

She shouldn't go to rush either. So the sorority was popular and, sure, she wanted Deedee to like her again, like she had once. Her thoughts flicked back and forth and the clock ticked.

She went to rush, after three hours of deep internal deliberation. Magic wasn't real. Conformity, sisterhood, those were real. She'd known all along, deep down, that Deedee hadn't really hated her. Just teasing, just a thing the girls did, and now they'd invited her. She could be one of them and being one of them was everything she'd ever wanted. She'd give DeeDee another chance, for the sake of a long-ago friendship, when they'd both been library girls.

* * *

The trees caught at Theca, scraping her bare shoulder, threatening to snatch her bra strap. Laughter trailed her, the high-pitched squeaks of the sorority, and how she could've been so stupid, so gullible, burned in her veins and her legs ached from running, topless. Why had they done this to her, the only girl to show up? It hit hard, this realization that they'd planned the whole thing, just to get her. That she, and only she, had been their intended target and they'd never meant to rush her at all, just strip her naked and set her loose on campus.

Ahead of her, shadowed by streetlights, two giant oaks guarded the marble steps of Wilson Library. The card, tucked into her bra, she wasn't sure how, nor how it had survived the run. She pulled it out again, her pace slowing to a walk, the laughter giving up the ghost behind her.

Well, there were lights on in the library, and a receptionist at the front portcullis. She straightened her shoulders, wishing for a sweater to put over her bra, and opened the door.

"Card please," the receptionist said, then disappeared behind the desk. There was a rustle, a desk drawer creaked, and she emerged with a purple cardigan, handing it over without a word. "Upstairs," she said. "Fear Reading Room."

Theca headed to the marble steps, curving up in wings from either side of the desk. At the top of the stairs, she hesitated. She knew the Wilson library, knew all its rooms, and she'd never heard of the Fear Reading Room. She'd also never seen a door at the top of the stairs, in the middle of the landing before. "Curiouser and curiouser," she muttered, and turned the handle. The massive door whispered open.

Her feet stopped inside. This room, oh, this was a marvel. This room had the gargoyles of Tolkien's Bodleian library, hovering over the wooden stacks, rows upon rows, vanishing into the depths. It had the grandeur of the columns of Rivendell, and rows of windows all showing the full moon hanging in the October sky. And, how it smelled of books. Books she hadn't yet read, the musty smell of worlds waiting to be opened, heads to roam through, forests yet to be hiked.

Overhead, constellations glowed in the domed ceiling, and stacks radiated out from a center rotunda. She longed to run into them, to lose herself in the printed word, but the Librarian pulled her forward and sat her down behind a reading desk on the rotunda. She ducked her head, aware of the eyes upon her.

Scattered throughout, reading desks loomed, each occupied by a robed and hooded figure. Like the library stretched, the rows continued, in wave upon dwindling wave, and each time her eyes met the horizon, the vantage shifted outward.

"Enter," said the Librarian, her hood slipping down, cat-eye glasses revealed. "Welcome to the library."

A brief clicking, snapping fingers, filled the room and roiled over her.

"Sit here," the Librarian said. "There's a ritual. Be patient."

There was indeed a rite, though most of it seemed to be official and rote. Boring. She let the talk of other libraries flow over her, too busy staring at the shelves and the books, and the other librarians, but they weren't as interesting as the rows upon rows, shelves upon shelves, of tomes, pamphlets, portfolios, periodicals, digests, compendiums, textbooks, and volumes of collections.

"Stand up," the Librarian hissed at her, and Theca jolted to attention, standing up and clutching the borrowed sweater tight.

"Our genes contain the library," the Librarian said. The hall echoed as the assembly repeated her words.

"To perpetuate the principles of our Order, we add to those the librarians who will maintain our ideals, our quests, and our communal library. You have been invited to pledge the Secret Society of Libraries. Should you choose to join us, you shall be tested as is our tradition.

"As Vivliothikarios, I ask you now: Will you, Theca Anne Belirus, be a true and faithful friend to the books, will you preserve them against the Logokritos and the flames, will you pledge to us and the three trials to come?"

Theca found herself standing tall. "Yes," she said, her knees shaking. She didn't need to think anymore. This was crazy and insane, and quite possible depraved, but libraries were her homes, and their inhabitants, her people. She took a deep breath, inhaling the perfume of dust and old paper. "I will." The clicking rang out across the room, figures standing, hoods dropping. "I will," she repeated.

"So be it, then. Fellow librarians, I present you to our newest candidate. Share with her your books, as you both will, harming none."

The hall echoed with the repetition.

The first librarian to approach her was the redheaded one with freckles. She liked his crooked smile, so she took his hand and let him lead her to a nook in the corner. He sat her down beside him on a red velvet couch, the touch of his hand on her arm prickling hairs with anticipation. When he licked the corner of her mouth, she shivered in Henry Miller delights, and his kisses tasted of smoky French cafés and Anaïs Nin.

Shy, she wasn't sure what to give back, how to please him in return. "Whatever you want," he said, in between breaths and gasps, so grasping for straws, she gave him back the rush of space and the self-assurance of Cordelia Naismith, the mischievous pleasures of Miles Vorkosigan, and the tremulous delights of Zelazny.

They shared books and hands, lips and flesh only, and when he gave her *Tropic of Cancer*, she trembled and burst apart.

Around the library, that vast endless room, the murmuring of lovers rippled through the smell of old paper and when she and the redhead had recovered their breaths, she turned to him. "What other books do you have?" she asked. He laughed with delight and pulled her down next to him.

"Once I've had a moment, I'll tempt you with Faulkner," he said.

She wrinkled her nose and he snorted. "Perhaps not Faulkner then. How about DeLillo?" He judged her reaction. "Philip Roth, then."

She ran a finger up his shin, lingering on his inner thigh, bare beneath the robe. "In return?"

"What's your specialty?" he asked, but his lips were already back on hers before she had a chance to answer that she didn't have a specialty. She wanted all the books and after she devoured what he had to offer, she switched partners and let the night carry her away in books and kisses.

* * *

The first test, a scavenger hunt for primary sources through the stacks, was easy and led to Mark, from whom she acquired on a lazy afternoon a complete set of Dickens and an increased appreciation for kissing.

The second test took longer.

"You've made an error," the Librarian said, a small smile flickering across her face, as though she took satisfaction in Theca's mistake. It'd taken her a day to complete the task – to read and then recreate, word for word, an ancient book of lists. And she had, word for word, but the Librarian smiled again and refused to tell her what she'd done wrong, and it took her a week to realize she'd added two commas.

Still, she'd succeeded, at last, and lost herself in Chanakya's library for a week in afternoons of Chai and rumpled patchouli bedsheets, until she'd drained him dry of the *Mahābhārata*, *Rāmāyana*, and *The God of Small Things*.

But no one would tell her what the third trial was, not even Jim the redhead with the Adam's apple, who she tried to seduce for information. He gave her all of DeLillo, which she didn't appreciate, and nothing else.

She longed for more, she wanted all the books, she wanted the hidden library, she wanted Atlantis and Alexandria. She wanted the head Librarian as much as she'd wanted Deedee, once upon a time.

* * *

In the world of Dewey Decimal, 398 is where fairy tales and folklore hide, and that's where in the stacks, she cornered the Librarian, leaning against the shelves for 398.2 – Atlantis.

She meant to say hello. Or something better then hello, something that was smart and sophisticated. Instead, all the anticipation rushed through her. "Is Atlantis really real?" She cringed.

The Librarian's cheeks tightened and a brief wrinkle creased her brow. "It is. Or rather it was, and it might be again. Only time and blood will tell. The Atlantis library is in all of us, really. They encoded it deep into the genes, to prevent the knowledge from being lost, but the key, that they hid in one gene line." She pulled out another book, flipped a page, then another. Flip. "Do you realize how much information is encoded in our DNA and if we could just access it…" Her red nails grabbed another book. 'But you haven't passed the final test yet. You're not one of us, yet."

"But I could be the one?" She knew it, deep in her bones. She was the chosen one, she would be the key to the library of Atlantis and she would share with the world. Her freakish reading ability, her eidetic memory, a heritage from long-ago lost ancestors.

"Possibly." The Librarian looked up from her page, another crease on her forehead. "I've been wrong before, though. Once I thought it was me."

The rush poured through her, a mixture of lust and books. "I want Atlantis," she said.

"So did I child. So do I. I've been waiting a long time for the next head Librarian. But you," she said, brow creased even deeper with a sigh, "You're not ready, even if you hold the key. You haven't passed the final test yet."

But she was the one. Theca knew it, it would be the only thing that made up for everything else, the ridicule of school, the loneliness she'd endured. "Why not?"

"No discipline. You're all over the place. You read anything." The librarian finished flipping and placed the book back on the shelf with a pale hand.

"I read everything," Theca said, stung. She'd read milk cartons and FDA daily dosage recommendations, and the ingredients list if there were no other words around. In Junior High, she went through the daily paper, the cereal box, and milk carton with breakfast, and a few chapters of whatever book was handy on the walk to school, having perfected the ability to read while walking up the long hill. Unless Deedee caught her.

"I am ready," she said.

"Shh," the Librarian said. "Not so loud. You're absolutely not ready for my library. Concentrate on something. Build your own." She coughed and lowered her voice, her rich contralto deep and vibrant. "Others have been complaining, you know. That you're stingy, that all you hold is just pieces of what everyone has, that you've nothing new to add. You don't specialize."

Theca stepped back, bracing herself against the bookshelves, shaking.

"I didn't mean to hurt you, child." The Librarian's voice was soft with regret and her hand cold on Theca's.

Pride had already hardened in her, something vast and red with fury, a beast swelling inside her stomach. Without meaning to, although she knew she did, she grabbed the Librarian's arm, raking her fingers into the forearm.

"You can't take a library by force," the Librarian said. The silence of the library grew. The incessant hum of air conditioning died; the faded murmurs of whispered conversations wilted away.

Together they watched the red scratches swell and beads of blood form.

"Perhaps I've erred. Perhaps you don't have the patience, the research skills, the true heart for knowledge." The Librarian removed Theca's hand. "Go acquire them. The library is closed."

The silence grew louder and the Librarian's blue eyes brighter until all she could see was sunshine and all she could hear was the roar of silence and then with a flapping of a million pages turning, the world spun around her, and her feet stumbled on the green grass of the quad.

* * *

She tried for the rest of the day to enter the library, but she couldn't. Her steps went wrong every time. She tried with her eyes closed, with her eyes fixed on a tree; she tried crawling and running and her pride turned to shame.

* * *

She soon found it was not only the Wilson Library that was forbidden to her, even Cathedral Mount's town library wouldn't let her in, nor, when she pounded on the glass, did anyone inside pay her any attention.

The bookstores on Franklin Street repelled her, the campus store let her in, but wouldn't let her near anything but textbooks. She finished those in a week.

None of the other librarians would talk to her, even DeLillo Jim lowered his shaggy head and walked away from her "Hello."

The Librarian she saw only once, on Halloween, crossing the quad with long strides, moving in a wave of silence. She did not even look at Theca, just altered her stride, her quietness shivering Theca to the bone when she passed.

She borrowed books from her suite mates, romances mostly, and devoured those. Two weeks later, she found herself in the quad before lunch, with the crisp snap of November biting at her cheek, leaning against an oak tree and contemplating asking strangers if she could borrow their books. Across the campus, against the afternoon light, she saw Deedee, and shrank back into the trunk.

"Hi," Deedee said.

She didn't respond. Deedee was alone, unusual, but still suspect. Still in pink, from scrunchie bow holding her ponytail to immaculate pink-striped Adidas.

"Look," Deedee said, placing a hand on Theca's shoulder. "I want to apologize."

She kept her silence. Deedee would go away, eventually. The lessons of high school had taught her to be quiet.

"I mean it. I've realized that I've been a total bitch to you, for too long. You were right, high school was another lifetime."

Theca had longed to hear those words. She shrugged.

"You ran away from us on rush. You do know it was just a prank. All the other girls did it." Deedee said, waving a large pink envelope. "But our Diokitis told us to give you a second chance, that you weren't really with those strange library science majors. I mean really, that redhead with the Adam's apple, what were you thinking?"

The mention of DeLillo Jim slapped her in her face with hot shame and when Deedee handed her the envelope, she took it.

"I want to make it up to you. I think you'd make an awesome sister. The council is willing to waive your rush. You can skip the pledge process. We could be friends again, just give me a chance."

Theca cracked the wax seal on the envelope.

The invitation felt heavier than paper should feel, it weighed her hand down, and was also pink. Swirls of blush and curlicues of coral, with fuchsia accents and the ornate typeface in bright salmon.

The Sisters of the Omega Chapter of the
Ithos Kai Ithiki
at the University of Cathedral Mount are pleased to invite Theca Anne Belirus to rush our Sisterhood on the TWENTY-FIRST of November Nineteen Hundred Eighty Eight at 11:00 p.m. Please accept this invitation by joining us in the Omega Suite at the Ithos Kai Ithiki House.

"But that's tonight," she said.

"Like you've got plans," Deedee said. Then in a rush, "Okay, so I was supposed to give this to you earlier, like I said, but it was the librarian's fault and you missed rush, but that's okay." Her words jumbled together, in a hurry of confession, perhaps. "They're really interested in you. I volunteered, cause I've known you so long. If you'd like, I could like help you pick out clothes, and do makeup. You know, if you'd like."

Theca read the invitation again. Did she really believe any of this, after the torment they'd already put her through?

DeLillo Jim walked past them without a word, again, and when Theca tried to catch his eye, he turned his head away, so that she could see only his scruffy profile and Adam's apple gulp.

"I know what you're thinking," Deedee said. "And you're right, I've been such a bitch. For so long. Just give me one last chance. We were good friends for so long."

"Theca, say yes!" A gaggle of the sorority clustered around, all perfumed and buoyant, sure of themselves and their pink uniformity.

"We're going to Alfonso's," another blonde added.

"You're coming with us, right?" Deedee asked Theca, grabbing her hand. "It'll give me a chance to say sorry some more."

"And talk about what we're all going to wear tonight."

"You'd look so pretty in pink."

And somehow, without ever quite not deciding, Theca found herself drawn into the swirl and by the end of a long lunch, she found herself thinking seriously about joining. All she wanted was a place and a people. Screw the Librarian. Screw the library. She'd go where she was wanted. Everyone deserved another chance.

After the lunch, she found herself at the chapter house, in the middle of a group of girls, all chattering away. Despite her protestations, Cindi and Mary were twirling her hair through a curler, while Wendy fluttered around with various makeup brushes and an intense crease on her forehead. The brushes felt like butterfly kisses and the room smelled of hot hair and floral perfume.

"You're really pretty," Wendy said, stepping back.

"You guys are doing too much," Theca said.

"We just want to spoil you," Deedee said from across the room, curled up in a wing chair by the fireplace. "Because that's what sisters do."

The afternoon droned on and Theca found herself telling them about the librarians, over another round of mimosas. She'd lost track of how many; enough to make the afternoon sun lazy, and the girls surrounding her fuzzy and warm.

"They're so weird," Deedee said, tossing back her hair. "That's awful, what they did to you. Forcing books on you like that."

A pang of guilt surfaced through the orange juice haze. They hadn't forced her to do anything. She'd been the one to use force and she swallowed the acid taste away.

* * *

And the afternoon faded and somehow she found herself saying yes, in the pink haze of sororal affection.

* * *

Which was how she found herself walking in a single-file line through the quiet campus night with a group mood suddenly solemn, carrying a book in her arms, dressed all in pink.

The aroma reached her before the heat did, all through the long silent, single-file march through the quad, with *A Wrinkle in Time* cradled in her arms – the smell of burning — not the toasty snap of wood, but a heavier, more acrid smell, like quills on a chicken; like burnt hair, or perhaps flesh; a smell that reached down her throat, and in her arms, *A Wrinkle in Time* grew heavier. They'd read it together, her and Deedee, once upon an elementary school time.

Her steps faltered.

"Don't lose your courage now," Deedee said, pushing her forward. "Just keep walking and do what the sister in front of you does. Trust us. It's just a book and I bet you've got it memorized anyways."

Flames flickered like fire lizards, and for a moment she saw this as a scene from a book: the courtyard with looming oak trees, the smoke spiraling gray and dirty against a clear dark blue sky, the edges only now fading into black. The circle of flames and the notch, which each woman stepped into to deposit her book, all varieties of pink and ponytail. If this were a book, a story, Theca'd be the heroine and she'd be brave and this moment would be just a paragraph she could skip past, to the point where the heroine came up with something, the plan, the great idea.

The night tasted of the ashes that floated like snowflakes in the air, fat and drifting down all around them, and when she brushed a flake off her shoulder it left a thumbprint smudge on the pink velour.

She kept following her future sisters. This was their ritual, the only thing she had to do to belong to them. It wasn't like books were alive, or they couldn't be replaced. This was just a symbol and she understood the price of admittance.

A piece of ash caught on her lip and she licked it away. Burning books tasted like a banquet gone stale and she yearned to read the words before they turned into smoke. Overlaying the flavor of tart ashes was a lingering nibble of ink, like a Bic pen chewed the wrong way inadvertently.

One step at a time, the line moved forward, each woman tossing a book into the fire. None spoke. None even stayed to watch the words wither.

Maus tasted like fear and guilt, and when *Beloved* burned, she almost wept as the soapy taste of summer roses burst and then faded away, replaced once again by heavy smoke. The words had gone.

Where were the librarians?

Books screamed when they burned, she could hear them, if no one else could. First there was a keening, as the pages struggled to resist, then a whoosh and roar of last resistance, then the pain, as ink fled, until finally only the oak trees were left moaning in the rising wind.

By the time it was her turn, the fire was a dragon roaring, an Orc creation, and the oaks had turned into Ents, and she wished the Shire was rising and she could turn the page and that the burning books would stop sighing, their mewling like injured kittens. The heat from the fire flickered over her chest and the hairs on her arm shriveled. Ribbons of heat shivered over her, followed by a breath of cool; the wind dancing the leaves into the fire with pops and sizzles.

"Your turn," Deedee said, prodding her forward. "Burn one book and we're your forever sisters." Her cheeks flickered with the shadows from the flames.

The heat pressed down on Theca, so intense she wanted to crouch away from the weight, as though flame were as implacable as stone.

"I don't think I can," she said.

"It's just a stupid book," Deedee said. "It doesn't mean anything. All you have to do is toss it into the fire and we can be friends. You can belong somewhere. I mean, they locked you out of the libraries, forced you to do things. This is just words on paper."

Deedee was absolutely right and utterly wrong. She'd done the forcing and books, well, books were more than words on paper, they brought worlds to life and restored history.

"I'm not going to," she said, finding her voice and her determination.

Deedee knocked the book out of her hands. *A Wrinkle in Time* flew through the air, and a tentacle snarled it down into the heart of the flames and before she could think, Theca followed the book.

And in the center of the fire, with the flames swirling around her and licking at her bare legs, crawling up her thighs, she met the Librarian's startled eyes.

"I thought you'd betrayed us," the Librarian said. "I hoped, but I had no faith."

"I made a mistake," she said.

The flames roared around them and though the heat still pressed in, though she could feel the tendrils swirling around her, the fire ate only the pink, the layers of clothing, the scrunchie in her hair. "I'm sorry," she said and bent down, picking up *A Wrinkle in Time*, unscarred except for one scorch mark on the cover. She handed it to the Librarian, who placed it on the stack in front of her. "But I could never burn a book."

Outside the bonfire, she could hear girls screaming. "Oh my god, she pushed her into the fire," Wendy said, her voice high. "Ohmygod," she repeated, over and over, the words running together higher and higher.

"I'll specialize," she said to the Librarian, her clothes burned away, naked before the woman, clutching her book. "I won't betray the books."

The flames wavered about the Librarian and Theca held her breath while the Librarian considered, the weight of her silence dousing the roar of the flames into quiet flickers, ribbons of light.

"You are received," she said, fracturing her silence. "Step forward."

She did and the Librarian kissed her on the forehead.

"You are now one with us in principle and purpose. May your reading never flag, may your sympathies grow deeper, may our regard increase as time shall heighten our appreciation of the noble books. May your union with the books forever resolve attainment of that goal of the true library of Atlantis, aspiration toward which is the sign and seal of our Fraternity. This concludes the Rite of Initiation and we welcome you to the library as a full associate librarian, with the duties and responsibilities that entails."

The Librarian's lips touched her forehead again, then each cheek, and finally, the beating pulse at the base of her neck. "Come," she said, holding out her hand. "There's someone who can tell us what you should be reading, but at any rate, you are truly one of us."

"What do I do about them?" Theca said, gesturing to the shadows rippling in turmoil outside the bonfire. Shouldn't she let them know she wasn't dead, or horribly burned, or scarred for life?

"Walk away. They'll figure it out eventually, their Diokitis knows I will have interfered. But it will take them a while and bring down the school's wrath for a moment. We can use that." The Librarian's hand remained and she took it.

Together, they walked through the fire and out the other side, away from the screams.

"I think that I shall introduce you to the Archivist," the Librarian said, their feet quiet on the grass, the dome of the Wilson Library shining in the night ahead of them, the marble steps waiting. "That can wait for another day though."

The library doors opened for them, and Theca walked inside, *A Wrinkle in Time* tight in her hands. This was her home, these her people. Maybe she wouldn't open the library of Atlantis, maybe she wasn't the chosen, but for tonight, it was enough to belong to the books and she'd never ever, fail to protect them again.

A Dream of Armageddon

H.G. Wells

THE MAN with the white face entered the carriage at Rugby. He moved slowly in spite of the urgency of his porter, and even while he was still on the platform I noted how ill he seemed. He dropped into the corner over against me with a sigh, made an incomplete attempt to arrange his travelling shawl, and became motionless, with his eyes staring vacantly. Presently he was moved by a sense of my observation, looked up at me, and put out a spiritless hand for his newspaper. Then he glanced again in my direction.

I feigned to read. I feared I had unwittingly embarrassed him, and in a moment I was surprised to find him speaking.

"I beg your pardon?" said I.

"That book," he repeated, pointing a lean finger, "is about dreams."

"Obviously," I answered, for it was Fortnum Roscoe's *Dream States*, and the title was on the cover.

He hung silent for a space as if he sought words. "Yes," he said at last, "but they tell you nothing."

I did not catch his meaning for a second.

"They don't know," he added.

I looked a little more attentively at his face.

"There are dreams," he said, "and dreams."

That sort of proposition I never dispute.

"I suppose—" he hesitated. "Do you ever dream? I mean vividly."

"I dream very little," I answered. "I doubt if I have three vivid dreams in a year."

"Ah!" he said, and seemed for a moment to collect his thoughts.

"Your dreams don't mix with your memories?" he asked abruptly. "You don't find yourself in doubt; did this happen or did it not?"

"Hardly ever. Except just for a momentary hesitation now and then. I suppose few people do."

"Does he say—?" He indicated the book.

"Says it happens at times and gives the usual explanation about intensity of impression and the like to account for its not happening as a rule. I suppose you know something of these theories—"

"Very little – except that they are wrong."

His emaciated hand played with the strap of the window for a time. I prepared to resume reading, and that seemed to precipitate his next remark. He leant forward almost as though he would touch me.

"Isn't there something called consecutive dreaming – that goes on night after night?"

"I believe there is. There are cases given in most books on mental trouble."

"Mental trouble! Yes. I daresay there are. It's the right place for them. But what I mean—" He looked at his bony knuckles. "Is that sort of thing always dreaming? Is it dreaming? Or is it something else? Mightn't it be something else?"

I should have snubbed his persistent conversation but for the drawn anxiety of his face. I remember now the look of his faded eyes and the lids red stained – perhaps you know that look.

"I'm not just arguing about a matter of opinion," he said. "The thing's killing me."

"Dreams?"

"If you call them dreams. Night after night. Vivid! – So vivid…this—" (he indicated the landscape that went streaming by the window) "seems unreal in comparison! I can scarcely remember who I am, what business I am on…."

He paused. "Even now—"

"The dream is always the same – do you mean?" I asked.

"It's over."

"You mean?"

"I died."

"Died?"

"Smashed and killed, and now, so much of me as that dream was, is dead. Dead forever. I dreamt I was another man, you know, living in a different part of the world and in a different time. I dreamt that night after night. Night after night I woke into that other life. Fresh scenes and fresh happenings – until I came upon the last—"

"When you died?"

"When I died."

"And since then—"

"No," he said. "Thank God! That was the end of the dream…."

It was clear I was in for this dream. And after all, I had an hour before me, the light was fading fast, and Fortnum Roscoe has a dreary way with him. "Living in a different time," I said: "do you mean in some different age?"

"Yes."

"Past?"

"No, to come – to come."

"The year three thousand, for example?"

"I don't know what year it was. I did when I was asleep, when I was dreaming, that is, but not now – not now that I am awake. There's a lot of things I have forgotten since I woke out of these dreams, though I knew them at the time when I was – I suppose it was dreaming. They called the year differently from our way of calling the year …What did they call it?" He put his hand to his forehead. "No," said he, "I forget."

He sat smiling weakly. For a moment I feared he did not mean to tell me his dream. As a rule I hate people who tell their dreams, but this struck me differently. I proffered assistance even. "It began—" I suggested.

"It was vivid from the first. I seemed to wake up in it suddenly. And it's curious that in these dreams I am speaking of I never remembered this life I am living now. It seemed as if the dream life was enough while it lasted. Perhaps – But I will tell you how I find myself when I do my best to recall it all. I don't remember anything clearly until I found myself sitting in a sort of loggia looking out over the sea. I had been dozing, and suddenly I woke up – fresh and vivid – not a bit dreamlike – because the girl had stopped fanning me."

"The girl?"

"Yes, the girl. You must not interrupt or you will put me out."

He stopped abruptly. "You won't think I'm mad?" he said.

"No," I answered. "You've been dreaming. Tell me your dream."

"I woke up, I say, because the girl had stopped fanning me. I was not surprised to find myself there or anything of that sort, you understand. I did not feel I had fallen into it suddenly. I simply took it up at that point. Whatever memory I had of this life, this nineteenth-century life, faded as I woke, vanished like a dream. I knew all about myself, knew that my name was no longer Cooper but Hedon, and all about my position in the world. I've forgotten a lot since I woke – there's a want of connection – but it was all quite clear and matter of fact then."

He hesitated again, gripping the window strap, putting his face forward and looking up to me appealingly.

"This seems bosh to you?"

"No, no!" I cried. "Go on. Tell me what this loggia was like!"

"It was not really a loggia – I don't know what to call it. It faced south. It was small. It was all in shadow except the semicircle above the balcony that showed the sky and sea and the corner where the girl stood. I was on a couch – it was a metal couch with light striped cushions – and the girl was leaning over the balcony with her back to me. The light of the sunrise fell on her ear and cheek. Her pretty white neck and the little curls that nestled there, and her white shoulder were in the sun, and all the grace of her body was in the cool blue shadow. She was dressed – how can I describe it? It was easy and flowing. And altogether there she stood, so that it came to me how beautiful and desirable she was, as though I had never seen her before. And when at last I sighed and raised myself upon my arm she turned her face to me—"

He stopped.

"I have lived three-and-fifty years in this world. I have had mother, sisters, friends, wife and daughters – all their faces, the play of their faces, I know. But the face of this girl – it is much more real to me. I can bring it back into memory so that I see it again – I could draw it or paint it. And after all—"

He stopped – but I said nothing.

"The face of a dream – the face of a dream. She was beautiful. Not that beauty which is terrible, cold, and worshipful, like the beauty of a saint; nor that beauty that stirs fierce passions; but a sort of radiation, sweet lips that softened into smiles, and grave grey eyes. And she moved gracefully, she seemed to have part with all pleasant and gracious things—"

He stopped, and his face was downcast and hidden. Then he looked up at me and went on, making no further attempt to disguise his absolute belief in the reality of his story.

"You see, I had thrown up my plans and ambitions, thrown up all I had ever worked for or desired for her sake. I had been a master man away there in the north, with influence and property and a great reputation, but none of it had seemed worth having beside her. I had come to the place, this city of sunny pleasures with her, and left all those things to wreck and ruin just to save a remnant at least of my life. While I had been in love with her before I knew that she had any care for me, before I had imagined that she would dare – that we should dare, all my life had seemed vain and hollow, dust and ashes. It was dust and ashes. Night after night and through the long days I had longed and desired – my soul had beaten against the thing forbidden!

"But it is impossible for one man to tell another just these things. It's emotion, it's a tint, a light that comes and goes. Only while it's there, everything changes, everything. The thing is I came away and left them in their Crisis to do what they could."

"Left whom?" I asked, puzzled.

"The people up in the north there. You see – in this dream, anyhow – I had been a big man, the sort of man men come to trust in, to group themselves about. Millions of men who had never seen me were ready to do things and risk things because of their confidence in me. I had been playing that game for years, that big laborious game, that vague, monstrous political game amidst intrigues and betrayals, speech and agitation. It was a vast weltering world, and at last I had a sort of leadership against the Gang – you know it was called the Gang – a sort of compromise of scoundrelly projects and base ambitions and vast public emotional stupidities and catch-words – the Gang that kept the world noisy and blind year by year, and all the while that it was drifting, drifting towards infinite disaster. But I can't expect you to understand the shades and complications of the year – the year something or other ahead. I had it all – down to the smallest details – in my dream. I suppose I had been dreaming of it before I awoke, and the fading outline of some queer new development I had imagined still hung about me as I rubbed my eyes. It was some grubby affair that made me thank God for the sunlight. I sat up on the couch and remained looking at the woman and rejoicing – rejoicing that I had come away out of all that tumult and folly and violence before it was too late. After all, I thought, this is life – love and beauty, desire and delight, are they not worth all those dismal struggles for vague, gigantic ends? And I blamed myself for having ever sought to be a leader when I might have given my days to love. But then, thought I, if I had not spent my early days sternly and austerely, I might have wasted myself upon vain and worthless women, and at the thought all my being went out in love and tenderness to my dear mistress, my dear lady, who had come at last and compelled me – compelled me by her invincible charm for me – to lay that life aside.

"'You are worth it,' I said, speaking without intending her to hear; 'you are worth it, my dearest one; worth pride and praise and all things. Love! To have you is worth them all together.' And at the murmur of my voice she turned about.

"'Come and see,' she cried – I can hear her now – 'come and see the sunrise upon Monte Solaro.'

"I remember how I sprang to my feet and joined her at the balcony. She put a white hand upon my shoulder and pointed towards great masses of limestone, flushing, as it were, into life. I looked. But first I noted the sunlight on her face caressing the lines of her cheeks and neck. How can I describe to you the scene we had before us? We were at Capri—"

"I have been there," I said. "I have clambered up Monte Solaro and drunk vero Capri – muddy stuff like cider – at the summit."

"Ah!" said the man with the white face; "Then perhaps you can tell me – you will know if this is indeed Capri. For in this life I have never been there. Let me describe it. We were in a little room, one of a vast multitude of little rooms, very cool and sunny, hollowed out of the limestone of a sort of cape, very high above the sea. The whole island, you know, was one enormous hotel, complex beyond explaining, and on the other side there were miles of floating hotels, and huge floating stages to which the flying machines came. They called it a pleasure city. Of course, there was none of that in your time – rather, I should say, is none of that now. Of course. Now! – Yes.

"Well, this room of ours was at the extremity of the cape, so that one could see east and west. Eastward was a great cliff – a thousand feet high perhaps – coldly grey except for one bright edge of gold, and beyond it the Isle of the Sirens, and a falling coast that faded and passed into the hot sunrise. And when one turned to the west, distinct and near was a little bay, a little beach still in shadow. And out of that shadow rose Solaro straight and tall, flushed and golden crested, like a beauty throned, and the white moon was floating behind her in the sky. And before us from east to west stretched the many-tinted sea all dotted with little sailing boats.

"To the eastward, of course, these little boats were grey and very minute and clear, but to the westward they were little boats of gold – shining gold – almost like little flames. And just below us was a rock with an arch worn through it. The blue sea-water broke to green and foam all round the rock, and a galley came gliding out of the arch."

"I know that rock." I said. "I was nearly drowned there. It is called the Faraglioni."

"I Faraglioni? Yes, she called it that," answered the man with the white face. "There was some story – but that—"

He put his hand to his forehead again. "No," he said, "I forget that story."

"Well, that is the first thing I remember, the first dream I had, that little shaded room and the beautiful air and sky and that dear lady of mine, with her shining arms and her graceful robe, and how we sat and talked in half whispers to one another. We talked in whispers not because there was any one to hear, but because there was still such a freshness of mind between us that our thoughts were a little frightened, I think, to find themselves at last in words. And so they went softly.

"Presently we were hungry and we went from our apartment, going by a strange passage with a moving floor, until we came to the great breakfast room – there was a fountain and music. A pleasant and joyful place it was, with its sunlight and splashing, and the murmur of plucked strings. And we sat and ate and smiled at one another, and I would not heed a man who was watching me from a table near by.

"And afterwards we went on to the dancing-hall. But I cannot describe that hall. The place was enormous – larger than any building you have ever seen – and in one place there was the old gate of Capri, caught into the wall of a gallery high overhead. Light girders, stems and threads of gold, burst from the pillars like fountains, streamed like an Aurora across the roof and interlaced, like – like conjuring tricks. All about the great circle for the dancers there were beautiful figures, strange dragons, and intricate and wonderful grotesques bearing lights. The place was inundated with artificial light that shamed the newborn day. And as we went through the throng the people turned about and looked at us, for all through the world my name and face were known, and how I had suddenly thrown up pride and struggle to come to this place. And they looked also at the lady beside me, though half the story of how at last she had come to me was unknown or mistold. And few of the men who were there, I know, but judged me a happy man, in spite of all the shame and dishonour that had come upon my name.

"The air was full of music, full of harmonious scents, full of the rhythm of beautiful motions. Thousands of beautiful people swarmed about the hall, crowded the galleries, sat in a myriad recesses; they were dressed in splendid colours and crowned with flowers; thousands danced about the great circle beneath the white images of the ancient gods, and glorious processions of youths and maidens came and went. We two danced, not the dreary monotonies of your days – of this time, I mean – but dances that were beautiful, intoxicating. And even now I can see my lady dancing – dancing joyously. She danced, you know, with a serious face; she danced with a serious dignity, and yet she was smiling at me and caressing me – smiling and caressing with her eyes.

"The music was different," he murmured. "It went – I cannot describe it; but it was infinitely richer and more varied than any music that has ever come to me awake.

"And then – it was when we had done dancing – a man came to speak to me. He was a lean, resolute man, very soberly clad for that place, and already I had marked his face watching me in the breakfasting hall, and afterwards as we went along the passage I had avoided his eye. But now, as we sat in a little alcove, smiling at the pleasure of all the people who went to and fro across the shining floor, he came and touched me, and spoke to me so that I was forced to listen. And he asked that he might speak to me for a little time apart.

"'No,' I said. 'I have no secrets from this lady. What do you want to tell me?'

"He said it was a trivial matter, or at least a dry matter, for a lady to hear.

"'Perhaps for me to hear,' said I.

"He glanced at her, as though almost he would appeal to her. Then he asked me suddenly if I had heard of a great and avenging declaration that Evesham had made? Now, Evesham had always before been the man next to myself in the leadership of that great party in the north. He was a forcible, hard, and tactless man, and only I had been able to control and soften him. It was on his account even more than my own, I think, that the others had been so dismayed at my retreat. So this question about what he had done reawakened my old interest in the life I had put aside just for a moment.

"'I have taken no heed of any news for many days,' I said. 'What has Evesham been saying?'

"And with that the man began, nothing loth, and I must confess even I was struck by Evesham's reckless folly in the wild and threatening words he had used. And this messenger they had sent to me not only told me of Evesham's speech, but went on to ask counsel and to point out what need they had of me. While he talked, my lady sat a little forward and watched his face and mine.

"My old habits of scheming and organising reasserted themselves. I could even see myself suddenly returning to the north, and all the dramatic effect of it. All that this man said witnessed to the disorder of the party indeed, but not to its damage. I should go back stronger than I had come. And then I thought of my lady. You see – how can I tell you? There were certain peculiarities of our relationship – as things are I need not tell you about that – which would render her presence with me impossible. I should have had to leave her; indeed, I should have had to renounce her clearly and openly, if I was to do all that I could do in the north. And the man knew that, even as he talked to her and me, knew it as well as she did, that my steps to duty were – first, separation, then abandonment. At the touch of that thought my dream of a return was shattered. I turned on the man suddenly, as he was imagining his eloquence was gaining ground with me.

"'What have I to do with these things now?' I said. 'I have done with them. Do you think I am coquetting with your people in coming here?'

"'No,' he said. 'But—'

"'Why cannot you leave me alone. I have done with these things. I have ceased to be anything but a private man.'

"'Yes,' he answered. 'But have you thought? – This talk of war, these reckless challenges, these wild aggressions—'

"I stood up.

"'No,' I cried. 'I won't hear you. I took count of all those things, I weighed them – and I have come away.'

"He seemed to consider the possibility of persistence. He looked from me to where the lady sat regarding us.

"'War,' he said, as if he were speaking to himself, and then turned slowly from me and walked away.

"I stood, caught in the whirl of thoughts his appeal had set going.

"I heard my lady's voice.

"'Dear,' she said; 'but if they had need of you—'

"She did not finish her sentence, she let it rest there. I turned to her sweet face, and the balance of my mood swayed and reeled.

"'They want me only to do the thing they dare not do themselves,' I said. 'If they distrust Evesham they must settle with him themselves.'

"She looked at me doubtfully.

"'But war—' she said.

"I saw a doubt on her face that I had seen before, a doubt of herself and me, the first shadow of the discovery that, seen strongly and completely, must drive us apart for ever.

"Now, I was an older mind than hers, and I could sway her to this belief or that.

"'My dear one,' I said, 'you must not trouble over these things. There will be no war. Certainly there will be no war. The age of wars is past. Trust me to know the justice of this case. They have no right upon me, dearest, and no one has a right upon me. I have been free to choose my life, and I have chosen this.'

"'But war—,' she said.

"I sat down beside her. I put an arm behind her and took her hand in mine. I set myself to drive that doubt away – I set myself to fill her mind with pleasant things again. I lied to her, and in lying to her I lied also to myself. And she was only too ready to believe me, only too ready to forget.

"Very soon the shadow had gone again, and we were hastening to our bathing-place in the Grotta del Bovo Marino, where it was our custom to bathe every day. We swam and splashed one another, and in that buoyant water I seemed to become something lighter and stronger than a man. And at last we came out dripping and rejoicing and raced among the rocks. And then I put on a dry bathing-dress, and we sat to bask in the sun, and presently I nodded, resting my head against her knee, and she put her hand upon my hair and stroked it softly and I dozed. And behold! As it were with the snapping of the string of a violin, I was awakening, and I was in my own bed in Liverpool, in the life of today.

"Only for a time I could not believe that all these vivid moments had been no more than the substance of a dream.

"In truth, I could not believe it a dream for all the sobering reality of things about me. I bathed and dressed as it were by habit, and as I shaved I argued why I of all men should leave the woman I loved to go back to fantastic politics in the hard and strenuous north. Even if Evesham did force the world back to war, what was that to me? I was a man with the heart of a man, and why should I feel the responsibility of a deity for the way the world might go?

"You know that is not quite the way I think about affairs, about my real affairs. I am a solicitor, you know, with a point of view.

"The vision was so real, you must understand, so utterly unlike a dream that I kept perpetually recalling little irrelevant details; even the ornament of the book-cover that lay on my wife's sewing-machine in the breakfast-room recalled with the utmost vividness the gilt line that ran about the seat in the alcove where I had talked with the messenger from my deserted party. Have you ever heard of a dream that had a quality like that?"

"Like—?"

"So that afterwards you remembered little details you had forgotten."

I thought. I had never noticed the point before, but he was right.

"Never," I said. "That is what you never seem to do with dreams."

"No," he answered. "But that is just what I did. I am a solicitor, you must understand, in Liverpool, and I could not help wondering what the clients and business people I found myself talking to in my office would think if I told them suddenly I was in love with a girl who would be born a couple of hundred years or so hence, and worried about the politics of my great-great-great-grandchildren. I was chiefly busy that day negotiating a ninety-nine-year building lease. It was a private builder in a hurry, and we wanted to tie him in every possible way. I had an interview with him, and he showed a certain want of temper that sent me to bed still irritated. That night I had no dream. Nor did I dream the next night, at least, to remember.

"Something of that intense reality of conviction vanished. I began to feel sure it was a dream. And then it came again.

"When the dream came again, nearly four days later, it was very different. I think it certain that four days had also elapsed in the dream. Many things had happened in the north, and the shadow of them was back again between us, and this time it was not so easily dispelled. I began I know with moody musings. Why, in spite of all, should I go back, go back for all the rest of my days to toil and stress, insults and perpetual dissatisfaction, simply to save hundreds of millions of common people, whom I did not love, whom too often I could do no other than despise, from the stress and anguish of war and infinite misrule? And after all I might fail. They all sought their own narrow ends, and why should not I – why should not I also live as a man? And out of such thoughts her voice summoned me, and I lifted my eyes.

"I found myself awake and walking. We had come out above the Pleasure City, we were near the summit of Monte Solaro and looking towards the bay. It was the late afternoon and very clear. Far away to the left Ischia hung in a golden haze between sea and sky, and Naples was coldly white against the hills, and before us was Vesuvius with a tall and slender streamer feathering at last towards the south, and the ruins of Torre dell' Annunziata and Castellammare glittering and near."

I interrupted suddenly: "You have been to Capri, of course?"

"Only in this dream," he said, "only in this dream. All across the bay beyond Sorrento were the floating palaces of the Pleasure City moored and chained. And northward were the broad floating stages that received the aeroplanes. Aeroplanes fell out of the sky every afternoon, each bringing its thousands of pleasure-seekers from the uttermost parts of the earth to Capri and its delights. All these things, I say, stretched below.

"But we noticed them only incidentally because of an unusual sight that evening had to show. Five war aeroplanes that had long slumbered useless in the distant arsenals of the Rhinemouth were manoeuvring now in the eastward sky. Evesham had astonished the world by producing them and others, and sending them to circle here and there. It was the threat material in the great game of bluff he was playing, and it had taken even me by surprise. He was one of those incredibly stupid energetic people who seem sent by heaven to create disasters. His energy to the first glance seemed so wonderfully like capacity! But he had no imagination, no invention, only a stupid, vast, driving force of will, and a mad faith in his stupid idiot 'luck' to pull him through. I remember how we stood upon the headland watching the squadron circling far away, and how I weighed the full meaning of the sight, seeing clearly the way things must go. And then even it was not too late. I might have gone back, I think, and saved the world. The people of the north would follow me, I knew, granted only that in one thing I respected their moral standards. The east and south would trust me as they would trust no other northern man. And I knew I had only to put it to her and she would have let me go … Not because she did not love me!

"Only I did not want to go; my will was all the other way about. I had so newly thrown off the incubus of responsibility: I was still so fresh a renegade from duty that the daylight clearness of what I ought to do had no power at all to touch my will. My will was to live, to gather pleasures and make my dear lady happy. But though this sense of vast neglected duties had no power to draw me, it could make me silent and preoccupied, it robbed the days I had spent of half their brightness and roused me into dark meditations in the silence of the night. And as I stood and watched Evesham's aeroplanes sweep to and fro – those birds of infinite ill omen – she stood beside me watching me, perceiving the trouble indeed, but not perceiving it clearly – her eyes questioning my face, her expression shaded with perplexity. Her face was grey because the sunset was fading out of the sky. It was no fault of hers that she held me. She had asked me to go from her, and again in the night time and with tears she had asked me to go.

"At last it was the sense of her that roused me from my mood. I turned upon her suddenly and challenged her to race down the mountain slopes. 'No,' she said, as if I had jarred with her gravity, but I was resolved to end that gravity, and make her run – no one can be very grey and sad who is out of breath – and when she stumbled I ran with my hand beneath her arm. We ran down past a couple of men, who turned back staring in astonishment at my behaviour – they must have recognised my face. And half way down the slope came a tumult in the air, clang-clank, clang-clank, and we stopped, and presently over the hill-crest those war things came flying one behind the other."

The man seemed hesitating on the verge of a description.

"What were they like?" I asked.

"They had never fought," he said. "They were just like our ironclads are nowadays; they had never fought. No one knew what they might do, with excited men inside them; few even cared to speculate. They were great driving things shaped like spear-heads without a shaft, with a propeller in the place of the shaft."

"Steel?"

"Not steel."

"Aluminum?"

"No, no, nothing of that sort. An alloy that was very common – as common as brass, for example. It was called – let me see—" He squeezed his forehead with the fingers of one hand. "I am forgetting everything," he said.

"And they carried guns?"

"Little guns, firing high explosive shells. They fired the guns backwards, out of the base of the leaf, so to speak, and rammed with the beak. That was the theory, you know, but they had never been fought. No one could tell exactly what was going to happen. And meanwhile I suppose it was very fine to go whirling through the air like a flight of young swallows, swift and easy. I guess the captains tried not to think too clearly what the real thing would be like. And these flying war machines, you know, were only one sort of the endless war contrivances that had been invented and had fallen into abeyance during the long peace. There were all sorts of these things that people were routing out and furbishing up; infernal things, silly things; things that had never been tried; big engines, terrible explosives, great guns. You know the silly way of these ingenious sort of men who make these things; they turn 'em out as beavers build dams, and with no more sense of the rivers they're going to divert and the lands they're going to flood!

"As we went down the winding stepway to our hotel again, in the twilight, I foresaw it all: I saw how clearly and inevitably things were driving for war in Evesham's silly, violent hands, and I had some inkling of what war was bound to be under these new conditions. And even then, though I knew it was drawing near the limit of my opportunity, I could find no will to go back."

He sighed.

"That was my last chance.

"We didn't go into the city until the sky was full of stars, so we walked out upon the high terrace, to and fro, and – she counselled me to go back.

"'My dearest,' she said, and her sweet face looked up to me, 'this is Death. This life you lead is Death. Go back to them, go back to your duty—'

"She began to weep, saying, between her sobs, and clinging to my arm as she said it, 'Go back – Go back.'

"Then suddenly she fell mute, and, glancing down at her face, I read in an instant the thing she had thought to do. It was one of those moments when one sees.

"'No!' I said.

"'No?' she asked, in surprise and I think a little fearful at the answer to her thought.

"'Nothing,' I said, 'shall send me back. Nothing! I have chosen. Love, I have chosen, and the world must go. Whatever happens I will live this life – I will live for you! It – nothing shall turn me aside; nothing, my dear one. Even if you died – even if you died—'

"'Yes?' she murmured, softly.

"'Then – I also would die.'

"And before she could speak again I began to talk, talking eloquently – as I could do in that life – talking to exalt love, to make the life we were living seem heroic and glorious; and the thing I was deserting something hard and enormously ignoble that it was a fine thing to set aside. I bent all my mind to throw that glamour upon it, seeking not only to convert her but myself to that. We talked, and she clung to me, torn too between all that she deemed noble and all that she knew was sweet. And at last I did make it heroic, made all the thickening disaster of the world only a sort of glorious setting to our unparalleled love, and we two poor foolish souls strutted there at last, clad in that splendid delusion, drunken rather with that glorious delusion, under the still stars.

"And so my moment passed.

"It was my last chance. Even as we went to and fro there, the leaders of the south and east were gathering their resolve, and the hot answer that shattered Evesham's bluffing for ever, took shape and waited. And, all over Asia, and the ocean, and the South, the air and the wires were throbbing with their warnings to prepare – prepare.

"No one living, you know, knew what war was; no one could imagine, with all these new inventions, what horror war might bring. I believe most people still believed it would be a matter of bright uniforms and shouting charges and triumphs and flags and bands – in a time when half the world drew its food supply from regions ten thousand miles away—"

The man with the white face paused. I glanced at him, and his face was intent on the floor of the carriage. A little railway station, a string of loaded trucks, a signal-box, and the back of a cottage, shot by the carriage window, and a bridge passed with a clap of noise, echoing the tumult of the train.

"After that," he said, "I dreamt often. For three weeks of nights that dream was my life. And the worst of it was there were nights when I could not dream, when I lay tossing on a bed in this accursed life; and there – somewhere lost to me – things were happening – momentous, terrible things… I lived at nights – my days, my waking days, this life I am living now, became a faded, far-away dream, a drab setting, the cover of the book."

He thought.

"I could tell you all, tell you every little thing in the dream, but as to what I did in the daytime – no. I could not tell – I do not remember. My memory – my memory has gone. The business of life slips from me—"

He leant forward, and pressed his hands upon his eyes. For a long time he said nothing.

"And then?" said I.

"The war burst like a hurricane."

He stared before him at unspeakable things.

"And then?" I urged again.

"One touch of unreality," he said, in the low tone of a man who speaks to himself, "and they would have been nightmares. But they were not nightmares – they were not nightmares. No!"

He was silent for so long that it dawned upon me that there was a danger of losing the rest of the story. But he went on talking again in the same tone of questioning self-communion.

"What was there to do but flight? I had not thought the war would touch Capri – I had seemed to see Capri as being out of it all, as the contrast to it all; but two nights after the whole place was shouting and bawling, every woman almost and every other man wore a badge – Evesham's badge – and there was no music but a jangling war-song over and over again, and everywhere men enlisting, and in the dancing halls they were drilling. The whole island was awhirl with rumours; it was said, again and again, that fighting had begun. I had not expected this. I had seen so little of the life of pleasure that I had failed to reckon with this violence of the amateurs. And as for me, I was out of it. I was like the man who might have prevented the firing of a magazine. The time had gone. I was no one; the vainest stripling with a badge counted for more than I. The crowd jostled us and bawled in our ears; that accursed song deafened us; a woman shrieked at my lady because no badge was on her, and we two went back to our own place again, ruffled and insulted – my lady white and silent, and I aquiver with rage. So furious was I, I could have quarrelled with her if I could have found one shade of accusation in her eyes.

"All my magnificence had gone from me. I walked up and down our rock cell, and outside was the darkling sea and a light to the southward that flared and passed and came again.

"'We must get out of this place,' I said over and over. 'I have made my choice, and I will have no hand in these troubles. I will have nothing of this war. We have taken our lives out of all these things. This is no refuge for us. Let us go.'

"And the next day we were already in flight from the war that covered the world.

"And all the rest was Flight – all the rest was Flight."

He mused darkly.

"How much was there of it?"

He made no answer.

"How many days?"

His face was white and drawn and his hands were clenched. He took no heed of my curiosity. I tried to draw him back to his story with questions.

"Where did you go?" I said.

"When?"

"When you left Capri."

"South-west," he said, and glanced at me for a second. "We went in a boat."

"But I should have thought an aeroplane?"

"They had been seized."

I questioned him no more. Presently I thought he was beginning again. He broke out in an argumentative monotone:

"But why should it be? If, indeed, this battle, this slaughter and stress is life, why have we this craving for pleasure and beauty? If there is no refuge, if there is no place of peace, and if all our dreams of quiet places are a folly and a snare, why have we such dreams? Surely it was no ignoble cravings, no base intentions, had brought us to this; it was Love had isolated us. Love had come to me with her eyes and robed in her beauty, more glorious than all else in life, in the very shape and colour of life, and summoned me away. I had silenced all the voices, I had answered all the questions – I had come to her. And suddenly there was nothing but War and Death!"

I had an inspiration. "After all," I said, "it could have been only a dream."

"A dream!" he cried, flaming upon me, "A dream – when, even now—"

For the first time he became animated. A faint flush crept into his cheek. He raised his open hand and clenched it, and dropped it to his knee. He spoke, looking away from me, and for all the rest of the time he looked away. "We are but phantoms!" he said, "And the phantoms of phantoms, desires like cloud-shadows and wills of straw that eddy in the wind; the days pass, use and wont carry us through as a train carries the shadow of its lights – so be it! But one thing is real and certain, one thing is no dream-stuff, but eternal and enduring. It is the centre of my life, and all other things about it are subordinate or altogether vain. I loved her, that woman of a dream. And she and I are dead together!

"A dream! How can it be a dream, when it drenched a living life with unappeasable sorrow, when it makes all that I have lived for and cared for, worthless and unmeaning?

"Until that very moment when she was killed I believed we had still a chance of getting away," he said. "All through the night and morning that we sailed across the sea from Capri to Salerno, we talked of escape. We were full of hope, and it clung about us to the end, hope for the life together we should lead, out of it all, out of the battle and struggle, the wild and empty passions, the empty arbitrary 'thou shalt' and 'thou shalt not' of the world. We were uplifted, as though our quest was a holy thing, as though love for another was a mission....

"Even when from our boat we saw the fair face of that great rock Capri – already scarred and gashed by the gun emplacements and hiding-places that were to make it a fastness – we reckoned nothing of the imminent slaughter, though the fury of preparation hung about in the puffs and clouds of dust at a hundred points amidst the grey; but, indeed, I made a text of that and talked. There, you know, was the rock, still beautiful for all its scars, with its countless windows and arches and ways, tier upon tier, for a thousand feet, a vast carving of grey, broken by vine-clad terraces, and lemon and orange groves, and masses of agave and prickly pear, and puffs of almond blossom. And out under the archway that is built over the Piccola Marina other boats were coming; and as we came round the cape and within sight of the mainland, another little string of boats came into view, driving before the wind towards the south-west. In a little while a multitude had come out, the remoter just little specks of ultramarine in the shadow of the eastward cliff.

"'It is love and reason,' I said, 'fleeing from all this madness of war.'

"And though we presently saw a squadron of aeroplanes flying across the southern sky we did not heed it. There it was – a line of little dots in the sky – and then more, dotting the south-eastern horizon, and then still more, until all that quarter of the sky was stippled with blue specks. Now they were all thin little strokes of blue, and now one and now a multitude would heel and catch the sun and become short flashes of light. They came, rising and falling and growing larger, like some huge flight of gulls or rooks or such-like birds, moving with a marvellous uniformity, and ever as they drew nearer they spread over a greater width of sky. The southward wind flung itself in an arrow-headed cloud athwart the sun. And then suddenly they swept round to the eastward and streamed eastward, growing smaller and smaller and clearer and clearer again until they vanished from the sky. And after that we noted to the northward and very high Evesham's fighting machines hanging high over Naples like an evening swarm of gnats.

"It seemed to have no more to do with us than a flight of birds.

"Even the mutter of guns far away in the south-east seemed to us to signify nothing....

"Each day, each dream after that, we were still exalted, still seeking that refuge where we might live and love. Fatigue had come upon us, pain and many distresses. For though we were dusty and stained by our toilsome tramping, and half starved and with the horror of the dead men we had seen and the flight of the peasants – for very soon a gust of fighting swept up the peninsula – with these things haunting our minds it still resulted only in a deepening resolution to escape. Oh, but she was brave and patient! She who had never faced hardship and exposure had courage for herself and me. We went to and fro seeking an outlet, over a country all commandeered and ransacked by the gathering hosts of war. Always we went on foot. At first there were other fugitives, but we did not mingle with them. Some escaped northward, some were caught in the torrent of peasantry that swept along the main roads; many gave themselves into the hands of the soldiery and were sent northward. Many of the men were impressed. But we kept away from these things; we had brought no money to bribe a passage north, and I feared for my lady at the hands of these conscript crowds. We had landed at Salerno, and we had been turned back from Cava, and we had tried to cross towards Taranto by a pass over Mount Alburno, but we had been driven back for want of food, and so we had come down among the marshes by Paestum, where those great temples stand alone. I had some vague idea that by Paestum it might be possible to find a boat or something, and take once more to sea. And there it was the battle overtook us.

"A sort of soul-blindness had me. Plainly I could see that we were being hemmed in; that the great net of that giant Warfare had us in its toils. Many times we had seen the levies that had come down from the north going to and fro, and had come upon them in the distance amidst the mountains making ways for the ammunition and preparing the mounting of the guns. Once we fancied they had fired at us, taking us for spies – at any rate a shot had gone shuddering over us. Several times we had hidden in woods from hovering aeroplanes.

"But all these things do not matter now, these nights of flight and pain… We were in an open place near those great temples at Paestum, at last, on a blank stony place dotted with spiky bushes, empty and desolate and so flat that a grove of eucalyptus far away showed to the feet of its stems. How I can see it! My lady was sitting down under a bush resting a little, for she was very weak and weary, and I was standing up watching to see if I could tell the distance of the firing that came and went. They were still, you know, fighting far from each other, with those terrible new weapons that had never before been used: guns that would carry beyond sight, and aeroplanes that would do – What they would do no man could foretell.

"I knew that we were between the two armies, and that they drew together. I knew we were in danger, and that we could not stop there and rest!

"Though all these things were in my mind, they were in the background. They seemed to be affairs beyond our concern. Chiefly, I was thinking of my lady. An aching distress filled me. For the first time she had owned herself beaten and had fallen a-weeping. Behind me I could hear her sobbing, but I would not turn round to her because I knew she had need of weeping, and had held herself so far and so long for me. It was well, I thought, that she would weep and rest and then we would toil on again, for I had no inkling of the thing that hung so near. Even now I can see her as she sat there, her lovely hair upon her shoulder, can mark again the deepening hollow of her cheek.

"'If we had parted,' she said, 'if I had let you go.'

"'No,' said I. 'Even now, I do not repent. I will not repent; I made my choice, and I will hold on to the end.'

"And then—

"Overhead in the sky flashed something and burst, and all about us I heard the bullets making a noise like a handful of peas suddenly thrown. They chipped the stones about us, and whirled fragments from the bricks and passed…."

He put his hand to his mouth, and then moistened his lips.

"At the flash I had turned about….

"You know – she stood up—

"She stood up, you know, and moved a step towards me – as though she wanted to reach me—

"And she had been shot through the heart."

He stopped and stared at me. I felt all that foolish incapacity an Englishman feels on such occasions. I met his eyes for a moment, and then stared out of the window. For a long space we kept silence. When at last I looked at him he was sitting back in his corner, his arms folded, and his teeth gnawing at his knuckles.

He bit his nail suddenly, and stared at it.

"I carried her," he said, "towards the temples, in my arms – as though it mattered. I don't know why. They seemed a sort of sanctuary, you know, they had lasted so long, I suppose.

"She must have died almost instantly. Only – I talked to her all the way."

Silence again.

"I have seen those temples," I said abruptly, and indeed he had brought those still, sunlit arcades of worn sandstone very vividly before me.

"It was the brown one, the big brown one. I sat down on a fallen pillar and held her in my arms… Silent after the first babble was over. And after a little while the lizards came out and ran about again, as though nothing unusual was going on, as though nothing had changed… It was tremendously still there, the sun high and the shadows still; even the shadows of the weeds upon the entablature were still – in spite of the thudding and banging that went all about the sky.

"I seem to remember that the aeroplanes came up out of the south, and that the battle went away to the west. One aeroplane was struck, and overset and fell. I remember that – though it didn't interest me in the least. It didn't seem to signify. It was like a wounded gull, you know – flapping for a time in the water. I could see it down the aisle of the temple – a black thing in the bright blue water.

"Three or four times shells burst about the beach, and then that ceased. Each time that happened all the lizards scuttled in and hid for a space. That was all the mischief done, except that once a stray bullet gashed the stone hard by – made just a fresh bright surface.

"As the shadows grew longer, the stillness seemed greater.

"The curious thing," he remarked, with the manner of a man who makes a trivial conversation, "is that I didn't *think* – at all. I sat with her in my arms amidst the stones – in a sort of lethargy – stagnant.

"And I don't remember waking up. I don't remember dressing that day. I know I found myself in my office, with my letters all slit open in front of me, and how I was struck by the absurdity of being there, seeing that in reality I was sitting, stunned, in that Paestum Temple with a dead woman in my arms. I read my letters like a machine. I have forgotten what they were about."

He stopped, and there was a long silence.

Suddenly I perceived that we were running down the incline from Chalk Farm to Euston. I started at this passing of time. I turned on him with a brutal question, with the tone of 'Now or never'.

"And did you dream again?"

"Yes."

He seemed to force himself to finish. His voice was very low.

"Once more, and as it were only for a few instants. I seemed to have suddenly awakened out of a great apathy, to have risen into a sitting position, and the body lay there on the stones beside me. A gaunt body. Not her, you know. So soon – it was not her....

"I may have heard voices. I do not know. Only I knew clearly that men were coming into the solitude and that that was a last outrage.

"I stood up and walked through the temple, and then there came into sight – first one man with a yellow face, dressed in a uniform of dirty white, trimmed with blue, and then several, climbing to the crest of the old wall of the vanished city, and crouching there. They were little bright figures in the sunlight, and there they hung, weapon in hand, peering cautiously before them.

"And further away I saw others and then more at another point in the wall. It was a long lax line of men in open order.

"Presently the man I had first seen stood up and shouted a command, and his men came tumbling down the wall and into the high weeds towards the temple. He scrambled down with them and led them. He came facing towards me, and when he saw me he stopped.

"At first I had watched these men with a mere curiosity, but when I had seen they meant to come to the temple I was moved to forbid them. I shouted to the officer.

"'You must not come here,' I cried, '*I* am here. I am here with my dead.'

"He stared, and then shouted a question back to me in some unknown tongue.

"I repeated what I had said.

"He shouted again, and I folded my arms and stood still. Presently he spoke to his men and came forward. He carried a drawn sword.

"I signed to him to keep away, but he continued to advance. I told him again very patiently and clearly: 'You must not come here. These are old temples and I am here with my dead.'

"Presently he was so close I could see his face clearly. It was a narrow face, with dull grey eyes, and a black moustache. He had a scar on his upper lip, and he was dirty and unshaven. He kept shouting unintelligible things, questions, perhaps, at me.

"I know now that he was afraid of me, but at the time that did not occur to me. As I tried to explain to him, he interrupted me in imperious tones, bidding me, I suppose, stand aside.

"He made to go past me, and I caught hold of him.

"I saw his face change at my grip.

"'You fool,' I cried. 'Don't you know? She is dead!'

"He started back. He looked at me with cruel eyes. I saw a sort of exultant resolve leap into them – delight. Then, suddenly, with a scowl, he swept his sword back – *so* – and thrust."

He stopped abruptly.

I became aware of a change in the rhythm of the train. The brakes lifted their voices and the carriage jarred and jerked. This present world insisted upon itself, became clamourous. I saw through the steamy window huge electric fights glaring down from tall masts upon a fog, saw rows of stationary empty carriages passing by, and then a signal-box hoisting its constellation of green and red into the murky London twilight, marched after them. I looked again at his drawn features.

"He ran me through the heart. It was with a sort of astonishment – no fear, no pain – but just amazement, that I felt it pierce me, felt the sword drive home into my body. It didn't hurt, you know. It didn't hurt at all."

The yellow platform lights came into the field of view, passing first rapidly, then slowly, and at last stopping with a jerk. Dim shapes of men passed to and fro without.

"Euston!" cried a voice.

"Do you mean—?"

"There was no pain, no sting or smart. Amazement and then darkness sweeping over everything. The hot, brutal face before me, the face of the man who had killed me, seemed to recede. It swept out of existence—"

"Euston!" clamoured the voices outside; "Euston!"

The carriage door opened admitting a flood of sound, and a porter stood regarding us. The sounds of doors slamming, and the hoof-clatter of cab-horses, and behind these things the featureless remote roar of the London cobble-stones, came to my ears. A truckload of lighted lamps blazed along the platform.

"A darkness, a flood of darkness that opened and spread and blotted out all things."

"Any luggage, sir?" said the porter.

"And that was the end?" I asked.

He seemed to hesitate. Then, almost inaudibly, he answered, "*No.*"

"You mean?"

"I couldn't get to her. She was there on the other side of the temple – and then—"

"Yes," I insisted. "Yes?"

"Nightmares," he cried; "nightmares indeed! My God! Great birds that fought and tore."

Bothon

Henry S. Whitehead and H.P. Lovecraft

POWERS MEREDITH, at his shower-bath before dinner in the bathroom adjoining his room in his New York City club, allowed the cake of soap to drop on the tiled floor. Stooping to recover it he rapped the side of his head against the marble sidewall. The resulting bruise was painful, and almost at once puffed up into a noticeable lump…

Meredith dined in the grill that evening. Having no after-dinner engagement he went into the quiet library of the club, empty at this hour, and settled himself with a new book beside a softly-shaded reading lamp.

From time to time a slight, inadvertent pressure of his head against the chair's leather upholstered back would remind him unpleasantly of his accident in the shower-bath. This, after it happened several times, became an annoyance, and Meredith shifted himself into a preventive attitude with his legs draped over one of the chair's rounded arms.

No one else came into the library. Faint, clicking noises came in from the nearby billiard-room where a couple of men were playing, but, absorbed in his book, he did not notice these. The only perceptible sound was that of the gentle, steady rain outside. This, in the form of a soothing, continuous murmur, came through the partly opened high windows. He read on.

Precisely as he turned over the ninety-sixth page of his book, he heard a dull sound, like a very large explosion coming from a vast distance.

Alert now, his finger holding his place in the book, he listened. Then he heard a rumbling roar, as though countless tons of wrecked masonry were falling; falling; clearly, unmistakably, the remote thunder of some catastrophic ruin. He dropped his book, and, obeying an almost automatic impulse, started for the door.

He met nobody as he rushed down the stairs. At the coatroom, which he had to pass on his way to the doorway, two fellow members were chatting easily as they took their checks. Meredith glanced at them, surprised. He rushed on, to the doorway, and out into the street, where he paused. An empty street!

The rain, reduced now to a mere drizzle, made the asphalt shimmer in the street lights. Over towards Broadway, certainly, there must be clamor! But when he reached it he found only the compound eleven o'clock bedlam of Times Square.

Along Sixth Avenue, countless taxi-cabs weaved in a many-hued stream, jockeying for position in the maelstrom of the night-traffic about the Hippodrome. On the corner, a solitary rubber-coated policeman swung long efficient arms like a pair of mechanical semaphores, and skillfully directed the crawling traffic. To his ever-increasing wonderment, everything seemed normal. But what then had been that catastrophic sound?

Returning to the club entrance, he hesitated, a frown creasing his brow. He mounted the three steps hesitatingly, and entered, pausing at the door-man's desk.

"Send me up an 'extra', please, if one comes out," he told the clerk. Then he went up to his bedroom completely puzzled.

Half an hour later as he lay in bed wakeful and trying to compose in his thoughts the varying, incongruous aspect of this strange affair, he was all at once acutely conscious of a distant, thin, confused, roaring hum. The most prominent element in this sound was the deep, soft, and insistently penetrating blending of countless voices. Through it ran a kind of dominant note – a note of horror. The sound chilled his blood. It was eerie. He found himself holding his breath as he listened, straining every faculty to take in that faint, distant, terrible clamor of fear and despair.

Of just when he fell asleep he had no recollection, but when he awakened the next morning there hung over his mind a shadow of remembered horror, not wholly dissipated until he had bathed and begun to dress. He heard none of the sounds at the time of his awakening.

No 'extra' lay outside his bedroom door, and a little later at breakfast he opened expectantly and scanned several newspapers vainly and with a mounting sense of wonderment for any account of a catastrophe which could have caused the sounds. Gradually the implication grew upon him. He had, actually, heard the convincing, unmistakable evidence of such a catastrophe – *and no one else knew anything about it!*

He fell asleep immediately after turning in.

The following morning was Sunday. The reading-room was full, and he carried his book up to his bedroom after late breakfast to read the rest of it in peace. Soon after he became immersed in it, his attention was distracted by the tapping of a window-shade, blown in and out by the breeze. It was annoying and he paused in his reading, intending to rise and adjust the shade.

As he withdrew his eyes, and part of his attention, from his book, all at once he heard a new sound. It was precisely as though a distant, sound-proof door had been abruptly opened.

As he listened, fascinated, there came back to him and grew upon him a paralyzing, cold fear. There seemed to be no stopping it. The faint penumbra of a slight nausea shook him. He could distinguish overtones now, high tones, cries of battle; the impact of a charge against a resistant horde; noise of plied weapons.

The window-shade tapped again against the window casing. He snapped back into the familiar environment of his bedroom. He felt a little sick and weak. He rose shakily, walked across the room and into the bathroom, and, noisily splashing the water about, washed his hands and face.

Then he paused suddenly to listen again, a towel gripped between clenched hands. But he could hear nothing now, nothing except the tapping of that window-shade in the fresh breeze blowing through the open window. He hung the towel on its porcelain rod and walked back to his chair.

It was an hour too early for lunch, but he wanted urgently to be where there were people about, even waiters, people who were not 'hearing things'!

In order to prolong his companionship with old Cavanagh, the only other early luncher, Meredith ate somewhat more than usual. The unaccustomed heavy meal at such an hour made him drowsy, and after lunch he stretched out on a davenport before one of the two open fireplaces in the now unoccupied reading-room, and fell at once into an uneasy sleep.

A little before three he awakened, stale, and as he came to conscious wakefulness he began to hear, at first quite distinctly, and then with increasing loudness and clarity as though a steady hand were opening up a loudspeaker, that same sound of fire and human conflict, and the dreadful, menacing roar of a thunderous ocean's incalculable anger.

Then, Old Cavanagh, napping on the other davenport, struggled with senile deliberation to his feet with many accompanying "hums" and "ha's", and began lumbering across the room towards him.

"Lords' sake, what's the matter?" he demanded.

Kindly goodwill looked out of the old man's distorted countenance. Meredith, unable to control himself any longer, stammered out his incredible story.

"Hm! Strange…" was the old man's comment when Meredith ended. He produced, lighted deliberately, and puffed upon an enormous cigar. He seemed to cogitate as the two sat side by side in a pregnant silence of many minutes. At last he spoke.

"You're upset, my boy, naturally. But, you can hear everything that's going on around you, can't you? Your actual hearing's all right, then. Hm! This other 'hearing' starts up and goes on only when everything's perfectly quiet. First time, you were here reading; second time, in bed; third time, reading again; this time – if I wasn't snoring – you were in perfect quiet once more. Let's test that out, now. Keep perfectly still, and I'll do the same. Let's see if you hear anything."

They fell silent once more, and for a while Meredith could hear nothing of the strange sounds. Then, as the silence deepened, once again came that complex of sounds indicating devastating battle, murder, and sudden death.

He nodded silently at Cavanagh, and at the old man's acquiescent murmur the sounds ceased abruptly.

It took urging before Meredith could be persuaded to consult an aurist. Medical men, Cavanagh reminded him, would keep quiet about anything strange or embarrassing. Professional ethics…

They went uptown together that afternoon to Dr. Gatefield, a noted specialist. The doctor heard the story with close-lipped, professional attention. Then he tested Meredith's hearing with various delicate instruments. Finally he gave an opinion.

"We are familiar with various 'ear-noises' Mr. Meredith. In some cases the location of one of the arteries too close to the ear-drum gives 'roaring' noises. There are others, similar. I have eliminated everything of that kind. Your physical organism is in excellent condition, and unusually acute. There is nothing wrong with your hearing. This is a case for a psychiatrist.

"I am not suggesting anything like mental derangement, you will please understand! But I recommend Dr. Cowlington. This seems to be a clear case of what is sometimes called 'clairaudience', or something similar – his department; not mine. The aural equivalent of 'clairvoyance' is what I am indicating, you see what I mean. 'Second-sight' has to do with the eyes, of course, but it is mental, although there is often some physical background, I have no knowledge of those phenomena. I hope you will take my advice and allow Dr. Cowling—"

"All right!" interrupted Meredith. "Where does he live? I might as well go through with the thing now as later."

Dr. Gatefield showed traces of sympathy under his rather frosty professional exterior. He dropped the diagnostician, became the obliging, courteous gentleman. He telephoned to his colleague, the psychiatrist, and then surprised both Meredith and Cavanagh by accompanying them to Dr. Cowlington's. The psychiatrist proved to be a tall, thin, and rather kindly person, with heavy, complex spectacles on a prominent nose, and then, sand-colored wisps of hair in a complication of cowlicks. He showed marked interest in the case from the start. After hearing Meredith's story and the aurist's report he subjected Meredith to an examination of more than an hour, from which, feeling more or less as though he had been dissected, he nevertheless derived a considerable sense of relief.

It was decided that Meredith should arrange at once to take several days off, come to Dr. Cowlington's house, and remain 'under observation'.

He arrived at the doctor's the next morning and was given a pleasant, upstairs room, with many books and a comfortable davenport on which, in a recumbent position, the psychiatrist suggested, he should spend most of his waking hours, reading.

During Monday and Tuesday, Meredith, now after Dr. Cowlington's skillful reassurances no longer upset at *hearing* the strange sounds, listened carefully for whatever might reach him from what seemed like another – and very restless – world! He *heard* as he *listened* for long periods uninterrupted by any aural distractions, the drama of a great community in the paralyzing grip of fear – fighting for its corporate life – against irresistible, impending, dreadful doom.

He began, about this time, at Dr. Cowlington's suggestion, to write down some of the syllabification of the cries and shouts as well as he could manage it, on a purely phonetic basis. The sounds corresponded to no language known to him. The words and phrases were blurred and marred by the continuous uproar of the fury of waters. This was invariably, and continued to be, the sustained, distinctive background for every sound he heard during the periods while he remained passive and quiet. The various words and phrases were entirely unintelligible. His notes looked like nothing which either he or Cowlington could relate to any modern or ancient tongue. When read aloud they made nothing but gibberish.

These strange terms were studied over very carefully by Dr. Cowlington, by Meredith himself, and by no less than three professors, of Archeology and Comparative Philology, one of whom, the Archeologist, was a friend of Cowlington's and the other two called in by him. All of these experts on ancient and obsolete languages listened with the greatest courtesy to Meredith's attempt to explain the apparent setting of the sounds – most of them were in the nature of battle – cries and what Meredith took to be fragments of desperately uttered prayer – some of the material having come to him in the form of uncouth, raucous howls – and with the greatest interest to his attempts at reproducing them orally. They studied his written notes with the most meticulous care. The verdict was unanimous, even emphatic on the part of the younger and more dogmatic philologist. These sounds were quite utterly at variance with any known speech, including Sanskrit, Indo-Iranian, and even the conjectural Akkadian and Sumerian spoken tongues. The transcribed syllables corresponded to nothing in any known language, ancient or modern. Emphatically they were not Japanese.

The three professors took their departure, and Meredith and the psychiatrist Dr. Cowlington went over the list again.

Meredith had written: "I, I, I, I; – R'ly-eh!—Ieh nya, —Ieh nya; —zoh, zoh-an-nuh!" There was only one grouping of the words which formed anything like a section of continuous speech, or sentence, and which Meredith had been able to capture more or less intact and write down – "Ióth, Ióth,—natcal-o, do yan kho thútthut."

There were many other cries and, as he believed, desperately uttered prayers quite as strange and off the beaten tracks of recognized human speech as those noted down.

It was quite possibly because of his concentration on this affair of the remembered words – his own interest in them being naturally enhanced by Dr. Cowlington's and that of the three experts – that Meredith's dream-state impressions just at this time, and suddenly, became markedly acute. These dreams had been continuous and consecutive since their beginning several nights before, but on this night after the rather elaborate investigation of the words and syllables, Meredith began in earnest to get the affair of his environment in the strange city of the flames and conflicts and confusion and of a roaring ocean, cleared up with a startling abruptness. His dream impression that night was so utterly vivid; so acutely identical with the terms of the waking state; that he couldn't tell the difference between his dream slumber and wakeful consciousness!

Everything that he had derived mentally out of that night's sleep was clearly and definitely present in his mind. It seemed to him precisely as though he had not been asleep; that he had not emerged from an ordinary night's rest into the accustomed circumstances of an early morning's awakening. It was, rather, as though he had very abruptly passed out of one quite definite life into another; as though, as it came to him afterwards, he had walked out of a theatre into the wholly unrelated after-theatre life of Times Square.

One of the radical phases of this situation was not only that the succession of dream experiences had been continuous, with time – allowances for the intervening periods of those days in-between which he had spent here in Dr. Cowlington's quiet house; not only that, extraordinary as this realization seemed to him. The nearly consecutive dream experiences *had been the events of the past few days in a life of thirty-two years,* spent in that same environment and civilization of which the cataclysmic conditions which he had been envisaging appeared to presage a direful end.

He was, to set out plainly what he had brought out of that last night's dream-experience, one Bothon, general of the military forces of the great district of Ludekta, the south-westerly provincial division of the continent of Atlantis, which had been colonized, as every Atlantean school child was well aware, some eighteen hundred years before by a series of emigrations from the mother continent. The Naacal language – with minor variations not unlike the differences between American speech and 'English English' – was the common language of both continents.

From his native Ludekta the General Bothon had made several voyages to the mother land. The first of these had been to Ghua, the central eastern province, a kind of grand tour made just after his finishing, at the age of twenty-two, his professional course in the Ludekta College of Military Training. He was thus familiar by experience, as were many other cultivated Atlanteans of the upper classes, with the very highly developed civilization of the mother continent. These cultural contacts had been aided by his second visit, and further enhanced not long before the present period of the dream-experiences when, at the age of thirty-one, Bothon, already of the rank of general, had been sent out as Ambassador to Aglad-Dho, joint capital of the confederated south-eastern provinces of Yish, Knan, and Buathon, one of the most strategic diplomatic posts, and the second most important provincial confederation of the mother continent.

He had served in his ambassadorial capacity for only four months, and then had been abruptly recalled without explanation, but, as he had soon discovered upon his arrival home, because of the privately communicated request of the Emperor himself. His diplomatic superiors at home offered him no censure. Such Imperial requests were not unknown. These gentlemen were, actually, quite unaware of the reasons behind the Imperial request. No explanations had been given them, but there had been no Imperial censure of any kind.

But the General Bothon knew the reasons very well, although he kept them strictly to himself. There was, indeed, only one reason, as he was acutely and very well aware.

The requirements of his office had taken him rather frequently to Alu, the continental capital, metropolis of the civilized world.

Here in the great city of Alu were assembled from all known parts of the terrestrial globe the world's diplomats, artists, philosophers, traders and shipmasters. Here in the great warehouses of solid stone and along the innumerable wharves were piled the world's goods – fabrics and perfumes; strange animals for the delectation of the untraveled curious. Here in the endless stalls and markets were dyed stuffs and silks; tubas and cymbals and musical rattles and lyres; choice woods and implements for the toilet – strigils, and curiously carved hand-fitting little blocks of soapstone, and oils innumerable for the freshening of beards and the anointing of bodies. Here were tunics and sandals and belts and thongs of soft-tanned, variously perfumed leathers. Here were displayed carved and cunningly wrought pieces of household furniture – glowing, burnished wall-mirrors of copper and tin and steel, bedsteads of an infinite range and design, cushions of swans' feathers, tables of plain and polished artizanship and of intarsia with metal scrolls set flush to their levels; marquetry work of contrasting woods-chairs and stools and cupboards and chests and foot-rests. Here were ornaments innumerable – fire-screens, and spindles for parchment-rolls, and tongs, and shades for lamps made of the scraped skins of animals; metal lamps of every design, and vegetable oils for the lamps in earthenware jars of many sizes and shapes. Here were foods and wines and dried fruits, and honey of many flavors; grains and dried meats and loaves of barley and wheat-meal past computation. Here in the great street of the armorers were maces and axes and swords and daggers of all the world's varieties and designs; armor of plate and chain-hauberks, and greaves and bassinets, and shelves with rows and rows of the heavy plate and helmets standardized for the use of such fighting men as Bothon himself commanded in their thousands.

Here were to be seen and examined costly canopies and the elaborate litters in which the slaves of the rich carried their masters through the narrow streets and broad, airy avenues of Alu. Rugs there were in an endless profusion of size and shape and design; rugs from distant Lemuria and from Atlantis and from tropical Antillea, and from the mountainous interior regions of the mother continent itself, where thousands of cunning weavers of fabrics worked at their looms; ordinary rugs of pressed felt, and gorgeous glowing rugs of silk from the southern regions where the mulberry trees grew; rugs, too, and thin, soft draperies of complex patterns made of the wool of lambs and of the long, silk-like hair of the mountain sheep.

Here in Alu, center of the world's culture, were philosophers with their groups of disciples, small or great, propounding their systems on the corners of streets and in the public squares, wrangling incessantly over the end of man, and the greatest good, and the origin of material things. Here were vast libraries containing the essence of all that had been written down concerning science and religion and engineering and the innumerable fine arts, of the civilization of forty thousand years. Here were the temples of religion where the hierarchs propounded the principles of life, colleges of priests studying incessantly more and more deeply into the mysteries of the four principles; teaching the people the endless applications of these esoteric affairs to their conduct and daily lives.

Into this fascinating treasure house of a great civilization the ambassador Bothon had penetrated as often as possible. The excellence of his family background, his own character and personal qualities, and his official position, all combined to make him a welcome guest in the mansions of the members of the emperor's court and of the highest stratum of social life in Alu.

An impressionable young man, most of whose life previous to his appointment as ambassador had been spent in hard training for his military duties and in the rigorous prosecution of these as he rose rapidly grade by grade by hard man's work in camp and field during his many campaigns in the standing army of Ludekta, the General Bothon revelled in these many high social contacts. Very soon he found within himself and growing apace, the strong and indeed natural desire for a type of life to which his backgrounds and achievements had amply entitled him, but of which he had been, so far, deprived because of the well-nigh incessant demands upon him of his almost continuous military service.

In short, the ambassador from Ludekta very greatly came to desire marriage, with some lady of his own caste and, preferably, of this metropolitan city of Alu with its sophistication and wide culture; a lady who might preside graciously over his ambassadorial establishment; who, when his term of office was concluded, would return with him to his native Ludekta in Atlantis, there permanently to grace the fine residence he had in his mind's eye when, a little later, he should retire from the Ludektan army and settle down as a senator into the type of life which he envisaged for his middle years.

He had been both fortunate and unfortunate in his actual falling in love. The lady, who reciprocated his ardent advances, was the Netvissa Ledda, daughter of the Netvis Toldon who was the emperor's brother. The fortunate aspect of this intense and sudden love affair which set all social Alu to commenting upon it, was the altogether human one of a virtually perfect compatability between the two. Their initial mutual attraction had become a settled regard for each other almost overnight. Within a few days thereafter they were very deeply in love. Humanly considered, the affair was perfection itself. Every circumstance save one, and that a merely artificial side of the case, gave promise of an ideal union.

The single difficulty in the way of this marriage was, however, most unfortunately, an insuperable one. The Netvissa Ledda, niece of the emperor, belonged of right to the very highest social caste of the empire. The rank and degree of Netvis lay next to Royalty itself and in the case of the family of the Netvis Toldon partook of royalty. Against this fact basic in the structure of the empire's long-established custom, the Ambassador, General Bothon of Ludekta – although a gentleman of the very highest attainments, character, and worth, whose family record reached back a thousand years into the dim past before the colonization of Atlantis, whose reputation was second to none in the empire – the General Bothon was a commoner. As such, according to the rigid system prevalent at the court in Alu, capital of the Empire, he was hopelessly ineligible. The marriage was simply out of the question.

The Emperor being called upon to settle this awkward affair, acted summarily, quite in the spirit of one who destroys a hopelessly wounded and suffering creature as an act of mercy. The Emperor took the one course open to him under these circumstances, and the General Bothon, without any choice being open to him save submission to an Imperial request which had the force of law, took ship for Ludekta, leaving behind him in Alu the highest and dearest hope of his life, irreparably shattered.

For the subsequent conduct of the General Bothon, recently Ludektan Ambassador to Aglad-Dho, there were three very definite contributing reasons. Of these the first and most prominent was the depth and intensity and genuineness of his love for the Netvissa Ledda. Beyond all possible things, he wanted her; and the proud soul of Bothon was very grievously racked and torn at the sudden unexpected and arbitrary separation from her which the Imperial request had brought about.

The voyage from Aglad-Dho to Ludetka, across two sections of the globe's great oceans and through the ship canals and lakes which bisected the southern continent of the western hemisphere, occupied seven weeks. During this period of enforced inaction the bitter chagrin and deep disappointment of Bothon crystallized itself by means of the sustained reflection inevitable under the circumstances. General Bothon arrived in Ludekta in a state of mind which made him ready for anything, provided only it was action. This state of mind was the second of these contributory factors. The third was the immediate satisfaction of his desire for activity. During the course of his voyage home the ghoulish and, indeed, sub-human factory slaves, the shockingly Simian Gyaa-Hau, had inaugurated a revolt. This had spread, by the time of Bothon's arrival, throughout the entire province of Ludekta. The state sorely needed the efficient services of this, the youngest and most brilliant of its generals, and his reception on landing was more nearly that of a savior of his country than what a virtually disgraced diplomat might expect.

Into this campaign, which he prosecuted with the utmost vigor and a thorough-going military effectiveness, Bothon threw himself with an abounding energy which even his most ardent Ludektan admirers had not anticipated. At the end of an intensive campaign of less than three weeks, with this very dangerous revolt completely crushed and the leaders of the Gyaa-Hua hanging to a man by great hooks through their neck muscles in dreadful rows along the outer city walls on either side of the great archway that pierced the defense of Ludekta's capital, the General Bothon found himself the hero of Ludekta and the idol of his admiring troops. A rigid disciplinarian; the attitude of the officers and men of the Ludektan standing army towards this general had hitherto been based upon the respect which his great abilities had always commanded. Now he found himself the recipient of something almost like worship because of this last brilliant campaign of his. It had been a *tour de force.*

Although it is highly probable that they would have advanced him because of this achievement in any event, the actual occasion for the action of the Ludektan Senate in rewarding Bothon with the supreme command of the standing army was the speech before that body of the aging generalissimo Tarba. Old Tarba ended his notable panegyric by laying his truncheon, emblem of the supreme command, on the great marble slab before the presiding senator, with a dramatic gesture.

Bothon thus found himself suddenly possessed of that intensive hero worship which would cause the state to acquiesce in anything which its object might suggest. He was, at the same time, in supreme command of the largest sectional standing army of the entire continent of Atlantis; an army, thanks chiefly to his own efficiency, probably the best trained and most effective fighting unit then extant.

Under the combined effect of the contributing causes and his new authority General Bothon made up his mind. On the eleventh day after his triumphal entry into Ludekta's capital city, forty-seven Ludektan war vessels freshly outfitted, their oar-slaves supplemented by a reserve of the Gyaa-Hau, selected for the power and endurance of their gorilla-like bodies, with new skin sails throughout the fleet, and the flower of the Ludektan army on board, sailed out from Ludekta westward for Alu under the command of the General Bothon.

It was precisely simultaneous with the arrival of this war fleet off the shores of the great city of Alu that there began unprecedented natural disturbances affecting the entire area of the mother continent. These were comparable to nothing recorded in the capital's carefully kept slate and parchment records, which went back over a period of thousands of years.

The first presage of these impending calamities took the form of a coppery tinge which replaced the blue of the sky. Without any warning the long ground-swell of this Western Ocean changed abruptly, along with the color of the water, into a kind of dull brick-grey, to short, choppy, spray-capped waves. These tossed even the great Ludektan war galleys so violently as to shatter many of the sweeps. The wind, to the consternation of several of Bothon's captains, appeared to come from every quarter at once! It tore the heavy skin sails of the Ludektan galleys away from their copper rings and bolts in some cases. In others it split the sails in clean straight lines as though they had been slit with sharp knives.

Undaunted by these manifestations and the reports of his augurs who had cast their lots and slain their sheep and fowls in a hasty series of divinations to account, if possible, for this unfavorable reception at the hands of the elements, the indomitable will of Bothon forced his fleet to an orderly landing. He sent forthwith as his herald to the Emperor himself, his highest ranking sub-general, accompanied by an imposing guard of honor. On slate tablets Bothon had set forth his demand in his own hand. This was in the form of a set of alternatives. The Emperor was asked to receive him as Generalissimo of the military forces of Ludekta, and to consent to his immediate marriage with the Netvissa Ledda; or, he, Bothon, would proceed forthwith to the siege of Alu and take the lady of his heart by force and arms.

The message prayed the Emperor to elect the first alternative. It also set forth briefly and in formal heraldic terms the status of the ancient family of Bothon.

The Emperor had been very seriously annoyed at this challenge, as he chose to regard it. He felt that his office and dignity had been outraged. He crucified Bothon's entire delegation.

The siege of Alu began forthwith under that menacing copper-tinted sky and to the accompaniment of a rumbling series of little earthquakes.

Not only not within the memory of living men, but, as the records indicated, during its entire history over thousands of years as the metropolis of the civilized world, had there been any previous hostile manifestations against the great city of Alu. That anything like this terrible campaign which the renowned General Bothon of Ludekta set in motion against her might come to pass, had never even remotely occurred to anyone in Alu. So promptly did Bothon launch his attack that the tortured bodies of the members of his delegation to the Emperor had not yet ceased writhing on their row of crosses before he had penetrated, at the head of his trained legionaries, to a point within two squares of the Imperial Palace which stood at the center of the great city.

There had been virtually no resistance. This intensive campaign would have been triumphantly concluded within twenty minutes, the Emperor probably captured along with all his Palace guards and household, the person of the Lady Ledda secured by this ardent lover of hers, and the entire objective of the expedition accomplished, save for what in modern legal phraseology would have been described as *An Act of God.*

The premonitory earth-shakings which had accompanied this armed invasion culminated, at that point in the advance of Bothon's army, in a terrific seismic cataclysm. The stone-paved streets opened in great gaping fissures. Massive buildings crashed tumultuously all about and upon the triumphantly advancing Ludektans. The General Bothon, at the head of his troops, dazed and deafened and hurled violently upon the ground, retained consciousness long enough to see three quarters of his devoted following engulfed, smashed, torn to fragments, crushed into unrecognizable heaps of bloody pulp; and this holocaust swiftly and mercifully obliterated from before his failing vision by the drifting dust from millions of tons of crumbled masonry.

He awakened in the innermost keep of the dungeon in Alu's citadel.

Coming quietly into Meredith's bedroom about ten o'clock in the morning, Dr. Cowlington, who had made up his mind overnight on a certain matter, quietly led his initial conversation with his observation-patient around to the subject which had been most prominent in his mind since their conference of yesterday over the strange linguistic terms which Meredith had noted down.

"It has occurred to me that I might very well tell you about something quite out of the ordinary which came under my notice seven or eight years ago. It happened while I was chief intern in the Connecticut State Hospital for the Insane. I served there for two years under Dr. Floyd Haviland before I went into private practice. We had a few private patients in the hospital, and one of these, who was in my particular charge, was a gentleman of middle-age who had come to us because of Haviland's enormous reputation, without commitment. This gentleman, whom I will call 'Smith', was neither legally nor actually 'insane'. His difficulty, which had interfered very seriously with the course of his life and affairs, would ordinarily be classified as 'delusions'. He was with us for nearly two months. As a voluntary patient of the institution, and being a man of means, he had private rooms. He was in every way normal except for his intensive mental preoccupation with what I have called his delusions. In daily contact with him during this period I became convinced *that Mr. Smith was not suffering from anything like a delusive affection of the mind.*

"I diagnosed his difficulty – and Dr. Haviland agreed with me – that this patient, Smith, *was suffering mentally from the effects of an ancestral memory.*

"Such a case is so rare as to be virtually unique. The average psychiatrist would go through a life-time working at his specialty without encountering anything of the sort. There are, however, recorded cases. We were able to send our patient home in a mental condition of almost complete normality. As sometimes occurs in mental cases, his virtual cure was accomplished by making our diagnosis very clear to him – impressing upon his mind through reiterated and very positive statements that he was in no sense of the word demented, and that his condition, while unusual, was not outside the range and limitations of complete normality."

"It must have been a very interesting case," said Meredith. His reply was dictated by nothing deeper than a desire to be courteous. For his mind was full of the affairs of the General Bothon, raging now in his prison-chamber; his mind harried, anxious over the fate of his surviving soldiers;

that lurid glare, dimmed by the remoteness of his flame-tinted prison-chamber, in his eyes; his mind tortured and his keen sense of hearing stultified by the sustained, dreadful roaring of that implacable sea. He, Meredith, for reasons far too deep for his own analysis, felt utterly incapable of telling Dr. Cowlington what was transpiring in those dreams of his. All his inmost basic instincts were warning him, though subconsciously, that what he might tell now, if he would, could not possibly be believed! Dr. Cowlington, looking at his patient, saw a face drawn and lined as though from some devastating mental stress; a deeply introspective expression in the eyes, which, professionally speaking, he did not like. The doctor considered a moment before resuming, erect in his chair, his knees crossed, his finger-tips joined in a somewhat judicial attitude.

"Frankly, Meredith, I emphasized the fact that the man I have called Smith was in no sense insane because I feel that I must go farther and tell you that the nature of his apparent 'delusions' was, in one striking particular, related to your own case. I did not wish to give you the slightest alarm over the perfect soundness of your own mentality! To put the matter plainly, Mr. Smith *remembered*, although rather vaguely and dimly, certain phases of those ancestral memories I mentioned, and was able to reproduce a number of the terms of some unknown and apparently prehistoric language. Meredith—" the doctor turned and looked intensely into the eyes of his now interested patient, *"—there were three or four of Smith's words identical with yours!"*

"Good God!" Meredith exclaimed, "What were the words, Doctor? Did you make notes of them?"

"Yes, I have them here," answered the psychiatrist.

Meredith was out of his chair and leaning eagerly over the doctor's shoulder long before Cowlington had his papers arranged. He gazed with a consuming intensity at the words and phrases carefully typed on several sheets of foolscap; listened, with an almost tremulous attention, while Dr. Cowlington carefully reproduced the sounds of these uncouth terms. Then, taking the sheets and resuming his chair, he read through all that had been written down, pronouncing the words, though very quietly, under his breath, his lips barely moving.

He was pale, and shaking from head to foot when he rose at last and handed back, hands trembling, the thin fascicle of papers to its owner. Dr. Cowlington looked at him anxiously, his professional mind alert, his fears somewhat aroused over the wisdom of this experiment of his in bringing his former case thus abruptly to his patient's attention. Dr. Cowlington felt, if he had cared to put his impression into words, somewhat baffled. He could not, despite his long and careful training in dealing with mental, nervous, and 'borderland' cases, quite put his acute professional finger upon just which one of the known simple and complex emotions was, for this moment, dominating this very interesting patient of his.

Dr. Cowlington would have been even more completely puzzled if he had known.

For Meredith, reading through the strange babblings of the patient, Smith, had recognized all the words and terms, and had lit upon the phrase:

"Our beloved Bothon has disappeared."

Dr. Cowlington, sensing accurately that it might be unwise to prolong this particular interview, concluded wisely that Meredith would most readily regain his normal poise and equanimity if left alone to cope with whatever, for the time-being, held possession of his mind, rose quietly and walked over to the bedroom door.

He paused there, however, for an instant, before leaving the room, and looked back at the man. Meredith had not, apparently, so much as noted the doctor's movements towards departure. His mind, very obviously, was turned inward. He was, it appeared, entirely oblivious to his surroundings.

And Dr. Cowlington, whose professional outward deportment, acquired through years of contact with abnormal people, had not wholly obliterated a kindly disposition, noted with a certain emotion of his own that there were unchecked tears plainly visible in his patient's inward-gazing eyes.

Summoned back to Meredith's room an hour later by one of his house nurses, Dr. Cowlington found his patient restored to his accustomed urbane normality.

"I asked you to come up for a moment, Doctor," began Meredith, "because I wanted to inquire if there is anything that you would care to give a patient to induce sleep." Then, with a deprecating smile: "The only such things I know about are morphine and laudanum! I don't know very much about medicine and naturally you wouldn't want to give me one of those any more than I would want to take it."

Dr. Cowlington resumed his judicial manner. He thought rapidly about this unexpected request. He took into consideration how his story about the patient Smith had appeared to upset Meredith. He deliberately refrained from inquiring why Meredith wanted a sleeping potion. Then he nodded his head.

"I use a very simple preparation;" he said. "It is non-habit-forming; based on a rather dangerous drug, chloral; but, as I use it for my patients, compounded with an aromatic syrup and diluted with half a tumbler of water, it works very well. I will send some up to you but remember, please, four teaspoonfuls of the syrup is the outside dose. Two will probably be enough. Never more than four at any time, and not more than one dose in twenty-four hours."

Dr. Cowlington rose, came over to Meredith, and looked at the place where he had struck the side of his head against the marble wall of his shower-bath. The bruise was still there. The doctor passed his fingers lightly over the contusion.

"It's beginning to go down,' he remarked. Then he smiled pleasantly, again nodded his head at Meredith, and, started to leave. Meredith stopped him as he was about to go out of the room.

"I wanted to ask you," said Meredith, "I wanted to ask you, Doctor, if you would be willing to put me in touch with the man to whom you referred as 'Smith'?"

The doctor shook his head. "I'm sorry, Mr. Smith died two years ago."

In ten minutes the house nurse fetched in a small tray. On it was a tumbler, a mixing spoon, and a freshly put up eight-ounce bottle containing a reddish colored, pleasant tasting syrup.

Twenty minutes later, Meredith, who had compromised on three teaspoons, was deeply asleep on his bed; and the General Bothon, in the innermost dungeon chamber of the great citadel of Alu, was standing poised in the center of that dungeon's smooth stone floor, tensed to leap in any direction; while all about him the rending crashes of thousands of tons of the riven and falling masonry of the citadel itself was deafening him against all other sounds except the incessant and indescribably thunderous fury of the now utterly maddened ocean. The lurid glare of the tires from without had been markedly heightened. Detonation after detonation came to Bothon's ears at frequent intervals. The Aluans were blowing up this central portion of their great city, in order to check the advance of the conflagration which had raged for days and nights and was utterly beyond control. These detonations seemed actually faint to the alert man in that prison room against the hideous crashing of the sections of the citadel itself, and the sustained roar of the ocean.

Abruptly the crisis for which he had been waiting arrived. The stone flooring beneath his feet buckled and sagged at his right. He whirled about and leaped far in the other direction, pressing himself, hands and arms stretched out above his head, against the wall of the prison-chamber, his heart pounding wildly, his breath coming in great gasps and sobs as the stifling, earthquake-deadened air about him shrank to a sudden and devastating attenuation. Then the solid wall opposite split in a tearing gap from top to bottom, and an even more stifling cloud of white dust sifted abruptly through the room as the ceiling was riven asunder.

Stifling, choking, fighting for breath and life, the General Bothon lowered his arms and whirled about again in the direction of this thunderous breakage, and groped his way across the now precarious flooring in the faint hope of discovering an avenue of escape. He struggled up a steep mound of debris through the grey darkness of the hanging dust where a few seconds before there had been a level floor of solid masonry. He groped his way through thicker clouds of the drifting, settling stone-dust, skirted the irregular edges of yawning holes and toiled up and down mounded heaps of rubble, far past the place where the confining wall of his dungeon had stood, onward and forward resolutely towards that vague goal of freedom.

At last, the resources of his mighty body spent, his eyes two tortured red holes, his mouth and throat one searing pain, Bothon emerged across the last hill of rubbish which had been the citadel of Alu and came out upon the corner edge of one of the largest of the city's great public squares.

For the first time in the course of his progress out of that death trap, Bothon suddenly trod on something soft and yielding. He paused. He could hardly see, and he crouched and felt with his hands, under the thickly mounded dust.

It was the body of a man, in chain mail. Bothon, exhaled a painful breath of satisfaction. He rolled the body over, freeing it from the pounds of dust upon it, and slid his hand along the copper-studded leather belt to where a short, heavy, one-handed battle-axe was attached. This he drew from its sheath.

Then from the dead man's silken tunic he tore off a large section and cleansed his eyes and mouth and wiped the sweat-caked dust from his face.

Finally he took from the corpse a heavy leathern purse. He lay down for a few moments beside the dead soldier on the soft dust for a brief rest. Some ten minutes later he rose, stretched himself, testing the heavy axe with three or four singing strokes through the clearing air, and dusted out and readjusted his garments, finally tightening a loosened sandal thong.

He stood free now in the center of Alu. He was adequately armed. A great gust of energy surged through him. He oriented himself; then he turned with an instinct as sure as a homing bee's in the direction he had been seeking, and began to march at the unhurrying, space-devouring pace of a Ludektan legionary, straight for the Imperial Palace.

Bothon had thoroughly settled in his mind the answer to a question which, for the first few days of his captivity had puzzled him greatly. Why had he been left alone and undisturbed in that confinement; food and water brought to him at regular intervals in accordance with the ordinary routine of the citadel? Why, to put the matter plainly, having been obviously captured by the Emperor's retainers while lying unconscious within two squares of the Imperial Palace, had he not been summarily crucified? His keen trained mind had apprised him that the answer was to be found in the hideous turmoil of the raging sea and in the fearful sounds of a disintegrating city. The Emperor had been too greatly occupied by those cataclysms even to command the punishment of this leader of such an armed attack against the world's metropolis as had not been known in all the long history of the mother continent.

Skirting its enormous outer walls, Bothon came at last to the massive chief entrance-way to the Imperial Palace. This enormous structure, its basic walls eight feet thick, stood massive, magnificent, intact. Without any hesitation he began mounting the many broad steps straight towards the magnificent entrance-gates of copper and gold and porphyry.

Before these gates, in the rigid line and under the command of an officer beneath whose corselet appeared the pale blue tunic of the Emperor's house-hold-guards, stood a dozen fully armed soldiers. One of these, at a word from the officer, ran down the steps to turn back this intruder. Bothon slew him with a single crashing stroke and continued to mount the steps. At this a shouted command of the officer sent the entire troop down the steps upon him in close order. Bothon paused, and waiting until the foremost was no more than the space of two of the broad steps above him, leaped lightly to his right. Then as the foremost four of the soldiers passed beyond him under the impetus of their downward charge, Bothon as lightly leaped back again, his heavy axe falling upon the troop's flank with deadly, short, quick-swinging blows.

Before they could collect themselves the officer and five of his men lay dead upon the steps. Leaving the demoralized remainder to gather themselves together as best they might, Bothon leaped up the intervening steps and was through the great entrance-doors, and, with a pair of lightning-like right-and-left strokes of his axe, had disposed of the two men-at-arms stationed just inside the doorway.

His way into the Palace now entirely unobstructed, Bothon sped through well-remembered rooms and along broad corridors into the heart of the Imperial Palace of Alu.

Within thirty seconds he had located the entrance to the brother of the Emperor, Netvis Toldon's apartments, and had passed through the doorway.

He discovered the family reclining about the horseshoe-shaped table in the refectory, for it was the hour of the evening meal. He paused in the doorway, was met with surprised glances, and bowed low to the Netvis Toldon.

"I beseech you to pardon this intrusion, my Lord Netvis. It would be inexcusable under other circumstances, at a more favorable time." The nobleman returned no answer, only stared in surprise. Then, the dear lady of his heart, the Netvissa Ledda, rose to her feet from her place at her father's table, her eyes wide with wonderment. A dawning realization of what this strange invasion might mean, made her lovely face suddenly the hue of the Aluan roses, She looked at this heroically formed lover of hers, her soul in her eyes.

"Come, my Lady Ledda," said Bothon quickly, and as lightly as a deer the Netvissa Ledda ran to him.

He took her arm, very quietly, and, before the assembled members of the family of Toldon had recovered from their surprise, the two were hastening along the corridor towards the palace entrance.

From around the first corner before them came then abrupt sounds of armed men. They paused, listening, and Bothon shifted his axe into his right hand and stepped before the Lady Ledda, but she laid firm hands upon his left arm. "This way, swiftly," she whispered, and led him down a narrow passageway at the wide corridor's left. This they traversed in haste, and had barely negotiated a sharp turn when they heard the guard-troop rush along the main corridor, and a voice, commanding:

"To the apartment of my Lord, the Netvis Toldon!"

The narrow passage-way led them past cook-rooms and scullery-chambers, and ended at a small door which opened upon a narrow court. Rapidly traversing this, they emerged upon a square at the west side of the palace, and well before any pursuit could have traced their course, were indistinguishable among the vast concourse of the people who thronged the wide avenues of Alu.

Bothon now resumed the direction of their course of escape. Leading the way across a larger adjacent square, he reached the secluded corner, mounded about with debris, where he had secured his weapon. It was not yet past the early dusk of a mid-summer evening, and now there was nothing to interfere with his keen vision.

Yes, it was as he had guessed from the quality of that torn fragment of silken tunic with which he had wiped his tortured eyes free of the stone-dust. The dead man was an officer of one of the Imperial Legions.

Seating the Lady Ledda upon a block of granite and requesting her to watch, Bothon knelt swiftly beside the dead body and busied himself upon it.

At the end of two intensive minutes the Netvissa Ledda looked up at his touch upon her shoulder to see her lover apparelled from head to foot in the uniform, armor, and accoutrements of an Elton of the Imperial Legion of the Hawk.

Then they hurried southward, side by side, across the great square with its desolation of shattered buildings, towards one of the few remaining residences of the rich before which four coal-black slaves in the livery of their household were lowering an ornamental litter to the ground.

From the luxurious vehicle, as they arrived beside it, there emerged a stout citizen who stared at them inquiringly, his initial fear disappearing at recognition of the Emperor's niece and the uniform of an Imperial Legion.

"We request the loan of your litter, my lord," said Bothon.

"Most willingly," returned the citizen, bowing. Bothon expressed thanks, handed his companion into the litter, distributed a handful of silver among the four slaves, and gave the destination to the Negro who stood beside the forward left-hand pole. Then he climbed in himself and drew the red silk curtains together.

The strong litter-poles strained and creaked as the load was hoisted to four brawny shoulders, and then the litter swung away from the residence of its still bowing and smirking owner towards the military enclosure which housed and guarded the flying-vessels of the Aluvian standing army.

"You may have observed how very completely I have entrusted my Imperial person to you," remarked the Netvissa Ledda, smiling. She was very well aware of the reasons for the Imperial request which had sent Bothon back to Ludekta, and for the first armed invasion against the Aluvian metropolis.

"I have not so much as inquired as to our destination!"

"It is my intention to seek safety to the northwest," answered Bothon gravely. "I am convinced the prediction of Bal, Lord of Fields, as to the destruction of the Mother Continent, is not a mere classic to be learned, as we learned it in our childhood, as a formal exercise in rhetoric. Here, all about us, is the evidence. More, my four augurs warned me of the continent's danger ere I brought my war-galleys up upon the beaches of Alu. The four great forces, they insisted, were in collusion to that end. Do we not see and hear them at work? Fire raging through the land; earth shaking mightily; winds such as never were encountered hitherto upon the planet, else the old records lie! Water, the commotion of which surpasses all experiences; – is it not so, my beloved? Am I not constrained to speak thus to be heard amidst this hellish tumult?"

The Lady Ledda nodded, grave now in her turn.

"There are many deafened in the palace," she remarked. "Where are we to go for refuge?"

"We depart straight this night, for the great mountains of A-Wah-Ii," answered Bothon, "if so be the four great forces allow us possession of a war chariot. And, to that end, your ring, my beloved."

The Lady Ledda nodded again, understandingly, and removed from the middle finger of her right hand the ring of the two suns and the eight-pointed star which, as a member of the Royal Family, she was entitled to wear. Bothon received it, and slipped it upon the little finger of his right hand.

The sentinel on guard before the barracks of the officer commanding the military enclosure of the Aluvian supply-barracks, saluted the commanding looking Elton of the Legion of the Hawk who stepped down from the ornamented litter. The Elton addressed him in formal military phrases.

"Report at once to the Ka-Kalbo Netro, the arrival of the Elton Barko of the Legion of the Hawk, conveying a member of the Imperial household into exile. I am requisitioning one battle-chariot of capacity for two persons, and officer's rations sufficient for fourteen days, together with the medicinal supply for a full kit-va of men. My authority, the Imperial Signet. Behold!"

The sentinel saluted the sun-and-star ring of the Emperor, repeated his orders like an efficient automaton, saluted the Elton of the Hawk Legion, and departed at the double to fetch the commandant, the Ka-Kalbo Netro.

The Ka-Kalbo arrived promptly in answer to this summons. He saluted the Imperial Signet, and, as a Ka-Kalbo outranked an Elton by one full grade, was punctiliously saluted according to military usage by the Elton Barko of the Legion of the Hawk, an officer whose personal acquaintance he had not previously made.

Within ten minutes the Netvissa Ledda had been ceremoniously carried to and placed upon her seat in the commandeered battle-chariot, and the Elton Barko had taken his place beside her. Then, the dozen sweating mechanicians who had carried out their commandant's orders in record time, standing in a stiff, saluting row, the battle-chariot started off at a stiff gallop, the driver standing and plying his long thong with loud, snapping reports over the horses' backs, while at the great chariot's rear the spare-horse leader whistled continuously to the four relay animals which galloped behind.

The heights of A-Wah-Ii, to the northwest, gave some promise, in Bothon's opinion, of security from the anciently predicted submersion of the continent. Those towering mountains would, at least, be among the last sections to sink, should the gas belts, hypothecated by the scientists of the mother continent, explode, and remove the underseas support of this great land of the globe's most ancient and noble civilization.

Shortly after daybreak, and accurately, according to the map and careful explanations of the painstaking Ka-Kalbo Netro, the chariot paused in the centre of a great level table-land one quarter of the way to his destination. The country was utterly uninhabited. They were relatively safe here in a region only lightly visited by the earthquakes, and not at all by fire. The roar of the north wind troubled the Netvissa Ledda severely. Bothon barely noticed it. He was now convinced that he was losing his sense of hearing.

They ate and slept and resumed their journey at noon after a readjustment of the provisions and a change of the now rested animals.

Their four days' journey steadily northwest was uneventful. The charioteer drove onward steadily. On the fourth day, as the coppery ball which was the smoking sun reached and touched a flat horizon, they caught their first view of the lofty summits of the A-Wah-Ii region, a goal of a possible immunity.

Dr. Cowlington, an anxious look on his face, was standing beside Meredith's bed when he awakened in mid-morning. He had slept twenty hours. However, what the doctor thought of as his patient's mental condition was so entirely normal, and his cheerfulness so pronounced after his protracted sleep, that Dr. Cowlington was reassured, and changed his mind about removing the bottle of sleeping medicine. Plainly it had had an excellent effect on Meredith.

Stretched out in his usual quiet-inducing attitude on the davenport just before lunch, Meredith suddenly ceased reading and put down his magazine. It had occurred to him that he had heard none of the turmoil of Alu during that waking period. He sat up, puzzled. Bothon, he remembered, had been hearing the sounds about him only dimly, a strange, perhaps a significant, coincidence.

He felt the bruise behind his right ear. It was no longer even slightly painful to the touch. He pressed his finger-tips firmly against the place. The contusion was now barely perceptible to the sense of touch.

He reported the apparent loss of what the ear-specialist Gatefield had named his 'clairaudience' to Dr. Cowlington after lunch.

"Your bruise is going down," said the doctor significantly. He examined the posterior edge of Meredith's right temporal area.

"I thought so," remarked the doctor, nodding. "Your secondary 'hearing' began with that injury to your head. As it goes down, some obscure stimulation of the auditory apparatus, which accounts for your ability to hear those sounds, diminishes accordingly. You could probably hear only some stupendous sound from there now. And in a day or so I predict that you will be hearing nothing more, and then you can go home!"

And, within an hour came the 'stupendous sound' in very truth. It broke in upon Meredith's quiet reading once more as though someone had opened that sound-proof door.

A curious, secondary, mental vision accompanied it. It was as though Meredith, in his own proper person, yet through the strange connection of his personality with the General Bothon, stood on the heights of Tharan-Yud, overlooking the stricken city of Alu. The utter fury of mountainous waves accompanied the now titanic rumblings of malignant earth, the wholesale crashing of the cyclopean masonry of Alu as the vast city crumbled and melted beneath his horrified eyes. With these hellish horrors went the wild roaring of ravaging flame, and the despairing, hysterical cacophony of Alu's doomed millions.

Then there came, at last, a sound as of the veritable yawning of the nethermost watery gulf of earth, and the high sun itself was blotted out by a monstrous green wall of advancing death. The sea rose up and fell upon accursed Alu, drowning forever the shrieks of utter despair, the piping and chittering of the obscurely gnawing Gyaa-Hua distracted at last from their loathsome banquet – hissings, roarings, shriekings, whinings, tearings, seethings – a cacophony more than human ears might bear, a sight of utter devastation more onerous than man might look upon, and live.

There came to Meredith a merciful stupor, as the waters of Mu-Iadon closed in forever over the mother continent, and as his consciousness failed him, he emerged once more out of that quiet bedroom – away from his overlooking of the world's major catastrophe, and as Bothon walked beside the Lady Ledda along a wooded ravine in A-Wah-Ii, goal of safety, among laden fruit trees, yet not, it seemed, upon the towering heights of those noble mountains but upon an island about the shores of which rolled and roared a brown and viscid ocean choked with the mud which had been the soil of the mother continent.

"We are safe here, it would appear, my Bothon," said the Netvissa Ledda. "Let us lie down and sleep, for I am very weary."

And after watching for a little space while the Lady Ledda reclined and slept, Bothon lay down beside her and fell at once into the deep and dreamless slumber of utter physical exhaustion.

Meredith awakened on his davenport. The room was dark, and when he had risen, switched on the lights and looked at his watch, he found that it was four o'clock in the morning. He undressed and went to bed and awakened three hours later without having dreamed.

A world and an era had come to its cataclysmic end, and he had been witness of it.

The contusion on his head had disappeared, Dr. Cowlington observed later in the morning.

"I think you can go home now, you'll never *hear* again," said the doctor, in his judicial manner. "But, by the way, Meredith, what, if you can remember, was the name of that 'mother continent' of yours?"

"We called it Mu," said Meredith. The doctor was silent for a while; then he nodded his head. He had made up his mind.

"I thought so," said he, gravely.

"Why?" Meredith asked.

"Because *Smith* called it that," replied the doctor.

Outsider

Lucy Zhang

THE OUTSIDER found the child deep within limestone cliffs that resembled petrified trees. It cracked open the limestone and plucked the girl out, carefully removing her from the jagged shell and chipped stone like prying lint from a wool sweater. After the girl lay cradled in its arm, it closed the limestone cliff, sealing the crack and jostling it until it fit back into place, a tiny hollow at the limestone's center where the girl had once been.

One month passed before the girl from the limestone cracked her eyes open. The Outsider knew little about how to raise children beyond what it had observed from human communities: children had to be fed, put to sleep, and occasionally taken outside to exercise so their bodies could maintain proper locomotive abilities. It gathered bundles of dandelions and blackberries and fed them to the girl. She ate whatever the Outsider could scavenge – even the shells of eggs stolen from neglectful birds' nests. She followed the Outsider on expeditions for water, her bare feet cushioned by surfaces of black dust that seemed to leak from the Outsider's body, spreading across the ground in thick waves, thinning the further out it spread. She slept when the sky turned dark and woke with the sun, an already awake Outsider sitting at the main table, curtains drawn close, the room dark, a mug of water held in its wisps of hands.

Another month passed when the girl began to speak.

"Where are your hands?" She asked, as they packed their few items in sacks and left their shelter for a new one. It was never safe to stay too long in one place or else risk crossing paths with humans. And humans were always prowling with weapons, trying to kill off the cursed.

The Outsider walked beside the girl, holding her hand so she wouldn't spring forward. She liked to chase after small critters, jumping at those that flew and stomping after those that crawled like lightning bolts streaking across the dirt.

"What do you mean? I've got hands," the Outsider replied.

"But you've got no fingers," the girl said, poking at the clouds of black dust pooling at the Outsider's wrists.

"I don't need fingers to have hands."

"Don't you?" The girl asked, staring skeptically as the dust swirled and spiraled.

"Look, I can still hold you." The Outsider lifted the girl into its arms and she squealed as she clutched to its arm, while its hand supported her legs.

"I can walk!" She demanded, and the Outsider set her back down.

"It's going to get bright soon, hurry up," the Outsider warned.

The girl nodded and began to speed up her pace, hitting each foot on the ground heel-to-toe with such deliberate precision that the Outsider wondered if she was mocking him.

"Don't wanna get caught! Don't wanna get caught!" She sang.

"No, you don't," the Outsider affirmed, even though the girl would probably be fine under sunlight. Only the Outsider's body risked evaporating under light – it was nearly impossible for the scattered particles to find their way back and reassemble into cohesive structures. It had lost its head that way – a careless mistake where rays struck its body from between the sparse branches of a warped tree. The Outsider's head had dispersed like aerosols before the rest of its body could find refuge behind a boulder. It was, of course, able to reform a head with the remainder of its mass, manifesting from memory a neck, the curve from neck to skull, the sharp jut of a chin, and facial features extruded from the remainder of its coherent form. But the newly constructed head could not substitute a true head – it could not think, guide, or provide a voice of reason. The head could only stand in place, an illusion for onlookers and itself. So adapted to the imitation and so accustomed to making decisions without a brain and only a heart, the Outsider occasionally forgot its head was not real.

When the Outsider lost its fingers to the sun, it didn't bother reconstructing them. Its particles had already filled in the gaps where its fingers had once been, its hands more like foam or water, fluid and easily adaptable to the current use case. The Outsider didn't need precision anyway – not to pick up heavy things, not to pull the limestone girl along, not to protect the girl from wolves that prowled at night, not to snatch entire nests of eggs to cook for breakfast.

"How are those people still fine under daylight?" The girl asked. She pointed downward at the hills below, where a person in a large, straw hat rode a mule along the road. The sunrise had already begun to warm the ground and was brightening the lower fields of wheat crops and olive trees.

"They must not be cursed," the Outsider answered.

"That's not fair. Curses should be for everyone."

The Outsider pushed the girl along, hurrying her to their next rest point, a shaded space behind a large, slanted slab of stone that resembled a mountain more than rock. "Probably because they are blessed by the Earth. Only those abandoned by the Earth get marked for removal. Curses are like garbage collectors."

"You should ask the garbage collectors for your fingers back. How else can I marry you when I grow up? You need a finger for a ring otherwise you can't get married."

"A ring doesn't dictate the feasibility of a marriage."

"That's what the book you got me said: the princess got a ring and then they could get married."

"To a prince. Not an Outsider."

"What's the difference?"

The Outsider shrugged. "Princes don't vanish so easily."

"Sure they do, they die when they get old or are killed in battle."

"They don't run the risk of disintegrating."

"I don't get it," the girl huffed, planting a foot on the ground and placing her hands on her waist. "Why can't I marry you?"

The Outsider sat behind the boulder as the sun rose and cast a long shadow over its body, the dark of the shadow blending with its particles, near black on black like it was truly invisible even though if you squinted, you could make out pockets of an abyss, like certain areas ended right there and others fell deep down, tunneling further and further away, forever.

"I don't love humans," the Outsider said.

"Then I don't need to be one."

"Well, it's good to have conviction." The Outsider lay on the ground, its body scattered at the crevasse of the boulder. It rested like a shadow pooling in cracks, sinking deeper and deeper until the crack itself was no longer a sanctuary, but rather a limitation on how far it could disappear. The girl dug her fingers into the dirt, drawing circles deeper and deeper until the dirt caked her nails. When she grew bored of drawing, she crawled to the edge of the boulder and peeked her head out toward the fields, the sprinkling of houses, the sunlight. Everything was moving: mules trekking up and down slopes, birds flitting sporadically from tree to shrub to ground, a human or two heaving their plows or walking along the river, soldiers stationed by the border with their tall guns and tall hats.

"There are more soldiers than normal humans," she commented.

"You need a lot of soldiers to fight the cursed," the Outsider replied.

"Will they come here?"

"This is probably too far. Even the soldiers aren't daring enough to venture so deep into cursed land."

The girl looked around. "Looks the same here to me. I'm not feeling any more or less cursed."

The Outsider extended an arm into the air, feeling the atmosphere. The air was heavier here, saturated with cursed ashes, Outsider bodies, and disintegrated biological matter that hadn't quite completed its transformation into an Outsider's shell before it had been eaten by the dawn. It smelled like copper and charcoal, like leather being tanned over a flame. "Of course not, it's all relative. We've yet to visit a proper, functional, untouched human town."

"Do you want to go?"

"We will go. It's a long way ahead so it'll take a while."

"Is it further than the limestone cliffs where I woke?"

"Much further, in a place where there are no limestone people, where people don't need to wait to come screaming to life, nor held in stone until someone can crack them free."

"I'm glad you found me," the girl nodded.

"It could've been a better time with fewer cursed. I'm sure your parents would've preferred that."

"Are they still my parents if I don't remember them?"

"No one in the limestone remembers their parents. But those parents are still parents."

The girl watched a soldier marching along the perimeter of a field, wondering if it was hot under that tall, dark blue hat under the sun. "I remember the limestone, the cool encasing, the rough surfaces that aligned with my arms and legs and back, the hard support. Don't you think the limestone birthed me?"

"I can't fault you for what you don't remember," the Outsider shrugged.

"Sit with me," she said. The girl retreated to the center behind the boulder, shifting her weight until she could lean her head on the Outsider's lap, which had materialized moments ago from the black particles like foam.

"How do I become like you?" She asked, closing her eyes and stretching her neck from side to side.

"Be born abandoned, get cursed, look at the sun too much even though it triggers the curse."

"I think I'm two-thirds of the way there. And then we'll be able to get married."

* * *

The Outsider had to carry the girl over most of the first mountain because the rocks were too slippery and steep for her to reach. It created a harness from its body, looping around her thighs and over her shoulders so she wouldn't peel away like dried bark. It could've formed a stronger, tighter hold if more of its mass remained, but at present, this would have to suffice. The girl napped. She was beginning to sleep for longer and longer hours, perhaps because of the cooling season. The Outsider had heard that limestone children took longer to adjust to consistent waking hours, having spent decades dormant and secluded from outside change. When the girl woke, it was only for several minutes – long enough the Outsider could ensure she ingested sufficient nutrition so her body could grow, but too short to hold their usual conversations.

"Are we almost there yet?" The girl had asked slowly as the Outsider set her down and prepared for her a handful of blackberries. They had nearly made it around the highest slope, but the rocks remained too jagged and too long, like sharpened and studded walls that'd only plummet creatures to the bottom.

"Almost," it said, but the girl had already fallen asleep, and it wrapped its particles of limbs around her as it continued the descent to the human town. It would need to hurry before it got too cold, as the town closed its entry during the winter when the curse was most contagious and humans most susceptible.

The Outsider continued to climb through day and night, its body thinning like dunes flayed by the wind. When it finally made it to town, the trees bared their branches like limbs crippled by winter and the gates remained propped open for visitors. The Outsider's body had dispersed and it appeared no different from dust kicked up from the ground. But it possessed enough strength and substance to lower the girl gently, parts of its arms flattened into a blanket to cushion the impact and prevent the hard pavement from waking her.

As the sun rose and people began to emerge from their homes, the Outsider watched and waited for someone to take her in.

Biographies & Sources

Ash Arya
A Promise in Bronze
(First Publication)
Ash Arya is an author of Fantasy and Science Fiction, born in New Delhi, India, where she pursued an M.A. in English and World Literature. A connoisseur of history and mythology, she enjoys reimagining legends from the Indian subcontinent, interspersing them with evergreen tropes, socio-cultural commentary, and unforeseen twists. Her literary influences run far and wide across time and genre – ranging from ancient Epics to modern Epic Fantasy, from Margaret Atwood to V.E. Schwab. Other than infusing her characters' lives with impossible choices, she likes reading, looking for her next TV obsession, and collecting trivia on just about anything.

Francis Bacon
The New Atlantis
(Originally Published in 1626)
Born in London, a leading courtier's son, Francis Bacon (1561–1626) was educated at a Cambridge which still saw scientific truth as resting with the 'authority' of ancient writings. His suggestion that conclusions should instead be drawn from the systematic observation of nature, experimentally tested, made him key to the development of the 'scientific method'. He is said to have died of pneumonia, caught when working on the preservative effects of freezing meat.

Rose Beardmore
Aging Ivy, Absent Sister
(First Publication)
Rose Beardmore is a writer and theatre artist living in the Boston area. She is currently a student at Suffolk University studying English literature and theatre. Though Rose began her artistic career as an actor, she has been writing for as long as she can remember. Her work is highly influenced by her experiences onstage. When she is not writing, directing, or acting, she's usually reading a book or taking the train to rehearsal.

Louis Becke
The Chilean Bluejacket
(Originally Published in *By Reef and Palm*, 1894)
Born in Port Macquarie, New South Wales, Louis Becke (1855–1913) moved to Sydney with his family for his teenage years. After a trip to San Francisco with an elder brother, he stowed away on a ship to Samoa and spent the rest of his life plying the Pacific as a trader. He wrote between voyages, starting with the short-story collection *By Reef and Palm*. Further stories followed, along with novels, travel writing and folktale anthologies.

Edward Bellamy
The Blindman's World
(Originally Published in *The Atlantic Monthly*, 1886)
Edward Bellamy (1850–98) was born in Chicopee, Massachusetts. He initially studied law in Germany, exposing him to the issues of the impoverished in the city. He eventually turned to

journalism, working as an editor for the *Springfield Union* and *The New York Evening Post*. Though he did not have much success with his early novels, he achieved immense fame with his utopian novel *Looking Backwards*, which promoted a socialist ideology that encouraged a harmonious world through cooperation and brotherhood.

Algernon Blackwood
Sand
(Originally Published in *Pan's Garden: A Volume of Nature Stories*, 1912)
Algernon Henry Blackwood (1869–1951) was a writer who crafted his tales with extraordinary vision. Born in Kent but working at numerous careers in America and Canada in his youth, he eventually settled back in England in his thirties. He wrote many novels and short stories including 'The Willows', which was rated by Lovecraft as one of his favourite stories, and he is credited by many scholars as a real master of imagery who wrote at a consistently high standard.

Samuel Butler
Erewhon: Chapters XIII–XV
(Originally Published as *Erewhon: or, Over the Range*, 1872)
Samuel Butler (1835–1902) was born in Nottinghamshire, England. He was a novelist, essayist and critic. His most famous works include *The Way of All Flesh*, an autobiographical novel largely considered his magnum opus, and *Erewhon*, a utopian satire of the mentality and lifestyles embraced by Victorian England. The inspiration for the first few chapters of the book came from Butler's own experiences in New Zealand, where he worked for several years as a sheep farmer.

Leah Cypess
Across the River
(Originally Published in *The Mythic Dream*, 2019)
Leah Cypess is the author of the middle grade *Sisters Ever After* series, which retells fairy tales from the points of view of forgotten younger sisters. The first three books in the series, *Thornwood*, *Glass Slippers*, and *The Piper's Promise*, are out now. Leah has also written four young adult fantasy novels and numerous works of short fiction. She is a three-time Nebula Award finalist and a World Fantasy Award finalist. You can learn more about her and her books at leahcypess.com.

Niya M.K. Davis
Whispers on the Wind
(First Publication)
Niya Munda Davis is an eclectic, intuitive, practitioner and creative soul. Through art, written and spoken word, her desire is to be a bridge between the gaps that appear to separate us – be they generationally, culturally, geographically and all the other labels designed to create pockets of separation. Her goal is to bring us all that little bit closer together. Niya has published two card decks, a colouring book, planner and original artworks. Come and join her over at AsheUnfolding.com.

Deborah L. Davitt
Under Hill, Under Dale
(First Publication)
Deborah L. Davitt was raised in Nevada, but currently lives in Houston, Texas with her husband and son. Her prize-winning poetry has appeared in over fifty journals, including *F&SF* and *Asimov's*. Her award-winning prose has appeared in venues such as *Analog*, *Lightspeed*, and Flame Tree

anthologies. For more on her work, including poetry collections *The Gates of Never* and *Bounded by Eternity*, and her forthcoming chapbook, *From Voyages Unending*, please see edda-earth.com.

Lord Dunsany
The Loot of Bombasharna
(Originally Published in *The Book of Wonder*, 1912. Reproduced with permission of Curtis Brown Ltd, London, on behalf of the Trustees of the Lord Dunsany Will Trust. Copyright © Lord Dunsany)
Edward John Moreton Drax Plunkett, 18th Baron of Dunsany (1878–1957), or Lord Dunsany, was born in London, but belonged to the Anglo-Irish ascendancy. His ancestral home was Dunsany Castle, Meath. He moved not just in aristocratic but in literary circles: in England he was a friend to Rudyard Kipling (1865–1936), in Ireland to the folklorist and dramatist Lady Gregory (1852–1932). He wrote over ninety books – largely collections of short stories.

Nictzin Dyalhis
Heart of Atlantan
(Originally Published in *Weird Tales*, September 1940)
The details of Nictzin Dyalhis' life (1873–1942) have always been uncertain, despite his being a sci-fi and fantasy writer of some repute. He is believed to have been born in Massachusetts but, after his service in the First World War, settled in Pennsylvania, with spells in Maryland. Many of his stories were published in the famous pulp fantasy magazine *Weird Tale*s, including 'The Sapphire Goddess' and the early space opera 'When the Green Star Waned'.

Tracy Fahey
Asylum
(First Publication)
Tracy Fahey is an Irish author of five books. She was twice shortlisted for Best Collection at the British Fantasy Awards in 2017 and 2022. Her short fiction is published in over thirty American, British, Australian and Irish anthologies. She holds a PhD on the Gothic in visual arts; her non-fiction work is published in Irish, English, Italian, Dutch and Australian edited collections. Fahey's writing is supported by residencies in Ireland and Greece. In 2022 she was awarded Saari Fellow status for 2023 by the Kone Foundation, Finland.

Dr. Jennifer Fuller
Lost Atlantis: Foreword
Jennifer Fuller is a Communications and Training Lead at Sierra 7 where she works to provide high-quality trainings and communications support for Veterans Affairs. Previously, she was a college professor serving at Jackson State University, Idaho State University, and Warner University. Her previous book *Dark Paradise* was a work of literary criticism that explored the Pacific islands through the lens of nineteenth-century literature. Her love of islands (and science fiction) is a theme that carries through much of her work, including her current co-authored project *Beyond Atlantis: Islands of Imagination*.

Isobel Granby
The Exiles
(First Publication)
Isobel Granby is a writer, artist, and actor living in St. John's, Newfoundland. While the focus of their academic work is currently on ghost ships, their previous writing has included the

medieval fantasy-comedy radio play *Corentin in Quarantine*, the ocean history podcast *The Deeps*, and the poetry map *Terra Precognita*. Along with pursuing a PhD in folklore, Isobel is part of the Practical Fantasists creative team (as Karin Murray-Bergquist).

John Linwood Grant
The Cities We Once Knew
(First Publication)
John Linwood Grant is a professional writer/editor from Yorkshire. He generally calls his work strange fictions, incorporating a range of weird, psychological and supernatural elements, and has had some eighty tales published in the last few years, including in award-winning anthologies. His second collection, *Where All is Night, and Starless* (2021, Trepidatio), was nominated for the Shirley Jackson Award. As an editor, he is responsible for the *Sherlock Holmes & the Occult Detectives* series (Belanger) and other anthologies, as well as the successful *Occult Detective Magazine*. He can be found regularly on Facebook, and at his eclectic website greydogtales.com/blog.

David Hankins
Where the Lost Things Are
(First Publication)
David Hankins is an award-winning author who writes from the thriving cornfields of Iowa where he lives with his wife, daughter, and two dragons disguised as cats. His stories have graced the pages of *Writers of the Future Volume 39*, *DreamForge Magazine*, *Unidentified Funny Objects* anthologies, *Third Flatiron* anthologies, and others. David devotes his time to his passions of writing, traveling with his family, and finding new ways to pay his mortgage. You can find him at davidhankins.com.

Lafcadio Hearn
The Dream of a Summer Day
(Originally Published in *The Japan Weekly Mail*, 1894)
Lafcadio Hearn (1850–1904) was a writer and translator best known in the English-speaking world for the works he wrote (as Koizumi Yakumo) on Japan, the adoptive homeland in which he spent the last years of his life. He'd previously lived in Ireland, the United States and the French West Indies, and was born in Lefkada, in the Ionian Islands, to an Irish father and Greek mother. The distinguished translator of modern French classics by Gautier, Flaubert, Zola and Maupassant, he was a literary force in his own right, with a longstanding interest in the supernatural.

Robert E. Howard
The Mirrors of Tuzun Thune
(Originally Published in *Weird Tales*, September 1929)
Robert Ervin Howard (1906–36) was born in Peaster, Texas. He is responsible for forming the subgenre within fantasy known as 'Sword and Sorcery', establishing him as a pulp fiction writer. Being a very intellectual and athletic man, Howard wrote within the genres of westerns, boxing, historical and horror fiction as well. Howard will perhaps always be known best for his association with the pulp magazine *Weird Tales*, in which he published many tales of a horror and fantasy nature. As well as Conan the Barbarian, Howard also created the character Kull of Atlantis, whose first appearance in a published story was in 'The Shadow Kingdom'.

M.K. Hutchins
The Temple's Posthole
(Originally Published in *Orson Scott Card's Intergalactic Medicine Show, Issue #32*, 2013)
M.K. Hutchins often draws on her background in archaeology when writing fantasy and science fiction. She's the author of several novels, including *Ana's Asteroid* and *The Redwood Palace*, along with over thirty short stories appearing in *Podcastle*, *Analog*, *Strange Horizons*, and elsewhere. When not writing, she's usually with her children as they grow veggies, bake, and play games together, though not usually all at the same time. Find her at linktr.ee/mkhutchins.

C.J. Cutcliffe Hyne
The Lost Continent: Chapters VI–VIII
(Originally Published by Hutchison, 1900)
Charles John Cutcliffe Wright Hyne (1866–1944) was a novelist. He is known primarily for *The Lost Continent*, the story of the lost city of Atlantis. The novel was first published in serial form in *Pearson's Magazine*, July–December 1899 and due to its success was published by Hutchison a year later in the form of a novel. It is widely considered a classic that combines elements of early myths. He also published many stories featuring Captain Kettle, a sea captain who had many adventures and which Joseph Conrad cites as one of his influences for *The Heart of Darkness*. Hyne wrote prolifically throughout his life, and died from wounds inflicted during the Battle of the Somme.

Karl Sade
Trouble in Paradise
(First Publication)
Karl Sade, an Indian-born writer from New Zealand, currently wanders across Europe in search of a publisher for his debut novel, *The Hysterical Immigrant*, while working on his second, *Hermit Phantasmagoria*. A ghostwriter by trade, he has authored several nonfiction books and has recently been published by the European Society of Literature for a short story called 'Mother, Engulf Me'. In addition to his writing pursuits, Sade is a devoted student of literary theory and you are likely to find him aimlessly trudging the globe, with a book tucked under his arm, waiting for another story to happen.

Silas Leavitt
All the Time in the World
(First Publication)
Silas Leavitt (pronouns he/him) grew up wandering the forests and mountains of Maine. He inhaled a steady diet of science-fiction and fantasy, finding joy in works that shake genre and gender conventions and push the bounds of the weird. He studied at the University of Saint Andrews in Scotland and has a Master of Arts in Urban and Environmental Planning from Tufts University, and many of his writings examine the interplay of environmental systems and societal change. He attended the Maine Writers and Publishers Alliance's Harvest Retreat for fiction in 2022. This is his first published piece.

H.P. Lovecraft
Bothon (written with Henry S. Whitehead)
(Originally Published in *Amazing Stories*, 1946)
Master of weird fiction Howard Phillips Lovecraft (1890–1937) was born in Providence, Rhode Island. Featuring unknown and otherworldly creatures, his stories were one of the

first to mix science fiction with horror. Plagued by nightmares from an early age, he was inspired to write his dark and strange fantasy tales; the isolation he must have experienced from suffering frequent illnesses can be felt as a prominent theme in his work. Lovecraft inspired many other authors, and his most famous story 'The Call of Cthulhu' has influenced many aspects of popular culture.

Kwame M.A. McPherson
The City of Warrior Queens
(First Publication)
Kwame is a 2007 Poetic Soul winner and 2020 Flash Fiction Bursary Awardee for The Bridport Prize: International Creative Writing Competition – the first Jamaican to do so. A qualified life-long learning trainer, he has conducted creative writing workshops internationally in Toronto, Canada; London, England; and Kingston, Jamaica; specifically, at the Kingston Book Festival as well as partnering with the National Library of Jamaica. His self-published books have been purchased by the University of West Indies Bookshop and his stories collected and displayed in the University's Archives Department. Kwame also assists others new to writing, to write and publish their own book. Kwame has a Postgraduate Certificate & Diploma in Management Studies (CertMS/DipMS); BTEC Higher National Certificate in Public Administration (HNC); BTEC National Certificate in Business & Finance (NC); MA in Business Administration (MBA).

Damien Mckeating
Waters of Avalon
(First Publication)
Damien Mckeating was born and a short time after that he developed a love of fantasy and the supernatural. He has written for radio, comics, film, prose, and worked as a lyricist and bass player for a peculiar folk band. He has short stories included in different anthologies, ranging from modern takes on Irish mythology to SF adventures for young readers. He is fond of corvids and is currently the oldest he has ever been. Sometimes he remembers to blog: skeletonbutler.wordpress.com.

John Moralee
Forgotten
(First Publication)
John Moralee was born in England, where his crime, horror and science-fiction stories have been published in various magazines and anthologies, including *The Mammoth Book of Jack the Ripper Stories*, *Clockwork Cairo* and *Crimewave*. His novels include the mystery thriller *Acting Dead*, the zombie apocalypse story *Journal of the Living*, and the humorous fantasy tale *Crowning Achievements: The Legend of King Arthur*.

Barry Neenan
Scavengers
(First Publication)
Barry Neenan is a librarian by trade, but hopes to have his own books on the shelf some day. A lifelong interest in stories has seen him dabble in a variety of genres, and an absolute inability to draw has left him focused on prose. He is a firm believer in the ability of genre fiction to resonate as strongly as the subtlest poem. He lives in Galway with his wife and, regrettably, no cats.

Douglas Newton
Sunken Cities
(Originally Published in *Munsey's Magazine*, 1923)
Little is known about Wilfrid Bernard Michael Newton (1884–1951) beyond the fact that he was born in London, and that he published over a thousand stories, mostly fantasy and science fiction. Our sense of his having lived largely in his written work is strengthened by the fact that he employed such a variety of noms de plume, including W.N. Douglas, Bernard Birmingham, John How and Ian Irons.

Spencer Orey
A Poison of Bodies Beneath the Water
(First Publication)
Spencer Orey is a graduate of the 2021 Odyssey Writing Workshop and a finalist for the Writers of the Future Contest. His short fiction is forthcoming in *Tales from Fiddler's Green*. He has a PhD in cultural anthropology, with academic interests in magic, mobility, and media dreams that he likes to weave into speculative stories. He grew up in dry New Mexico and dry California and is happy to live in rainy Denmark with his wife and kids. Find him online at spencerorey.com or on Twitter @spencerorey.

Barry Pain
The New Gulliver
(Originally Published in *The New Gulliver and Other Stories*, 1913)
A regular contributor to *Punch* and other magazines, Cambridge-born Barry Pain (1864–1928) was renowned first and foremost as a comic writer. Like his friend and fellow-humourist Jerome K. Jerome (1859–1927), however, he had a longstanding interest in the supernatural and the gothic. His mad-scientist shocker *The Octave of Claudius* (1897) was to become a pioneering Hollywood Horror movie, in the form of *A Blind Bargain*, with Lon Chaney and Raymond McKee, in 1922.

Plato
Critias
(This translation by Jowett originally published in *The Dialogues of Plato*, 1871)
Among the founders of western thought, Plato (*c.* 428–348 BCE) came from Athens, where he established the original Academy. His most celebrated student was Aristotle (348–22 BCE). So central were intellectual exchange and questioning for Plato that he wrote his works as dialogues, one voice being that of his own true-life tutor Socrates (*c.* 470–399 BCE). The translator Benjamin Jowett (1817–93) was an Anglican clergyman and classical scholar and for many years master of Balliol College, Oxford.

Phylos the Thibetan
A Dweller on Two Planets: Part III, Chapter IV – The Fall of Atlantis
(Originally Published in 1905)
A physician's son, Frederick S. Oliver (1866–99) was born in Washington DC, but was brought up first in California then in Oregon. *A Dweller on Two Planets* was his first and for a long time his only book, which Oliver claims to have written automatically between 1883 and 1886, by dictation from a spirit named 'Phylos the Thibetan'. He copyrighted this text in 1894, and an expanded version five years later, though it would be published only posthumously, in 1905.

Erica Ruppert
To Selareme
(First Publication)
Erica Ruppert, HWA, SFWA. lives in northern New Jersey with her husband and too many cats. Her novella *Sisters in Arms* was released in 2021. Her short stories have appeared in magazines including *Vastarien*, *Lamplight*, and *Nightmare*, on podcasts including *PodCastle*, and in multiple anthologies. Her collection *Imago and Other Transformations* will be released by Trepidatio Publishing in March 2023. When she is not writing, she runs, bakes, and gardens with more enthusiasm than skill.

C.R. Serajeddini
Issa and the Gryphon
(First Publication)
C.R. Serajeddini is a British-Kurdish author of fantasy and science fiction. Inspired by her background, her work borrows from Kurdish history, and Mesopotamian and Persian mythology, often interwoven with fantastical and extra-terrestrial elements. Her writing has appeared – or is forthcoming – in several anthologies, including *Immigrant Sci-Fi* and *Spirits & Ghouls* from Flame Tree Publishing, and *Gargantua* from Air & Nothingness Press. She's currently working on her first novel, a YA Space Fantasy featuring a kick-ass heroine. When she's not busy exploring imaginary worlds, she enjoys hiking the mountains and coast with her family and gazing up at the stars.

Zach Shephard
The Tower Calls
(First Publication)
Zach Shephard lives in Enumclaw, Washington, where he writes fantasy, science fiction and horror stories. When not scribbling words down, he can often be found playing board games – even, occasionally, all by himself. (It's not weird.) Zach's fiction has appeared in places like *Fantasy & Science Fiction*, the Unidentified Funny Objects anthology series, and several of Flame Tree Publishing's Gothic Fantasy books. He's particularly fond of his contribution to *Lost Atlantis*, because it was written for someone who, quite frankly, deserves to have a story written for them. For more of Zach's work, check out zachshephard.com.

Clark Ashton Smith
A Vintage from Atlantis
(Originally Published in *Weird Tales*, September 1933. Published with permission of CASiana Enterprises, the Literary Estate of Clark Ashton Smith.)
Clark Ashton Smith (1893–1961) was born in Long Valley, California. He is well regarded as both a poet and a writer of horror, fantasy and science fiction stories. Along with H.P. Lovecraft and Robert E. Howard, he was a prolific contributor to the magazine *Weird Tales*. His stories are full of dark and imaginative creations, and glimpses into the worlds beyond. His unique writing style and incredible vision have led to many of his stories influencing later fantasy writers.

Jules Verne
Twenty Thousand Leagues Under the Sea: Part II, Chapters IX–XI
(Originally Published as *Vingt mille lieues sous les mers: Tour du monde sous-marin* in *Magasin d'éducation et de récréation*, 1869–70; this translation published in 1873)

Jules Verne (1828–1905) was born in Nantes, France. As a novelist, poet and playwright, he wrote adventure novels and had a big impact on the science fiction genre. Along with H.G. Wells, Verne is considered to be one of the founding fathers of science fiction. His most famous adventure novels formed the series *Voyages Extraordinaires*, and include *Journey to the Centre of the Earth* and *Twenty Thousand Leagues Under the Sea*. His works continue to be popular today, and Verne ranks as the most translated science fiction author to date, with his tales often reprinted and adapted for film.

Calie Voorhis
The Librarian's Secret Society, 1988
(First Publication)
Calie Voorhis is a short story author, poet, and editor. She has work appearing or forthcoming in over thirty venues around the world. She's a lifelong fan of the fantastical, an Odyssey Workshop Alumna, and holds an MFA in Writing Popular Fiction from Seton Hill University. In her spare time, she enjoys reading and stabbing fabric. You can visit her at the world's fourth worst writer's website: calievoorhis.com.

H.G. Wells
A Dream of Armageddon
(Originally Published in *Black and White*, 1901)
Herbert George Wells (1866–1946) was born in Kent, England. Novelist, journalist, social reformer and historian, Wells is one of the greatest ever science fiction writers and along with Jules Verne is sometimes referred to as a 'founding father' of the genre. With Aldous Huxley and, later, George Orwell, he defined the adventurous, social concern of early speculative fiction where the human condition was played out on a greater stage. Wells created over fifty novels, including his famous works *The Time Machine*, *The Invisible Man*, *The Island of Dr. Moreau* and *The War of the Worlds*, as well as a fantastic array of short stories.

Henry S. Whitehead
Bothon (written with H.P. Lovecraft)
(Originally Published in *Amazing Stories*, 1946)
Born in Elizabeth, New Jersey, into the upper middle class, Henry S. Whitehead (1882–1932) grew up to go to Harvard, and then take orders as an Episcopalian clergyman. By no means a conventional one, however. 'He has nothing of the musty cleric about him,' wrote an approving H.P. Lovecraft, who became a great friend and encouraged Whitehead's other vocation as a writer of fantasy and horror fiction – even collaborating with him in the writing of 'Bothon'.

Lucy Zhang
Outsider
(First Publication)
Lucy Zhang writes, codes, and watches anime. Her work has appeared in *CRAFT*, *The Spectacle*, *Redivider*, and elsewhere. She is the author of the chapbooks *Hollowed* (Thirty West Publishing) and *Absorption* (Harbor Review). Her work is anthologised in *Best Microfiction*, *Best Small Fictions*, and *Best of the Net*, and was longlisted in the Wigleaf Top 50. She edits for Heavy Feather Review. When not stressing about feature deadlines, she can be found stressing about finishing her novel. Find her at lucyzhang.tech or on Twitter @Dango_Ramen.